A Collection distributed by Heron Books

CHARLES DICKENS

COMPLETE
WORKS

CENTENNIAL EDITION

Charles Dickens

CHARLES DICKENS

BLEAK HOUSE
I

Introduction by
Sir Osbert Sitwell

Illustrations
by Phiz

Distributed by
HERON BOOKS

I.S.B.N. for this volume:
0 86225 089 7

INTRODUCTION

Any author who writes of Charles Dickens's novels must preface his remarks with the axiom that Dickens was a genius. He must add – for even to-day this is sometimes denied – that he was a great artist, albeit the most inartistic, the least precious, who ever created a work of art. Indeed, it is this very quality which makes his use of words so interesting, and, together with the fire which he infuses into his novels, ensures that they will be read as long as the language he yet so often maltreated shall continue to exist. But, of latter years, it has been the character of Dickens, rather than his achievements, that have been decried and denigrated, and so it may be well to write a few lines about the author of Bleak House *before proceeding to discuss the book itself.*

It is alleged, then, that in several respects the life of this great man fell short of the ideals he upheld with such vigour in his books. This may well be. Nobody, no human being, could live up to them. Nevertheless, whether or no he behaved, after many years, with some calculated hardness toward the tiresome, untidy, repining Mrs. Dickens (part of her untidiness was the trick of catching her foot in public and falling, which plainly irritated her husband beyond bearing), whether he was a harsh, unindulgent parent, disappointed at his children's lack of character, and perhaps disinclined to welcome childish bumpings and yellings when he was trying to work, in order to support them, nevertheless the immense attraction and sympathy of his whole being shines through every line of every book he wrote, and inevitably draws the reader to him. There is no mistaking the warmth of his nature, his hatred of cruelty, and the genuine feeling that permeates his denunciations of oppression: nor is there any limit, even though in private he may sometimes have been testy, to the good humour of his creations. Recent writers truly have found in him the most singular causes of offence. For example, he has been blamed for the pleasure he derived – and the money he made – towards the end of his career from giving public readings of specially adapted versions of his novels and short stories: but, when one remembers the love of drama so evident in them, his love, too, of acting and all that pertained to the theatre, and when one also takes into consideration how wonderfully effective he was – as all who heard him read, testify – in the various parts he assigned to himself, it is hard to condemn him in this respect, though the strain he thus put upon himself may well have helped to shorten his life. Another able critic, in a book concerned with Dickens, denounces him roundly for having gout – a disease he shared with many other eminent writers and artists. As well hold him up to excoriation for suffering from hay-fever, a kindred ailment! This critic also explains that Dickens's mastery of the effects of horror were due to secret feelings of guilt and dissatisfaction with himself. If so, it is a pity that a great many other writers do not cultivate these same emotions in their natures.

Certainly Dickens did excel in evoking feelings of suspense and horror. The murders in his books are among the most effective in literature. Yet his subtleties are no whit the less to be noticed than his strong outlines, and his general atmosphere is equally effective with his most brilliant definition of character. Smollett and Fielding had dealt with London before him: but it was a different London: though Bleak House *contains no steam-engine, after the manner of Zola's* La Bête humaine, *it was, in contradistinction to his earlier novels, written in the Coal Age. As was fitting in*

INTRODUCTION

one who had been driven by his greedy mother and weak father into a blacking factory, when he still should have been at school, Dickens became the first novelist – and the first poet – of the great industrial city; the dark enormous cities dedicated to enshrouding a submerged proletariat, among which dwelt a whole nation of brutalized criminals and of the forgotten, feeble, and despised. When the great eighteenth-century novelists wrote their works London, though already the largest and busiest of European capitals, was a place into which countrymen still wandered, gaping at the view from the brigdes, where the river was still pure and where peasants in smocks could still be seen driving their sheep and oxen to market through the streets. But now, in the age of Dickens:

‘... Smoke lowering down from chimney-pots, making a soft, black drizzle, with flakes of soot in it as big as full-grown snow-flakes – gone into mourning, one might imagine, for the death of the sun. Dogs, undistinguishable in mire, Horses, scarcely better; splashed to their very blinkers.... Fog everywhere. Fog up the river, where it flows among green aits and meadows; fog down the river, where it rolls defiled among the tiers of shipping, and the waterside pollutions of a great (and dirty) city. Fog on the Essex marshes, fog on the Kentish heights. Fog creeping into the cabooses of collier-brigs; fog lying out on the yards, and hovering in the rigging of great ships; fog drooping on the gunwales of barges and small boats. Fog in the eyes and throats of ancient Greenwich pensioners, wheezing by the firesides of their wards; fog in the stem and bowl of the afternoon pipe of the wrathful skipper, down in his close cabin; fog cruelly pinching the toes and fingers of his shivering little ’prentice boy on deck. Chance people on the bridges peeping over the parapets into a nether sky of fog, with fog all round them, as if they were up in a balloon, and hanging in the misty clouds.... Gas looming through the fog in divers places in the streets, much as the sun may, from the spongy fields, be seen to loom by husbandman and ploughboy. Most of the shops lighted two hours before their time – as the gas seems to know, for it has a haggard and unwilling look.’

So runs the description of London, on the first page of Bleak House, perhaps my own favourite among Dickens's great novels – even though it may not possess the perfection of David Copperfield, a work of the same middle period, or the promise contained in such books of his last years as Great Expectations and The

BLEAK HOUSE

Mystery of Edwin Drood, *novels which exhibit a whole new range of power and understanding: (for the final books of an elderly author to show promise, as well as the mastery to be expected from them, constitutes the rarest and most patent sign of genius.)* Bleak House *has a major theme – or rather, two connected major themes – running through it; the iniquities committed by the obsolete English legal machine, and the wilful and wicked blindness shown by our Mote-Beam school of Philanthropy, the members of which rescue, clothe, and feed savages in islands lost among the Antipodes, but allow their own children to grow up totally neglected and those of their neighbours to die of starvation. Round these themes, carried through triumphantly to the end of the book, modulated, disguised, transformed, but always reappearing, swarms a whole population of city weeds, hypocrites and philanthropists, villains and heroes; a great crowd of individuals that could only have been created by this author. It is on these beings that in the main I propose to dwell, for in this direction there are still two or three points that should be made, discussed and scrutinized though his novels have been for three generations.*

I delight in the people of this book: though to my mind it contains the most detestable of all Dickens's heroines. Esther Summerson is odious, so sweet, so sweetly spiteful – especially about Mr. Skimpole – so tenderly cocksure, so coy and subacid; on the other hand, one would welcome entire stories devoted to Mrs. Jellyby, old Mr. Turveydrop, his son Prince, and his daughter-in-law Caddy: one clamours for more concerning Tony Jobling, alias Weevle, Mr. Guppy, the Snagsbys, Mr. and Mrs. Bayham Badger, and the Chadbands. (I wonder if, as a charitable type, the Chadbands still exist: at one time I used to meet quantities of them – and of Mrs. Jellybys – in my philanthropic grandmother's house, but she died in 1911, and I have lost touch.) In passing, we may note that Mrs. Jellyby contradicts the theory, so often advanced, that Dickens 'exaggerates' or 'caricatures'; the cool and kindly aloofness of this lady when her daughter breaks the news of her engagement to Prince is much more true to life than would be the more vehement attitude that we might have expected. The truth is, as I have written elsewhere, that this great novelist distorts, as a great painter may distort, for the purpose of emphasizing the design and of bringing

x

out other qualities: he did not caricature. Similarly with the alleged exaggeration of themes on a large scale; I suppose, for example, the Circumlocution Office in Little Dorrit *may by some be deemed an exaggeration: but by means of it he presented to the public one of the chief evils in English political life, and the main cause, hitherto unidentified, of delayed or frustrated action.*

Bleak House *is (with the possible exception of* Little Dorrit, *in the pages of which can be found Mrs. Murdle, 'positively rustic to a degree') the novel in which the author carries to its highest pitch his observation of fashionable life. Often it has been denied – usually by 'real ladies and gentlemen' – that he could describe such personages. I hold that their objection on this score may have been founded on the very truthfulness of his unflattering portraiture. In this book his study of the Dedlocks, for example, is superb: how accurately he summons it all up, the atmosphere of Dedlock Hall, its desolate beauty in the rain, Sir Leicester, with his formal manner, the glacial beauty of Lady Dedlock, the slurred accents of the sporting cousin, above all, the poor, ageing ensconced relation, Miss Volumnia Dedlock, with her Spanish songs, to an accompaniment coquettishly scratched upon a guitar, her French conundrums, 'her profusion in the article of rouge, and persistency in an obsolete pearl necklace like a rosary of little birds-eggs'. As a type, Miss Volumnia is dead to-day, but her sprightly, petrified foolishness will always spring to life within the covers of this novel. And about these particular portraits there remains something more to be said. It was not, I think, until the publication of Dame Una Pope-Hennessy's recent book on Charles Dickens, that it became generally known that the great novelist was the grandson, on each side, of domestic servants: in the eyes that observed, there may have lingered something of the malice of a then depressed class. To-day, he would, it may be, have told the story in a different manner; with Sir Leicester and Lady Dedlock finding themselves obliged to do all the housework, or he might have given us an account of the non-stop grumbling in the depopulated Servants' Hall, the loud voices therein raised against an unalterable background of raging wireless: while Miss Volumnia and her guitar would have become, I suspect, a star-turn of Broadcasting House.*

BLEAK HOUSE

Most of all in Bleak House *do the exquisite conversations of Mr. Skimpole entrance me. Seldom, if ever, has the talk of a brilliant conversationalist been wafted across to us so naturally, so successfully from the printed page: (how much better it is than the reporting of Whistler's or Wilde's discourse that occurs in various novels and memoirs of the '90s!) And, bear in mind, this talking was usually wasted on the deserving Miss Summerson – there was no kindred spirit to call it out. If Harold Skimpole is, indeed, Leigh Hunt, what an incomparable companion he must have been: if Dickens invented the character, what a superb creation is he! The description of him when he first enters the narrative is unforgettable:*

'He was a little bright creature, with a rather large head; but a delicate face and a sweet voice, and there was a perfect charm in him. All he said was so free from effort and spontaneous and was said with such a captivating gaiety, that it was fascinating to hear him talk. . . . Indeed, he had more the appearance in all respects, of a damaged young man, than a well-preserved elderly one. There was an easy negligence in his manner, and even in his dress (his hair carelessly disposed, and his neck-kerchief loose and flowing, as I have seen artists paint their own portraits), which I could not separate from the idea of a romantic youth who had undergone some unique process of depreciation. . . .'

As for the passages and flights of his conversation, they are so lightly modulated, so perfect in rhythm, that I know many of them by heart.

'Mr. Skimpole was as agreeable at breakfast, as he had been over-night. There was honey on the table, and it led him into a discourse about Bees. He had no objection to honey, he said (and . . . he seemed to like it), but he protested against the overweening assumptions of Bees. He didn't at all see why the busy Bee should be proposed as a model to him; he supposed the Bee liked to make honey or he wouldn't do it – nobody asked him. It was not necessary for the Bee to make such a merit of his tastes. If every confectioner went buzzing about the world, banging against everything that came in his way, and egotistically calling upon everybody to take notice that he was going to his work and must not be interrupted, the world would be quite an unsupportable place. Then, after all, it was a ridiculous position, to be smoked out of your fortune with brimstone, as soon as you had made it. You

INTRODUCTION

would have a very mean opinion of a Manchester man, if he spun cotton for no other purpose. He must say he thought a Drone the embodiment of a pleasanter and wiser idea. The Drone said, unaffectedly, "You will excuse me, I really cannot attend to the shop! I find myself in a world in which there is so much to see, and so short a time to see it in, that I must take the liberty of looking about me, and begging to be provided for by somebody who doesn't want to look about him." This appeared to Mr. Skimpole to be the Drone philosophy, and he thought it a very good philosophy – always supposing the Drone to be willing to be on good terms with the Bee: which, so far as he knew, the easy fellow always was, if the consequential creature would only let him, and not be so conceited about his honey!'

Again, how gay and how true to life is the scene where he asks 'particularly' to see Charley, or 'Little Couvinses', as he called her, the bailiff's daughter. He

'told her with a patriarchal air, that he had given her late father all the business in his power; and that if one of her little brothers would make haste to get set-up in the same profession, he hoped he should still be able to put a good deal of employment in his way.

"For I am constantly being taken in these nets," said Mr. Skimpole, looking beamingly at us over a glass of wine-and-water, "and am constantly being bailed out – like a boat. Or paid off – like a ship's company. Somebody always does it for me. I can't do it, you know, for I never have any money. But Somebody does it. I get out by Somebody's means; I am not like the starling; I get out. If you were to ask me who Somebody is, upon my word I couldn't tell you. Let us drink to Somebody. God bless him!"...'

Even the author can only bring himself, one would hazard, to dislike the heartless, gay, little man towards the end of the book. And it has sometimes seemed hard to me that he may have based his final loathing for Skimpole on that airy being's attempt to eject a sufferer from smallpox from the house in which he was finding shelter. After all, Skimpole, we are told, had been a doctor, though he had never practised, and his advice, that if they did not turn the boy out, they should take him to a loft, give him cooling medicine, and sprinkle him with vinegar, was sound counsel for the time when it was offered. It has to be admitted that the next morning he connived, behind his host's back, at the victim being removed; but already two persons had caught the infection.

BLEAK HOUSE

Unlike Skimpole, Charles Dickens is great in his weaknesses, in his unfairnesses; they are merely typical of his greatness. Thus, for example, when a villain or villainess has to appear, and murder to be committed, it is enough to make him (the bearded ruffian, who assumes so many aliases and pops in and out of the story so often and without reason in Little Dorrit*), or her (Mademoiselle Hortense of* Bleak House*) of French nationality: no motive, then – or at the most the very slightest – is required, for the commission of the crime. To-day, were Dickens writing, the villain would have to be a German. Thus is crystallized one of the English contemporary prejudices; but all the more strangely, in that Dickens himself was never so happy as when in Paris, and possessed, furthermore, a most keen appreciation of the French genius, and of the French attitude towards their authors.*

I have tried elsewhere to emphasize the brilliance of the writing, the snap and modernity of Dickens's descriptions, that can be found in no other novelist of his time: read, in Little Dorrit*, the account of Mrs. General, sitting on a chair on a strip of carpet, in a huge apartment in Mr. Dorrit's Venetian Palazzo, or reconsider the virtuosity of his picture of Miss Volumnia's bedroom in the Dedlock mansion in London, a*

'room up a retired landing on the staircase – the second turning past the carving and gilding – a cousinly room containing a fearful abortion of a portrait of Sir Leicester, banished for its crimes, and commanding in the day a solemn yard, planted with dried-up shrubs like antediluvian specimens of black tea....'

These last words sum up for ever a certain kind of London garden.

After many readings, Bleak House *still has the same spell: it is impossible to put it down, impossible not to look forward to returning to it. Criticism can, no doubt, uncover inconsequences in the plot – but who cares? Who would stop reading the book to argue about the scientific probality of spontaneous combustion in a human being, or to discuss the likelihood of Mr. Tulkinghorn's death, under his dusty, painted ceiling? The excitement of the whole story, the icy terror inspired by the lawyer, the humour of the Snagsbys and the rest, the pathos of poor Miss Flite with her caged birds, are too vital and profound, the panorama the book provides*

XIV

INTRODUCTION

too vivid to allow any pause for critical reasoning. The power is extraordinary, such as only genius can supply. And, besides this, and by means of it, the novelist nails the noses of the smug and comfortable to the reek of the slums: he revealed whole vistas of suffering it had hitherto been impolite to notice – just as the author was too great-hearted to allow himself really to enjoy the fun of his creation, Skimpole, so he refused to blind himself to injustice, cruelty, and oppression. After his writings, the lives of the poor in England were lifted, with every passing decade, to a more humane level. His books thus visibly altered their lives. But to achieve this, he had to romanticize poverty, to try and make people regard it as a virtue (just as Shaw, with the same high object in view, has been obliged to denounce it as a crime). And so, from Dickens's characters, energetic even in their virtue or their laziness, are descended the listless, cretinous heroes and heroines of the novels of to-day, the fatigued, valorous, erotic charwomen, the A.R.P. worker who escaped from a mental home, all those border-line cases from asylums and work-houses who have in fiction now assumed the position of the Byronic heroes and heroines, haughty, high-bred, and misunderstood, of a hundred years ago.

Sir Osbert Sitwell

PREFACE

A CHANCERY Judge once had the kindness to inform me, as one of a company of some hundred and fifty men and women not labouring under any suspicions of lunacy, that the Court of Chancery, though the shining subject of much popular prejudice (at which point I thought the Judge's eye had a cast in my direction), was almost immaculate. There had been, he admitted, a trivial blemish or so in its rate of progress, but this was exaggerated, and had been entirely owing to the "parsimony of the public;" which guilty public, it appeared, had been until lately bent in the most determined manner on by no means enlarging the number of Chancery Judges appointed—I believe by Richard the Second, but any other King will do as well.

This seemed to me too profound a joke to be inserted in the body of this book, or I should have restored it to Conversation Kenge or to Mr. Vholes, with one or other of whom I think it must have originated. In such mouths I might have coupled it with an apt quotation from one of SHAKSPEARE's Sonnets:

> My nature is subdued
> To what it works in, like the dyer's hand:
> Pity me then, and wish I were renew'd!

XVII

PREFACE

But as it is wholesome that the parsimonious public should know what has been doing, and still is doing, in this connexion, I mention here that everything set forth in these pages concerning the Court of Chancery is substantially true, and within the truth. The case of Gridley is in no essential altered from one of actual occurrence, made public by a disinterested person who was professionally acquainted with the whole of the monstrous wrong from beginning to end. At the present moment * there is a suit before the Court which was commenced nearly twenty years ago; in which from thirty to forty counsel have been known to appear at one time; in which costs have been incurred to the amount of seventy thousand pounds; which is *a friendly suit;* and which is (I am assured) no nearer to its termination now than when it was begun. There is another well-known suit in Chancery, not yet decided, which was commenced before the close of the last century, and in which more than double the amount of seventy thousand pounds has been swallowed up in costs. If I wanted other authorities for JARNDYCE AND JARNDYCE, I could rain them on these pages, to the shame of—a parsimonious public.

There is only one other point on which I offer a word of remark. The possibility of what is called Spontaneous Combustion has been denied since the death of Mr. Krook; and my good friend MR. LEWES (quite mistaken, as he soon found, in supposing the thing to have been abandoned by all authorities) published some ingenious letters to me at the time when that event was chronicled, arguing that Spontaneous Combustion could not possibly be. I have no need to observe that I do not wilfully or negligently mislead my readers, and that before I wrote that description I took pains to investigate

* In August, 1853.

PREFACE

the subject. There are about thirty cases on record, of which the most famous, that of the Countess Cornelia de Bandi Cesenate, was minutely investigated and described by Giuseppe Bianchini, a prebendary of Verona, otherwise distinguished in letters, who published an account of it at Verona, in 1731, which he afterwards republished at Rome. The appearances beyond all rational doubt observed in that case, are the appearances observed in Mr. Krook's case. The next most famous instance happened at Rheims, six years earlier; and the historian in that case is LE CAT, one of the most renowned surgeons produced by France. The subject was a woman, whose husband was ignorantly convicted of having murdered her; but, on solemn appeal to a higher court, he was acquitted, because it was shown upon the evidence that she had died the death to which this name of Spontaneous Combustion is given. I do not think it necessary to add to these notable facts, and that general reference to the authorities which will be found at page 31, vol. ii.,* the recorded opinions and experiences of distinguished medical professors, French, English, and Scotch, in more modern days; contenting myself with observing, that I shall not abandon the facts until there shall have been a considerable Spontaneous Combustion of the testimony on which human occurrences are usually received.

In Bleak House, I have purposely dwelt upon the romantic side of familiar things.

* Another case, very clearly described by a dentist, occurred at the town of Columbus, in the United States of America, quite recently. The subject was a German, who kept a liquor-shop, and was an inveterate drunkard.

CONTENTS

XXI

CONTENTS

CHAPTER VIII

CONTENTS

CONTENTS

CHAPTER XXVIII

CHAPTER XXIX

CHAPTER XXX

CHAPTER XXXI

XXIV

LIST OF ILLUSTRATIONS

CHAPTER I

LONDON. Michaelmas Term lately over, and the Lord Chancellor sitting in Lincoln's Inn Hall. Implacable November weather. As much mud in the streets, as if the waters had but newly retired from the face of the earth, and it would not be wonderful to meet a Megalosaurus, forty feet long or so, waddling like an elephantine lizard up Holborn Hill. Smoke lowering down from chimney-pots, making a soft black drizzle, with flakes of soot in it as big as full-grown snow-flakes—gone into mourning, one might imagine, for the death of the sun. Dogs, undistinguishable in mire. Horses, scarcely better; splashed to their very blinkers. Foot passengers, jostling one another's umbrellas, in a general infection of ill-temper, and losing their foot-hold at street-corners, where tens of thousands of other foot passengers have been slipping and sliding since the day broke (if this day ever broke), adding new deposits to the crust upon crust of mud, sticking at those points tenaciously to the pavement, and accumulating at compound interest.

Fog everywhere. Fog up the river, where it flows among green aits and meadows; fog down the river, where it rolls defiled among the tiers of shipping, and the waterside pollutions of a great (and dirty) city. Fog on the Essex marshes,

1

fog on the Kentish heights. Fog creeping into the cabooses of collier-brigs; fog lying out on the yards, and hovering in the rigging of great ships; fog drooping on the gunwales of barges and small boats. Fog in the eyes and throats of ancient Greenwich pensioners, wheezing by the firesides of their wards; fog in the stem and bowl of the afternoon pipe of the wrathful skipper, down in his close cabin; fog cruelly pinching the toes and fingers of his shivering little 'prentice boy on deck. Chance people on the bridges peeping over the parapets into a nether sky of fog, with fog all round them, as if they were up in a balloon, and hanging in the misty clouds.

Gas looming through the fog in divers places in the streets, much as the sun may, from the spongy fields, be seen to loom by husbandman and ploughboy. Most of the shops lighted two hours before their time—as the gas seems to know, for it has a haggard and unwilling look.

The raw afternoon is rawest, and the dense fog is densest, and the muddy streets are muddiest, near that leaden-headed old obstruction, appropriate ornament for the threshold of a leaden-headed old corporation : Temple Bar. And hard by Temple Bar, in Lincoln's Inn Hall, at the very heart of the fog, sits the Lord High Chancellor in his High Court of Chancery.

Never can there come fog too thick, never can there come mud and mire too deep, to assort with the groping and floundering condition which this High Court of Chancery, most pestilent of hoary sinners, holds, this day, in the sight of heaven and earth.

On such an afternoon, if ever, the Lord High Chancellor ought to be sitting here—as here he is—with a foggy glory round his head, softly fenced in with crimson cloth and curtains, addressed by a large advocate with great whiskers, a little voice, and an interminable brief, and outwardly directing his contemplation to the lantern in the roof, where he can see nothing but fog. On such an afternoon, some score of members of the High Court of Chancery bar ought

2

Bleak House

to be—as here they are—mistily engaged in one of the ten thousand stages of an endless cause, tripping one another up on slippery precedents, groping knee-deep in technicalities, running their goat-hair and horse-hair warded heads against walls of words, and making a pretence of equity with serious faces, as players might. On such an afternoon, the various solicitors in the cause, some two or three of whom have inherited it from their fathers, who made a fortune by it, ought to be—as are they not?—ranged in a line, in a long matted well (but you might look in vain for Truth at the bottom of it), between the registrar's red table and the silk gowns, with bills, cross-bills, answers, rejoinders, injunctions, affidavits, issues, references to masters, masters' reports, mountains of costly nonsense, piled before them. Well may the court be dim, with wasting candles here and there; well may the fog hang heavy in it as if it would never get out; well may the stained glass windows lose their colour, and admit no light of day into the place; well may the uninitiated from the streets, who peep in through the glass panes in the door, be deterred from entrance by its owlish aspect, and by the drawl languidly echoing to the roof from the padded dais where the Lord High Chancellor looks into the lantern that has no light in it, and where the attendant wigs are all stuck in a fog-bank! This is the Court of Chancery; which has its decaying houses and its blighted lands in every shire; which has its worn-out lunatic in every madhouse, and its dead in every churchyard; which has its ruined suitor, with his slipshod heels and threadbare dress, borrowing and begging through the round of every man's acquaintance; which gives to monied might the means abundantly of wearying out the right; which so exhausts finances, patience, courage, hope; so overthrows the brain and breaks the heart; that there is not an honourable man among its practitioners who would not give—who does not often give—the warning, "Suffer any wrong that can be done you rather than come here!"

3

Who happen to be in the Lord Chancellor's court this murky afternoon besides the Lord Chancellor, the counsel in the cause, two or three counsel who are never in any cause, and the well of solicitors before mentioned? There is the registrar below the Judge, in wig and gown; and there are two or three maces, or petty-bags, or privy purses, or whatever they may be, in legal court suits. These are all yawning; for no crumb of amusement ever falls from JARNDYCE AND JARNDYCE (the cause in hand), which was squeezed dry years upon years ago. The short-hand writers, the reporters of the court, and the reporters of the newspapers, invariably decamp with the rest of the regulars when Jarndyce and Jarndyce comes on. Their places are a blank. Standing on a seat at the side of the hall, the better to peer into the curtained sanctuary, is a little mad old woman in a squeezed bonnet, who is always in court, from its sitting to its rising, and always expecting some incomprehensible judgment to be given in her favour. Some say she really is, or was, a party to a suit; but no one knows for certain, because no one cares. She carries some small litter in a reticule which she calls her documents; principally consisting of paper matches and dry lavender. A sallow prisoner has come up, in custody, for the half-dozenth time, to make a personal application "to purge himself of his contempt;" which, being a solitary surviving executor who has fallen into a state of conglomeration about accounts of which it is not pretended that he had ever any knowledge, he is not at all likely ever to do. In the meantime his prospects in life are ended. Another ruined suitor, who periodically appears from Shropshire, and breaks out into efforts to address the Chancellor at the close of the day's business, and who can by no means be made to understand that the Chancellor is legally ignorant of his existence after making it desolate for a quarter of a century, plants himself in a good place and keeps an eye on the Judge, ready to call out "My Lord!" in a voice of sonorous complaint, on the instant of his rising.

JARNDYCE AND JARNDYCE

A few lawyers' clerks and others who know this suitor by sight, linger, on the chance of his furnishing some fun, and enlivening the dismal weather a little.

Jarndyce and Jarndyce drones on. This scarecrow of a suit has, in course of time, become so complicated, that no man alive knows what it means. The parties to it understand it least; but it has been observed that no two Chancery lawyers can talk about it for five minutes, without coming to a total disagreement as to all the premises. Innumerable children have been born into the cause; innumerable young people have married into it; innumerable old people have died out of it. Scores of persons have deliriously found themselves made parties in Jarndyce and Jarndyce, without knowing how or why; whole families have inherited legendary hatreds with the suit. The little plaintiff or defendant, who was promised a new rocking-horse when Jarndyce and Jarndyce should be settled, has grown up, possessed himself of a real horse, and trotted away into the other world. Fair wards of court have faded into mothers and grandmothers; a long procession of Chancellors has come in and gone out; the legion of bills in the suit have been transformed into mere bills of mortality; there are not three Jarndyces left upon the earth perhaps, since old Tom Jarndyce in despair blew his brains out at a coffee-house in Chancery Lane; but Jarndyce and Jarndyce still drags its dreary length before the Court, perennially hopeless.

Jarndyce and Jarndyce has passed into a joke. That is the only good that has ever come of it. It has been death to many, but it is a joke in the profession. Every master in Chancery has had a reference out of it. Every Chancellor was " in it," for somebody or other, when he was counsel at the bar. Good things have been said about it by blue-nosed, bulbous-shoed old benchers, in select port-wine committee after dinner in hall. Articled clerks have been in the habit of fleshing their legal wit upon it. The last Lord Chancellor handled it neatly, when, correcting Mr. Blowers the eminent silk gown who said that such a thing might happen when the sky rained potatoes, he observed, " or when we get through Jarndyce and Jarndyce, Mr. Blowers ; "—a pleasantry that particularly tickled the maces, bags, and purses.

How many people out of the suit, Jarndyce and Jarndyce has stretched forth its unwholesome hand to spoil and corrupt, would be a very wide question. From the master, upon whose impaling files reams of dusty warrants in Jarndyce and Jarndyce have grimly writhed into many shapes ; down to the copying-clerk in the Six Clerks' Office, who has copied his tens of thousands of Chancery-folio-pages under that eternal heading ; no man's nature has been made better by it. In trickery, evasion, procrastination, spoliation, bothera-tion, under false pretences of all sorts, there are influences that can never come to good. The very solicitors' boys who have kept the wretched suitors at bay, by protesting time out of mind that Mr. Chizzle, Mizzle, or otherwise, was particularly engaged and had appointments until dinner, may have got an extra moral twist and shuffle into themselves out of Jarndyce and Jarndyce. The receiver in the cause has acquired a goodly sum of money by it, but has acquired too a distrust of his own mother, and a contempt for his own kind. Chizzle, Mizzle, and otherwise, have lapsed into a habit of vaguely promising themselves that they will look into that outstanding little matter, and see what can be done for Drizzle—who was not well used—when Jarndyce and Jarndyce shall be got out of the office. Shirking and sharking, in all their many varieties, have been sown broad-cast by the ill-fated cause ; and even those who have con-templated its history from the outermost circle of such evil, have been insensibly tempted into a loose way of letting bad things alone to take their own bad course, and a loose belief that if the world go wrong, it was, in some off-hand manner, never meant to go right.

Thus, in the midst of the mud and at the heart of the

fog, sits the Lord High Chancellor in his High Court of Chancery.

"Mr. Tangle," says the Lord High Chancellor, latterly something restless under the eloquence of that learned gentleman.

"Mlud," says Mr. Tangle. Mr. Tangle knows more of Jarndyce and Jarndyce than anybody. He is famous for it—supposed never to have read anything else since he left school.

"Have you nearly concluded your argument?"

"Mlud, no—variety of points—feel it my duty tsubmit —ludship," is the reply that slides out of Mr. Tangle.

"Several members of the bar are still to be heard, I believe?" says the Chancellor, with a slight smile.

Eighteen of Mr. Tangle's learned friends, each armed with a little summary of eighteen hundred sheets, bob up like eighteen hammers in a pianoforte, make eighteen bows, and drop into their eighteen places of obscurity.

"We will proceed with the hearing on Wednesday fort-night," says the Chancellor. For, the question at issue is only a question of costs, a mere bud on the forest tree of the parent suit, and really will come to a settlement one of these days.

The Chancellor rises; the bar rises; the prisoner is brought forward in a hurry; the man from Shropshire cries, "My lord!" Maces, bags, and purses, indignantly proclaim silence, and frown at the man from Shropshire.

"In reference," proceeds the Chancellor, still on Jarndyce and Jarndyce, "to the young girl——"

"Begludship's pardon—boy," says Mr. Tangle, prematurely.

"In reference," proceeds the Chancellor, with extra dis-tinctness, "to the young girl and boy, the two young people,"

(Mr. Tangle crushed.)

"Whom I directed to be in attendance to-day, and who are now in my private room, I will see them and satisfy myself as to the expediency of making the order for their residing with their uncle."

7

Mr. Tangle on his legs again.

"Begludship's pardon—dead."

"With their," Chancellor looking through his double eye-glass at the papers on his desk, "grandfather."

"Begludship's pardon—victim of rash action—brains."

Suddenly a very little counsel, with a terrific bass voice, arises, fully inflated, in the back settlements of the fog, and says, "Will your lordship allow me? I appear for him. He is a cousin, several times removed. I am not at the moment prepared to inform the Court in what exact remove he is a cousin; but he *is* a cousin."

Leaving this address (delivered like a sepulchral message) ringing in the rafters of the roof, the very little counsel drops, and the fog knows him no more. Everybody looks for him. Nobody can see him.

"I will speak with both the young people," says the Chancellor anew, "and satisfy myself on the subject of their residing with their cousin. I will mention the matter to-morrow morning when I take my seat."

The Chancellor is about to bow to the bar, when the prisoner is presented. Nothing can possibly come of the prisoner's conglomeration, but his being sent back to prison; which is soon done. The man from Shropshire ventures another demonstrative "My lord!" but the Chancellor, being aware of him, has dexterously vanished. Everybody else quickly vanishes too. A battery of blue bags is loaded with heavy charges of papers and carried off by clerks; the little mad old woman marches off with her documents; the empty court is locked up. If all the injustice it has committed, and all the misery it has caused, could only be locked up with it, and the whole burnt away in a great funeral pyre,—why so much the better for other parties than the parties in Jarndyce and Jarndyce!

CHAPTER II

It is but a glimpse of the world of fashion that we want on this same miry afternoon. It is not so unlike the Court of Chancery, but that we may pass from the one scene to the other, as the crow flies. Both the world of fashion and the Court of Chancery are things of precedent and usage; over-sleeping Rip Van Winkles, who have played at strange games through a deal of thundery weather; sleeping beauties, whom the Knight will wake one day, when all the stopped spits in the kitchen shall begin to turn prodigiously!

It is not a large world. Relatively even to this world of ours, which has its limits too (as your Highness shall find when you have made the tour of it, and are come to the brink of the void beyond), it is a very little speck. There is much good in it; there are many good and true people in it; it has its appointed place. But the evil of it is, that it is a world wrapped up in too much jeweller's cotton and fine wool, and cannot hear the rushing of the larger worlds, and cannot see them as they circle round the sun. It is a deadened world, and its growth is sometimes unhealthy for want of air.

My Lady Dedlock has returned to her house in town for a few days previous to her departure for Paris, where her ladyship intends to stay some weeks; after which her movements are uncertain. The fashionable intelligence says so, for the comfort of the Parisians, and it knows all fashionable

9

things. To know things otherwise, were to be unfashionable. My Lady Dedlock has been down at what she calls, in familiar conversation, her "place" in Lincolnshire. The waters are out in Lincolnshire. An arch of the bridge in the park has been sapped and sopped away. The adjacent low-lying ground, for half a mile in breadth, is a stagnant river, with melancholy trees for islands in it, and a surface punctured all over, all day long, with falling rain. My Lady Dedlock's "place" has been extremely dreary. The weather, for many a day and night, has been so wet that the trees seem wet through, and the soft loppings and prunings of the woodman's axe can make no crash or crackle as they fall. The deer, looking soaked, leave quagmires, where they pass. The shot of a rifle loses its sharpness in the moist air, and its smoke moves in a tardy little cloud towards the green rise, coppice-topped, that makes a background for the falling rain. The view from my Lady Dedlock's own windows is alternately a lead-coloured view, and a view in Indian ink. The vases on the stone terrace in the foreground catch the rain all day; and the heavy drops fall, drip, drip, drip, upon the broad flagged pavement, called, from old time, the Ghost's Walk, all night. On Sundays, the little church in the park is mouldy; the oaken pulpit breaks out into a cold sweat; and there is a general smell and taste as of the ancient Dedlocks in their graves. My Lady Dedlock (who is childless), looking out in the early twilight from her boudoir at a keeper's lodge, and seeing the light of a fire upon the latticed panes, and smoke rising from the chimney, and a child, chased by a woman, running out into the rain to meet the shining figure of a wrapped-up man coming through the gate, has been put quite out of temper. My Lady Dedlock says she has been "bored to death."

Therefore my Lady Dedlock has come away from the place in Lincolnshire, and has left it to the rain, and the crows, and the rabbits, and the deer, and the partridges and pheasants. The pictures of the Dedlocks past and gone have seemed to vanish into the damp walls in mere lowness of spirits, as the housekeeper has passed along the old rooms, shutting up the shutters. And when they will next come forth again, the fashionable intelligence—which, like the fiend, is omniscient of the past and present, but not the future—cannot yet undertake to say.

Sir Leicester Dedlock is only a baronet, but there is no mightier baronet than he. His family is as old as the hills, and infinitely more respectable. He has a general opinion that the world might get on without hills, but would be done up without Dedlocks. He would on the whole admit Nature to be a good idea (a little low, perhaps, when not enclosed with a park-fence), but an idea dependent for its execution on your great county families. He is a gentleman of strict conscience, disdainful of all littleness and mean-ness, and ready, on the shortest notice, to die any death you may please to mention rather than give occasion for the least impeachment of his integrity. He is an honour-able, obstinate, truthful, high-spirited, intensely prejudiced, perfectly unreasonable man.

Sir Leicester is twenty years, full measure, older than my Lady. He will never see sixty-five again, nor perhaps sixty-six, nor yet sixty-seven. He has a twist of the gout now and then, and walks a little stiffly. He is of a worthy presence, with his light grey hair and whiskers, his fine shirt-frill, his pure white waistcoat, and his blue coat with bright buttons always buttoned. He is ceremonious, stately, most polite on every occasion to my Lady, and holds her personal attractions in the highest estimation. His gallantry to my Lady, which has never changed since he courted her, is the one little touch of romantic fancy in him.

Indeed, he married her for love. A whisper still goes about, that she had not even family; howbeit, Sir Leicester had so much family that perhaps he had enough, and could dispense with any more. But she had beauty, pride, ambition, insolent resolve, and sense enough to portion out a legion of fine ladies. Wealth and station, added to these, soon floated her upward ; and for years, now, my Lady Dedlock has been at the centre of the fashionable intelligence, and at the top of the fashionable tree.

How Alexander wept when he had no more worlds to conquer, everybody knows—or has some reason to know by this time, the matter having been rather frequently mentioned. My Lady Dedlock, having conquered *her* world, fell, not into the melting, but rather into the freezing mood. An exhausted composure, a worn-out placidity, an equanimity of fatigue not to be ruffled by interest or satisfaction, are the trophies of her victory. She is perfectly well-bred. If she could be translated to Heaven to-morrow, she might be expected to ascend without any rapture.

She has beauty still, and, if it be not in its heyday, it is not yet in its autumn. She has a fine face—originally of a character that would be rather called very pretty than handsome, but improved into classicality by the acquired expression of her fashionable state. Her figure is elegant, and has the effect of being tall. Not that she is so, but that "the most is made," as the Honourable Bob Stables has frequently asserted upon oath, "of all her points." The same authority observes, that she is perfectly got up ; and remarks, in commendation of her hair especially, that she is the best-groomed woman in the whole stud.

With all her perfections on her head, my Lady Dedlock has come up from her place in Lincolnshire (hotly pursued by the fashionable intelligence), to pass a few days at her house in town previous to her departure for Paris, where her ladyship intends to stay some weeks, after which her movements are uncertain. And at her house in town, upon this muddy, murky afternoon, presents himself an old-fashioned old gentleman, attorney-at-law, and eke solicitor of the High Court of Chancery, who has the honour of acting as legal adviser of the Dedlocks, and has as many cast-iron boxes in his office with that name outside, as if the present baronet were the coin of the conjurer's trick, and were constantly being juggled through the whole set. Across the hall, and up the stairs, and along the passages, and through the rooms, which are very brilliant in ·the season and very dismal out of it—Fairy-land to visit, but a desert to live in —the old gentleman is conducted, by a Mercury in powder, to my Lady's presence.

The old gentleman is rusty to look at, but is reputed to have made good thrift out of aristocratic marriage settlements and aristocratic wills, and to be very rich. He is surrounded by a mysterious halo of family confidences; of which he is known to be the silent depository. There are noble Mausoleums rooted for centuries in retired glades of parks, among the growing timber and the fern, which perhaps hold fewer noble secrets than walk abroad among men, shut up in the breast of Mr. Tulkinghorn. He is of what is called the old school—a phrase generally meaning any school that seems never to have been young—and wears knee breeches tied with ribbons, and gaiters or stockings. One peculiarity of his black clothes, and of his black stockings, be they silk or worsted, is, that they never shine. Mute, close, irresponsive to any glancing light, his dress is like himself. He never converses, when not professionally consulted. He is found sometimes, speechless but quite at home, at corners of dinner-tables in great country houses, and near doors of drawing-rooms, concerning which the fashionable intelligence is eloquent: where everybody knows him, and where half the Peerage stops to say " How do you do, Mr. Tulkinghorn ? " he receives these salutations with gravity, and buries them along with the rest of his knowledge.

Sir Leicester Dedlock is with my Lady, and is happy to see Mr. Tulkinghorn. There is an air of prescription about him which is always agreeable to Sir Leicester ; he receives it as a kind of tribute. He likes Mr. Tulkinghorn's dress ; there is a kind of tribute in that too. It is eminently respectable, and likewise, in a general way, retainer-like. It expresses, as it were, the steward of the legal mysteries, the butler of the legal cellar, of the Dedlocks.

Has Mr. Tulkinghorn any idea of this himself? It may be so, or it may not; but there is this remarkable circumstance to be noted in everything associated with my Lady Dedlock as one of a class—as one of the leaders and representatives of her little world. She supposes herself to be an inscrutable Being, quite out of the reach and ken of ordinary mortals—seeing herself in her glass, where indeed she looks so. Yet, every dim little star revolving about her, from her maid to the manager of the Italian Opera, knows her weaknesses, prejudices, follies, haughtinesses, and caprices; and lives upon as accurate a calculation and as nice a measure of her moral nature, as her dressmaker takes of her physical proportions. Is a new dress, a new custom, a new singer, a new dancer, a new form of jewellery, a new dwarf or giant, a new chapel, a new anything, to be set up? There are deferential people, in a dozen callings, whom my Lady Dedlock suspects of nothing but prostration before her, who can tell you how to manage her as if she were a baby; who do nothing but nurse her all their lives; who, humbly affecting to follow with profound subservience, lead her and her whole troop after them; who, in hooking one, hook all and bear them off, as Lemuel Gulliver bore away the stately fleet of the majestic Lilliput. "If you want to address our people, sir," say Blaze and Sparkle the jewellers—meaning by our people, Lady Dedlock and the rest—"you must remember that you are not dealing with the general public; you must hit our people in their weakest place, and their weakest place is such a place." "To make this article go down, gentlemen," say Sheen and Gloss the mercers, to their friends the manufacturers, "you must come to us, because we know where to have the fashionable people, and we can make it fashionable." "If you want to get this print upon the tables of my high connexion, sir," says Mr. Sladdery the librarian, "or if you want to get this dwarf or giant into the houses of my high connexion, sir, or if you want to secure to this entertainment, the patronage of my high connexion, sir, you must leave it, if you please, to me ; for I have been accustomed to study the leaders of my high connexion, sir ; and I may tell you, without vanity, that I can turn them round my finger,"—in which Mr. Sladdery, who is an honest man, does not exaggerate at all.

Therefore, while Mr. Tulkinghorn may not know what is passing in the Dedlock mind at present, it is very possible that he may.

" My Lady's cause has been again before the Chancellor, has it, Mr. Tulkinghorn ? " says Sir Leicester, giving him his hand.

" Yes. It has been on again to-day," Mr. Tulkinghorn replies ; making one of his quiet bows to my Lady who is on a sofa near the fire, shading her face with a hand-screen.

" It would be useless to ask," says my Lady, with the dreariness of the place in Lincolnshire still upon her, " whether anything has been done."

" Nothing that *you* would call anything, has been done to-day," replies Mr. Tulkinghorn.

" Nor ever will be," says my Lady.

Sir Leicester has no objection to an interminable Chancery suit. It is a slow, expensive, British, constitutional kind of thing. To be sure, he has not a vital interest in the suit in question, her part in which was the only property my Lady brought him ; and he has a shadowy impression that for his name—the name of Dedlock—to be in a cause, and not in the title of that cause, is a most ridiculous accident. But he regards the Court of Chancery, even if it should involve an occasional delay of justice and a trifling amount of confusion, as a something, devised in conjunction with a variety of other somethings, by the perfection of human wisdom, for the eternal settlement (humanly speaking) of everything. And he is upon the whole of a fixed opinion, that to give the sanction of his countenance to any complaints respecting it, would be to encourage some person in the lower classes to rise up somewhere—like Wat Tyler.

"As a few fresh affidavits have been put upon the file," says Mr. Tulkinghorn, "and as they are short, and as I proceed upon the troublesome principle of begging leave to possess my clients with any new proceedings in a cause;" cautious man Mr. Tulkinghorn, taking no more responsibility than necessary; "and further, as I see you are going to Paris; I have brought them in my pocket."

(Sir Leicester was going to Paris too. by-the-bye, but the delight of the fashionable intelligence was in his Lady.)

Mr. Tulkinghorn takes out his papers, asks permission to place them on a golden talisman of a table at my Lady's elbow, puts on his spectacles, and begins to read by the light of a shaded lamp.

"'In Chancery. Between John Jarndyce——'"

My Lady interrupts, requesting him to miss as many of the formal horrors as he can.

Mr. Tulkinghorn glances over his spectacles, and begins again lower down. My Lady carelessly and scornfully abstracts her attention. Sir Leicester in a great chair looks at the fire, and appears to have a stately liking for the legal repetitions and prolixities, as ranging among the national bulwarks. It happens that the fire is hot, where my Lady sits; and that the hand-screen is more beautiful than useful, being priceless but small. My Lady, changing her position, sees the papers on the table—looks at them nearer—looks at them nearer still—asks impulsively:

"Who copied that?"

Mr. Tulkinghorn stops short, surprised by my Lady's animation and her unusual tone.

"Is it what you people call law-hand?" she asks, looking full at him in her careless way again, and toying with her screen.

"Not quite. Probably"—Mr. Tulkinghorn examines it as he speaks—"the legal character which it has, was acquired after the original hand was formed. Why do you ask?"

"Anything to vary this detestable monotony. O, go on, do!"

Mr. Tulkinghorn reads again. The heat is greater, my Lady screens her face. Sir Leicester dozes, starts up suddenly, and cries "Eh? what do you say?"

"I say I am afraid," says Mr. Tulkinghorn, who had risen hastily, "that Lady Dedlock is ill."

"Faint," my Lady murmurs, with white lips, "only that; but it is like the faintness of death. Don't speak to me. Ring, and take me to my room!"

Mr. Tulkinghorn retires into another chamber; bells ring, feet shuffle and patter, silence ensues. Mercury at last begs Mr. Tulkinghorn to return.

"Better now," quoth Sir Leicester, motioning the lawyer to sit down and read to him alone. "I have been quite alarmed. I never knew my Lady swoon before. But the weather is extremely trying—and she really has been bored to death down at our place in Lincolnshire."

CHAPTER III

I HAVE a great deal of difficulty in beginning to write my portion of these pages, for I know I am not clever. I always knew that. I can remember, when I was a very little girl indeed, I used to say to my doll, when we were alone together, "Now, Dolly, I am not clever, you know very well, and you must be patient with me, like a dear!" And so she used to sit propped up in a great arm-chair, with her beautiful complexion and rosy lips, staring at me—or not so much at me, I think, as at nothing—while I busily stitched away, and told her every one of my secrets.

My dear old doll! I was such a shy little thing that I seldom dared to open my lips, and never dared to open my heart, to anybody else. It almost makes me cry to think what a relief it used to be to me, when I came home from school of a day, to run up-stairs to my room, and say, "O you dear faithful Dolly, I knew you would be expecting me!" and then to sit down on the floor, leaning on the elbow of her great chair, and tell her all I had noticed since we parted. I had always rather a noticing way—not a quick way, O no!—a silent way of noticing what passed before me, and thinking I should like to understand it better. I have not by any means a quick understanding. When I love a person very tenderly indeed, it seems to brighten. But even that may be my vanity.

I was brought up, from my earliest remembrance—like

18

some of the princesses in the fairy stories, only I was not charming—by my godmother. At least I only knew her as such. She was a good, good woman! She went to church three times every Sunday, and to morning prayers on Wednesdays and Fridays, and to lectures whenever there were lectures; and never missed. She was handsome; and if she had ever smiled, would have been (I used to think) like an angel—but she never smiled. She was always grave, and strict. She was so very good herself, I thought, that the badness of other people made her frown all her life. I felt so different from her, even making every allowance for the differences between a child and a woman; I felt so poor, so trifling, and so far off; that I never could be unrestrained with her—no, could never even love her as I wished. It made me very sorry to consider how good she was, and how unworthy of her I was; and I used ardently to hope that I might have a better heart; and I talked it over very often with the dear old doll; but I never loved my godmother as I ought to have loved her, and as I felt I must have loved her if I had been a better girl.

This made me, I dare say, more timid and retiring than I naturally was, and cast me upon Dolly as the only friend with whom I felt at ease. But something happened when I was still quite a little thing, that helped it very much.

I had never heard my mama spoken of. I had never heard of my papa either, but I felt more interested about my mama. I had never worn a black frock, that I could recollect. I had never been shown my mama's grave. I had never been told where it was. Yet I had never been taught to pray for any relation but my godmother. I had more than once approached this subject of my thoughts with Mrs. Rachael, our only servant, who took my light away when I was in bed (another very good woman, but austere to me), and she had only said, "Esther, good night!" and gone away and left me.

Although there were seven girls at the neighbouring school

19

where I was a day boarder, and although they called me little Esther Summerson, I knew none of them at home. All of them were older than I, to be sure (I was the youngest there by a good deal), but there seemed to be some other separation between us besides that, and besides their being far more clever than I was, and knowing much more than I did. One of them, in the first week of my going to the school (I remember it very well), invited me home to a little party, to my great joy. But my godmother wrote a stiff letter declining for me, and I never went. I never went out at all.

It was my birthday. There were holidays at school on other birthdays—none on mine. There were rejoicings at home on other birthdays, as I knew from what I heard the girls relate to one another—there were none on mine. My birthday was the most melancholy day at home, in the whole year.

I have mentioned, that, unless my vanity should deceive me (as I know it may, for I may be very vain, without suspecting it—though indeed I don't), my comprehension is quickened when my affection is. My disposition is very affectionate; and perhaps I might still feel such a wound, if such a wound could be received more than once, with the quickness of that birthday.

Dinner was over, and my godmother and I were sitting at the table before the fire. The clock ticked, the fire clicked; not another sound had been heard in the room, or in the house, for I don't know how long. I happened to look timidly up from my stitching, across the table, at my godmother, and I saw in her face, looking gloomily at me, "It would have been far better, little Esther, that you had had no birthday; that you had never been born!"

I broke out crying and sobbing, and I said "O, dear godmother, tell me, pray do tell me, did mama die on my birthday?"

"No," she returned. "Ask me no more, child!"

DIFFERENT FROM OTHER CHILDREN

" O, do pray tell me something of her. Do now, at last, dear godmother, if you please! What did I do to her? How did I lose her? Why am I so different from other children, and why is it my fault, dear godmother? No, no, no, don't go away. O, speak to me!"

I was in a kind of fright beyond my grief; and I caught hold of her dress, and was kneeling to her. She had been saying all the while, "Let me go!" But now she stood still.

Her darkened face had such power over me, that it stopped me in the midst of my vehemence. I put up my trembling little hand to clasp hers, or to beg her pardon with what earnestness I might, but withdrew it as she looked at me, and laid it on my fluttering heart. She raised me, sat in her chair, and standing me before her, said, slowly, in a cold, low voice—I see her knitted brow, and pointed finger:

"Your mother, Esther, is your disgrace, and you were hers. The time will come—and soon enough—when you will understand this better, and will feel it too, as no one save a woman can. I have forgiven her;" but her face did not relent; "the wrong she did to me, and I say no more of it, though it was greater than you will ever know—than any one will ever know, but I, the sufferer. For yourself, unfortunate girl, orphaned and degraded from the first of these evil anniversaries, pray daily that the sins of others be not visited upon your head, according to what is written. Forget your mother, and leave all other people to forget her who will do her unhappy child that greatest kindness. Now, go!"

She checked me, however, as I was about to depart from her—so frozen as I was!—and added this:

"Submission, self-denial, diligent work, are the preparations for a life begun with such a shadow on it. You are different from other children, Esther, because you were not born, like them, in common sinfulness and wrath. You are set apart."

I went up to my room, and crept to bed, and laid my
doll's cheek against mine wet with tears; and holding that
solitary friend upon my bosom, cried myself to sleep. Imperfect as my understanding of my sorrow was, I knew that
I had brought no joy, at any time, to anybody's heart, and
that I was to no one upon earth what Dolly was to me.

Dear, dear, to think how much time we passed alone
together afterwards, and how often I repeated to the doll
the story of my birthday, and confided to her that I would
try, as hard as ever I could, to repair the fault I had been
born with (of which I confessedly felt guilty and yet innocent),
and would strive as I grew up to be industrious, contented,
and kind-hearted, and to do some good to some one, and
win some love to myself if I could. I hope it is not self-
indulgent to shed these tears as I think of it. I am very
thankful, I am very cheerful, but I cannot quite help their
coming to my eyes.

There! I have wiped them away now, and can go on
again properly.

I felt the distance between my godmother and myself so
much more after the birthday, and felt so sensible of filling
a place in her house which ought to have been empty, that
I found her more difficult of approach, though I was fervently
grateful to her in my heart, than ever. I felt in the same
way towards my school companions; I felt in the same way
towards Mrs. Rachael, who was a widow; and O, towards her
daughter, of whom she was proud, who came to see her once
a fortnight! I was very retired and quiet, and tried to be
very diligent.

One sunny afternoon, when I had come home from school
with my books and portfolio, watching my long shadow at
my side, and as I was gliding up-stairs to my room as usual,
my godmother looked out of the parlour-door, and called me
back. Sitting with her, I found—which was very unusual
indeed—a stranger. A portly important-looking gentleman,
dressed all in black, with a white cravat, large gold watch

seals, a pair of gold eye-glasses, and a large seal-ring upon his little finger.

"This," said my godmother in an under-tone, "is the child." Then she said, in her naturally stern way of speaking, "This is Esther, sir."

The gentleman put up his eye-glasses to look at me, and said, "Come here, my dear!" He shook hands with me, and asked me to take off my bonnet—looking at me all the while. When I had complied, he said, "Ah!" and afterwards "Yes!" And then, taking off his eye-glasses, and folding them in a red case, and leaning back in his arm-chair, turning the case about in his two hands he gave my godmother a nod. Upon that, my godmother said, "You may go up-stairs, Esther!" and I made him my curtsey and left him.

It must have been two years afterwards, and I was almost fourteen, when one dreadful night my godmother and I sat at the fireside. I was reading aloud, and she was listening. I had come down at nine o'clock, as I always did, to read the Bible to her; and was reading, from St. John, how our Saviour stooped down, writing with his finger in the dust, when they brought the sinful woman to him.

"'So when they continued asking him, he lifted up himself and said unto them, He that is without sin among you, let him first cast a stone at her!'"

I was stopped by my godmother's rising, putting her hand to her head, and crying out, in an awful voice, from quite another part of the book:

"'Watch ye therefore! lest coming suddenly he find you sleeping. And what I say unto you, I say unto all, Watch!'"

In an instant, while she stood before me repeating these words, she fell down on the floor. I had no need to cry out; her voice had sounded through the house, and been heard in the street.

She was laid upon her bed. For more than a week she

lay there, little altered outwardly; with her old handsome resolute frown that I so well knew, carved upon her face. Many and many a time, in the day and in the night, with my head upon the pillow by her that my whispers might be plainer to her, I kissed her, thanked her, prayed for her, asked her for her blessing and forgiveness, entreated her to give me the least sign that she knew or heard me. No, no, no. Her face was immoveable. To the very last, and even afterwards, her frown remained unsoftened.

On the day after my poor good godmother was buried, the gentleman in black with the white neckcloth reappeared. I was sent for by Mrs. Rachael, and found him in the same place, as if he had never gone away.

"My name is Kenge," he said; "you may remember it, my child; Kenge and Carboy, Lincoln's Inn."

I replied that I remembered to have seen him once before.

"Pray be seated—here near me. Don't distress yourself; it's of no use. Mrs. Rachael, I needn't inform you who were acquainted with the late Miss Barbary's affairs, that her means die with her; and that this young lady, now her aunt is dead——"

"My aunt, sir!"

"It is really of no use carrying on a deception when no object is to be gained by it," said Mr. Kenge, smoothly. "Aunt in fact, though not in law. Don't distress yourself! Don't weep! Don't tremble! Mrs. Rachael, our young friend has no doubt heard of—the—a—Jarndyce and Jarndyce."

"Never," said Mrs. Rachael.

"Is it possible," pursued Mr. Kenge, putting up his eye-glasses, "that our young friend—I *beg* you won't distress yourself!—never heard of Jarndyce and Jarndyce!"

I shook my head, wondering even what it was.

"Not of Jarndyce and Jarndyce?" said Mr. Kenge, looking over his glasses at me, and softly turning the case about and about, as if he were petting something. "Not of one of the greatest Chancery suits known? Not of Jarndyce and

Jarndyce—the—a—in itself a monument of Chancery practice. In which (I would say) every difficulty, every contingency, every masterly fiction, every form of procedure known in that court, is represented over and over again? It is a cause that could not exist, out of this free and great country. I should say that the aggregate of costs in Jarndyce and Jarndyce, Mrs. Rachael;" I was afraid he addressed himself to her, because I appeared inattentive; "amounts at the present hour to from six-ty to seven-ty thousand pounds!" said Mr. Kenge, leaning back in his chair.

I felt very ignorant, but what could I do? I was so entirely unacquainted with the subject, that I understood nothing about it even then.

"And she really never heard of the cause!" said Mr. Kenge. "Surprising!"

"Miss Barbary, sir," returned Mrs. Rachael, "who is now among the Seraphim——"

("I hope so, I am sure," said Mr. Kenge politely.)

"—Wished Esther only to know what would be serviceable to her. And she knows, from any teaching she has had here, nothing more."

"Well!" said Mr. Kenge. "Upon the whole, very proper. Now to the point," addressing me. "Miss Barbary, your sole relation (in fact, that is; for I am bound to observe that in law you had none), being deceased, and it naturally not being to be expected that Mrs. Rachael——"

"O dear no!" said Mrs. Rachael, quickly.

"Quite so," assented Mr. Kenge;—"that Mrs. Rachael should charge herself with your maintenance and support (I beg you won't distress yourself), you are in a position to receive the renewal of an offer which I was instructed to make to Miss Barbary some two years ago, and which, though rejected then, was understood to be renewable under the lamentable circumstances that have since occurred. Now, if I avow, that I represent, in Jarndyce and Jarndyce, and otherwise, a highly humane, but at the same time singular

25

man, shall I compromise myself by any stretch of my professional caution?" said Mr. Kenge, leaning back in his
chair again, and looking calmly at us both.

He appeared to enjoy beyond everything the sound of
his own voice. I couldn't wonder at that, for it was mellow
and full, and gave great importance to every word he uttered.
He listened to himself with obvious satisfaction, and sometimes gently beat time to his own music with his head, or
rounded a sentence with his hand. I was very much impressed by him—even then, before I knew that he formed
himself on the model of a great lord who was his client, and
that he was generally called Conversation Kenge.

"Mr. Jarndyce," he pursued, "being aware of the—I
would say, desolate—position of our young friend, offers to
place her at a first-rate establishment; where her education
shall be completed, where her comfort shall be secured,
where her reasonable wants shall be anticipated, where she
shall be eminently qualified to discharge her duty in that
station of life unto which it has pleased—shall I say Providence?—to call her."

My heart was filled so full, both by what he said, and by
his affecting manner of saying it, that I was not able to
speak, though I tried.

"Mr. Jarndyce," he went on, "makes no condition, beyond
expressing his expectation, that our young friend will not
at any time remove herself from the establishment in question without his knowledge and concurrence. That she will
faithfully apply herself to the acquisition of those accomplishments, upon the exercise of which she will be ultimately
dependent. That she will tread in the paths of virtue and
honour, and—the—a——so forth."

I was still less able to speak, than before.

"Now, what does our young friend say?" proceeded Mr.
Kenge. "Take time, take time! I pause for her reply.
But take time!"

What the destitute subject of such an offer tried to say,

I need not repeat. What she did say, I could more easily tell, if it were worth the telling. What she felt, and will feel to her dying hour, I could never relate.

This interview took place at Windsor, where I had passed (as far as I knew) my whole life. On that day week, amply provided with all necessaries, I left it, inside the stage-coach, for Reading.

Mrs. Rachael was too good to feel any emotion at parting, but I was not so good, and wept bitterly. I thought that I ought to have known her better after so many years, and ought to have made myself enough of a favourite with her to make her sorry then. When she gave me one cold parting kiss upon my forehead, like a thaw-drop from the stone porch—it was a very frosty day—I felt so miserable and self-reproachful, that I clung to her and told her it was my fault, I knew, that she could say good-bye so easily!

"No, Esther!" she returned. "It is your misfortune!"

The coach was at the little lawn-gate—we had not come out until we heard the wheels—and thus I left her, with a sorrowful heart. She went in before my boxes were lifted to the coach-roof, and shut the door. As long as I could see the house, I looked back at it from the window, through my tears. My godmother had left Mrs. Rachael all the little property she possessed; and there was to be a sale; and an old hearthrug with roses on it, which always seemed to me the first thing in the world I had ever seen, was hanging outside in the frost and snow. A day or two before, I had wrapped the dear old doll in her own shawl, and quietly laid her—I am half ashamed to tell it—in the garden-earth, under the tree that shaded my old window. I had no companion left but my bird, and him I carried with me in his cage.

When the house was out of sight, I sat, with my bird-cage in the straw at my feet, forward on the low seat, to look out of the high window; watching the frosty trees, that were like beautiful pieces of spar; and the fields all smooth and white with last night's snow; and the sun, so red but yielding so little heat; and the ice, dark like metal, where the skaters and sliders had brushed the snow away. There was a gentleman in the coach who sat on the opposite seat, and looked very large in a quantity of wrappings; but he sat gazing out of the other window, and took no notice of me.

I thought of my dead godmother; of the night when I read to her; of her frowning so fixedly and sternly in her bed; of the strange place I was going to; of the people I should find there, and what they would be like, and what they would say to me; when a voice in the coach gave me a terrible start.

It said, "What the de-vil are you crying for?"

I was so frightened that I lost my voice, and could only answer in a whisper. "Me, sir?" For of course I knew it must have been the gentleman in the quantity of wrappings, though he was still looking out of his window.

"Yes, you," he said, turning round.

"I didn't know I was crying, sir," I faltered.

"But you are!" said the gentleman. "Look here!" He came quite opposite to me from the other corner of the coach, brushed one of his large furry cuffs across my eyes (but without hurting me), and showed me that it was wet.

"There! Now you know you are," he said. "Don't you?"

"Yes, sir," I said.

"And what are you crying for?" said the gentleman. "Don't you want to go there?"

"Where, sir?"

"Where? Why, wherever you are going," said the gentleman.

"I am very glad to go there, sir," I answered.

"Well, then! Look glad!" said the gentleman.

I thought he was very strange; or at least that what I could see of him was very strange, for he was wrapped up to the chin, and his face was almost hidden in a fur cap, with broad fur straps at the side of his head, fastened under his chin ; but I was composed again, and not afraid of him. So I told him that I thought I must have been crying, because of my godmother's death, and because of Mrs. Rachael's not being sorry to part with me.

"Con-found Mrs. Rachael !" said the gentleman. "Let her fly away in a high wind on a broomstick !"

I began to be really afraid of him now, and looked at him with the greatest astonishment. But I thought that he had pleasant eyes, although he kept on muttering to himself in an angry manner, and calling Mrs. Rachael names.

After a little while, he opened his outer wrapper, which appeared to me large enough to wrap up the whole coach, and put his arm down into a deep pocket in the side.

"Now, look here !" he said. "In this paper," which was nicely folded, "is a piece of the best plum-cake that can be got for money—sugar on the outside an inch thick, like fat on mutton chops. Here's a little pie (a gem this is, both for size and quality), made in France. And what do you suppose it's made of ? Livers of fat geese. There's a pie ! Now let's see you eat 'em."

"Thank you, sir," I replied, "thank you very much indeed, but I hope you won't be offended ; they are too rich for me."

"Floored again !" said the gentleman, which I didn't at all understand ; and threw them both out of window.

He did not speak to me any more, until he got out of the coach a little way short of Reading, when he advised me to be a good girl, and to be studious ; and shook hands with me. I must say I was relieved by his departure. We left him at a milestone. I often walked past it afterwards, and never for a long time, without thinking of him, and half expecting to meet him. But I never did ; and so, as time went on, he passed out of my mind.

When the coach stopped, a very neat lady looked up at the window, and said :

" Miss Donny."

" No, ma'am, Esther Summerson."

" That is quite right," said the lady, " Miss Donny."

I now understood that she introduced herself by that name, and begged Miss Donny's pardon for my mistake, and pointed out my boxes at her request. Under the direction of a very neat maid, they were put outside a very small green carriage; and then Miss Donny, the maid, and I, got inside, and were driven away.

"Everything is ready for you, Esther," said Miss Donny; "and the scheme of your pursuits has been arranged in exact accordance with the wishes of your guardian, Mr. Jarndyce."

" Of —— did you say, ma'am ? "

" Of your guardian, Mr. Jarndyce," said Miss Donny.

I was so bewildered that Miss Donny thought the cold had been too severe for me, and lent me her smelling-bottle.

" Do you know my—guardian, Mr. Jarndyce, ma'am ? " I asked, after a good deal of hesitation.

" Not personally, Esther," said Miss Donny; "merely through his solicitors, Messrs. Kenge and Carboy, of London. A very superior gentleman, Mr. Kenge. Truly eloquent indeed. Some of his periods quite majestic ! "

I felt this to be very true, but was too confused to attend to it. Our speedy arrival at our destination, before I had time to recover myself, increased my confusion; and I never shall forget the uncertain and the unreal air of everything at Greenleaf (Miss Donny's house), that afternoon !

But I soon became used to it. I was so adapted to the routine of Greenleaf before long, that I seemed to have been there a great while : and almost to have dreamed rather than really lived, my old life at my godmother's. Nothing could be more precise, exact, and orderly, than Greenleaf. There was a time for everything all round the dial of the clock, and everything was done at its appointed moment.

We were twelve boarders, and there were two Miss Donnys,

twins. It was understood that I would have to depend, by-and-by, on my qualifications as a governess; and I was not only instructed in everything that was taught at Greenleaf, but was very soon engaged in helping to instruct others. Although I was treated in every other respect like the rest of the school, this single difference was made in my case from the first. As I began to know more, I taught more, and so in course of time I had plenty to do, which I was very fond of doing, because it made the dear girls fond of me. At last, whenever a new pupil came who was a little downcast and unhappy, she was so sure—indeed I don't know why— to make a friend of me, that all new-comers were confided to my care. They said I was so gentle; but I am sure *they* were! I often thought of the resolution I had made on my birthday, to try to be industrious, contented, and true-hearted, and to do some good to some one, and win some love if I could; and indeed, indeed, I felt almost ashamed to have done so little and have won so much.

I passed at Greenleaf six happy, quiet years. I never saw in any face there, thank Heaven, on my birthday, that it would have been better if I had never been born. When the day came round, it brought me so many tokens of affectionate remembrance that my room was beautiful with them from New Year's Day to Christmas.

In those six years I had never been away, except on visits at holiday time in the neighbourhood. After the first six months or so, I had taken Miss Donny's advice in reference to the propriety of writing to Mr. Kenge, to say that I was happy and grateful; and with her approval I had written such a letter. I had received a formal answer acknowledging its receipt, and saying, "We note the contents thereof, which shall be duly communicated to our client." After that, I sometimes heard Miss Donny and her sister mention how regular my accounts were paid; and about twice a year I ventured to write a similar letter. I always received by return of post exactly the same answer, in the same round hand; with the signature of Kenge and Carboy in another writing, which I supposed to be Mr. Kenge's.

It seems so curious to me to be obliged to write all this about myself! As if this narrative were the narrative of *my* life! But my little body will soon fall into the background now.

Six quiet years (I find I am saying it for the second time) I had passed at Greenleaf, seeing in those around me, as it might be in a looking-glass, every stage of my own growth and change there, when, one November morning, I received this letter. I omit the date.

Old Square, Lincoln's Inn.

Madam,

Jarndyce and Jarndyce.

Our c̄l̄t̄ Mr. Jarndyce being ā̄b̄t̄ to r̄ēc̄ē into his house, under an Order of the C̄t̄ of C̄h̄ȳ, a Ward o̲f̲ the C̄t̄ in this cause, for whom he wishes to secure an e̲l̲g̲b̲l̲e̲ c̲o̲m̲p̲n̲, directs u̲s̲ t̲o̲ inform you that he will be glad of your s̲e̲r̲c̲e̲s̲ in the āf̄s̄d̄ capacity.

We have ār̄r̄n̄ḡd̄ for your being f̄ōr̄d̄ēd̄, carriage free, p̄r̄ eight o'clock coach from Reading, on Monday morning next, to White Horse Cellar, Piccadilly, London, w̲h̲e̲r̲e̲ o̲n̲e̲ o̲f̲ our c̄l̄k̄s̄ will be in waiting to convey you to our ōf̄f̄ē as above.

We are, Madam, Your obed̄t̄ Serv̄ᵃ̄,

Kenge and Carboy.

Miss Esther Summerson.

O, never, never, never shall I forget the emotion this letter caused in the house! It was so tender in them to care so much for me; it was so gracious in that Father who had not forgotten me, to have made my orphan way so smooth and easy, and to have inclined so many youthful natures towards me; that I could hardly bear it. Not that I would have had them less sorry—I am afraid not; but the pleasure of it, and the pain of it, and the pride and joy of it, and the humble regret of it, were so blended, that my heart seemed almost breaking while it was full of rapture.

The letter gave me only five days' notice of my removal. When every minute added to the proofs of love and kindness that were given me in those five days; and when at last the morning came, and when they took me through all the rooms that I might see them for the last time; and when some cried, " Esther, dear, say good-bye to me here, at my bedside, where you first spoke so kindly to me!" and when others asked me only to write their names, " With Esther's love;" and when they all surrounded me with their parting presents, and clung to me weeping, and cried, " What shall we do when dear, dear Esther's gone!" and when I tried to tell them how forbearing, and how good they had all been to me, and how I blessed, and thanked them every one; what a heart I had!

And when the two Miss Donnys grieved as much to part with me, as the least among them; and when the maids said, " Bless you, miss, wherever you go!" and when the ugly lame old gardener, who I thought had hardly noticed me in all those years, came panting after the coach to give me a little nosegay of geraniums, and told me I had been the light of his eyes—indeed the old man said so!—what a heart I had then!

And could I help it, if with all this, and the coming to the little school, and the unexpected sight of the poor children outside waving their hats and bonnets to me, and of a grey-haired gentleman and lady, whose daughter I had helped to teach and at whose house I had visited (who were said to be the proudest people in all that country), caring for nothing but calling out, " Good-bye, Esther. May you be very happy!"—could I help it if I was quite bowed down in the coach by myself, and said, " O, I am so thankful, I am so thankful!" many times over!

But of course I soon considered that I must not take tears where I was going, after all that had been done for me. Therefore, of course, I made myself sob less, and persuaded myself to be quiet by saying very often, "Esther, now you really must! This *will not* do!" I cheered myself up pretty well at last, though I am afraid I was longer about it than I ought to have been; and when I had cooled my eyes with lavender water, it was time to watch for London.

I was quite persuaded that we were there, when we were ten miles off; and when we really were there, that we should never get there. However, when we began to jolt upon a stone pavement, and particularly when every other conveyance seemed to be running into us, and we seemed to be running into every other conveyance, I began to believe that we really were approaching the end of our journey. Very soon afterwards we stopped.

A young gentleman who had inked himself by accident, addressed me from the pavement, and said, "I am from Kenge and Carboy's, miss, of Lincoln's Inn."

"If you please, sir," said I.

He was very obliging; and as he handed me into a fly, after superintending the removal of my boxes, I asked him whether there was a great fire anywhere? For the streets were so full of dense brown smoke that scarcely anything was to be seen.

"O dear no, miss," he said. "This is a London particular."

I had never heard of such a thing.

"A fog, miss," said the young gentleman.

"O indeed!" said I.

We drove slowly through the dirtiest and darkest streets that ever were seen in the world (I thought), and in such a distracting state of confusion that I wondered how the people kept their senses, until we passed into sudden quietude under an old gateway, and drove on through a silent square until we came to an odd nook in a corner, where there was an entrance up a steep, broad flight of stairs, like an entrance to a church. And there really was a churchyard, outside under some cloisters, for I saw the gravestones from the staircase window.

GOING BEFORE THE CHANCELLOR

This was Kenge and Carboy's. The young gentleman showed me through an outer office into Mr. Kenge's room —there was no one in it—and politely put an arm-chair for me by the fire. He then called my attention to a little looking-glass, hanging from a nail on one side of the chimney-piece.

"In case you should wish to look at yourself, miss, after the journey, as you're going before the Chancellor. Not that it's requisite, I am sure," said the young gentleman civilly.

"Going before the Chancellor?" I said, startled for a moment.

"Only a matter of form, miss," returned the young gentleman. "Mr. Kenge is in Court now. He left his compliments, and would you partake of some refreshment;" there were biscuits and a decanter of wine on a small table; "and look over the paper;" which the young gentleman gave me as he spoke. He then stirred the fire, and left me.

Everything was so strange—the stranger from its being night in the day-time, the candles burning with a white flame, and looking raw and cold—that I read the words in the newspaper without knowing what they meant, and found myself reading the same words repeatedly. As it was of no use going on in that way, I put the paper down, took a peep at my bonnet in the glass to see if it was neat, and looked at the room which was not half lighted, and at the shabby dusty tables, and at the piles of writings, and at a bookcase full of the most inexpressive-looking books that ever had anything to say for themselves. Then I went on, thinking, thinking, thinking; and the fire went on, burning, burning, burning; and the candles went on flickering and guttering, and there were no snuffers—until the young gentleman by-and-by brought a very dirty pair; for two hours.

At last Mr. Kenge came. *He* was not altered; but he was surprised to see how altered I was; and appeared quite pleased. "As you are going to be the companion of the young lady who is now in the Chancellor's private room,

Miss Summerson," he said, "we thought it well that you should be in attendance also. You will not be discomposed by the Lord Chancellor, I dare say?"

"No, sir," I said, "I don't think I shall." Really not seeing, on consideration, why I should be.

So Mr. Kenge gave me his arm, and we went round the corner, under a colonnade, and in at a side door. And so we came, along a passage, into a comfortable sort of room, where a young lady and a young gentleman were standing near a great, loud-roaring fire. A screen was interposed between them and it, and they were leaning on the screen, talking.

They both looked up when I came in, and I saw in the young lady, with the fire shining upon her, such a beautiful girl! With such rich golden hair, such soft blue eyes, and such a bright, innocent, trusting face!

"Miss Ada," said Mr. Kenge, "this is Miss Summerson."

She came to meet me with a smile of welcome and her hand extended, but seemed to change her mind in a moment, and kissed me. In short, she had such a natural, captivating, winning manner, that in a few minutes we were sitting in the window-seat, with the light of the fire upon us, talking together, as free and happy as could be.

What a load off my mind! It was so delightful to know that she could confide in me, and like me! it was so good of her, and so encouraging to me!

The young gentleman was her distant cousin, she told me, and his name Richard Carstone. He was a handsome youth, with an ingenuous face, and a most engaging laugh; and after she had called him up to where we sat, he stood by us, in the light of the fire too, talking gaily, like a light-hearted boy. He was very young; not more than nineteen then, if quite so much, but nearly two years older than she was. They were both orphans, and (what was very unexpected and curious to me) had never met before that day. Our all three coming together for the first time, in such an unusual place, was a thing to talk about; and we talked about it; and the fire, which had left off roaring, winked its red eyes at us— as Richard said—like a drowsy old Chancery lion.

We conversed in a low tone, because a full-dressed gentleman in a bag wig frequently came in and out, and when he did so, we could hear a drawling sound in the distance, which he said was one of the counsel in our case addressing the Lord Chancellor. He told Mr. Kenge that the Chancellor would be up in five minutes; and presently we heard a bustle, and a tread of feet, and Mr. Kenge said that the Court had risen, and his lordship was in the next room.

The gentleman in the bag wig opened the door almost directly, and requested Mr. Kenge to come in. Upon that, we all went into the next room; Mr. Kenge first, with my darling—it is so natural to me now, that I can't help writing it; and there, plainly dressed in black, and sitting in an arm-chair at a table near the fire, was his lordship, whose robe, trimmed with beautiful gold-lace, was thrown upon another chair. He gave us a searching look as we entered, but his manner was both courtly and kind.

The gentleman in the bag wig laid bundles of papers on his lordship's table, and his lordship silently selected one, and turned over the leaves.

"Miss Clare," said the Lord Chancellor. "Miss Ada Clare?"

Mr. Kenge presented her, and his lordship begged her to sit down near him. That he admired her, and was interested by her, even *I* could see in a moment. It touched me, that the home of such a beautiful young creature should be represented by that dry official place. The Lord High Chancellor, at his best, appeared so poor a substitute for the love and pride of parents.

"The Jarndyce in question," said the Lord Chancellor, still turning over leaves, "is Jarndyce of Bleak House."

"Jarndyce of Bleak House, my lord," said Mr. Kenge.

"A dreary name," said the Lord Chancellor.

37

"But not a dreary place at present, my lord," said Mr. Kenge.

"And Bleak House," said his lordship, "is in—— "

"Hertfordshire, my lord."

"Mr. Jarndyce of Bleak House is not married?" said his lordship.

"He is not, my lord," said Mr. Kenge.

A pause.

"Young Mr. Richard Carstone is present?" said the Lord Chancellor, glancing towards him.

Richard bowed and stepped forward.

"Hum!" said the Lord Chancellor, turning over more leaves.

"Mr. Jarndyce of Bleak House, my lord," Mr. Kenge observed, in a low voice, "if I may venture to remind your lordship, provides a suitable companion for—— "

"For Mr. Richard Carstone?" I thought (but I am not quite sure) I heard his lordship say, in an equally low voice, and with a smile.

"For Miss Ada Clare. This is the young lady. Miss Summerson."

His lordship gave me an indulgent look, and acknowledged my curtsey very graciously.

"Miss Summerson is not related to any party in the cause, I think?"

"No, my lord."

Mr. Kenge leant over before it was quite said, and whispered. His lordship, with his eyes upon his papers, listened, nodded twice or thrice, turned over more leaves, and did not look towards me again, until we were going away.

Mr. Kenge now retired, and Richard with him, to where I was, near the door, leaving my pet (it is so natural to me that again I can't help it!) sitting near the Lord Chancellor; with whom his lordship spoke a little apart; asking her, as she told me afterwards, whether she had well reflected on

The Little Old Lady

the proposed arrangement, and if she thought she would be happy under the roof of Mr. Jarndyce of Bleak House, and why she thought so? Presently he rose courteously and released her, and then he spoke for a minute or two with Richard Carstone; not seated, but standing, and altogether with more ease and less ceremony—as if he still knew, though he *was* Lord Chancellor, how to go straight to the candour of a boy.

"Very well!" said his lordship aloud. "I shall make the order. Mr. Jarndyce of Bleak House has chosen, so far as I may judge," and this was when he looked at me, "a very good companion for the young lady, and the arrangement altogether seems the best of which the circumstances admit."

He dismissed us pleasantly, and we all went out, very much obliged to him for being so affable and polite; by which he had certainly lost no dignity, but seemed to us to have gained some.

When we got under the colonnade, Mr. Kenge remembered that he must go back for a moment, to ask a question; and left us in the fog, with the Lord Chancellor's carriage and servants waiting for him to come out.

"Well!" said Richard Carstone, "*that's* over! And where do we go next, Miss Summerson?"

"Don't you know?" I said.

"Not in the least," said he.

"And don't *you* know, my love?" I asked Ada.

"No!" said she. "Don't you?"

"Not at all!" said I.

We looked at one another, half laughing at our being like the children in the wood, when a curious little old woman in a squeezed bonnet, and carrying a reticule, came curtseying and smiling up to us, with an air of great ceremony.

"O!" said she. "The wards in Jarndyce! Ve-ry happy, I am sure, to have the honour! It is a good omen for youth, and hope, and beauty, when they find themselves in this place, and don't know what's to come of it."

"Mad!" whispered Richard, not thinking she could hear him.

"Right! Mad, young gentleman," she returned so quickly that he was quite abashed. "I was a ward myself. I was not mad at that time," curtseying low, and smiling between every little sentence. "I had youth and hope. I believe, beauty. It matters very little now. Neither of the three served, or saved me. I have the honour to attend Court regularly. With my documents. I expect a judgment. Shortly. On the Day of Judgment. I have discovered that the sixth seal mentioned in the Revelations is the Great Seal. It has been open a long time! Pray accept my blessing."

As Ada was a little frightened, I said, to humour the poor old lady, that we were much obliged to her.

"Ye-es!" she said mincingly. "I imagine so. And here is Conversation Kenge. With *his* documents! How does your honourable worship do?"

"Quite well, quite well! Now don't be troublesome, that's a good soul!" said Mr. Kenge, leading the way back.

"By no means," said the poor old lady, keeping up with Ada and me. "Anything but troublesome. I shall confer estates on both,—which is not being troublesome, I trust? I expect a judgment. Shortly. On the Day of Judgment. This is a good omen for you. Accept my blessing!"

She stopped at the bottom of the steep, broad flight of stairs; but we looked back as we went up, and she was still there, saying, still with a curtsey and a smile between every little sentence, "Youth. And hope. And beauty. And Chancery. And Conversation Kenge! Ha! Pray accept my blessing!"

CHAPTER IV

WE were to pass the night, Mr. Kenge told us when we arrived in his room, at Mrs. Jellyby's; and then he turned to me, and said he took it for granted I knew who Mrs. Jellyby was?

"I really don't, sir," I returned. "Perhaps Mr. Carstone —or Miss Clare—— "

But no, they knew nothing whatever about Mrs. Jellyby.

"In-deed! Mrs. Jellyby," said Mr. Kenge, standing with his back to the fire, and casting his eyes over the dusty hearth-rug as if it were Mrs. Jellyby's biography, "is a lady of very remarkable strength of character, who devotes herself entirely to the public. She has devoted herself to an extensive variety of public subjects, at various times, and is at present (until something else attracts her) devoted to the subject of Africa; with a view to the general cultivation of the coffee berry—*and* the natives—and the happy settlement, on the banks of the African rivers, of our superabundant home population. Mr. Jarndyce, who is desirous to aid any work that is considered likely to be a good work, and who is much sought after by philanthropists, has, I believe, a very high opinion of Mrs. Jellyby."

Mr. Kenge, adjusting his cravat, then looked at us.

"And Mr. Jellyby, sir?" suggested Richard.

"Ah! Mr. Jellyby," said Mr. Kenge, "is—a—I don't

know that I can describe him to you better than by saying that he is the husband of Mrs. Jellyby."

"A nonentity, sir?" said Richard, with a droll look.

"I don't say that," returned Mr. Kenge, gravely. "I can't say that, indeed, for I know nothing whatever *of* Mr. Jellyby. I never, to my knowledge, had the pleasure of seeing Mr. Jellyby. He may be a very superior man ; but he is, so to speak, merged—Merged—in the more shining qualities of his wife." Mr. Kenge proceeded to tell us that as the road to Bleak House would have been very long, dark, and tedious, on such an evening, and as we had been travelling already, Mr. Jarndyce had himself proposed this arrangement. A carriage would be at Mrs. Jellyby's to convey us out of town, early in the forenoon of to-morrow.

He then rang a little bell, and the young gentleman came in. Addressing him by the name of Guppy, Mr. Kenge inquired whether Miss Summerson's boxes and the rest of the baggage had been "sent round." Mr. Guppy said yes, they had been sent round, and a coach was waiting to take us round too, as soon as we pleased.

"Then it only remains," said Mr. Kenge, shaking hands with us, "for me to express my lively satisfaction in (good day, Miss Clare!) the arrangement this day concluded, and my (*good* bye to you, Miss Summerson!) lively hope that it will conduce to the happiness, the (glad to have had the honour of making your acquaintance, Mr. Carstone!) welfare, the advantage in all points of view, of all concerned! Guppy, see the party safely there."

"Where *is* 'there,' Mr. Guppy?" said Richard, as we went down-stairs.

"No distance," said Mr. Guppy; "round in Thavies Inn, you know."

"I can't say I know where it is, for I come from Winchester, and am strange in London."

"Only round the corner," said Mr. Guppy. "We just twist up Chancery Lane, and cut along Holborn, and there

42

we are in four minutes' time, as near as a toucher. This is about a London particular *now*, ain't it, miss?" He seemed quite delighted with it on my account.

"The fog is very dense, indeed!" said I.

"Not that it affects you, though, I'm sure," said Mr. Guppy, putting up the steps. "On the contrary, it seems to do you good, miss, judging from your appearance."

I knew he meant well in paying me this compliment, so I laughed at myself for blushing at it, when he had shut the door and got upon the box; and we all three laughed, and chatted about our inexperience, and the strangeness of London, until we turned up under an archway, to our destination: a narrow street of high houses, like an oblong cistern to hold the fog. There was a confused little crowd of people, principally children, gathered about the house at which we stopped, which had a tarnished brass plate on the door, with the inscription, JELLYBY.

"Don't be frightened!" said Mr. Guppy, looking in at the coach-window. "One of the young Jellybys been and got his head through the area railings!"

"O poor child," said I, "let me out, if you please!"

"Pray be careful of yourself, miss. The young Jellybys are always up to something," said Mr. Guppy.

I made my way to the poor child, who was one of the dirtiest little unfortunates I ever saw, and found him very hot and frightened, and crying loudly, fixed by the neck between two iron railings, while a milkman and a beadle, with the kindest intentions possible, were endeavouring to drag him back by the legs, under a general impression that his skull was compressible by those means. As I found (after pacifying him), that he was a little boy, with a naturally large head, I thought that, perhaps, where his head could go, his body could follow, and mentioned that the best mode of extrication might be to push him forward. This was so favourably received by the milkman and beadle, that he would immediately have been pushed into the area,

43

if I had not held his pinafore, while Richard and Mr. Guppy ran down through the kitchen, to catch him when he should be released. At last he was happily got down without any accident, and then he began to beat Mr. Guppy with a hoop-stick in quite a frantic manner.

Nobody had appeared belonging to the house, except a person in pattens, who had been poking at the child from below with a broom; I don't know with what object, and I don't think she did. I therefore supposed that Mrs. Jellyby was not at home; and was quite surprised when the person appeared in the passage without the pattens, and going up to the back room on the first floor, before Ada and me, announced us as, "Them two young ladies, Missis Jellyby!" We passed several more children on the way up, whom it was difficult to avoid treading on in the dark; and as we came into Mrs. Jellyby's presence, one of the poor little things fell down-stairs—down a whole flight (as it sounded to me), with a great noise.

Mrs. Jellyby, whose face reflected none of the uneasiness which we could not help showing in our own faces, as the dear child's head recorded its passage with a bump on every stair —Richard afterwards said he counted seven, besides one for the landing—received us with perfect equanimity. She was a pretty, very diminutive, plump woman, of from forty to fifty, with handsome eyes, though they had a curious habit of seeming to look a long way off. As if—I am quoting Richard again—they could see nothing nearer than Africa!

"I am very glad indeed," said Mrs. Jellyby, in an agreeable voice, "to have the pleasure of receiving you. I have a great respect for Mr. Jarndyce; and no one in whom he is interested can be an object of indifference to me."

We expressed our acknowledgments, and sat down behind the door where there was a lame invalid of a sofa. Mrs. Jellyby had very good hair, but was too much occupied with her African duties to brush it. The shawl in which she had been loosely muffled, dropped on to her chair when she advanced to us; and as she turned to resume her seat, we could not help noticing that her dress didn't nearly meet up the back, and that the open space was railed across with a lattice-work of stay-lace—like a summer-house.

The room, which was strewn with papers and nearly filled by a great writing-table covered with similar litter, was, I must say, not only very untidy, but very dirty. We were obliged to take notice of that with our sense of sight, even while, with our sense of hearing, we followed the poor child who had tumbled down-stairs: I think into the back kitchen, where somebody seemed to stifle him.

But what principally struck us was a jaded, and unhealthy-looking, though by no means plain girl, at the writing-table, who sat biting the feather of her pen, and staring at us. I suppose nobody ever was in such a state of ink. And, from her tumbled hair to her pretty feet, which were disfigured with frayed and broken satin slippers trodden down at heel, she really seemed to have no article of dress upon her, from a pin upwards, that was in its proper condition or its right place.

"You find me, my dears," said Mrs. Jellyby, snuffing the two great office candles in tin candlesticks which made the room taste strongly of hot tallow (the fire had gone out, and there was nothing in the grate but ashes, a bundle of wood, and a poker), "you find me, my dears, as usual, very busy; but that you will excuse. The African project at present employs my whole time. It involves me in correspondence with public bodies, and with private individuals anxious for the welfare of their species all over the country. I am happy to say it is advancing. We hope by this time next year to have from a hundred and fifty to two hundred healthy families cultivating coffee and educating the natives of Borrioboola-Gha, on the left bank of the Niger."

As Ada said nothing, but looked at me, I said it must be very gratifying,

"It *is* gratifying," said Mrs. Jellyby. "It involves the

45

devotion of all my energies, such as they are ; but that is nothing, so that it succeeds ; and I am more confident of success every day. Do you know, Miss Summerson, I almost wonder that *you* never turned your thoughts to Africa."

This application of the subject was really so unexpected to me, that I was quite at a loss how to receive it. I hinted that the climate——

"The finest climate in the world!" said Mrs. Jellyby.

" Indeed, ma'am ? "

"Certainly. With precaution," said Mrs. Jellyby. " You may go into Holborn, without precaution, and be run over. You may go into Holborn, with precaution, and never be run over. Just so with Africa."

I said, " No doubt."—I meant as to Holborn.

" If you would like," said Mrs. Jellyby, putting a number of papers towards us, " to look over some remarks on that head, and on the general subject (which have been extensively circulated), while I finish a letter I am now dictating—to my eldest daughter, who is my amanuensis—— "

The girl at the table left off biting her pen, and made a return to our recognition, which was half bashful and half sulky.

" —I shall then have finished for the present," proceeded Mrs. Jellyby, with a sweet smile ; " though my work is never done. Where are you, Caddy ? "

" ' Presents her compliments to Mr. Swallow, and begs—— ' " said Caddy.

" ' And begs,' " said Mrs. Jellyby, dictating, " ' to inform him, in reference to his letter of inquiry on the African project.'—No, Peepy ! Not on any account ! "

Peepy (so self-named) was the unfortunate child who had fallen down-stairs, who now interrupted the correspondence by presenting himself, with a strip of plaister on his forehead, to exhibit his wounded knees, in which Ada and I did not know which to pity most—the bruises or the dirt. Mrs.

Jellyby merely added, with the serene composure with which she said everything, "Go along, you naughty Peepy!" and fixed her fine eyes on Africa again.

However, as she at once proceeded with her dictation, and as I interrupted nothing by doing it, I ventured quietly to stop poor Peepy as he was going out, and to take him up to nurse. He looked very much astonished at it, and at Ada's kissing him; but soon fell fast asleep in my arms, sobbing at longer and longer intervals, until he was quiet. I was so occupied with Peepy that I lost the letter in detail, though I derived such a general impression from it of the momentous importance of Africa, and the utter insignificance of all other places and things, that I felt quite ashamed to have thought so little about it.

"Six o'clock!" said Mrs. Jellyby. "And our dinner hour is nominally (for we dine at all hours) five! Caddy, show Miss Clare and Miss Summerson their rooms. You will like to make some change, perhaps? You will excuse me, I know, being so much occupied. O, that very bad child! Pray put him down, Miss Summerson!"

I begged permission to retain him, truly saying that he was not at all troublesome; and carried him up-stairs and laid him on my bed. Ada and I had two upper rooms, with a door of communication between. They were excessively bare and disorderly, and the curtain to my window was fastened up with a fork.

"You would like some hot water, wouldn't you?" said Miss Jellyby, looking round for a jug with a handle to it, but looking in vain.

"If it is not being troublesome," said we.

"O, it's not the trouble," returned Miss Jellyby; "the question is, if there *is* any."

The evening was so very cold, and the rooms had such a marshy smell, that I must confess it was a little miserable; and Ada was half crying. We soon laughed, however, and were busily unpacking, when Miss Jellyby came back to say, that she was sorry there was no hot water ; but they couldn't find the kettle, and the boiler was out of order.

We begged her not to mention it, and made all the haste we could to get down to the fire again. But all the little children had come up to the landing outside, to look at the phenomenon of Peepy lying on my bed ; and our attention was distracted by the constant apparition of noses and fingers, in situations of danger between the hinges of the doors. It was impossible to shut the door of either room ; for my lock, with no knob to it, looked as if it wanted to be wound up ; and though the handle of Ada's went round and round with the greatest smoothness, it was attended with no effect whatever on the door. Therefore I proposed to the children that they should come in and be very good at my table, and I would tell them the story of Little Red Riding Hood while I dressed ; which they did, and were as quiet as mice, including Peepy, who awoke opportunely before the appearance of the wolf.

When we went down-stairs we found a mug, with " A Present from Tunbridge Wells " on it, lighted up in the staircase window with a floating wick ; and a young woman, with a swelled face bound up in a flannel bandage, blowing the fire of the drawing-room (now connected by an open door with Mrs. Jellyby's room), and choking dreadfully. It smoked to that degree in short, that we all sat coughing and crying with the windows open for half an hour ; during which Mrs. Jellyby, with the same sweetness of temper, directed letters about Africa. Her being so employed was, I must say, a great relief to me ; for Richard told us that he had washed his hands in a pie-dish, and that they had found the kettle on his dressing-table ; and he made Ada laugh so, that they made me laugh in the most ridiculous manner.

Soon after seven o'clock we went down to dinner ; carefully, by Mrs. Jellyby's advice ; for the stair-carpets, besides being very deficient in stair-wires, were so torn as to be absolute traps. We had a fine cod-fish, a piece of roast beef, a dish

48

of cutlets, and a pudding; an excellent dinner, if it had had any cooking to speak of, but it was almost raw. The young woman with the flannel bandage waited, and dropped everything on the table wherever it happened to go, and never moved it again until she put it on the stairs. The person I had seen in pattens (who I suppose to have been the cook), frequently came and skirmished with her at the door, and there appeared to be ill-will between them.

All through dinner; which was long, in consequence of such accidents as the dish of potatoes being mislaid in the coal scuttle, and the handle of the corkscrew coming off, and striking the young woman in the chin; Mrs. Jellyby preserved the evenness of her disposition. She told us a great deal that was interesting about Borrioboola-Gha and the natives; and received so many letters that Richard, who sat by her, saw four envelopes in the gravy at once. Some of the letters were proceedings of ladies' committees, or resolutions of ladies' meetings, which she read to us; others were applications from people excited in various ways about the cultivation of coffee, and natives; others required answers, and these she sent her eldest daughter from the table three or four times to write. She was full of business, and undoubtedly was, as she had told us, devoted to the cause.

I was a little curious to know who a mild bald gentleman in spectacles was, who dropped into a vacant chair (there was no top or bottom in particular) after the fish was taken away, and seemed passively to submit himself to Borrioboola-Gha, but not to be actively interested in that settlement. As he never spoke a word, he might have been a native, but for his complexion. It was not until we left the table, and he remained alone with Richard, that the possibility of his being Mr. Jellyby ever entered my head. But he *was* Mr. Jellyby; and a loquacious young man called Mr. Quale, with large shining knobs for temples, and his hair all brushed to the back of his head, who came in the evening, and told Ada

49

he was a philanthropist, also informed her that he called the matrimonial alliance of Mrs. Jellyby with Mr. Jellyby the union of mind and matter.

This young man, besides having a great deal to say for himself about Africa, and a project of his for teaching the coffee colonists to teach the natives to turn piano-forte legs and establish an export trade, delighted in drawing Mrs. Jellyby out by saying, "I believe now, Mrs. Jellyby, you have received as many as from one hundred and fifty to two hundred letters respecting Africa in a single day, have you not?" or, "If my memory does not deceive me, Mrs. Jellyby, you once mentioned that you had sent off five thousand circulars from one post-office at one time?"—always repeating Mrs. Jellyby's answer to us like an interpreter. During the whole evening, Mr. Jellyby sat in a corner with his head against the wall, as if he were subject to low spirits. It seemed that he had several times opened his mouth when alone with Richard, after dinner, as if he had something on his mind; but had always shut it again, to Richard's extreme confusion, without saying anything.

Mrs. Jellyby, sitting in quite a nest of waste paper, drank coffee all the evening, and dictated at intervals to her eldest daughter. She also held a discussion with Mr. Quale; of which the subject seemed to be—if I understood it—the Brotherhood of Humanity; and gave utterance to some beautiful sentiments. I was not so attentive an auditor as I might have wished to be, however, for Peepy and the other children came flocking about Ada and me in a corner of the drawing-room to ask for another story; so we sat down among them, and told them in whispers Puss in Boots and I don't know what else, until Mrs. Jellyby accidentally remembering them, sent them to bed. As Peepy cried for me to take him to bed, I carried him up-stairs, where the young woman with the flannel bandage charged into the midst of the little family like a dragon, and overturned them into cribs.

After that, I occupied myself in making our room a little tidy, and in coaxing a very cross fire that had been lighted, to burn; which at last it did, quite brightly. On my return down-stairs, I felt that Mrs. Jellyby looked down upon me rather, for being so frivolous; and I was sorry for it; though at the same time I knew that I had no higher pretensions.

It was nearly midnight before we found an opportunity of going to bed; and even then we left Mrs. Jellyby among her papers drinking coffee, and Miss Jellyby biting the feather of her pen.

"What a strange house!" said Ada, when we got up-stairs. "How curious of my cousin Jarndyce to send us here!"

"My love," said I, "it quite confuses me. I want to understand it, and I can't understand it at all."

"What?" asked Ada, with her pretty smile.

"All this, my dear," said I. "It *must* be very good of Mrs. Jellyby to take such pains about a scheme for the benefit of Natives—and yet—Peepy and the housekeeping!"

Ada laughed; and put her arm about my neck, as I stood looking at the fire; and told me I was a quiet, dear, good creature, and had won her heart. "You are so thoughtful, Esther," she said, "and yet so cheerful! and you do so much, so unpretendingly! You would make a home out of even this house."

My simple darling! She was quite unconscious that she only praised herself, and that it was in the goodness of her own heart that she made so much of me!

"May I ask you a question?" said I, when we had sat before the fire a little while.

"Five hundred," said Ada.

"Your cousin, Mr. Jarndyce. I owe so much to him. Would you mind describing him to me?"

Shaking her golden hair, Ada turned her eyes upon me with such laughing wonder, that I was full of wonder too—partly at her beauty, partly at her surprise.

"Esther!" she cried.

"My dear!"

"You want a description of my cousin Jarndyce?"

"My dear, I never saw him."

"And *I* never saw him!" returned Ada.

Well, to be sure!

No, she had never seen him. Young as she was when her mama died, she remembered how the tears would come into her eyes, when she spoke of him, and of the noble generosity of his character, which she had said was to be trusted above all earthly things; and Ada trusted it. Her cousin Jarndyce had written to her a few months ago,—"a plain, honest letter," Ada said—proposing the arrangement we were now to enter on, and telling her that, "in time it might heal some of the wounds made by the miserable Chancery suit." She had replied, gratefully accepting his proposal. Richard had received a similar letter, and had made a similar response. He *had* seen Mr. Jarndyce once, but only once, five years ago, at Winchester school. He had told Ada, when they were leaning on the screen before the fire where I found them, that he recollected him as "a bluff, rosy fellow." This was the utmost description Ada could give me.

It set me thinking so, that when Ada was asleep, I still remained before the fire, wondering and wondering about Bleak House, and wondering and wondering that yesterday morning should seem so long ago. I don't know where my thoughts had wandered, when they were recalled by a tap at the door.

I opened it softly, and found Miss Jellyby shivering there, with a broken candle in a broken candlestick in one hand, and an egg-cup in the other.

"Good night!" she said, very sulkily.

"Good night!" said I.

"May I come in?" she shortly and unexpectedly asked me in the same sulky way.

"Certainly," said I. "Don't wake Miss Clare."

Miss Jellyby

She would not sit down, but stood by the fire, dipping her inky middle finger in the egg-cup, which contained vinegar, and smearing it over the ink stains on her face; frowning, the whole time, and looking very gloomy.

"I wish Africa was dead!" she said, on a sudden.

I was going to remonstrate.

"I do!" she said. "Don't talk to me, Miss Summerson. I hate it and detest it. It's a beast!"

I told her she was tired, and I was sorry. I put my hand upon her head, and touched her forehead, and said it was hot now, but would be cool to-morrow. She still stood, pouting and frowning at me; but presently put down her egg-cup, and turned softly towards the bed where Ada lay.

"She is very pretty!" she said, with the same knitted brow, and in the same uncivil manner.

I assented with a smile.

"An orphan. Ain't she?"

"Yes."

"But knows a quantity, I suppose? Can dance, and play music, and sing? She can talk French, I suppose, and do geography, and globes, and needlework, and everything?"

"No doubt," said I.

"*I* can't," she returned. "I can't do anything hardly, except write. I'm always writing for Ma. I wonder you two were not ashamed of yourselves to come in this after-noon, and see me able to do nothing else. It was like your ill-nature. Yet you think yourselves very fine, I dare say!"

I could see that the poor girl was near crying, and I resumed my chair without speaking, and looked at her (I hope) as mildly as I felt towards her.

"It's disgraceful," she said. "You know it is. The whole house is disgraceful. The children are disgraceful. *I*'m disgraceful. Pa's miserable, and no wonder! Priscilla drinks —she's always drinking. It's a great shame and a great story of you, if you say you didn't smell her to-day. It was

53

as bad as a public-house, waiting at dinner; you know
it was!"

"My dear, I don't know it," said I.

"You do," she said, very shortly. "You shan't say you
don't. You do!"

"O, my dear!" said I, "if you won't let me speak——"

"You're speaking now. You know you are. Don't tell
stories, Miss Summerson."

"My dear," said I, "as long as you won't hear me
out——"

"I don't want to hear you out."

"O yes, I think you do," said I, "because that would be
so very unreasonable. I did not know what you tell me,
because the servant did not come near me at dinner; but I
don't doubt what you tell me, and I am sorry to hear it."

"You needn't make a merit of that," said she.

"No, my dear," said I. "That would be very foolish."

She was still standing by the bed, and now stooped down
(but still with the same discontented face) and kissed Ada.
That done, she came softly back, and stood by the side of
my chair. Her bosom was heaving in a distressful manner
that I greatly pitied; but I thought it better not to speak.

"I wish I was dead!" she broke out. "I wish we were
all dead. It would be a great deal better for us."

In a moment afterwards, she knelt on the ground at my
side, hid her face in my dress, passionately begged my pardon,
and wept. I comforted her, and would have raised her, but
she cried, No, no; she wanted to stay there!

"You used to teach girls," she said. "If you could only
have taught me, I could have learnt from you! I am so
very miserable, and I like you so much!"

I could not persuade her to sit by me, or to do anything
but move a ragged stool to where she was kneeling, and
take that, and still hold my dress in the same manner. By
degrees, the poor tired girl fell asleep; and then I contrived to raise her head so that it should rest on my lap,

and to cover us both with shawls. The fire went out, and all night long she slumbered thus before the ashy grate. At first I was painfully awake, and vainly tried to lose myself, with my eyes closed, among the scenes of the day. At length, by slow degrees, they became indistinct and mingled. I began to lose the identity of the sleeper resting on me. Now it was Ada; now, one of my old Reading friends from whom I could not believe I had so recently parted. Now, it was the little mad woman worn out with curtseying and smiling; now, some one in authority at Bleak House. Lastly, it was no one, and I was no one.

The purblind day was feebly struggling with the fog, when I opened my eyes to encounter those of a dirty-faced little spectre fixed upon me. Peepy had scaled his crib, and crept down in his bedgown and cap, and was so cold that his teeth were chattering as if he had cut them all.

CHAPTER V

ALTHOUGH the morning was raw, and although the fog still seemed heavy—I say seemed, for the windows were so encrusted with dirt, that they would have made Midsummer sunshine dim—I was sufficiently forewarned of the discomfort within doors at that early hour, and sufficiently curious about London, to think it a good idea on the part of Miss Jellyby when she proposed that we should go out for a walk.

"Ma won't be down for ever so long," she said, "and then it's a chance if breakfast's ready for an hour afterwards, they dawdle so. As to Pa, he gets what he can, and goes to the office. He never has what you would call a regular breakfast. Priscilla leaves him out the loaf and some milk, when there is any, over-night. Sometimes there isn't any milk, and sometimes the cat drinks it. But I'm afraid you must be tired, Miss Summerson; and perhaps you would rather go to bed."

"I am not at all tired, my dear," said I, "and would much prefer to go out."

"If you're sure you would," returned Miss Jellyby, "I'll get my things on."

Ada said she would go too, and was soon astir. I made a proposal to Peepy, in default of being able to do anything better for him, that he should let me wash him, and afterwards lay him down on my bed again. To this he submitted with the best grace possible; staring at me during the whole operation, as if he never had been, and never could again be, so astonished in his life—looking very miserable also, certainly, but making no complaint, and going snugly to sleep as soon as it was over. At first I was in two minds about taking such a liberty, but I soon reflected that nobody in the house was likely to notice it.

What with the bustle of despatching Peepy, and the bustle of getting myself ready, and helping Ada, I was soon quite in a glow. We found Miss Jellyby trying to warm herself at the fire in the writing-room, which Priscilla was then lighting with a smutty parlour candlestick—throwing the candle in to make it burn better. Everything was just as we had left it last night, and was evidently intended to remain so. Below-stairs the dinner-cloth had not been taken away, but had been left ready for breakfast. Crumbs, dust, and waste paper were all over the house. Some pewter-pots and a milk-can hung on the area railings; the door stood open; and we met the cook round the corner coming out of a public-house, wiping her mouth. She mentioned, as she passed us, that she had been to see what o'clock it was.

But before we met the cook, we met Richard, who was dancing up and down Thavies Inn to warm his feet. He was agreeably surprised to see us stirring so soon, and said he would gladly share our walk. So he took care of Ada, and Miss Jellyby and I went first. I may mention that Miss Jellyby had relapsed into her sulky manner, and that I really should not have thought she liked me much, unless she had told me so.

"Where would you wish to go?" she asked.

"Anywhere, my dear?" I replied.

"Anywhere's nowhere," said Miss Jellyby, stopping perversely.

"Let us go somewhere at any rate," said I.

She then walked me on very fast.

"I don't care!" she said. "Now, you are my witness, Miss Summerson, I say I don't care—but if he was to come to our house, with his great shining lumpy forehead, night after night, till he was as old as Methuselah, I wouldn't have anything to say to him. Such Asses as he and Ma make of themselves!

"My dear!" I remonstrated, in allusion to the epithet, and the vigorous emphasis Miss Jellyby set upon it. "Your duty as a child——"

"O! don't talk of duty as a child, Miss Summerson; where's Ma's duty as a parent? All made over to the public and Africa, I suppose! Then let the public and Africa show duty as a child; it's much more their affair than mine. You are shocked, I dare say! Very well, so am I shocked too; so we are both shocked, and there's an end of it!"

She walked me on faster yet.

"But for all that, I say again, he may come, and come, and come, and I won't have anything to say to him. I can't bear him. If there's any stuff in the world that I hate and detest, it's the stuff he and Ma talk. I wonder the very paving-stones opposite our house can have the patience to stay there, and be a witness of such inconsistencies and contradictions as all that sounding nonsense, and Ma's management!"

I could not but understand her to refer to Mr. Quale, the young gentleman who had appeared after dinner yesterday. I was saved the disagreeable necessity of pursuing the subject by Richard and Ada coming up at a round pace, laughing, and asking us if we meant to run a race? Thus interrupted, Miss Jellyby became silent, and walked moodily on at my side; while I admired the long successions and varieties of streets, the quantity of people already going to and fro, the number of vehicles passing and repassing, the busy preparations in the setting forth of shop windows and the sweeping out of shops, and the extraordinary creatures in rags, secretly groping among the swept-out rubbish for pins and other refuse.

"So, cousin," said the cheerful voice of Richard to Ada,

behind me. "We are never to get out of Chancery! We have come by another way to our place of meeting yesterday, and—by the Great Seal, here's the old lady again!"

Truly, there she was, immediately in front of us, curtseying, and smiling, and saying, with her yesterday's air of patronage:

"The wards in Jarndyce! Ve-ry happy, I am sure!"

"You are out early, ma'am," said I, as she curtseyed to me.

"Ye-es! I usually walk here early. Before the Court sits. It's retired. I collect my thoughts here for the business of the day," said the old lady, mincingly. "The business of the day requires a great deal of thought. Chancery justice is so ve-ry difficult to follow."

"Who's this, Miss Summerson?" whispered Miss Jellyby, drawing my arm tighter through her own.

The little old lady's hearing was remarkably quick. She answered for herself directly.

"A suitor, my child. At your service. I have the honour to attend court regularly. With my documents. Have I the pleasure of addressing another of the youthful parties in Jarndyce?" said the old lady, recovering herself, with her head on one side, from a very low curtsey.

Richard, anxious to atone for his thoughtlessness of yesterday, good-naturedly explained that Miss Jellyby was not connected with the suit.

"Ha!" said the old lady. "She does not expect a judgment? She will still grow old. But not so old. O dear, no! This is the garden of Lincoln's Inn. I call it my garden. It is quite a bower in the summer-time. Where the birds sing melodiously. I pass the greater part of the long vacation here. In contemplation. You find the long vacation exceedingly long, don't you?"

We said yes, as she seemed to expect us to say so.

"When the leaves are falling from the trees, and there are no more flowers in bloom to make up into nosegays for the

59

Lord Chancellor's court," said the old lady, "the vacation is fulfilled; and the sixth seal, mentioned in the Revelations, again prevails. Pray come and see my lodging. It will be a good omen for me. Youth, and hope, and beauty, are very seldom there. It is a long long time since I had a visit from either."

She had taken my hand, and, leading me and Miss Jellyby away, beckoned Richard and Ada to come too. I did not know how to excuse myself, and looked to Richard for aid. As he was half amused and half curious, and all in doubt how to get rid of the old lady without offence, she continued to lead us away, and he and Ada continued to follow; our strange conductress informing us all the time, with much smiling condescension, that she lived close by.

It was quite true, as it soon appeared. She lived so close by, that we had not time to have done humouring her for a few moments, before she was at home. Slipping us out at a little side gate, the old lady stopped most unexpectedly in a narrow back street, part of some courts and lanes immediately outside the wall of the Inn, and said, "This is my lodging. Pray walk up!"

She had stopped at a shop, over which was written, KROOK, RAG AND BOTTLE WAREHOUSE. Also, in long thin letters, KROOK, DEALER IN MARINE STORES. In one part of the window was a picture of a red paper mill, at which a cart was unloading a quantity of sacks of old rags. In another, was the inscription, BONES BOUGHT. In another, KITCHEN-STUFF BOUGHT. In another, OLD IRON BOUGHT. In another, WASTE PAPER BOUGHT. In another, LADIES' AND GENTLEMEN'S WARDROBES BOUGHT. Everything seemed to be bought, and nothing to be sold there. In all parts of the window, were quantities of dirty bottles: blacking bottles, medicine bottles, ginger-beer and soda-water bottles, pickle bottles, wine bottles, ink bottles: I am reminded by mentioning the latter, that the shop had, in several little particulars, the air of being in a legal neighbourhood, and of being, as it were, a dirty hanger-on and disowned relation of the law. There were a great many ink bottles. There was a little tottering bench of shabby old volumes, outside the door, labelled "Law Books, all at 9*d*." Some of the inscriptions I have enumerated were written in law-hand, like the papers I had seen in Kenge and Carboy's office, and the letters I had so long received from the firm. Among them was one, in the same writing, having nothing to do with the business of the shop, but announcing that a respectable man aged forty-five wanted engrossing or copying to execute with neatness and despatch : Address to Nemo, care of Mr. Krook within. There were several second-hand bags, blue and red, hanging up. A little way within the shop-door, lay heaps of old crackled parchment scrolls, and discoloured and dog's-eared law-papers. I could have fancied that all the rusty keys, of which there must have been hundreds huddled together as old iron, had once belonged to doors of rooms or strong chests in lawyers' offices. The litter of rags tumbled partly into and partly out of a one-legged wooden scale, hanging without any counterpoise from a beam, might have been counsellors' bands and gowns torn up. One had only to fancy, as Richard whispered to Ada and me while we all stood looking in, that yonder bones in a corner, piled together and picked very clean, were the bones of clients, to make the picture complete.

As it was still foggy and dark, and as the shop was blinded besides by the wall of Lincoln's Inn, intercepting the light within a couple of yards, we should not have seen so much but for a lighted lantern that an old man in spectacles and a hairy cap was carrying about in the shop. Turning towards the door, he now caught sight of us. He was short, cadaverous, and withered ; with his head sunk sideways between his shoulders, and the breath issuing in visible smoke from his mouth, as if he were on fire within. His throat, chin, and eyebrows were so frosted with white hairs, and so gnarled with veins and puckered skin, that he looked from his breast upward, like some old root in a fall of snow.

"Hi hi!" said the old man coming to the door. "Have you anything to sell?"

We naturally drew back and glanced at our conductress, who had been trying to open the house-door with a key she had taken from her pocket, and to whom Richard now said, that, as we had had the pleasure of seeing where she lived, we would leave her, being pressed for time. But she was not to be so easily left. She became so fantastically and pressingly earnest in her entreaties that we would walk up, and see her apartment for an instant; and was so bent, in her harmless way, on leading me in, as part of the good omen she desired; that I (whatever the others might do) saw nothing for it but to comply. I suppose we were all more or less curious;—at any rate, when the old man added his persuasions to hers, and said, "Aye, aye! Please her! It won't take a minute! Come in, come in! Come in through the shop, if t'other door's out of order!" we all went in, stimulated by Richard's laughing encouragement, and relying on his protection.

"My landlord, Krook," said the little old lady, condescending to him from her lofty station, as she presented him to us. "He is called among the neighbours the Lord Chancellor. His shop is called the Court of Chancery. He is a very eccentric person. He is very odd. Oh, I assure you he is very odd!"

She shook her head a great many times, and tapped her forehead with her finger, to express to us that we must have the goodness to excuse him, "For he is a little—you know! —M—!" said the old lady, with great stateliness. The old man overheard, and laughed.

"It's true enough," he said, going before us with the lantern, "that they call me the Lord Chancellor, and call my shop Chancery. And why do you think they call me the Lord Chancellor, and my shop Chancery?"

"I don't know, I am sure!" said Richard, rather carelessly.

"You see," said the old man, stopping and turning round, "they—Hi! Here's lovely hair! I have got three sacks of ladies' hair below, but none so beautiful and fine as this. What colour, and what texture!"

"That'll do, my good friend!" said Richard, strongly disapproving of his having drawn one of Ada's tresses through his yellow hand. "You can admire as the rest of us do, without taking that liberty."

The old man darted at him a sudden look, which even called my attention from Ada, who, startled and blushing, was so remarkably beautiful that she seemed to fix the wandering attention of the little old lady herself. But as Ada interposed, and laughingly said she could only feel proud of such genuine admiration, Mr. Krook shrunk into his former self as suddenly as he had leaped out of it.

"You see I have so many things here," he resumed, holding up the lantern, "of so many kinds, and all, as the neighbours think (but *they* know nothing), wasting away and going to rack and ruin, that that's why they have given me and my place a christening. And I have so many old parchmentses and papers in my stock. And I have a liking for rust and must and cobwebs. And all's fish that comes to my net. And I can't abear to part with anything I once lay hold of (or so my neighbours think, but what do *they* know?) or to alter anything, or to have any sweeping, nor scouring, nor cleaning, nor repairing going on about me. That's the way I've got the ill name of Chancery. *I* don't mir l. I go to see my noble and learned brother pretty well every day, when he sits in the Inn. He don't notice me, but I notice him. There's no great odds betwixt us. We both grub on in a muddle. Hi, Lady Jane!"

A large grey cat leaped from some neighbouring shelf on his shoulder, and startled us all.

"Hi! show 'em how you scratch. Hi! Tear, my lady!" said her master.

The cat leaped down, and ripped at a bundle of rags with

her tigerish claws, with a sound that it set my teeth on edge to hear.

"She'd do as much for any one I was to set her on," said the old man. "I deal in cat-skins among other general matters, and hers was offered to me. It's a very fine skin, as you may see, but I didn't have it stripped off! *That* warn't like Chancery practice though, says you!"

He had by this time led us across the shop, and now opened a door in the back part of it, leading to the house-entry. As he stood with his hand upon the lock, the little old lady graciously observed to him before passing out:

"That will do, Krook. You mean well, but are tiresome. My young friends are pressed for time. I have none to spare myself, having to attend court very soon. My young friends are the wards in Jarndyce."

"Jarndyce!" said the old man with a start.

"Jarndyce and Jarndyce. The great suit, Krook," returned his lodger.

"Hi!" exclaimed the old man, in a tone of thoughtful amazement, and with a wider stare than before. "Think of it!"

He seemed so rapt all in a moment, and looked so curiously at us, that Richard said:

"Why you appear to trouble yourself a good deal about the causes before your noble and learned brother, the other Chancellor!"

"Yes," said the old man abstractedly. "Sure! *Your* name now will be——"

"Richard Carstone."

"Carstone," he repeated, slowly checking off that name upon his forefinger; and each of the others he went on to mention, upon a separate finger. "Yes. There was the name of Barbary, and the name of Clare, and the name of Dedlock, too, I think."

"He knows as much of the cause as the real salaried Chancellor!" said Richard, quite astonished, to Ada and me.

THE STORY OF TOM JARNDYCE'S DEATH

"Ay!" said the old man, coming slowly out of his abstraction. "Yes! Tom Jarndyce—you'll excuse me, being related; but he was never known about court by any other name, and was as well known there, as—she is now;" nodding slightly at his lodger; "Tom Jarndyce was often in here. He got into a restless habit of strolling about when the cause was on, or expected, talking to the little shop-keepers, and telling 'em to keep out of Chancery, whatever they did. 'For,' says he, 'it's being ground to bits in a slow mill; it's being roasted at a slow fire; it's being stung to death by single bees; it's being drowned by drops; it's going mad by grains.' He was as near making away with himself, just where the young lady stands, as near could be."

We listened with horror.

"He come in at the door," said the old man, slowly pointing an imaginary track along the shop, "on the day he did it—the whole neighbourhood had said for months before, that he would do it, of a certainty sooner or later—he come in at the door that day, and walked along there, and sat himself on a bench that stood there, and asked me (you'll judge I was a mortal sight younger then) to fetch him a pint of wine. 'For,' says he, 'Krook, I am much depressed; my cause is on again, and I think I'm nearer judgment than I ever was.' I hadn't a mind to leave him alone; and I persuaded him to go to the tavern over the way there, t'other side my lane (I mean Chancery Lane); and I followed and looked in at the window, and saw him, comfortable as I thought, in the arm-chair by the fire, and company with him. I hadn't hardly got back here, when I heard a shot go echoing and rattling right away into the inn. I ran out—neighbours ran out—twenty of us cried at once, 'Tom Jarndyce!'"

The old man stopped, looked hard at us, looked down into the lantern, blew the light out, and shut the lantern up.

"We were right, I needn't tell the present hearers. Hi! To be sure, how the neighbourhood poured into court that

65

afternoon while the cause was on! How my noble and learned brother, and all the rest of 'em, grubbed and muddled away as usual, and tried to look as if they hadn't heard a word of the last fact in the case; or as if they had—O dear me!—nothing at all to do with it, if they had heard of it by any chance!"

Ada's colour had entirely left her, and Richard was scarcely less pale. Nor could I wonder, judging even from my emotions, and I was no party in the suit, that to hearts so untried and fresh, it was a shock to come into the inheritance of a protracted misery, attended in the minds of many people with such dreadful recollections. I had another uneasiness, in the application of the painful story to the poor half-witted creature who had brought us there; but, to my surprise, she seemed perfectly unconscious of that, and only led the way up-stairs again; informing us, with the toleration of a superior creature for the infirmities of a common mortal, that her landlord was "a little—M—, you know!"

She lived at the top of the house, in a pretty large room, from which she had a glimpse of Lincoln's Inn Hall. This seemed to have been her principal inducement, originally, for taking up her residence there. She could look at it, she said, in the night: especially in the moonshine. Her room was clean, but very, very bare. I noticed the scantiest necessaries in the way of furniture; a few old prints from books, of Chancellors and barristers, wafered against the wall; and some half-dozen reticules and work-bags, "containing documents," as she informed us. There were neither coals nor ashes in the grate, and I saw no articles of clothing anywhere, nor any kind of food. Upon a shelf in an open cupboard were a plate or two, a cup or two, and so forth; but all dry and empty. There was a more affecting meaning in her pinched appearance, I thought as I looked round, than I had understood before.

"Extremely honoured, I am sure," said our poor hostess, with the greatest suavity, "by this visit from the wards in

Jarndyce. And very much indebted for the omen. It is a retired situation. Considering. I am limited as to situation. In consequence of the necessity of attending on the Chancellor. I have lived here many years. I pass my days in court; my evenings and my nights here. I find the nights long, for I sleep but little, and think much. That is, of course, unavoidable; being in Chancery. I am sorry I cannot offer chocolate. I expect a judgment shortly, and shall then place my establishment on a superior footing. At present, I don't mind confessing to the wards in Jarndyce (in strict confidence), that I sometimes find it difficult to keep up a genteel appearance. I have felt the cold here. I have felt something sharper than cold. It matters very little. Pray excuse the introduction of such mean topics."

She partly drew aside the curtain of the long low garret-window, and called our attention to a number of bird-cages hanging there: some, containing several birds. There were larks, linnets, and goldfinches—I should think at least twenty.

"I began to keep the little creatures," she said, "with an object that the wards will readily comprehend. With the intention of restoring them to liberty. When my judgment should be given. Ye-es! They die in prison, though. Their lives, poor silly things, are so short in comparison with Chancery proceedings, that, one by one, the whole collection has died over and over again. I doubt, do you know, whether one of these, though they are all young, will live to be free! Ve-ry mortifying, is it not?"

Although she sometimes asked a question, she never seemed to expect a reply; but rambled on as if she were in the habit of doing so, when no one but herself was present.

"Indeed," she pursued, "I positively doubt sometimes, I do assure you, whether while matters are still unsettled, and the sixth or Great Seal still prevails, *I* may not one day be found lying stark and senseless here, as I have found so many birds!"

Richard, answering what he saw in Ada's compassionate eyes, took the opportunity of laying some money, softly and unobserved, on the chimney-piece. We all drew nearer to the cages, feigning to examine the birds.

"I can't allow them to sing much," said the little old lady, "for (you'll think this curious) I find my mind confused by the idea that they are singing, while I am following the arguments in Court. And my mind requires to be so very clear, you know! Another time, I'll tell you their names. Not at present. On a day of such good omen, they shall sing as much as they like. In honour of youth," a smile and curtsey; "hope," a smile and curtsey; "and beauty," a smile and curtsey. "There! We'll let in the full light."

The birds began to stir and chirp.

"I cannot admit the air freely," said the little old lady; the room was close, and would have been the better for it; "because the cat you saw down-stairs—called Lady Jane—is greedy for their lives. She crouches on the parapet outside for hours and hours. I have discovered," whispering mysteriously, "that her natural cruelty is sharpened by a jealous fear of their regaining their liberty. In consequence of the judgment I expect being shortly given. She is sly, and full of malice. I half believe, sometimes, that she is no cat, but the wolf of the old saying. It is so very difficult to keep her from the door."

Some neighbouring bells, reminding the poor soul that it was half-past nine, did more for us in the way of bringing our visit to an end, than we could easily have done for ourselves. She hurriedly took up her little bag of documents, which she had laid upon the table on coming in, and asked if we were also going into Court? On our answering no, and that we would on no account detain her, she opened the door to attend us down-stairs.

"With such an omen, it is even more necessary than usual that I should be there before the Chancellor comes in," said she, "for he might mention my case the first thing. I have

68

a presentiment that he *will* mention it the first thing this morning."

She stopped to tell us, in a whisper, as we were going down, that the whole house was filled with strange lumber which her landlord had bought piecemeal, and had no wish to sell, in consequence of being a little—M—. This was on the first floor. But she had made a previous stoppage on the second floor, and had silently pointed at a dark door there.

"The only other lodger," she now whispered, in explanation; "a law-writer. The children in the lanes here, say he has sold himself to the devil. I don't know what he can have done with the money. Hush!"

She appeared to mistrust that the lodger might hear her, even there; and repeating "Hush!" went before us on tip-toe, as though even the sound of her footsteps might reveal to him what she had said.

Passing through the shop on our way out, as we had passed through it on our way in, we found the old man storing a quantity of packets of waste paper, in a kind of well in the floor. He seemed to be working hard, with the perspiration standing on his forehead, and had a piece of chalk by him; with which, as he put each separate package or bundle down, he made a crooked mark on the panelling of the wall.

Richard and Ada, and Miss Jellyby, and the little old lady, had gone by him, and I was going, when he touched me on the arm to stay me, and chalked the letter J upon the wall—in a very curious manner, beginning with the end of the letter, and shaping it backward. It was a capital letter, not a printed one, but just such a letter as any clerk in Messrs. Kenge and Carboy's office would have made.

"Can you read it?" he asked me with a keen glance.

"Surely," said I. "It's very plain."

"What is it?"

"J."

With another glance at me, and a glance at the door, he

rubbed it out, and turned an a in its place (not a capital letter this time), and said, "What's that?"

I told him. He then rubbed that out, and turned the letter r, and asked me the same question. He went on quickly, until he had formed, in the same curious manner, beginning at the ends and bottoms of the letters, the word JARNDYCE, without once leaving two letters on the wall together.

"What does that spell?" he asked me.

When I told him, he laughed. In the same odd way, yet with the same rapidity, he then produced singly, and rubbed out singly, the letters forming the words BLEAK HOUSE. These, in some astonishment, I also read; and he laughed again.

"Hi!" said the old man, laying aside the chalk, "I have a turn for copying from memory, you see, miss, though I can neither read nor write."

He looked so disagreeable, and his cat looked so wickedly at me, as if I were a blood-relation of the birds up-stairs, that I was quite relieved by Richard's appearing at the door and saying:

"Miss Summerson, I hope you are not bargaining for the sale of your hair. Don't be tempted. Three sacks below are quite enough for Mr. Krook!"

I lost no time in wishing Mr. Krook good morning, and joining my friends outside, where we parted with the little old lady, who gave us her blessing with great ceremony, and renewed her assurance of yesterday in reference to her intention of settling estates on Ada and me. Before we finally turned out of those lanes, we looked back, and saw Mr. Krook standing at his shop-door, in his spectacles, looking after us, with his cat upon his shoulder, and her tail sticking up on one side of his hairy cap, like a tall feather.

"Quite an adventure for a morning in London!" said Richard, with a sigh. "Ah, cousin, cousin, it's a weary word, this Chancery!"

The Lord Chancellor copies from Memory

"It is to me, and has been ever since I can remember," returned Ada. "I am grieved that I should be the enemy —as I suppose I am—of a great number of relations and others; and that they should be my enemies—as I suppose they are; and that we should all be ruining one another, without knowing how or why, and be in constant doubt and discord all our lives. It seems very strange, as there must be right somewhere, that an honest judge in real earnest has not been able to find out through all these years where it is."

"Ah, cousin!" said Richard. "Strange, indeed! all this wasteful wanton chess-playing *is* very strange. To see that composed Court yesterday jogging on so serenely, and to think of the wretchedness of the pieces on the board, gave me the headache and the heartache both together. My head ached with wondering how it happened, if men were neither fools nor rascals; and my heart ached to think they could possibly be either. But at all events, Ada—I may call you Ada?"

"Of course you may, cousin Richard."

"At all events, Chancery will work none of its bad influences on *us*. We have happily been brought together, thanks to our good kinsman, and it can't divide us now!"

"Never, I hope, cousin Richard!" said Ada, gently.

Miss Jellyby gave my arm a squeeze, and me a very significant look. I smiled in return, and we made the rest of the way back very pleasantly.

In half an hour after our arrival, Mrs. Jellyby appeared; and in the course of an hour the various things necessary for breakfast straggled one by one into the dining-room. I do not doubt that Mrs. Jellyby had gone to bed, and got up in the usual manner, but she presented no appearance of having changed her dress. She was greatly occupied during breakfast; for the morning's post brought a heavy correspondence relative to Borrioboola-Gha, which would occasion her (she said) to pass a busy day. The children tumbled about, and notched memoranda of their accidents in their legs, which

71

were perfect little calendars of distress; and Peepy was lost for an hour and a half, and brought home from Newgate market by a policeman. The equable manner in which Mrs. Jellyby sustained both his absence, and his restoration to the family circle, surprised us all.

She was by that time perseveringly dictating to Caddy, and Caddy was fast relapsing into the inky condition in which we had found her. At one o'clock an open carriage arrived for us, and a cart for our luggage. Mrs. Jellyby charged us with many remembrances to her good friend, Mr. Jarndyce; Caddy left her desk to see us depart, kissed me in the passage, and stood, biting her pen, and sobbing on the steps; Peepy, I am happy to say, was asleep, and spared the pain of separation (I was not without misgivings that he had gone to Newgate market in search of me); and all the other children got up behind the barouche and fell off, and we saw them with great concern, scattered over the surface of Thavies Inn, as we rolled out of its precincts.

CHAPTER VI

THE day had brightened very much, and still brightened as
we went westward. We went our way through the sunshine
and the fresh air, wondering more and more at the extent of
the streets, the brilliancy of the shops, the great traffic, and
the crowds of people whom the pleasanter weather seemed to
have brought out like many-coloured flowers. By-and-by we
began to leave the wonderful city, and to proceed through
suburbs which, of themselves, would have made a pretty large
town, in my eyes; and at last we got into a real country road
again, with windmills, rickyards, milestones, farmers' waggons,
scents of old hay, swinging signs and horse troughs: trees,
fields, and hedgerows. It was delightful to see the green
landscape before us, and the immense metropolis behind; and
when a waggon with a train of beautiful horses, furnished
with red trappings and clear-sounding bells, came by us with
its music, I believe we could all three have sung to the bells,
so cheerful were the influences around.

"The whole road has been reminding me of my namesake
Whittington," said Richard, "and that waggon is the finishing
touch. Halloa! what's the matter?"

We had stopped, and the waggon had stopped too. Its
music changed as the horses came to a stand, and subsided
to a gentle tinkling, except when a horse tossed his head, or
shook himself, and sprinkled off a little shower of bell-
ringing.

73

"Our postilion is looking after the waggoner," said Richard; "and the waggoner is coming back after us. Good day, friend!" The waggoner was at our coach-door. "Why, here's an extraordinary thing!" added Richard, looking closely at the man. "He has got your name, Ada, in his hat!"

He had all our names in his hat. Tucked within the band were three small notes; one, addressed to Ada; one, to Richard; one, to me. These the waggoner delivered to each of us respectively, reading the name aloud first. In answer to Richard's inquiry from whom they came, he briefly answered, "Master, sir, if you please;" and putting on his hat again (which was like a soft bowl), cracked his whip, re-awakened his music, and went melodiously away.

"Is that Mr. Jarndyce's waggon?" said Richard, calling to our post-boy.

"Yes, sir," he replied. "Going to London."

We opened the notes. Each was a counterpart of the other, and contained these words, in a solid, plain hand.

"I look forward, my dear, to our meeting easily, and without constraint on either side. I therefore have to propose that we meet as old friends, and take the past for granted. It will be a relief to you possibly, and to me certainly, and so my love to you.

"JOHN JARNDYCE."

I had perhaps less reason to be surprised than either of my companions, having never yet enjoyed an opportunity of thanking one who had been my benefactor and sole earthly dependence through so many years. I had not considered how I could thank him, my gratitude lying too deep in my heart for that; but I now began to consider how I could meet him without thanking him, and felt it would be very difficult indeed.

The notes revived, in Richard and Ada, a general impression that they both had, without quite knowing how they came by it, that their cousin Jarndyce could never bear acknowledgments for any kindness he performed, and that, sooner than receive any, he would resort to the most singular expedients and evasions, or would even run away. Ada dimly remembered to have heard her mother tell, when she was a very little child, that he had once done her an act of uncommon generosity, and that on her going to his house to thank him, he happened to see her through a window coming to the door, and immediately escaped by the back gate, and was not heard of for three months. This discourse led to a great deal more on the same theme, and indeed it lasted us all day, and we talked of scarcely anything else. If we did, by any chance, diverge into another subject, we soon returned to this; and wondered what the house would be like, and when we should get there, and whether we should see Mr. Jarndyce as soon as we arrived, or after a delay, and what he would say to us, and what we should say to him. All of which we wondered about, over and over again.

The roads were very heavy for the horses, but the pathway was generally good; so we alighted and walked up all the hills, and liked it so well that we prolonged our walk on the level ground when we got to the top. At Barnet there were other horses waiting for us; but as they had only just been fed, we had to wait for them too, and got a long fresh walk, over a common and an old battle-field, before the carriage came up. These delays so protracted the journey, that the short day was spent and the long night had closed in, before we came to St. Albans; near to which town Bleak House was, we knew.

By that time we were so anxious and nervous, that even Richard confessed, as we rattled over the stones of the old street, to feeling an irrational desire to drive back again. As to Ada and me, whom he had wrapped up with great care, the night being sharp and frosty, we trembled from head to foot. When we turned out of the town, round a corner, and Richard told us that the post-boy, who had for a long time sympathised with our heightened expectation, was looking back and nodding, we both stood up in the carriage (Richard holding Ada, lest she should be jolted down), and gazed round upon the open country and the starlight night, for our destination. There was a light sparkling on the top of a hill before us, and the driver, pointing to it with his whip, and crying, "That's Bleak House!" put his horses into a canter, and took us forward at such a rate, up-hill though it was, that the wheels sent the road drift flying about our heads like spray from a water-mill. Presently we lost the light, presently saw it, presently lost it, presently saw it, and turned into an avenue of trees, and cantered up towards where it was beaming brightly. It was in a window of what seemed to be an old-fashioned house, with three peaks in the roof in front, and a circular sweep leading to the porch. A bell was rung as we drew up, and amidst the sound of its deep voice in the still air, and the distant barking of some dogs, and a gush of light from the opened door, and the smoking and steaming of the heated horses, and the quickened beating of our own hearts, we alighted in no inconsiderable confusion.

"Ada, my love, Esther, my dear, you are welcome. I rejoice to see you! Rick, if I had a hand to spare at present, I would give it you!"

The gentleman who said these words in a clear, bright, hospitable voice, had one of his arms round Ada's waist, and the other round mine, and kissed us both in a fatherly way, and bore us across the hall into a ruddy little room, all in a glow with a blazing fire. Here he kissed us again, and, opening his arms, made us sit down side by side, on a sofa ready drawn out near the hearth. I felt that if we had been at all demonstrative, he would have run away in a moment.

"Now, Rick!" said he, "I have a hand at liberty. A word in earnest is as good as a speech. I am heartily glad to see you. You are at home. Warm yourself!"

Richard shook him by both hands with an intuitive mixture of respect and frankness, and only saying (though with an earnestness that rather alarmed me, I was so afraid of Mr. Jarndyce's suddenly disappearing), "You are very kind, sir! We are very much obliged to you!" laid aside his hat and coat, and came up to the fire:

"And how did you like the ride? And how did you like Mrs. Jellyby, my dear?" said Mr. Jarndyce to Ada.

While Ada was speaking to him in reply, I glanced (I need not say with how much interest) at his face. It was a handsome, lively, quick face, full of change and motion; and his hair was a silvered iron-grey. I took him to be nearer sixty than fifty, but he was upright, hearty, and robust. From the moment of his first speaking to us, his voice had connected itself with an association in my mind that I could not define; but now, all at once, a something sudden in his manner, and a pleasant expression in his eyes, recalled the gentleman in the stage-coach, six years ago, on the memorable day of my journey to Reading. I was certain it was he. I never was so frightened in my life as when I made the discovery, for he caught my glance, and appearing to read my thoughts, gave such a look at the door that I thought we had lost him.

However, I am happy to say he remained where he was, and asked me what I thought of Mrs. Jellyby?

"She exerts herself very much for Africa, sir," I said.

"Nobly!" returned Mr. Jarndyce. "But you answer like Ada." Whom I had not heard. "You all think something else, I see."

"We rather thought," said I, glancing at Richard and Ada, who entreated me with their eyes to speak, "that perhaps she was a little unmindful of her home."

"Floored!" cried Mr. Jarndyce.

I was rather alarmed again.

"Well! I want to know your real thoughts, my dear. I may have sent you there on purpose."

"We thought that, perhaps," said I, hesitating, "it is right to begin with the obligations of home, sir; and that, perhaps, while those are overlooked and neglected, no other duties can possibly be substituted for them."

"The little Jellybys," said Richard, coming to my relief, "are really—I can't help expressing myself strongly, sir—in a devil of a state."

"She means well," said Mr. Jarndyce, hastily. "The wind's in the east."

"It was in the north, sir, as we came down," observed Richard.

"My dear Rick," said Mr. Jarndyce, poking the fire; "I'll take an oath it's either in the east, or going to be. I am always conscious of an uncomfortable sensation now and then when the wind is blowing in the east."

"Rheumatism, sir?" said Richard.

"I dare say it is, Rick. I believe it is. And so the little Jell—I had my doubts about 'em—are in a—oh, Lord, yes, it's easterly!" said Mr. Jarndyce.

He had taken two or three undecided turns up and down while uttering these broken sentences, retaining the poker in one hand and rubbing his hair with the other, with a good-natured vexation, at once so whimsical and so loveable, that I am sure we were more delighted with him than we could possibly have expressed in any words. He gave an arm to Ada and an arm to me, and bidding Richard bring a candle, was leading the way out, when he suddenly turned us all back again.

"Those little Jellybys. Couldn't you—didn't you—now, if it had rained sugar-plums, or three-cornered raspberry tarts, or anything of that sort!" said Mr. Jarndyce.

"O, cousin—!" Ada hastily began.

"Good, my pretty pet. I like cousin. Cousin John, perhaps, is better."

"Then, cousin John!—— " Ada laughingly began again.

"Ha, ha! Very good indeed!" said Mr. Jarndyce, with great enjoyment. "Sounds uncommonly natural. Yes, my dear?"

"It did better than that. It rained Esther."

"Ay?" said Mr. Jarndyce. "What did Esther do?"

"Why, cousin John," said Ada, clasping her hands upon his arm, and shaking her head at me across him—for I wanted her to be quiet: "Esther was their friend directly. Esther nursed them, coaxed them to sleep, washed and dressed them, told them stories, kept them quiet, bought them keepsakes"—My dear girl! I had only gone out with Peepy, after he was found, and given him a little, tiny horse! —"and, cousin John, she softened poor Caroline, the eldest one, so much, and was so thoughtful for me and so amiable! —No, no, I won't be contradicted, Esther dear! You know, you know, it's true!"

The warm-hearted darling leaned across her cousin John, and kissed me; and then looking up in his face, boldly said, "At all events, cousin John, I *will* thank you for the companion you have given me." I felt as if she challenged him to run away. But he didn't.

"Where did you say the wind was, Rick?" asked Mr. Jarndyce.

"In the north, as we came down, sir."

"You are right. There's no east in it. A mistake of mine. Come, girls, come and see your home!"

It was one of those delightfully irregular houses where you go up and down steps out of one room into another, and where you come upon more rooms when you think you have seen all there are, and where there is a bountiful provision of little halls and passages, and where you find still older cottage-rooms in unexpected places, with lattice windows and green growth pressing through them. Mine, which we entered first, was of this kind, with an up-and-down roof, that had more corners in it than I ever counted afterwards, and a chimney (there was a wood-fire on the hearth) paved all around with pure white tiles, in every one of which a bright miniature of the fire was blazing. Out of this room, you went down two steps, into a charming little sitting-room, looking down upon a flower-garden, which room was henceforth to belong to Ada and me. Out of this you went up three steps, into Ada's bed-room, which had a fine broad window, commanding a beautiful view (we saw a great expanse of darkness lying underneath the stars), to which there was a hollow window-seat, in which, with a spring-lock, three dear Adas might have been lost at once. Out of this room, you passèd into a little gallery, with which the other best rooms (only two) communicated, and so, by a little staircase of shallow steps, with a number of corner stairs in it, considering its length, down into the hall. But if, instead of going out at Ada's door, you came back into my room, and went out at the door by which you had entered it, and turned up a few crooked steps that branched off in an unexpected manner from the stairs, you lost your-self in passages, with mangles in them, and three-cornered tables, and a Native-Hindoo chair, which was also a sofa, a box, and a bedstead, and looked in every form, something between a bamboo skeleton and a great bird-cage, and had been brought from India nobody knew by whom or when. From these, you came on Richard's room, which was part library, part sitting-room, part bed-room, and seemed indeed a comfortable compound of many rooms. Out of that, you went straight, with a little interval of passage, to the plain room where Mr. Jarndyce slept, all the year round, with his window open, his bedstead without any furniture standing in the middle of the floor for more air, and his cold-bath gaping for him in a smaller room adjoining. Out of that, you came into another passage, where there were back-stairs, and where you could hear the horses being rubbed down, outside the stable, and being told to Hold up, and Get over, as they slipped about very much on the uneven stones. Or you might, if you came out at another door (every room had at least two doors), go straight down to the hall again by half-a-dozen steps and a low archway, wondering how you got back there, or had ever got out of it.

OLD-FASHIONED FURNITURE

The furniture, old-fashioned rather than old, like the house, was as pleasantly irregular. Ada's sleeping-room was all flowers—in chintz and paper, in velvet, in needlework, in the brocade of two stiff courtly chairs, which stood, each attended by a little page of a stool for greater state, on either side of the fireplace. Our sitting-room was green; and had, framed and glazed, upon the walls, numbers of surprising and surprised birds, staring out of pictures at a real trout in a case, as brown and shining as if it had been served with gravy; at the death of Captain Cook; and at the whole process of preparing tea in China, as depicted by Chinese artists. In my room there were oval engravings of the months—ladies haymaking, in short waists, and large hats tied under the chin, for June—smooth-legged noblemen, pointing, with cocked-hats, to village steeples, for October. Half-length portraits, in crayons, abounded all through the house; but were so dispersed that I found the brother of a youthful officer of mine in the china-closet, and the grey old age of my pretty young bride, with a flower in her bodice, in the breakfast-room. As substitutes, I had four angels, of Queen Anne's reign, taking a complacent gentleman to heaven, in festoons, with some difficulty; and a composition in needlework, representing fruit, a kettle, and an alphabet. All the moveables, from the wardrobes to the chairs and tables, hangings, glasses, even to the pincushions and scent-bottles on the dressing-tables, displayed the same quaint variety. They agreed in nothing but their perfect neatness, their display of the whitest linen, and their storing-up, wheresoever the existence of a drawer, small or large, rendered it possible, of quantities of rose-leaves and sweet lavender. Such, with its illuminated windows, softened here and there by shadows of curtains, shining out upon the star-light night; with its light, and warmth, and comfort; with its hospitable jingle, at a distance, of preparations for dinner; with the face of its generous master brightening everything we saw; and just wind enough without to sound a low

81

accompaniment to everything we heard; were our first impressions of Bleak House.

"I am glad you like it," said Mr. Jarndyce, when he had brought us round again to Ada's sitting-room. "It makes no pretensions; but it is a comfortable little place, I hope, and will be more so with such bright young looks in it. You have barely half an hour before dinner. There's no one here but the finest creature upon earth—a child."

"More children, Esther!" said Ada.

"I don't mean literally a child," pursued Mr. Jarndyce; "not a child in years. He is grown up—he is at least as old as I am—but in simplicity, and freshness, and enthusiasm, and a fine guileless inaptitude for all worldly affairs, he is a perfect child."

We felt that he must be very interesting.

"He knows Mrs. Jellyby," said Mr. Jarndyce. "He is a musical man; an Amateur, but might have been a Professional. He is an Artist, too; an Amateur, but might have been a Professional. He is a man of attainments and of captivating manners. He has been unfortunate in his affairs, and unfortunate in his pursuits, and unfortunate in his family; but he don't care—he's a child!"

"Did you imply that he has children of his own, sir?" inquired Richard.

"Yes, Rick! Half-a-dozen. More! Nearer a dozen, I should think. But he has never looked after them. How could he? He wanted somebody to look after *him*. He is a child, you know!" said Mr. Jarndyce.

"And have the children looked after themselves at all, sir?" inquired Richard.

"Why, just as you may suppose," said Mr. Jarndyce: his countenance suddenly falling. "It is said that the children of the very poor are not brought up, but dragged up. Harold Skimpole's children have tumbled up somehow or other.—The wind's getting round again, I am afraid. I feel it rather!"

Richard observed that the situation was exposed on a sharp night.

"It *is* exposed," said Mr. Jarndyce. "No doubt that's the cause. Bleak House has an exposed sound. But you are coming my way. Come along!"

Our luggage having arrived, and being all at hand, I was dressed in a few minutes, and engaged in putting my worldly goods away, when a maid (not the one in attendance upon Ada, but another whom I had not seen) brought a basket into my room, with two bunches of keys in it, all labelled.

"For you, miss, if you please," said she.

"For me?" said I.

"The housekeeping keys, miss."

I showed my surprise; for she added with some little surprise on her own part: "I was told to bring them as soon as you was alone, miss. Miss Summerson, if I don't deceive myself?"

"Yes," said I. "That is my name."

"The large bunch is the housekeeping, and the little bunch is the cellars, miss. Any time you was pleased to appoint to-morrow morning, I was to show you the presses and things they belong to."

I said I would be ready at half-past six; and, after she was gone, stood looking at the basket, quite lost in the magnitude of my trust. Ada found me thus; and had such a delightful confidence in me when I showed her the keys and told her about them, that it would have been insensibility and ingratitude not to feel encouraged. I knew, to be sure, that it was the dear girl's kindness; but I liked to be so pleasantly cheated.

When we went down-stairs, we were presented to Mr. Skimpole, who was standing before the fire, telling Richard how fond he used to be, in his school-time, of football. He was a little bright creature, with a rather large head; but a delicate face, and a sweet voice, and there was a perfect charm in him. All he said was so free from effort and spontaneous, and was said with such a captivating gaiety, that it was fascinating to hear him talk. Being of a more slender figure than Mr. Jarndyce, and having a richer complexion, with browner hair, he looked younger. Indeed, he had more the appearance, in all respects, of a damaged young man, than a well-preserved elderly one. There was an easy negligence in his manner, and even in his dress (his hair carelessly disposed, and his neck-kerchief loose and flowing, as I have seen artists paint their own portraits), which I could not separate from the idea of a romantic youth who had undergone some unique process of depreciation. It struck me as being not at all like the manner or appearance of a man who had advanced in life, by the usual road of years, cares, and experiences.

I gathered from the conversation, that Mr. Skimpole had been educated for the medical profession, and had once lived, in his professional capacity, in the household of a German prince. He told us, however, that as he had always been a mere child in point of weights and measures, and had never known anything about them (except that they disgusted him), he had never been able to prescribe with the requisite accuracy of detail. In fact, he said, he had no head for detail. And he told us, with great humour, that when he was wanted to bleed the prince, or physic any of his people, he was generally found lying on his back, in bed, reading the newspapers, or making fancy-sketches in pencil, and couldn't come. The prince, at last objecting to this, "in which," said Mr. Skimpole, in the frankest manner, "he was perfectly right," the engagement terminated, and Mr. Skimpole having (as he added with delightful gaiety) "nothing to live upon but love, fell in love, and married, and surrounded himself with rosy cheeks." His good friend Jarndyce and some other of his good friends then helped him, in quicker or slower succession, to several openings in life; but to no purpose, for he must confess to two of the oldest infirmities in the world: one was, that he had no idea of time; the other, that he had no idea of money. In consequence of which he never kept an appointment, never could transact any business, and never knew the value of anything! Well! So he had got on in life, and here he was! He was very fond of reading the papers, very fond of making fancy-sketches with a pencil, very fond of nature, very fond of art. All he asked of society was, to let him live. *That* wasn't much. His wants were few. Give him the papers, conversation, music, mutton, coffee, landscape, fruit in the season, a few sheets of Bristol-board, and a little claret, and he asked no more. He was a mere child in the world, but he didn't cry for the moon. He said to the world, " Go your several ways in peace! Wear red coats, blue coats, lawn sleeves, put pens behind your ears, wear aprons; go after glory, holiness, commerce, trade, any object you prefer; only —let Harold Skimpole live!"

All this, and a great deal more, he told us, not only with the utmost brilliancy and enjoyment, but with a certain vivacious candour—speaking of himself as if he were not at all his own affair, as if Skimpole were a third person, as if he knew that Skimpole had his singularities, but still had his claims too, which were the general business of the community and must not be slighted. He was quite enchanting. If I felt at all confused at that early time, in endeavouring to reconcile anything he said with anything I had thought about the duties and accountabilities of life (which I am far from sure of), I was confused by not exactly understanding why he was free of them. That he *was* free of them, I scarcely doubted; he was so very clear about it himself.

"I covet nothing," said Mr. Skimpole, in the same light way. "Possession is nothing to me. Here is my friend Jarndyce's excellent house. I feel obliged to him for possessing it. I can sketch it, and alter it. I can set it to music. When I am here, I have sufficient possession of it, and have neither trouble, cost, nor responsibility. My steward's name, in short, is Jarndyce, and he can't cheat me. We have been mentioning Mrs. Jellyby. There is a bright-eyed woman, of a strong will and immense power of business-detail, who throws herself into objects with surprising ardour! I don't regret that *I* have not a strong will and an immense power of business-detail, to throw myself into objects with surprising ardour. I can admire her without envy. I can sympathise with the objects. I can dream of them. I can lie down on the grass—in fine weather—and float along an African river, embracing all the natives I meet, as sensible of the deep silence, and sketching the dense overhanging tropical growth as accurately, as if I were there. I don't know that it's of any direct use my doing so, but it's all I can do, and I do it thoroughly. Then, for Heaven's sake, having Harold Skimpole, a confiding child, petitioning you, the world, an agglomeration of practical people of business habits, to let him live and admire the human family, do it somehow or other, like good souls, and suffer him to ride his rocking-horse!"

It was plain enough that Mr. Jarndyce had not been neglectful of the adjuration.

Mr. Skimpole's general position there would have rendered it so, without the addition of what he presently said.

"It's only you, the generous creatures, whom I envy," said Mr. Skimpole, addressing us, his new friends, in an impersonal manner. "I envy you your power of doing what you do. It is what I should revel in, myself. I don't feel any vulgar gratitude to you. I almost feel as if *you* ought to be grateful to *me*, for giving you the opportunity of enjoying the luxury of generosity. I know you like it. For anything I can tell, I may have come into the world expressly for the purpose of increasing your stock of happiness. I may have been born to be a benefactor to you, by sometimes giving you an opportunity of assisting me in my little perplexities. Why should I regret my incapacity for details and worldly affairs, when it leads to such pleasant consequences? I don't regret it therefore."

THE CHILD OF THE UNIVERSE

Of all his playful speeches (playful, yet always fully meaning what they expressed) none seemed to be more to the taste of Mr. Jarndyce than this. I had often new temptations, afterwards, to wonder whether it was really singular, or only singular to me, that he, who was probably the most grateful of mankind upon the least occasion, should so desire to escape the gratitude of others.

We were all enchanted. I felt it a merited tribute to the engaging qualities of Ada and Richard, that Mr. Skimpole, seeing them for the first time, should be so unreserved, and should lay himself out to be so exquisitely agreeable. They (and especially Richard) were naturally pleased for similar reasons, and considered it no common privilege to be so freely confided in by such an attractive man. The more we listened, the more gaily Mr. Skimpole talked. And what with his fine hilarious manner, and his engaging candour, and his genial way of lightly tossing his own weaknesses about, as if he had said, "I am a child, you know! You are designing people compared with me;" (he really made me consider myself in that light;) "but I am gay and innocent; forget your worldly arts and play with me!"— the effect was absolutely dazzling.

He was so full of feeling too, and had such a delicate sentiment for what was beautiful or tender, that he could have won a heart by that alone. In the evening when I was preparing to make tea, and Ada was touching the piano in the adjoining room and softly humming a tune to her cousin Richard, which they had happened to mention, he came and sat down on the sofa near me, and so spoke of Ada that I almost loved him.

"She is like the morning," he said. "With that golden hair, those blue eyes, and that fresh bloom on her cheek, she is like the summer morning. The birds here will mistake her for it. We will not call such a lovely young creature as that, who is a joy to all mankind, an orphan. She is the child of the universe."

Mr. Jarndyce, I found, was standing near us, with his hands behind him, and an attentive smile upon his face.

"The universe," he observed, "makes rather an indifferent parent, I am afraid."

"O! I don't know!" cried Mr. Skimpole, buoyantly.

"I think I do know," said Mr. Jarndyce.

"Well!" cried Mr. Skimpole, "you know the world (which in your sense is the universe), and I know nothing of it, so you shall have your way. But if I had mine," glancing at the cousins, "there should be no brambles of sordid realities in such a path as that. It should be strewn with roses; it should lie through bowers, where there was no spring, autumn, nor winter, but perpetual summer. Age or change should never wither it. The base word money should never be breathed near it!"

Mr. Jarndyce patted him on the head with a smile, as if he had been really a child; and passing a step or two on, and stopping a moment, glanced at the young cousins. His look was thoughtful, but had a benignant expression in it which I often (how often!) saw again: which has long been engraven on my heart. The room in which they were, communicating with that in which he stood, was only lighted by the fire. Ada sat at the piano; Richard stood beside her, bending down. Upon the wall, their shadows blended together, surrounded by strange forms, not without a ghostly motion caught from the unsteady fire, though reflecting from motionless objects. Ada touched the notes so softly, and sang so low, that the wind, sighing away to the distant hills, was as audible as the music. The mystery of the future, and the little clue afforded to it by the voice of the present, seemed expressed in the whole picture.

But it is not to recall this fancy, well as I remember it, that I recall the scene. First, I was not quite unconscious of the contrast in respect of meaning and intention, between the silent look directed that way, and the flow of words that had preceded it. Secondly, though Mr. Jarndyce's glance, as he withdrew it, rested for but a moment on me, I felt as if, in that moment, he confided to me—and knew that he confided to me, and that I received the confidence—his hope that Ada and Richard might one day enter on a dearer relationship.

Mr. Skimpole could play on the piano, and the violoncello; and he was a composer—had composed half an opera once, but got tired of it—and played what he composed with taste. After tea we had quite a little concert, in which Richard—who was enthralled by Ada's singing, and told me that she seemed to know all the songs that ever were written—and Mr. Jarndyce, and I, were the audience. After a little while I missed, first Mr. Skimpole, and afterwards Richard; and while I was thinking how could Richard stay away so long, and lose so much, the maid who had given me the keys looked in at the door, saying, "If you please, miss, could you spare a minute?"

When I was shut out with her in the hall, she said, holding up her hands, "Oh if you please, miss, Mr. Carstone says would you come up-stairs to Mr. Skimpole's room. He has been took, miss!"

"Took?" said I.

"Took, miss. Sudden," said the maid.

I was apprehensive that his illness might be of a dangerous kind; but of course, I begged her to be quiet and not disturb any one; and collected myself, as I followed her quickly up-stairs, sufficiently to consider what were the best remedies to be applied if it should prove to be a fit. She threw open a door, and I went into a chamber; where, to my unspeakable surprise, instead of finding Mr. Skimpole stretched upon the bed, or prostrate on the floor, I found him standing before the fire smiling at Richard, while Richard, with a face of great embarrassment, looked at a person on the sofa, in a white great-coat, with smooth hair upon his head and not much of it, which he was wiping smoother, and making less of, with a pocket-handkerchief.

" Miss Summerson," said Richard, hurriedly, " I am glad you are come. You will be able to advise us. Our friend, Mr. Skimpole—don't be alarmed!—is arrested for debt."

" And, really, my dear Miss Summerson," said Mr. Skimpole, with his agreeable candour, " I never was in a situation, in which that excellent sense, and quiet habit of method and usefulness, which anybody must observe in you who has the happiness of being a quarter of an hour in your society, was more needed."

The person on the sofa, who appeared to have a cold in his head, gave such a very loud snort, that he startled me.

" Are you arrested for much, sir?" I inquired of Mr. Skimpole.

" My dear Miss Summerson," said he, shaking his head pleasantly, " I don't know. Some pounds, odd shillings, and half-pence, I think, were mentioned."

" It's twenty-four pound, sixteen, and seven-pence ha'penny," observed the stranger. " That's wot it is."

" And it sounds—somehow it sounds," said Mr. Skimpole, " like a small sum?"

The strange man said nothing, but made another snort. It was such a powerful one, that it seemed quite to lift him out of his seat.

" Mr. Skimpole," said Richard to me, " has a delicacy in applying to my cousin Jarndyce, because he has lately—I think, sir, I understood you that you had lately—— "

" Oh, yes!" returned Mr. Skimpole, smiling. " Though I forgot how much it was, and when it was. Jarndyce would readily do it again; but I have the epicure-like feeling that I would prefer a novelty in help; that I would rather," and he looked at Richard and me, " develop generosity in a new soil, and in a new form of flower."

" What do you think will be best, Miss Summerson?" said Richard, aside.

I ventured to inquire, generally, before replying, what would happen if the money were not produced.

"Jail," said the strange man, coolly putting his handkerchief into his hat, which was on the floor at his feet. "Or Coavinses."

"May I ask, sir, what is——"

"Coavinses?" said the strange man. "A 'ouse."

Richard and I looked at one another again. It was a most singular thing that the arrest was our embarrassment, and not Mr. Skimpole's. He observed us with a genial interest; but there seemed, if I may venture on such a contradiction, nothing selfish in it. He had entirely washed his hands of the difficulty, and it had become ours.

"I thought," he suggested, as if good-naturedly to help us out, "that being parties in a Chancery suit concerning (as people say) a large amount of property, Mr. Richard or his beautiful cousin, or both, could sign something, or make over something, or give some sort of undertaking, or pledge, or bond? I don't know what the business name of it may be, but I suppose there is some instrument within their power that would settle this?"

"Not a bit on it," said the strange man.

"Really?" returned Mr. Skimpole. "That seems odd, now, to one who is no judge of these things!"

"Odd or even," said the stranger, gruffly, "I tell you, not a bit on it!"

"Keep your temper, my good fellow, keep your temper!" Mr. Skimpole gently reasoned with him, as he made a little drawing of his head on the fly-leaf of a book. "Don't be ruffled by your occupation. We can separate you from your office; we can separate the individual from the pursuit. We are not so prejudiced as to suppose that in private life you are otherwise than a very estimable man, with a great deal of poetry in your nature, of which you may not be conscious."

The stranger only answered with another violent snort; whether in acceptance of the poetry-tribute, or in disdainful rejection of it, he did not express to me.

"Now, my dear Miss Summerson, and my dear Mr.

91

Richard," said Mr. Skimpole, gaily, innocently, and confidingly, as he looked at his drawing with his head on one side; "here you see me utterly incapable of helping myself, and entirely in your hands! I only ask to be free. The butterflies are free. Mankind will surely not deny to Harold Skimpole what it concedes to the butterflies!"

"My dear Miss Summerson," said Richard, in a whisper, "I have ten pounds that I received from Mr. Kenge. I must try what that will do."

I possessed fifteen pounds, odd shillings, which I had saved from my quarterly allowance during several years. I had always thought that some accident might happen which would throw me, suddenly, without any relation, or any property, on the world; and had always tried to keep some little money by me, that I might not be quite penniless. I told Richard of my having this little store, and having no present need of it; and I asked him delicately to inform Mr. Skimpole, while I should be gone to fetch it, that we would have the pleasure of paying his debt.

When I came back, Mr. Skimpole kissed my hand, and seemed quite touched. Not on his own account (I was again aware of that perplexing and extraordinary contradiction), but on ours; as if personal considerations were impossible with him, and the contemplation of our happiness alone affected him. Richard, begging me, for the greater grace of the transaction, as he said, to settle with Coavinses (as Mr. Skimpole now jocularly called him), I counted out the money and received the necessary acknowledgment. This, too, delighted Mr. Skimpole.

His compliments were so delicately administered, that I blushed less than I might have done; and settled with the stranger in the white coat, without making any mistakes. He put the money in his pocket, and shortly said, "Well, then, I'll wish you a good evening, miss."

"My friend," said Mr. Skimpole, standing with his back to the fire, after giving up the sketch when it was half

Coavinses

finished, "I should like to ask you something, without offence."

I think the reply was, "Cut away, then!"

"Did you know this morning, now, that you were coming out on this errand?" said Mr. Skimpole.

"Know'd it yes'day aft'noon at tea-time," said Coavinses.

"It didn't affect your appetite? Didn't make you at all uneasy?"

"Not a bit," said Coavinses. "I know'd if you wos missed to-day, you wouldn't be missed to-morrow. A day makes no such odds."

"But when you came down here," proceeded Mr. Skimpole, "it was a fine day. The sun was shining, the wind was blowing, the lights and shadows were passing across the fields, the birds were singing."

"Nobody said they warn't, in *my* hearing," returned Coavinses.

"No," observed Mr. Skimpole. "But what did you think upon the road?"

"Wot do you mean?" growled Coavinses, with an appearance of strong resentment. "Think! I've got enough to do, and little enough to get for it, without thinking. Thinking!" (with profound contempt).

"Then you didn't think, at all events," proceeded Mr. Skimpole, "to this effect. 'Harold Skimpole loves to see the sun shine; loves to hear the wind blow; loves to watch the changing lights and shadows; loves to hear the birds, those choristers in Nature's great cathedral. And does it seem to me that I am about to deprive Harold Skimpole of his share in such possessions, which are his only birthright!' You thought nothing to that effect?"

"I—certainly—did—NOT," said Coavinses, whose doggedness in utterly renouncing the idea was of that intense kind, that he could only give adequate expression to it by putting a long interval between each word, and accompanying the last with a jerk that might have dislocated his neck.

"Very odd and very curious, the mental process is, in you men of business!" said Mr. Skimpole, thoughtfully. "Thank you, my friend. Good night."

As our absence had been long enough already to seem strange down-stairs, I returned at once, and found Ada sitting at work by the fireside talking to her cousin John. Mr. Skimpole presently appeared, and Richard shortly after him. I was sufficiently engaged, during the remainder of the evening, in taking my first lesson in backgammon from Mr. Jarndyce, who was very fond of the game, and from whom I wished of course to learn it as quickly as I could, in order that I might be of the very small use of being able to play when he had no better adversary. But I thought, occasionally when Mr. Skimpole played some fragments of his own compositions; or when, both at the piano and the violoncello, and at our table, he preserved, with an absence of all effort, his delightful spirits and his easy flow of conversation; that Richard and I seemed to retain the transferred impression of having been arrested since dinner, and that it was very curious altogether.

It was late before we separated : for when Ada was going at eleven o'clock, Mr. Skimpole went to the piano, and rattled, hilariously, that the best of all ways, to lengthen our days, was to steal a few hours from Night, my dear! It was past twelve before he took his candle and his radiant face out of the room ; and I think he might have kept us there, if he had seen fit, until daybreak. Ada and Richard were lingering for a few moments by the fire, wondering whether Mrs. Jellyby had yet finished her dictation for the day, when Mr. Jarndyce, who had been out of the room, returned.

"Oh, dear me, what's this, what's this!" he said, rubbing his head and walking about with his good-humoured vexation. "What's this they tell me? Rick, my boy, Esther, my dear, what have you been doing? Why did you do it? How could you do it? How much apiece was it?—The wind's round again. I feel it all over me!"

We neither of us quite knew what to answer.

"Come, Rick, come! I must settle this before I sleep. How much are you out of pocket? You two made the money up, you know! Why did you? How could you?— O Lord, yes, it's due east—must be!"

"Really, sir," said Richard, "I don't think it would be honourable in me to tell you. Mr. Skimpole relied upon us——"

"Lord bless you, my dear boy! He relies upon everybody!" said Mr. Jarndyce, giving his head a great rub, and stopping short.

"Indeed, sir?"

"Everybody! And he'll be in the same scrape again, next week!" said Mr. Jarndyce, walking again at a great pace, with a candle in his hand that had gone out. "He's always in the same scrape. He was born in the same scrape. I verily believe that the announcement in the newspapers when his mother was confined, was 'On Tuesday last, at her residence in Botheration Buildings, Mrs. Skimpole of a son in difficulties.'"

Richard laughed heartily, but added, "Still, sir, I don't want to shake his confidence, or to break his confidence; and if I submit to your better knowledge again, that I ought to keep his secret, I hope you will consider before you press me any more. Of course, if you do press me, sir, I shall know I am wrong, and will tell you."

"Well!" cried Mr. Jarndyce, stopping again, and making several absent endeavours to put his candlestick in his pocket. "I—here! Take it away, my dear. I don't know what I am about with it; it's all the wind—invariably has that effect —I won't press you, Rick; you may be right. But really— to get hold of you and Esther—and to squeeze you like a couple of tender young Saint Michael's oranges!—It'll blow a gale in the course of the night!"

He was now alternately putting his hands into his pockets, as if he were going to keep them there a long time; and taking them out again, and vehemently rubbing them all over his head.

I ventured to take this opportunity of hinting that Mr. Skimpole, being in all such matters, quite a child—

"Eh, my dear?" said Mr. Jarndyce, catching at the word.

" —Being quite a child, sir," said I, "and so different from other people—— "

"You are right!" said Mr. Jarndyce, brightening. "Your woman's wit hits the mark. He is a child—an absolute child. I told you he was a child, you know, when I first mentioned him."

Certainly! certainly! we said.

"And he *is* a child. Now, isn't he?" asked Mr. Jarndyce, brightening more and more.

He was indeed, we said.

"When you come to think of it, it's the height of childishness in you—I mean me— " said Mr. Jarndyce, "to regard him for a moment as a man. You can't make *him* responsible. The idea of Harold Skimpole with designs or plans, or knowledge of consequences! Ha, ha, ha!"

It was so delicious to see the clouds about his bright face clearing, and to see him so heartily pleased, and to know, as it was impossible not to know, that the source of his pleasure was the goodness which was tortured by condemning, or mistrusting, or secretly accusing any one, that I saw the tears in Ada's eyes, while she echoed his laugh, and felt them in my own.

"Why, what a cod's head and shoulders I am," said Mr. Jarndyce, "to require reminding of it! The whole business shows the child from beginning to end. Nobody but a child would have thought of singling *you* two out for parties in the affair! Nobody but a child would have thought of *your* having the money! If it had been a thousand pounds, it would have been just the same!" said Mr. Jarndyce, with his whole face in a glow.

We all confirmed it from our night's experience.

"To be sure, to be sure!" said Mr. Jarndyce. "However, Rick, Esther, and you too, Ada, for I don't know that even your little purse is safe from his inexperience—I must have a promise all round, that nothing of this sort shall ever be done any more. No advances! Not even sixpences."

We all promised faithfully; Richard, with a merry glance at me, touching his pocket, as if to remind me that there was no danger of *our* transgressing.

"As to Skimpole," said Mr. Jarndyce, "a habitable doll's house, with good board, and a few tin people to get into debt with and borrow money of, would set the boy up in life. He is in a child's sleep by this time, I suppose; it's time I should take my craftier head to my more worldly pillow. Good night, my dears. God bless you!"

He peeped in again, with a smiling face, before we had lighted our candles, and said, "O! I have been looking at the weather-cock. I find it was a false alarm about the wind. It's in the south!" And went away singing to himself.

Ada and I agreed, as we talked together for a little while up-stairs, that this caprice about the wind was a fiction; and that he used the pretence to account for any disappointment he could not conceal, rather than he would blame the real cause of it, or disparage or depreciate any one. We thought this very characteristic of his eccentric gentleness; and of the difference between him and those petulant people who make the weather and the winds (particularly that unlucky wind which he had chosen for such a different purpose) the stalking-horses of their splenetic and gloomy humours.

Indeed, so much affection for him had been added in this one evening to my gratitude, that I hoped I already began to understand him through that mingled feeling. Any seeming inconsistencies in Mr. Skimpole, or in Mrs. Jellyby, I could not expect to be able to reconcile; having so little experience or practical knowledge. Neither did I try; for my thoughts were busy when I was alone, with Ada and Richard, and with the confidence I had seemed to receive concerning them. My fancy, made a little wild by the wind perhaps, would not consent to be all unselfish, either, though I would have persuaded it to be so if I could. It wandered back to my godmother's house, and came along the intervening track, raising up shadowy speculations which had sometimes trembled there in the dark, as to what knowledge Mr. Jarndyce had of my earliest history—even as to the possibility of his being my father—though that idle dream was quite gone now.

It was all gone now, I remembered, getting up from the fire. It was not for me to muse over bygones, but to act with a cheerful spirit and a grateful heart. So I said to myself, "Esther, Esther, Esther! Duty, my dear!" and gave my little basket of housekeeping keys such a shake, that they sounded like little bells, and rang me hopefully to bed.

CHAPTER VII

WHILE Esther sleeps, and while Esther wakes, it is still wet weather down at the place in Lincolnshire. The rain is ever falling, drip, drip, drip, by day and night, upon the broad flagged terrace-pavement, The Ghost's Walk. The weather is so very bad, down in Lincolnshire, that the liveliest imagination can scarcely apprehend its ever being fine again. Not that there is any superabundant life of imagination on the spot, for Sir Leicester is not here (and, truly, even if he were, would not do much for it in that particular), but is in Paris, with my Lady; and solitude, with dusky wings, sits brooding upon Chesney Wold.

There may be some motions of fancy among the lower animals at Chesney Wold. The horses in the stables—the long stables in a barren, red-brick courtyard, where there is a great bell in a turret, and a clock with a large face, which the pigeons who live near it, and who love to perch upon its shoulders, seem to be always consulting—*they* may contemplate some mental pictures of fine weather on occasions, and may be better artists at them than the grooms. The old roan, so famous for cross-country work, turning his large eyeball to the grated window near his rack, may remember the fresh leaves that glisten there at other times, and the scents that stream in, and may have a fine run with the hounds, while the human helper, clearing out the next stall, never stirs beyond his pitchfork and birch-broom. The grey, whose place is opposite the door, and who, with an impatient rattle of his halter, pricks his ears and turns his head so wistfully when it is opened, and to whom the opener says, " Woa, grey, then, steady ! Noabody wants you to-day !" may know it quite as well as the man. The whole seemingly monotonous and uncompanionable half-dozen, stabled together, may pass the long wet hours, when the door is shut, in livelier communication than is held in the servants' hall, or at the Dedlock Arms ;— or may even beguile the time by improving (perhaps corrupting) the pony in the loose-box in the corner.

So the mastiff, dozing in his kennel, in the courtyard, with his large head on his paws, may think of the hot sunshine, when the shadows of the stable-buildings tire his patience out by changing, and leave him, at one time of the day, no broader refuge than the shadow of his own house, where he sits on end, panting and growling short, and very much wanting something to worry, besides himself and his chain. So, now, half-waking and all-winking, he may recall the house full of company, the coach-houses full of vehicles, the stables full of horses, and the out-buildings full of attendants upon horses, until he is undecided about the present, and comes forth to see how it is. Then, with that impatient shake of himself, he may growl in the spirit, " Rain, rain, rain ! Nothing but rain—and no family here !" as he goes in again, and lies down with a gloomy yawn.

So with the dogs in the kennel-buildings across the park, who have their restless fits, and whose doleful voices, when the wind has been very obstinate, have even made it known in the house itself: up-stairs, down-stairs, and in my lady's chamber. They may hunt the whole country-side, while the raindrops are pattering round their inactivity. So the rabbits with their self-betraying tails, frisking in and out of holes at roots of trees, may be lively with ideas of the breezy days when their ears are blown about, or of those seasons of interest when there are sweet young plants to gnaw. The turkey in the poultry-yard, always troubled with a class-grievance (probably Christmas), may be reminiscent of that summer-morning wrongfully taken from him, when he got into the lane among the felled trees, where there was a barn and barley. The discontented goose, who stoops to pass under the old gateway, twenty feet high, may gabble out, if we only knew it, a waddling preference for weather when the gateway casts its shadow on the ground.

Be this as it may, there is not much fancy otherwise stirring at Chesney Wold. If there be a little at any odd moment, it goes, like a little noise in that old echoing place, a long way, and usually leads off to ghosts and mystery.

It has rained so hard and rained so long, down in Lincolnshire, that Mrs. Rouncewell, the old housekeeper at Chesney Wold, has several times taken off her spectacles and cleaned them, to make certain that the drops were not upon the glasses. Mrs. Rouncewell might have been sufficiently assured by hearing the rain, but that she is rather deaf, which nothing will induce her to believe. She is a fine old lady, handsome, stately, wonderfully neat, and has such a back and such a stomacher, that if her stays should turn out when she dies to have been a broad old-fashioned family fire-grate, nobody who knows her would have cause to be surprised. Weather affects Mrs. Rouncewell little. The house is there in all weathers, and the house, as she expresses it, " is what she looks at." She sits in her room (in a side passage on the ground floor, with an arched window commanding a smooth quadrangle, adorned at regular intervals with smooth round trees and smooth round blocks of stone, as if the trees were going to play at bowls with the stones), and the whole house reposes on her mind. She can open it on occasion, and be busy and fluttered ; but it is shut-up now, and lies on the breadth of Mrs. Rouncewell's iron-bound bosom, in a majestic sleep.

It is the next difficult thing to an impossibility to imagine Chesney Wold without Mrs. Rouncewell, but she has only been here fifty years. Ask her how long, this rainy day, and she shall answer "fifty year three months and a fortnight, by the blessing of Heaven, if I live till Tuesday." Mr. Rouncewell died some time before the decease of the pretty fashion of pig-tails, and modestly hid his own (if he took it with him) in a corner of the churchyard in the park, near the mouldy porch. He was born in the market-town, and so was his young widow. Her progress in the family began in the time of the last Sir Leicester, and originated in the still-room.

The present representative of the Dedlocks is an excellent master. He supposes all his dependants to be utterly bereft of individual characters, intentions, or opinions, and is persuaded that he was born to supersede the necessity of their having any. If he were to make a discovery to the contrary, he would be simply stunned—would never recover himself, most likely, except to gasp and die. But he is an excellent master still, holding it a part of his state to be so. He has a great liking for Mrs. Rouncewell; he says she is a most respectable, creditable woman. He always shakes hands with her, when he comes down to Chesney Wold, and when he goes away; and if he were very ill, or if he were knocked down by accident, or run over, or placed in any situation expressive of a Dedlock at a disadvantage, he would say if he could speak, "Leave me, and send Mrs. Rouncewell here!" feeling his dignity, at such a pass, safer with her than with anybody else.

Mrs. Rouncewell has known trouble. She has had two sons, of whom the younger ran wild, and went for a soldier, and never came back. Even to this hour, Mrs. Rouncewell's calm hands lose their composure when she speaks of him, and unfolding themselves from her stomacher, hover about her in an agitated manner, as she says, what a likely lad, what a fine lad, what a gay, good-humoured, clever lad he was! Her second son would have been provided for at Chesney Wold, and would have been made steward in due season; but he took, when he was a schoolboy, to constructing steam-engines out of saucepans, and setting birds to draw their own water, with the least possible amount of labour; so assisting them with artful contrivance of hydraulic pressure, that a thirsty canary had only, in a literal sense, to put his shoulder to the wheel, and the job was done. This propensity gave Mrs. Rouncewell great uneasiness. She felt it with a mother's anguish, to be a move in the Wat Tyler direction: well knowing that Sir Leicester had that general impression of an aptitude for any art to which smoke and a tall chimney might be considered essential. But the doomed young rebel (otherwise a mild youth, and very persevering), showing no sign of grace as he got older; but, on the contrary, constructing a model of a power-loom, she was fain, with many tears, to mention his backslidings to the baronet. "Mrs. Rouncewell," said Sir Leicester, "I can never consent to argue, as you know, with any one on any subject. You had better get rid of your boy; you had better get him into some Works. The Iron country farther north is, I suppose, the congenial direction for a boy with these tendencies." Farther north he went, and farther north he grew up; and if Sir Leicester Dedlock ever saw him, when he came to Chesney Wold to visit his mother, or ever thought of him afterwards, it is certain that he only regarded him as one of a body of some odd thousand conspirators, swarthy and grim, who were in the habit of turning out by torchlight, two or three nights in the week, for unlawful purposes.

Nevertheless Mrs. Rouncewell's son has, in the course of nature and art, grown up, and established himself, and married, and called unto him Mrs. Rouncewell's grandson: who, being out of his apprenticeship, and home from a journey in far countries, whither he was sent to enlarge his knowledge and complete his preparations for the venture of this life, stands leaning against the chimney-piece this very day, in Mrs. Rouncewell's room at Chesney Wold.

"And, again and again, I am glad to see you, Watt! And, once again, I am glad to see you, Watt!" says Mrs. Rouncewell. "You are a fine young fellow. You are like your poor uncle George. Ah!" Mrs. Rouncewell's hands unquiet, as usual, on this reference.

"They say I am like my father, grandmother."

"Like him, also, my dear,—but most like your poor uncle George! And your dear father." Mrs. Rouncewell folds her hands again. "He is well?"

"Thriving, grandmother, in every way."

"I am thankful!" Mrs. Rouncewell is fond of her son, but has a plaintive feeling towards him—much as if he were a very honourable soldier, who had gone over to the enemy.

"He is quite happy?" says she.

"Quite."

"I am thankful! So he has brought you up to follow in his ways, and has sent you into foreign countries and the like? Well, he knows best. There may be a world beyond Chesney Wold that I don't understand. Though I am not young, either. And I have seen a quantity of good company too!"

"Grandmother," says the young man, changing the subject, "what a very pretty girl that was, I found with you just now. You called her Rosa?"

"Yes, child. She is daughter of a widow in the village. Maids are so hard to teach, now-a-days, that I have put her about me young. She's an apt scholar, and will do well. She shows the house already, very pretty. She lives with me at my table here."

"I hope I have not driven her away?"

"She supposes we have family affairs to speak about, I dare say. She is very modest. It is a fine quality in a young woman. And scarcer," says Mrs. Rouncewell, expanding her stomacher to its utmost limits, "than it formerly was!"

The young man inclines his head, in acknowledgment of the precepts of experience. Mrs. Rouncewell listens.

"Wheels!" says she. They have long been audible to the younger ears of her companion. "What wheels on such a day as this, for gracious sake?"

After a short interval a tap at the door. "Come in!" A dark-eyed, dark-haired, shy, village beauty comes in—so fresh in her rosy and yet delicate bloom, that the drops of rain, which have beaten on her hair, look like the dew upon a flower fresh gathered.

"What company is this, Rosa?" says Mrs. Rouncewell.

"It's two young men in a gig, ma'am, who want to see the house—yes, and if you please, I told them so!" in quick reply to a gesture of dissent from the housekeeper. "I went to the hall-door, and told them it was the wrong day, and the wrong hour; but the young man who was driving took off his hat in the wet, and begged me to bring this card to you."

"Read it, my dear Watt," says the housekeeper.

Rosa is so shy as she gives it to him, that they drop it between them, and almost knock their foreheads together as they pick it up. Rosa is shyer than before.

"Mr. Guppy" is all the information the card yields.

"Guppy!" repeats Mrs. Rouncewell. "*Mr.* Guppy! Nonsense, I never heard of him!"

"If you please, he told *me* that!" says Rosa. "But he said that he and the other young gentleman came from London only last night by the mail, on business at the magistrates' meeting, ten miles off, this morning; and that as their business was soon over, and they had heard a great deal said of Chesney Wold, and really didn't know what to do with themselves, they had come through the wet to see it. They are lawyers. He says he is not in Mr. Tulkinghorn's office, but he is sure he may make use of Mr. Tulkinghorn's name, if necessary." Finding, now she leaves off, that she has been making quite a long speech, Rosa is shyer than ever.

Now, Mr. Tulkinghorn is, in a manner, part and parcel of the place; and, besides, is supposed to have made Mrs.

Rouncewell's will. The old lady relaxes, consents to the
admission of the visitors as a favour, and dismisses Rosa.
The grandson, however, being smitten by a sudden wish to
see the house himself, proposes to join the party. The
grandmother, who is pleased that he should have that interest,
accompanies him—though to do him justice, he is exceedingly
unwilling to trouble her.

"Much obliged to you, ma'am!" says Mr. Guppy, divesting
himself of his wet dreadnought in the hall. "Us London
lawyers don't often get an out; and when we do, we like to
make the most of it, you know."

The old housekeeper, with a gracious severity of deportment, waves her hand towards the great staircase. Mr.
Guppy and his friend follow Rosa, Mrs. Rouncewell and her
grandson follow them, a young gardener goes before to open
the shutters.

As is usually the case with people who go over houses,
Mr. Guppy and his friend are dead beat before they have
well begun. They straggle about in wrong places, look at
wrong things, don't care for the right things, gape when
more rooms are opened, exhibit profound depression of spirits,
and are clearly knocked up. In each successive chamber that
they enter, Mrs. Rouncewell, who is as upright as the house
itself, rests apart in a window-seat, or other such nook, and
listens with stately approval to Rosa's exposition. Her grandson is so attentive to it, that Rosa is shyer than ever—and
prettier. Thus they pass on from room to room, raising
the pictured Dedlocks for a few brief minutes as the young
gardener admits the light, and reconsigning them to their
graves as he shuts it out again. It appears to the afflicted
Mr. Guppy and his inconsolable friend, that there is no end
to the Dedlocks, whose family greatness seems to consist in
their never having done anything to distinguish themselves,
for seven hundred years.

Even the long drawing-room of Chesney Wold cannot
revive Mr. Guppy's spirits. He is so low that he droops

on the threshold, and has hardly strength of mind to enter. But a portrait over the chimney-piece, painted by the fashionable artist of the day, acts upon him like a charm. He recovers in a moment. He stares at it with uncommon interest; he seems to be fixed and fascinated by it.

"Dear me!" says Mr. Guppy. "Who's that?"

"The picture over the fireplace," says Rosa, "is the portrait of the present Lady Dedlock. It is considered a perfect likeness, and the best work of the master."

"'Blest!" says Mr. Guppy, staring in a kind of dismay at his friend, "if I can ever have seen her. Yet I know her! Has the picture been engraved, miss?"

"The picture has never been engraved. Sir Leicester has always refused permission."

"Well!" says Mr. Guppy in a low voice, "I'll be shot if it ain't very curious how well I know that picture! So that's Lady Dedlock, is it!"

"The picture on the right is the present Sir Leicester Dedlock. The picture on the left is his father, the late Sir Leicester."

Mr. Guppy has no eyes for either of these magnates. "It's unaccountable to me," he says, still staring at the portrait, "how well I know that picture! I'm dashed!" adds Mr. Guppy, looking round, "if I don't think I must have had a dream of that picture, you know!"

As no one present takes any especial interest in Mr. Guppy's dreams, the probability is not pursued. But he still remains so absorbed by the portrait, that he stands immoveable before it until the young gardener has closed the shutters; when he comes out of the room in a dazed state, that is an odd though a sufficient substitute for interest, and follows into the succeeding rooms with a confused stare, as if he were looking everywhere for Lady Dedlock again.

He sees no more of her. He sees her rooms, which are the last shown, as being very elegant, and he looks out of the windows from which she looked out, not long ago, upon the weather that bored her to death. All things have an end—even houses that people take infinite pains to see, and are tired of before they begin to see them. He has come to the end of the sight, and the fresh village beauty to the end of her description; which is always this:

"The terrace below is much admired. It is called, from an old story in the family, The Ghost's Walk."

"No?" says Mr. Guppy, greedily curious; "what's the story, miss? Is it anything about a picture?"

"Pray tell us the story," says Watt, in a half whisper.

"I don't know it, sir." Rosa is shyer than ever.

"It is not related to visitors; it is almost forgotten," says the housekeeper, advancing. "It has never been more than a family anecdote."

"You'll excuse my asking again if it has anything to do with a picture, ma'am," observes Mr. Guppy, "because I do assure you that the more I think of that picture the better I know it, without knowing how I know it!"

The story has nothing to do with a picture; the housekeeper can guarantee that. Mr. Guppy is obliged to her for the information; and is, moreover, generally obliged. He retires with his friend, guided down another staircase by the young gardener; and presently is heard to drive away. It is now dusk. Mrs. Rouncewell can trust to the discretion of her two young hearers, and may tell *them* how the terrace came to have that ghostly name. She seats herself in a large chair by the fast-darkening window, and tells them:

"In the wicked days, my dears, of King Charles the First —I mean, of course, in the wicked days of the rebels who leagued themselves against that excellent King—Sir Morbury Dedlock was the owner of Chesney Wold. Whether there was any account of a ghost in the family before those days, I can't say. I should think it very likely indeed."

Mrs. Rouncewell holds this opinion, because she considers that a family of such antiquity and importance has a right to a ghost. She regards a ghost as one of the privileges of the upper classes; a genteel distinction to which the common people have no claim.

"Sir Morbury Dedlock," says Mrs. Rouncewell, "was, I have no occasion to say, on the side of the blessed martyr. But it *is* supposed that his Lady, who had none of the family blood in her veins, favoured the bad cause. It is said that she had relations among King Charles's enemies: that she was in correspondence with them; and that she gave them information. When any of the country gentlemen who followed His Majesty's cause met here, it is said that my Lady was always nearer to the door of their council-room than they supposed. Do you hear a sound like a footstep passing along the terrace, Watt?"

Rosa draws nearer to the housekeeper.

"I hear the rain-drip on the stones," replies the young man, "and I hear a curious echo—I suppose an echo—which is very like a halting step."

The housekeeper gravely nods and continues:

"Partly on account of this division between them, and partly on other accounts, Sir Morbury and his Lady led a troubled life. She was a lady of a haughty temper. They were not well suited to each other in age or character, and they had no children to moderate between them. After her favourite brother, a young gentleman, was killed in the civil wars (by Sir Morbury's near kinsman), her feeling was so violent that she hated the race into which she had married. When the Dedlocks were about to ride out from Chesney Wold in the King's cause, she is supposed to have more than once stolen down into the stables in the dead of night, and lamed their horses: and the story is, that once, at such an hour, her husband saw her gliding down the stairs and followed her into the stall where his own favourite horse stood. There he seized her by the wrist; and in a struggle or in a fall, or through the horse being frightened and lashing out, she was lamed in the hip, and from that hour began to pine away."

The housekeeper has dropped her voice to a little more than a whisper.

"She had been a lady of a handsome figure and a noble carriage. She never complained of the change; she never spoke to any one of being crippled, or of being in pain; but, day by day, she tried to walk upon the terrace; and with the help of the stone balustrade, went up and down, up and down, up and down, in sun and shadow, with greater difficulty every day. At last, one afternoon, her husband (to whom she had never, on any persuasion, opened her lips since that night), standing at the great south window, saw her drop upon the pavement. He hastened down to raise her, but she repulsed him as he bent over her, and looking at him fixedly and coldly, said 'I will die here where I have walked. And I will walk here, though I am in my grave. I will walk here, until the pride of this house is humbled. And when calamity, or when disgrace is coming to it, let the Dedlocks listen for my step!'"

Watt looks at Rosa. Rosa in the deepening gloom looks down upon the ground, half frightened and half shy.

"There and then she died. And from those days," says Mrs. Rouncewell, "the name has come down—The Ghost's Walk. If the tread is an echo, it is an echo that is only heard after dark, and is often unheard for a long while together. But it comes back, from time to time; and so sure as there is sickness or death in the family, it will be heard then."

"—And disgrace, grandmother—" says Watt.

"Disgrace never comes to Chesney Wold," returns the housekeeper.

Her grandson apologises, with "True. True."

"That is the story. Whatever the sound is, it is a worrying sound," says Mrs. Rouncewell, getting up from her chair, "and what is to be noticed in it, is, that it *must be heard*. My Lady, who is afraid of nothing, admits that when it is there, it must be heard. You cannot shut it out.

Watt, there is a tall French clock behind you (placed there, 'a purpose) that has a loud beat when it is in motion, and can play music. You understand how those things are managed?"

"Pretty well, grandmother, I think."

"Set it a-going."

Watt sets it a-going—music and all.

"Now, come hither," says the housekeeper. "Hither, child, towards my Lady's pillow. I am not sure that it is dark enough yet, but listen! Can you hear the sound upon the terrace, through the music, and the beat, and everything?"

"I certainly can!"

"So my Lady says."

CHAPTER VIII

COVERING A MULTITUDE OF SINS

IT was interesting when I dressed before daylight, to peep
out of window, where my candles were reflected in the
black panes like two beacons, and, finding all beyond still
enshrouded in the indistinctness of last night, to watch how
it turned out when the day came on. As the prospect
gradually revealed itself, and disclosed the scene over which
the wind had wandered in the dark, like my memory over
my life, I had a pleasure in discovering the unknown objects
that had been around me in my sleep. At first they were
faintly discernible in the mist, and above them the later
stars still glimmered. That pale interval over, the picture
began to enlarge and fill up so fast, that, at every new peep,
I could have found enough to look at for an hour. Imper-
ceptibly, my candles became the only incongruous part of
the morning, the dark places in my room all melted away,
and the day shone bright upon a cheerful landscape, prominent
in which the old Abbey Church, with its massive tower,
threw a softer train of shadow on the view than seemed
compatible with its rugged character. But so from rough
outsides (I hope I have learnt), serene and gentle influences
often proceed.

Every part of the house was in such order, and every one
was so attentive to me, that I had no trouble with my two
bunches of keys : though what with trying to remember the
contents of each little store-room drawer, and cupboard ;

112

and what with making notes on a slate about jams, and pickles, and preserves, and bottles, and glass, and china, and a great many other things ; and what with being generally a methodical, old-maidish sort of foolish little person ; I was so busy that I could not believe it was breakfast-time when I heard the bell ring. Away I ran, however, and made tea, as I had already been installed into the responsibility of the teapot ; and then, as they were all rather late, and nobody was down yet, I thought I would take a peep at the garden and get some knowledge of that too. I found it quite a delightful place ; in front, the pretty avenue and drive by which we had approached (and where, by-the-bye, we had cut up the gravel so terribly with our wheels that I asked the gardener to roll it); at the back, the flower-garden, with my darling at her window up there, throwing it open to smile out at me, as if she would have kissed me from that distance. Beyond the flower-garden was a kitchen-garden, and then a paddock, and then a snug little rick-yard, and then a dear little farm-yard. As to the House itself, with its three peaks in the roof ; its various-shaped windows, some so large, some so small, and all so pretty ; its trellis-work, against the south-front for roses and honey-suckle, and its homely, comfortable, welcoming look : it was, as Ada said, when she came out to meet me with her arm through that of its master, worthy of her cousin John—a bold thing to say, though he only pinched her dear cheek for it.

Mr. Skimpole was as agreeable at breakfast, as he had been over-night. There was honey on the table, and it led him into a discourse about Bees. He had no objection to honey, he said (and I should think he had not, for he seemed to like it), but he protested against the overweening assumptions of Bees. He didn't at all see why the busy Bee should be proposed as a model to him ; he supposed the Bee liked to make honey, or he wouldn't do it—nobody asked him. It was not necessary for the Bee to make such a merit of his tastes. If every confectioner went buzzing about the world, banging

113

against everything that came in his way, and egotistically calling upon everybody to take notice that he was going to his work and must not be interrupted, the world would be quite an unsupportable place. Then, after all, it was a ridiculous position, to be smoked out of your fortune with brimstone, as soon as you had made it. You would have a very mean opinion of a Manchester man, if he spun cotton for no other purpose. He must say he thought a Drone the embodiment of a pleasanter and wiser idea. The Drone said, unaffectedly, "You will excuse me; I really cannot attend to the shop! I find myself in a world in which there is so much to see, and so short a time to see it in, that I must take the liberty of looking about me, and begging to be provided for by somebody who doesn't want to look about him." This appeared to Mr. Skimpole to be the Drone philosophy, and he thought it a very good philosophy—always supposing the Drone to be willing to be on good terms with the Bee: which, so far as he knew, the easy fellow always was, if the consequential creature would only let him, and not be so conceited about his honey!

He pursued this fancy with the lightest foot over a variety of ground, and made us all merry; though again he seemed to have as serious a meaning in what he said as he was capable of having. I left them still listening to him, when I withdrew to attend to my new duties. They had occupied me for some time, and I was passing through the passages on my return with my basket of keys on my arm, when Mr. Jarndyce called me into a small room next his bed-chamber, which I found to be in part a little library of books and papers, and in part quite a little museum of his boots and shoes, and hat-boxes.

"Sit down, my dear," said Mr. Jarndyce. "This, you must know, is the Growlery. When I am out of humour, I come and growl here."

"You must be here very seldom, sir," said I.

"O, you don't know me!" he returned. "When I am

deceived or disappointed in—the wind, and it's Easterly, I take refuge here. The Growlery is the best-used room in the house. You are not aware of half my humours yet. My dear, how you are trembling!"

I could not help it: I tried very hard: but being alone with that benevolent presence, and meeting his kind eyes, and feeling so happy, and so honoured there, and my heart so full——

I kissed his hand. I don't know what I said, or even that I spoke. He was disconcerted, and walked to the window; I almost believed with an intention of jumping out, until he turned, and I was reassured by seeing in his eyes what he had gone there to hide. He gently patted me on the head, and I sat down.

"There! There!" he said. "That's over. Pooh! Don't be foolish."

"It shall not happen again, sir," I returned, "but at first it is difficult——"

"Nonsense!" he said, "it's easy, easy. Why not? I hear of a good little orphan girl without a protector, and I take it into my head to be that protector. She grows up, and more than justifies my good opinion, and I remain her guardian and her friend. What is there in all this? So, so! Now, we have cleared off old scores, and I have before me thy pleasant, trusting, trusty face again."

I said to myself, "Esther, my dear, you surprise me! This really is not what I expected of you!" and it had such a good effect, that I folded my hands upon my basket and quite recovered myself. Mr. Jarndyce, expressing his approval in his face, began to talk to me as confidentially as if I had been in the habit of conversing with him every morning for I don't know how long. I almost felt as if I had.

"Of course, Esther," he said, "you don't understand this Chancery business?"

And of course I shook my head.

"I don't know who does," he returned. "The Lawyers

have twisted it into such a state of bedevilment that the original merits of the case have long disappeared from the face of the earth. It's about a Will, and the trusts under a Will—or it was, once. It's about nothing but Costs, now. We are always appearing, and disappearing, and swearing, and interrogating, and filing, and cross-filing, and arguing, and sealing, and motioning, and referring, and reporting, and revolving about the Lord Chancellor and all his satellites, and equitably waltzing ourselves off to dusty death, about Costs. That's the great question. All the rest, by some extraordinary means, has melted away."

"But it was, sir," said I, to bring him back, for he began to rub his head, "about a Will?"

"Why, yes, it was about a Will when it was about anything," he returned. "A certain Jarndyce, in an evil hour, made a great fortune, and made a great Will. In the question how the trusts under that Will are to be administered, the fortune left by the Will is squandered away; the legatees under the Will are reduced to such a miserable condition that they would be sufficiently punished, if they had committed an enormous crime in having money left them; and the Will itself is made a dead letter. All through the deplorable cause, everything that everybody in it, except one man, knows already, is referred to that only one man who don't know it, to find out—all through the deplorable cause, everybody must have copies, over and over again, of everything that has accumulated about it in the way of cartloads of papers (or must pay for them without having them, which is the usual course, for nobody wants them); and must go down the middle and up again, through such an infernal country-dance of costs and fees and nonsense and corruption, as was never dreamed of in the wildest visions of a Witch's Sabbath. Equity sends questions to Law, Law sends questions back to Equity; Law finds it can't do this, Equity finds it can't do that; neither can so much as say it can't do anything, without this solicitor instructing and this counsel appearing for A, and that solicitor instructing and that counsel appearing for B; and so on through the whole alphabet, like the history of the Apple Pie. And thus, through years and years, and lives and lives, everything goes on, constantly beginning over and over again, and nothing ever ends. And we can't get out of the suit on any terms, for we are made parties to it, and *must be* parties to it, whether we like it or not. But it won't do to think of it! When my great uncle, poor Tom Jarndyce, began to think of it, it was the beginning of the end!"

"The Mr. Jarndyce, sir, whose story I have heard?"

He nodded gravely. "I was his heir, and this was his house, Esther. When I came here, it was bleak, indeed. He had left the signs of his misery upon it."

"How changed it must be now!" I said.

"It had been called, before his time, the Peaks. He gave it its present name, and lived here shut up: day and night poring over the wicked heaps of papers in the suit, and hoping against hope to disentangle it from its mystification and bring it to a close. In the meantime, the place became dilapidated, the wind whistled through the cracked walls, the rain fell through the broken roof, the weeds choked the passage to the rotting door. When I brought what remained of him home here, the brains seemed to me to have been blown out of the house too; it was so shattered and ruined."

He walked a little to and fro, after saying this to himself with a shudder, and then looked at me, and brightened, and came and sat down again with his hands in his pockets.

"I told you this was the Growlery, my dear. Where was I?"

I reminded him, at the hopeful change he had made in Bleak House.

"Bleak House: true. There is, in that city of London there, some property of ours, which is much at this day what Bleak House was then,—I say property of ours, meaning of the Suit's, but I ought to call it the property of Costs; for

Costs is the only power on earth that will ever get anything out of it now, or will ever know it for anything but an eyesore and a heartsore. It is a street of perishing blind houses, with their eyes stoned out; without a pane of glass, without so much as a window-frame, with the bare blank shutters tumbling from their hinges and falling asunder; the iron rails peeling away in flakes of rust; the chimneys sinking in; the stone steps to every door (and every door might be Death's Door) turning stagnant green; the very crutches on which the ruins are propped, decaying. Although Bleak House was not in Chancery, its master was, and it was stamped with the same seal. These are the Great Seal's impressions, my dear, all over England—the children know them!"

"How changed it is!" I said again.

"Why, so it is," he answered much more cheerfully; "and it is wisdom in you to keep me to the bright side of the picture." (The idea of my wisdom!) "These are things I never talk about, or even think about, excepting in the Growlery here. If you consider it right to mention them to Rick and Ada," looking seriously at me, "you can. I leave it to your discretion, Esther."

"I hope, sir"—said I.

"I think you had better call me Guardian, my dear."

I felt that I was choking again—I taxed myself with it, "Esther, now, you know you are!"—when he feigned to say this slightly, as if it were a whim, instead of a thoughtful tenderness. But I gave the housekeeping keys the least shake in the world as a reminder to myself, and folding my hands in a still more determined manner on the basket, looked at him quietly.

"I hope, Guardian," said I, "that you may not trust too much to my discretion. I hope you may not mistake me. I am afraid it will be a disappointment to you to know that I am not clever—but it really is the truth; and you would soon find it out if I had not the honesty to confess it."

WIGLOMERATION

He did not seem at all disappointed : quite the contrary. He told me, with a smile all over his face, that he knew me very well indeed, and that I was quite clever enough for him.

"I hope I may turn out so," said I, "but I am much afraid of it, Guardian."

"You are clever enough to be the good little woman of our lives here, my dear," he returned, playfully ; "the little old woman of the Child's (I don't mean Skimpole's) Rhyme.

> "'Little old woman, and whither so high ?'—
> 'To sweep the cobwebs out of the sky.'

You will sweep them so neatly out of *our* sky, in the course of your housekeeping, Esther, that one of these days, we shall have to abandon the Growlery, and nail up the door."

This was the beginning of my being called Old Woman, and Little Old Woman, and Cobweb, and Mrs. Shipton, and Mother Hubbard, and Dame Durden, and so many names of that sort, that my own name soon became quite lost among them.

"However," said Mr. Jarndyce, "to return to our gossip. Here's Rick, a fine young fellow full of promise. What's to be done with him ?"

O my goodness, the idea of asking my advice on such a point!

"Here he is, Esther," said Mr. Jarndyce, comfortably putting his hands into his pockets and stretching out his legs. "He must have a profession ; he must make some choice for himself. There will be a world more Wiglomeration about it, I suppose, but it must be done."

"More what, Guardian?" said I.

"More Wiglomeration," said he. "It's the only name I know for the thing. He is a ward in Chancery, my dear. Kenge and Carboy will have something to say about it ; Master Somebody—a sort of ridiculous Sexton, digging graves for the merits of causes in a back room at the end

119

of Quality Court, Chancery Lane—will have something to say about it; Counsel will have something to say about it; the Chancellor will have something to say about it; the Satellites will have something to say about it; they will all have to be handsomely fee'd, all round, about it; the whole thing will be vastly ceremonious, wordy, unsatisfactory, and expensive, and I call it, in general, Wiglomeration. How mankind ever came to be afflicted with Wiglomeration, or for whose sins these young people ever fell into a pit of it, I don't know; so it is."

He began to rub his head again, and to hint that he felt the wind. But it was a delightful instance of his kindness towards me, that whether he rubbed his head, or walked about, or did both, his face was sure to recover its benignant expression as it looked at mine; and he was sure to turn comfortable again, and put his hands in his pockets and stretch out his legs.

"Perhaps it would be best, first of all," said I, "to ask Mr. Richard what he inclines to himself."

"Exactly so," he returned. "That's what I mean! You know, just accustom yourself to talk it over, with your tact and in your quiet way, with him and Ada, and see what you all make of it. We are sure to come at the heart of the matter by your means, little woman."

I really was frightened at the thought of the importance I was attaining, and the number of things that were being confided to me. I had not meant this at all; I had meant that he should speak to Richard. But of course I said nothing in reply, except that I would do my best, though I feared (I really felt it necessary to repeat this) that he thought me much more sagacious than I was. At which my guardian only laughed the pleasantest laugh I ever heard.

"Come!" he said, rising and pushing back his chair. "I think we may have done with the Growlery for one day! Only a concluding word. Esther, my dear, do you wish to ask me anything?"

He looked so attentively at me, that I looked attentively at him, and felt sure I understood him.

"About myself, sir?" said I.

"Yes."

"Guardian," said I, venturing to put my hand, which was suddenly colder than I could have wished, in his, "nothing! I am quite sure that if there were anything I ought to know, or had any need to know, I should not have to ask you to tell it to me. If my whole reliance and confidence were not placed in you, I must have a hard heart indeed. I have nothing to ask you; nothing in the world."

He drew my hand through his arm, and we went away to look for Ada. From that hour I felt quite easy with him, quite unreserved, quite content to know no more, quite happy.

We lived, at first, rather a busy life at Bleak House; for we had to become acquainted with many residents in and out of the neighbourhood who knew Mr. Jarndyce. It seemed to Ada and me that everybody knew him, who wanted to do anything with anybody else's money. It amazed us, when we began to sort his letters, and to answer some of them for him in the Growlery of a morning, to find how the great object of the lives of nearly all his correspondents appeared to be to form themselves into committees for getting in and laying out money. The ladies were as desperate as the gentlemen; indeed, I think they were even more so. They threw themselves into committees in the most impassioned manner, and collected subscriptions with a vehemence quite extraordinary. It appeared to us that some of them must pass their whole lives in dealing out subscription-cards to the whole Post-office Directory—shilling cards, half-crown cards, half-sovereign cards, penny cards. They wanted everything. They wanted wearing apparel, they wanted linen rags, they wanted money, they wanted coals, they wanted soup, they wanted interest, they wanted autographs, they wanted flannel, they wanted whatever Mr.

121

Jarndyce had—or had not. Their objects were as various as their demands. They were going to raise new buildings, they were going to pay off debts on old buildings, they were going to establish in a picturesque building (engraving of proposed West Elevation attached) the Sisterhood of Mediæval Marys; they were going to give a testimonial to Mrs. Jellyby; they were going to have their Secretary's portrait painted, and presented to his mother-in-law, whose deep devotion to him was well known; they were going to get up everything, I really believe, from five hundred thousand tracts to an annuity, and from a marble monument to a silver teapot. They took a multitude of titles. They were the Women of England, the Daughters of Britain, the Sisters of all the Cardinal Virtues separately, the Females of America, the Ladies of a hundred denominations. They appeared to be always excited about canvassing and electing. They seemed to our poor wits, and according to their own accounts, to be constantly polling people by tens of thousands, yet never bringing their candidates in for anything. It made our heads ache to think, on the whole, what feverish lives they must lead.

Among the ladies who were most distinguished for this rapacious benevolence (if I may use the expression), was a Mrs. Pardiggle, who seemed, as I judged from the number of her letters to Mr. Jarndyce, to be almost as powerful a correspondent as Mrs. Jellyby herself. We observed that the wind always changed, when Mrs. Pardiggle became the subject of conversation: and that it invariably interrupted Mr. Jarndyce, and prevented his going any farther, when he had remarked that there were two classes of charitable people; one, the people who did a little and made a great deal of noise; the other, the people who did a great deal and made no noise at all. We were therefore curious to see Mrs. Pardiggle, suspecting her to be a type of the former class; and were glad when she called one day with her five young sons.

A VISITING LADY AND FAMILY

She was a formidable style of lady, with spectacles, a prominent nose, and a loud voice, who had the effect of wanting a great deal of room. And she really did, for she knocked down little chairs with her skirts that were quite a great way off. As only Ada and I were at home, we received her timidly; for she seemed to come in like cold weather, and to make the little Pardiggles blue as they followed.

"These, young ladies," said Mrs. Pardiggle, with great volubility, after the first salutations, "are my five boys. You may have seen their names in a printed subscription list (perhaps more than one), in the possession of our esteemed friend, Mr. Jarndyce. Egbert, my eldest (twelve), is the boy who sent out his pocket-money, to the amount of five-and-threepence, to the Tockahoopo Indians. Oswald, my second (ten-and-a-half), is the child who contributed two-and-ninepence to the Great National Smithers Testimonial. Francis, my third (nine), one-and-sixpence-halfpenny; Felix, my fourth (seven), eightpence to the Superannuated Widows; Alfred, my youngest (five), has voluntarily enrolled himself in the Infant Bonds of Joy, and is pledged never, through life, to use tobacco in any form."

We had never seen such dissatisfied children. It was not merely that they were weazened and shrivelled—though they were certainly that too—but they looked absolutely ferocious with discontent. At the mention of the Tockahoopo Indians, I could really have supposed Egbert to be one of the most baleful members of that tribe, he gave me such a savage frown. The face of each child, as the amount of his contribution was mentioned, darkened in a peculiarly vindictive manner, but his was by far the worst. I must except, however, the little recruit into the Infant Bonds of Joy, who was stolidly and evenly miserable.

"You have been visiting, I understand," said Mrs. Pardiggle, "at Mrs. Jellyby's?"

We said yes, we had passed one night there.

123

" Mrs. Jellyby," pursued the lady, always speaking in the same demonstrative, loud, hard tone, so that her voice impressed my fancy as if it had a sort of spectacles on too— and I may take the opportunity of remarking that her spectacles were made the less engaging by her eyes being what Ada called " choking eyes," meaning very prominent: " Mrs. Jellyby is a benefactor to society, and deserves a helping hand. My boys have contributed to the African project—Egbert, one-and six, being the entire allowance of nine weeks; Oswald, one-and-a-penny-halfpenny, being the same; the rest, according to their little means. Nevertheless, I do not go with Mrs. Jellyby in all things. I do not go with Mrs. Jellyby in her treatment of her young family. It has been noticed. It has been observed that her young family are excluded from participation in the objects to which she is devoted. She may be right, she may be wrong; but, right or wrong, this is not my course with *my* young family. I take them everywhere."

I was afterwards convinced (and so was Ada) that from the ill-conditioned eldest child, these words extorted a sharp yell. He turned it off into a yawn, but it began as a yell.

" They attend Matins with me (very prettily done), at half-past six o'clock in the morning all the year round, including of course the depth of winter," said Mrs. Pardiggle rapidly, " and they are with me during the revolving duties of the day. I am a School lady, I am a Visiting lady, I am a Reading lady, I am a Distributing lady; I am on the local Linen Box Committee, and many general Committees; and my canvassing alone is very extensive—perhaps no one's more so. But they are my companions everywhere; and by these means they acquire that knowledge of the poor, and that capacity of doing charitable business in general—in short, that taste for the sort of thing—which will render them in after life a service to their neighbours, and a satisfaction to themselves. My young family are not frivolous; they expend the entire amount of their allowance, in subscriptions, under my direction; and they have attended as many public meetings, and listened to as many lectures, orations, and discussions, as generally fall to the lot of few grown people. Alfred (five), who, as I mentioned, has of his own election joined the Infant Bonds of Joy, was one of the very few children who manifested consciousness on that occasion, after a fervid address of two hours from the chairman of the evening."

Alfred glowered at us as if he never could, or would, forgive the injury of that night.

"You may have observed, Miss Summerson," said Mrs. Pardiggle, "in some of the lists to which I have referred, in the possession of our esteemed friend Mr. Jarndyce, that the names of my young family are concluded with the name of O. A. Pardiggle, F.R.S., one pound. That is their father. We usually observe the same routine. I put down my mite first; then my young family enrol their contributions, according to their ages and their little means; and then Mr. Pardiggle brings up the rear. Mr. Pardiggle is happy to throw in his limited donation, under my direction; and thus things are made, not only pleasant to ourselves, but, we trust, improving to others."

Suppose Mr. Pardiggle were to dine with Mr. Jellyby, and suppose Mr. Jellyby were to relieve his mind after dinner to Mr. Pardiggle, would Mr. Pardiggle, in return, make any confidential communication to Mr. Jellyby? I was quite confused to find myself thinking this, but it came into my head.

"You are very pleasantly situated here!" said Mrs. Pardiggle.

We were glad to change the subject; and, going to the window, pointed out the beauties of the prospect, on which the spectacles appeared to me to rest with curious indifference.

"You know Mr. Gusher?" said our visitor.

We were obliged to say that we had not the pleasure of Mr. Gusher's acquaintance.

"The loss is yours, I assure you," said Mrs. Pardiggle,

with her commanding deportment. "He is a very fervid impassioned speaker—full of fire·! Stationed in a waggon on this lawn, now, which, from the shape of the land, is naturally adapted to a public meeting, he would improve almost any occasion you could mention for hours and hours! By this time, young ladies," said Mrs. Pardiggle, moving back to her chair, and overturning, as if by invisible agency, a little round table at a considerable distance with my work-basket on it, "by this time you have found me out, I dare say?"

This was really such a confusing question that Ada looked at me in perfect dismay. As to the guilty nature of my own consciousness, after what I had been thinking, it must have been expressed in the colour of my cheeks.

"Found out, I mean," said Mrs. Pardiggle, "the prominent point in my character. I am aware that it is so prominent as to be discoverable immediately. I lay myself open to detection, I know. Well! I freely admit, I am a woman of business. I love hard work; I enjoy hard work. The excitement does me good. I am so accustomed and inured to hard work that I don't know what fatigue is."

We murmured that it was very astonishing and very gratifying; or something to that effect. I don't think we knew what it was either, but this is what our politeness expressed.

"I do not understand what it is to be tired; you cannot tire me if you try!" said Mrs. Pardiggle. "The quantity of exertion (which is no exertion to me), the amount of business (which I regard as nothing), that I go through, sometimes astonishes myself. I have seen my young family, and Mr. Pardiggle, quite worn out with witnessing it, when I may truly say I have been as fresh as a lark!"

If that dark-visaged eldest boy could look more malicious than he had already looked, this was the time when he did it. I observed that he doubled his right fist, and delivered a secret blow into the crown of his cap, which was under his left arm.

MRS. PARDIGGLE'S PATRONAGE

"This gives me a great advantage when I am making my rounds," said Mrs. Pardiggle. "If I find a person unwilling to hear what I have to say, I tell that person directly, 'I am incapable of fatigue, my good friend, I am never tired, and I mean to go on until I have done.' It answers admirably! Miss Summerson, I hope I shall have your assistance in my visiting rounds immediately, and Miss Clare's very soon?"

At first I tried to excuse myself, for the present, on the general ground of having occupations to attend to, which I must not neglect. But as this was an ineffectual protest, I then said, more particularly, that I was not sure of my qualifications. That I was inexperienced in the art of adapting my mind to minds very differently situated, and addressing them from suitable points of view. That I had not that delicate knowledge of the heart which must be essential to such a work. That I had much to learn, myself, before I could teach others, and that I could not confide in my good intentions alone. For these reasons, I thought it best to be as useful as I could, and to render what kind services I could, to those immediately about me; and to try to let that circle of duty gradually and naturally expand itself. All this I said, with anything but confidence; because Mrs. Pardiggle was much older than I, and had great experience, and was so very military in her manners.

"You are wrong, Miss Summerson," said she: "but perhaps you are not equal to hard work, or the excitement of it; and that makes a vast difference. If you would like to see how I go through my work, I am now about—with my young family—to visit a brickmaker in the neighbourhood (a very bad character), and shall be glad to take you with me. Miss Clare also, if she will do me the favour."

Ada and I interchanged looks, and; as we were going out in any case, accepted the offer. When we hastily returned from putting on our bonnets, we found the young family languishing in a corner, and Mrs. Pardiggle sweeping about the room, knocking down nearly all the light objects it contained. Mrs. Pardiggle took possession of Ada, and I followed with the family.

Ada told me afterwards that Mrs. Pardiggle talked in the same loud tone (that, indeed, I overheard), all the way to the brickmaker's, about an exciting contest which she had for two or three years waged against another lady, relative to the bringing in of their rival candidates for a pension somewhere. There had been a quantity of printing, and promising, and proxying, and polling; and it appeared to have imparted great liveliness to all concerned, except the pensioners—who were not elected yet.

I am very fond of being confided in by children, and am happy in being usually favoured in that respect, but on this occasion it gave me great uneasiness. As soon as we were out of doors, Egbert, with the manner of a little footpad, demanded a shilling of me, on the ground that his pocket-money was "boned" from him. On my pointing out the great impropriety of the word, especially in connexion with his parent (for he added sulkily "By her!"), he pinched me and said "O then! Now! Who are you! *You* wouldn't like it, I think? What does she make a sham for, and pretend to give me money, and take it away again? Why do you call it *my* allowance, and never let me spend it?" These exasperating questions so inflamed his mind, and the minds of Oswald and Francis, that they all pinched me at once, and in a dreadfully expert way: screwing up such little pieces of my arms that I could hardly forbear crying out. Felix, at the same time, stamped upon my toes. And the Bond of Joy, who, on account of always having the whole of his little income anticipated, stood in fact pledged to abstain from cakes as well as tobacco, so swelled with grief and rage when we passed a pastry-cook's shop, that he terrified me by becoming purple. I never underwent so much, both in body and mind, in the course of a walk with young people, as from these unnaturally constrained children, when they paid me the compliment of being natural.

A VISIT TO THE BRICKMAKER'S

I was glad when we came to the brickmaker's house; though it was one of a cluster of wretched hovels in a brick-field, with pigsties close to the broken windows, and miserable little gardens before the doors, growing nothing but stagnant pools. Here and there, an old tub was put to catch the droppings of rain-water from a roof, or they were banked up with mud into a little pond like a large dirt-pie. At the doors and windows, some men and women lounged or prowled about, and took little notice of us, except to laugh to one another, or to say something as we passed, about gentlefolks minding their own business, and not troubling their heads and muddying their shoes with coming to look after other people's.

Mrs. Pardiggle, leading the way with a great show of moral determination, and talking with much volubility about the untidy habits of the people (though I doubted if the best of us could have been tidy in such a place), conducted us into a cottage at the farthest corner, the ground-floor room of which we nearly filled. Besides ourselves, there were in this damp offensive room—a woman with a black eye, nursing a poor little gasping baby by the fire; a man, all stained with clay and mud, and looking very dissipated, lying at full length on the ground, smoking a pipe; a powerful young man, fastening a collar on a dog; and a bold girl, doing some kind of washing in very dirty water. They all looked up at us as we came in, and the woman seemed to turn her face towards the fire, as if to hide her bruised eye; nobody gave us any welcome.

"Well, my friends," said Mrs. Pardiggle; but her voice had not a friendly sound, I thought; it was much too business-like and systematic. "How do you do, all of you? I am here again. I told you, you couldn't tire me, you know. I am fond of hard work, and am true to my word."

"There an't," growled the man on the floor, whose head rested on his hand as he stared at us, "any more on you to come in, is there?"

"No, my friend," said Mrs. Pardiggle, seating herself on one stool, and knocking down another. "We are all here."

"Because I thought there warn't enough of you, perhaps?" said the man, with his pipe between his lips, as he looked round upon us.

The young man and the girl both laughed. Two friends of the young man whom we had attracted to the doorway, and who stood there with their hands in their pockets, echoed the laugh noisily.

"You can't tire me, good people," said Mrs. Pardiggle to these latter. "I enjoy hard work; and the harder you make mine, the better I like it."

"Then make it easy for her!" growled the man upon the floor. "I wants it done, and over. I wants a end of these liberties took with my place. I wants a end of being drawed like a badger. Now you're a-going to poll-pry and question according to custom—I know what you're a-going to be up to. Well! You haven't got no occasion to be up to it. I'll save you the trouble. Is my daughter a-washin? Yes, she *is* a-washin. Look at the water. Smell it! That's wot we drinks. How do you like it, and what do you think of gin, instead! An't my place dirty? Yes, it is dirty—it's nat'rally dirty, and it's nat'rally onwholesome; and we've had five dirty and onwholesome children, as is all dead infants, and so much the better for them, and for us besides. Have I read the little book wot you left? No, I an't read the little book wot you left. There an't nobody here as knows how to read it; and if there wos, it wouldn't be suitable to me. It's a book fit for a babby, and I'm not a babby. If you was to leave me a doll, I shouldn't nuss it. How have I been conducting of myself? Why, I've been drunk for three days; and I'd a been drunk four, if I'd a had the money. Don't I never mean for to go to church? No, I don't never mean for to go to church. I shouldn't be expected there, if I did; the beadle's too gen-teel for me.

The Visit to the Brickmaker's

And how did my wife get that black eye? Why, I giv' it her; and if she says I didn't, she's a Lie!"

He had pulled his pipe out of his mouth to say all this, and he now turned over on his other side, and smoked again. Mrs. Pardiggle, who had been regarding him through her spectacles with a forcible composure, calculated, I could not help thinking, to increase his antagonism, pulled out a good book, as if it were a constable's staff, and took the whole family into custody. I mean into religious custody, of course; but she really did it, as if she were an inexorable moral Policeman carrying them all off to a station-house.

Ada and I were very uncomfortable. We both felt intrusive and out of place; and we both thought that Mrs. Pardiggle would have got on infinitely better, if she had not had such a mechanical way of taking possession of people. The children sulked and stared; the family took no notice of us whatever, except when the young man made the dog bark: which he usually did when Mrs. Pardiggle was most emphatic. We both felt painfully sensible that between us and these people there was an iron barrier, which could not be removed by our new friend. By whom, or how, it could be removed, we did not know; but we knew that. Even what she read and said, seemed to us to be ill chosen for such auditors, if it had been imparted ever so modestly and with ever so much tact. As to the little book to which the man on the floor had referred, we acquired a knowledge of it afterwards; and Mr. Jarndyce said he doubted if Robinson Crusoe could have read it, though he had had no other on his desolate island.

We were much relieved, under these circumstances, when Mrs. Pardiggle left off. The man on the floor then turning his head round again, said morosely,

" Well! You've done, have you?"

" For to-day, I have, my friend. But I am never fatigued. I shall come to you again, in your regular order," returned Mrs. Pardiggle with demonstrative cheerfulness.

" So long as you goes now," said he, folding his arms and

131

shutting his eyes with an oath, "you may do wot you like!"

Mrs. Pardiggle accordingly rose, and made a little vortex in the confined room from which the pipe itself very narrowly escaped. Taking one of her young family in each hand, and telling the others to follow closely, and expressing her hope that the brickmaker and all his house would be improved when she saw them next, she then proceeded to another cottage. I hope it is not unkind in me to say that she certainly did make, in this, as in everything else, a show that was not conciliatory, of doing charity by wholesale, and of dealing in it to a large extent.

She supposed that we were following her; but as soon as the space was left clear, we approached the woman sitting by the fire, to ask if the baby were ill.

She only looked at it as it lay on her lap. We had observed before, that when she looked at it she covered her discoloured eye with her hand, as though she wished to separate any association with noise and violence and ill-treatment, from the poor little child.

Ada, whose gentle heart was moved by its appearance, bent down to touch its little face. As she did so, I saw what happened and drew her back. The child died.

"O Esther!" cried Ada, sinking on her knees beside it. "Look here! O Esther, my love, the little thing! The suffering, quiet, pretty little thing! I am so sorry for it. I am so sorry for the mother. I never saw a sight so pitiful as this before! O baby, baby!"

Such compassion, such gentleness, as that with which she bent down weeping, and put her hand upon the mother's, might have softened any mother's heart that ever beat. The woman at first gazed at her in astonishment, and then burst into tears.

Presently I took the light burden from her lap; did what I could to make the baby's rest the prettier and gentler; laid it on a shelf, and covered it with my own handkerchief. We tried to comfort the mother, and we whispered to her what Our Saviour said of children. She answered nothing, but sat weeping—weeping very much.

When I turned, I found that the young man had taken out the dog, and was standing at the door looking in upon us; with dry eyes, but quiet. The girl was quiet too, and sat in a corner looking on the ground. The man had risen. He still smoked his pipe with an air of defiance, but he was silent.

An ugly woman, very poorly clothed, hurried in while I was glancing at them, and coming straight up to the mother, said, "Jenny! Jenny!" The mother rose on being so addressed, and fell upon the woman's neck.

She also had upon her face and arms the marks of ill-usage. She had no kind of grace about her, but the grace of sympathy; but when she condoled with the woman, and her own tears fell, she wanted no beauty. I say condoled, but her only words were "Jenny! Jenny!" All the rest was in the tone in which she said them.

I thought it very touching to see these two women, coarse and shabby and beaten, so united; to see what they could be to one another; to see how they felt for one another; how the heart of each to each was softened by the hard trials of their lives. I think the best side of such people is almost hidden from us. What the poor are to the poor is little known, excepting to themselves and GOD.

We felt it better to withdraw and leave them uninterrupted. We stole out quietly, and without notice from any one except the man. He was leaning against the wall near the door; and finding that there was scarcely room for us to pass, went out before us. He seemed to want to hide that he did this on our account, but we perceived that he did, and thanked him. He made no answer.

Ada was so full of grief all the way home, and Richard, whom we found at home, was so distressed to see her in tears (though he said to me when she was not present, how beautiful it was too!) that we arranged to return at night with some little comforts, and repeat our visit at the brickmaker's house. We said as little as we could to Mr. Jarndyce, but the wind changed directly.

Richard accompanied us at night to the scene of our morning expedition. On our way there, we had to pass a noisy drinking-house, where a number of men were flocking about the door. Among them, and prominent in some dispute, was the father of the little child. At a short distance, we passed the young man and the dog, in congenial company. The sister was standing laughing and talking with some other young women, at the corner of the row of cottages; but she seemed ashamed, and turned away as we went by.

We left our escort within sight of the brickmaker's dwelling, and proceeded by ourselves. When we came to the door, we found the woman who had brought such consolation with her, standing there, looking anxiously out.

"It's you, young ladies, is it?" she said in a whisper. "I'm a-watching for my master. My heart's in my mouth. If he was to catch me away from home, he'd pretty near murder me."

"Do you mean your husband?" said I.

"Yes, miss, my master. Jenny's asleep, quite worn out. She's scarcely had the child off her lap, poor thing, these seven days and nights, except when I've been able to take it for a minute or two."

As she gave way for us, she went softly in, and put what we had brought, near the miserable bed on which the mother slept. No effort had been made to clean the room—it seemed in its nature almost hopeless of being clean; but the small waxen form, from which so much solemnity diffused itself, had been composed afresh, and washed, and neatly dressed in some fragments of white linen; and on my handkerchief, which still covered the poor baby, a little bunch of sweet herbs had been laid by the same rough scarred hands, so lightly, so tenderly!

"May Heaven reward you!" we said to her. "You are a good woman."

"Me, young ladies?" she returned with surprise. "Hush! Jenny, Jenny!"

The mother had moaned in her sleep, and moved. The sound of the familiar voice seemed to calm her again. She was quiet once more.

How little I thought, when I raised my handkerchief to look upon the tiny sleeper underneath, and seemed to see a halo shine around the child through Ada's drooping hair as her pity bent her head—how little I thought in whose unquiet bosom that handkerchief would come to lie, after covering the motionless and peaceful breast! I only thought that perhaps the Angel of the child might not be all unconscious of the woman who replaced it with so compassionate a hand; not all unconscious of her presently, when we had taken leave, and left her at the door, by turns looking, and listening in terror for herself, and saying in her old soothing manner, "Jenny, Jenny!"

CHAPTER IX

SIGNS AND TOKENS

I DON'T know how it is, I seem to be always writing about myself. I mean all the time to write about other people, and I try to think about myself as little as possible, and I am sure, when I find myself coming into the story again, I am really vexed and say, " Dear, dear, you tiresome little creature, I wish you wouldn't ! " but it is all of no use. I hope any one who may read what I write, will understand that if these pages contain a great deal about me, I can only suppose it must be because I have really something to do with them, and can't be kept out.

My darling and I read together, and worked, and practised ; and found so much employment for our time, that the winter days flew by us like bright-winged birds. Generally in the afternoons, and always in the evenings, Richard gave us his company. Although he was one of the most restless creatures in the world, he certainly was very fond of our society.

He was very, very, very fond of Ada. I mean it, and I had better say it at once. I had never seen any young people falling in love before, but I found them out quite soon. I could not say so, of course, or show that I knew anything about it. On the contrary, I was so demure, and used to seem so unconscious, that sometimes I considered within myself while I was sitting at work, whether I was not growing quite deceitful.

But there was no help for it. All I had to do was to be

quiet, and I was as quiet as a mouse. They were as quiet as mice, too, so far as any words were concerned; but the innocent manner in which they relied more and more upon me, as they took more and more to one another, was so charming, that I had great difficulty in not showing how it interested me.

"Our dear little old woman is such a capital old woman," Richard would say, coming up to meet me in the garden early, with his pleasant laugh and perhaps the least tinge of a blush, "that I can't get on without her. Before I begin my harum-scarum day—grinding away at those books and instruments, and then galloping up hill and down dale, all the country round, like a highwayman—it does me so much good to come and have a steady walk with our comfortable friend, that here I am again!"

"You know, Dame Durden, dear," Ada would say at night, with her head upon my shoulder, and the firelight shining in her thoughtful eyes, "I don't want to talk when we come up-stairs here. Only to sit a little while, thinking, with your dear face for company; and to hear the wind, and remember the poor sailors at sea—— "

Ah! Perhaps Richard was going to be a sailor. We had talked it over very often, now, and there was some talk of gratifying the inclination of his childhood for the sea. Mr. Jarndyce had written to a relation of the family, a great Sir Leicester Dedlock, for his interest in Richard's favour, generally; and Sir Leicester had replied in a gracious manner, "that he would be happy to advance the prospects of the young gentleman if it should ever prove to be within his power, which was not at all probable—and that my Lady sent her compliments to the young gentleman (to whom she perfectly remembered that she was allied by remote consanguinity), and trusted that he would ever do his duty in any honourable profession to which he might devote himself."

"So I apprehend it's pretty clear," said Richard to me, "that I shall have to work my own way. Never mind!

Plenty of people have had to do that before now, and have done it. I only wish I had the command of a clipping privateer, to begin with, and could carry off the Chancellor and keep him on short allowance until he gave judgment in our cause. He'd find himself growing thin, if he didn't look sharp!"

With a buoyancy and hopefulness and a gaiety that hardly ever flagged, Richard had a carelessness in his character that quite perplexed me—principally because he mistook it, in such a very odd way, for prudence. It entered into all his calculations about money, in a singular manner, which I don't think I can better explain than by reverting for a moment to our loan to Mr. Skimpole.

Mr. Jarndyce had ascertained the amount, either from Mr. Skimpole himself or from Coavinses, and had placed the money in my hands with instructions to me to retain my own part of it and hand the rest to Richard. The number of little acts of thoughtless expenditure which Richard justified by the recovery of his ten pounds, and the number of times he talked to me as if he had saved or realised that amount, would form a sum in simple addition.

" My prudent Mother Hubbard, why not ? " he said to me, when he wanted, without the least consideration, to bestow five pounds on the brickmaker. " I made ten pounds, clear, out of Coavinses' business."

" How was that ? " said I.

" Why, I got rid of ten pounds which I was quite content to get rid of, and never expected to see any more. You don't deny that ? "

" No," said I.

" Very well ! then I came into possession of ten pounds— "

" The same ten pounds," I hinted.

" That has nothing to do with it ! " returned Richard. " I have got ten pounds more than I expected to have, and consequently I can afford to spend it without being particular."

In exactly the same way, when he was persuaded out of the sacrifice of these five pounds by being convinced that it would do no good, he carried that sum to his credit and drew upon it.

"Let me see!" he would say. "I saved five pounds out of the brickmaker's affair; so, if I have a good rattle to London and back in a post-chaise, and put that down at four pounds, I shall have saved one. And it's a very good thing to save one, let me tell you: a penny saved, is a penny got!"

I believe Richard's was as frank and generous a nature as there possibly can be. He was ardent and brave, and, in the midst of all his wild restlessness, was so gentle, that I knew him like a brother in a few weeks. His gentleness was natural to him, and would have shown itself abundantly, even without Ada's influence; but, with it, he became one of the most winning of companions, always so ready to be interested, and always so happy, sanguine, and light-hearted. I am sure that I, sitting with them, and walking with them, and talking with them, and noticing from day to day how they went on, falling deeper and deeper in love, and saying nothing about it, and each shyly thinking that this love was the greatest of secrets, perhaps not yet suspected even by the other—I am sure that I was scarcely less enchanted than they were, and scarcely less pleased with the pretty dream.

We were going on in this way, when one morning at breakfast Mr. Jarndyce received a letter, and looking at the superscription said, "From Boythorn? Aye, aye!" and opened and read it with evident pleasure, announcing to us, in a parenthesis, when he was about half-way through, that Boythorn was "coming down" on a visit. Now, who was Boythorn? we all thought. And I dare say we all thought, too—I am sure I did, for one—would Boythorn at all interfere with what was going forward?

"I went to school with this fellow, Lawrence Boythorn," said Mr. Jarndyce, tapping the letter as he laid it on the table, "more than five-and-forty years ago. He was then the most impetuous boy in the world, and he is now the most impetuous man. He was then the loudest boy in the world, and he is now the loudest man. He was then the heartiest and sturdiest boy in the world, and he is now the heartiest and sturdiest man. He is a tremendous fellow."

"In stature, sir!" asked Richard.

"Pretty well, Rick, in that respect," said Mr. Jarndyce; "being some ten years older than I, and a couple of inches taller, with his head thrown back like an old soldier, his stalwart chest squared, his hands like a clean blacksmith's, and his lungs!—there's no simile for his lungs. Talking, laughing, or snoring, they make the beams of the house shake."

As Mr. Jarndyce sat enjoying the image of his friend Boythorn, we observed the favourable omen that there was not the least indication of any change in the wind.

"But it's the inside of the man, the warm heart of the man, the passion of the man, the fresh blood of the man, Rick—and Ada, and little Cobweb too, for you are all interested in a visitor!—that I speak of," he pursued. "His language is as sounding as his voice. He is always in extremes; perpetually in the superlative degree. In his condemnation he is all ferocity. You might suppose him to be an Ogre, from what he says; and I believe he has the reputation of one with some people. There! I tell you no more of him beforehand. You must not be surprised to see him take me under his protection; for he has never forgotten that I was a low boy at school, and that our friendship began in his knocking two of my head tyrant's teeth out (he says six) before breakfast. Boythorn and his man," to me, "will be here this afternoon, my dear."

I took care that the necessary preparations were made for Mr. Boythorn's reception, and we looked forward to his arrival with some curiosity. The afternoon wore away, however, and he did not appear. The dinner-hour arrived, and still he did not appear. The dinner was put back an hour, and we were sitting round the fire with no light but the blaze, when the hall-door suddenly burst open, and the hall resounded with these words, uttered with the greatest vehemence and in a stentorian tone :

"We have been misdirected, Jarndyce, by a most abandoned ruffian, who told us to take the turning to the right instead of to the left. He is the most intolerable scoundrel on the face of the earth. His father must have been a most consummate villain, ever to have such a son. I would have had that fellow shot without the least remorse!"

"Did he do it on purpose?" Mr. Jarndyce inquired.

"I have not the slightest doubt that the scoundrel has passed his whole existence in misdirecting travellers!" returned the other. "By my soul, I thought him the worst-looking dog I had ever beheld, when he was telling me to take the turning to the right. And yet I stood before that fellow face to face, and didn't knock his brains out!"

"Teeth, you mean?" said Mr. Jarndyce.

"Ha, ha, ha!" laughed Mr. Lawrence Boythorn, really making the whole house vibrate. "What, you have not forgotten it yet! Ha, ha, ha!—And that was another most consummate vagabond! By my soul, the countenance of that fellow, when he was a boy, was the blackest image of perfidy, cowardice, and cruelty ever set up as a scarecrow in a field of scoundrels. If I were to meet that most unparalleled despot in the streets to-morrow, I would fell him like a rotten tree!"

"I have no doubt of it," said Mr. Jarndyce. "Now, will you come up-stairs?"

"By my soul, Jarndyce," returned his guest, who seemed to refer to his watch, "if you had been married, I would have turned back at the garden-gate, and gone away to the remotest summits of the Himalaya Mountains, sooner than I would have presented myself at this unseasonable hour."

"Not quite so far, I hope?" said Mr. Jarndyce.

"By my life and honour, yes!" cried the visitor. "I wouldn't be guilty of the audacious insolence of keeping a lady of the house waiting all this time, for any earthly consideration. I would infinitely rather destroy myself—infinitely rather!"

Talking thus, they went up-stairs; and presently we heard him in his bedroom thundering "Ha, ha, ha!" and again "Ha, ha, ha!" until the flattest echo in the neighbourhood seemed to catch the contagion, and to laugh as enjoyingly as he did, or as we did when we heard him laugh.

We all conceived a prepossession in his favour; for there was a sterling quality in this laugh, and in his vigorous healthy voice, and in the roundness and fulness with which he uttered every word he spoke, and in the very fury of his superlatives, which seemed to go off like blank cannons and hurt nothing. But we were hardly prepared to have it so confirmed by his appearance, when Mr. Jarndyce presented him. He was not only a very handsome old gentleman—upright and stalwart as he had been described to us—with a massive grey head, a fine composure of face when silent, a figure that might have become corpulent but for his being so continually in earnest that he gave it no rest, and a chin that might have subsided into a double chin but for the vehement emphasis in which it was constantly required to assist; but he was such a true gentleman in his manner, so chivalrously polite, his face was lighted by a smile of so much sweetness and tenderness, and it seemed so plain that he had nothing to hide, but showed himself exactly as he was—incapable (as Richard said) of anything on a limited scale, and firing away with those blank great guns, because he carried no small arms whatever—that really I could not help looking at him with equal pleasure as he sat at dinner, whether he smilingly conversed with Ada and me, or was led by Mr. Jarndyce into some great volley of superlatives, or threw up his head like a bloodhound, and gave out that tremendous Ha, ha, ha!

" You have brought your bird with you, I suppose?" said Mr. Jarndyce.

" By Heaven, he is the most astonishing bird in Europe!" replied the other. " He *is* the most wonderful creature! I wouldn't take ten thousand guineas for that bird. I have left an annuity for his sole support, in case he should outlive me. He is, in sense and attachment, a phenomenon. And his father before him was one of the most astonishing birds that ever lived!"

The subject of this laudation was a very little canary, who was so tame that he was brought down by Mr. Boythorn's man, on his forefinger, and, after taking a gentle flight round the room, alighted on his master's head. To hear Mr. Boythorn presently expressing the most implacable and passionate sentiments, with this fragile mite of a creature quietly perched on his forehead, was to have a good illustration of his character, I thought.

" By my soul, Jarndyce," he said, very gently holding up a bit of bread to the canary to peck at, " if I were in your place, I would seize every Master in Chancery by the throat to-morrow morning, and shake him until his money rolled out of his pockets, and his bones rattled in his skin. I would have a settlement out of somebody, by fair means or by foul. If you would empower me to do it, I would do it for you with the greatest satisfaction!" (All this time the very small canary was eating out of his hand.)

" I thank you, Lawrence, but the suit is hardly at such a point at present," returned Mr. Jarndyce, laughing, " that it would be greatly advanced, even by the legal process of shaking the Bench and the whole Bar."

" There never was such an infernal cauldron as that Chancery, on the face of the earth!" said Mr. Boythorn. " Nothing but a mine below it on a busy day in term time, with all its records, rules, and precedents collected in it, and every functionary belonging to it also, high and low, upward and downward, from its son the Accountant-General to its father the Devil, and the whole blown to atoms with ten thousand hundred-weight of gunpowder, would reform it in the least!"

It was impossible not to laugh at the energetic gravity with which he recommended this strong measure of reform. When we laughed, he threw up his head, and shook his broad chest, and again the whole country seemed to echo to his Ha, ha, ha! It had not the least effect in disturbing the bird, whose sense of security was complete; and who hopped about the table with its quick head now on this side and now on that, turning its bright sudden eye on its master, as if he were no more than another bird.

"But how do you and your neighbour get on about the disputed right of way?" said Mr. Jarndyce. "You are not free from the toils of the law yourself!"

"The fellow has brought actions against *me* for trespass, and I have brought actions against *him* for trespass," returned Mr. Boythorn. "By Heaven, he is the proudest fellow breathing. It is morally impossible that his name can be Sir Leicester. It must be Sir Lucifer."

"Complimentary to our distant relation!" said my Guardian laughingly, to Ada and Richard.

"I would beg Miss Clare's pardon and Mr. Carstone's pardon," resumed our visitor, "if I were not reassured by seeing in the fair face of the lady, and the smile of the gentleman, that it is quite unnecessary, and that they keep their distant relation at a comfortable distance."

"Or he keeps us," suggested Richard.

"By my soul!" exclaimed Mr. Boythorn, suddenly firing another volley, "that fellow is, and his father was, and his grandfather was, the most stiff-necked, arrogant, imbecile, pig-headed numskull, ever, by some inexplicable mistake of Nature, born in any station of life but a walking-stick's! The whole of that family are the most solemnly conceited and consummate blockheads!—But it's no matter; he should not shut up my path if he were fifty baronets melted into one, and living in a hundred Chesney Wolds, one within another, like the ivory balls in a Chinese carving. The fellow, by his agent, or secretary, or somebody, writes to me, 'Sir Leicester Dedlock, Baronet, presents his compliments to Mr. Lawrence Boythorn, and has to call his attention to the fact that the green pathway by the old parsonage-house, now the property of Mr. Lawrence Boythorn, is Sir Leicester's right of way, being in fact a portion of the park of Chesney Wold; and that Sir Leicester finds it convenient to close up the same.' I write to the fellow, 'Mr. Lawrence Boythorn presents his compliments to Sir Leicester Dedlock, Baronet, and has to call *his* attention to the fact that he totally denies the whole of Sir Leicester Dedlock's positions on every possible subject, and has to add, in reference to closing up the pathway, that he will be glad to see the man who may undertake to do it.' The fellow sends a most abandoned villain with one eye, to construct a gateway. I play upon that execrable scoundrel with a fire-engine, until the breath is nearly driven out of his body. The fellow erects a gate in the night. I chop it down and burn it in the morning. He sends his myrmidons to come over the fence, and pass and repass. I catch them in humane man traps, fire split peas at their legs, play upon them with the engine—resolve to free mankind from the insupportable burden of the existence of those lurking ruffians. He brings actions for trespass; I bring actions for trespass. He brings actions for assault and battery; I defend them, and continue to assault and batter. Ha, ha, ha!'"

To hear him say all this with unimaginable energy, one might have thought him the angriest of mankind. To see him at the very same time, looking at the bird now perched upon his thumb, and softly smoothing its feathers with his forefinger, one might have thought him the gentlest. To hear him laugh, and see the broad good nature of his face then, one might have supposed that he had not a care in the world, or a dispute, or a dislike, but that his whole existence was a summer joke.

145

"No, no," he said, "no closing up of my paths, by any Dedlock! Though I willingly confess," here he softened in a moment, "that Lady Dedlock is the most accomplished lady in the world, to whom I would do any homage that a plain gentleman, and no baronet with a head seven hundred years thick, may. A man who joined his regiment at twenty, and, within a week, challenged the most imperious and presumptuous coxcomb of a commanding officer that ever drew the breath of life through a tight waist—and got broke for it—is not the man to be walked over, by all the Sir Lucifers, dead or alive, locked or unlocked. Ha, ha, ha!"

"Nor the man to allow his junior to be walked over, either?" said my Guardian.

"Most assuredly not!" said Mr. Boythorn, clapping him on the shoulder with an air of protection, that had some-thing serious in it, though he laughed. "He will stand by the low boy, always. Jarndyce, you may rely upon him! But, speaking of this trespass—with apologies to Miss Clare and Miss Summerson for the length at which I have pursued so dry a subject—is there nothing for me from your men, Kenge and Carboy?"

"I think not, Esther?" said Mr. Jarndyce.

"Nothing, Guardian."

"Much obliged!" said Mr. Boythorn. "Had no need to ask, after even my slight experience of Miss Summerson's forethought for every one about her." (They all encouraged me; they were determined to do it.) "I inquired because, coming from Lincolnshire, I of course have not yet been in town, and I thought some letters might have been sent down here. I dare say they will report progress to-morrow morning."

I saw him so often, in the course of the evening, which passed very pleasantly, contemplate Richard and Ada with an interest and a satisfaction that made his fine face remark-ably agreeable as he sat at a little distance from the piano listening to the music—and he had small occasion to tell us that he was passionately fond of music, for his face showed it—that I asked my Guardian, as we sat at the backgammon board, whether Mr. Boythorn had ever been married.

" No," said he. " No."

" But he meant to be!" said I.

" How did you find out that?" he returned, with a smile.

" Why, Guardian," I explained, not without reddening a little at hazarding what was in my thoughts, " there is something so tender in his manner, after all, and he is so very courtly and gentle to us, and—— "

Mr. Jarndyce directed his eyes to where he was sitting, as I have just described him.

I said no more.

" You are right, little woman," he answered. " He was all but married, once. Long ago. And once."

" Did the lady die?"

" No—but·she died to him. That time has had its influence on all his later life. Would you suppose him to have a head and a heart full of romance yet?"

" I think, Guardian, I might have supposed so. But it is easy to say that, when you have told me so."

" He has never since been what he might have been," said Mr. Jarndyce, " and now you see him in his age with no one near him but his servant, and his little yellow friend.—It's your throw, my dear!"

I felt, from my Guardian's manner, that beyond this point I could not pursue the subject without changing the wind. I therefore forbore to ask any further questions. I was interested, but not curious. I thought a little while about this old love story in the night, when I was awakened by Mr. Boythorn's lusty snoring; and I tried to do that very difficult thing, imagine old people young again, and invested with the graces of youth. But I fell asleep before I had succeeded, and dreamed of the days when I lived in my godmother's house. I am not sufficiently acquainted with such subjects to know whether it is at all remarkable that I almost always dreamed of that period of my life.

With the morning, there came a letter from Messrs. Kenge and Carboy to Mr. Boythorn, informing him that one of their clerks would wait upon him at noon. As it was the day of the week on which I paid the bills, and added up my books, and made all the household affairs as compact as possible, I remained at home while Mr. Jarndyce, Ada, and Richard, took advantage of a very fine day to make a little excursion. Mr. Boythorn was to wait for Kenge and Carboy's clerk, and then was to go on foot to meet them on their return.

Well! I was full of business, examining tradesmen's books, adding up columns, paying money, filing receipts, and I dare say making a great bustle about it, when Mr. Guppy was announced and shown in. I had had some idea that the clerk who was to be sent down, might be the young gentleman who had met me at the coach-office; and I was glad to see him, because he was associated with my present happiness.

I scarcely knew him again, he was so uncommonly smart. He had an entirely new suit of glossy clothes on, a shining hat, lilac-kid gloves, a neckerchief of a variety of colours, a large hot-house flower in his button-hole, and a thick gold ring on his little finger. Besides which, he quite scented the dining-room with bear's-grease and other perfumery. He looked at me with an attention that quite confused me, when I begged him to take a seat until the servant should return; and as he sat there, crossing and uncrossing his legs in a corner, and I asked him if he had had a pleasant ride, and hoped that Mr. Kenge was well, I never looked at him, but I found him looking at me, in the same scrutinising and curious way.

When the request was brought to him that he would go up-stairs to Mr. Boythorn's room, I mentioned that he would find lunch prepared for him when he came down, of which Mr. Jarndyce hoped he would partake. He said with some embarrassment, holding the handle of the door, "Shall I have the honour of finding you here, miss ? " I replied yes, I should be there; and he went out with a bow and another look.

I thought him only awkward and shy, for he was evidently much embarrassed; and I fancied that the best thing I could do, would be to wait until I saw that he had everything he wanted, and then to leave him to himself. The lunch was soon brought, but it remained for some time on the table. The interview with Mr. Boythorn was a long one—and a stormy one too, I should think; for although his room was at some distance, I heard his loud voice every now and then like a high wind, and evidently blowing perfect broadsides of denunciation.

At last Mr. Guppy came back, looking something the worse for the conference. "My eye, miss," he said in a low voice, "he's a Tartar!"

"Pray take some refreshment, sir," said I.

Mr. Guppy sat down at the table, and began nervously sharpening the carving-knife on the carving-fork; still looking at me (as I felt quite sure without looking at him), in the same unusual manner. The sharpening lasted so long, that at last I felt a kind of obligation on me to raise my eyes, in order that I might break the spell under which he seemed to labour, of not being able to leave off.

He immediately looked at the dish, and began to carve.

"What will you take yourself, miss? You'll take a morsel of something?"

"No, thank you," said I.

"Shan't I give you a piece of anything at all, miss?" said Mr. Guppy, hurriedly drinking off a glass of wine.

"Nothing, thank you," said I. "I have only waited to see that you have everything you want. Is there anything I can order for you?"

"No, I am much obliged to you, miss, I'm sure. I've everything that I can require to make me comfortable—at least I—not comfortable—I'm never that:" he drank off two more glasses of wine, one after another.

I thought I had better go.

"I beg your pardon, miss!" said Mr. Guppy, rising, when he saw me rise. "But would you allow me the favour of a minute's private conversation?"

Not knowing what to say, I sat down again.

"What follows is without prejudice, miss?" said Mr. Guppy, anxiously bringing a chair towards my table.

"I don't understand what you mean," said I, wondering.

"It's one of our law terms, miss. You won't make any use of it to my detriment, at Kenge and Carboy's, or elsewhere. If our conversation shouldn't lead to anything, I am to be as I was, and am not to be prejudiced in my situation or worldly prospects. In short, it's in total confidence."

"I am at a loss, sir," said I, "to imagine what you can have to communicate in total confidence to me, whom you have never seen but once; but I should be very sorry to do you any injury."

"Thank you, miss. I'm sure of it—that's quite sufficient." All this time Mr. Guppy was either planing his forehead with his handkerchief, or tightly rubbing the palm of his left hand with the palm of his right. "If you would excuse my taking another glass of wine, miss, I think it might assist me in getting on, without a continual choke that cannot fail to be mutually unpleasant."

He did so, and came back again. I took the opportunity of moving well behind my table.

"You wouldn't allow me to offer you one, would you, miss?" said Mr. Guppy, apparently refreshed.

"Not any," said I.

"Not half a glass?" said Mr. Guppy; "quarter? No! Then, to proceed. My present salary, Miss Summerson, at Kenge and Carboy's, is two pound a-week. When I first had the happiness of looking upon you, it was one-fifteen, and had stood at that figure for a lengthened period. A rise of five has since taken place, and a further rise of five is guaranteed at the expiration of a term not exceeding twelve months from

In Re Guppy. Extraordinary Proceedings

the present date. My mother has a little property, which takes the form of a small life annuity; upon which she lives in an independent though unassuming manner, in the Old Street Road. She is eminently calculated for a mother-in-law. She never interferes, is all for peace, and her disposition easy. She has her failings—as who has not?—but I never knew her do it when company was present; at which time you may freely trust her with wines, spirits, or malt liquors. My own abode is lodgings at Penton Place, Pentonville. It is lowly, but airy, open at the back, and considered one of the 'ealthiest outlets. Miss Summerson! In the mildest language, I adore you. Would you be so kind as to allow me (as I may say) to file a declaration—to make an offer!"

Mr. Guppy went down on his knees. I was well behind my table, and not much frightened. I said, "Get up from that ridiculous position immediately, sir, or you will oblige me to break my implied promise and ring the bell!"

"Hear me out, miss!" said Mr. Guppy, folding his hands.

"I cannot consent to hear another word, sir," I returned, "unless you get up from the carpet directly, and go and sit down at the table, as you ought to do if you have any sense at all."

He looked piteously, but slowly rose and did so.

"Yet what a mockery it is, miss," he said, with his hand upon his heart, and shaking his head at me in a melancholy manner over the tray, "to be stationed behind food at such a moment. The soul recoils from food at such a moment, miss."

"I beg you to conclude," said I; "you have asked me to hear you out, and I beg you to conclude."

"I will, miss," said Mr. Guppy. "As I love and honour, so likewise I obey. Would that I could make Thee the subject of that vow, before the shrine!"

"That is quite impossible," said I, "and entirely out of the question."

"I am aware," said Mr. Guppy, leaning forward over the

151

tray, and regarding me, as I again strangely felt, though my eyes were not directed to him, with his late intent look, " I am aware that in a worldly point of view, according to all appearances, my offer is a poor one. But, Miss Summerson! Angel!—No, don't ring—I have been brought up in a sharp school, and am accustomed to a variety of general practice. Though a young man, I have ferreted out evidence, got up cases, and seen lots of life. Blest with your hand, what means might I not find of advancing your interests, and pushing your fortunes! What might I not get to know, nearly concerning you? I know nothing now, certainly; but what *might* I not, if I had your confidence, and you set me on ? "

I told him that he addressed my interest, or what he supposed to be my interest, quite as unsuccessfully as he addressed my inclination; and he would now understand that I requested him, if he pleased, to go away immediately.

" Cruel miss," said Mr. Guppy, " hear but another word ! I think you must have seen that I was struck with those charms, on the day when I waited at the Whytorseller. I think you must have remarked that I could not forbear a tribute to those charms when I put up the steps of the 'ackney-coach. It was a feeble tribute to Thee, but it was well meant. Thy image has ever since been fixed in my breast. I have walked up and down, of an evening, opposite Jellyby's house, only to look upon the bricks that once contained Thee. This out of to-day, quite an unnecessary out so far as the attendance, which was its pretended object, went, was planned by me alone for Thee alone. If I speak of interest, it is only to recommend myself and my respectful wretchedness. Love was before it, and is before it."

" I should be pained, Mr. Guppy," said I, rising and putting my hand upon the bell-rope, " to do you, or any one who was sincere, the injustice of slighting any honest feeling, however disagreeably expressed. If you have really meant to give me a proof of your good opinion, though

ill-timed and misplaced, I feel that I ought to thank you. I
have very little reason to be proud, and I am not proud.
I hope," I think I added, without very well knowing what I
said, "that you will now go away as if you had never been
so exceedingly foolish, and attend to Messrs. Kenge and
Carboy's business."

"Half a minute, miss!" cried Mr. Guppy, checking me as
I was about to ring. "This has been without prejudice?"

"I will never mention it," said I, "unless you should give
me future occasion to do so."

"A quarter of a minute, miss! In case you should think
better—at any time, however distant, *that's* no consequence,
for my feelings can never alter—of anything I have said,
particularly what might I not do—Mr. William Guppy,
eighty-seven, Penton Place, or if removed, or dead (of
blighted hopes or anything of that sort), care of Mrs. Guppy,
three hundred and two, Old Street Road, will be sufficient."

I rang the bell, the servant came, and Mr. Guppy, laying
his written card upon the table, and making a dejected bow,
departed. Raising my eyes as he went out, I once more saw
him looking at me after he had passed the door.

I sat there for another hour or more, finishing my books
and payments, and getting through plenty of business. Then,
I arranged my desk, and put everything away, and was so
composed and cheerful that I thought I had quite dismissed
this unexpected incident. But, when I went up-stairs to my
own room, I surprised myself by beginning to laugh about
it, and then surprised myself still more by beginning to cry
about it. In short, I was in a flutter for a little while; and
felt as if an old chord had been more coarsely touched than
it ever had been since the days of the dear old doll, long
buried in the garden.

CHAPTER X

THE LAW-WRITER

On the eastern borders of Chancery Lane, that is to say, more particularly in Cook's Court, Cursitor Street, Mr. Snagsby, Law-Stationer, pursues his lawful calling. In the shade of Cook's Court, at most times a shady place, Mr. Snagsby has dealt in all sorts of blank forms of legal process; in skins and rolls of parchment; in paper—foolscap, brief, draft, brown, white, whitey-brown, and blotting; in stamps; in office-quills, pens, ink, India-rubber, pounce, pins, pencils, sealing-wax, and wafers; in red tape and green ferret; in pocket-books, almanacks, diaries, and law lists; in string boxes, rulers, inkstands—glass and leaden, penknives, scissors, bodkins, and other small office-cutlery; in short, in articles too numerous to mention; ever since he was out of his time, and went into partnership with Peffer. On that occasion, Cook's Court was in a manner revolutionised by the new inscription in fresh paint, PEFFER and SNAGSBY, displacing the time-honoured and not easily to be deciphered legend, PEFFER, only. For smoke, which is the London ivy, had so wreathed itself round Peffer's name, and clung to his dwelling-place, that the affectionate parasite quite overpowered the parent tree.

Peffer is never seen in Cook's Court now. He is not expected there, for he has been recumbent this quarter of a century in the churchyard of St. Andrew's, Holborn, with the waggons and hackney-coaches roaring past him, all the day and half the night, like one great dragon. If he ever steal forth when the dragon is at rest, to air himself again in Cook's Court, until admonished to return by the crowing of the sanguine cock in the cellar at the little dairy in Cursitor Street, whose ideas of daylight it would be curious to ascertain, since he knows from his personal observation next to nothing about it—if Peffer ever do revisit the pale glimpses of Cook's Court, which no law-stationer in the trade can positively deny, he comes invisibly, and no one is the worse or wiser.

In his lifetime, and likewise in the period of Snagsby's "time" of seven long years, there dwelt with Peffer, in the same law-stationering premises, a niece—a short, shrewd niece, something too violently compressed about the waist, and with a sharp nose like a sharp autumn evening, inclining to be frosty towards the end. The Cook's-Courtiers had a rumour flying among them, that the mother of this niece did, in her daughter's childhood, moved by too jealous a solicitude that her figure should approach perfection, lace her up every morning with her maternal foot against the bed-post for a stronger hold and purchase ; and further, that she exhibited internally pints of vinegar and lemon-juice : which acids, they held, had mounted to the nose and temper of the patient. With whichsoever of the many tongues of Rumour this frothy report originated, it either never reached, or never influenced, the ears of young Snagsby ; who, having wooed and won its fair subject on his arrival at man's estate, entered into two partnerships at once. So now, in Cook's Court, Cursitor Street, Mr. Snagsby and the niece are one ; and the niece still cherishes her figure—which, however tastes may differ, is unquestionably so far precious, that there is mighty little of it.

Mr. and Mrs. Snagsby are not only one bone and one flesh, but, to the neighbours' thinking, one voice too. That voice, appearing to proceed from Mrs. Snagsby alone, is heard in Cook's Court very often. Mr. Snagsby, otherwise than as he finds expression through these dulcet tones, is rarely heard. He is a mild, bald, timid man, with a shining head, and a scrubby clump of black hair sticking out at the back. He tends to meekness and obesity. As he stands at his door in Cook's Court, in his grey shop-coat and black calico sleeves, looking up at the clouds; or stands behind a desk in his dark shop, with a heavy flat ruler, snipping and slicing at sheepskin, in company with his two 'prentices; he is emphatically a retiring and unassuming man. From beneath his feet, at such times, as from a shrill ghost unquiet in its grave, there frequently arise complainings and lamentations in the voice already mentioned; and haply, on some occasions, when these reach a sharper pitch than usual, Mr. Snagsby mentions to the 'prentices, "I think my little woman is a-giving it to Guster!"

This proper name, so used by Mr. Snagsby, has before now sharpened the wit of the Cook's-Courtiers to remark that it ought to be the name of Mrs. Snagsby; seeing that she might with great force and expression be termed a Guster, in compliment to her stormy character. It is, however, the possession, and the only possession, except fifty shillings per annum and a very small box indifferently filled with clothing, of a lean young woman from a workhouse (by some supposed to have been christened Augusta); who, although she was farmed or contracted for, during her growing time, by an amiable benefactor of his species resident at Tooting, and cannot fail to have been developed under the most favourable circumstances, " has fits "—which the parish can't account for.

Guster, really aged three or four and twenty, but looking a round ten years older, goes cheap with this unaccountable drawback of fits; and is so apprehensive of being returned on the hands of her patron saint, that except when she is found with her head in the pail, or the sink, or the copper, or the dinner, or anything else that happens to be near her at the time of her seizure, she is always at work. She is a satisfaction to the parents and guardians of the 'prentices, who feel that there is little danger of her inspiring tender emotions in the breast of youth; she is a satisfaction to Mrs. Snagsby, who can always find fault with her; she is a satisfaction to Mr. Snagsby, who thinks it a charity to keep her. The law-stationer's establishment is, in Guster's eyes, a Temple of plenty and splendour. She believes the little drawing-room up-stairs, always kept, as one may say, with its hair in papers and its pinafore on, to be the most elegant apartment in Christendom. The view it commands of Cook's Court at one end (not to mention a squint into Cursitor Street), and of Coavinses' the sheriff's officer's back-yard at the other, she regards as a prospect of unequalled beauty. The portraits it displays in oil—and plenty of it too—of Mr. Snagsby looking at Mrs. Snagsby, and of Mrs. Snagsby looking at Mr. Snagsby, are in her eyes as achievements of Raphael or Titian. Guster has some recompenses for her many privations.

Mr. Snagsby refers everything not in the practical mysteries of the business to Mrs. Snagsby. She manages the money, reproaches the Tax-gatherers, appoints the times and places of devotion on Sundays, licenses Mr. Snagsby's entertainments, and acknowledges no responsibility as to what she thinks fit to provide for dinner; insomuch that she is the high standard of comparison among the neighbouring wives, a long way down Chancery Lane on both sides, and even out in Holborn, who, in any domestic passages of arms, habitually call upon their husbands to look at the difference between their (the wives') position and Mrs. Snagsby's, and their (the husbands') behaviour and Mr. Snagsby's. Rumour, always flying, bat-like, about Cook's Court, and skimming in and out at everybody's windows, does say that Mrs. Snagsby is jealous and inquisitive; and that Mr. Snagsby is sometimes worried out of house and home, and that if he had the spirit of a mouse he wouldn't stand it. It is even observed, that the wives who quote him to their self-willed husbands as a shining example, in reality look down upon him; and that nobody does so, with greater superciliousness than one particular lady, whose lord is more than suspected of laying his umbrella on her as an instrument of correction. But these vague whisperings may arise from Mr. Snagsby's being, in his way, rather a meditative and poetical man ; loving to walk in Staple Inn in the summer time, and to observe how countrified the sparrows and the leaves are ; also to lounge about the Rolls Yard of a Sunday afternoon, and to remark (if in good spirits) that there were old times once, and that you'd find a stone coffin or two, now, under that chapel, he'll be bound, if you was to dig for it. He solaces his imagination, too, by thinking of the many Chancellors and Vices, and Masters of the Rolls, who are deceased ; and he gets such a flavour of the country out of telling the two 'prentices how he *has* heard say that a brook " as clear as crystial " once ran right down the middle of Holborn, when Turnstile really was a turnstile, leading slap away into the meadows—gets such a flavour of the country out of this, that he never wants to go there.

The day is closing in and the gas is lighted, but is not yet fully effective, for it is not quite dark. Mr. Snagsby standing at his shop-door looking up at the clouds, sees a crow, who is out late, skim westward over the slice of sky belonging to Cook's Court. The crow flies straight across Chancery Lane and Lincoln's Inn Garden, into Lincoln's Inn Fields.

Here, in a large house, formerly a house of state, lives Mr. Tulkinghorn. It is let off in sets of chambers now ; and in those shrunken fragments of its greatness, lawyers lie like maggots in nuts. But its roomy staircases, passages, and ante-chambers still remain ; and even its painted ceilings, where Allegory, in Roman helmet and celestial linen, sprawls among balustrades and pillars, flowers, clouds. and big-legged boys, and makes the head ache—as would seem to be Allegory's object always, more or less. Here, among his many boxes labelled with transcendent names, lives Mr. Tulkinghorn, when not speechlessly at home in country-houses where the great ones of the earth are bored to death. Here he is to-day, quiet at his table. An Oyster of the old school, whom nobody can open.

MR. TULKINGHORN'S HOUSE AND OFFICE

Like as he is to look at, so is his apartment in the dusk of the present afternoon. Rusty, out of date, withdrawing from attention, able to afford it. Heavy broad-backed old-fashioned mahogany and horsehair chairs, not easily lifted, obsolete tables with spindle-legs and dusty baize covers, presentation prints of the holders of great titles in the last generation, or the last but one, environ him. A thick and dingy Turkey-carpet muffles the floor where he sits, attended by two candles in old-fashioned silver candlesticks, that give a very insufficient light to his large room. The titles on the backs of his books have retired into the binding; everything that can have a lock has got one; no key is visible. Very few loose papers are about. He has some manuscript near him, but is not referring to it. With the round top of an inkstand, and two broken bits of sealing-wax, he is silently and slowly working out whatever train of indecision is in his mind. Now, the inkstand top is in the middle: now, the red bit of sealing-wax, now the black bit. That's not it. Mr. Tulkinghorn must gather them all up and begin again.

Here, beneath the painted ceiling, with foreshortened Allegory staring down at his intrusion as if it meant to swoop upon him, and he cutting it dead, Mr. Tulkinghorn has at once his house and office. He keeps no staff; only one middle-aged man, usually a little out at elbows, who sits in a high Pew in the hall, and is rarely overburdened with business. Mr. Tulkinghorn is not in a common way. He wants no clerks. He is a great reservoir of confidences, not to be so tapped. His clients want *him*; he is all in all. Drafts that he requires to be drawn, are drawn by special-pleaders in the Temple on mysterious instructions; fair copies that he requires to be made, are made at the stationers', expense being no consideration. The middle-aged man in the Pew knows scarcely more of the affairs of the Peerage than any crossing-sweeper in Holborn.

The red bit, the black bit, the inkstand top, the other inkstand top, the little sand-box. So! You to the middle, you to the right, you to the left. This train of indecision must surely be worked out now or never.—Now! Mr. Tulkinghorn gets up, adjusts his spectacles, puts on his hat, puts the manuscript in his pocket, goes out, tells the middle-aged man out at elbows, "I shall be back presently." Very rarely tells him anything more explicit.

Mr. Tulkinghorn goes, as the crow came—not quite so straight, but nearly—to Cook's Court, Cursitor Street. To Snagsby's, Law-Stationer's, Deeds engrossed and copied, Law-Writing executed in all its branches, &c., &c., &c.

It is somewhere about five or six o'clock in the afternoon, and a balmy fragrance of warm tea hovers in Cook's Court. It hovers about Snagsby's door. The hours are early there; dinner at half-past one, and supper at half-past nine. Mr. Snagsby was about to descend into the subterranean regions to take tea, when he looked out of his door just now, and saw the crow who was out late.

"Master at home?"

Guster is minding the shop, for the 'prentices take tea in the kitchen, with Mr. and Mrs. Snagsby; consequently, the robe-maker's two daughters, combing their curls at the two glasses in the two second-floor windows of the opposite house, are not driving the two 'prentices to distraction, as they fondly suppose, but are merely awakening the unprofitable admiration of Guster, whose hair won't grow, and never would, and, it is confidently thought, never will.

"Master at home?" says Mr. Tulkinghorn.

Master is at home, and Guster will fetch him. Guster disappears, glad to get out of the shop, which she regards with mingled dread and veneration as a storehouse of awful implements of the great torture of the law; a place not to be entered after the gas is turned off.

Mr. Snagsby appears: greasy, warm, herbaceous, and chewing. Bolts a bit of bread and butter. Says, "Bless my soul, sir! Mr. Tulkinghorn!"

"I want half a word with you, Snagsby."

160

A VISITOR TO MR. SNAGSBY

"Certainly, sir! Dear me, sir, why didn't you send your young man round for me? Pray walk into the back shop, sir." Snagsby has brightened in a moment.

The confined room, strong of parchment-grease, is warehouse, counting-house, and copying-office. Mr. Tulkinghorn sits, facing round, on a stool at the desk.

"Jarndyce and Jarndyce, Snagsby."

"Yes, sir." Mr. Snagsby turns up the gas, and coughs behind his hand, modestly anticipating profit. Mr. Snagsby, as a timid man, is accustomed to cough with a variety of expressions, and so to save words.

"You copied some affidavits in that cause for me lately."

"Yes, sir, we did."

"There was one of them," says Mr. Tulkinghorn, carelessly feeling—tight, unopenable Oyster of the old school!—in the wrong coat-pocket, "the handwriting of which is peculiar, and I rather like. As I happened to be passing, and thought I had it about me, I looked in to ask you—but I haven't got it. No matter, any other time will do—Ah! here it is! —I looked in to ask you who copied this?"

"Who copied this, sir?" says Mr. Snagsby, taking it, laying it flat on the desk, and separating all the sheets at once with a twirl and a twist of the left hand peculiar to law-stationers. "We gave this out, sir. We were giving out rather a large quantity of work just at that time. I can tell you in a moment who copied it, sir, by referring to my Book."

Mr. Snagsby takes his Book down from the safe, makes another bolt of the bit of bread and butter which seemed to have stopped short, eyes the affidavit aside, and brings his right forefinger travelling down a page of the Book. "Jewby —Packer—Jarndyce."

"Jarndyce! Here we are, sir," says Mr. Snagsby. "To be sure! I might have remembered it. This was given out, sir, to a Writer who lodges just over on the opposite side of the lane."

Mr. Tulkinghorn has seen the entry, found it before the

Law-stationer, read it while the forefinger was coming down the hill.

"*What* do you call him? Nemo?" says Mr. Tulkinghorn.

"Nemo, sir. Here it is. Forty-two folio. Given out on the Wednesday night, at eight o'clock; brought in on the Thursday morning, at half after nine."

"Nemo!" repeats Mr. Tulkinghorn. "Nemo is Latin for no one."

"It must be English for some one, sir, I think," Mr. Snagsby submits, with his deferential cough. "It is a person's name. Here it is, you see, sir! Forty-two folio. Given out Wednesday night, eight o'clock; brought in Thursday morning, half after nine."

The tail of Mr. Snagsby's eye becomes conscious of the head of Mrs. Snagsby looking in at the shop-door to know what he means by deserting his tea. Mr. Snagsby addresses an explanatory cough to Mrs. Snagsby, as who should say, "My dear, a customer!"

"Half after nine, sir," repeats Mr. Snagsby. "Our law-writers, who live by job-work, are a queer lot; and this may not be his name, but it's the name he goes by. I remember now, sir, that he gives it in a written advertisement he sticks up down at the Rule Office, and the King's Bench Office, and the Judges' Chambers, and so forth. You know the kind of document, sir—wanting employ?"

Mr. Tulkinghorn glances through the little window at the back of Coavinses', the sheriff's officer's, where lights shine in Coavinses' windows. Coavinses' coffee-room is at the back, and the shadows of several gentlemen under a cloud loom cloudily upon the blinds. Mr. Snagsby takes the opportunity of slightly turning his head, to glance over his shoulder at his little woman, and to make apologetic motions with his mouth to this effect: "Tul-king-horn—rich—in-flu-en-tial!"

"Have you given this man work before!" asks Mr. Tulkinghorn.

"O dear, yes, sir! Work of yours."

"Thinking of more important matters, I forget where you said he lived?"

"Across the lane, sir. In fact, he lodges at a—" Mr. Snagsby makes another bolt, as if the bit of bread and butter were insurmountable—"at a rag and bottle shop."

"Can you show me the place as I go back?"

"With the greatest pleasure, sir!"

Mr. Snagsby pulls off his sleeves and his grey coat, pulls on his black coat, takes his hat from its peg. "Oh! here is my little woman!" he says aloud. "My dear, will you be so kind as to tell one of the lads to look after the shop, while I step across the lane with Mr. Tulkinghorn? Mrs. Snagsby, sir—I shan't be two minutes, my love!"

Mrs. Snagsby bends to the lawyer, retires behind the counter, peeps at them through the window-blind, goes softly into the back office, refers to the entries in the book still lying open. Is evidently curious.

"You will find that the place is rough, sir," says Mr. Snagsby, walking deferentially in the road, and leaving the narrow pavement to the lawyer; "and the party is very rough. But they're a wild lot in general, sir. The advantage of this particular man is, that he never wants sleep. He'll go at it right on end, if you want him to, as long as ever you like."

It is quite dark now, and the gas-lamps have acquired their full effect. Jostling against clerks going to post the day's letters, and against counsel and attorneys going home to dinner, and against plaintiffs and defendants, and suitors of all sorts, and against the general crowd, in whose way the forensic wisdom of ages has interposed a million of obstacles to the transaction of the commonest business of life—diving through law and equity, and through that kindred mystery, the street mud, which is made of nobody knows what, and collects about us nobody knows whence or how: we only knowing in general that when there is too much of it, we find it necessary to shovel it away—the lawyer and the law-stationer come to a Rag and Bottle shop, and general emporium of much disregarded merchandise, lying and being in the shadow of the wall of Lincoln's Inn, and kept, as is announced in paint, to all whom it may concern, by one Krook.

"This is where he lives, sir," says the law-stationer.

"This is where he lives, is it?" says the lawyer unconcernedly. "Thank you."

"Are you not going in, sir?"

"No, thank you, no; I am going on to the Fields at present. Good evening. Thank you!" Mr. Snagsby lifts his hat, and returns to his little woman and his tea.

But Mr. Tulkinghorn does not go on to the Fields at present. He goes a short way, turns back, comes again to the shop of Mr. Krook, and enters it straight. It is dim enough, with a blot-headed candle or so in the windows, and an old man and a cat sitting in the back part by a fire. The old man rises and comes forward, with another blot-headed candle in his hand.

"Pray is your lodger within?"

"Male or female, sir?" says Mr. Krook.

"Male. The person who does copying."

Mr. Krook has eyed his man narrowly. Knows him by sight. Has an indistinct impression of his aristocratic repute.

"Did you wish to see him, sir?"

"Yes."

"It's what I seldom do myself," says Mr Krook with a grin. "Shall I call him down? But it's a weak chance if he'd come, sir!"

"I'll go up to him, then," says Mr. Tulkinghorn.

"Second floor, sir. Take the candle. Up there!" Mr. Krook, with his cat beside him, stands at the bottom of the staircase, looking after Mr. Tulkinghorn. "Hi—hi!" he says, when Mr. Tulkinghorn has nearly disappeared. The lawyer looks down over the hand-rail. The cat expands her wicked mouth, and snarls at him.

"Order, Lady Jane! Behave yourself to visitors, my lady! You know what they say of my lodger?" whispers Krook, going up a step or two.

"What do they say of him?"

"They say he has sold himself to the Enemy; but you and I know better—he don't buy. I'll tell you what, though; my lodger is so black-humoured and gloomy that I believe he'd as soon make that bargain as any other. Don't put him out, sir. That's my advice!"

Mr. Tulkinghorn with a nod goes on his way. He comes to the dark door on the second floor. He knocks, receives no answer, opens it, and accidentally extinguishes his candle in doing so.

The air of the room is almost bad enough to have extinguished it, if he had not. It is a small room, nearly black with soot, and grease, and dirt. In the rusty skeleton of a grate, pinched at the middle as if Poverty had gripped it, a red coke fire burns low. In the corner by the chimney, stand a deal table and a broken desk; a wilderness marked with a rain of ink. In another corner, a ragged old portmanteau on one of the two chairs, serves for cabinet or wardrobe; no larger one is needed, for it collapses like the cheeks of a starved man. The floor is bare; except that one old mat, trodden to shreds of rope-yarn, lies perishing upon the hearth. No curtain veils the darkness of the night, but the discoloured shutters are drawn together; and through the two gaunt holes pierced in them, famine might be staring in—the Banshee of the man upon the bed.

For, on a low bed opposite the fire, a confusion of dirty patchwork, lean-ribbed ticking, and coarse sacking, the lawyer, hesitating just within the doorway, sees a man. He lies there, dressed in shirt and trousers, with bare feet. He has a yellow look in the spectral darkness of a candle that has guttered down, until the whole length of its wick (still burning) has doubled over, and left a tower of winding-sheet above it. His hair is ragged, mingling with his whiskers and his beard

—the latter, ragged too, and grown, like the scum and mist around him, in neglect. Foul and filthy as the room is, foul and filthy as the air is, it is not easy to perceive what fumes those are which most oppress the senses in it; but through the general sickliness and faintness, and the odour of stale tobacco, there comes into the lawyer's mouth the bitter, vapid taste of opium.

"Hallo, my friend!" he cries, and strikes his iron candle-stick against the door.

He thinks he has awakened his friend. He lies a little turned away, but his eyes are surely open.

"Hallo, my friend!" he cries again. "Hallo! Hallo!"

As he rattles on the door, the candle which has drooped so long, goes out, and leaves him in the dark; with the gaunt eyes in the shutters staring down upon the bed.

CHAPTER XI

A TOUCH on the lawyer's wrinkled hand, as he stands in the dark room, irresolute, makes him start and say "What's that?"

"It's me," returns the old man of the house, whose breath is in his ear. "Can't you wake him?"

"No."

"What have you done with your candle?"

"It's gone out. Here it is."

Krook takes it, goes to the fire, stoops over the red embers, and tries to get a light. The dying ashes have no light to spare, and his endeavours are vain. Muttering, after an ineffectual call to his lodger, that he will go down-stairs and bring a lighted candle from the shop, the old man departs. Mr. Tulkinghorn, for some new reason that he has, does not await his return in the room, but on the stairs outside.

The welcome light soon shines upon the wall, as Krook comes slowly up, with his green-eyed cat following at his heels. "Does the man generally sleep like this?" inquires the lawyer, in a low voice. "Hi! I don't know," says Krook, shaking his head and lifting his eyebrows. "I know next to nothing of his habits, except that he keeps himself very close."

Thus whispering, they both go in together. As the light goes in, the great eyes in the shutters, darkening, seem to close. Not so the eyes upon the bed.

167

"God save us!" exclaims Mr. Tulkinghorn. "He is dead!"
Krook drops the heavy hand he has taken up, so suddenly
that the arm swings over the bedside.

They look at one another for a moment.

"Send for some doctor! Call for Miss Flite up the stairs,
sir. Here's poison by the bed! Call out for Flite, will you?"
says Krook, with his lean hands spread out above the body
like a vampire's wings.

Mr. Tulkinghorn hurries to the landing, and calls "Miss
Flite! Flite! Make haste, here, whoever you are! Flite!"
Krook follows him with his eyes, and, while he is calling,
finds opportunity to steal to the old portmanteau, and steal
back again.

"Run, Flite, run! The nearest doctor! Run!" So Mr.
Krook addresses a crazy little woman, who is his female lodger:
who appears and vanishes in a breath: who soon returns,
accompanied by a testy medical man, brought from his dinner
—with a broad snuffy upper lip, and a broad Scotch tongue.

"Ey! Bless the hearts o' ye," says the medical man,
looking up at them after a moment's examination. "He's
just as dead as Phairy!"

Mr. Tulkinghorn (standing by the old portmanteau) inquires if he has been dead any time?

"Any time, sir?" says the medical gentleman. "It's
probable he wull have been dead aboot three hours."

"About that time, I should say," observes a dark young
man, on the other side of the bed.

"Air you in the maydickle prayfession yourself, sir?"
inquires the first.

The dark young man says yes.

"Then I'll just tak' my depairture," replies the other; "for
I'm nae gude here!" With which remark, he finishes his
brief attendance, and returns to finish his dinner. The dark
young surgeon passes the candle across and across the face,
and carefully examines the law-writer, who has established
his pretensions to his name by becoming indeed No one.

168

"I knew this person by sight, very well," says he. "He has purchased opium of me, for the last year and a half. Was anybody present related to him?" glancing round upon the three bystanders.

"I was his landlord," grimly answers Krook, taking the candle from the surgeon's outstretched hand. "He told me once, I was the nearest relation he had."

"He has died," says the surgeon, "of an over-dose of opium, there is no doubt. The room is strongly flavoured with it. There is enough here now," taking an old teapot from Mr. Krook, "to kill a dozen people."

"Do you think he did it on purpose?" asks Krook.

"Took the over-dose?"

"Yes!" Krook almost smacks his lips with the unction of a horrible interest.

"I can't say. I should think it unlikely, as he has been in the habit of taking so much. But nobody can tell. He was very poor, I suppose?"

"I suppose he was. His room—don't look rich," says Krook, who might have changed eyes with his cat, as he casts his sharp glance around. "But I have never been in it since he had it, and he was too close to name his circumstances to me."

"Did he owe you any rent?"

"Six weeks."

"He will never pay it!" says the young man, resuming his examination. "It is beyond a doubt that he is indeed as dead as Pharaoh; and to judge from his appearance and condition, I should think it a happy release. Yet he must have been a good figure when a youth, and I dare say, good-looking." He says this, not unfeelingly, while sitting on the bedstead's edge, with his face towards that other face, and his hand upon the region of the heart. "I recollect once thinking there was something in his manner, uncouth as it was, that denoted a fall in life. Was that so?" he continues, looking round.

Krook replies, "You might as well ask me to describe the ladies whose heads of hair I have got in sacks down-stairs. Than that he was my lodger for a year and a half, and lived —or didn't live—by law-writing, I know no more of him."

During this dialogue, Mr. Tulkinghorn has stood aloof by the old portmanteau, with his hands behind him, equally removed, to all appearance, from all three kinds of interest exhibited near the bed—from the young surgeon's professional interest in death, noticeable as being quite apart from his remarks on the deceased as an individual; from the old man's unction; and the little crazy woman's awe. His imperturbable face has been as inexpressive as his rusty clothes. One could not even say he has been thinking all this while. He has shown neither patience nor impatience, nor attention nor abstraction. He has shown nothing but his shell. As easily might the tone of a delicate musical instrument be inferred from its case, as the tone of Mr. Tulkinghorn from *his* case.

He now interposes; addressing the young surgeon, in his unmoved, professional way.

"I looked in here," he observes, "just before you, with the intention of giving this deceased man, whom I never saw alive, some employment at his trade of copying. I had heard of him from my stationer—Snagsby of Cook's Court. Since no one here knows anything about him, it might be as well to send for Snagsby. Ah!" to the little crazy woman, who has often seen him in Court, and whom he has often seen, and who proposes, in frightened dumb-show, to go for the law-stationer. "Suppose you do!"

While she is gone, the surgeon abandons his hopeless investigation, and covers its subject with the patchwork counterpane. Mr. Krook and he interchange a word or two. Mr. Tulkinghorn says nothing; but stands, ever, near the old portmanteau.

Mr. Snagsby arrives hastily, in his grey coat and his black sleeves. "Dear me, dear me," he says; "and it has come to this, has it! Bless my soul!"

"Can you give the person of the house any information about this unfortunate creature, Snagsby?" inquires Mr. Tulkinghorn. "He was in arrears with his rent, it seems. And he must be buried, you know."

"Well, sir," says Mr. Snagsby, coughing his apologetic cough behind his hand; "I really don't know what advice I could offer, except sending for the beadle."

"I don't speak of advice," returns Mr. Tulkinghorn. "*I* could advise——"

("No one better, sir, I am sure," says Mr. Snagsby, with his deferential cough.)

"I speak of affording some clue to his connexions, or to where he came from, or to anything concerning him."

"I assure you, sir," says Mr. Snagsby, after prefacing his reply with his cough of general propitiation, "that I no more know where he came from than I know——"

"Where he has gone to, perhaps," suggests the surgeon, to help him out.

A pause. Mr. Tulkinghorn looking at the law-stationer. Mr. Krook, with his mouth open, looking for somebody to speak next.

"As to his connexions, sir," says Mr. Snagsby, "if a person was to say to me, 'Snagsby, here's twenty thousand pound down, ready for you in the Bank of England, if you'll only name one of 'em,' I couldn't do it, sir! About a year and a half ago—to the best of my belief at the time when he first came to lodge at the present rag and bottle shop——"

"That was the time!" says Krook, with a nod.

"About a year and a half ago," says Mr. Snagsby, strengthened, "he came into our place one morning after breakfast, and, finding my little woman (which I name Mrs. Snagsby when I use that appellation) in our shop, produced a specimen of his handwriting, and gave her to understand that he was in want of copying work to do, and was—not to put too fine a point upon it—" a favourite apology for plain-speaking with

171

Mr. Snagsby, which he always offers with a sort of argumentative frankness, "hard up! My little woman is not in general partial to strangers, particular—not to put too fine a point upon it—when they want anything. But she was rather took by something about this person; whether by his being unshaved, or by his hair being in want of attention, or by what other ladies' reasons, I leave you to judge; and she accepted of the specimen, and likewise of the address. My little woman hasn't a good ear for names," proceeds Mr. Snagsby, after consulting his cough of consideration behind his hand, "and she considered Nemo equally the same as Nimrod. In consequence of which, she got into a habit of saying to me at meals, 'Mr. Snagsby, you haven't found Nimrod any work yet!' or 'Mr. Snagsby, why didn't you give that eight-and-thirty Chancery folio in Jarndyce, to Nimrod?' or such like. And that is the way he gradually fell into job-work at our place; and that is the most I know of him, except that he was a quick hand, and a hand not sparing of night-work; and that if you gave him out, say five-and-forty folio on the Wednesday night, you would have it brought in on the Thursday morning. All of which—" Mr. Snagsby concludes by politely motioning with his hat towards the bed, as much as to add, "I have no doubt my honourable friend would confirm, if he were in a condition to do it."

"Hadn't you better see," says Mr. Tulkinghorn to Krook, "whether he had any papers that may enlighten you? There will be an Inquest, and you will be asked the question. You can read?"

"No, I can't," returns the old man, with a sudden grin.

"Snagsby," says Mr. Tulkinghorn, "look over the room for him. He will get into some trouble or difficulty, otherwise. Being here, I'll wait, if you make haste; and then I can testify on his behalf, if it should ever be necessary, that all was fair and right. If you will hold the candle for Mr. Snagsby, my friend, he'll soon see whether there is anything to help you."

A FRUITLESS SEARCH

"In the first place, here's an old portmanteau, sir," says Snagsby.

Ah, to be sure, so there is! Mr. Tulkinghorn does not appear to have seen it before, though he is standing so close to it, and though there is very little else, Heaven knows.

The marine-store merchant holds the light, and the law-stationer conducts the search. The surgeon leans against the corner of the chimney-piece; Miss Flite peeps and trembles just within the door. The apt old scholar of the old school, with his dull black breeches tied with ribbons at the knees, his large black waistcoat, his long-sleeved black coat, and his wisp of limp white neckerchief tied in the bow the Peerage knows so well, stands in exactly the same place and attitude.

There are some worthless articles of clothing in the old portmanteau; there is a bundle of pawnbrokers' duplicates, those turnpike tickets on the road of Poverty; there is a crumpled paper, smelling of opium, on which are scrawled rough memoranda—as, took, such a day, so many grains; took, such another day, so many more—begun some time ago, as if with the intention of being regularly continued, but soon left off. There are a few dirty scraps of newspapers, all referring to Coroners' Inquests; there is nothing else. They search the cupboard, and the drawer of the ink-splashed table. There is not a morsel of an old letter, or of any other writing, in either. The young surgeon examines the dress on the law-writer. A knife and some odd halfpence are all he finds. Mr. Snagsby's suggestion is the practical suggestion after all, and the beadle must be called in.

So the little crazy lodger goes for the beadle, and the rest come out of the room. "Don't leave the cat there!" says the surgeon: "that won't do!" Mr. Krook therefore drives her out before him; and she goes furtively down-stairs, winding her lithe tail and licking her lips.

"Good night!" says Mr. Tulkinghorn; and goes home to Allegory and meditation.

By this time the news has got into the court. Groups of

its inhabitants assemble to discuss the thing; and the out-posts of the army of observation (principally boys) are pushed forward to Mr. Krook's window, which they closely invest. A policeman has already walked up to the room, and walked down again to the door, where he stands like a tower, only condescending to see the boys at his base occasionally; but whenever he does see them, they quail and fall back. Mrs. Perkins, who has not been for some weeks on speaking terms with Mrs. Piper, in consequence of an unpleasantness origin-ating in young Perkins having "fetched" young Piper "a crack," renews her friendly intercourse on this auspicious occasion. The potboy at the corner, who is a privileged amateur, as possessing official knowledge of life, and having to deal with drunken men occasionally, exchanges confidential communications with the policeman, and has the appearance of an impregnable youth, unassailable by truncheons and unconfinable in station-houses. People talk across the court out of window, and bare-headed scouts come hurrying in from Chancery Lane to know what's the matter. The general feeling seems to be that it's a blessing Mr. Krook warn't made away with first, mingled with a little natural disappointment that he was not. In the midst of this sensation, the beadle arrives.

The beadle, though generally understood in the neighbour-hood to be a ridiculous institution, is not without a certain popularity for the moment, if it were only as a man who is going to see the body. The policeman considers him an imbecile civilian, a remnant of the barbarous watchmen-times; but gives him admission, as something that must be borne with until Government shall abolish him. The sensation is heightened, as the tidings spread from mouth to mouth that the beadle is on the ground, and has gone in.

By-and-by the beadle comes out, once more intensifying the sensation, which has rather languished in the interval. He is understood to be in want of witnesses, for the Inquest to-morrow, who can tell the Coroner and Jury anything

whatever respecting the deceased. Is immediately referred
to innumerable people who can tell nothing whatever. Is
made more imbecile by being constantly informed that Mrs.
Green's son " was a law-writer his-self, and knowed him better
than anybody "—which son of Mrs. Green's appears, on inquiry, to be at the present time aboard a vessel bound for
China, three months out, but considered accessible by telegraph,
on application to the Lords of the Admiralty. Beadle goes
into various shops and parlours, examining the inhabitants ;
always shutting the door first, and by exclusion, delay, and
general idiotcy, exasperating the public. Policeman seen
to smile to potboy. Public loses interest, and undergoes
reaction. Taunts the beadle, in shrill youthful voices, with
having boiled a boy ; choruses fragments of a popular song
to that effect, and importing that the boy was made into
soup for the workhouse. Policeman at last finds it necessary
to support the law, and seize a vocalist ; who is released upon
the flight of the rest, on condition of his getting out of this
then, come ! and cutting it—a condition he immediately
observes. So the sensation dies off for the time ; and the
unmoved policeman (to whom a little opium, more or less, is
nothing), with his shining hat, stiff stock, inflexible great-coat,
stout belt and bracelet, and all things fitting, pursues his
lounging way with a heavy tread : beating the palms of his
white gloves one against the other, and stopping now and
then, at a street-corner, to look casually about for anything
between a lost child and a murder.

Under cover of the night, the feeble-minded beadle comes
flitting about Chancery Lane with his summonses, in which
every Juror's name is wrongly spelt, and nothing rightly
spelt but the beadle's own name, which nobody can read or
wants to know. The summonses served, and his witnesses
forewarned, the beadle goes to Mr. Krook's, to keep a small
appointment he has made with certain paupers ; who, presently arriving, are conducted up-stairs ; where they leave
the great eyes in the shutter something new to stare at,

in that last shape which earthly lodgings take for No one—
and for Every one.

And, all that night, the coffin stands ready by the old
portmanteau; and the lonely figure on the bed, whose path
in life has lain through five-and-forty years, lies there, with
no more track behind him, that any one can trace, than a
deserted infant.

Next day the court is all alive—is like a fair, as Mrs.
Perkins, more than reconciled to Mrs. Piper, says, in amicable
conversation with that excellent woman. The Coroner is to
sit in the first-floor room at the Sol's Arms, where the Harmonic Meetings take place twice a-week, and where the chair
is filled by a gentleman of professional celebrity, faced by
Little Swills, the comic vocalist, who hopes (according to the
bill in the window) that his friends will rally round him, and
support first-rate talent. The Sol's Arms does a brisk stroke
of business all the morning. Even children so require sustain-
ing, under the general excitement, that a pieman who has
established himself for the occasion at the corner of the court,
says his brandy-balls go off like smoke. What time the
beadle, hovering between the door of Mr. Krook's establishment and the door of the Sol's Arms, shows the curiosity in
his keeping to a few discreet spirits, and accepts the compliment of a glass of ale or so in return.

At the appointed hour arrives the Coroner, for whom the
Jurymen are waiting, and who is received with a salute of
skittles from the good dry skittle-ground attached to the Sol's
Arms. The Coroner frequents more public-houses than any
man alive. The smell of sawdust, beer, tobacco-smoke, and
spirits, is inseparable in his vocation from death in its most
awful shapes. He is conducted by the beadle and the landlord to the Harmonic Meeting Room, where he puts his hat
on the piano, and takes a Windsor-chair at the head of a
long table, formed of several short tables put together, and
ornamented with glutinous rings in endless involutions, made
by pots and glasses. As many of the Jury as can crowd

together at the table sit there. The rest get among the spittoons and pipes, or lean against the piano. Over the Coroner's head is a small iron garland, the pendant handle of a bell, which rather gives the Majesty of the Court the appearance of going to be hanged presently.

Call over and swear the Jury! While the ceremony is in progress, sensation is created by the entrance of a chubby little man in a large shirt-collar, with a moist eye, and an inflamed nose, who modestly takes a position near the door as one of the general public, but seems familiar with the room too. A whisper circulates that this is Little Swills. It is considered not unlikely that he will get up an imitation of the Coroner, and make it the principal feature of the Harmonic Meeting in the evening.

"Well, gentlemen—" the Coroner begins.

"Silence there, will you!" says the beadle. Not to the Coroner, though it might appear so.

"Well, gentlemen," resumes the Coroner. "You are impanelled here, to inquire into the death of a certain man. Evidence will be given before you, as to the circumstances attending that death, and you will give your verdict according to the—skittles; they must be stopped, you know, beadle!— evidence, and not according to anything else. The first thing to be done, is to view the body."

"Make way there!" cries the beadle.

So they go out in a loose procession, something after the manner of a straggling funeral, and make their inspection in Mr. Krook's back second floor. from which a few of the Jurymen retire pale and precipitately. The beadle is very careful that two gentlemen not very neat about the cuffs and buttons (for whose accommodation he has provided a special little table near the Coroner, in the Harmonic Meeting Room) should see all that is to be seen. For they are the public chroniclers of such inquiries, by the line; and he is not superior to the universal human infirmity, but hopes to read in print what "Mooney, the active and intelligent beadle of the district," said and did; and even aspires to see the name of Mooney as familiarly and patronisingly mentioned as the name of the Hangman is, according to the latest examples.

Little Swills is waiting for the Coroner and Jury on their return. Mr. Tulkinghorn, also. Mr. Tulkinghorn is received with distinction, and seated near the Coroner; between that high judicial officer, a bagatelle-board, and the coal-box. The inquiry proceeds. The Jury learn how the subject of their inquiry died, and learn no more about him. "A very eminent solicitor is in attendance, gentlemen," says the Coroner, "who, I am informed, was accidentally present, when discovery of the death was made; but he could only repeat the evidence you have already heard from the surgeon, the landlord, the lodger, and the law-stationer; and it is not necessary to trouble him. Is anybody in attendance who knows anything more?"

Mrs. Piper pushed forward by Mrs. Perkins. Mrs. Piper sworn.

Anastasia Piper, gentlemen. Married woman. Now, Mrs. Piper—what have you got to say about this?

Why, Mrs. Piper has a good deal to say, chiefly in parentheses and without punctuation, but not much to tell. Mrs. Piper lives in the court (which her husband is a cabinet-maker), and it has long been well beknown among the neighbours (counting from the day next but one before the half-baptising of Alexander James Piper aged eighteen months and four days old on accounts of not being expected to live such was the sufferings gentlemen of that child in his gums) as the Plaintive—so Mrs. Piper insists on calling the deceased—was reported to have sold himself. Thinks it was the Plaintive's air in which that report originatinin. See the Plaintive often and considered as his air was feariocious and not to be allowed to go about some children being timid (and if doubted hoping Mrs. Perkins may be brought forard for she is here and will do credit to her husband and herself and family). Has seen the Plaintive wexed and

worrited by the children (for children they will ever be
and you cannot expect them specially if of playful disposi-
tions to be Methoozellers which you was not yourself). On
accounts of this and his dark looks has often dreamed as she
see him take a pick-axe from his pocket and split Johnny's
head (which the child knows not fear and has repeatually
called after him close at his eels). Never however see the
Plaintive take a pick-axe or any other wepping far from it.
Has seen him hurry away when run and called after as if
not partial to children and never see him speak to neither
child nor grown person at any time (excepting the boy that
sweeps the crossing down the lane over the way round the
corner which if he was here would tell you that he has been
seen a-speaking to him frequent).

Says the Coroner, is that boy here? Says the beadle, no,
sir, he is not here. Says the Coroner, go and fetch him
then. In the absence of the active and intelligent, the
Coroner converses with Mr. Tulkinghorn.

O! Here's the boy, gentlemen!

Here he is, very muddy, very hoarse, very ragged. Now,
boy!—But stop a minute. Caution. This boy must be
put through a few preliminary paces.

Name, Jo. Nothing else that he knows on. Don't know
that everybody has two names. Never heerd of sich a think.
Don't know that Jo is short for a longer name. Thinks it
long enough for *him*. *He* don't find no fault with it. Spell
it? No. *He* can't spell it. No father, no mother, no
friends. Never been to school. What's home? Knows a
broom's a broom, and knows it's wicked to tell a lie. Don't
recollect who told him about the broom, or about the lie,
but knows both. Can't exactly say what'll be done to him
arter he's dead if he tells a lie to the gentlemen here, but
believes it'll be something wery bad to punish him, and serve
him right—and so he'll tell the truth.

"This won't do, gentlemen!" said the Coroner, with a
melancholy shake of the head.

179

"Don't you think you can receive his evidence, sir?" asks an attentive Juryman.

"Out of the question," says the Coroner. "You have heard the boy. 'Can't exactly say' won't do, you know. We can't take *that*, in a Court of Justice, gentlemen. It's terrible depravity. Put the boy aside."

Boy put aside; to the great edification of the audience;— especially of Little Swills, the Comic Vocalist.

Now. Is there any other witness? No other witness.

Very well, gentlemen! Here's a man unknown, proved to have been in the habit of taking opium in large quantities for a year and a half, found dead of too much opium. If you think you have any evidence to lead you to the con- clusion that he committed suicide, you will come to that conclusion. If you think it is a case of accidental death, you will find a Verdict accordingly.

Verdict accordingly. Accidental death. No doubt. Gentlemen, you are discharged. Good afternoon.

While the Coroner buttons his great-coat, Mr. Tulking- horn and he give private audience to the rejected witness in a corner.

That graceless creature only knows that the dead man (whom he recognised just now by his yellow face and black hair) was sometimes hooted and pursued about the streets. That one cold winter night, when he, the boy, was shivering in a doorway near his crossing, the man turned to look at him, and came back, and, having questioned him and found that he had not a friend in the world, said, "Neither have I. Not one!" and gave him the price of a supper and a night's lodging. That the man had often spoken to him since; and asked him whether he slept sound at night, and how he bore cold and hunger, and whether he ever wished to die; and similar strange questions. That when the man had no money, he would say in passing, "I am as poor as you to-day, Jo;" but that when he had any, he had always (as the boy most heartily believes) been glad to give him some.

"He was wery good to me," says the boy, wiping his eyes
with his wretched sleeve. "Wen I see him a-layin' so stritched
out just now, I wished he could have heerd me tell him so.
He wos wery good to me, he wos!"

As he shuffles down-stairs, Mr. Snagsby, lying in wait for
him, puts a half-crown in his hand. "If you ever see me
coming past your crossing with my little woman—I mean a
lady—" says Mr. Snagsby, with his finger on his nose,
"don't allude to it!"

For some little time the Jurymen hang about the Sol's
Arms colloquially. In the sequel, half-a-dozen are caught up
in a cloud of pipe-smoke that pervades the parlour of the
Sol's Arms; two stroll to Hampstead; and four engage to go
half-price to the play at night, and top up with oysters.
Little Swills is treated on several hands. Being asked what
he thinks of the proceedings; characterises them (his strength
lying in a slangular direction) as "a rummy start." The
landlord of the Sol's Arms, finding Little Swills so popular,
commends him highly to the Jurymen and public; observing
that, for a song in character, he don't know his equal, and
that that man's character-wardrobe would fill a cart.

Thus, gradually the Sol's Arms melts into the shadowy
night, and then flares out of it strong in gas. The
Harmonic Meeting hour arriving, the gentleman of professional celebrity takes the chair; is faced (red-faced) by
Little Swills; their friends rally round them, and support
first-rate talent. In the zenith of the evening, Little Swills
says, Gentlemen, if you'll permit me, I'll attempt a short
description of a scene of real life that came off here to-day.
Is much applauded and encouraged; goes out of the room
as Swills; comes in as the Coroner (not the least in the
world like him); describes the Inquest, with recreative
intervals of piano-forte accompaniment to the refrain—With
his (the Coroner's) tippy tol li doll, tippy tol lo doll, tippy
tol li doll, Dee!

The jingling piano at last is silent, and the Harmonic

friends rally round their pillows. Then there is rest around the lonely figure, now laid in its last earthly habitation; and it is watched by the gaunt eyes in the shutters through some quiet hours of night. If this forlorn man could have been prophetically seen lying here, by the mother at whose breast he nestled, a little child, with eyes upraised to her loving face, and soft hand scarcely knowing how to close upon the neck to which it crept, what an impossibility the vision would have seemed! O, if, in brighter days, the now-extinguished fire within him ever burned for one woman who held him in her heart, where is she, while these ashes are above the ground!

It is anything but a night of rest at Mr. Snagsby's, in Cook's Court; where Guster murders sleep, by going, as Mr. Snagsby himself allows—not to put too fine a point upon it —out of one fit into twenty. The occasion of this seizure is, that Guster has a tender heart, and a susceptible something that possibly might have been imagination, but for Tooting and her patron saint. Be it what it may, now, it was so direfully impressed at tea-time by Mr. Snagsby's account of the inquiry at which he had assisted, that at supper-time she projected herself into the kitchen, preceded by a flying Dutch-cheese, and fell into a fit of unusual duration: which she only came out of to go into another, and another, and so on through a chain of fits, with short intervals between, of which she has pathetically availed herself by consuming them in entreaties to Mrs. Snagsby not to give her warning "when she quite comes to;" and also in appeals to the whole establishment to lay her down on the stones, and go to bed. Hence, Mr. Snagsby, at last hearing the cock at the little dairy in Cursitor Street go into that disinterested ecstasy of his on the subject of daylight, says, drawing a long breath, though the most patient of men, "I thought you was dead, I am sure!"

What question this enthusiastic fowl supposes he settles when he strains himself to such an extent, or why he should

thus crow (so men crow on various triumphant public occasions, however) about what cannot be of any moment to him,
is his affair. It is enough that daylight comes, morning
comes, noon comes.

Then the active and intelligent, who has got into the
morning papers as such, comes with his pauper company to
Mr. Krook's, and bears off the body of our dear brother here
departed, to a hemmed-in churchyard, pestiferous and obscene,
whence malignant diseases are communicated to the bodies of
our dear brothers and sisters who have not departed ; while
our dear brothers and sisters who hang about official back-
stairs—would to Heaven they *had* departed !—are very complacent and agreeable. Into a beastly scrap of ground which
a Turk would reject as a savage abomination, and a Caffre
would shudder at, they bring our dear brother here departed,
to receive Christian burial.

With houses looking on, on every side, save where a reeking little tunnel of a court gives access to the iron gate—
with every villainy of life in action close on death, and every
poisonous element of death in action close on life—here, they
lower our dear brother down a foot or two : here, sow him in
corruption, to be raised in corruption : an avenging ghost at
many a sick-bedside : a shameful testimony to future ages, how
civilisation and barbarism walked this boastful island together.

Come night, come darkness, for you cannot come too soon,
or stay too long, by such a place as this ! Come, straggling
lights into the windows of the ugly houses ; and you who do
iniquity therein, do it at least with this dread scene shut
out ! Come, flame of gas, burning so sullenly above the iron
gate, on which the poisoned air deposits its witch-ointment
slimy to the touch ! It is well that you should call to every
passer-by, " Look here ! "

With the night, comes a slouching figure through the
tunnel-court, to the outside of the iron gate. It holds the
gate with its hands, and looks in between the bars ; stands
looking in, for a little while.

It then, with an old broom it carries, softly sweeps the step, and makes the archway clean. It does so, very busily and trimly; looks in again, a little while; and so departs.

Jo, is it thou? Well, well! Though a rejected witness, who "can't exactly say" what will be done to him in greater hands than men's, thou art not quite in outer darkness. There is something like a distant ray of light in thy muttered reason for this:

"He wos wery good to me, he wos!"

CHAPTER XII

It has left off raining down in Lincolnshire, at last, and Chesney Wold has taken heart. Mrs. Rouncewell is full of hospitable cares, for Sir Leicester and my Lady are coming home from Paris. The fashionable intelligence has found it out, and communicates the glad tidings to benighted England. It has also found out, that they will entertain a brilliant and distinguished circle of the *élite* of the *beau monde* (the fashionable intelligence is weak in English, but a giant refreshed in French), at the ancient and hospitable family seat in Lincolnshire.

For the greater honour of the brilliant and distinguished circle, and of Chesney Wold into the bargain, the broken arch of the bridge in the park is mended; and the water, now retired within its proper limits and again spanned gracefully, makes a figure in the prospect from the house. The clear cold sunshine glances into the brittle woods, and approvingly beholds the sharp wind scattering the leaves and drying the moss. It glides over the park after the moving shadows of the clouds, and chases them, and never catches them, all day. It looks in at the windows, and touches the ancestral portraits with bars and patches of brightness, never contemplated by the painters. Athwart the picture of my Lady, over the great chimney-piece, it throws a broad bend-sinister of light that strikes down crookedly into the hearth, and seems to rend it.

185

Through the same cold sunshine, and the same sharp wind, my Lady and Sir Leicester, in their travelling chariot (my Lady's woman, and Sir Leicester's man affectionate in the rumble), start for home. With a considerable amount of jingling and whip-cracking, and many plunging demonstrations on the part of two bare-backed horses, and two Centaurs with glazed hats, jack-boots, and flowing manes and tails, they rattle out of the yard of the Hôtel Bristol in the Place Vendôme, and canter between the sun-and-shadow-chequered colonnade of the Rue de Rivoli and the garden of the ill-fated palace of a headless king and queen, off by the Place of Concord, and the Elysian Fields, and the Gate of the Star, out of Paris.

Sooth to say, they cannot go away too fast; for, even here, my Lady Dedlock has been bored to death. Concert, assembly, opera, theatre, drive, nothing is new to my Lady, under the worn-out heavens. Only last Sunday, when poor wretches were gay—within the walls, playing with children among the clipped trees and the statues in the Palace Garden; walking, a score abreast, in the Elysian Fields, made more Elysian by performing dogs and wooden horses; between whiles filtering (a few) through the gloomy Cathedral of our Lady, to say a word or two at the base of a pillar, within flare of a rusty little gridiron-full of gusty little tapers —without the walls, encompassing Paris with dancing, love-making, wine-drinking, tobacco-smoking, tomb-visiting, billiard, card, and domino playing, quack-doctoring, and much murderous refuse, animate and inanimate—only last Sunday, my Lady, in the desolation of Boredom and the clutch of Giant Despair, almost hated her own maid for being in spirits.

She cannot, therefore, go too fast from Paris. Weariness of soul lies before her, as it lies behind—her Ariel has put a girdle of it round the whole earth, and it cannot be unclasped —but the imperfect remedy is always to fly, from the last place where it has been experienced. Fling Paris back into the distance, then, exchanging it for endless avenues and cross-avenues of wintry trees! And, when next beheld, let it be some leagues away, with the Gate of the Star a white speck glittering in the sun, and the city a mere mound in a plain : two dark square towers rising out of it, and light and shadow descending on it aslant, like the angels in Jacob's dream!

Sir Leicester is generally in a complacent state, and rarely bored. When he has nothing else to do, he can always contemplate his own greatness. It is a considerable advantage to a man, to have so inexhaustible a subject. After reading his letters, he leans back in his corner of the carriage, and generally reviews his importance to society.

"You have an unusual amount of correspondence this morning?" says my Lady, after a long time. She is fatigued with reading. Has almost read a page in twenty miles.

"Nothing in it, though. Nothing whatever."

"I saw one of Mr. Tulkinghorn's long effusions, I think?"

"You see everything," says Sir Leicester, with admiration.

"Ha!" sighs my Lady. "He is the most tiresome of men!"

"He sends—I really beg your pardon—he sends," says Sir Leicester, selecting the letter, and unfolding it, "a message to you. Our stopping to change horses, as I came to his postscript, drove it out of my memory. I beg you'll excuse me. He says—" Sir Leicester is so long in taking out his eye-glass and adjusting it, that my Lady looks a little irritated. "He says, 'In the matter of the right of way—' I beg your pardon, that's not the place. He says—yes! Here I have it! He says, 'I beg my respectful compliments to my Lady, who, I hope, has benefited by the change. Will you do me the favour to mention (as it may interest her), that I have something to tell her on her return, in reference to the person who copied the affidavit in the Chancery suit, which so powerfully stimulated her curiosity. I have seen him.'"

My Lady, leaning forward, looks out of her window.

"That's the message," observes Sir Leicester.

"I should like to walk a little," says my Lady, still looking out of her window.

"Walk!" repeats Sir Leicester, in a tone of surprise.

"I should like to walk a little," says my Lady, with unmistakable distinctness. "Please to stop the carriage."

The carriage is stopped, the affectionate man alights from the rumble, opens the door, and lets down the steps, obedient to an impatient motion of my Lady's hand. My Lady alights so quickly, and walks away so quickly, that Sir Leicester, for all his scrupulous politeness, is unable to assist her, and is left behind. A space of a minute or two has elapsed before he comes up with her. She smiles, looks very handsome, takes his arm, lounges with him for a quarter of a mile, is very much bored, and resumes her seat in the carriage.

The rattle and clatter continue through the greater part of three days, with more or less of bell-jingling and whip-cracking, and more or less plunging of Centaurs and bare-backed horses. Their courtly politeness to each other, at the Hotels where they tarry, is the theme of general admiration. Though my Lord *is* a little aged for my Lady, says Madame, the hostess of the Golden Ape, and though he might be her amiable father, one can see at a glance that they love each other. One observes my Lord with his white hair, standing, hat in hand, to help my Lady to and from the carriage. One observes my Lady, how recognisant of my Lord's politeness, with an inclination of her gracious head, and the concession of her so-genteel fingers! It is ravishing!

The sea has no appreciation of great men, but knocks them about like the small fry. It is habitually hard upon Sir Leicester, whose countenance it greenly mottles in the manner of sage-cheese, and in whose aristocratic system it effects a dismal revolution. It is the Radical of Nature to him. Nevertheless, his dignity gets over it, after stopping to refit: and he goes on with my Lady for Chesney Wold, lying only one night in London on the way to Lincolnshire.

Through the same cold sunlight—colder as the day declines,

—and through the same sharp wind—sharper as the separate shadows of bare trees gloom together in the woods, and as the Ghost's Walk, touched at the western corner by a pile of fire in the sky, resigns itself to coming night,—they drive into the park. The Rooks, swinging in their lofty houses in the elm-tree avenue, seem to discuss the question of the occupancy of the carriage as it passes underneath; some agreeing that Sir Leicester and my Lady are come down; some arguing with malcontents who won't admit it; now, all consenting to consider the question disposed of; now, all breaking out again in violent debate, incited by one obstinate and drowsy bird, who will persist in putting in a last contradictory croak. Leaving them to swing and caw, the travelling chariot rolls on to the house; where fires gleam warmly through some of the windows, though not through so many as to give an inhabited expression to the darkening mass of front. But the brilliant and distinguished circle will soon do that.

Mrs. Rouncewell is in attendance, and receives Sir Leicester's customary shake of the hand with a profound curtsey.

" How do you do, Mrs. Rouncewell? I am glad to see you."

" I hope I have the honour of welcoming you in good health, Sir Leicester ? "

" In excellent health, Mrs. Rouncewell."

" My Lady is looking charmingly well," says Mrs. Rouncewell, with another curtsey.

My Lady signifies, without profuse expenditure of words, that she is as wearily well as she can hope to be.

But Rosa is in the distance, behind the housekeeper; and my Lady, who has not subdued the quickness of her observation, whatever else she may have conquered, asks :

" Who is that girl ? "

" A young scholar of mine, my Lady. Rosa."

" Come here, Rosa ! " Lady Dedlock beckons her, with even an appearance of interest. " Why, do you know how pretty you are, child?" she says, touching her shoulder with her two forefingers.

Rosa, very much abashed, says, "No, if you please, my Lady!" and glances up, and glances down, and don't know where to look, but looks all the prettier.

"How old are you?"

"Nineteen, my Lady.'

"Nineteen," repeats my Lady thoughtfully. "Take care they don't spoil you by flattery."

"Yes, my Lady."

My Lady taps her dimpled cheek with the same delicate gloved fingers, and goes on to the foot of the oak staircase, where Sir Leicester pauses for her as her knightly escort. A staring old Dedlock in a panel, as large as life and as dull, looks as if he didn't know what to make of it—which was probably his general state of mind in the days of Queen Elizabeth.

That evening, in the housekeeper's room, Rosa can do nothing but murmur Lady Dedlock's praises. She is so affable, so graceful, so beautiful, so elegant; has such a sweet voice and such a thrilling touch, that Rosa can feel it yet! Mrs. Rouncewell confirms all this, not without personal pride, reserving only the one point of affability. Mrs. Rouncewell is not quite sure as to that. Heaven forbid that she should say a syllable in dispraise of any member of that excellent family; above all, of my Lady, whom the whole world admires; but if my Lady would only be "a little more free," not quite so cold and distant, Mrs. Rouncewell thinks she would be more affable.

" Tis almost a pity," Mrs. Rouncewell adds—only " almost," because it borders on impiety to suppose that anything could be better than it is, in such an express dispensation as the Dedlock affairs ; " that my Lady has no family. If she had had a daughter now, a grown young lady, to interest her, I think she would have had the only kind of excellence she wants."

"Might not that have made her still more proud, grandmother?" says Watt; who has been home and come back again, he is such a good grandson.

"More and most, my dear," returns the housekeeper with dignity, "are words it's not my place to use—nor so much as to hear—applied to any drawback on my Lady."

"I beg your pardon, grandmother. But she *is* proud, is she not?"

"If she is, she has reason to be. The Dedlock family have always reason to be."

"Well!" says Watt, "it's to be hoped they line out of their Prayer-Books a certain passage for the common people about pride and vainglory. Forgive me, grandmother! Only a joke!"

"Sir Leicester and Lady Dedlock, my dear, are not fit subjects for joking."

"Sir Leicester is no joke by any means," says Watt; "and I humbly ask his pardon. I suppose, grandmother, that even with the family and their guests down here, there is no objection to my prolonging my stay at the Dedlock Arms for a day or two, as any other traveller might?"

"Surely, none in the world, child."

"I am glad of that," says Watt, "because I have an inexpressible desire to extend my knowledge of this beautiful neighbourhood."

He happens to glance at Rosa, who looks down, and is very shy, indeed. But, according to the old superstition, it should be Rosa's ears that burn, and not her fresh bright cheeks; for my Lady's maid is holding forth about her at this moment, with surpassing energy.

My Lady's maid is a Frenchwoman of two-and-thirty, from somewhere in the southern country about Avignon and Marseilles—a large-eyed brown woman with black hair; who would be handsome, but for a certain feline mouth, and general uncomfortable tightness of face, rendering the jaws too eager, and the skull too prominent. There is something

191

indefinably keen and wan about her anatomy; and she has a watchful way of looking out of the corners of her eyes without turning her head, which could be pleasantly dispensed with—especially when she is in an ill-humour and near knives. Through all the good taste of her dress and little adornments, these objections so express themselves, that she seems to go about like a very neat She-Wolf imperfectly tamed. Besides being accomplished in all the knowledge appertaining to her post, she is almost an Englishwoman in her acquaintance with the language—consequently, she is in no want of words to shower upon Rosa for having attracted my Lady's attention; and she pours them out with such grim ridicule as she sits at dinner, that her companion, the affectionate man, is rather relieved when she arrives at the spoon stage of that performance.

Ha, ha, ha! She, Hortense, been in my Lady's service since five years, and always kept at the distance, and this doll, this puppet, caressed—absolutely caressed—by my Lady on the moment of her arriving at the house! Ha, ha, ha! "And do you know how pretty you are, child?"—"No, my Lady."—You are right there! "And how old are you, child? And take care they do not spoil you by flattery, child!" O how droll! It is the *best* thing altogether.

In short, it is such an admirable thing, that Mademoiselle Hortense can't forget it; but at meals for days afterwards, even among her countrywomen and others attached in like capacity to the troop of visitors, relapses into silent enjoyment of the joke—an enjoyment expressed, in her own convivial manner, by an additional tightness of face, thin elongation of compressed lips, and sidewise look: which intense appreciation of humour is frequently reflected in my Lady's mirrors, when my Lady is not among them.

All the mirrors in the house are brought into action now: many of them after a long blank. They reflect handsome faces, simpering faces, youthful faces, faces of threescore-and ten that will not submit to be old; the entire collection of

faces that have come to pass a January week or two at
Chesney Wold, and which the fashionable intelligence, a
mighty hunter before the Lord, hunts with a keen scent, from
their breaking cover at the Court of St. James's to their
being run down to Death. The place in Lincolnshire is all
alive. By day, guns and voices are heard ringing in the
woods, horsemen and carriages enliven the park roads, servants
and hangers-on pervade the Village and the Dedlock Arms.
Seen by night, from distant openings in the trees, the row
of windows in the long drawing-room, where my Lady's
picture hangs over the great chimney-piece, is like a row
of jewels set in a black frame. On Sunday, the chill little
church is almost warmed by so much gallant company, and
the general flavour of the Dedlock dust is quenched in
delicate perfumes.

The brilliant and distinguished circle comprehends within
it, no contracted amount of education, sense, courage, honour,
beauty, and virtue. Yet there is something a little wrong about
it, in despite of its immense advantages. What can it be?

Dandyism? There is no King George the Fourth now
(more's the pity!) to set the dandy fashion; there are no
clear-starched jack-towel neckcloths, no short-waisted coats,
no false calves, no stays. There are no caricatures, now, of
effeminate Exquisites so arrayed, swooning in opera boxes
with excess of delight, and being revived by other dainty
creatures, poking long-necked scent-bottles at their noses.
There is no beau whom it takes four men at once to shake
into his buckskins, or who goes to see all the executions, or
who is troubled with the self-reproach of having once consumed a pea. But is there Dandyism in the brilliant and
distinguished circle notwithstanding, Dandyism of a more
mischievous sort, that has got below the surface and is doing
less harmless things than jack-towelling itself and stopping
its own digestion, to which no rational person need particularly object?

Why, yes. It cannot be disguised. There *are*, at Chesney

Wold this January week, some ladies and gentlemen of the newest fashion, who have set up a Dandyism—in Religion, for instance. Who, in mere lackadaisical want of an emotion, have agreed upon a little dandy talk about the Vulgar wanting faith in things in general ; meaning, in the things that have been tried and found wanting, as though a low fellow should unaccountably lose faith in a bad shilling, after finding it out ! Who would make the Vulgar very picturesque and faithful, by putting back the hands upon the Clock of Time, and cancelling a few hundred years of history.

There are also ladies and gentlemen of another fashion, not so new, but very elegant, who have agreed to put a smooth glaze on the world, and to keep down all its realities. For whom everything must be languid and pretty. Who have found out the perpetual stoppage. Who are to rejoice at nothing, and be sorry for nothing. Who are not to be disturbed by ideas. On whom even the Fine Arts, attending in powder and walking backward like the Lord Chamberlain, must array themselves in the milliners' and tailors' patterns of past generations, and be particularly careful not to be in earnest, or to receive any impress from the moving age.

Then there is my Lord Boodle, of considerable reputation with his party, who has known what office is, and who tells Sir Leicester Dedlock with much gravity, after dinner, that he really does not see to what the present age is tending. A debate is not what a debate used to be; the House is not what the House used to be ; even a Cabinet is not what it formerly was. He perceives with astonishment, that supposing the present Government to be overthrown, the limited choice of the Crown, in the formation of a new Ministry, would lie between Lord Coodle and Sir Thomas Doodle— supposing it to be impossible for the Duke of Foodle to act with Goodle, which may be assumed to be the case in consequence of the breach arising out of that affair with Hoodle. Then, giving the Home Department and the Leadership of the House of Commons to Joodle, the Exchequer to Koodle, the Colonies to Loodle, and the Foreign Office to Moodle, what are you to do with Noodle? You can't offer him the Presidency of the Council; that is reserved for Poodle. You can't put him in the Woods and Forests; that is hardly good enough for Quoodle. What follows? That the country is shipwrecked, lost, and gone to pieces (as is made manifest to the Patriotism of Sir Leicester Dedlock), because you can't provide for Noodle!

On the other hand, the Right Honourable William Buffy, M.P., contends across the table with some one else, that the shipwreck of the country—about which there is no doubt; it is only the manner of it that is in question—is attributable to Cuffy. If you had done with Cuffy what you ought to have done when he first came into Parliament, and had prevented him from going over to Duffy, you would have got him into alliance with Fuffy, you would have had with you the weight attaching as a smart debater to Guffy, you would have brought to bear upon the elections the wealth of Huffy, you would have got in for three counties Juffy, Kuffy, and Luffy, and you would have strengthened your administration by the official knowledge and the business habits of Muffy. All this, instead of being as you now are, dependent on the mere caprice of Puffy!

As to this point, and as to some minor topics, there are differences of opinion; but it is perfectly clear to the brilliant and distinguished circle, all round, that nobody is in question but Boodle and his retinue, and Buffy and *his* retinue. These are the great actors for whom the stage is reserved. A People there are, no doubt—a certain large number of supernumeraries, who are to be occasionally addressed, and relied upon for shouts and choruses, as on the theatrical stage; but Boodle and Buffy, their followers and families, their heirs, executors, administrators, and assigns, are the born first-actors, managers, and leaders, and no others can appear upon the scene for ever and ever.

In this, too, there is perhaps more Dandyism at Chesney

Wold than the brilliant and distinguished circle will find good for itself in the long run. For it is, even with the stillest and politest circles, as with the circle the necromancer draws around him—very strange appearances may be seen in active motion outside. With this difference; that, being realities and not phantoms, there is the greater danger of their breaking in.

Chesney Wold is quite full, anyhow; so full, that a burning sense of injury arises in the breasts of ill-lodged ladies'-maids, and is not to be extinguished. Only one room is empty. It is a turret chamber of the third order of merit, plainly but comfortably furnished, and having an old-fashioned business air. It is Mr. Tulkinghorn's room, and is never bestowed on anybody else, for he may come at any time. He is not come yet. It is his quiet habit to walk across the park from the village, in fine weather; to drop into this room, as if he had never been out of it since he was last seen there; to request a servant to inform Sir Leicester that he is arrived, in case he should be wanted; and to appear ten minutes before dinner, in the shadow of the library-door. He sleeps in his turret, with a complaining flag-staff over his head; and has some leads outside, on which, any fine morning when he is down here, his black figure may be seen walking before breakfast like a larger species of rook.

Every day before dinner, my Lady looks for him in the dusk of the library, but he is not there. Every day at dinner, my Lady glances down the table for the vacant place, that would be waiting to receive him if he had just arrived; but there is no vacant place. Every night, my Lady casually asks her maid:

"Is Mr. Tulkinghorn come?"

Every night the answer is, "No, my Lady, not yet."

One night, while having her hair undressed, my Lady loses herself in deep thought after this reply, until she sees her own brooding face, in the opposite glass, and a pair of black eyes curiously observing her.

" Be so good as to attend," says my Lady then, addressing the reflection of Hortense, " to your business. You can contemplate your beauty at another time."

" Pardon ! It was your Ladyship's beauty."

" That," says my Lady, " you needn't contemplate at all."

At length, one afternoon a little before sunset, when the bright groups of figures, which have for the last hour or two enlivened the Ghost's Walk, are all dispersed, and only Sir Leicester and my Lady remain upon the terrace, Mr. Tulkinghorn appears. He comes towards them at his usual methodical pace, which is never quickened, never slackened. He wears his usual expressionless mask—if it be a mask— and carries family secrets in every limb of his body, and every crease of his dress. Whether his whole soul is devoted to the great, or whether he yields them nothing beyond the services he sells, is his personal secret. He keeps it, as he keeps the secrets of his clients ; he is his own client in that matter, and will never betray himself.

" How do you do, Mr. Tulkinghorn ?" says Sir Leicester, giving him his hand.

Mr. Tulkinghorn is quite well. Sir Leicester is quite well. My Lady is quite well. All highly satisfactory. The lawyer, with his hands behind him, walks, at Sir Leicester's side, along the terrace. My Lady walks upon the other side.

" We expected you before," says Sir Leicester. A gracious observation. As much as to say, " Mr. Tulkinghorn, we remember your existence when you are not here to remind us of it by your presence. We bestow a fragment of our minds upon you, sir, you see !"

Mr. Tulkinghorn, comprehending it, inclines his head, and says he is much obliged.

" I should have come down sooner," he explains, " but that I have been much engaged with those matters in the several suits between yourself and Boythorn."

" A man of a very ill-regulated mind," observes Sir Leicester, with severity. " An extremely dangerous person in any community. A man of a very low character of mind."

" He is obstinate," says Mr. Tulkinghorn.

" It is natural to such a man to be so," says Sir Leicester, looking most profoundly obstinate himself. " I am not at all surprised to hear it."

" The only question is," pursues the lawyer, " whether you will give up anything."

" No, sir," replies Sir Leicester. " Nothing. *I* give up ? "

" I don't mean anything of importance. That, of course, I know you would not abandon. I mean any minor point."

" Mr. Tulkinghorn," returns Sir Leicester, " there can be no minor point between myself and Mr. Boythorn. If I go farther, and observe that I cannot readily conceive how *any* right of mine can be a minor point, I speak not so much in reference to myself as an individual, as in reference to the family position I have it in charge to maintain."

Mr. Tulkinghorn inclines his head again. " I have now my instructions," he says. " Mr. Boythorn will give us a good deal of trouble——"

" It is the character of such a mind, Mr. Tulkinghorn," Sir Leicester interrupts him, " *to* give trouble. An exceedingly ill-conditioned, levelling person. A person who, fifty years ago, would probably have been tried at the Old Bailey for some demagogue proceeding, and severely punished—if not," adds Sir Leicester, after a moment's pause, " if not hanged, drawn, and quartered."

Sir Leicester appears to discharge his stately breast of a burden, in passing this capital sentence ; as if it were the next satisfactory thing to having the sentence executed.

" But night is coming on," says he, " and my Lady will take cold. My dear, let us go in."

As they turn towards the hall-door, Lady Dedlock addresses Mr. Tulkinghorn for the first time.

" You sent me a message respecting the person whose

writing I happened to inquire about. It was like you to remember the circumstance ; I had quite forgotten it. Your message reminded me of it again. I can't imagine what association I had, with a hand like that ; but I surely had some."

"You had some ? " Mr. Tulkinghorn repeats.

"O yes!" returns my Lady, carelessly. "I think I must have had some. And did you really take the trouble to find out the writer of that actual thing—what is it !—Affidavit ? "

"Yes."

"How very odd ! "

They pass into a sombre breakfast-room on the ground floor, lighted in the day by two deep windows. It is now twilight. The fire glows brightly on the panelled wall, and palely on the window-glass, where, through the cold reflection of the blaze, the colder landscape shudders in the wind, and a grey mist creeps along : the only traveller besides the waste of clouds.

My Lady lounges in a great chair in the chimney-corner, and Sir Leicester takes another great chair opposite. The lawyer stands before the fire, with his hand out at arm's length, shading his face. He looks across his arm at my Lady.

"Yes," he says, "I inquired about the man, and found him. And, what is very strange, I found him—— "

"Not to be any out-of-the-way person, I am afraid !" Lady Dedlock languidly anticipates.

"I found him dead."

"O dear me !" remonstrated Sir Leicester. Not so much shocked by the fact, as by the fact of the fact being mentioned.

"I was directed to his lodging—a miserable, poverty-stricken place—and I found him dead."

"You will excuse me, Mr. Tulkinghorn," observes Sir Leicester. "I think the less said—— "

"Pray, Sir Leicester, let me hear the story out" (it is my Lady speaking). "It is quite a story for twilight. How very shocking ! Dead ? "

199

Mr. Tulkinghorn re-asserts it by another inclination of his head. "Whether by his own hand——"

"Upon my honour!" cries Sir Leicester. "Really!"

"Do let me hear the story!" says my Lady.

"Whatever you desire, my dear. But, I must say——"

"No, you mustn't say! Go on, Mr. Tulkinghorn."

Sir Leicester's gallantry concedes the point; though he still feels that to bring this sort of squalor among the upper classes is really—really——

"I was about to say," resumes the lawyer, with undisturbed calmness, "that whether he had died by his own hand or not, it was beyond my power to tell you. I should amend that phrase, however, by saying that he had unquestionably died of his own act; though whether by his own deliberate intention, or by mischance, can never certainly be known. The Coroner's jury found that he took the poison accidentally."

"And what kind of man," my Lady asks, "was this deplorable creature?"

"Very difficult to say," returns the lawyer, shaking his head. "He had lived so wretchedly, and was so neglected, with his gipsy colour, and his wild black hair and beard, that I should have considered him the commonest of the common. The surgeon had a notion that he had once been something better, both in appearance and condition."

"What did they call the wretched being?"

"They called him what he had called himself, but no one knew his name."

"Not even any one who had attended on him?"

"No one had attended on him. He was found dead. In fact, I found him."

"Without any clue to anything more?"

"Without any; there was," says the lawyer meditatively, "an old portmanteau; but—No, there were no papers."

During the utterance of every word of this short dialogue, Lady Dedlock and Mr. Tulkinghorn, without any other alteration in their customary deportment, have looked very steadily at one another—as was natural, perhaps, in the discussion of so unusual a subject. Sir Leicester has looked at the fire, with the general expression of the Dedlock on the staircase. The story being told, he renews his stately protest, saying, that as it is quite clear that no association in my Lady's mind can possibly be traceable to this poor wretch (unless he was a begging-letter writer); he trusts to hear no more about a subject so far removed from my Lady's station.

"Certainly, a collection of horrors," says my Lady, gathering up her mantles and furs; "but they interest one for the moment! Have the kindness, Mr. Tulkinghorn, to open the door for me."

Mr. Tulkinghorn does so with deference, and holds it open while she passes out. She passes close to him, with her usual fatigued manner, and insolent grace. They meet again at dinner—again, next day—again, for many days in succession. Lady Dedlock is always the same exhausted deity, surrounded by worshippers, and terribly liable to be bored to death, even while presiding at her own shrine. Mr. Tulkinghorn is always the same speechless repository of noble confidences: so oddly out of place, and yet so perfectly at home. They appear to take as little note of one another, as any two people, enclosed within the same walls, could. But, whether each evermore watches and suspects the other, evermore mistrustful of some great reservation; whether each is evermore prepared at all points for the other, and never to be taken unawares; what each would give to know how much the other knows—all this is hidden, for the time, in their own hearts.

CHAPTER XIII

\

ESTHER'S NARRATIVE

WE held many consultations about what Richard was to be; first, without Mr. Jarndyce, as he had requested, and afterwards with him; but it was a long time before we seemed to make progress. Richard said he was ready for anything. When Mr. Jarndyce doubted whether he might not already be too old to enter the Navy, Richard said he had thought of that, and perhaps he was. When Mr. Jarndyce asked him what he thought of the Army, Richard said he had thought of that, too, and it wasn't a bad idea. When Mr. Jarndyce advised him to try and decide within himself, whether his old preference for the sea was an ordinary boyish inclination, or a strong impulse, Richard answered, Well, he really *had* tried very often, and he couldn't make out.

"How much of this indecision of character," Mr. Jarndyce said to me, "is chargeable on that incomprehensible heap of uncertainty and procrastination on which he has been thrown from his birth, I don't pretend to say; but that Chancery, among its other sins, is responsible for some of it, I can plainly see. It has engendered or confirmed in him a habit of putting off—and trusting to this, that, and the other chance, without knowing what chance—and dismissing everything as unsettled, uncertain, and confused. The character of much older and steadier people may be even changed by the circumstances surrounding them. It would be too much

202

to expect that a boy's, in its formation, should be the subject of such influences, and escape them."

I felt this to be true; though, if I may venture to mention what I thought besides, I thought it much to be regretted that Richard's education had not counteracted those influences, or directed his character. He had been eight years at a public school, and had learnt, I understood, to make Latin Verses of several sorts, in the most admirable manner. But I never heard that it had been anybody's business to find out what his natural bent was, or where his failings lay, or to adapt any kind of knowledge to *him*. *He* had been adapted to the Verses, and had learnt the art of making them to such perfection, that if he had remained at school until he was of age, I suppose he could only have gone on making them over and over again, unless he had enlarged his education by forgetting how to do it. Still, although I had no doubt that they were very beautiful, and very improving, and very sufficient for a great many purposes of life, and always remembered all through life, I did doubt whether Richard would not have profited by some one studying him a little, instead of his studying them quite so much.

To be sure, I knew nothing of the subject, and do not even now know whether the young gentlemen of classic Rome or Greece made verses to the same extent—or whether the young gentlemen of any country ever did.

"I haven't the least idea," said Richard, musing, "what I had better be. Except that I am quite sure I don't want to go into the Church, it's a toss-up."

"You have no inclination in Mr. Kenge's way?" suggested Mr. Jarndyce.

"I don't know that, sir!" replied Richard. "I am fond of boating. Articled clerks go a good deal on the water. It's a capital profession!"

"Surgeon—" suggested Mr. Jarndyce.

"That's the thing, sir!" cried Richard.

I doubt if he had ever once thought of it before.

"That's the thing, sir!" repeated Richard, with the greatest enthusiasm. "We have got it at last. M.R.C.S.!"

He was not to be laughed out of it, though he laughed at it heartily. He said he had chosen his profession, and the more he thought of it, the more he felt that his destiny was clear; the art of healing was the art of all others for him. Mistrusting that he only came to this conclusion, because, having never had much chance of finding out for himself what he was fitted for, and having never been guided to the discovery, he was taken by the newest idea, and was glad to get rid of the trouble of consideration, I wondered whether the Latin Verses often ended in this, or whether Richard's was a solitary case.

Mr. Jarndyce took great pains to talk with him, seriously, and to put it to his good sense not to deceive himself in so important a matter. Richard was a little grave after these interviews; but invariably told Ada and me "that it was all right," and then began to talk about something else.

"By Heaven!" cried Mr. Boythorn, who interested himself strongly in the subject—though I need not say that, for he could do nothing weakly; "I rejoice to find a young gentleman of spirit and gallantry devoting himself to that noble profession! The more spirit there is in it, the better for mankind, and the worse for those mercenary task-masters and low tricksters who delight in putting that illustrious art at a disadvantage in the world. By all that is base and despicable," cried Mr. Boythorn, "the treatment of Surgeons aboard ship is such, that I would submit the legs—both legs—of every member of the Admiralty Board to a compound fracture, and render it a transportable offence in any qualified practitioner to set them, if the system were not wholly changed in eight-and-forty hours!"

"Wouldn't you give them a week?" asked Mr. Jarndyce.

"No!" cried Mr. Boythorn, firmly. "Not on any consideration! Eight-and-forty hours! As to Corporations, Parishes, Vestry-Boards, and similar gatherings of jolterheaded clods, who assemble to exchange such speeches that, by Heaven! they ought to be worked in quicksilver mines for the short remainder of their miserable existence, if it were only to prevent their detestable English from contaminating a language spoken in the presence of the Sun—as to those fellows, who meanly take advantage of the ardour of gentlemen in the pursuit of knowledge, to recompense the inestimable services of the best years of their lives, their long study, and their expensive education, with pittances too small for the acceptance of clerks, I would have the necks of every one of them wrung, and their skulls arranged in Surgeons' Hall for the contemplation of the whole profession—in order that its younger members might understand from actual measurement, in early life, *how* thick skulls may become!"

He wound up this vehement declaration by looking round upon us with a most agreeable smile, and suddenly thundering, Ha, ha, ha! over and over again, until anybody else might have been expected to be quite subdued by the exertion.

As Richard still continued to say that he was fixed in his choice, after repeated periods for consideration had been recommended by Mr. Jarndyce, and had expired; and he still continued to assure Ada and me, in the same final manner, that it was "all right;" it became advisable to take Mr. Kenge into council. Mr. Kenge, therefore, came down to dinner one day, and leaned back in his chair, and turned his eye-glasses over and over, and spoke in a sonorous voice, and did exactly what I remembered to have seen him do when I was a little girl.

"Ah!" said Mr. Kenge. "Yes. Well! A very good profession, Mr. Jarndyce; a very good profession."

"The course of study and preparation requires to be diligently pursued," observed my Guardian, with a glance at Richard.

"O, no doubt," said Mr. Kenge. "Diligently."

"But that being the case, more or less, with all pursuits,

that are worth much," said Mr. Jarndyce, "it is not a special consideration which another choice would be likely to escape."

"Truly," said Mr. Kenge. "And Mr. Richard Carstone, who has so meritoriously acquitted himself in the—shall I say the classic shades?—in which his youth had been passed, will, no doubt, apply the habits, if not the principles and practice, of versification in that tongue in which a poet was said (unless I mistake) to be born, not made, to the more eminently practical field of action on which he enters."

"You may rely upon it," said Richard, in his off-hand manner, "that I shall go at it and do my best."

"Very well, Mr. Jarndyce!" said Mr. Kenge, gently nodding his head. "Really, when we are assured by Mr. Richard that he means to go at it, and to do his best," nodding feelingly and smoothly over those expressions; "I would submit to you, that we have only to inquire into the best mode of carrying out the object of his ambition. Now, with reference to placing Mr. Richard with some sufficiently eminent practitioner. Is there any one in view at present?"

"No one, Rick, I think?" said my Guardian.

"No one, sir," said Richard.

"Quite so!" observed Mr. Kenge. "As to situation, now. Is there any particular feeling on that head?"

"N—no," said Richard.

"Quite so!" observed Mr. Kenge again.

"I should like a little variety," said Richard; "—I mean a good range of experience."

"Very requisite, no doubt," returned Mr. Kenge. "I think this may be easily arranged, Mr. Jarndyce? We have only, in the first place, to discover a sufficiently eligible practitioner; and, as soon as we make our want—and, shall I add, our ability to pay a premium?—known, our only difficulty will be in the selection of one from a large number. We have only, in the second place, to observe those little formalities which are rendered necessary by our time of life, and our being under the guardianship of the Court. We shall soon be—shall I say, in Mr. Richard's own light-hearted manner, 'going at it'—to our heart's content. It is a coincidence," said Mr. Kenge, with a tinge of melancholy in his smile, "one of those coincidences which may or may not require an explanation beyond our present limited faculties, that I have a cousin in the medical profession. He might be deemed eligible by you, and might be disposed to respond to this proposal. I can answer for him as little as for you; but he *might!*"

As this was an opening in the prospect, it was arranged that Mr. Kenge should see his cousin. And as Mr. Jarndyce had before proposed to take us to London for a few weeks, it was settled next day that we should make our visit at once, and combine Richard's business with it.

Mr. Boythorn leaving us within a week, we took up our abode at a cheerful lodging near Oxford Street, over an up-holsterer's shop. London was a great wonder to us, and we were out for hours and hours at a time; seeing the sights; which appeared to be less capable of exhaustion than we were. We made the round of the principal theatres, too, with great delight, and saw all the plays that were worth seeing. I mention this, because it was at the theatre that I began to be made uncomfortable again, by Mr. Guppy.

I was sitting in front of the box one night with Ada; and Richard was in the place he liked best, behind Ada's chair; when, happening to look down into the pit, I saw Mr. Guppy, with his hair flattened down upon his head, and woe depicted in his face, looking up at me. I felt, all through the performance, that he never looked at the actors, but constantly looked at me, and always with a carefully pre-pared expression of the deepest misery and the profoundest dejection.

It quite spoiled my pleasure for that night, because it was so very embarrassing and so very ridiculous. But, from that time forth, we never went to the play without my seeing

Mr. Guppy in the pit, always with his hair straight and flat, his shirt-collar turned down, and a general feebleness about him. If he were not there when we went in, and I began to hope he would not come, and yielded myself for a little while to the interest of the scene, I was certain to encounter his languishing eyes when I least expected it, and, from that time, to be quite sure that they were fixed upon me all the evening.

I really cannot express how uneasy this made me. If he would only have brushed up his hair, or turned up his collar, it would have been bad enough; but to know that that absurd figure was always gazing at me, and always in that demonstrative state of despondency, put such a constraint upon me that I did not like to laugh at the play, or to cry at it, or to move or to speak. I seemed able to do nothing naturally. As to escaping Mr. Guppy by going to the back of the box, I could not bear to do that; because I knew Richard and Ada relied on having me next them, and that they could never have talked together so happily if anybody else had been in my place. So there I sat, not knowing where to look—for wherever I looked, I knew Mr. Guppy's eyes were following me—and thinking of the dreadful expense to which this young man was putting himself on my account.

Sometimes I thought of telling Mr. Jarndyce. Then I feared that the young man would lose his situation, and that I might ruin him. Sometimes, I thought of confiding in Richard; but was deterred by the possibility of his fighting Mr. Guppy, and giving him black eyes. Sometimes, I thought, should I frown at him, or shake my head. Then I felt I could not do it. Sometimes, I considered whether I should write to his mother, but that ended in my being convinced that to open a correspondence would be to make the matter worse. I always came to the conclusion, finally, that I could do nothing. Mr. Guppy's perseverance, all this time, not only produced him regularly at any theatre to which we went, but caused him to appear in the crowd as we were

Mr. Guppy's Desolation

coming out, and even to get up behind our fly—where I am sure I saw him, two or three times, struggling among the most dreadful spikes. After we got home, he haunted a post opposite our house. The upholsterer's where we lodged, being at the corner of two streets, and my bedroom window being opposite the post, I was afraid to go near the window when I went up-stairs, lest I should see him (as I did one moonlight night) leaning against the post, and evidently catching cold. If Mr. Guppy had not been, fortunately for me, engaged in the day-time, I really should have had no rest from him.

While we were making this round of gaieties, in which Mr. Guppy so extraordinarily participated, the business which had helped to bring us to town was not neglected. Mr. Kenge's cousin was a Mr. Bayham Badger, who had a good practice at Chelsea, and attended a large public Institution besides. He was quite willing to receive Richard into his house, and to superintend his studies ; and as it seemed that those could be pursued advantageously under Mr. Badger's roof, and Mr. Badger liked Richard, and as Richard said he liked Mr. Badger "well enough," an agreement was made, the Lord Chancellor's consent was obtained, and it was all settled.

On the day when matters were concluded between Richard and Mr. Badger, we were all under engagement to dine at Mr. Badger's house. We were to be "merely a family party," Mrs. Badger's note said ; and we found no lady there but Mrs. Badger herself. She was surrounded in the drawing-room by various objects, indicative of her painting a little, playing the piano a little, playing the guitar a little, playing the harp a little, singing a little, working a little, reading a little, writing poetry a little, and botanising a little. She was a lady of about fifty, I should think, youthfully dressed, and of a very fine complexion. If I add, to the little list of her accomplishments, that she rouged a little, I do not mean that there was any harm in it.

Mr. Bayham Badger himself was a pink, fresh-faced, crisp-looking gentleman, with a weak voice, white teeth, light hair, and surprised eyes: some years younger, I should say, than Mrs. Bayham Badger. He admired her exceedingly, but principally, and to begin with, on the curious ground (as it seemed to us) of her having had three husbands. We had barely taken our seats, when he said to Mr. Jarndyce quite triumphantly,

" You would hardly suppose that I am Mrs. Bayham Badger's third ! "

" Indeed ? " said Mr. Jarndyce.

" Her third ! " said Mr. Badger. " Mrs. Bayham Badger has not the appearance, Miss Summerson, of a lady who has had two former husbands ? "

I said " Not at all ! "

" And most remarkable men ! " said Mr. Badger, in a tone of confidence. " Captain Swosser of the Royal Navy, who was Mrs. Badger's first husband, was a very distinguished officer indeed. The name of Professor Dingo my immediate predecessor, is one of European reputation."

Mrs. Badger overheard him, and smiled.

" Yes, my dear ! " Mr. Badger replied to the smile, " I was observing to Mr. Jarndyce and Miss Summerson, that you had had two former husbands—both very distinguished men. And they found it, as people generally do, difficult to believe."

" I was barely twenty," said Mrs. Badger, " when I married Captain Swosser of the Royal Navy. I was in the Mediterranean with him ; I am quite a Sailor. On the twelfth anniversary of my wedding-day, I became the wife of Professor Dingo."

(" Of European reputation," added Mr. Badger in an under-tone.)

" And when Mr. Badger and myself were married," pursued Mrs. Badger, " we were married on the same day of the year. I had become attached to the day."

" So that Mrs. Badger has been married to three husbands —two of them highly distinguished men," said Mr. Badger, summing up the facts ; " and, each time, upon the twenty-first of March at Eleven in the forenoon ! "

We all expressed our admiration.

" But for Mr. Badger's modesty," said Mr. Jarndyce, " I would take leave to correct him, and say three distinguished men."

" Thank you, Mr. Jarndyce ! What I always tell him ! " observed Mrs. Badger.

" And, my dear," said Mr. Badger, " what do *I* always tell you ? That without any affectation of disparaging such professional distinction as I may have attained (which our friend Mr. Carstone will have many opportunities of estimating), I am not so weak—no, really," said Mr. Badger to us generally, " so unreasonable—as to put my reputation on the same footing with such first-rate men as Captain Swosser and Professor Dingo. Perhaps you may be interested, Mr. Jarndyce," continued Mr. Bayham Badger, leading the way into the next drawing-room, " in this portrait of Captain Swosser. It was taken on his return home from the African Station, where he had suffered from the fever of the country. Mrs. Badger considers it too yellow. But it's a very fine head. A very fine head ! "

We all echoed " A very fine head ! "

" I feel when I look at it," said Mr. Badger, " ' that's a man I should like to have seen ! ' It strikingly bespeaks the first-class man that Captain Swosser pre-eminently was. On the other side, Professor Dingo. I knew him well—attended him in his last illness—a speaking likeness ! Over the piano, Mrs. Bayham Badger when Mrs. Swosser. Over the sofa, Mrs. Bayham Badger when Mrs. Dingo. Of Mrs. Bayham Badger *in esse*, I possess the original, and have no copy."

Dinner was now announced, and we went down-stairs. It was a very genteel entertainment, very handsomely served. But the Captain and the Professor still ran in Mr. Badger's

211

head, and, as Ada and I had the honour of being under his particular care, we had the full benefit of them.

"Water, Miss Summerson? Allow me! Not in that tumbler, pray. Bring me the Professor's goblet, James!"

Ada very much admired some artificial flowers, under a glass.

"Astonishing how they keep!" said Mr. Badger. "They were presented to Mrs. Bayham Badger when she was in the Mediterranean."

He invited Mr. Jarndyce to take a glass of claret.

"Not that claret!" he said. "Excuse me! This is an occasion, and *on* an occasion I produce some very special claret I happen to have. (James, Captain Swosser's wine!) Mr. Jarndyce, this is a wine that was imported by the Captain, we will not say how many years ago. You will find it very curious. My dear, I shall be happy to take some of this wine with you. (Captain Swosser's claret to your mistress, James!) My love, your health!"

After dinner, when we ladies retired, we took Mrs. Badger's first and second husband with us. Mrs. Badger gave us, in the drawing-room, a Biographical sketch of the life and services of Captain Swosser before his marriage, and a more minute account of him dating from the time when he fell in love with her, at a ball on board the Crippler, given to the officers of that ship when she lay in Plymouth Harbour.

"The dear old Crippler!" said Mrs. Badger, shaking her head. "She was a noble vessel. Trim, ship-shape, all a taunto, as Captain Swosser used to say. You must excuse me if I occasionally introduce a nautical expression; I was quite a sailor once. Captain Swosser loved that craft for my sake. When she was no longer in commission, he frequently said that if he were rich enough to buy her old hulk, he would have an inscription let into the timbers of the quarter-deck where we stood as partners in the dance, to mark the spot where he fell—raked fore and aft (Captain Swosser used to say) by the fire from my tops. It was his naval way of mentioning my eyes."

The Family Portraits at Mr. Bayham Badger's

ADA'S GREAT SECRET

Mrs. Badger shook her head, sighed, and looked in the glass.

"It was a great change from Captain Swosser to Professor Dingo," she resumed, with a plaintive smile. "I felt it a good deal at first. Such an entire revolution in my mode of life! But custom, combined with science—particularly science —inured me to it. Being the Professor's sole companion in his botanical excursions, I almost forgot that I had ever been afloat, and became quite learned. It is singular that the Professor was the Antipodes of Captain Swosser, and that Mr. Badger is not in the least like either!"

We then passed into a narrative of the deaths of Captain Swosser and Professor Dingo, both of whom seem to have had very bad complaints. In the course of it, Mrs. Badger signified to us that she had never madly loved but once; and that the object of that wild affection, never to be recalled in its fresh enthusiasm, was Captain Swosser. The Professor was yet dying by inches in the most dismal manner, and Mrs. Badger was giving us imitations of his way of saying, with great difficulty, "Where is Laura? Let Laura give me my toast and water!" when the entrance of the gentlemen consigned him to the tomb.

Now, I observed that evening, as I had observed for some days past, that Ada and Richard were more than ever attached to each other's society; which was but natural, seeing that they were going to be separated so soon. I was therefore not very much surprised, when we got home, and Ada and I retired up-stairs, to find Ada more silent than usual; though I was not quite prepared for her coming into my arms, and beginning to speak to me, with her face hidden.

"My darling Esther!" murmured Ada. "I have a great secret to tell you!"

A mighty secret, my pretty one, no doubt!

"What is it, Ada?"

"O Esther, you would never guess!"

"Shall I try to guess?" said I.

213

"O no! Don't! Pray don't!" cried Ada, very much startled by the idea of my doing so.

"Now, I wonder who it can be about?" said I, pretending to consider.

"It's about," said Ada, in a whisper. "It's about—my cousin Richard!"

"Well, my own!" said I, kissing her bright hair, which was all I could see. "And what about him?"

"O Esther, you would never guess!"

It was so pretty to have her clinging to me in that way, hiding her face; and to know that she was not crying in sorrow, but in a little glow of joy, and pride, and hope; that I would not help her just yet.

"He says—I know it's very foolish, we are both so young —but he says," with a burst of tears, "that he loves me dearly, Esther."

"Does he indeed?" said I. "I never heard of such a thing! Why, my pet of pets, I could have told you that weeks and weeks ago!"

To see Ada lift up her flushed face in joyful surprise, and hold me round the neck, and laugh, and cry, and blush, and laugh, was so pleasant!

"Why, my darling!" said I, "what a goose you must take me for! Your cousin Richard has been loving you as plainly as he could, for I don't know how long!"

"And yet you never said a word about it!" cried Ada, kissing me.

"No, my love," said I. "I waited to be told."

"But now I have told you, you don't think it wrong of me; do you?" returned Ada. She might have coaxed me to say No, if I had been the hardest-hearted Duenna in the world. Not being that yet, I said No, very freely.

"And now," said I, "I know the worst of it."

"O, that's not quite the worst of it, Esther dear!" cried Ada, holding me tighter, and laying down her face again upon my breast.

"No?" said I. "Not even that?"

"No, not even that!" said Ada, shaking her head.

"Why, you never mean to say—!" I was beginning in joke.

But Ada, looking up, and smiling through her tears, cried, "Yes, I do! You know, you know I do!" and then sobbed out, "With all my heart I do! With all my whole heart, Esther!"

I told her, laughing, why I had known that, too, just as well as I had known the other! And we sat before the fire, and I had all the talking to myself for a little while (though there was not much of it); and Ada was soon quiet and happy.

"Do you think my cousin John knows, dear Dame Durden?" she asked.

"Unless my cousin John is blind, my pet," said I, "I should think my cousin John knows pretty well as much as we know."

"We want to speak to him before Richard goes," said Ada, timidly, "and we wanted you to advise us, and to tell him so. Perhaps you wouldn't mind Richard's coming in, Dame Durden?"

"O! Richard is outside, is he, my dear?" said I.

"I am not quite certain," returned Ada, with a bashful simplicity that would have won my heart, if she had not won it long before; "but I think he's waiting at the door."

There he was, of course. They brought a chair on either side of me, and put me between them, and really seemed to have fallen in love with me, instead of one another; they were so confiding, and so trustful, and so fond of me. They went on in their own wild way for a little while—*I* never stopped them; I enjoyed it too much myself—and then we gradually fell to considering how young they were, and how there must be a lapse of several years before this early love could come to anything, and how it could come to happiness only if it were real and lasting, and inspired them with a steady resolution to do their duty to each other, with constancy, fortitude, and perseverance : each always for the other's sake. Well! Richard said that he would work his fingers to the bone for Ada, and Ada said that she would work her fingers to the bone for Richard, and they called me all sorts of endearing and sensible names, and we sat there, advising and talking, half the night. Finally, before we parted, I gave them my promise to speak to their cousin John to-morrow.

So, when to-morrow came, I went to my Guardian after breakfast, in the room that was our town-substitute for the Growlery, and told him that I had it in trust to tell him something.

"Well, little woman," said he, shutting up his book, "if you have accepted the trust, there can be no harm in it."

"I hope not, Guardian," said I. "I can guarantee that there is no secrecy in it. For it only happened yesterday."

"Aye? And what is it, Esther?"

"Guardian," said I, "you remember the happy night when first we came down to Bleak House? When Ada was singing in the dark room?"

I wished to call to his remembrance the look he had given me then. Unless I am much mistaken, I saw that I did so.

"Because," said I, with a little hesitation.

"Yes, my dear!" said he. "Don't hurry."

"Because," said I, "Ada and Richard have fallen in love. And have told each other so."

"Already!" cried my Guardian, quite astonished.

"Yes!" said I, "and to tell you the truth, Guardian, I rather expected it."

"The deuce you did!" said he.

He sat considering for a minute or two; with his smile, at once so handsome and so kind, upon his changing face; and then requested me to let them know that he wished to see them. When they came, he encircled Ada with one arm, in his fatherly way, and addressed himself to Richard with a cheerful gravity.

216

"Rick," said Mr. Jarndyce, "I am glad to have won your confidence. I hope to preserve it. When I contemplated these relations between us four which have so brightened my life, and so invested it with new interests and pleasures, I certainly did contemplate, afar off, the possibility of you and your pretty cousin here (don't be shy, Ada, don't be shy, my dear!) being in a mind to go through life together. I saw, and do see, many reasons to make it desirable. But that was afar off, Rick, afar off!"

"We look afar off, sir," returned Richard.

"Well!" said Mr. Jarndyce. "That's rational. Now, hear me, my dears! I might tell you that you don't know your own minds yet; that a thousand things may happen to divert you from one another; that it is well this chain of flowers you have taken up is very easily broken, or it might become a chain of lead. But I will not do that. Such wisdom will come soon enough, I dare say, if it is to come at all. I will assume that, a few years hence, you will be in your hearts to one another, what you are to-day. All I say before speaking to you according to that assumption is, if you *do* change —if you *do* come to find that you are more commonplace cousins to each other as man and woman, than you were as boy and girl (your manhood will excuse me, Rick!)—don't be ashamed still to confide in me, for there will be nothing monstrous or uncommon in it. I am only your friend and distant kinsman. I have no power over you whatever. But I wish and hope to retain your confidence, if I do nothing to forfeit it."

"I am very sure, sir," returned Richard, "that I speak for Ada, too, when I say that you have the strongest power over us both—rooted in respect, gratitude, and affection— strengthening every day."

"Dear cousin John," said Ada, on his shoulder, "my father's place can never be empty again. All the love and duty I could ever have rendered to him, is transferred to you."

"Come!" said Mr. Jarndyce. "Now for our assumption,

Now we lift our eyes up, and look hopefully at the distance! Rick, the world is before you; and it is most probable that as you enter it, so it will receive you. Trust in nothing but in Providence and your own efforts. Never separate the two, like the heathen waggoner. Constancy in love is a good thing; but it means nothing, and is nothing, without constancy in every kind of effort. If you had the abilities of all the great men, past and present, you could do nothing well, without sincerely meaning it, and setting about it. If you entertain the supposition that any real success, in great things or in small, ever was or could be, ever will or can be, wrested from Fortune by fits and starts, leave that wrong idea here, or leave your cousin Ada here."

"I will leave *it* here, sir," replied Richard, smiling, "if I brought it here just now (but I hope I did not), and will work my way on to my cousin Ada in the hopeful distance."

"Right!" said Mr. Jarndyce. "If you are not to make her happy, why should you pursue her?"

"I wouldn't make her unhappy—no, not even for her love," retorted Richard, proudly.

"Well said!" cried Mr. Jarndyce; "that's well said! She remains here, in her home with me. Love her, Rick, in your active life, no less than in her home when you revisit it, and all will go well. Otherwise, all will go ill. That's the end of my preaching. I think you and Ada had better take a walk."

Ada tenderly embraced him, and Richard heartily shook hands with him, and then the cousins went out of the room —looking back again directly, though, to say that they would wait for me.

The door stood open, and we both followed them with our eyes, as they passed down the adjoining room on which the sun was shining, and out at its farther end. Richard with his head bent, and her hand drawn through his arm, was talking to her very earnestly; and she looked up in his face, listening, and seemed to see nothing else. So young, so beautiful, so full of hope and promise, they went on lightly through the sunlight, as their own happy thoughts might then be traversing the years to come, and making them all years of brightness. So they passed away into the shadow, and were gone. It was only a burst of light that had been so radiant. The room darkened as they went out, and the sun was clouded over.

"Am I right, Esther?" said my Guardian, when they were gone.

He who was so good and wise, to ask *me* whether he was right!

"Rick may gain, out of this, the quality he wants. Wants, at the core of so much that is good!" said Mr. Jarndyce, shaking his head. "I have said nothing to Ada, Esther. She has her friend and counsellor always near." And he laid his hand lovingly upon my head.

I could not help showing that I was a little moved, though I did all I could to conceal it.

"Tut, tut!" said he. "But we must take care, too, that our little woman's life is not all consumed in care for others."

"Care? My dear Guardian, I believe I am the happiest creature in the world!"

"I believe so, too," said he. "But some one may find out, what Esther never will,—that the little woman is to be held in remembrance above all other people!"

I have omitted to mention in its place, that there was some one else at the family dinner party. It was not a lady. It was a gentleman. It was a gentleman of a dark complexion —a young surgeon. He was rather reserved, but I thought him very sensible and agreeable. At least, Ada asked me if I did not, and I said yes.

CHAPTER XIV

DEPORTMENT

RICHARD left us on the very next evening, to begin his new career, and committed Ada to my charge with great love for her, and great trust in me. It touched me then to reflect, and it touches me now, more nearly, to remember (having what I have to tell) how they both thought of me, even at that engrossing time. I was a part of all their plans, for the present and the future. I was to write to Richard once a week, making my faithful report of Ada, who was to write to him every alternate day. I was to be informed, under his own hand, of all his labours and successes; I was to observe how resolute and persevering he would be; I was to be Ada's bridesmaid when they were married; I was to live with them afterwards; I was to keep all the keys of their house; I was to be made happy for ever and a day.

"And if the suit *should* make us rich, Esther—which it may, you know!" said Richard, to crown all.

A shade crossed Ada's face.

"My dearest Ada," asked Richard, "why not?"

"It had better declare us poor at once," said Ada.

"O! I don't know about that," returned Richard; "but, at all events, it won't declare anything at once. It hasn't declared anything in Heaven knows how many years."

"Too true," said Ada.

"Yes, but," urged Richard, answering what her look

suggested rather than her words, "the longer it goes on, dear cousin, the nearer it must be to a settlement one way or other. Now, is not that reasonable?"

"You know best, Richard. But I am afraid if we trust to it, it will make us unhappy."

"But, my Ada, we are not going to trust to it!" cried Richard. "We know it better than to trust to it. We only say that if it *should* make us rich, we have no constitutional objection to being rich. The Court is, by solemn settlement of law, our grim old guardian, and we are to suppose that what it gives us (when it gives us anything) is our right. It is not necessary to quarrel with our right."

"No," said Ada, "but it may be better to forget all about it."

"Well, well!" cried Richard, "then we will forget all about it! We consign the whole thing to oblivion. Dame Durden puts on her approving face, and it's done!"

"Dame Durden's approving face," said I, looking out of the box in which I was packing his books, "was not very visible when you called it by that name; but it does approve, and she thinks you can't do better."

So, Richard said there was an end of it,—and immediately began, on no other foundation, to build as many castles in the air as would man the great wall of China. He went away in high spirits. Ada and I, prepared to miss him very much, commenced our quieter career.

On our arrival in London, we had called with Mr. Jarndyce at Mrs. Jellyby's, but had not been so fortunate as to find her at home. It appeared that she had gone somewhere, to a tea-drinking, and had taken Miss Jellyby with her. Besides the tea-drinking, there was to be some considerable speech-making and letter-writing on the general merits of the cultivation of coffee, conjointly with natives, at the Settlement of Borrioboola-Gha. All this involved, no doubt, sufficient active exercise of pen and ink, to make her daughter's part in the proceedings anything but a holiday.

It being, now, beyond the time appointed for Mrs. Jellyby's return, we called again. She was in town, but not at home, having gone to Mile End, directly after breakfast, on some Borrioboolan business, arising out of a Society called the East London Branch Aid Ramification. As I had not seen Peepy on the occasion of our last call (when he was not to be found anywhere; and when the cook rather thought he must have strolled away with the dustman's cart), I now inquired for him again. The oyster-shells he had been building a house with, were still in the passage, but he was nowhere discoverable, and the cook supposed that he had "gone after the sheep." When we repeated, with some surprise, "The sheep?" she said, O yes, on market days he sometimes followed them quite out of town, and came back in such a state as never was!

I was sitting at the window with my guardian, on the following morning, and Ada was busy writing—of course to Richard—when Miss Jellyby was announced, and entered, leading the identical Peepy, whom she had made some endeavours to render presentable, by wiping the dirt into corners of his face and hands, and making his hair very wet and then violently frizzling it with her fingers. Everything the dear child wore, was either too large for him or too small. Among his other contradictory decorations he had the hat of a Bishop, and the little gloves of a baby. His boots were, on a small scale, the boots of a ploughman : while his legs, so crossed and recrossed with scratches that they looked like maps, were bare, below a very short pair of plaid drawers finished off with two frills of perfectly different patterns. The deficient buttons on his plaid frock had evidently been supplied from one of Mr. Jellyby's coats, they were so extremely brazen and so much too large. Most extraordinary specimens of needlework appeared on several parts of his dress, where it had been hastily mended ; and I recognised the same hand on Miss Jellyby's. She was, however, unaccountably improved in her appearance, and looked very pretty. She was conscious of poor little Peepy being but a failure after all her trouble, and she showed it as she came in, by the way in which she glanced, first at him and then at us.

"O dear me!" said my guardian. "Due East!"

Ada and I gave her a cordial welcome, and presented her to Mr. Jarndyce; to whom she said, as she sat down:

"Ma's compliments, and she hopes you'll excuse her, because she's correcting proofs of the plan. She's going to put out five thousand new circulars, and she knows you'll be interested to hear that. I have brought one of them with me. Ma's compliments." With which she presented it sulkily enough.

"Thank you," said my guardian. "I am much obliged to Mrs. Jellyby. O dear me! This is a very trying wind!"

We were busy with Peepy; taking off his clerical hat; asking him if he remembered us; and so on. Peepy retired behind his elbow at first, but relented at the sight of sponge-cake, and allowed me to take him on my lap, where he sat munching quietly. Mr. Jarndyce then withdrawing into the temporary Growlery, Miss Jellyby opened a conversation with her usual abruptness.

"We are going on just as bad as ever in Thavies Inn," said she. "I have no peace of my life. Talk of Africa! I couldn't be worse off if I was a what's-his-name—man and a brother!"

I tried to say something soothing.

"O, it's of no use, Miss Summerson," exclaimed Miss Jellyby, "though I thank you for the kind intention all the same. I know how I am used, and I am not to be talked over. *You* wouldn't be talked over, if you were used so. Peepy, go and play at Wild Beasts under the piano!"

"I sha'n't!" said Peepy.

"Very well, you ungrateful, naughty, hard-hearted boy!" returned Miss Jellyby, with tears in her eyes. "I'll never take pains to dress you any more."

"Yes, I will go, Caddy!" cried Peepy, who was really a

good child, and who was so moved by his sister's vexation that he went at once.

"It seems a little thing to cry about," said poor Miss Jellyby, apologetically, "but I am quite worn out. I was directing the new circulars till two this morning. I detest the whole thing so, that that alone makes my head ache till I can't see out of my eyes. And look at that poor unfortunate child! Was there ever such a fright as he is!"

Peepy, happily unconscious of the defects in his appearance, sat on the carpet behind one of the legs of the piano, looking calmly out of his den at us, while he ate his cake.

"I have sent him to the other end of the room," observed Miss Jellyby, drawing her chair nearer ours, "because I don't want him to hear the conversation. Those little things are so sharp! I was going to say, we really are going on worse than ever. Pa will be a bankrupt before long, and then I hope Ma will be satisfied. There'll be nobody but Ma to thank for it."

We said we hoped Mr. Jellyby's affairs were not in so bad a state as that.

"It's of no use hoping, though it's very kind of you," returned Miss Jellyby, shaking her head. "Pa told me, only yesterday morning (and dreadfully unhappy he is), that he couldn't weather the storm. I should be surprised if he could. When all our tradesmen send into our house any stuff they like, and the servants do what they like with it, and I have no time to improve things if I knew how, and Ma don't care about anything, I should like to make out how Pa *is* to weather the storm. I declare if I was Pa, I'd run away."

"My dear!" said I, smiling. "Your papa, no doubt, considers his family."

"O yes, his family is all very fine, Miss Summerson," replied Miss Jellyby; "but what comfort is his family to him? His family is nothing but bills, dirt, waste, noise, tumbles down-stairs, confusion, and wretchedness. His scrambling home, from week's-end to week's-end, is like one great washing-day—only nothing's washed!"

Miss Jellyby tapped her foot upon the floor, and wiped her eyes.

"I am sure I pity Pa to that degree," she said, "and am so angry with Ma, that I can't find words to express myself! However, I am not going to bear it, I am determined. I won't be a slave all my life, and I won't submit to be proposed to by Mr. Quale. A pretty thing, indeed, to marry a Philanthropist. As if I hadn't had enough of *that!*" said poor Miss Jellyby.

I must confess that I could not help feeling rather angry with Mrs. Jellyby, myself; seeing and hearing this neglected girl, and knowing how much of bitterly satirical truth there was in what she said.

"If it wasn't that we had been intimate when you stopped at our house," pursued Miss Jellyby, "I should have been ashamed to come here to-day, for I know what a figure I must seem to you two. But, as it is, I made up my mind to call: especially as I am not likely to see you again, the next time you come to town."

She said this with such great significance that Ada and I glanced at one another, foreseeing something more.

"No!" said Miss Jellyby, shaking her head. "Not at all likely! I know I may trust you two. I am sure you won't betray me. I am engaged."

"Without their knowledge at home?" said I.

"Why, good gracious me, Miss Summerson," she returned, justifying herself in a fretful but not angry manner, "how can it be otherwise? You know what Ma is—and I needn't make poor Pa more miserable by telling *him*."

"But would it not be adding to his unhappiness, to marry without his knowledge or consent, my dear?" said I.

"No," said Miss Jellyby, softening. "I hope not. I should try to make him happy and comfortable when he came to see me; and Peepy and the others should take it in turns to come and stay with me; and they should have some care taken of them, then."

There was a good deal of affection in poor Caddy. She softened more and more while saying this, and cried so much over the unwonted little home-picture she had raised in her mind, that Peepy, in his cave under the piano, was touched, and turned himself over on his back with loud lamentations. It was not until I had brought him to kiss his sister, and had restored him to his place on my lap, and had shown him that Caddy was laughing (she laughed expressly for the purpose), that we could recall his peace of mind; even then, it was for some time conditional on his taking us in turns by the chin, and smoothing our faces all over with his hand. At last, as his spirits were not equal to the piano, we put him on a chair to look out of window; and Miss Jellyby, holding him by one leg, resumed her confidence.

" It began in your coming to our house," she said.

We naturally asked how?

" I felt I was so awkward," she replied, " that I made up my mind to be improved in that respect, at all events, and to learn to dance. I told Ma I was ashamed of myself, and I must be taught to dance. Ma looked at me in that provoking way of hers as if I wasn't in sight; but, I was quite determined to be taught to dance, and so I went to Mr. Turveydrop's Academy in Newman Street."

" And was it there, my dear——" I began.

" Yes, it was there," said Caddy, " and I am engaged to Mr. Turveydrop. There are two Mr. Turveydrops, father and son. My Mr. Turveydrop is the son, of course. I only wish I had been better brought up, and was likely to make him a better wife; for I am very fond of him."

" I am sorry to hear this," said I, " I must confess."

" I don't know why you should be sorry," she retorted a little anxiously, " but I am engaged to Mr. Turveydrop, whether or no, and he is very fond of me. It's a secret as yet, even on his side, because old Mr. Turveydrop has a share in the connexion, and it might break his heart, or give him some other shock, if he was told of it abruptly. Old Mr. Turveydrop is a very gentlemanly man indeed—very gentlemanly."

"Does his wife know of it?" asked Ada.

"Old Mr. Turveydrop's wife, Miss Clare?" returned Miss Jellyby, opening her eyes. "There's no such person. He is a widower."

We were here interrupted by Peepy, whose leg had undergone so much on account of his sister's unconsciously jerking it like a bell-rope whenever she was emphatic, that the afflicted child now bemoaned his sufferings with a very low-spirited noise. As he appealed to me for compassion, and as I was only a listener, I undertook to hold him. Miss Jellyby proceeded, after begging Peepy's pardon with a kiss, and assuring him that she hadn't meant to do it.

"That's the state of the case," said Caddy. "If I ever blame myself, I still think it's Ma's fault. We are to be married whenever we can, and then I shall go to Pa at the office and write to Ma. It won't much agitate Ma; I am only pen and ink to *her*. One great comfort is," said Caddy, with a sob, "that I shall never hear of Africa after I am married. Young Mr. Turveydrop hates it for my sake; and if old Mr. Turveydrop knows there is such a place, it's as much as he does."

"It was he who was very gentlemanly, I think!" said I.

"Very gentlemanly, indeed," said Caddy. "He is celebrated, almost everywhere, for his Deportment."

"Does he teach?" asked Ada.

"No, he don't teach anything in particular," replied Caddy. "But his Deportment is beautiful."

Caddy went on to say, with considerable hesitation and reluctance, that there was one thing more she wished us to know, and felt we ought to know, and which she hoped would not offend us. It was, that she had improved her acquaintance with Miss Flite, the little crazy old lady; and that she frequently went there early in the morning, and met her lover for a few minutes before breakfast—only for a few minutes. "*I* go there, at other times," said Caddy, "but Prince does not come then. Young Mr. Turveydrop's name is Prince; I wish it wasn't, because it sounds like a dog, but of course he didn't christen himself. Old Mr. Turveydrop had him christened Prince, in remembrance of the Prince Regent. Old Mr. Turveydrop adored the Prince Regent on account of his Deportment. I hope you won't think the worse of me for having made these little appointments at Miss Flite's, where I first went with you; because I like the poor thing for her own sake, and I believe she likes me. If you could see young Mr. Turveydrop, I am sure you would think well of him—at least, I am sure you couldn't possibly think any ill of him. I am going there now, for my lesson. I couldn't ask you to go with me, Miss Summerson; but if you would," said Caddy, who had said all this, earnestly and tremblingly, "I should be very glad—very glad."

It happened that we had arranged with my guardian to go to Miss Flite's that day. We had told him of our former visit, and our account had interested him; but something had always happened to prevent our going there again. As I trusted that I might have sufficient influence with Miss Jellyby to prevent her taking any very rash step, if I fully accepted the confidence she was so willing to place in me, poor girl, I proposed that she and I and Peepy should go to the Academy, and afterwards meet my guardian and Ada at Miss Flite's—whose name I now learnt for the first time. This was on condition that Miss Jellyby and Peepy should come back with us to dinner. The last article of the agreement being joyfully acceded to by both, we smartened Peepy up a little, with the assistance of a few pins, some soap and water, and a hair-brush; and went out: bending our steps towards Newman Street, which was very near.

I found the Academy established in a sufficiently dingy house at the corner of an archway, with busts in all the staircase windows. In the same house there were also established, as I gathered from the plates on the door, a drawing-master, a coal-merchant (there was, certainly, no room for his coals), and a lithographic artist. On the plate which, in size and situation, took precedence of all the rest, I read, Mr. TURVEYDROP. The door was open, and the hall was blocked up by a grand piano, a harp, and several other musical instruments in cases, all in progress of removal, and all looking rakish in the daylight. Miss Jellyby informed me that the Academy had been lent, last night, for a concert.

We went up-stairs—it had been quite a fine house once, when it was anybody's business to keep it clean and fresh, and nobody's business to smoke in it all day—and into Mr. Turveydrop's great room, which was built out into a mews at the back, and was lighted by a skylight. It was a bare, resounding room, smelling of stables; with cane forms along the walls; and the walls ornamented at regular intervals with painted lyres, and little cut-glass branches for candles, which seemed to be shedding their old-fashioned drops as other branches might shed autumn leaves. Several young lady pupils, ranging from thirteen or fourteen years of age to two or three and twenty, were assembled; and I was looking among them for their instructor, when Caddy, pinching my arm, repeated the ceremony of introduction. "Miss Summerson, Mr. Prince Turveydrop!"

I curtseyed to a little blue-eyed fair man of youthful appearance, with flaxen hair parted in the middle, and curling at the ends all round his head. He had a little fiddle, which we used to call at school a kit, under his left arm, and its little bow in the same hand. His little dancing-shoes were particularly diminutive, and he had a little innocent, feminine manner, which not only appealed to me in an amiable way, but made this singular effect upon me : that I received the impression that he was like his mother, and that his mother had not been much considered or well used.

"I am very happy to see Miss Jellyby's friend," he said,

bowing low to me. " I began to fear," with timid tenderness, "as it was past the usual time, that Miss Jellyby was not coming."

"I beg you will have the goodness to attribute that to me, who have detained her, and to receive my excuses, sir," said I.

"O dear!" said he.

" And pray," I entreated, " do not allow me to be the cause of any more delay."

With that apology I withdrew to a seat between Peepy (who, being well used to it, had already climbed into a corner place) and an old lady of a censorious countenance, whose two nieces were in the class, and who was very indignant with Peepy's boots. Prince Turveydrop then tinkled the strings of his kit with his fingers, and the young ladies stood up to dance. Just then, there appeared from a side door, old Mr. Turveydrop, in the full lustre of his Deportment.

He was a fat old gentleman with a false complexion, false teeth, false whiskers, and a wig. He had a fur collar, and he had a padded breast to his coat, which only wanted a star or a broad blue ribbon to be complete. He was pinched in, and swelled out, and got up, and strapped down, as much as he could possibly bear. He had such a neckcloth on (puffing his very eyes out of their natural shape), and his chin and even his ears so sunk into it, that it seemed as though he must inevitably double up, if it were cast loose. He had, under his arm, a hat of great size and weight, shelving downward from the crown to the brim; and in his hand a pair of white gloves, with which he flapped it, as he stood poised on one leg, in a high-shouldered, round-elbowed state of elegance not to be surpassed. He had a cane, he had an eye-glass, he had a snuff-box, he had rings, he had wristbands, he had everything but any touch of nature; he was not like youth, he was not like age, he was not like anything in the world but a model of Deportment.

"Father! A visitor. Miss Jellyby's friend, Miss Summerson."

The Dancing School

A MODEL OF DEPORTMENT

"Distinguished," said Mr. Turveydrop, "by Miss Summerson's presence." As he bowed to me in that tight state, I almost believe I saw creases come into the whites of his eyes.

"My father," said the son, aside, to me, with quite an affecting belief in him, "is a celebrated character. My father is greatly admired."

"Go on, Prince! Go on!" said Mr. Turveydrop, standing with his back to the fire, and waving his gloves condescendingly. "Go on, my son!"

At this command, or by this gracious permission, the lesson went on. Prince Turveydrop sometimes played the kit, dancing; sometimes played the piano, standing; sometimes hummed the tune with what little breath he could spare, while he set a pupil right; always conscientiously moved with the least proficient through every step and every part of the figure; and never rested for an instant. His distinguished father did nothing whatever, but stand before the fire, a model of Deportment.

"And he never does anything else," said the old lady of the censorious countenance. "Yet would you believe that it's *his* name on the door-plate?"

"His son's name is the same, you know," said I.

"He wouldn't let his son have any name, if he could take it from him," returned the old lady. "Look at the son's dress!" It certainly was plain—threadbare—almost shabby. "Yet the father must be garnished and tricked out," said the old lady, "because of his Deportment. I'd deport him! Transport him would be better!"

I felt curious to know more, concerning this person. I asked, "Does he give lessons in Deportment, now?"

"Now!" returned the old lady, shortly. "Never did."

After a moment's consideration, I suggested that perhaps fencing had been his accomplishment?

"I don't believe he can fence at all, ma'am," said the old lady.

I looked surprised and inquisitive. The old lady, becoming

more and more incensed against the Master of Deportment as she dwelt upon the subject, gave me some particulars of his career, with strong assurances that they were mildly stated.

He had married a meek little dancing-mistress, with a tolerable connexion (having never in his life before done anything but deport himself), and had worked her to death, or had, at the best, suffered her to work herself to death, to maintain him in those expenses which were indispensable to his position. At once to exhibit his Deportment to the best models, and to keep the best models constantly before himself, he had found it necessary to frequent all public places of fashionable and lounging resort; to be seen at Brighton and elsewhere at fashionable times; and to lead an idle life in the very best clothes. To enable him to do this, the affectionate little dancing-mistress had toiled and laboured, and would have toiled and laboured to that hour, if her strength had lasted so long. For, the mainspring of the story was, that, in spite of the man's absorbing selfishness, his wife (over-powered by his Deportment) had, to the last, believed in him, and had, on her death-bed, in the most moving terms, confided him to their son as one who had an inextinguishable claim upon him, and whom he could never regard with too much pride and deference. The son, inheriting his mother's belief, and having the Deportment always before him, had lived and grown in the same faith, and now, at thirty years of age, worked for his father twelve hours a-day, and looked up to him with veneration on the old imaginary pinnacle.

"The airs the fellow gives himself!" said my informant, shaking her head at old Mr. Turveydrop with speechless indignation as he drew on his tight gloves: of course unconscious of the homage she was rendering. "He fully believes he is one of the aristocracy! And he is so condescending to the son he so egregiously deludes, that you might suppose him the most virtuous of parents. O!" said the old lady, apostrophising him with infinite vehemence, "I could bite you!"

I could not help being amused, though I heard the old

lady out with feelings of real concern. It was difficult to doubt her, with the father and son before me. What I might have thought of them without the old lady's account, or what I might have thought of the old lady's account without them, I cannot say. There was a fitness of things in the whole that carried conviction with it.

My eyes were yet wandering, from young Mr. Turveydrop working so hard, to old Mr. Turveydrop deporting himself so beautifully, when the latter came ambling up to me, and entered into conversation.

He asked me, first of all, whether I conferred a charm and a distinction on London by residing in it? I did not think it necessary to reply that I was perfectly aware I should not do that, in any case, but merely told him where I did reside.

"A lady so graceful and accomplished," he said, kissing his right glove, and afterwards extending it towards the pupils, "will look leniently on the deficiencies here. We do our best to polish—polish—polish!"

He sat down beside me; taking some pains to sit on the form, I thought, in imitation of the print of his illustrious model on the sofa. And really he did look very like it.

"To polish—polish—polish!" he repeated, taking a pinch of snuff and gently fluttering his fingers. "But we are not—if I may say so, to one formed to be graceful both by Nature and Art;" with the high-shouldered bow, which it seemed impossible for him to make without lifting up his eyebrows and shutting his eyes—"we are not what we used to be in point of Deportment."

"Are we not, sir?" said I.

"We have degenerated," he returned, shaking his head, which he could do, to a very limited extent, in his cravat. "A levelling age is not favourable to Deportment. It develops vulgarity. Perhaps I speak with some little partiality. It may not be for me to say that I have been called, for some years now, Gentleman Turveydrop; or that His Royal

Highness the Prince Regent did me the honour to inquire, on my removing my hat as he drove out of the Pavilion at Brighton (that fine building), 'Who is he? Who the Devil is he? Why don't I know him? Why hasn't he thirty thousand a-year?' But these are little matters of anecdote —the general property, ma'am,—still repeated, occasionally, among the upper classes."

" Indeed ? " said I.

He replied with the high-shouldered bow. " Where what is left among us of Deportment," he added, " still lingers. England—alas, my country !—has degenerated very much, and is degenerating every day. She has not many gentlemen left. We are few. I see nothing to succeed us, but a race of weavers."

" One might hope that the race of gentlemen would be perpetuated here," said I.

" You are very good," he smiled, with the high-shouldered bow again. " You flatter me. But, no—no ! I have never been able to imbue my poor boy with that part of his art. Heaven forbid that I should disparage my dear child, but he has—no Deportment."

" He appears to be an excellent master," I observed.

" Understand me, my dear madam, he *is* an excellent master. All that can be acquired, he has acquired. All that can be imparted, he can impart. But there *are* things "—he took another pinch of snuff and made the bow again, as if to add, " this kind of thing, for instance."

I glanced towards the centre of the room, where Miss Jellyby's lover, now engaged with single pupils, was undergoing greater drudgery than ever.

" My amiable child," murmured Mr. Turveydrop, adjusting his cravat.

" Your son is indefatigable," said I.

" It is my reward," said Mr. Turveydrop, " to hear you say so. In some respects, he treads in the footsteps of his sainted mother. She was a devoted creature. But Wooman, lovely

Wooman," said Mr. Turveydrop, with very disagreeable gallantry, "what a sex you are!"

I rose and joined Miss Jellyby, who was, by this time, putting on her bonnet. The time allotted to a lesson having fully elapsed, there was a general putting on of bonnets. When Miss Jellyby and the unfortunate Prince found an opportunity to become betrothed I don't know, but they certainly found none, on this occasion, to exchange a dozen words.

"My dear," said Mr. Turveydrop benignly to his son, "do you know the hour?"

"No, father." The son had no watch. The father had a handsome gold one, which he pulled out, with an air that was an example to mankind.

"My son," said he, "it's two o'clock. Recollect your school at Kensington at three."

"That's time enough for me, father," said Prince. "I can take a morsel of dinner, standing, and be off."

"My dear boy," returned his father, "you must be very quick. You will find the cold mutton on the table."

"Thank you, father. Are *you* off now, father?"

"Yes, my dear. I suppose," said Mr. Turveydrop, shutting his eyes and lifting up his shoulders, with modest consciousness, "that I must show myself, as usual, about town."

"You had better dine out comfortably, somewhere," said his son.

"My dear child, I intend to. I shall take my little meal, I think, at the French house, in the Opera Colonnade."

"That's right. Good-bye, father!" said Prince, shaking hands.

"Good-bye, my son. Bless you!"

Mr. Turveydrop said this in quite a pious manner, and it seemed to do his son good; who, in parting from him, was so pleased with him, so dutiful to him, and so proud of him, that I almost felt as if it were an unkindness to the younger man not to be able to believe implicitly in the elder. The few moments that were occupied by Prince in taking leave of us (and particularly of one of us, as I saw, being in the secret), enhanced my favourable impression of his almost childish character. I felt a liking for him, and a compassion for him, as he put his little kit in his pocket—and with it his desire to stay a little while with Caddy—and went away good-humouredly to his cold mutton and his school at Kensington, that made me scarcely less irate with his father than the censorious old lady.

The father opened the room-door for us, and bowed us out, in a manner, I must acknowledge, worthy of his shining original. In the same style he presently passed us on the other side of the street, on his way to the aristocratic part of the town, where he was going to show himself among the few other gentlemen left. For some moments, I was so lost in reconsidering what I had heard and seen in Newman Street, that I was quite unable to talk to Caddy, or even to fix my attention on what she said to me : especially when I began to inquire in my mind whether there were, or ever had been, any other gentlemen, not in the dancing profession, who lived and founded a reputation entirely on their Deportment. This became so bewildering, and suggested the possibility, of so many Mr. Turveydrops, that I said, "Esther, you must make up your mind to abandon this subject altogether, and attend to Caddy." I accordingly did so, and we chatted all the rest of the way to Lincoln's Inn.

Caddy told me that her lover's education had been so neglected, that it was not always easy to read his notes. She said, if he were not so anxious about his spelling, and took less pains to make it clear, he would do better; but he put so many unnecessary letters into short words, that they sometimes quite lost their English appearance. "He does it with the best intention," observed Caddy, "but it hasn't the effect he means, poor fellow!" Caddy then went on to reason, how could he be expected to be a scholar, when he had passed his whole life in the dancing-school, and had done nothing but teach and fag, fag and teach, morning, noon, and night!

And what did it matter? She could write letters enough for both, as she knew to her cost, and it was far better for him to be amiable than learned. "Besides, it's not as if I was an accomplished girl, who had any right to give herself airs," said Caddy. "I know little enough, I am sure, thanks to Ma!"

"There's another thing I want to tell you, now we are alone," continued Caddy, "which I should not have liked to mention unless you had seen Prince, Miss Summerson. You know what a house ours is. It's of no use my trying to learn anything that it would be useful for Prince's wife to know, in *our* house. We live in such a state of muddle that it's impossible, and I have only been more disheartened whenever I have tried. So, I get a little practice with—who do you think? Poor Miss Flite! Early in the morning, I help her to tidy her room, and clean her birds; and I make her cup of coffee for her (of course she taught me), and I have learnt to make it so well that Prince says it's the very best coffee he ever tasted, and would quite delight old Mr. Turveydrop, who is very particular indeed about his coffee. I can make little puddings too; and I know how to buy neck of mutton, and tea, and sugar, and butter, and a good many house-keeping things. I am not clever at my needle, yet," said Caddy, glancing at the repairs on Peepy's frock, "but perhaps I shall improve, and since I have been engaged to Prince, and have been doing all this, I have felt better-tempered, I hope, and more forgiving to Ma. It rather put me out, at first this morning, to see you and Miss Clare looking so neat and pretty, and to feel ashamed of Peepy and myself too; but, on the whole, I hope I am better-tempered than I was, and more forgiving to Ma."

The poor girl, trying so hard, said it from her heart, and touched mine. "Caddy, my love," I replied, "I begin to have a great affection for you, and I hope we shall become friends." "Oh, do you?" cried Caddy; "how happy that would make me!" "My dear Caddy," said I, "let us be friends from this time, and let us often have a chat about these matters, and try to find the right way through them." Caddy was overjoyed. I said everything I could, in my old-fashioned way, to comfort and encourage her; and I would not have objected to old Mr. Turveydrop, that day, for any smaller consideration than a settlement on his daughter-in-law.

By this time, we were come to Mr. Krook's, whose private door stood open. There was a bill, pasted on the door-post, announcing a room to let on the second floor. It reminded Caddy to tell me as we proceeded up-stairs, that there had been a sudden death there, and an inquest; and that our little friend had been ill of the fright. The door and window of the vacant room being open, we looked in. It was the room with the dark door, to which Miss Flite had secretly directed my attention when I was last in the house. A sad and desolate place it was; a gloomy, sorrowful place, that gave me a strange sensation of mournfulness and even dread. "You look pale," said Caddy, when we came out, "and cold!" I felt as if the room had chilled me.

We had walked slowly, while we were talking; and my guardian and Ada were here before us. We found them in Miss Flite's garret. They were looking at the birds, while a medical gentleman who was so good as to attend Miss Flite with much solicitude and compassion, spoke with her cheerfully by the fire.

"I have finished my professional visit," he said, coming forward. "Miss Flite is much better, and may appear in Court (as her mind is set upon it) to-morrow. She has been greatly missed there, I understand."

Miss Flite received the compliment with complacency, and dropped a general curtsey to us.

"Honoured, indeed," said she, "by another visit from the wards in Jarndyce! Ve-ry happy to receive Jarndyce of Bleak House beneath my humble roof!" with a special curtsey. "Fitz-Jarndyce, my dear;" she had bestowed that name on Caddy, it appeared, and always called her by it; "a double welcome!"

"Has she been very ill?" asked Mr. Jarndyce of the gentleman whom we had found in attendance on her. She answered for herself directly, though he had put the question in a whisper.

"O decidedly unwell! O very unwell indeed," she said, confidentially. "Not pain, you know—trouble. Not bodily so much as nervous, nervous! The truth is," in a subdued voice and trembling, "we have had death here. There was poison in the house. I am very susceptible to such horrid things. It frightened me. Only Mr. Woodcourt knows how much. My physician, Mr. Woodcourt!" with great stateliness. "The wards in Jarndyce—Jarndyce of Bleak House—Fitz-Jarndyce!"

"Miss Flite," said Mr. Woodcourt, in a grave kind of voice, as if he were appealing to her while speaking to us; and laying his hand gently on her arm; "Miss Flite describes her illness with her usual accuracy. She was alarmed by an occurrence in the house which might have alarmed a stronger person, and was made ill by the distress and agitation. She brought me here, in the first hurry of the discovery, though too late for me to be of any use to the unfortunate man. I have compensated myself for that disappointment by coming here since, and being of some small use to her."

"The kindest physician in the college," whispered Miss Flite to me. "I expect a Judgment. On the day of Judgment. And shall then confer estates."

"She will be as well, in a day or two," said Mr. Woodcourt, looking at her with an observant smile, "as she ever will be. In other words, quite well of course. Have you heard of her good fortune?"

"Most extraordinary!" said Miss Flite, smiling brightly. "You never heard of such a thing, my dear! Every Saturday, Conversation Kenge, or Guppy (clerk to Conversation K.), places in my hand a paper of shillings. Shillings. I assure you! Always the same number in the paper. Always one for every day in the week. Now you know, really! So well-timed, is it not? Ye-es! From whence do these papers come, you say? That is the great question. Naturally. Shall I tell you what *I* think? *I* think," said Miss Flite, drawing herself back with a very shrewd look, and shaking her right forefinger in a most significant manner, "that the Lord Chancellor, aware of the length of time during which the Great Seal has been open, (for it has been open a long time!) forwards them. Until the Judgment I expect, is given. Now that's very creditable, you know. To confess in that way that he *is* a little slow for human life. So delicate! Attending Court the other day—I attend it regularly—with my documents—I taxed him with it, and he almost confessed. That is, I smiled at him from my bench, and *he* smiled at me from his bench. But it's great good fortune, is it not? And Fitz-Jarndyce lays the money out for me to great advantage. O, I assure you to the greatest advantage!"

I congratulated her (as she addressed herself to me) upon this fortunate addition to her income, and wished her a long continuance of it. I did not speculate upon the source from which it came, or wonder whose humanity was so considerate. My guardian stood before me, contemplating the birds, and I had no need to look beyond him.

"And what do you call these little fellows, ma'am?" said he in his pleasant voice. "Have they any names?"

"I can answer for Miss Flite that they have," said I, "for she promised to tell us what they were. Ada remembers?"

Ada remembered very well.

"Did I?" said Miss Flite—"Who's that at my door? What are you listening at my door for, Krook?"

The old man of the house, pushing it open before him, appeared there with his fur-cap in his hand, and his cat at his heels.

"I warn't listening, Miss Flite," he said. "I was going to give a rap with my knuckles, only you're so quick!"

"Make your cat go down. Drive her away!" the old lady angrily exclaimed.

"Bah, bah!—There ain't no danger, gentlefolks," said Mr. Krook, looking slowly and sharply from one to another, until he had looked at all of us; "she'd never offer at the birds when I was here, unless I told her to it."

"You will excuse my landlord," said the old lady with a dignified air. "M, quite M! What do you want, Krook, when I have company?"

"Hi!" said the old man. "You know I am the Chancellor."

"Well?" returned Miss Flite. "What of that?"

"For the Chancellor," said the old man, with a chuckle, "not to be acquainted with a Jarndyce is queer, ain't it, Miss Flite? Mightn't I take the liberty?—Your servant, sir. I know Jarndyce and Jarndyce a'most as well as you do, sir. I knowed old Squire Tom, sir. I never to my knowledge see you afore though, not even in Court. Yet, I go there a mortal sight of times in the course of the year, taking one day with another."

"I never go there," said Mr. Jarndyce (which he never did on any consideration). "I would sooner go—somewhere else."

"Would you though?" returned Krook, grinning. "You're bearing hard upon my noble and learned brother in your meaning, sir; though, perhaps, it is but nat'ral in a Jarndyce. The burnt child, sir! What, you're looking at my lodger's birds, Mr. Jarndyce?" The old man had come by little and little into the room, until he now touched my guardian with his elbow, and looked close up into his face with his spectacled eyes. "It's one of her strange ways, that she'll never tell the names of these birds if she can help it, though she named 'em all." This was in a whisper. "Shall I run 'em over, Flite?" he asked aloud, winking at us and pointing at her as she turned away, affecting to sweep the grate.

" If you like," she answered hurriedly.

The old man, looking up at the cages, after another look at us, went through the list.

" Hope, Joy, Youth, Peace, Rest, Life, Dust, Ashes, Waste, Want, Ruin, Despair, Madness, Death, Cunning, Folly, Words, Wigs, Rags, Sheepskin, Plunder, Precedent, Jargon, Gammon, and Spinach. That's the whole collection," said the old man, " all cooped up together, by my noble and learned brother."

" This is a bitter wind ! " muttered my guardian.

" When my noble and learned brother gives his Judgment, they're to be let go free," said Krook, winking at us again. " And then," he added, whispering and grinning, " if that ever was to happen—which it won't—the birds that have never been caged would kill 'em."

" If ever the wind was in the east," said my guardian, pretending to look out of the window for a weathercock, " I think it's there to-day ! "

We found it very difficult to get away from the house. It was not Miss Flite who detained us; she was as reasonable a little creature in consulting the convenience of others, as there possibly could be. It was Mr. Krook. He seemed unable to detach himself from Mr. Jarndyce. If he had been linked to him, he could hardly have attended him more closely. He proposed to show us his Court of Chancery, and all the strange medley it contained ; during the whole of our inspection (prolonged by himself) he kept close to Mr. Jarndyce, and sometimes detained him, under one pretence or other, until we had passed on, as if he were tormented by an inclination to enter upon some secret subject, which he could not make up his mind to approach. I cannot imagine a countenance and manner more singularly expressive of caution and indecision, and a perpetual impulse to do something he could not resolve to venture on, than Mr. Krook's was, that day. His watchfulness of my guardian was incessant. He rarely removed his eyes from his face. If he went on beside him, he observed him with the slyness of an old white fox. If he went before, he looked back. When we stood still, he got opposite to him, and drawing his hand across and across his open mouth with a curious expression of a sense of power, and turning up his eyes, and lowering his grey eyebrows until they appeared to be shut, seemed to scan every lineament of his face.

At last, having been (always attended by the cat) all over the house, and having seen the whole stock of miscellaneous lumber, which was certainly curious, we came into the back part of the shop. Here, on the head of an empty barrel stood on end, were an ink-bottle, some old stumps of pens, and some dirty playbills ; and, against the wall, were pasted several large printed alphabets in several plain hands.

" What are you doing here ? " asked my guardian.

" Trying to learn myself to read and write," said Krook.

" And how do you get on ? "

" Slow. Bad," returned the old man, impatiently. " It's hard at my time of life."

" It would be easier to be taught by some one," said my guardian.

" Aye, but they might teach me wrong ! " returned the old man, with a wonderfully suspicious flash of his eye. " I don't know what I may have lost, by not being learnd afore. I wouldn't like to lose anything by being learnd wrong now."

" Wrong ? " said my guardian, with his good-humoured smile. " Who do you suppose would teach you wrong ? "

" I don't know, Mr. Jarndyce of Bleak House ! " replied the old man, turning up his spectacles on his forehead, and rubbing his hands. " I don't suppose as anybody would—but I'd rather trust my own self than another ! "

These answers, and his manner, were strange enough to cause my guardian to inquire of Mr. Woodcourt, as we all walked across Lincoln's Inn together, whether Mr. Krook were really, as his lodger represented him, deranged ? The young surgeon replied, no, he had seen no reason to think so. He was exceedingly distrustful, as ignorance usually was, and he was always more or less under the influence of raw gin : of which he drank great quantities, and of which he and his back-shop, as we might have observed, smelt strongly ; but he did not think him mad, as yet.

On our way home, I so conciliated Peepy's affections by buying him a windmill and two flour-sacks, that he would suffer nobody else to take off his hat and gloves, and would sit nowhere at dinner but at my side. Caddy sat upon the other side of me, next to Ada, to whom we imparted the whole history of the engagement as soon as we got back. We made much of Caddy, and Peepy too ; and Caddy brightened exceedingly ; and my guardian was as merry as we were ; and we were all very happy indeed ; until Caddy went home at night in a hackney-coach, with Peepy fast asleep, but holding tight to the windmill.

I have forgotten to mention—at least I have not mentioned —that Mr. Woodcourt was the same dark young surgeon whom we had met at Mr. Badger's. Or, that Mr. Jarndyce invited him to dinner that day. Or, that he came. Or, that when they were all gone, and I said to Ada, "Now, my darling, let us have a little talk about Richard!" Ada laughed and said——

But, I don't think it matters what my darling said. She was always merry.

CHAPTER XV

WHILE we were in London, Mr. Jarndyce was constantly beset by the crowd of excitable ladies and gentlemen whose proceedings had so much astonished us. Mr. Quale, who presented himself soon after our arrival, was in all such excitements. He seemed to project those two shining knobs of temples of his into everything that went on, and to brush his hair farther and farther back, until the very roots were almost ready to fly out of his head in inappeasable philanthropy. All objects were alike to him, but he was always particularly ready for anything in the way of a testimonial to any one. His great power seemed to be his power of indiscriminate admiration. He would sit, for any length of time, with the utmost enjoyment, bathing his temples in the light of any order of luminary. Having first seen him perfectly swallowed up in admiration of Mrs. Jellyby, I had supposed her to be the absorbing object of his devotion. I soon discovered my mistake, and found him to be train-bearer and organ-blower to a whole procession of people.

Mrs. Pardiggle came one day for a subscription to something—and with her, Mr. Quale. Whatever Mrs. Pardiggle said, Mr. Quale repeated to us; and just as he had drawn Mrs. Jellyby out, he drew Mrs. Pardiggle out. Mrs. Pardiggle wrote a letter of introduction to my guardian, in behalf of her eloquent friend, Mr. Gusher. With Mr.

245

Gusher, appeared Mr. Quale again. Mr. Gusher, being a flabby gentleman with a moist surface, and eyes so much too small for his moon of a face that they seemed to have been originally made for somebody else, was not at first sight prepossessing; yet, he was scarcely seated, before Mr. Quale asked Ada and me, not inaudibly, whether he was not a great creature—which he certainly was, flabbily speaking; though Mr. Quale meant in intellectual beauty—and whether we were not struck by his massive configuration of brow? In short, we heard of a great many Missions of various sorts, among this set of people; but, nothing respecting them was half so clear to us, as that it was Mr. Quale's mission to be in ecstasies with everybody else's mission, and that it was the most popular mission of all.

Mr. Jarndyce had fallen into this company, in the tenderness of his heart and his earnest desire to do all the good in his power; but, that he felt it to be too often an unsatisfactory company, where benevolence took spasmodic forms; where charity was assumed, as a regular uniform, by loud professors and speculators in cheap notoriety, vehement in profession, restless and vain in action, servile in the last degree of meanness to the great, adulatory of one another, and intolerable to those who were anxious quietly to help the weak from falling, rather than with a great deal of bluster and self-laudation to raise them up a little way when they were down; he plainly told us. When a testimonial was originated to Mr. Quale, by Mr. Gusher (who had already got one, originated by Mr. Quale), and when Mr. Gusher spoke for an hour and a half on the subject to a meeting, including two charity schools of small boys and girls, who were specially reminded of the widow's mite, and requested to come forward with halfpence and be acceptable sacrifices; I think the wind was in the east for three whole weeks.

I mention this, because I am coming to Mr. Skimpole again. It seemed to me, that his off-hand professions of childishness and carelessness were a great relief to my guardian, by contrast with such things, and were the more readily believed in; since, to find one perfectly undesigning and candid man, among many opposites, could not fail to give him pleasure. I should be sorry to imply that Mr. Skimpole divined this, and was politic: I really never understood him well enough to know. What he was to my guardian, he certainly was to the rest of the world.

He had not been very well; and thus, though he lived in London, we had seen nothing of him until now. He appeared one morning, in his usual agreeable way, and as full of pleasant spirits as ever.

Well, he said, here he was! He had been bilious, but rich men were often bilious, and therefore he had been persuading himself that he was a man of property. So he was, in a certain point of view—in his expansive intentions. He had been enriching his medical attendant in the most lavish manner. He had always doubled, and sometimes quadrupled, his fees. He had said to the doctor, "Now, my dear doctor, it is quite a delusion on your part to suppose that you attend me for nothing. I am overwhelming you with money—in my expansive intentions—if you only knew it!" And really (he said) he meant it to that degree, that he thought it much the same as doing it. If he had had those bits of metal or thin paper, to which mankind attached so much importance, to put in the doctor's hand, he would have put them in the doctor's hand. Not having them, he substituted the will for the deed. Very well! If he really meant it—if his will were genuine and real: which it was—it appeared to him that it was the same as coin, and cancelled the obligation.

"It may be, partly, because I know nothing of the value of money," said Mr. Skimpole, "but I often feel this. It seems so reasonable! My butcher says to me, he wants that little bill. It's a part of the pleasant unconscious poetry of the man's nature, that he always calls it a 'little' bill—to make the payment appear easy to both of us. I reply to the butcher, My good friend, if you knew it you are paid. You

247

haven't had the trouble of coming to ask for the little bill. You are paid. I mean it."

"But, suppose," said my guardian, laughing, "he had meant the meat in the bill, instead of providing it?"

"My dear Jarndyce," he returned, "you surprise me. You take the butcher's position. A butcher I once dealt with, occupied that very ground. Says he, 'Sir, why did you eat spring lamb at eighteen-pence a pound?' 'Why did I eat spring lamb at eighteen-pence a pound, my honest friend?' said I, naturally amazed by the question. 'I like spring lamb!' This was so far convincing. 'Well, sir,' says he, 'I wish I had meant the lamb as you mean the money!' 'My good fellow,' said I, 'pray let us reason like intellectual beings. How could that be? It was impossible. You *had* got. the lamb, and I have *not* got the money. You couldn't really mean the lamb without sending it in, whereas I can, and do, really mean the money without paying it!' He had not a word. There was an end of the subject."

"Did he take no legal proceedings?" inquired my guardian.

"Yes, he took legal proceedings," said Mr. Skimpole. "But, in that, he was influenced by passion; not by reason. Passion reminds me of Boythorn. He writes me that you and the ladies have promised him a short visit at his bachelor-house in Lincolnshire."

"He is a great favourite with my girls," said Mr. Jarndyce, "and I have promised for them."

"Nature forgot to shade him off, I think?" observed Mr. Skimpole to Ada and me. "A little too boisterous—like the sea? A little too vehement—like a bull, who has made up his mind to consider every colour scarlet? But, I grant a sledge-hammering sort of merit in him!"

I should have been surprised if those two could have thought very highly of one another; Mr. Boythorn attaching so much importance to many things, and Mr. Skimpole caring so little for anything. Besides which, I had noticed Mr. Boythorn more than once on the point of breaking out into some strong opinion, when Mr. Skimpole was referred to. Of course I merely joined Ada in saying that we had been greatly pleased with him.

"He has invited me," said Mr. Skimpole; "and if a child may trust himself in such hands: which the present child is encouraged to do, with the united tenderness of two angels to guard him: I shall go. He proposes to frank me down and back again. I suppose it will cost money? Shillings perhaps? Or pounds? Or something of that sort? By-the-bye. Coavinses. You remember our friend Coavinses, Miss Summerson?"

He asked me, as the subject arose in his mind, in his graceful light-hearted manner, and without the least embarrassment.

"O yes!" said I.

"Coavinses has been arrested by the great Bailiff," said Mr. Skimpole. "He will never do violence to the sunshine any more."

It quite shocked me to hear it; for, I had already recalled, with anything but a serious association, the image of the man sitting on the sofa that night, wiping his head.

"His successor informed me of it yesterday," said Mr. Skimpole. "His successor is in my house now—in possession, I think he calls it. He came yesterday, on my blue-eyed daughter's birthday. I put it to him, 'This is unreasonable and inconvenient. If you had a blue-eyed daughter you wouldn't like *me* to come, uninvited, on *her* birthday?' But, he stayed."

Mr. Skimpole laughed at the pleasant absurdity, and lightly touched the piano by which he was seated.

"And he told me," he said, playing little chords where I shall put full stops, "That Coavinses had left. Three children. No mother. And that Coavinses' profession. Being unpopular. The rising Coavinses. Were at a considerable disadvantage."

Mr. Jarndyce got up, rubbing his head, and began to walk

about. Mr. Skimpole played the melody of one of Ada's favourite songs. Ada and I both looked at Mr. Jarndyce, thinking that we knew what was passing in his mind.

After walking and stopping, and several times leaving off rubbing his head, and beginning again, my guardian put his hand upon the keys and stopped Mr. Skimpole's playing. "I don't like this, Skimpole," he said thoughtfully.

Mr. Skimpole, who had quite forgotten the subject, looked up surprised.

"The man was necessary," pursued my guardian, walking backward and forward in the very short space between the piano and the end of the room, and rubbing his hair up from the back of his head as if a high east wind had blown it into that form. "If we make such men necessary by our faults and follies, or by our want of worldly knowledge, or by our misfortunes, we must not revenge ourselves upon them. There was no harm in his trade. He maintained his children. One would like to know more about this."

"O! Coavinses?" cried Mr. Skimpole, at length perceiving what he meant. "Nothing easier. A walk to Coavinses' head-quarters, and you can know what you will."

Mr. Jarndyce nodded to us, who were only waiting for the signal. "Come! We will walk that way, my dears. Why not that way, as soon as another!" We were quickly ready, and went out. Mr. Skimpole went with us, and quite enjoyed the expedition. It was so new and so refreshing, he said, for him to want Coavinses, instead of Coavinses wanting him!

He took us, first, to Cursitor Street, Chancery Lane, where there was a house with barred windows, which he called Coavinses' Castle. On our going into the entry and ringing a bell, a very hideous boy came out of a sort of office, and looked at us over a spiked wicket.

"Who did you want?" said the boy, fitting two of the spikes into his chin.

"There was a follower, or an officer, or something, here," said Mr. Jarndyce, "who is dead."

" Yes ? " said the boy. " Well ? "

" I want to know his name, if you please ? "

" Name of Neckett," said the boy. .

" And his address ? "

" Bell Yard," said the boy. " Chandler's shop, left hand side, name of Blinder."

" Was he—I don't know how to shape the question," murmured my guardian—" industrious ? "

" Was Neckett ? " said the boy. " Yes, wery much so. He was never tired of watching. He'd set upon a post at a street corner, eight or ten hours at a stretch, if he undertook to do it."

" He might have done worse," I heard my guardian soliloquize. " He might have undertaken to do it, and not done it. Thank you. That's all I want."

We left the boy, with his head on one side, and his arms on the gate, fondling and sucking the spikes; and went back to Lincoln's Inn, where Mr. Skimpole, who had not cared to remain nearer Coavinses, awaited us. Then, we all went to Bell Yard : a narrow alley, at a very short distance. We soon found the chandler's shop. In it, was a good-natured-looking old woman, with a dropsy, or an asthma, or perhaps both.

" Neckett's children ? " said she, in reply to my inquiry. " Yes, surely, miss. Three pair, if you please. Door right opposite the stairs." And she handed me the key across the counter.

I glanced at the key, and glanced at her ; but she took it for granted that I knew what to do with it. As it could only be intended for the children's door, I came out, without asking any more questions, and led the way up the dark stairs. We went as quietly as we could ; but, four of us made some noise on the aged boards ; and, when we came to the second story, we found we had disturbed a man who was standing there, looking out of his room.

" Is it Gridley that's wanted ? " he said, fixing his eyes on me with an angry stare.

"No, sir," said I, "I am going higher up."

He looked at Ada, and at Mr. Jarndyce, and at Mr. Skimpole: fixing the same angry stare on each in succession, as they passed and followed me. Mr. Jarndyce gave him good day. "Good day!" he said, abruptly and fiercely. He was a tall sallow man, with a careworn head, on which but little hair remained, a deeply lined face, and prominent eyes. He had a combative look; and a chafing, irritable manner, which, associated with his figure—still large and powerful, though evidently in its decline—rather alarmed me. He had a pen in his hand, and, in the glimpse I caught of his room in passing, I saw that it was covered with a litter of papers.

Leaving him standing there, we went up to the top room. I tapped at the door, and a little shrill voice inside said, "We are locked in. Mrs. Blinder's got the key!"

I applied the key on hearing this, and opened the door. In a poor room, with a sloping ceiling, and containing very little furniture, was a mite of a boy, some five or six years old, nursing and hushing a heavy child of eighteen months. There was no fire, though the weather was cold; both children were wrapped in some poor shawls and tippets, as a substitute. Their clothing was not so warm, however, but that their noses looked red and pinched, and their small figures shrunken, as the boy walked up and down, nursing and hushing the child with its head on his shoulder.

"Who has locked you up here alone?" we naturally asked.

"Charley," said the boy, standing still to gaze at us.

"Is Charley your brother?"

"No. She's my sister, Charlotte. Father called her Charley."

"Are there any more of you besides Charley?"

"Me," said the boy, "and Emma," patting the limp bonnet of the child he was nursing. "And Charley."

"Where is Charley now?"

252

"Out a-washing," said the boy, beginning to walk up and down again, and taking the nankeen bonnet much too near the bedstead, by trying to gaze at us at the same time.

We were looking at one another, and at these two children, when there came into the room a very little girl, childish in figure but shrewd and older-looking in the face—pretty-faced too—wearing a womanly sort of bonnet much too large for her, and drying her bare arms on a womanly sort of apron. Her fingers were white and wrinkled with washing, and the soap-suds were yet smoking which she wiped off her arms. But for this, she might have been a child, playing at washing, and imitating a poor working-woman with a quick observation of the truth.

She had come running from some place in the neighbourhood, and had made all the haste she could. Consequently, though she was very light, she was out of breath, and could not speak at first, as she stood panting, and wiping her arms, and looking quietly at us.

"O, here's Charley!" said the boy.

The child he was nursing, stretched forth its arms, and cried out to be taken by Charley. The little girl took it, in a womanly sort of manner belonging to the apron and the bonnet, and stood looking at us over the burden that clung to her most affectionately.

"Is it possible," whispered my guardian, as we put a chair for the little creature, and got her to sit down with her load : the boy keeping close to her, holding to her apron, "that this child works for the rest? Look at this! For God's sake look at this!"

It was a thing to look at. The three children close together, and two of them relying solely on the third, and the third so young and yet with an air of age and steadiness that sat so strangely on the childish figure.

"Charley, Charley!" said my guardian. "How old are you?"

"Over thirteen, sir," replied the child.

"O! What a great age!" said my guardian. "What a great age, Charley!"

I cannot describe the tenderness with which he spoke to her; half playfully, yet all the more compassionately and mournfully.

"And do you live alone here with these babies, Charley?" said my guardian.

"Yes, sir," returned the child, looking up into his face with perfect confidence, "since father died."

"And how do you live, Charley? O! Charley," said my guardian, turning his face away for a moment, "how do you live?"

"Since father died, sir, I've gone out to work. I'm out washing to-day."

"God help you, Charley!" said my guardian. "You're not tall enough to reach the tub!"

"In pattens I am, sir," she said quickly. "I've got a high pair as belonged to mother."

"And when did mother die? Poor mother!"

"Mother died, just after Emma was born," said the child, glancing at the face upon her bosom. "Then father said I was to be as good a mother to her as I could. And so I tried. And so I worked at home, and did cleaning and nursing and washing, for a long time before I began to go out. And that's how I know how; don't you see, sir?"

"And do you often go out?"

"As often as I can," said Charley, opening her eyes, and smiling, "because of earning sixpences and shillings!"

"And do you always lock the babies up when you go out?"

"To keep 'em safe, sir, don't you see?" said Charley. "Mrs. Blinder comes up now and then, and Mr. Gridley comes up sometimes, and perhaps I can run in sometimes, and they can play you know, and Tom an't afraid of being locked up, are you, Tom?"

"No-o!" said Tom, stoutly.

"When it comes on dark, the lamps are lighted down in

254

the court, and they show up here quite bright—almost quite bright. Don't they, Tom?"

"Yes, Charley," said Tom, "almost quite bright."

"Then he's as good as gold," said the little creature—O! in such a motherly, womanly way! "And when Emma's tired, he puts her to bed. And when he's tired he goes to bed himself. And when I come home and light the candle, and has a bit of supper, he sits up again and has it with me. Don't you, Tom?"

"O yes, Charley!" said Tom. "That I do!" And either in this glimpse of the great pleasure of his life, or in gratitude and love for Charley, who was all in all to him, he laid his face among the scanty folds of her frock, and passed from laughing into crying.

It was the first time since our entry, that a tear had been shed among these children. The little orphan girl had spoken of their father, and their mother, as if all that sorrow were subdued by the necessity of taking courage, and by her childish importance in being able to work, and by her bustling busy way. But, now, when Tom cried; although she sat quite tranquil, looking quietly at us, and did not by any movement disturb a hair of the head of either of her little charges: I saw two silent tears fall down her face.

I stood at the window with Ada, pretending to look at the housetops, and the blackened stack of chimneys, and the poor plants, and the birds in little cages belonging to the neighbours, when I found that Mrs. Blinder, from the shop below, had come in (perhaps it had taken her all this time to get up-stairs) and was talking to my guardian.

"It's not much to forgive 'em the rent, sir," she said: "who could take it from them!"

"Well, well!" said my guardian to us two. "It is enough that the time will come when this good woman will find that it *was* much, and that forasmuch as she did it unto the least of these—! This child," he added, after a few moments, "could she possibly continue this?"

255

" Really, sir, I think she might," said Mrs. Blinder, getting her heavy breath by painful degrees. " She's as handy as it's possible to be. Bless you, sir, the way she tended them two children, after the mother died, was the talk of the yard ! And it was a wonder to see her with him after he was took ill, it really was ! ' Mrs. Blinder,' he said to me the very last he spoke—he was lying there—' Mrs. Blinder, whatever my calling may have been, I see a Angel sitting in this room last night along with my child, and I trust her to Our Father !' "

" He had no other calling ? " said my guardian.

" No, sir," returned Mrs. Blinder, " he was nothing but a follerer. When he first came to lodge here, I didn't know what he was, and I confess that when I found out I gave him notice. It wasn't liked in the yard. It wasn't approved by the other lodgers. It is *not* a genteel calling," said Mrs. Blinder, " and most people do object to it. Mr. Gridley objected to it, very strong ; and he is a good lodger, though his temper has been hard tried."

" So you gave him notice ? " said my guardian.

" So I gave him notice," said Mrs. Blinder. " But really when the time came, and I knew no other ill of him, I was in doubts. He was punctual and diligent ; he did what he had to do, sir," said Mrs. Blinder, unconsciously fixing Mr. Skimpole with her eye ; " and it's something in this world, even to do that."

" So you kept him after all ? "

" Why, I said that if he could arrange with Mr. Gridley, I could arrange it with the other lodgers, and should not so much mind its being liked or disliked in the yard. Mr. Gridley gave his consent gruff—but gave it. He was always gruff with him, but he has been kind to the children since. A person is never known till a person is proved."

" Have many people been kind to the children ? " asked Mr. Jarndyce.

" Upon the whole, not so bad, sir," said Mrs. Blinder :

"but, certainly not so many as would have been, if their father's calling had been different. Mr. Coavins gave a guinea, and the follerers made up a little purse. Some neighbours in the yard, that had always joked and tapped their shoulders when he went by, came forward with a little subscription, and—in general—not so bad. Similarly with Charlotte. Some people won't employ her, because she was a follerer's child; some people that do employ her, cast it at her; some make a merit of having her to work for them, with that and all her drawbacks upon her: and perhaps pay her less and put upon her more. But she's patienter than others would be, and is clever too, and always willing, up to the full mark of her strength and over. So I should say, in general, not so bad, sir, but might be better."

Mrs. Blinder sat down to give herself a more favourable opportunity of recovering her breath, exhausted anew by so much talking before it was fully restored. Mr. Jarndyce was turning to speak to us, when his attention was attracted, by the abrupt entrance into the room of the Mr. Gridley who had been mentioned, and whom we had seen on our way up.

"I don't know what you may be doing here, ladies and gentlemen," he said, as if he resented our presence, "but you'll excuse my coming in. I don't come in to stare about me. Well, Charley! Well, Tom! Well, little one! How is it with us all to-day?"

He bent over the group, in a caressing way, and clearly was regarded as a friend by the children, though his face retained its stern character, and his manner to us was as rude as it could be. My guardian noticed it, and respected it.

"No one, surely, would come here to stare about him," he said mildly.

"May be so, sir, may be so," returned the other, taking Tom upon his knee, and waving him off impatiently. "I don't want to argue with ladies and gentlemen. I have had enough of arguing, to last one man his life."

"You have sufficient reason, I dare say," said Mr. Jarndyce, "for being chafed and irritated——"

"There again!" exclaimed the man, becoming violently angry. "I am of a quarrelsome temper. I am irascible. I am not polite!"

"Not very, I think."

"Sir," said Gridley, putting down the child, and going up to him as if he meant to strike him. "Do you know anything of Courts of Equity?"

"Perhaps I do, to my sorrow.

"To your sorrow?" said the man, pausing in his wrath. "If so, I beg your pardon. I am not polite, I know. I beg your pardon! Sir," with renewed violence, "I have been dragged for five-and-twenty years over burning iron, and I have lost the habit of treading upon velvet. Go into the Court of Chancery yonder, and ask what is one of the standing jokes that brighten up their business sometimes, and they will tell you that the best joke they have, is the man from Shropshire. I," he said, beating one hand on the other, passionately, "am the man from Shropshire."

"I believe, I and my family have also had the honour of furnishing some entertainment in the same grave place," said my guardian, composedly. "You may have heard my name —Jarndyce."

"Mr. Jarndyce," said Gridley, with a rough sort of salutation, "you bear your wrongs more quietly than I can bear mine. More than that, I tell you—and I tell this gentleman, and these young ladies, if they are friends of yours—that if I took my wrongs in any other way, I should be driven mad! It is only by resenting them, and by revenging them in my mind, and by angrily demanding the justice I never get, that I am able to keep my wits together. It is only that!" he said, speaking in a homely, rustic way, and with great vehemence. "You may tell me that I over-excite myself. I answer that it's in my nature to do it, under wrong, and I must do it. There's nothing between doing it, and sinking into the smiling state of the poor little mad woman that haunts the Court. If I was once to sit down under it, I should become imbecile."

The passion and heat in which he was, and the manner in which his face worked, and the violent gestures with which he accompanied what he said, were most painful to see.

" Mr. Jarndyce," he said, " consider my case. As true as there is a Heaven above us, this is my case. I am one of two brothers. My father (a farmer) made a will, and left his farm and stock, and so forth, to my mother, for her life. After my mother's death, all was to come to me, except a legacy of three hundred pounds that I was then to pay my brother. My mother died. My brother, some time afterwards, claimed his legacy. I, and some of my relations, said that he had had a part of it already, in board and lodging, and some other things. Now mind! That was the question, and nothing else. No one disputed the will; no one disputed anything but whether part of that three hundred pounds had been already paid or not. To settle that question, my brother filing a bill, I was obliged to go into this accursed Chancery; I was forced there, because the law forced me, and would let me go nowhere else. Seventeen people were made defendants to that simple suit! It first came on, after two years. It was then stopped for another two years, while the Master (may his head rot off!) inquired whether I was my father's son—about which, there was no dispute at all with any mortal creature. He then found out, that there were not defendants enough—remember, there were only seventeen as yet!—but, that we must have another who had been left out; and must begin all over again. The costs at that time— before the thing was begun!—were three times the legacy. My brother would have given up the legacy, and joyful, to escape more costs. My whole estate, left to me in that will of my father's, has gone in costs. The suit, still undecided, has fallen into rack, and ruin, and despair, with everything else—and here I stand, this day! Now, Mr. Jarndyce, in your suit there are thousands and thousands involved where in mine there are hundreds. Is mine less hard to bear, or is it harder to bear, when my whole living was in it, and has been thus shamefully sucked away?"

Mr. Jarndyce said that he condoled with him with all his heart, and that he set up no monopoly, himself, in being unjustly treated by this monstrous system.

"There again!" said Mr. Gridley, with no diminution of his rage. "The system! I am told, on all hands, it's the system. I mustn't look to individuals. It's the system. I mustn't go into Court, and say, 'My Lord, I beg to know this from you—is this right or wrong? Have you the face to tell me I have received justice, and therefore am dismissed?' My Lord knows nothing of it. He sits there, to administer the system. I mustn't go to Mr. Tulkinghorn, the solicitor in Lincoln's Inn Fields, and say to him when he makes me furious, by being so cool and satisfied—as they all do; for I know they gain by it while I lose, don't I?—I mustn't say to him, I will have something out of some one for my ruin, by fair means or foul! *He* is not responsible. It's the system. But, if I do no violence to any of them, here—I may! I don't know what may happen if I am carried beyond myself at last!—I will accuse the individual workers of that system against me, face to face, before the great eternal bar!"

His passion was fearful. I could not have believed in such rage without seeing it.

"I have done!" he said, sitting down and wiping his face. "Mr. Jarndyce, I have done! I am violent, I know. I ought to know it. I have been in prison for contempt of Court. I have been in prison for threatening the solicitor. I have been in this trouble, and that trouble, and shall be again. I am the man from Shropshire, and I sometimes go beyond amusing them —though they have found it amusing, too, to see me committed into custody, and brought up in custody, and all that. It would be better for me, they tell me, if I restrained myself. I tell them, that if I did restrain myself, I should become imbecile. I was a good-enough-tempered man once, I believe. People in my part of the country, say, they remember me so; but, now, I must have this vent under my sense of injury, or nothing could hold my wits together. 'It would be far better for you, Mr. Gridley,' the Lord Chancellor told me last week, 'not to waste your time here, and to stay, usefully employed, down in Shropshire.' 'My Lord, my Lord, I know it would,' said I to him, 'and it would have been far better for me never to have heard the name of your high office; but, unhappily for me, I can't undo the past, and the past drives me here!' —Besides," he added, breaking fiercely out, "I'll shame them. To the last, I'll show myself in that Court to its shame. If I knew when I was going to die, and could be carried there, and had a voice to speak with, I would die there, saying, 'You have brought me here, and sent me from here, many and many a time. Now send me out, feet foremost!'"

His countenance had, perhaps for years, become so set in its contentious expression that it did not soften, even now when he was quiet.

"I came to take these babies down to my room for an hour," he said, going to them again, "and let them play about. I didn't mean to say all this, but it don't much signify. You're not afraid of me, Tom; are you?"

"No!" said Tom. "You ain't angry with *me*."

"You are right, my child. You're going back, Charley? Aye? Come then, little one!" He took the youngest child on his arm, where she was willing enough to be carried. "I shouldn't wonder if we found a ginger-bread soldier down-stairs. Let's go and look for him!"

He made his former rough salutation, which was not deficient in a certain respect, to Mr. Jarndyce; and bowing slightly to us, went down-stairs to his room.

Upon that, Mr. Skimpole began to talk, for the first time since our arrival, in his usual gay strain. He said, Well, it was really very pleasant to see how things lazily adapted themselves to purposes. Here was this Mr. Gridley, a man of a robust will, and surprising energy—intellectually speaking, a sort of inharmonious blacksmith—and he could easily imagine that there Gridley was, years ago, wandering about in life for something to expend his superfluous combativeness upon—a sort of Young Love among the thorns—when the Court of Chancery came in his way, and accommodated him with the exact thing he wanted. There they were, matched, ever afterwards! Otherwise he might have been a great general, blowing up all sorts of towns, or he might have been a great politician, dealing in all sorts of parliamentary rhetoric; but, as it was, he and the Court of Chancery had fallen upon each other in the pleasantest way, and nobody was much the worse, and Gridley was, so to speak, from that hour provided for. Then look at Coavinses! How delightfully poor Coavinses (father of these charming children) illustrated the same principle! He, Mr. Skimpole, himself, had sometimes repined at the existence of Coavinses. He had found Coavinses in his way. He could have dispensed with Coavinses. There had been times when, if he had been a Sultan, and his Grand Vizier had said one morning, " What does the Commander of the Faithful require at the hands of his slave? " he might have even gone so far as to reply, " The head of Coavinses! " But what turned out to be the case? That, all that time, he had been giving employment to a most deserving man; that he had been a benefactor to Coavinses; that he had actually been enabling Coavinses to bring up these charming children in this agreeable way, developing these social virtues! Insomuch that his heart had just now swelled, and the tears had come into his eyes, when he had looked round the room, and thought, " I was the great patron of Coavinses, and his little comforts were *my* work! "

There was something so captivating in his light way of touching these fantastic strings, and he was such a mirthful child by the side of the graver childhood we had seen, that he made my guardian smile even as he turned towards us from a little private talk with Mrs. Blinder. We kissed

Charley, and took her down-stairs with us, and stopped out-side the house to see her run away to her work. I don't know where she was going, but we saw her run, such a little, little creature, in her womanly bonnet and apron, through a covered way at the bottom of the court; and melt into the city's strife and sound, like a dewdrop in an ocean.

CHAPTER XVI

TOM-ALL-ALONE'S

My Lady Dedlock is restless, very restless. The astonished fashionable intelligence hardly knows where to have her. To-day, she is at Chesney Wold; yesterday she was at her house in town; to-morrow, she may be abroad, for anything the fashionable intelligence can with confidence predict. Even Sir Leicester's gallantry has some trouble to keep pace with her. It would have more, but that his other faithful ally, for better and for worse—the gout—darts into the old oak bed-chamber at Chesney Wold, and grips him by both legs.

Sir Leicester receives the gout as a troublesome demon, but still a demon of the patrician order. All the Dedlocks, in the direct male line, through a course of time during and beyond which the memory of man goeth not to the contrary, have had the gout. It can be proved, sir. Other men's fathers may have died of the rheumatism, or may have taken base contagion from the tainted blood of the sick vulgar, but the Dedlock family have communicated something exclusive, even to the levelling process of dying, by dying of their own family gout. It has come down, through the illustrious line, like the plate, or the pictures, or the place in Lincolnshire. It is among their dignities. Sir Leicester is, perhaps, not wholly without an impression, though he has never resolved it into words, that the angel of death in the discharge of his necessary duties may observe to the shades of the aristocracy,

" My lords and gentlemen, I have the honour to present to you another Dedlock certified to have arrived per the family gout."

Hence, Sir Leicester yields up his family legs to the family disorder, as if he held his name and fortune on that feudal tenure. He feels, that for a Dedlock to be laid upon his back and spasmodically twitched and stabbed in his extremities, is a liberty taken somewhere; but, he thinks, " We have all yielded to this; it belongs to us; it has, for some hundreds of years, been understood that we are not to make the vaults in the park interesting on more ignoble terms; and I submit myself to the compromise."

And a goodly show he makes, lying in a flush of crimson and gold, in the midst of the great drawing-room, before his favourite picture of my Lady, with broad strips of sunlight shining in, down the long perspective, through the long line of windows, and alternating with soft reliefs of shadow. Outside, the stately oaks, rooted for ages in the green ground which has never known ploughshare, but was still a Chase when kings rode to battle with sword and shield, and rode a-hunting with bow and arrow; bear witness to his greatness. Inside, his forefathers, looking on him from the walls, say, " Each of us was a passing reality here, and left this coloured shadow of himself, and melted into remembrance as dreamy as the distant voices of the rooks now lulling you to rest;" and bear their testimony to his greatness, too. And he is very great, this day. And woe to Boythorn, or other daring wight, who shall presumptuously contest an inch with him!

My Lady is at present represented, near Sir Leicester, by her portrait. She has flitted away to town, with no intention of remaining there, and will soon flit hither again, to the confusion of the fashionable intelligence. The house in town is not prepared for her reception. It is muffled and dreary. Only one Mercury in powder, gapes disconsolate at the hall-window; and he mentioned last night to another Mercury of his acquaintance, also accustomed to good society, that if that sort of thing was to last—which it couldn't, for a man of his spirits couldn't bear it, and a man of his figure couldn't be expected to bear it—there would be no resource for him, upon his honour, but to cut his throat!

What connexion can there be, between the place in Lincoln-shire, the house in town, the Mercury in powder, and the whereabout of Jo the outlaw with the broom, who had that distant ray of light upon him when he swept the churchyard-step? What connexion can there have been between many people in the innumerable histories of this world, who, from opposite sides of great gulfs, have, nevertheless, been very curiously brought together!

Jo sweeps his crossing all day long, unconscious of the link, if any link there be. He sums up his mental condition, when asked a question, by replying that he "don't know nothink." He knows that it's hard to keep the mud off the crossing in dirty weather, and harder still to live by doing it. Nobody taught him, even that much; he found it out.

Jo lives—that is to say, Jo has not yet died—in a ruinous place, known to the like of him by the name of Tom-all-Alone's. It is a black, dilapidated street, avoided by all decent people; where the crazy houses were seized upon, when their decay was far advanced, by some bold vagrants, who, after establishing their own possession, took to letting them out in lodgings. Now, these tumbling tenements contain, by night, a swarm of misery. As, on the ruined human wretch, vermin parasites appear, so, these ruined shelters have bred a crowd of foul existence that crawls in and out of gaps in walls and boards; and coils itself to sleep, in maggot numbers, where the rain drips in; and comes and goes, fetching and carrying fever, and sowing more evil in its every footprint than Lord Coodle, and Sir Thomas Doodle, and the Duke of Foodle, and all the fine gentlemen in office, down to Zoodle, shall set right in five hundred years—though born expressly to do it.

Twice, lately, there has been a crash and a cloud of dust, like the springing of a mine, in Tom-all-Alone's; and, each time, a house has fallen. These accidents have made a paragraph in the newspapers, and have filled a bed or two in the nearest hospital. The gaps remain, and there are not unpopular lodgings among the rubbish. As several more houses are nearly ready to go, the next crash in Tom-all-Alone's may be expected to be a good one.

This desirable property is in Chancery, of course. It would be an insult to the discernment of any man with half an eye, to tell him so. Whether "Tom" is the popular representative of the original plaintiff or defendant in Jarndyce and Jarndyce; or, whether Tom lived here when the suit had laid the street waste, all alone, until other settlers came to join him; or, whether the traditional title is a comprehensive name for a retreat cut off from honest company and put out of the pale of hope; perhaps nobody knows. Certainly, Jo don't know.

"For *I* don't," says Jo, "*I* don't know nothink."

It must be a strange state to be like Jo! To shuffle through the streets, unfamiliar with the shapes, and in utter darkness as to the meaning, of those mysterious symbols, so abundant over the shops, and at the corners of streets, and on the doors, and in the windows! To see people read, and to see people write, and to see the postmen deliver letters, and not to have the least idea of all that language—to be, to every scrap of it, stone blind and dumb! It must be very puzzling to see the good company going to the churches on Sundays, with their books in their hands, and to think (for perhaps Jo *does* think, at odd times) what does it all mean, and if it means anything to anybody, how comes it that it means nothing to me? To be hustled, and jostled, and moved on; and really to feel that it would appear to be perfectly true that I have no business, here, or there, or anywhere; and yet to be perplexed by the consideration that I *am* here somehow, too, and everybody overlooked me until I

267

became the creature that I am! It must be a strange state, not merely to be told that I am scarcely human (as in the case of my offering myself for a witness), but to feel it of my own knowledge all my life! To see the horses, dogs, and cattle, go by me, and to know that in ignorance I belong to them, and not to the superior beings in my shape, whose delicacy I offend! Jo's ideas of a Criminal Trial, or a Judge, or a Bishop, or a Government, or that inestimable jewel to him (if he only knew it) the Constitution, should be strange! His whole material and immaterial life is wonderfully strange; his death, the strangest thing of all.

Jo comes out of Tom-all-Alone's, meeting the tardy morning which is always late in getting down there, and munches his dirty bit of bread as he comes along. His way lying through many streets, and the houses not yet being open, he sits down to breakfast on the door-step of the Society for the Propagation of the Gospel in Foreign Parts, and gives it a brush when he has finished, as an acknowledgment of the accommodation. He admires the size of the edifice, and wonders what it's all about. He has no idea, poor wretch, of the spiritual destitution of a coral reef in the Pacific, or what it costs to look up the precious souls among the cocoa-nuts and bread-fruit.

He goes to his crossing, and begins to lay it out for the day. The town awakes; the great tee-totum is set up for its daily spin and whirl; all that unaccountable reading and writing, which has been suspended for a few hours, re-commences. Jo, and the other lower animals, get on in the unintelligible mess as they can. It is market-day. The blinded oxen, over-goaded, over-driven, never guided, run into wrong places and are beaten out; and plunge, red-eyed and foaming, at stone walls; and often sorely hurt the innocent, and often sorely hurt themselves. Very like Jo and his order; very, very like!

A band of music comes and plays. Jo listens to it. So does a dog—a drover's dog, waiting for his master outside a butcher's shop, and evidently thinking about those sheep he has had upon his mind for some hours, and is happily rid of. He seems perplexed respecting three or four; can't remember where he left them; looks up and down the street, as half expecting to see them astray; suddenly pricks up his ears and remembers all about it. A thoroughly vagabond dog, accustomed to low company and public-houses; a terrific dog to sheep; ready at a whistle to scamper over their backs, and tear out mouthfuls of their wool; but an educated, improved, developed dog, who has been taught his duties and knows how to discharge them. He and Jo listen to the music, probably with much the same amount of animal satisfaction; likewise, as to awakened association, aspiration or regret, melancholy or joyful reference to things beyond the senses, they are probably upon a par. But, otherwise, how far above the human listener is the brute!

Turn that dog's descendants wild, like Jo, and in a very few years they will so degenerate that they will lose even their bark—but not their bite.

The day changes as it wears itself away, and becomes dark and drizzly. Jo fights it out, at his crossing, among the mud and wheels, the horses, whips, and umbrellas, and gets but a scanty sum to pay for the unsavoury shelter of Tom-all-Alone's. Twilight comes on; gas begins to start up in the shops; the lamplighter, with his ladder, runs along the margin of the pavement. A wretched evening is beginning to close in.

In his chambers, Mr. Tulkinghorn sits meditating an application to the nearest magistrate to-morrow morning for a warrant. Gridley, a disappointed suitor, has been here to-day, and has been alarming. We are not to be put in bodily fear, and that ill-conditioned fellow shall be held to bail again. From the ceiling, foreshortened Allegory, in the person of one impossible Roman upside down, points with the arm of Samson (out of joint, and an odd one) obtrusively towards the window. Why should Mr. Tulkinghorn, for such no reason, look out of window? Is the hand not always pointing there? So he does not look out of window.

And if he did, what would it be to see a woman going by? There are women enough in the world, Mr. Tulking-horn thinks—too many; they are at the bottom of all that goes wrong in it, though, for the matter of that, they create business for lawyers. What would it be to see a woman going by, even though she were going secretly? They are all secret. Mr. Tulkinghorn knows that, very well.

But they are not all like the woman who now leaves him and his house behind; between whose plain dress, and her refined manner, there is something exceedingly inconsistent. She should be an upper servant by her attire, yet, in her air and step, though both are hurried and assumed—as far as she can assume in the muddy streets, which she treads with an unaccustomed foot—she is a lady. Her face is veiled, and still she sufficiently betrays herself to make more than one of those who pass her look round sharply.

She never turns her head. Lady or servant, she has a purpose in her, and can follow it. She never turns her head, until she comes to the crossing where Jo plies with his broom. He crosses with her, and begs. Still, she does not turn her head until she has landed on the other side. Then, she slightly beckons to him, and says "Come here!"

Jo follows her, a pace or two, into a quiet court.

"Are you the boy I've read of in the papers?" she asked behind her veil.

"I don't know," says Jo, staring moodily at the veil, "nothink about no papers. I don't know nothink about nothink at all."

"Were you examined at an Inquest?"

"I don't know nothink about no—where I was took by the beadle, do you mean?" says Jo. "Was the boy's name at the Inkwhich, Jo?"

"Yes."

"That's me!" says Jo.

"Come farther up."

"You mean about the man?" says Jo, following. "Him as wos dead?"

"Hush! Speak in a whisper! Yes. Did he look, when he was living, so very ill and poor?"

"O jist!" says Jo.

"Did he look like—not like *you*?" says the woman with abhorrence.

"O not so bad as me," says Jo. "I'm a reg'lar one *I* am! You didn't know him, did you?"

"How dare you ask me if I knew him?"

"No offence, my lady," says Jo, with much humility; for even he has got at the suspicion of her being a lady.

"I am not a lady. I am a servant."

"You are a jolly servant!" says Jo; without the least idea of saying anything offensive; merely as a tribute of admiration.

"Listen and be silent. Don't talk to me, and stand farther from me! Can you show me all those places that were spoken of in the account I read? The place he wrote for, the place he died at, the place where you were taken to, and the place where he was buried? Do you know the place where he was buried?"

Jo answers with a nod; having also nodded as each other place was mentioned.

"Go before me, and show me all those dreadful places. Stop opposite to each, and don't speak to me unless I speak to you. Don't look back. Do what I want, and I will pay you well."

Jo attends closely while the words are being spoken; tells them off on his broom-handle, finding them rather hard; pauses to consider their meaning; considers it satisfactory, and nods his ragged head.

"I'm fly," says Jo. "But fen larks, you know! Stow hooking it!"

271

" What does the horrible creature mean ? " exclaims the servant, recoiling from him.

" Stow cutting away, you know ! " says Jo.

" I don't understand you. Go on before ! I will give you more money than you ever had in your life."

Jo screws up his mouth into a whistle, gives his ragged head a rub, takes his broom under his arm, and leads the way ; passing deftly, with his bare feet, over the hard stones, and through the mud and mire.

Cook's Court. Jo stops. A pause.

" Who lives here ? "

" Him wot give him his writing, and give me half a bull," says Jo, in a whisper, without looking over his shoulder.

" Go on to the next."

Krook's house. Jo stops again. A longer pause.

" Who lives here ? "

" *He* lived here," Jo answers as before.

After a silence he is asked " In which room ? "

" In the back room up there. You can see the winder from this corner. Up there ! That's where I see him stritched out. This is the public ouse where I was took to."

" Go on to the next ! "

It is a longer walk to the next ; but Jo, relieved of his first suspicions, sticks to the forms imposed upon him, and does not look round. By many devious ways, reeking with offence of many kinds, they come to the little tunnel of a court, and to the gas-lamp (lighted now), and to the iron gate.

" He was put there," says Jo, holding to the bars and looking in.

" Where ? O, what a scene of horror ! "

" There ! " says Jo, pointing. " Over yinder. Among them piles of bones, and close to that there kitchin winder ! They put him wery nigh the top. They was obliged to stamp upon it to git it in. I could unkiver it for you with my broom, if the gate was open. That's why they locks it.

Consecrated Ground

I s'pose," giving it a shake. "It's always locked. Look at the rat!" cries Jo, excited. "Hi! Look! There he goes! Ho! Into the ground!"

The servant shrinks into a corner—into a corner of that hideous archway, with its deadly stains contaminating her dress; and putting out her two hands, and passionately telling him to keep away from her, for he is loathsome to her, so remains for some moments. Jo stands staring, and is still staring when she recovers herself.

"Is this place of abomination. consecrated ground?"

"I don't know nothink of consequential ground," says Jo, still staring.

"Is it blessed?"

"WHICH?" says Jo, in the last degree amazed.

"Is it blessed?"

"I'm blest if I know," says Jo, staring more than ever; "but I shouldn't think it warn't. Blest?" repeats Jo, something troubled in his mind. "It an't done it much good if it is. Blest? I should think it was t'othered myself. But I don't know nothink!"

The servant takes as little heed of what he says, as she seems to take of what she has said herself. She draws off her glove, to get some money from her purse. Jo silently notices how white and small her hand is, and what a jolly servant she must be to wear such sparkling rings.

She drops a piece of money in his hand, without touching it, and shuddering as their hands approach. "Now," she adds, "show me the spot again!"

Jo thrusts the handle of his broom between the bars of the gate, and, with his utmost power of elaboration, points it out. At length, looking aside to see if he has made himself intelligible, he finds that he is alone.

His first proceeding, is, to hold the piece of money to the gas-light, and to be overpowered at finding that it is yellow—gold. His next, is, to give it a one-sided bite at the edge, as a test of its quality. His next, to put it in his mouth for safety, and to sweep the step and passage with great care. His job done, he sets off for Tom-all-Alone's; stopping in the light of innumerable gas-lamps to produce the piece of gold, and give it another one-sided bite, as a reassurance of its being genuine.

The Mercury in powder is in no want of society to-night, for my Lady goes to a grand dinner, and three or four balls. Sir Leicester is fidgety, down at Chesney Wold, with no better company than the gout; he complains to Mrs. Rouncewell that the rain makes such a monotonous pattering on the terrace, that he can't read the paper, even by the fireside in his own snug dressing-room.

"Sir Leicester would have done better to try the other side of the house, my dear," says Mrs. Rouncewell to Rosa. "His dressing-room is on my Lady's side. And in all these years I never heard the step upon the Ghost's Walk, more distinct than it is to-night!"

CHAPTER XVII

RICHARD very often came to see us while we remained in London (though he soon failed in his letter-writing), and with his quick abilities, his good spirits, his good temper, his gaiety and freshness, was always delightful. But, though I liked him more and more, the better I knew him, I still felt more and more, how much it was to be regretted that he had been educated in no habits of application and concentration. The system which had addressed him in exactly the same manner as it had addressed hundreds of other boys, all varying in character and capacity, had enabled him to dash through his tasks, always with fair credit, and often with distinction; but in a fitful, dazzling way that had confirmed his reliance on those very qualities in himself, which it had been most desirable to direct and train. They were good qualities, without which no high place can be meritoriously won; but, like fire and water, though excellent servants, they were very bad masters. If they had been under Richard's direction, they would have been his friends; but Richard being under their direction, they became his enemies.

I write down these opinions, not because I believe that this or any other thing was so, because I thought so; but only because I did think so, and I want to be quite candid about all I thought and did. These were my thoughts about

Richard. I thought I often observed besides, how right my guardian was in what he had said; and that the uncertainties and delays of the Chancery suit had imparted to his nature something of the careless spirit of a gamester, who felt that he was part of a great gaming system.

Mr. and Mrs. Bayham Badger coming one afternoon, when my guardian was not at home, in the course of conversation I naturally inquired after Richard.

"Why, Mr. Carstone," said Mrs. Badger, "is very well, and is, I assure you, a great acquisition to our society. Captain Swosser used to say of me that I was always better than land a-head and a breeze a-starn to the midshipmen's mess when the purser's junk had become as tough as the fore-topsel weather earrings. It was his naval way of mentioning generally that I was an acquisition to any society. I may render the same tribute, I am sure, to Mr. Carstone. But I—you won't think me premature if I mention it?"

I said no, as Mrs. Badger's insinuating tone seemed to require such an answer.

"Nor Miss Clare?" said Mrs. Bayham Badger, sweetly.

Ada said no, too, and looked uneasy.

"Why, you see, my dears," said Mrs. Badger—"you'll excuse me calling you my dears?"

We entreated Mrs. Badger not to mention it.

"Because you really are, if I may take the liberty of saying so," pursued Mrs. Badger, "so perfectly charming. You see, my dears, that although I am still young—or Mr. Bayham Badger pays me the compliment of saying so—"

"No," Mr. Badger called out, like some one contradicting at a public meeting. "Not at all!"

"Very well," smiled Mrs. Badger, "we will say still young."

("Undoubtedly," said Mr. Badger.)

"My dears, though still young, I have had many opportunities of observing young men. There were many such on board the dear old Crippler, I assure you. After that, when I was with Captain Swosser in the Mediterranean, I embraced

276

every opportunity of knowing and befriending the midshipmen under Captain Swosser's command. *You* never heard them called the young gentlemen, my dears, and probably would not understand allusions to their pipe-claying their weekly accounts; but it is otherwise with me, for blue water has been a second home to me, and I have been quite a sailor. Again, with Professor Dingo."

("A man of European reputation," murmured Mr. Badger.)

"When I lost my dear first," and became the wife of my dear second," said Mrs. Badger, speaking of her former husbands as if they were parts of a charade, "I still enjoyed opportunities of observing youth. The class attendant on Professor Dingo's lectures was a large one, and it became my pride, as the wife of an eminent scientific man seeking herself in science the utmost consolation it could impart, to throw our house open to the students, as a kind of Scientific Exchange. Every Tuesday evening there was lemonade and a mixed · biscuit, for all who chose to partake of those refreshments. And there was science to an unlimited extent."

("Remarkable assemblies those, Miss Summerson," said Mr. Badger, reverentially. "There must have been great intellectual friction going on there, under the auspices of such a man!")

"And now," pursued Mrs. Badger, "now that I am the wife of my dear third, Mr. Badger, I still pursue those habits of observation which were formed during the lifetime of Captain Swosser, and adapted to new and unexpected purposes during the lifetime of Professor Dingo. I therefore have not come to the consideration of Mr. Carstone as a Neophyte. And yet I am very much of the opinion, my dears, that he has not chosen his profession advisedly."

Ada looked so very anxious now, that I asked Mrs. Badger on what she founded her supposition?

"My dear Miss Summerson," she replied, "on Mr. Carstone's character and conduct. He is of such a very easy disposition, that probably he would never think it worth while to mention how he really feels; but, he feels languid about the profession. He has not that positive interest in it which makes it his vocation. If he has any decided impression in reference to it, I should say it was that it is a tiresome pursuit. Now, this is not promising. Young men, like Mr. Allan Wood-court, who take it from a strong interest in all that it can do, will find some reward in it through a great deal of work for a very little money, and through years of considerable endurance and disappointment. But I am quite convinced that this would never be the case with Mr. Carstone."

"Does Mr. Badger think so too?" asked Ada, timidly.

"Why," said Mr. Badger, "to tell the truth, Miss Clare, this view of the matter had not occurred to me until Mrs. Badger mentioned it. But, when Mrs. Badger put it in that light, I naturally gave great consideration to it; knowing that Mrs. Badger's mind, in addition to its natural advantages, has had the rare advantage of being formed by two such very distinguished (I will even say illustrious) public men as Captain Swosser of the Royal Navy and Professor Dingo. The conclusion at which I have arrived is—in short, is Mrs. Badger's conclusion."

"It was a maxim of Captain Swosser's," said Mrs. Badger, "speaking in his figurative naval manner, that when you make pitch hot, you cannot make it too hot; and that if you only have to swab a plank, you should swab it as if Davy Jones were after you. It appears to me that this maxim is applicable to the medical, as well as to the nautical profession."

"To all professions," observed Mr. Badger. "It was admirably said by Captain Swosser. Beautifully said."

"People objected to Professor Dingo, when we were staying in the North of Devon, after our marriage," said Mrs. Badger, "that he disfigured some of the houses and other buildings, by chipping off fragments of those edifices with his little geological hammer. But the Professor replied, that he knew of no building, save the Temple of Science. The principle is the same, I think?"

"Precisely the same," said Mr. Badger. "Finely expressed! The Professor made the same remark, Miss Summerson, in his last illness; when (his mind wandering) he insisted on keeping his little hammer under the pillow, and chipping at the countenances of the attendants. The ruling passion!"

Although we could have dispensed with the length at which Mr. and Mrs. Badger pursued the conversation, we both felt that it was disinterested in them to express the opinion they had communicated to us, and that there was a great probability of its being sound. We agreed to say nothing to Mr. Jarndyce until we had spoken to Richard; and, as he was coming next evening, we resolved to have a very serious talk with him.

So, after he had been a little while with Ada, I went in and found my darling (as I knew she would be) prepared to consider him thoroughly right in whatever he said.

"And how do you get on, Richard?" said I. I always sat down on the other side of him. He made quite a sister of me.

"O! well enough!" said Richard.

"He can't say better than that, Esther, can he?" cried my pet, triumphantly.

I tried to look at my pet in the wisest manner, but of course I couldn't.

"Well enough?" I repeated.

"Yes," said Richard, "well enough. It's rather jog-trotty and humdrum. But it'll do as well as anything else!"

"O! my dear Richard!" I remonstrated.

"What's the matter?" said Richard.

"Do as well as anything else!"

"I don't think there's any harm in that, Dame Durden," said Ada, looking so confidingly at me across him; "because if it will do as well as anything else, it will do very well, I hope."

"O yes, I hope so," returned Richard, carelessly tossing his hair from his forehead. "After all, it may be only a kind of probation till our suit is—I forgot though. I am not to mention the suit. Forbidden ground! O yes, it's all right enough. Let us talk about something else."

Ada would have done so, willingly, and with a full persuasion that we had brought the question to a most satisfactory state. But I thought it would be useless to stop there, so I began again.

"No, but, Richard," said I, "and my dear Ada! Consider how important it is to you both, and what a point of honour it is towards your cousin, that you, Richard, should be quite in earnest without any reservation. I think we had better talk about this, really, Ada. It will be too late, very soon."

"O yes! We must talk about it!" said Ada. "But I think Richard is right."

What was the use of my trying to look wise, when she was so pretty, and so engaging, and so fond of him!

"Mr. and Mrs. Badger were here yesterday, Richard," said I, "and they seemed disposed to think that you had no great liking for the profession."

"Did they though?" said Richard. "O! Well, that rather alters the case, because I had no idea that they thought so, and I should not have liked to disappoint or inconvenience them. The fact is, I don't care much about it. But O, it don't matter! It'll do as well as anything else!"

"You hear him, Ada!" said I.

"The fact is," Richard proceeded, half thoughtfully and half jocosely, "it is not quite in my way. I don't take to it. And I get too much of Mrs. Bayham Badger's first and second."

"I am sure *that's* very natural!" cried Ada, quite delighted. "The very thing we both said yesterday, Esther!"

"Then," pursued Richard, "it's monotonous, and to-day is too like yesterday, and to-morrow is too like to-day."

"But I am afraid," said I, "this is an objection to all kinds of application—to life itself, except under some very uncommon circumstances."

"Do you think so?" returned Richard, still considering. "Perhaps! Ha! Why, then, you know," he added, suddenly becoming gay again, "we travel outside a circle, to what I said just now. It'll do as well as anything else. O, it's all right enough! Let us talk about something else."

But, even Ada, with her loving face—and if it had seemed innocent and trusting, when I first saw it in that memorable November fog, how much more did it seem now, when I knew her innocent and trusting heart—even Ada shook her head at this, and looked serious. So I thought it a good opportunity to hint to Richard, that if he were sometimes a little careless of himself, I was very sure he never meant to be careless of Ada; and that it was a part of his affectionate consideration for her, not to slight the importance of a step that might influence both their lives. This made him almost grave.

"My dear Mother Hubbard," he said, "that's the very thing! I have thought of that, several times; and have been quite angry with myself for meaning to be so much in earnest, and—somehow—not exactly being so. I don't know how it is; I seem to want something or other to stand by. Even you have no idea how fond I am of Ada (my darling cousin, I love you, so much!), but I don't settle down to constancy in other things. It's such uphill work, and it takes such a time!" said Richard, with an air of vexation.

"That may be," I suggested, "because you don't like what you have chosen."

"Poor fellow!" said Ada. "I am sure I don't wonder at it!"

No. It was not of the least use my trying to look wise. I tried again; but how could I do it, or how could it have any effect if I could, while Ada rested her clasped hands upon his shoulder, and while he looked at her tender blue eyes, and while they looked at him!

"You see, my precious girl," said Richard, passing her golden curls through and through his hand, "I was a little hasty, perhaps; or I misunderstood my own inclinations, perhaps. They don't seem to lie in that direction. I couldn't tell, till I tried. Now the question is, whether it's worth while to undo all that has been done. It seems like making a great disturbance about nothing particular."

"My dear Richard," said I, "how *can* you say about nothing particular?"

"I don't mean absolutely that," he returned. "I mean that it *may* be nothing particular, because I may never want it."

Both Ada and I urged, in reply, not only that it was decidedly worth while to undo what had been done, but that it must be undone. I then asked Richard whether he had thought of any more congenial pursuit?

"There, my dear Mrs. Shipton," said Richard, "you touch me home. Yes, I have. I have been thinking that the law is the boy for me."

"The law!" repeated Ada, as if she were afraid of the name.

"If I went into Kenge's office," said Richard, "and if I were placed under articles to Kenge, I should have my eye on the—hum!—the forbidden ground—and should be able to study it, and master it, and to satisfy myself that it was not neglected, and was being properly conducted. I should be able to look after Ada's interests, and my own interests (the same thing!); and I should peg away at Blackstone and all those fellows with the most tremendous ardour."

I was not by any means so sure of that; and I saw how his hankering after the vague things yet to come of those long-deferred hopes, cast a shade on Ada's face. But I thought it best to encourage him in any project of continuous exertion, and only advised him to be quite sure that his mind was made up now.

"My dear Minerva," said Richard, "I am as steady as you are. I made a mistake; we are all liable to mistakes; I won't do so any more, and I'll become such a lawyer as is not often seen. That is, you know," said Richard, relapsing into doubt, " if it really is worth while, after all, to make such a disturbance about nothing particular ! "

This led to our saying again, with a great deal of gravity, all that we had said already, and to our coming to much the same conclusion afterwards. But, we so strongly advised Richard to be frank and open with Mr. Jarndyce, without a moment's delay; and his disposition was naturally so opposed to concealment; that he sought him out at once (taking us with him), and made a full avowal. " Rick," said my guardian, after hearing him attentively, " we can retreat with honour, and we will. But we must be careful—for our cousin's sake, Rick, for our cousin's sake—that we make no more such mistakes. Therefore, in the matter of the law, we will have a good trial before we decide. We will look before we leap, and take plenty of time about it."

Richard's energy was of such an impatient and fitful kind, that he would have liked nothing better than to have gone to Mr. Kenge's office in that hour, and to have entered into articles with him on the spot. Submitting, however, with a good grace to the caution that we had shown to be so necessary, he contented himself with sitting down among us in his lightest spirits, and talking as if his one unvarying purpose in life from childhood had been that one which now held possession of him. My guardian was very kind and cordial with him, but rather grave ; enough so to cause Ada, when he had departed and we were going up-stairs to bed, to say :

" Cousin John, I hope you don't think the worse of Richard ? "

" No, my love," said he.

" Because it was very natural that Richard should be mistaken in such a difficult case. It is not uncommon."

" No, no, my love," said he. " Don't look unhappy."

" O, I am not unhappy, cousin John ! " said Ada, smiling cheerfully, with her hand upon his shoulder, where she had put it in bidding him good night. " But I should be a little so, if you thought at all the worse of Richard."

"My dear," said Mr. Jarndyce. "I should think the worse of him only if you were ever in the least unhappy through his means. I should be more disposed to quarrel with myself, even then, than with poor Rick, for I brought you together. But, tut, all this is nothing! He has time before him, and the race to run. *I* think the worse of him? Not I, my loving cousin! And not you, I swear!"

"No, indeed, cousin John," said Ada, "I am sure I could not—I am sure I would not—think any ill of Richard, if the whole world did. I could, and I would, think better of him then, than at any other time!"

So quietly and honestly she said it, with her hands upon his shoulders—both hands now—and looking up into his face, like the picture of Truth!

"I think," said my guardian, thoughtfully regarding her, "I think it must be somewhere written that the virtues of the mothers shall, occasionally, be visited on the children, as well as the sins of the fathers. Good night, my rosebud. Good night, little woman. Pleasant slumbers! Happy dreams!"

This was the first time I ever saw him follow Ada with his eyes, with something of a shadow on their benevolent expression. I well remembered the look with which he had contemplated her and Richard, when she was singing in the fire-light; it was but a very little while since he had watched them passing down the room in which the sun was shining, and away into the shade; but his glance was changed, and even the silent look of confidence in me which now followed it once more, was not quite so hopeful and untroubled as it had originally been.

Ada praised Richard more to me, that night, than ever she had praised him yet. She went to sleep with a little bracelet he had given her clasped upon her arm. I fancied she was dreaming of him when I kissed her cheek after she had slept an hour, and saw how tranquil and happy she looked.

For I was so little inclined to sleep, myself, that night, that I sat up working. It would not be worth mentioning for its own sake, but I was wakeful and rather low-spirited. I don't know why. At least I don't think I know why. At least, perhaps I do, but I don't think it matters.

At any rate, I made up my mind to be so dreadfully industrious that I would leave myself not a moment's leisure to be low-spirited. For I naturally said, "Esther! You to be low-spirited. *You!*" And it really was time to say so, for I—yes, I really did see myself in the glass, almost crying. "As if you had anything to make you unhappy, instead of everything to make you happy, you ungrateful heart!" said I.

If I could have made myself go to sleep, I would have done it directly; but, not being able to do that, I took out of my basket some ornamental work for our house (I mean Bleak House) that I was busy with at that time, and sat down to it with great determination. It was necessary to count all the stitches in that work, and I resolved to go on with it until I couldn't keep my eyes open, and then to go to bed.

I soon found myself very busy. But I had left some silk down-stairs in a work-table drawer in the temporary Growlery; and coming to a stop for want of it, I took my candle and went softly down to get it. To my great surprise, on going in, I found my guardian still there, and sitting looking at the ashes. He was lost in thought, his book lay unheeded by his side, his silvered iron-grey hair was scattered confusedly upon his forehead as though his hand had been wandering among it while his thoughts were elsewhere, and his face looked worn. Almost frightened by coming upon him so unexpectedly, I stood still for a moment; and should have retired without speaking, had he not, in again passing his hand abstractedly through his hair, seen me and started.

"Esther!"

I told him what I had come for.

"At work so late, my dear?"

"I am working late to-night," said I, "because I couldn't sleep, and wished to tire myself. But, dear Guardian, you are late too, and look weary. You have no trouble, I hope, to keep you waking?"

"None, little woman, that *you* would readily understand," said he.

He spoke in a regretful tone so new to me, that I inwardly repeated, as if that would help me to his meaning, "That *I* could readily understand!"

"Remain a moment, Esther," said he. "You were in my thoughts."

"I hope I was not the trouble, Guardian?"

He slightly waved his hand, and fell into his usual manner. The change was so remarkable, and he appeared to make it by dint of so much self-command, that I found myself again inwardly repeating, "None that *I* could understand!"

"Little woman," said my guardian, "I was thinking—that is, I have been thinking since I have been sitting here—that you ought to know, of your own history, all I know. It is very little. Next to nothing."

"Dear Guardian," I replied, "when you spoke to me before on that subject——"

"But since then," he gravely interposed, anticipating what I meant to say, "I have reflected that your having anything to ask me, and my having anything to tell you, are different considerations, Esther. It is perhaps my duty to impart to you the little I know."

"If you think so, Guardian, it is right."

"I think so," he returned, very gently, and kindly, and very distinctly. "My dear, I think so now. If any real disadvantage can attach to your position, in the mind of any man or woman worth a thought, it is right that you, at least, of all the world should not magnify it to yourself, by having vague impressions of its nature."

I sat down; and said, after a little effort to be as calm as I ought to be, "One of my earliest remembrances, Guardian, is of these words: 'Your mother, Esther, is your disgrace, and you were hers. The time will come, and soon enough, when you will understand this better, and will feel it too, as no one save a woman can.'" I had covered my face with my hands, in repeating the words; but I took them away now with a better kind of shame, I hope, and told him, that to him I owed the blessing that I had from my childhood to that hour never, never, never felt it. He put up his hand as if to stop me. I well knew that he was never to be thanked, and said no more.

"Nine years, my dear," he said, after thinking for a little while, "have passed since I received a letter from a lady living in seclusion, written with a stern passion and power that rendered it unlike all other letters I have ever read. It was written to me (as it told me in so many words), perhaps, because it was the writer's idiosyncrasy to put that trust in me: perhaps, because it was mine to justify it. It told me of a child, an orphan girl then twelve years old, in some such cruel words as those which live in your remembrance. It told me that the writer had bred her in secrecy from her birth, had blotted out all trace of her existence, and that if the writer were to die before the child became a woman, she would be left entirely friendless, nameless, and unknown. It asked me, to consider if I would, in that case, finish what the writer had begun?"

I listened in silence, and looked attentively at him.

"Your early recollection, my dear, will supply the gloomy medium through which all this was seen and expressed by the writer, and the distorted religion which clouded her mind with impressions of the need there was for the child to expiate an offence of which she was quite innocent. I felt concerned for the little creature, in her darkened life; and replied to the letter."

I took his hand and kissed it.

"It laid the injunction on me that I should never propose to see the writer, who had long been estranged from all

287

intercourse with the world, but who would see a confidential agent if I would appoint one. I accredited Mr. Kenge. The lady said, of her own accord, and not of his seeking, that her name was an assumed one. That she was, if there were any ties of blood in such a case, the child's aunt. That more than this she would never (and he was well persuaded of the steadfastness of her resolution), for any human consideration, disclose. My dear, I have told you all."

I held his hand for a little while in mine.

"I saw my ward oftener than she saw me," he added, cheerily making light of it, "and I always knew she was beloved, useful, and happy. She repays me twenty-thousand-fold, and twenty more to that, every hour in every day!"

"And oftener still," said I, "she blesses the Guardian who is a Father to her!"

At the word Father, I saw his former trouble come into his face. He subdued it as before, and it was gone in an instant; but, it had been there, and it had come so swiftly upon my words that I felt as if they had given him a shock. I again inwardly repeated, wondering, "That *I* could readily understand. None that *I* could readily understand!" No, it was true. I did not understand it. Not for many and many a day.

"Take a fatherly good night, my dear," said he, kissing me on the forehead, "and so to rest. These are late hours for working and thinking. You do that for all of us, all day long, little housekeeper!"

I neither worked nor thought, any more, that night. I opened my grateful heart to Heaven in thankfulness for its Providence to me and its care of me, and fell asleep.

We had a visitor next day. Mr. Allan Woodcourt came. He came to take leave of us; he had settled to do so beforehand. He was going to China, and to India, as a surgeon on board ship. He was to be away a long, long time.

I believe—at least I know—that he was not rich. All his

Caddy's Flowers

widowed mother could spare had been spent in qualifying
him for his profession. It was not lucrative to a young
practitioner, with very little influence in London; and
although he was, night and day, at the service of numbers
of poor people, and did wonders of gentleness and skill for
them, he gained very little by it in money. He was seven
years older than I. Not that I need mention it, for it
hardly seems to belong to anything.

I think—I mean, he told us—that he had been in practice
three or four years, and that if he could have hoped to
contend through three or four more, he would not have
made the voyage on which he was bound. But he had no
fortune or private means, and so he was going away. He
had been to see us several times altogether. We thought
it a pity he should go away. Because he was distinguished
in his art among those who knew it best, and some of the
greatest men belonging to it had a high opinion of him.

When he came to bid us good-bye, he brought his mother
with him for the first time. She was a pretty old lady, with
bright black eyes, but she seemed proud. She came from
Wales; and had had, a long time ago, an eminent person
for an ancestor, of the name of Morgan ap-Kerrig—of some
place that sounded like Gimlet—who was the most illustrious
person that ever was known, and all of whose relations were
a sort of Royal Family. He appeared to have passed his
life in always getting up into mountains, and fighting somebody; and a Bard whose name sounded like Crumlinwallinwer
had sung his praises, in a piece which was called, as nearly
as I could catch it, Mewlinnwillinwodd.

Mrs. Woodcourt, after expatiating to us on the fame of her
great kinsman, said that, no doubt, wherever her son Allan
went, he would remember his pedigree, and would on no
account form an alliance below it. She told him that there
were many handsome English ladies in India who went out
on speculation, and that there were some to be picked up
with property; but, that neither charms nor wealth would

suffice for the descendant from such a line, without birth: which must ever be the first consideration. She talked so much about birth, that, for a moment, I half fancied, and with pain—but, what an idle fancy to suppose that she could think or care what *mine* was!

Mr. Woodcourt seemed a little distressed by her prolixity, but he was too considerate to let her see it, and contrived delicately to bring the conversation round to making his acknowledgments to my guardian for his hospitality, and for the very happy hours—he called them the very happy hours—she had passed with us. The recollection of them, he said, would go with him wherever he went, and would be always treasured. And so we gave him our hands, one after another—at least, they did—and I did; and so he put his lips to Ada's hand—and to mine; and so he went away upon his long, long voyage!

I was very busy indeed, all day, and wrote directions home to the servants, and wrote notes for my guardian, and dusted his books and papers, and jingled my housekeeping keys a good deal, one way and another. I was still busy between the lights, singing and working by the window, when who should come in but Caddy, whom I had no expectation of seeing!

"Why, Caddy, my dear," said I, "what beautiful flowers!" She had such an exquisite little nosegay in her hand.

"Indeed, I think so, Esther," replied Caddy. "They are the loveliest I ever saw."

"Prince, my dear?" said I, in a whisper.

"No," answered Caddy, shaking her head, and holding them to me to smell. "Not Prince."

"Well, to be sure, Caddy!" said I. "You must have two lovers!"

"What? Do they look like that sort of thing?" said Caddy.

"Do they look like that sort of thing?" I repeated, pinching her cheek.

Caddy only laughed in return; and telling me that she had come for half-an-hour, at the expiration of which time Prince would be waiting for her at the corner, sat chatting with me and Ada in the window: every now and then, handing me the flowers again, or trying how they looked against my hair. At last, when she was going, she took me into my room, and put them in my dress.

" For me ? " said I, surprised.

" For you," said Caddy, with a kiss. " They were left behind by Somebody."

" Left behind ? "

" At poor Miss Flite's," said Caddy. " Somebody who has been very good to her, was hurrying away an hour ago, to join a ship, and left these flowers behind. No, no ! Don't take them out. Let the pretty little things lie here ! " said Caddy, adjusting them with a careful hand, " because I was present myself, and I ' shouldn't wonder if Somebody left them·on purpose ! "

" Do they look like that sort of thing ? " said Ada, coming laughingly behind me, and clasping me merrily round the waist. " O, yes, indeed they do, Dame Durden ! They look very, very like that sort of thing. O, very like it indeed, my dear ! "

CHAPTER XVIII

LADY DEDLOCK

It was not so easy as it had appeared at first, to arrange for Richard's making a trial of Mr. Kenge's office. Richard himself was the chief impediment. As soon as he had it in his power to leave Mr. Badger at any moment, he began to doubt whether he wanted to leave him at all. He didn't know, he said, really. It wasn't a bad profession; he couldn't assert that he disliked it; perhaps he liked it as well as he liked any other—suppose he gave it one more chance! Upon that, he shut himself up, for a few weeks, with some books and some bones, and seemed to acquire a considerable fund of information with great rapidity. His fervour, after lasting about a month, began to cool; and when it was quite cooled, began to grow warm again. His vacillations between law and medicine lasted so long, that Midsummer arrived before he finally separated from Mr. Badger, and entered on an experimental course of Messrs. Kenge and Carboy. For all his waywardness, he took great credit to himself as being determined to be in earnest " this time." And he was so good-natured throughout, and in such high spirits, and so fond of Ada, that it was very difficult indeed to be otherwise than pleased with him.

" As to Mr. Jarndyce," who, I may mention, found the wind much given, during this period, to stick in the east;

"As to Mr. Jarndyce," Richard would say to me, "he is the finest fellow in the world, Esther! I must be particularly careful, if it were only for his satisfaction, to take myself well to task, and have a regular wind-up of this business now."

The idea of his taking himself well to task, with that laughing face and heedless manner, and with a fancy that everything could catch and nothing could hold, was ludicrously anomalous. However, he told us between-whiles, that he was doing it to such an extent, that he wondered his hair didn't turn grey. His regular wind-up of the business was (as I have said), that he went to Mr. Kenge's about Midsummer, to try how he liked it.

All this time he was, in money affairs, what I have described him in a former illustration : generous, profuse, wildly careless, but fully persuaded that he was rather calculating and prudent. I happened to say to Ada, in his presence, half-jestingly, half-seriously, about the time of his going to Mr. Kenge's, that he needed to have Fortunatus's purse, he made so light of money, which he answered in this way :

"My jewel of a·dear cousin, you hear this old woman! Why does she say that? Because I gave eight pounds odd (or whatever it was) for a certain neat waistcoat and buttons a few days ago. Now, if I had stayed at Badger's I should have been obliged to spend twelve pounds at a blow, for some heart-breaking lecture-fees. So I make four pounds—in a lump—by the transaction!"

It was a question much discussed between him and my guardian what arrangements should be made for his living in London, while he experimented on the law; for, we had long since gone back to Bleak House, and it was too far off to admit of his coming there oftener than once a week. My guardian told me that if Richard were to settle down at Mr. Kenge's he would take some apartments or chambers, where we, too, could occasionally stay for a few days at a time;

293

"but, little woman," he added, rubbing his head very significantly, "he hasn't settled down there yet!" The discussions ended in our hiring for him, by the month, a neat little furnished lodging in a quiet old house near Queen Square. He immediately began to spend all the money he had, in buying the oddest little ornaments and luxuries for this lodging; and so often as Ada and I dissuaded him from making any purchase that he had in contemplation which was particularly unnecessary and expensive, he took credit for what it would have cost, and made out that to spend anything less on something else was to save the difference.

While these affairs were in abeyance, our visit to Mr. Boythorn's was postponed. At length, Richard having taken possession of his lodging, there was nothing to prevent our departure. He could have gone with us at that time of the year, very well; but he was in the full novelty of his new position, and was making most energetic attempts to unravel the mysteries of the fatal suit. Consequently we went without him; and my darling was delighted to praise him for being so busy.

We made a pleasant journey down into Lincolnshire by the coach, and had an entertaining companion in Mr. Skimpole. His furniture had been all cleared off, it appeared, by the person who took possession of it on his blue-eyed daughter's birthday; but, he seemed quite relieved to think that it was gone. Chairs and tables, he said, were wearisome objects; they were monotonous ideas, they had no variety of expression, they looked you out of countenance, and you looked them out of countenance. How pleasant, then, to be bound to no particular chairs and tables, but to sport like a butterfly among all the furniture on hire, and to flit from rosewood to mahogany, and from mahogany to walnut, and from this shape to that, as the humour took one!

"The oddity of the thing is," said Mr. Skimpole, with a quickened sense of the ludicrous, "that my chairs and tables were not paid for, and yet my landlord walks off with them as composedly as possible. Now, that seems droll! There is something grotesque in it. The chair and table merchant never engaged to pay my landlord my rent. Why should my landlord quarrel with *him?* If I have a pimple on my nose which is disagreeable to my landlord's peculiar ideas of beauty, my landlord has no business to scratch my chair and table merchant's nose, which has no pimple on it. His reasoning seems defective!"

"Well," said my guardian, good-humouredly, "it's pretty clear that whoever became security for those chairs and tables will have to pay for them."

"Exactly!" returned Mr. Skimpole. "That's the crowning point of unreason in the business! I said to my landlord, 'My good man, you are not aware that my excellent friend Jarndyce will have to pay for those things that you are sweeping off in that indelicate manner. Have you no consideration for *his* property?' He hadn't the least."

"And refused all proposals," said my guardian.

"Refused all proposals," returned Mr. Skimpole. "I made him business proposals. I had him into my room. I said, 'You are a man of business, I believe?' He replied, 'I am.' 'Very well,' said I, 'now let us be business-like. Here is an inkstand, here are pens and paper, here are wafers. What do you want? I have occupied your house for a considerable period, I believe to our mutual satisfaction until this unpleasant misunderstanding arose; let us be at once friendly and business-like. What do you want?' In reply to this, he made use of the figurative expression—which has something Eastern about it—that he had never seen the colour of my money. 'My amiable friend,' said I, 'I never have any money. I never know anything about money.' 'Well, sir,' said he, 'what do you offer if I give you time?' 'My good fellow,' said I, 'I have no idea of time; but, you say you are a man of business, and whatever you can suggest to be done in a business-like way with pen, and ink, and paper—and wafers —I am ready to do. Don't pay yourself at another man's expense (which is foolish), but be business-like!' However, he wouldn't be, and there was an end of it."

If these were some of the inconveniences of Mr. Skimpole's childhood, it assuredly possessed its advantages too. On the journey he had a very good appetite for such refreshment as came in our way (including a basket of choice hot-house peaches), but never thought of paying for anything. So when the coachman came round for his fee, he pleasantly asked him what he considered a very good fee indeed, now— a liberal one—and, on his replying, half-a-crown for a single passenger, said it was little enough too, all things considered; and left Mr. Jarndyce to give it him.

It was delightful weather. The green corn waved so beautifully, the larks sang so joyfully, the hedges were so full of wild flowers, the trees were so thickly out in leaf, the bean-fields, with a light wind blowing over them, filled the air with such a delicious fragrance! Late in the afternoon we came to the market-town where we were to alight from the coach—a dull little town, with a church-spire, and a market-place, and a market-cross, and one intensely sunny street, and a pond with an old horse cooling his legs in it, and a very few men sleepily lying and standing about in narrow little bits of shade. After the rustling of the leaves and the waving of the corn all along the road, it looked as still, as hot, as motionless a little town as England could produce.

At the inn, we found Mr. Boythorn on horseback, waiting with an open carriage, to take us to his house, which was a few miles off. He was overjoyed to see us, and dismounted with great alacrity.

"By Heaven!" said he, after giving us a courteous greeting, "this is a most infamous coach. It is the most flagrant example of an abominable public vehicle that ever encumbered the face of the earth. It is twenty-five minutes after its time, this afternoon. The coachman ought to be put to death!"

"*Is* he after his time?" said Mr. Skimpole, to whom he happened to address himself. "You know my infirmity."

"Twenty-five minutes! Twenty-six minutes!" replied Mr. Boythorn, referring to his watch. "With two ladies in the coach, this scoundrel has deliberately delayed his arrival six-and-twenty minutes. Deliberately! It is impossible that it can be accidental! But his father—and his uncle—were the most profligate coachmen that ever sat upon a box."

While he said this in tones of the greatest indignation, he handed us into the little phaeton with the utmost gentleness, and was all smiles and pleasure.

"I am sorry, ladies," he said, standing bare-headed at the carriage-door, when all was ready, "that I am obliged to conduct you nearly two miles out of the way. But, our direct road lies through Sir Leicester Dedlock's park; and, in that fellow's property, I have sworn never to set foot of mine, or horse's foot of mine, pending the present relations between us, while I breathe the breath of life!" And here, catching my guardian's eye, he broke into one of his tremendous laughs, which seemed to shake even the motion-less little market-town.

"Are the Dedlocks down here, Lawrence?" said my guardian as we drove along, and Mr. Boythorn trotted on the green turf by the roadside.

"Sir Arrogant Numskull is here," replied Mr. Boythorn. "Ha ha ha! Sir Arrogant is here, and I am glad to say, has been laid by the heels here. My Lady," in naming whom he always made a courtly gesture as if particularly to exclude her from any part in the quarrel, "is expected, I believe, daily. I am not in the least surprised that she postpones her appearance as long as possible. Whatever can have induced that transcendent woman to marry that effigy and figure-head of a baronet, is one of the most impenetrable mysteries that ever baffled human inquiry. Ha ha ha ha!"

"I suppose," said my guardian laughing, "we may set foot in the park while we are here? The prohibition does not extend to us, does it?"

"I can lay no prohibition on my guests," he said, bending

his head to Ada and me, with the smiling politeness which sat so gracefully upon him, "except in the matter of their departure. I am only sorry that I cannot have the happiness of being their escort about Chesney Wold, which is a very fine place! But, by the light of this summer day, Jarndyce, if you call upon the owner, while you stay with me, you are likely to have but a cool reception. He carries himself like an eight-day clock at all times; like one of a race of eight-day clocks in gorgeous cases that never go and never went —Ha ha ha!—but he will have some extra stiffness, I can promise you, for the friends of his friend and neighbour, Boythorn!"

"I shall not put him to the proof," said my guardian. "He is as indifferent to the honour of knowing me, I dare say, as I am to the honour of knowing him. The air of the grounds, and perhaps such a view of the house as any other sight-seer might get, are quite enough for me."

"Well!" said Mr. Boythorn, "I am glad of it on the whole. It's in better keeping. I am looked upon, about here, as a second Ajax defying the lightning. Ha ha ha ha! When I go into our little church on a Sunday, a considerable part of the inconsiderable congregation expect to see me drop, scorched and withered, on the pavement under the Dedlock displeasure. Ha ha ha ha! I have no doubt he is surprised that I don't. For he is, by Heaven! the most self-satisfied, and the shallowest, and the most coxcombical and utterly brainless ass!"

Our coming to the ridge of a hill we had been ascending, enabled our friend to point out Chesney Wold itself to us, and diverted his attention from its master.

It was a picturesque old house, in a fine park richly wooded. Among the trees, and not far from the residence, he pointed out the spire of the little church of which he had spoken. O, the solemn woods over which the light and shadow travelled swiftly, as if Heavenly wings were sweeping on benignant errands through the summer air; the smooth green slopes, the glittering water, the garden where the flowers were so symmetrically arranged in clusters of the richest colours, how beautiful they looked! The house, with gable and chimney, and tower, and turret, and dark doorway, and broad terrace-walk, twining among the balustrades of which, and lying heaped upon the vases, there was one great flush of roses, seemed scarcely real in its light solidity, and in the serene and peaceful hush that rested on all around it. To Ada and to me, that, above all, appeared the pervading influence. On everything, house, garden, terrace, green slopes, water, old oaks, fern, moss, woods again, and far away across the openings in the prospect, to the distance lying wide before us with a purple bloom upon it, there seemed to be such undisturbed repose.

When we came into the little village, and passed a small inn with the sign of the Dedlock Arms swinging over the road in front, Mr. Boythorn interchanged greetings with a young gentleman sitting on a bench outside the inn-door, who had some fishing-tackle lying beside him.

"That's the housekeeper's grandson, Mr. Rouncewell by name," said he; "and he is in love with a pretty girl up at the House. Lady Dedlock has taken a fancy to the pretty girl, and is going to keep her about her own fair person— an honour which my young friend himself does not at all appreciate. However, he can't marry just yet, even if his Rosebud were willing; so he is fain to make the best of it. In the meanwhile, he comes here pretty often, for a day or two at a time, to—fish. Ha ha ha ha!"

"Are he and the pretty girl engaged, Mr. Boythorn?" asked Ada.

"Why, my dear Miss Clare," he returned, "I think they may perhaps understand each other; but you will see them soon, I dare say, and I must learn from you on such a point —not you from me."

Ada blushed; and Mr. Boythorn, trotting forward on his comely grey horse, dismounted at his own door, and stood ready, with extended arm and uncovered head, to welcome us when we arrived.

He lived in a pretty house, formerly the Parsonage-house, with a lawn in front, a bright flower-garden at the side, and a well-stocked orchard and kitchen-garden in the rear, enclosed with a venerable wall that had of itself a ripened ruddy look. But, indeed, everything about the place wore an aspect of maturity and abundance. The old lime-tree walk was like green cloisters, the very shadows of the cherry-trees and apple-trees were heavy with fruit, the gooseberry-bushes were so laden that their branches arched and rested on the earth, the strawberries and raspberries grew in like profusion, and the peaches basked by the hundred on the wall. Tumbled about among the spread nets and the glass frames sparkling and winking in the sun, there were such heaps of drooping pods, and marrows, and cucumbers, that every foot of ground appeared a vegetable treasury, while the smell of sweet herbs and all kinds of wholesome growth (to say nothing of the neighbouring meadows where the hay was carrying) made the whole air a great nosegay. Such stillness and composure reigned within the orderly precincts of the old red wall, that even the feathers hung in garlands to scare the birds hardly stirred; and the wall had such a ripening influence that where, here and there high up, a disused nail and scrap of list still clung to it, it was easy to fancy that they had mellowed with the changing seasons, and that they had rusted and decayed according to the common fate.

The house, though a little disorderly in comparison with the garden, was a real old house, with settles in the chimney of the brick-floored kitchen, and great beams across the ceilings. On one side of it was the terrible piece of ground in dispute, where Mr. Boythorn maintained a sentry in a smock-frock, day and night, whose duty was supposed to be, in cases of aggression, immediately to ring a large bell hung up there for the purpose, to unchain a great bull-dog established in a kennel as his ally, and generally to deal destruction on the enemy. Not content with these precautions, Mr. Boythorn had himself composed and posted there, on painted boards to which his name was attached in large letters, the following solemn warnings: "Beware of the Bull-dog. He is most ferocious. Lawrence Boythorn." "The blunderbuss is loaded with slugs. Lawrence Boythorn." "Man-traps and spring-guns are set here at all times of the day and night. Lawrence Boythorn." "Take notice. That any person or persons audaciously presuming to trespass on this property, will be punished with the utmost severity of private chastisement, and prosecuted with the utmost rigour of the law. Lawrence Boythorn." These he showed us, from the drawing-room window, while his bird was hopping about his head; and he laughed, "Ha ha ha ha! Ha ha ha ha!" to that extent as he pointed them out, that I really thought he would have hurt himself.

"But this is taking a good deal of trouble," said Mr. Skimpole in his light way, "when you are not in earnest after all?"

"Not in earnest!" returned Mr. Boythorn, with unspeakable warmth. "Not in earnest! If I could have hoped to train him, I would have bought a Lion instead of that dog, and would have turned him loose upon the first intolerable robber who should dare to make an encroachment on my rights. Let Sir Leicester Dedlock consent to come out and decide this question by single combat, and I will meet him with any weapon known to mankind in any age or country. I am that much in earnest. Not more!"

We arrived at his house on a Saturday. On the Sunday morning we all set forth to walk to the little church in the park. Entering the park, almost immediately by the disputed ground, we pursued a pleasant footpath winding among the verdant turf and the beautiful trees, until it brought us to the church-porch.

The congregation was extremely small and quite a rustic one, with the exception of a large muster of servants from the House, some of whom were already in their seats, while others were yet dropping in. There were some stately footmen; and there was a perfect picture of an old coachman, who looked as if he were the official representative of all the pomps and vanities that had ever been put into his coach. There was a very pretty show of young women; and above them, the handsome old face and fine responsible portly figure of the housekeeper, towered pre-eminent. The pretty girl, of whom Mr. Boythorn had told us, was close by her. She was so very pretty, that I might have known her by her beauty, even if I had not seen how blushingly conscious she was of the eyes of the young fisherman, whom I discovered not far off. One face, and not an agreeable one, though it was handsome, seemed maliciously watchful of this pretty girl, and indeed of every one and everything there. It was a Frenchwoman's.

As the bell was yet ringing and the great people were not yet come, I had leisure to glance over the church, which smelt as earthy as a grave, and to think what a shady, ancient, solemn little church it was. The windows, heavily shaded by trees, admitted a subdued light that made the faces around me pale, and darkened the old brasses in the pavement, and the time and damp-worn monuments, and rendered the sunshine in the little porch, where a monotonous ringer was working at the bell, inestimably bright. But a stir in that direction, a gathering of reverential awe in the rustic faces, and a blandly-ferocious assumption on the part of Mr. Boythorn of being resolutely unconscious of somebody's existence, forewarned me that the great people were come, and that the service was going to begin.

"'Enter not into judgment with thy servant, O Lord, for in thy sight——'"

Shall I ever forget the rapid beating at my heart, occasioned by the look I met, as I stood up! Shall I ever forget the manner in which those handsome proud eyes seemed to spring out of their languor, and to hold mine! It was only a

The Little Church in the Park

moment before I cast mine down—released again, if I may
say so—on my book; but, I knew the beautiful face quite
well in that short space of time.

And, very strangely, there was something quickened within
me, associated with the lonely days at my godmother's; yes,
away even to the days when I had stood on tiptoe to dress
myself at my little glass, after dressing my doll. And this,
although I had never seen this lady's face before in all my
life—I was quite sure of it—absolutely certain.

It was easy to know that the ceremonious, gouty, grey-
haired gentleman, the only other occupant of the great pew,
was Sir Leicester Dedlock; and that the lady was Lady
Dedlock. But why her face should be, in a confused way,
like a broken glass to me, in which I saw scraps of old
remembrances; and why I should be so fluttered and troubled
(for I was still), by having casually met her eyes; I could not
think.

I felt it to be an unmeaning weakness in me, and tried to
overcome it by attending to the words I heard. Then,
very strangely, I seemed to hear them, not in the reader's
voice, but in the well-remembered voice of my godmother.
This made me think, did Lady Dedlock's face accidentally
resemble my godmother's? It might be that it did, a little;
but, the expression was so different, and the stern decision
which had worn into my godmother's face, like weather into
rocks, was so completely wanting in the face before me, that
it could not be that resemblance which had struck me.
Neither did I know the loftiness and haughtiness of Lady
Dedlock's face, at all, in any one. And yet I—I, little
Esther Summerson, the child who lived a life apart, and on
whose birthday there was no rejoicing—seemed to arise before
my own eyes, evoked out of the past by some power in this
fashionable lady, whom I not only entertained no fancy that
I had ever seen, but whom I perfectly well knew I had never
seen until that hour.

It made me tremble so, to be thrown into this unaccountable

303

agitation, that I was conscious of being distressed even by the observation of the French maid, though I knew she had been looking watchfully here, and there, and everywhere, from the moment of her coming into the church. By degrees, though very slowly, I at last overcame my strange emotion. After a long time, I looked towards Lady Dedlock again. It was while they were preparing to sing, before the sermon. She took no heed of me, and the beating at my heart was gone. Neither did it revive for more than a few moments, when she once or twice afterwards glanced at Ada or at me through her glass.

The service being concluded, Sir Leicester gave his arm with much taste and gallantry to Lady Dedlock—though he was obliged to walk by the help of a thick stick—and escorted her out of church to the pony carriage in which they had come. The servants then dispersed, and so did the congregation; whom Sir Leicester had contemplated all along (Mr. Skimpole said to Mr. Boythorn's infinite delight), as if he were a considerable landed proprietor in Heaven.

" He believes he is ! " said Mr. Boythorn. " He firmly believes it. So did his father, and his grandfather, and his great-grandfather ! "

" Do you know," pursued Mr. Skimpole, very unexpectedly, to Mr. Boythorn, " it's agreeable to me to see a man of that sort."

" *Is* it ! " said Mr. Boythorn.

" Say that he wants to patronise me," pursued Mr. Skimpole. " Very well ! I don't object."

" *I* do," said Mr. Boythorn, with great vigour.

" Do you really ? " returned Mr. Skimpole, in his easy light vein. " But, that's taking trouble, surely. And why should you take trouble ? Here am I, content to receive things childishly, as they fall out : and I never take trouble ! I come down here, for instance, and I find a mighty potentate, exacting homage. Very well ! I say, ' Mighty potentate, here *is* my homage ! It's easier to give it, than to withhold it.

Here it is. If you have anything of an agreeable nature to show me, I shall be happy to see it; if you have anything of an agreeable nature to give me, I shall be happy to accept it.' Mighty potentate replies in effect, 'This is a sensible fellow. I find him accord with my digestion and my bilious system. He doesn't impose upon me the necessity of rolling myself up like a hedgehog with my points outward. I expand, I open, I turn my silver lining outward like Milton's cloud, and it's more agreeable to both of us.' That's my view of such things: speaking as a child!"

"But suppose you went down somewhere else to-morrow," said Mr. Boythorn, "where there was the opposite of that fellow—or of this fellow—How then?"

"How then?" said Mr. Skimpole, with an appearance of the utmost simplicity and candour. "Just the same then! I should say, 'My esteemed. Boythorn'—to make you the personification of our imaginary friend—'my esteemed Boythorn, you object to the mighty potentate? Very good. So do I. I take it that my business in the social system is to be agreeable; I take it that everybody's business in the social system is to be agreeable. It's a system of harmony, in short. Therefore if you object, I object. Now, excellent Boythorn, let us go to dinner!'"

"But excellent Boythorn might say," returned our host, swelling and growing very red, "I'll be——"

"I understand," said Mr. Skimpole. "Very likely he would."

"——if I *will* go to dinner!" cried Mr. Boythorn, in a violent burst, and stopping to strike his stick upon the ground. "And he would probably add, 'Is there such a thing as principle, Mr. Harold Skimpole?'"

"To which Harold Skimpole would reply, you know," he returned in his gayest manner, and with his most ingenious smile, "'Upon my life I have not the least idea! I don't know what it is you call by that name, or where it is, or who possesses it. If you possess it, and find it comfortable,

I am quite delighted, and congratulate you heartily. But I know nothing about it, I assure you ; for I am a mere child, and I lay no claim to it, and I don't want it !' So, you see, excellent Boythorn and I would go to dinner after all !"

This was one of many little dialogues between them, which I always expected to end, and which I dare say would have ended under other circumstances, in some violent explosion on the part of our host. But he had so high a sense of his hospitable and responsible position as our entertainer, and my guardian laughed so sincerely at and with Mr. Skimpole, as a child who blew bubbles and broke them all day long, that matters never went beyond this point. Mr. Skimpole, who always seemed quite unconscious of having been on delicate ground, then betook himself to beginning some sketch in the park which he never finished, or to playing fragments of airs on the piano, or to singing scraps of songs, or to lying down on his back under a tree, and looking at the sky—which he couldn't help thinking, he said, was what he was meant for ; it suited him so exactly.

"Enterprise and effort," he would say to us (on his back), "are delightful to me. I believe I am truly cosmopolitan. I have the deepest sympathy with them. I lie in a shady place like this, and think of adventurous spirits going to the North Pole, or penetrating to the heart of the Torrid Zone, with admiration. Mercenary creatures ask, ' What is the use of a man's going to the North Pole ! What good does it do ?' I can't say ; but, for anything I *can* say, he may go for the purpose—though he don't know it—of employing my thoughts as I lie here. Take an extreme case. Take the case of the Slaves on American plantations. I dare say they are worked hard, I dare say they don't altogether like it, I dare say theirs is an unpleasant experience on the whole ; but, they people the landscape for me, they give it a poetry for me, and perhaps that is one of the pleasanter objects of their existence. I am very sensible of it, if it be, and I shouldn't wonder if it were !"

I always wondered on these occasions whether he ever thought of Mrs. Skimpole and the children, and in what point of view they presented themselves to his cosmopolitan mind. So far as I could understand, they rarely presented themselves at all.

The week had gone round to the Saturday following that beating of my heart in the church; and every day had been so bright and blue, that to ramble in the woods, and to see the light striking down among the transparent leaves, and sparkling in the beautiful interlacings of the shadows of the trees, while the birds poured out their songs, and the air was drowsy with the hum of insects, had been most delightful. We had one favourite spot, deep in moss and last year's leaves, where there were some felled trees from which the bark was all stripped off. Seated among these, we looked through a green vista supported by thousands of natural columns, the whitened stems of trees, upon a distant prospect made so radiant by its contrast with the shade in which we sat, and made so precious by the arched perspective through which we saw it, that it was like a glimpse of the better land. Upon the Saturday we sat here, Mr. Jarndyce, Ada, and I, until we heard thunder muttering in the distance, and felt the large rain-drops rattle through the leaves.

The weather had been all the week extremely sultry; but, the storm broke so suddenly—upon us, at least, in that sheltered spot—that before we reached the outskirts of the wood, the thunder and lightning were frequent, and the rain came plunging through the leaves, as if every drop were a great leaden bead. As it was not a time for standing among trees, we ran out of the wood, and up and down the moss-grown steps which crossed the plantation-fence like two broad-staved ladders placed back to back, and made for a keeper's lodge which was close at hand. We had often noticed the dark beauty of this lodge standing in a deep twilight of trees, and how the ivy clustered over it, and how there was a steep hollow near, where we had once seen the keeper's dog dive down into the fern as if it were water.

The lodge was so dark within, now the sky was over-cast, that we only clearly saw the man who came to the door when we took shelter there, and put two chairs for Ada and me. The lattice-windows were all thrown open, and we sat, just within the doorway, watching the storm. It was grand to see how the wind awoke, and bent the trees, and drove the rain before it like a cloud of smoke; and to hear the solemn thunder, and to see the lightning; and while thinking with awe of the tremendous powers by which our little lives are encompassed, to consider how beneficent they are, and how upon the smallest flower and leaf there was already a freshness poured from all this seeming rage, which seemed to make creation new again.

" Is it not dangerous to sit in so exposed a place?"

" O no, Esther dear!" said Ada, quietly.

Ada said it to me; but, *I* had not spoken.

The beating of my heart came back again. I had never heard the voice, as I had never seen the face, but it affected me in the same strange way. Again, in a moment, there arose before my mind innumerable pictures of myself.

Lady Dedlock had taken shelter in the lodge, before our arrival there, and had come out of the gloom within. She stood behind my chair, with her hand upon it. I saw her with her hand close to my shoulder, when I turned my head.

"I have frightened you?" she said.

No. It was not fright. Why should I be frightened!

" I believe," said Lady Dedlock to my guardian, " I have the pleasure of speaking to Mr. Jarndyce."

" Your remembrance does me more honour than I had supposed it would, Lady Dedlock," he returned.

" I recognised you in church on Sunday. I am sorry that any local disputes of Sir Leicester's—they are not of his seeking, however, I believe—should render it a matter of some absurd difficulty to show you any attention here."

" I am aware of the circumstances," returned my guardian with a smile, " and am sufficiently obliged."

She had given him her hand, in an indifferent way that seemed habitual to her, and spoke in a correspondingly indifferent manner, though in a very pleasant voice. She was as graceful as she was beautiful; perfectly self-possessed; and had the air, I thought, of being able to attract and interest any one, if she had thought it worth her while. The keeper had brought her a chair, on which she sat, in the middle of the porch between us.

"Is the young gentleman disposed of, whom you wrote to Sir Leicester about, and whose wishes Sir Leicester was sorry not to have it in his power to advance in any way?" she said, over her shoulder, to my guardian.

"I hope so," said he.

She seemed to respect him, and even to wish to conciliate him. There was something very winning in her haughty manner; and it became more familiar—I was going to say more easy, but that could hardly be—as she spoke to him over her shoulder.

"I presume this is your other ward, Miss Clare?"

He presented Ada, in form.

"You will lose the disinterested part of your Don Quixote character," said Lady Dedlock to Mr. Jarndyce, over her shoulder again, "if you only redress the wrongs of beauty like this. But present me," and she turned full upon me, "to this young lady too!"

"Miss Summerson really is my ward," said Mr. Jarndyce. "I am responsible to no Lord Chancellor in her case."

"Has Miss Summerson lost both her parents?" said my Lady.

"Yes."

"She is very fortunate in her guardian."

Lady Dedlock looked at me, and I looked at her, and said I was indeed. All at once she turned from me with a hasty air, almost expressive of displeasure or dislike, and spoke to him over her shoulder again.

"Ages have passed since we were in the habit of meeting, Mr. Jarndyce."

"A long time. At least I thought it was a long time, until I saw you last Sunday," he returned.

"What! Even you are a courtier, or think it necessary to become one to me!" she said, with some disdain. "I have achieved that reputation, I suppose."

"You have achieved so much, Lady Dedlock," said my guardian, "that you pay some little penalty, I dare say. But none to me."

"So much!" she repeated, slightly laughing. "Yes!"

With her air of superiority, and power, and fascination, and I know not what, she seemed to regard Ada and me as little more than children. So, as she slightly laughed, and afterwards sat looking at the rain, she was as self-possessed, and as free to occupy herself with her own thoughts, as if she had been alone.

"I think you knew my sister, when we were abroad together, better than you knew me?" she said, looking at him again.

"Yes, we happened to meet oftener," he returned.

"We went our several ways," said Lady Dedlock, "and had little in common even before we agreed to differ. It is to be regretted, I suppose, but it could not be helped."

Lady Dedlock again sat looking at the rain. The storm soon began to pass upon its way. The shower greatly abated, the lightning ceased, the thunder rolled among the distant hills, and the sun began to glisten on the wet leaves and the falling rain. As we sat there, silently, we saw a little pony phaeton coming towards us at a merry pace.

"The messenger is coming back, my Lady," said the keeper, "with the carriage."

As it drove up, we saw that there were two people inside. There alighted from it, with some cloaks and wrappers, first the Frenchwoman whom I had seen in church, and secondly the pretty girl; the Frenchwoman, with a defiant confidence; the pretty girl confused and hesitating.

"What now?" said Lady Dedlock. "Two!"

310

"I am your maid, my Lady, at the present," said the Frenchwoman. "The message was for the attendant."

"I was afraid you might mean me, my Lady," said the pretty girl.

"I did mean you, child," replied her mistress, calmly. "Put that shawl on me."

She slightly stooped her shoulders to receive it, and the pretty girl lightly dropped it in its place. The French-woman stood unnoticed, looking on with her lips very tightly set.

"I am sorry," said Lady Dedlock to Mr. Jarndyce, "that we are not likely to renew our former acquaintance. You will allow me to send the carriage back for your two wards. It shall be here directly."

But, as he would on no account accept this offer, she took a graceful leave of Ada—none of me—and put her hand upon his proffered arm, and got into the carriage; which was a little, low, park carriage, with a hood.

"Come in, child," she said to the pretty girl, "I shall want you. Go on!"

The carriage rolled away; and the Frenchwoman, with the wrappers she had brought hanging over her arm, remained standing where she had alighted.

I suppose there is nothing Pride can so little bear with as Pride itself, and that she was punished for her imperious manner. Her retaliation was the most singular I could have imagined. She remained perfectly still until the carriage had turned into the drive, and then, without the least discomposure of countenance, slipped off her shoes, left them on the ground, and walked deliberately in the same direction, through the wettest of the wet grass.

"Is that young woman mad?" said my guardian.

"O no, sir!" said the keeper, who, with his wife, was looking after her. "Hortense is not one of that sort. She has as good a head-piece as the best. But she's mortal high and passionate—powerful high and passionate; and what with having notice to leave, and having others put above her, she don't take kindly to it."

"But why should she walk shoeless, through all that water?" said my guardian.

"Why, indeed, sir, unless it is to cool her down!" said the man.

"Or unless she fancies it's blood," said the woman. "She'd as soon walk through that as anything else, I think, when her own's up!"

We passed not far from the House, a few minutes afterwards. Peaceful as it had looked when we first saw it, it looked even more so now, with a diamond spray glittering all about it, a light wind blowing, the birds no longer hushed but singing strongly, everything refreshed by the late rain, and the little carriage shining at the doorway like a fairy carriage made of silver. Still, very steadfastly and quietly walking towards it, a peaceful figure too in the landscape, went Mademoiselle Hortense, shoeless, through the wet grass.

CHAPTER XIX

It is the long vacation in the regions of Chancery Lane. The good ships Law and Equity, those teak-built, copper-bottomed, iron-fastened, brazen-faced, and not by any means fast-sailing Clippers, are laid up in ordinary. The Flying Dutchman, with a crew of ghostly clients imploring all whom they may encounter to peruse their papers, has drifted, for the time being, Heaven knows where. The Courts are all shut up; the public offices lie in a hot sleep; Westminster Hall itself is a shady solitude where nightingales might sing, and a tenderer class of suitors than is usually found there, walk.

The Temple, Chancery Lane, Serjeants' Inn, and Lincoln's Inn even unto the Fields, are like tidal harbours at low water; where stranded proceedings, offices at anchor, idle clerks lounging on lop-sided stools that will not recover their perpendicular until the current of Term sets in, lie high and dry upon the ooze of the long vacation. Outer doors of chambers are shut up by the score, messages and parcels are to be left at the Porter's Lodge by the bushel. A crop of grass would grow in the chinks of the stone pavement outside Lincoln's Inn Hall, but that the ticket-porters, who have nothing to do beyond sitting in the shade there, with their white aprons over their heads to keep the flies off, grub it up and eat it thoughtfully.

There is only one Judge in town. Even he only comes twice a-week to sit in chambers. If the country folks of those assize towns on his circuit could see him now! No full-bottomed wig, no red petticoats, no fur, no javelin-men, no white wands. Merely a close-shaved gentleman in white trousers and a white hat, with sea-bronze on the judicial countenance, and a strip of bark peeled by the solar rays from the judicial nose, who calls in at the shell-fish shop as he comes along, and drinks iced ginger-beer!

The bar of England is scattered over the face of the earth. How England can get on through four long summer months without its bar—which is its acknowledged refuge in adversity, and its only legitimate triumph in prosperity—is beside the question; assuredly that shield and buckler of Britannia are not in present wear. The learned gentleman who is always so tremendously indignant at the unprecedented outrage committed on the feelings of his client by the opposite party, that he never seems likely to recover it, is doing infinitely better than might be expected, in Switzerland. The learned gentleman who does the withering business, and who blights all opponents with his gloomy sarcasm, is as merry as a grig at a French watering-place. The learned gentleman who weeps by the pint on the smallest provocation, has not shed a tear these six weeks. The very learned gentleman who has cooled the natural heat of his gingery complexion in pools and fountains of law, until he has become great in knotty arguments for term-time, when he poses the drowsy Bench with legal "chaff," inexplicable to the uninitiated and to most of the initiated too, is roaming, with a characteristic delight in aridity and dust, about Constantinople. Other dispersed fragments of the same great Palladium are to be found on the canals of Venice, at the second cataract of the Nile, in the baths of Germany, and sprinkled on the sea-sand all over the English coast. Scarcely one is to be encountered in the deserted region of Chancery Lane. If such a lonely member of the bar do flit across the waste, and come upon a prowling suitor who is unable to leave off haunting the scenes of his anxiety, they frighten one another, and retreat into opposite shades.

It is the hottest long vacation known for many years. All the young clerks are madly in love, and, according to their various degrees, pine for bliss with the beloved object, at Margate, Ramsgate, or Gravesend. All the middle-aged clerks think their families too large. All the unowned dogs who stray into the Inns of Court, and pant about staircases and other dry places, seeking water, give short howls of aggravation. All the blind men's dogs in the streets draw their masters against pumps, or trip them over buckets. A shop with a sun-blind, and a watered pavement, and a bowl of gold and silver fish in the window, is a sanctuary. Temple Bar gets so hot, that it is, to the adjacent Strand and Fleet Street, what a heater is in an urn, and keeps them simmering all night.

There are offices about the Inns of Court in which a man might be cool, if any coolness were worth purchasing at such a price in dulness; but, the little thoroughfares immediately outside those retirements seem to blaze. In Mr. Krook's court, it is so hot that the people turn their houses inside out, and sit in chairs upon the pavement—Mr. Krook included, who there pursues his studies, with his cat (who never is too hot) by his side. The Sol's Arms has discontinued the harmonic meetings for the season, and Little Swills is engaged at the Pastoral Gardens down the river, where he comes out in quite an innocent manner, and sings comic ditties of a juvenile complexion, calculated (as the bill says) not to wound the feelings of the most fastidious mind.

Over all the legal neighbourhood, there hangs, like some great veil of rust, or gigantic cobweb, the idleness and pensiveness of the long vacation. Mr. Snagsby, law-stationer of Cook's Court, Cursitor Street, is sensible of the influence; not only in his mind as a sympathetic and contemplative man, but also in his business as a law-stationer aforesaid. He

315

has more leisure for musing in Staple Inn and in the Rolls Yard, during the long vacation, than at other seasons; and he says to the two 'prentices, what a thing it is in such hot weather to think that you live in an island, with the sea a-rolling and a-bowling right round you.

Guster is busy in the little drawing-room, on this present afternoon in the long vacation, when Mr. and Mrs. Snagsby have it in contemplation to receive company. The expected guests are rather select than numerous, being Mr. and Mrs. Chadband, and no more. From Mr. Chadband's being much given to describe himself, both verbally and in writing, as a vessel, he is occasionally mistaken by strangers for a gentleman connected with navigation; but, he is, as he expresses it, "in the ministry." Mr. Chadband is attached to no particular denomination; and is considered by his persecutors to have nothing so very remarkable to say on the greatest of subjects as to render his volunteering, on his own account, at all incumbent on his conscience; but, he has his followers, and Mrs. Snagsby is of the number. Mrs. Snagsby has but recently taken a passage upward by the vessel, Chadband; and her attention was attracted to that Bark A 1, when she was something flushed by the hot weather.

"My little woman," says Mr. Snagsby to the sparrows in Staple Inn, "likes to have her religion rather sharp, you see!"

So, Guster, much impressed by regarding herself for the time as the handmaid of Chadband, whom she knows to be endowed with the gift of holding forth for four hours at a stretch, prepares the little drawing-room for tea. All the furniture is shaken and dusted, the portraits of Mr. and Mrs. Snagsby are touched up with a wet cloth, the best tea-service is set forth, and there is excellent provision made of dainty new bread, crusty twists, cool fresh butter, thin slices of ham, tongue and German sausage, and delicate little rows of anchovies nestling in parsley; not to mention new-laid eggs, to be brought up warm in a napkin, and hot buttered toast.

MR. AND MRS. CHADBAND

For, Chadband is rather a consuming vessel—the persecutors say a gorging vessel; and can wield such weapons of the flesh as a knife and fork, remarkably well.

Mr. Snagsby in his best coat, looking at all the preparations when they are completed, and coughing his cough of deference behind his hand, says to Mrs. Snagsby, "At what time did you expect Mr. and Mrs. Chadband, my love?"

"At six," says Mrs. Snagsby.

Mr. Snagsby observes in a mild and casual way, that "it's gone that."

"Perhaps you'd like to begin without them," is Mrs. Snagsby's reproachful remark.

Mr. Snagsby does look as if he would like it very much, but he says, with his cough of mildness, "No, my dear, no. I merely named the time."

"What's time," says Mrs. Snagsby, "to eternity?"

"Very true, my dear," says Mr. Snagsby. "Only when a person lays in victuals for tea, a person does it with a view—perhaps—more to time. And when a time is named for having tea, it's better to come up to it."

"To come up to it!" Mrs. Snagsby repeats with severity. "Up to it! As if Mr. Chadband was a fighter!"

"Not at all, my dear," says Mr. Snagsby.

Here, Guster, who had been looking out of the bedroom window, comes rustling and scratching down the little staircase like a popular ghost, and, falling flushed into the drawing-room, announces that Mr. and Mrs. Chadband have appeared in the court. The bell at the inner door in the passage immediately thereafter tinkling, she is admonished by Mrs. Snagsby, on pain of instant reconsignment to her patron saint, not to omit the ceremony of announcement. Much discomposed in her nerves (which were previously in the best order) by this threat, she so fearfully mutilates that point of state as to announce "Mr. and Mrs. Cheeseming, least which, Imeantersay, whatsername!" and retires conscience-stricken from the presence.

Mr. Chadband is a large yellow man, with a fat smile, and a general appearance of having a good deal of train oil in his system. Mrs. Chadband is a stern, severe-looking, silent woman. Mr. Chadband moves softly and cumbrously, not unlike a bear who has been taught to walk upright. He is very much embarrassed about the arms, as if they were inconvenient to him, and he wanted to grovel; is very much in a perspiration about the head; and never speaks without first putting up his great hand, as delivering a token to his hearers that he is going to edify them.

" My friends," says Mr. Chadband, " Peace be on this house! On the master thereof, on the mistress thereof, on the young maidens, and on the young men! My friends, why do I wish for peace? What is peace? Is it war? No. Is it strife? No. Is it lovely, and gentle, and beautiful, and pleasant, and serene, and joyful? O yes! Therefore, my friends, I wish for peace, upon you and upon yours."

In consequence of Mrs. Snagsby looking deeply edified, Mr. Snagsby thinks it expedient on the whole to say Amen, which is well received.

" Now, my friends," proceeds Mr. Chadband, " since I am upon this theme—— "

Guster presents herself. Mrs. Snagsby, in a spectral bass voice, and without removing her eyes from Chadband, says, with dread distinctness, " Go away! "

" Now, my friends," says Chadband, " since I am upon this theme, and in my lowly path improving it—— "

Guster is heard unaccountably to murmur " one thousing seven hundred and eighty-two." The spectral voice repeats more solemnly, " Go away! "

" Now, my friends," says Mr. Chadband, " we will inquire in a spirit of love—— "

Still Guster reiterates " one thousing seven hundred and eighty-two."

Mr. Chadband, pausing with the resignation of a man accustomed to be persecuted, and languidly folding up his chin into his fat smile, says, "Let us hear the maiden! Speak, maiden!"

"One thousing seven hundred and eighty-two, if you please, sir. Which he wish to know what the shilling ware for," says Guster, breathless.

"For?" returns Mrs. Chadband. "For his fare!"

Guster replies that "he insistes on one and eightpence, or on summonsizzing the party." Mrs. Snagsby and Mrs. Chadband are proceeding to grow shrill in indignation, when Mr. Chadband quiets the tumult by lifting up his hand.

"My friends," says he, "I remember a duty unfulfilled yesterday. It is right that I should be chastened in some penalty. I ought not to murmur. Rachael, pay the eightpence!"

While Mrs. Snagsby, drawing her breath, looks hard at Mr. Snagsby, as who should· say, "You hear this Apostle!" and while.Mr. Chadband glows with humility and train oil, Mrs. Chadband pays the money. It is Mr. Chadband's habit —it is the head and front of his pretensions indeed—to keep this sort of debtor and creditor account in the smallest items, and to post it publicly on the most trivial occasions.

"My friends," says Chadband, "eightpence is not much; it might justly have been one and fourpence; it might justly have been half-a-crown. O let us be joyful, joyful! O let us be joyful!"

With which remark, which appears from its sound to be an extract in verse, Mr. Chadband stalks to the table, and, before taking a chair, lifts up his admonitory hand.

"My friends," says he, "what is this which we now behold as being spread before us? Refreshment. Do we need refreshment then, my friends? We do. And why do we need refreshment, my friends? Because we are but mortal, because we are but sinful, because we are but of the earth, because we are not of the air. Can we fly, my friends? We cannot. Why can we not fly, my friends?"

Mr. Snagsby, presuming on the success of his last point,

ventures to observe in a cheerful and rather knowing tone, "No wings." But, is immediately frowned down by Mrs. Snagsby.

"I say, my friends," pursues Mr. Chadband, utterly rejecting and obliterating Mr. Snagsby's suggestion, "why can we not fly? Is it because we are calculated to walk? It is. Could we walk, my friends, without strength? We could not. What should we do without strength, my friends? Our legs would refuse to bear us, our knees would double up, our ankles would turn over, and we should come to the ground. Then from whence, my friends, in a human point of view, do we derive the strength that is necessary to our limbs? Is it," says Chadband, glancing over the table, "from bread in various forms, from butter which is churned from the milk which is yielded untoe us by the cow, from the eggs which are laid by the fowl, from ham, from tongue, from sausage, and from such like? It is. Then let us partake of the good things which are set before us!"

The persecutors denied that there was any particular gift in Mr. Chadband's piling verbose flights of stairs, one upon another, after this fashion. But this can only be received as a proof of their determination to persecute, since it must be within everybody's experience, that the Chadband style of oratory is widely received and much admired.

Mr. Chadband, however, having concluded for the present, sits down at Mr. Snagsby's table, and lays about him prodigiously. The conversion of nutriment of any sort into oil of the quality already mentioned, appears to be a process so inseparable from the constitution of this exemplary vessel, that in beginning to eat and drink, he may be described as always becoming a kind of considerable Oil Mills, or other large factory for the production of that article on a wholesale scale. On the present evening of the long vacation, in Cook's Court, Cursitor Street, he does such a powerful stroke of business, that the warehouse appears to be quite full when the works cease.

At this period of the entertainment, Guster, who has never recovered her first failure, but has neglected no possible or impossible means of bringing the establishment and herself into contempt—among which may be briefly enumerated her unexpectedly performing clashing military music on Mr. Chadband's head with plates, and afterwards crowning that gentleman with muffins—at which period of the entertainment, Guster whispers Mr. Snagsby that he is wanted.

"And being wanted in the—not to put too fine a point upon it—in the shop!" says Mr. Snagsby rising, "perhaps this good company will excuse me for half a minute."

Mr. Snagsby descends, and finds the two 'prentices intently contemplating a police constable, who holds a ragged boy by the arm.

"Why, bless my heart," says Mr. Snagsby, "what's the matter!"

"This boy," says the constable, "although he's repeatedly told to, won't move on——"

"I'm always a-moving on, sir," cries the boy, wiping away his grimy tears with his arm. "I've always been a-moving and a-moving on, ever since I was born. Where can I possible move to, sir, more nor I do move!"

"He won't move on," says the constable, calmly, with a slight professional hitch of his neck involving its better settlement in his stiff stock, "although he has been repeatedly cautioned, and therefore I am obliged to take him into custody. He's as obstinate a young gonoph as I know. He won't move on."

"O my eye! Where can I move to!" cries the boy, clutching quite desperately at his hair, and beating his bare feet upon the floor of Mr. Snagsby's passage.

"Don't you come none of that, or I shall make blessed short work of you!" says the constable, giving him a passionless shake. "My instructions are, that you are to move on. I have told you so five hundred times."

"But where?" cries the boy.

"Well! Really, constable, you know," says Mr. Snagsby wistfully, and coughing behind his hand his cough of great perplexity and doubt; "really that does seem a question. Where, you know?"

"My instructions don't go to that," replies the constable. "My instructions are that this boy is to move on."

Do you hear, Jo? It is nothing to you or to any one else, that the great lights of the parliamentary sky have failed for some few years, in this business, to set you the example of moving on. The one grand recipe remains for you—the profound philosophical prescription—the be-all and the end-all of your strange existence upon earth. Move on! You are by no means to move off, Jo, for the great lights can't at all agree about that. Move on!

Mr. Snagsby says nothing to this effect; says nothing at all, indeed; but coughs his forlornest cough, expressive of no thoroughfare in any direction. By this time Mr. and Mrs. Chadband, and Mrs. Snagsby, hearing the altercation, have appeared upon the stairs. Guster having never left the end of the passage, the whole household are assembled.

"The simple question is, sir," says the constable, "whether you know this boy. He says you do."

Mrs. Snagsby, from her elevation, instantly cries out, "No he don't!"

"My lit-tle woman!" says Mr. Snagsby, looking up the staircase. "My love, permit me! Pray have a moment's patience, my dear. I do know something of this lad, and in what I know of him, I can't say that there's any harm; perhaps on the contrary, constable." To whom the law-stationer relates his Joful and woful experience, suppressing the half-crown fact.

"Well!" says the constable, "so far, it seems, he had grounds for what he said. When I took him into custody up in Holborn, he said you knew him. Upon that, a young man who was in the crowd said he was acquainted with you, and you were a respectable housekeeper, and if I'd call and make the inquiry, he'd appear. The young man don't seem inclined to keep his word, but—Oh! Here *is* the young man!"

Enter Mr. Guppy, who nods to Mr. Snagsby, and touches his hat with the chivalry of clerkship to the ladies on the stairs.

"I was strolling away from the office just now, when I found this row going on," says Mr. Guppy to the law-stationer; "and as your name was mentioned, I thought it was right the thing should be looked into."

"It was very good-natured of you, sir," says Mr. Snagsby, "and I am obliged to you." And Mr. Snagsby again relates his experience, again suppressing the half-crown fact.

"Now, I know where you live," says the constable, then, to Jo. "You live down in Tom-all-Alone's. That's a nice innocent place to live in, ain't it?"

"I can't go and live in no nicer place, sir," replies Jo. "They wouldn't have nothink to say to me if I wos to go to a nice innocent place fur to live. Who ud go and let a nice innocent lodging to such a reg'lar one as me!"

"You are very poor, ain't you?" says the constable.

"Yes, I am indeed, sir, wery poor in gin'ral," replies Jo.

"I leave you to judge now! I shook these two half-crowns out of him," says the constable, producing them to the company, "in only putting my hand upon him!"

"They're wot's left, Mr. Snagsby," says Jo, "out of a sov'ring as wos give me by a lady in a wale as sed she wos a servant and as come to my crossin one night and asked to be showd this 'ere ouse and the ouse wot him as you giv the writin to died at, and the berrin-ground wot he's berrid in. She ses to me she ses 'are you the boy at the Inkwhich?' she ses. I ses 'yes' I ses. She ses to me she ses 'can you show me all them places?' I ses 'yes I can' I ses. And she ses to me 'do it' and I dun it and she giv me a sov'ring and hooked it. And I an't had much of the sov'ring neither," says Jo, with dirty tears, "fur I had to pay five bob, down in Tom-all-Alone's, afore they'd square it fur to give me change, and then a young man he thieved another five while I was asleep and another boy he thieved ninepence and the landlord he stood drains round with a lot more on it."

"You don't expect anybody to believe this, about the lady and the sovereign, do you?" says the constable, eyeing him aside with ineffable disdain.

"I don't know as I do, sir," replies Jo. "I don't expect nothink at all, sir, much, but that's the true hist'ry on it."

"You see what he is!" the constable observes to the audience. "Well, Mr. Snagsby, if I don't lock him up this time, will you engage for his moving on?"

"No!" cries Mrs. Snagsby from the stairs.

"My little woman!" pleads her husband. "Constable, I have no doubt he'll move on. You know you really must do it," says Mr. Snagsby.

"I'm everyways agreeable, sir," says the hapless Jo.

"Do it, then," observes the constable. "You know what you have got to do. Do it! And recollect you won't get off so easy next time. Catch hold of your money. Now, the sooner you're five mile off, the better for all parties."

With this farewell hint, and pointing generally to the setting sun, as a likely place to move on to, the constable bids his auditors good afternoon; and makes the echoes of Cook's Court perform slow music for him as he walks away on the shady side, carrying his iron-bound hat in his hand for a little ventilation.

Now, Jo's improbable story concerning the lady and the sovereign has awakened more or less the curiosity of all the company. Mr. Guppy, who has an inquiring mind in matters of evidence, and who has been suffering severely from the lassitude of the long vacation, takes that interest in the case, that he enters on a regular cross-examination of the witness, which is found so interesting by the ladies that Mrs. Snagsby politely invites him to step up-stairs, and drink a cup of tea, if he will excuse the disarranged state of the tea-table, consequent on their previous exertions. Mr. Guppy yielding his assent to this proposal, Jo is requested to follow into the drawing-room doorway, where Mr. Guppy takes him in hand as a witness, patting him into this shape, that shape, and the other shape, like a butterman dealing with so much butter, and worrying him according to the best models. Nor is the examination unlike many such model displays, both in respect of its eliciting nothing, and of its being lengthy; for, Mr. Guppy is sensible of his talent, and Mrs. Snagsby feels, not only that it gratifies her inquisitive disposition, but that it lifts her husband's establishment higher up in the law. During the progress of this keen encounter, the vessel Chadband, being merely engaged in the oil trade, gets aground, and waits to be floated off.

"Well!" says Mr. Guppy, "either this boy sticks to it like cobbler's-wax, or there is something out of the common here that beats anything that ever came into my way at Kenge and Carboy's."

Mrs. Chadband whispers Mrs. Snagsby, who exclaims, "You don't say so!"

"For years!" replies Mrs. Chadband.

"Has known Kenge and Carboy's office for years," Mrs. Snagsby triumphantly explains to Mr. Guppy. "Mrs. Chadband—this gentleman's wife—Reverend Mr. Chadband."

"Oh, indeed!" says Mr. Guppy.

"Before I married my present husband," says Mrs. Chadband.

"Was you a party in anything, ma'am?" says Mr. Guppy, transferring his cross-examination.

"No."

"*Not* a party in anything, ma'am?" says Mr. Guppy.

Mrs. Chadband shakes her head.

"Perhaps you were acquainted with somebody who was a party in something, ma'am?" says Mr. Guppy, who likes nothing better than to model his conversation on forensic principles.

"Not exactly that, either," replies Mrs. Chadband, humouring the joke with a hard-favoured smile.

"Not exactly that, either!" repeats Mr. Guppy. "Very good. Pray, ma'am, was it a lady of your acquaintance who had some transactions (we will not at present say what transactions) with Kenge and Carboy's office, or was it a gentleman of your acquaintance? Take time, ma'am. We shall come to it presently. Man or woman, ma'am?"

"Neither," says Mrs. Chadband, as before.

"Oh! A child!" says Mr. Guppy, throwing on the admiring Mrs. Snagsby the regular acute professional eye which is thrown on British jurymen. "Now, ma'am, perhaps you'll have the kindness to tell us *what* child."

"You have got it at last, sir," says Mrs. Chadband, with another hard-favoured smile. "Well, sir, it was before your time, most likely, judging from your appearance. I was left in charge of a child named Esther Summerson, who was put out in life by Messrs. Kenge and Carboy."

"Miss Summerson, ma'am!" cries Mr. Guppy, excited.

"*I* call her Esther Summerson," says Mrs. Chadband, with austerity. "There was no Miss-ing of the girl in my time. It was Esther. 'Esther, do this! Esther, do that!' and she was made to do it."

"My dear ma'am," returns Mr. Guppy, moving across the small apartment, "the humble individual who now addresses you received that young lady in London, when she first came here from the establishment to which you have alluded. Allow me to have the pleasure of taking you by the hand."

Mr. Chadband, at last seeing his opportunity, makes his accustomed signal, and rises with a smoking head, which he dabs with his pocket-handkerchief. Mrs. Snagsby whispers "Hush!"

"My friends," says Chadband, "we have partaken in moderation" (which was certainly not the case so far as he was concerned), "of the comforts which have been provided for us. May this house live upon the fatness of the land; may corn and wine be plentiful therein; may it grow, may it ·thrive, may it prosper, may it advance, may it proceed, may it press forward! But, my friends, have we partaken of anything else? We have. My friends, of what else have we partaken? Of spiritual profit? Yes. From whence have we derived that spiritual profit? My young friend, stand forth!"

Jo, thus apostrophised, gives a slouch backward, and another slouch forward, and another slouch to each side, and confronts the eloquent Chadband, with evident doubts of his intentions.

"My young friend," says Chadband, "you are to us a pearl, you are to us a diamond, you are to us a gem, you are to us a jewel. And why, my young friend?"

"*I* don't know," replies Joe. "I don't know nothink."

"My young friend," says Chadband, "it is because you know nothing that you are to us a gem and jewel. For what are you, my young friend? Are you a beast of the field? No. A bird of the air? No. A fish of the sea or river? No. You are a human boy, my young friend. A human boy. O glorious to be a human boy! And why glorious, my young friend? Because you are capable of receiving the lessons of wisdom, because you are capable of profiting by this discourse which I now deliver for your good, because you are not a stick, or a staff, or a stock, or a stone, or a post, or a pillar.

> O running stream of sparkling joy
> To be a soaring human boy!

And do you cool yourself in that stream now, my young friend? No. Why do you not cool yourself in that stream now? Because you are in a state of darkness, because you are in a state of obscurity, because you are in a state of sinfulness, because you are in a state of bondage. My young friend, what *is* bondage? Let us, in a spirit of love, inquire."

At this threatening stage of the discourse, Jo, who seems

to have been gradually going out of his mind, smears his right arm over his face, and gives a terrible yawn. Mrs. Snagsby indignantly expresses her belief that he is a limb of the arch-fiend.

"My friends," says Mr. Chadband, with his persecuted chin folding itself into its fat smile again as he looks round, "it is right that I should be humbled, it is right that I should be tried, it is right that I should be mortified, it is right that I should be corrected. I stumbled, on Sabbath last, when I thought with pride of my three hours' improving. The account is now favourably balanced: my creditor has accepted a composition. O let us be joyful, joyful! O let us be joyful!"

Great sensation on the part of Mrs. Snagsby.

"My friends," says Chadband, looking round him in conclusion, "I will not proceed with my young friend now. Will you come to-morrow, my young friend, and inquire of this good lady where I am to be found to deliver a discourse untoe you, and will you come like the thirsty swallow upon the next day, and upon the day after that, and upon the day after that, and upon many pleasant days, to hear discourses?" (This, with a cow-like lightness.)

Jo, whose immediate object seems to be to get away on any terms, gives a shuffling nod. Mr. Guppy then throws him a penny, and Mrs. Snagsby calls to Guster to see him safely out of the house. But, before he goes down-stairs, Mr. Snagsby loads him with some broken meats from the table, which he carries away, hugging in his arms.

So, Mr. Chadband—of whom the persecutors say that it is no wonder he should go on for any length of time uttering such abominable nonsense, but that the wonder rather is that he should ever leave off, having once the audacity to begin—retires into private life until he invests a little capital of supper in the oil-trade. Jo moves on, through the long vacation, down to Blackfriars Bridge, where he finds a baking stony corner, wherein to settle to his repast.

ANOTHER "MOVE ON"

And there he sits, munching and gnawing, and looking up at the great Cross on the summit of St. Paul's Cathedral, glittering above a red and violet-tinted cloud of smoke. From the boy's face one might suppose that sacred emblem to be, in his eyes, the crowning confusion of the great, confused city; so golden, so high up, so far out of his reach. There he sits, the sun going down, the river rnnning fast, the crowd flowing by him in two streams—everything moving on to some purpose and to one end—until he is stirred up, and told to "move on" too.

CHAPTER XX

THE long vacation saunters on towards term-time, like an idle river very leisurely strolling down a flat country to the sea. Mr. Guppy saunters along with it congenially. He has blunted the blade of his penknife, and broken the point off, by sticking that instrument into his desk in every direction. Not that he bears the desk any ill-will, but he must do something, and it must be something of an unexciting nature, which will lay neither his physical nor his intellectual energies under too heavy contribution. He finds that nothing agrees with him so well, as to make little gyrations on one leg of his stool, and stab his desk, and gape.

Kenge and Carboy are out of town, and the articled clerk has taken out a shooting licence, and gone down to his father's, and Mr. Guppy's two fellow-stipendiaries are away on leave. Mr. Guppy, and Mr. Richard Carstone, divide the dignity of the office. But Mr. Carstone is for the time being established in Kenge's room, whereat Mr. Guppy chafes. So exceedingly, that he with biting sarcasm informs his mother, in the confidential moments when he sups with her off a lobster and lettuce, in the Old Street Road, that he is afraid the office is hardly good enough for swells, and that if he had known there was a swell coming, he would have got it painted.

Mr. Guppy suspects everybody who enters on the occupation of a stool in Kenge and Carboy's office, of entertaining, as a matter of course, sinister designs upon him. He is clear that every such person wants to depose him. If he be ever asked how, why, when, or wherefore, he shuts up one eye and shakes his head. On the strength of these profound views, he in the most ingenious manner takes infinite pains to counterplot, when there is no plot; and plays the deepest games of chess without any adversary.

It is a source of much gratification to Mr. Guppy, therefore, to find the new-comer constantly poring over the papers in Jarndyce and Jarndyce; for he well knows that nothing but confusion and failure can come of that. His satisfaction communicates itself to a third saunterer through the long vacation in Kenge and Carboy's office; to wit, Young Smallweed.

Whether Young Smallweed (metaphorically called Small and eke Chick Weed, as it were jocularly to express a fledgling,) was ever a boy, is much doubted in Lincoln's Inn. He is now something under fifteen, and an old limb of the law. He is facetiously understood to entertain a passion for a lady at a cigar-shop, in the neighbourhood of Chancery Lane, and for her sake to have broken off a contract with another lady, to whom he had been engaged some years. He is a town-made article, of small stature and weazen features; but may be perceived from a considerable distance by means of his very tall hat. To become a Guppy is the object of his ambition. He dresses at that gentleman (by whom he is patronized), talks at him, walks at him, founds himself entirely on him. He is honoured with Mr. Guppy's particular confidence, and occasionally advises him, from the deep wells of his experience, on difficult points in private life.

Mr. Guppy has been lolling out of window all the morning, after trying all the stools in succession and finding none of them easy, and after several times putting his head into the iron safe with a notion of cooling it. Mr. Smallweed has been twice despatched for effervescent drinks, and

331

has twice mixed them in the two official tumblers and stirred them up with the ruler. Mr. Guppy propounds, for Mr. Smallweed's consideration, the paradox that the more you drink the thirstier you are; and reclines his head upon the window-sill in a state of hopeless languor.

While thus looking out into the shade of Old Square, Lincoln's Inn, surveying the intolerable bricks and mortar, Mr. Guppy becomes conscious of a manly whisker emerging from the cloistered walk below, and turning itself up in the direction of his face. At the same time, a low whistle is wafted through the Inn, and a suppressed voice cries, " Hip! Gup-py!"

"Why, you don't mean it?" says Mr. Guppy, aroused. "Small! Here's Jobling!" Small's head looks out of window too, and nods to Jobling.

"Where have you sprung up from?" inquires Mr. Guppy.

"From the market-gardens down by Deptford. I can't stand it any longer. I must enlist. I say! I wish you'd lend me half-a-crown. Upon my soul I'm hungry."

Jobling looks hungry, and also has the appearance of having run to seed in the market-gardens down by Deptford.

"I say! Just throw out half-a-crown, if you have got one to spare. I want to get some dinner."

"Will you come and dine with me?" says Mr. Guppy, throwing out the coin, which Mr. Jobling catches neatly.

"How long should I have to hold out?" says Jobling.

"Not half an hour. I am only waiting here till the enemy goes," returns Mr. Guppy, butting inward with his head.

"What enemy?"

"A new one. Going to be articled. Will you wait?"

"Can you give a fellow anything to read in the meantime?" says Mr. Jobling.

Smallweed suggests the Law List. But Mr. Jobling declares, with much earnestness, that he "can't stand it."

" You shall have the paper," says Mr. Guppy. " He shall bring it down. But you had better not be seen about here. Sit on our staircase and read. It's a quiet place."

Jobling nods intelligence and acquiescence. The sagacious Smallweed supplies him with the newspaper, and occasionally drops his eye upon him from the landing as a precaution against his becoming disgusted with waiting, and making an untimely departure. At last the enemy retreats, and then Smallweed fetches Mr. Jobling up.

" Well, and how are you ? " says Mr. Guppy, shaking hands with him.

" So, so. How are you ? "

Mr. Guppy replying that he is not much to boast of, Mr. Jobling ventures on the question, " How is *she?* " This Mr. Guppy resents as a liberty ; retorting, " Jobling, there *are* chords in the human mind—— " Jobling begs pardon.

" Any subject but that ! " says Mr. Guppy, with a gloomy enjoyment of his injury. " For there *are* chords, Jobling—— "

Mr. Jobling begs pardon again.

During this short colloquy, the active Smallweed, who is of the dinner party, has written in legal characters on a slip of paper, " Return immediately." This notification to all whom it may concern, he inserts in the letter-box ; and then putting on the tall hat, at the angle of inclination at which Mr. Guppy wears his, informs his patron that they may now make themselves scarce.

Accordingly they betake themselves to a neighbouring dining-house, of the class known among its frequenters by the denomination Slap-Bang, where the waitress, a bouncing young female of forty, is supposed to have made some impression on the susceptible Smallweed ; of whom it may be remarked that he is a weird changeling, to whom years are nothing. He stands precociously possessed of centuries of owlish wisdom. If he ever lay in a cradle, it seems as if he must have lain there in a tail-coat. He has an old, old eye, has Smallweed: and he drinks and smokes, in a monkeyish way; and his neck is stiff in his collar; and he is never to be taken in; and he knows all about it, whatever it is. In short, in his bringing up, he has been so nursed by Law and Equity that he has become a kind of fossil Imp, to account for whose terrestrial existence it is reported at the public offices that his father was John Doe, and his mother the only female member of the Roe family: also that his first long-clothes were made from a blue bag.

Into the dining-house, unaffected by the seductive show in the window, of artificially whitened cauliflowers and poultry, verdant baskets of peas, coolly blooming cucumbers, and joints ready for the spit, Mr. Smallweed leads the way. They know him there, and defer to him. He has his favourite box, he bespeaks all the papers, he is down upon bald patriarchs, who keep them more than ten minutes afterwards. It is of no use trying him with anything less than a full-sized "bread," or proposing to him any joint in cut, unless it is in the very best cut. In the matter of gravy he is adamant.

Conscious of his elfin power, and submitting to his dread experience, Mr. Guppy consults him in the choice of that day's banquet; turning an appealing look towards him as the waitress repeats the catalogue of viands, and saying "What do *you* take, Chick?" Chick, out of the profundity of his artfulness, preferring "veal and ham and French beans —And don't you forget the stuffing, Polly," (with an unearthly cock of his venerable eye); Mr. Guppy and Mr. Jobling give the like order. Three pint pots of half-and-half are superadded. Quickly the waitress returns, bearing what is apparently a model of the tower of Babel, but what is really a pile of plates and flat tin dish-covers. Mr. Smallweed, approving of what is set before him, conveys intelligent benignity into his ancient eye, and winks upon her. Then, amid a constant coming in, and going out, and running about, and a clatter of crockery, and a rumbling up and down of

Mr. Guppy's Entertainment

the machine which brings the nice cuts from the kitchen, and a shrill crying for more nice cuts down the speaking-pipe, and a shrill reckoning of the cost of nice cuts that have been disposed of, and a general flush and steam of hot joints, cut and uncut, and a considerably heated atmosphere in which the soiled knives and table-cloths seem to break out spontaneously into eruptions of grease and blotches of beer, the legal triumvirate appease their appetites.

Mr. Jobling is buttoned up closer than mere adornment might require. His hat presents at the rims a peculiar appearance of a glistening nature, as if it had been a favourite snail-promenade. The same phenomenon is visible on some parts of his coat, and particularly at the seams. He has the faded appearance of a gentleman in embarrassed circumstances; even his light whiskers droop with something of a shabby air.

His appetite is so vigorous, that it suggests spare living for some little time back. He makes such a speedy end of his plate of veal and ham, bringing it to a close while his companions are yet midway in theirs, that Mr. Guppy proposes another. "Thank you, Guppy," says Mr. Jobling, "I really don't know but what I *will* take another."

Another being brought, he falls to with great good will.

Mr. Guppy takes silent notice of him at intervals, until he is half way through this second plate and stops to take an enjoying pull at his pint pot of half-and-half (also renewed), and stretches out his legs and rubs his hands. Beholding him in which glow of contentment, Mr. Guppy says:

"You are a man again, Tony!"

"Well, not quite, yet," says Mr. Jobling. "Say, just born."

"Will you take any other vegetables? Grass? Peas? Summer cabbage?"

"Thank you, Guppy," says Mr. Jobling. "I really don't know but what I *will* take summer cabbage."

Order given; with the sarcastic addition (from Mr. Small-weed) of "Without slugs, Polly!" And cabbage produced.

"I am growing up, Guppy," says Mr. Jobling, plying his knife and fork with a relishing steadiness.

"Glad to hear it."

"In fact, I have just turned into my teens," says Mr. Jobling.

He says no more until he has performed his task, which he achieves as Messrs. Guppy and Smallweed finish theirs; thus getting over the ground in excellent style, and beating those two gentlemen easily by a veal and ham and a cabbage.

"Now, Small," says Mr. Guppy, "what would you recommend about pastry?"

"Marrow puddings," says Mr. Smallweed, instantly.

"Aye, aye!" cries Mr. Jobling, with an arch look. "You're there, are you? Thank you, Mr. Guppy, I don't know but what I *will* take a marrow pudding."

Three marrow puddings being produced, Mr. Jobling adds, in a pleasant humour, that he is coming of age fast. To these succeed, by command of Mr. Smallweed, "three Cheshires;" and to those, "three small rums." This apex of the entertainment happily reached, Mr. Jobling puts up his legs on the carpeted seat (having his own side of the box to himself), leans against the wall, and says, "I am grown up, now, Guppy. I have arrived at maturity."

"What do you think, now," says Mr. Guppy, "about—you don't mind Smallweed?"

"Not the least in the world. I have the pleasure of drinking his good health."

"Sir, to you!" says Mr. Smallweed.

"I was saying, what do you think *now*," pursues Mr. Guppy, "of enlisting?"

"Why, what I may think after dinner," returns Mr. Jobling, "is one thing, my dear Guppy, and what I may think before dinner is another thing. Still, even after dinner, I ask myself the question, What am I to do? How am I to live? Ill fo manger, you know," says Mr. Jobling, pronouncing that word as if he meant a necessary fixture in an English stable. "Ill fo manger. That's the French saying, and mangering is as necessary to me as it is to a Frenchman. Or more so."

Mr. Smallweed is decidedly of opinion "much more so."

"If any man had told me," pursues Jobling, "even so lately as when you and I had the frisk down in Lincolnshire, Guppy, and drove over to see that house at Castle Wold——"

Mr. Smallweed corrects him—Chesney Wold.

"Chesney Wold. (I thank my honourable friend for that cheer.) If any man had told me, then, that I should be as hard up at the present time as I literally find myself, I should have—well, I should have pitched into him," says Mr. Jobling, taking a little rum-and-water with an air of desperate resignation; "I should have let fly at his head."

"Still, Tony, you were on the wrong side of the post then," remonstrates Mr. Guppy. "You were talking about nothing else in the gig."

"Guppy," says Mr. Jobling, "I will not deny it. I was on the wrong side of the post. But I trusted to things coming round."

That very popular trust in flat things coming round! Not in their being beaten round, or worked round, but in their "coming" round! As though a lunatic should trust in the world's "coming" triangular!

"I had confident expectations that things would come round and be all square," says Mr. Jobling, with some vagueness of expression, and perhaps of meaning, too. "But I was disappointed. They never did. And when it came to creditors making rows at the office, and to people that the office dealt with making complaints about dirty trifles of borrowed money, why there was an end of that connexion. And of any new professional connexion, too; for if I was to give a reference to-morrow, it would be mentioned, and would sew me up. Then, what's a fellow to do? I have been keeping out of the way, and living cheap, down about the market-gardens; but what's the use of living cheap when you have got no money? You might as well live dear."

"Better," Mr. Smallweed thinks.

"Certainly. It's the fashionable way; and fashion and whiskers have been my weaknesses, and I don't care who knows it," says Mr. Jobling. "They are great weaknesses—Damme, sir, they are great. Well!" proceeds Mr. Jobling, after a defiant visit to his rum-and-water, "what can a fellow do, I ask you, *but* enlist?"

Mr. Guppy comes more fully into the conversation, to state what, in his opinion, a fellow can do. His manner is the gravely impressive manner of a man who has not committed himself in life, otherwise than as he has become the victim of a tender sorrow of the heart.

"Jobling," says Mr. Guppy, "myself and our mutual friend Smallweed—— "

(Mr. Smallweed modestly observes "Gentlemen both!" and drinks.)

"Have had a little conversation on this matter more than once, since you—— "

"Say, got the sack!" cries Mr. Jobling, bitterly. "Say it, Guppy. You mean it."

"N-o-o! Left the Inn," Mr. Smallweed delicately suggests.

"Since you left the Inn, Jobling," says Mr. Guppy; "and I have mentioned, to our mutual friend Smallweed, a plan I have lately thought of proposing. You know Snagsby the stationer?"

"I know there is such a stationer," returns Mr. Jobling. "He was not ours, and I am not acquainted with him."

"He *is* ours, Jobling, and I *am* acquainted with him," Mr. Guppy retorts. "Well, sir! I have lately become better acquainted with him, through some accidental circumstances that have made me a visitor of his in private life. Those circumstances it is not necessary to offer in argument. They may—or they may not—have some reference to a subject,

338

which may—or may not—have cast its shadow on my existence."

As it is Mr. Guppy's perplexing way, with boastful misery to tempt his particular friends into this subject, and the moment they touch it, to turn on them with that trenchant severity about the chords in the human mind; both Mr. Jobling and Mr. Smallweed decline the pitfall, by remaining silent.

"Such things may be," repeats Mr. Guppy, "or they may not be. They are no part of the case. It is enough to mention, that both Mr. and Mrs. Snagsby are very willing to oblige me; and that Snagsby has, in busy times, a good deal of copying work to give out. He has all Tulkinghorn's, and an excellent business besides. I believe, if our mutual friend Smallweed were put into the box, he could prove this?"

Mr. Smallweed nods, and appears greedy to be sworn.

"Now, gentlemen of the jury," says Mr. Guppy, "—I mean, now Jobling—you may say this is a poor prospect of a living. Granted. But it's better than nothing, and better than enlistment. You want time. There must be time for these late affairs to blow over. You might live through it on much worse terms than by writing for Snagsby."

Mr. Jobling is about to interrupt, when the sagacious Smallweed checks him with a dry cough, and the words, "Hem! Shakspeare!"

"There are two branches to this subject, Jobling," says Mr. Guppy. "That is the first. I come to the second. You know Krook, the Chancellor, across the lane. Come, Jobling," says Mr. Guppy, in his encouraging cross-examination-tone, "I think you know Krook, the Chancellor, across the lane?"

"I know him by sight," says Mr. Jobling.

"You know him by sight. Very well. And you know little Flite?"

"Everybody knows her," says Mr. Jobling.

"Everybody knows her. *Very* well. Now it has been one

of my duties of late, to pay Flite a certain weekly allowance, deducting from it the amount of her weekly rent: which I have paid (in consequence of instructions I have received) to Krook himself, regularly in her presence. This has brought me into communication with Krook, and into a knowledge of his house and his habits. I know he has a room to let. You may live there at a very low charge, under any name you like; as quietly as if you were a hundred miles off. He'll ask no questions; and would accept you as a tenant, at a word from me—before the clock strikes, if you chose. And I tell you another thing, Jobling," says Mr. Guppy, who has suddenly lowered his voice, and become familiar again, "he's an extraordinary old chap—always rummaging among a litter of papers, and grubbing away at teaching himself to read and write; without getting on a bit, as it seems to me. He is a most extraordinary old chap, sir. I don't know but what it might be worth a fellow's while to look him up a bit."

"You don't mean——?" Mr. Jobling begins.

"I mean," returns Mr. Guppy, shrugging his shoulders with becoming modesty, "that *I* can't make him out. I appeal to our mutual friend Smallweed whether he has or has not heard me remark, that I can't make him out."

Mr. Smallweed bears the concise testimony, "A few!"

"I have seen something of the profession, and something of life, Tony," says Mr. Guppy, "and it's seldom I can't make a man out, more or less. But such an old card as this; so deep, so sly, and secret (though I don't believe he is ever sober), I never came across. Now, he must be precious old, you know, and he has not a soul about him, and he is reported to be immensely rich; and whether he is a smuggler, or a receiver, or an unlicensed pawnbroker, or a money-lender—all of which I have thought likely at different times—it might pay you to knock up a sort of knowledge of him. I don't see why you shouldn't go in for it, when everything else suits."

Mr. Jobling, Mr. Guppy, and Mr. Smallweed, all lean their

elbows on the table, and their chins upon their hands, and look at the ceiling. After a time, they all drink, slowly lean back, put their hands in their pockets, and look at one another.

"If I had the energy I once possessed, Tony!" says Mr. Guppy, with a sigh. "But there are chords in the human mind——"

Expressing the remainder of the desolate sentiment in rum-and-water, Mr. Guppy concludes by resigning the adventure to Tony Jobling, and informing him that during the vacation and while things are slack, his purse, "as far as three or four or even five pound goes," will be at his disposal. "For never shall it be said," Mr. Guppy adds with emphasis, "that William Guppy turned his back upon his friend!"

The latter part of the proposal is so directly to the purpose, that Mr. Jobling says with emotion, "Guppy, my trump, your fist!" Mr. Guppy presents it, saying, "Jobling, my boy, there it is!" Mr. Jobling returns, "Guppy, we have been pals now for some years!" Mr. Guppy replies, "Jobling, we have."

They then shake hands, and Mr. Jobling adds in a feeling manner, "Thank you, Guppy, I don't know but what I *will* take another glass for old acquaintance sake."

"Krook's last lodger died there," observes Mr. Guppy, in an incidental way.

"Did he though!" says Mr. Jobling.

"There was a verdict. Accidental death. You don't mind that?"

"No," says Mr. Jobling, "I don't mind it; but he might as well have died somewhere else. It's devilish odd that he need go and die at *my* place!" Mr. Jobling quite resents this liberty; several times returning to it with such remarks as, "There are places enough to die in, I should think!" or, "He wouldn't have liked my dying at *his* place, I dare say!"

However, the compact being virtually made, Mr. Guppy

341

proposes to despatch the trusty Smallweed to ascertain if Mr. Krook is at home, as in that case they may complete the negotiation without delay. Mr. Jobling approving, Smallweed puts himself under the tall hat and conveys it out of the dining-rooms in the Guppy manner. He soon returns with the intelligence that Mr. Krook is at home, and that he has seen him through the shop-door, sitting in the back premises, sleeping, "like one o'clock."

"Then I'll pay," says Mr. Guppy, "and we'll go and see him. Small, what will it be?"

Mr. Smallweed, compelling the attendance of the waitress with one hitch of his eyelash, instantly replies as follows: "Four veals and hams is three, and four potatoes is three and four, and one summer cabbage is three and six, and three marrows is four and six, and six breads is five, and three Cheshires is five and three, and four half-pints of half-and-half is six and three, and four small rums is eight and three, and three Pollys is eight and six. Eight and six in half a sovereign, Polly, and eighteenpence out!"

Not at all excited by these stupendous calculations, Smallweed dismisses his friends with a cool nod, and remains behind to take a little admiring notice of Polly, as opportunity may serve, and to read the daily papers: which are so very large in proportion to himself, shorn of his hat, that when he holds up The Times to run his eye over the columns, he seems to have retired for the night, and to have disappeared under the bedclothes.

Mr. Guppy and Mr. Jobling repair to the rag and bottle shop, where they find Krook still sleeping like one o'clock; that is to say, breathing stertorously with his chin upon his breast, and quite insensible to any external sounds, or even to gentle shaking. On the table beside him, among the usual lumber, stand an empty gin-bottle and a glass. The unwholesome air is so stained with this liquor, that even the green eyes of the cat upon her shelf, as they open and shut and glimmer on the visitors, look drunk.

"Hold up here!" says Mr. Guppy, giving the relaxed figure of the old man another shake. "Mr. Krook! Halloa, sir!"

But it would seem as easy to wake a bundle of old clothes, with a spirituous heat smouldering in it. "Did you ever see such a stupor as he falls into, between drink and sleep?" says Mr. Guppy.

"If this is his regular sleep," returns Jobling, rather alarmed, "it'll last a long time one of these days, I am thinking."

"It's always more like a fit than a nap," says Mr. Guppy, shaking him again. "Halloa, your lordship! Why he might be robbed, fifty times over! Open your eyes!"

After much ado, he opens them, but without appearing to see his visitors, or any other objects. Though he crosses one leg on another, and folds his hands, and several times closes and opens his parched lips, he seems to all intents and purposes as insensible as before.

"He is alive, at any rate," says Mr. Guppy. "How are you, my Lord Chancellor? I have brought a friend of mine, sir, on a little matter of business."

The old man still sits, often smacking his dry lips without the least consciousness. After some minutes, he makes an attempt to rise. They help him up, and he staggers against the wall, and stares at them.

"How do you do, Mr. Krook?" says Mr. Guppy, in some discomfiture. "How do you do, sir? You are looking charming, Mr. Krook. I hope you are pretty well?"

The old man, in aiming a purposeless blow at Mr. Guppy, or at nothing, feebly swings himself round, and comes with his face against the wall. So he remains for a minute or two, heaped up against it; and then staggers down the shop to the front door. The air, the movement in the court, the lapse of time, or the combination of these things, recovers him. He comes back pretty steadily, adjusting his fur-cap on his head, and looking keenly at them.

343

"Your servant, gentlemen; I've been dozing. Hi! I am hard to wake, odd times."

"Rather so, indeed, sir," responds Mr. Guppy.

"What? You've been a-trying to do it, have you?" says the suspicious Krook.

"Only a little," Mr. Guppy explains.

The old man's eye resting on the empty bottle, he takes it up, examines it, and slowly tilts it upside down.

"I say!" he cries, like the Hobgoblin in the story. "Somebody's been making free here!"

"I assure you we found it so," says Mr. Guppy. "Would you allow me to get it filled for you?"

"Yes, certainly I would!" cries Krook, in high glee. "Certainly I would! Don't mention it! Get it filled next door—Sol's Arms—the Lord Chancellor's fourteenpenny. Bless you, they know *me*!"

He so presses the empty bottle upon Mr. Guppy, that that gentleman, with a nod to his friend, accepts the trust, and hurries out and hurries in again with the bottle filled. The old man receives it in his arms like a beloved grandchild, and pats it tenderly.

"But, I say!" he whispers, with his eyes screwed up, after tasting it, "this ain't the Lord Chancellor's fourteenpenny. This is eighteenpenny!"

"I thought you might like that better," says Mr. Guppy.

"You're a nobleman, sir," returns Krook, with another taste—and his hot breath seems to come towards them like a flame. "You're a baron of the land."

Taking advantage of this auspicious moment, Mr. Guppy presents his friend under the impromptu name of Mr. Weevle, and states the object of their visit. Krook with his bottle under his arm (he never gets beyond a certain point of either drunkenness or sobriety), takes time to survey his proposed lodger, and seems to approve of him. "You'd like to see the room, young man?" he says. "Ah! It's a good room! Been whitewashed. Been cleaned down with soft soap and soda.

Hi! It's worth twice the rent; letting alone my company when you want it, and such a cat to keep the mice away."

Commending the room after this manner, the old man takes them up-stairs, where indeed they do find it cleaner than it used to be, and also containing some old articles of furniture which he has dug up from his inexhaustible stores. The terms are easily concluded—for the Lord Chancellor cannot be hard on Mr. Guppy, associated as he is with Kenge and Carboy, Jarndyce and Jarndyce, and other famous claims on his professional consideration—and it is agreed that Mr. Weevle shall take possession on the morrow. Mr. Weevle and Mr. Guppy then repair to Cook's Court, Cursitor Street, where the personal introduction of the former to Mr. Snagsby is effected, and (more important) the vote and interest of Mrs. Snagsby are secured. They then report progress to the eminent Smallweed, waiting at the office in his tall hat for that purpose, and separate; Mr. Guppy explaining that he would terminate his little entertainment by standing treat at the play, but that there are chords in the human mind which would render it a hollow mockery.

On the morrow, in the dusk of evening, Mr. Weevle modestly appears at Krook's, by no means incommoded with luggage, and establishes himself in his new lodging; where the two eyes in the shutters stare at him in his sleep, as if they were full of wonder. On the following day Mr. Weevle, who is a handy good-for-nothing kind of young fellow, borrows a needle and thread of Miss Flite, and a hammer of his land-lord, and goes to work devising apologies for window-curtains, and knocking up apologies for shelves, and hanging up his two teacups, milkpot, and crockery sundries on a pennyworth of little hooks, like a shipwrecked sailor making the best of it.

But what Mr. Weevle prizes most, of all his few possessions (next after his light whiskers, for which he has an attachment that only whiskers can awaken in the breast of man), is a choice collection of copper-plate impressions from that truly national work, The Divinities of Albion, or Galaxy Gallery of British Beauty, representing ladies of title and fashion in every variety of smirk that art, combined with capital, is capable of producing. With these magnificent portraits, unworthily confined in a band-box during his seclusion among the market-gardens, he decorates his apartment; and as the Galaxy Gallery of British Beauty wears every variety of fancy dress, plays every variety of musical instrument, fondles every variety of dog, ogles every variety of prospect, and is backed up by every variety of flower-pot and balustrade, the result is very imposing.

But, fashion is Mr. Weevle's, as it was Tony Jobling's weakness. To borrow yesterday's paper from the Sol's Arms of an evening, and read about the brilliant and distinguished meteors that are shooting across the fashionable sky in every direction, is unspeakable consolation to him. To know what member of what brilliant and distinguished circle accomplished the brilliant and distinguished feat of joining it yesterday, or contemplates the no less brilliant and distinguished feat of leaving it to-morrow, gives him a thrill of joy. To be informed what the Galaxy Gallery of British Beauty is about, and means to be about, and what Galaxy marriages are on the tapis, and what Galaxy rumours are in circulation, is to become acquainted with the most glorious destinies of mankind. Mr. Weevle reverts from this intelligence, to the Galaxy portraits implicated; and seems to know the originals, and to be known of them.

For the rest he is a quiet lodger, full of handy shifts and devices as before mentioned, able to cook and clean for himself as well as to carpenter, and developing social inclinations after the shades of evening have fallen on the court. At those times, when he is not visited by Mr. Guppy, or by a small light in his likeness quenched in a dark hat, he comes out of his dull room—where he has inherited the deal wilderness of desk bespattered with a rain of ink—and talks to Krook, or is "very free," as they call it in the court, commendingly.

346

with any one disposed for conversation. Wherefore, Mrs. Piper, who leads the court, is impelled to offer two remarks to Mrs. Perkins: Firstly, that if her Johnny was to have whiskers, she could wish 'em to be identically like that young man's; and secondly, Mark my words, Mrs. Perkins, ma'am, and don't you be surprised Lord bless you, if that young man comes in at last for old Krook's money!

CHAPTER XXI

In a rather ill-favoured and ill-savoured neighbourhood, though one of its rising grounds bears the name of Mount Pleasant, the Elfin Smallweed, christened Bartholomew, and known on the domestic hearth as Bart, passes that limited portion of his time on which the office and its contingencies have no claim. He dwells in a little narrow street, always solitary, shady, and sad, closely bricked in on all sides like a tomb, but where there yet lingers the stump of an old forest tree, whose flavour is about as fresh and natural as the Smallweed smack of youth.

There has been only one child in the Smallweed family for several generations. Little old men and women there have been, but no child, until Mr. Smallweed's grandmother, now living, became weak in her intellect, and fell (for the first time) into a childish state. With such infantine graces as a total want of observation, memory, understanding and interest, and an eternal disposition to fall asleep over the fire and into it, Mr. Smallweed's grandmother has undoubtedly brightened the family.

Mr. Smallweed's grandfather is likewise of the party. He is in a helpless condition as to his lower, and nearly so as to his upper limbs; but his mind is unimpaired. It holds, as well as it ever held, the first four rules of arithmetic, and a certain small collection of the hardest facts. In respect of

348

ideality, reverence, wonder, and other such phrenological attributes, it is no worse off than it used to be. Everything that Mr. Smallweed's grandfather ever put away in his mind was a grub at first, and is a grub at last. In all his life he has never bred a single butterfly.

The father of this pleasant grandfather, of the neighbourhood of Mount Pleasant, was a horny-skinned, two-legged, money-getting species of spider, who spun webs to catch unwary flies, and retired into holes until they were entrapped. The name of this old pagan's God was Compound Interest. He lived for it, married it, died of it. Meeting with a heavy loss in an honest little enterprise in which all the loss was intended to have been on the other side, he broke something —something necessary to his existence; therefore it couldn't have been his heart—and made an end of his career. As his character was not good, and he had been bred at a Charity School, in a complete course, according to question and answer, of those ancient people the Amorites and Hittites, he was frequently quoted as an example of the failure of education.

His spirit shone through his son, to whom he had always preached of "going out" early in life, and whom he made a clerk in a sharp scrivener's office at twelve years old. There, the young gentleman improved his mind, which was of a lean and anxious character; and, developing the family gifts, gradually elevated himself into the discounting profession. Going out early in life, and marrying late, as his father had done before him, he too begat a lean and anxious-minded son; who, in his turn, going out early in life and marrying late, became the father of Bartholomew and Judith Smallweed, twins. During the whole time consumed in the slow growth of this family tree, the house of Smallweed, always early to go out and late to marry, has strengthened itself in its practical character, has discarded all amusements, discountenanced all story-books, fairy tales, fictions, and fables, and banished all levities whatsoever. Hence the gratifying fact, that it has had no child born to it, and that the complete little men and women whom it has produced, have been observed to bear a likeness to old monkeys with something depressing on their minds.

At the present time, in the dark little parlour certain feet below the level of the street—a grim, hard, uncouth parlour, only ornamented with the coarsest of baize table-covers, and the hardest of sheet-iron tea-trays, and offering in its decorative character no bad allegorical representation of Grandfather Smallweed's mind—seated in two black horse-hair porter's chairs, one on each side of the fireplace, the superannuated Mr. and Mrs. Smallweed while away the rosy hours. On the stove are a couple of trivets for the pots and kettles which it is Grandfather Smallweed's usual occupation to watch, and projecting from the chimney-piece between them is a sort of brass gallows for roasting, which he also superintends when it is in action. Under the venerable Mr. Smallweed's seat, and guarded by his spindle legs, is a drawer in his chair, reported to contain property to a fabulous amount. Beside him is a spare cushion, with which he is always provided, in order that he may have something to throw at the venerable partner of his respected age whenever she makes an allusion to money—a subject on which he is particularly sensitive.

" And where's Bart ? " Grandfather Smallweed inquires of Judy, Bart's twin-sister.

" He ain't come in yet," says Judy.

" It's his tea-time, isn't it ? "

" No."

" How much do you mean to say it wants then ? "

" Ten minutes."

" Hey ? "

" Ten minutes."—(Loud on the part of Judy.)

" Ho ! " says Grandfather Smallweed. " Ten minutes."

Grandmother Smallweed, who has been mumbling and shaking her head at the trivets, hearing figures mentioned, connects them with money, and screeches, like a horrible old parrot without any plumage, "Ten ten-pound notes!"

Grandfather Smallweed immediately throws the cushion at her.

"Drat you, be quiet!" says the good old man.

The effect of this act of jaculation is twofold. It not only doubles up Mrs. Smallweed's head against the side of her porter's chair, and causes her to present, when extricated by her grand-daughter, a highly unbecoming state of cap, but the necessary exertion recoils on Mr. Smallweed himself, whom it throws back into *his* porter's chair, like a broken puppet. The excellent old gentleman being, at these times, a mere clothes-bag with a black skull-cap on the top of it, does not present a very animated appearance, until he has undergone the two operations at the hands of his grand-daughter, of being shaken up like a great bottle, and poked and punched like a great bolster. Some indication of a neck being developed in him by these means, he and the sharer of his life's evening again sit fronting one another in their two porter's chairs, like a couple of sentinels long forgotten on their post by the Black Serjeant, Death.

Judy the twin is worthy company for these associates. She is so indubitably sister to Mr. Smallweed the younger, that the two kneaded into one would hardly make a young person of average proportions ; while she so happily exemplifies the before-mentioned family likeness to the monkey tribe, that, attired in a spangled robe and cap, she might walk about the table-land on the top of a barrel-organ without exciting much remark as an unusual specimen. Under existing circumstances, however, she is dressed in a plain, spare gown of brown stuff.

Judy never owned a doll, never heard of Cinderella, never played at any game. She once or twice fell into children's company when she was about ten years old, but the children couldn't get on with Judy, and Judy couldn't get on with them. She seemed like an animal of another species, and there was instinctive repugnance on both sides. It is very doubtful whether Judy knows how to laugh. She has so rarely seen the thing done, that the probabilities are strong the other way. Of anything like a youthful laugh, she certainly can have no conception. If she were to try one, she would find her teeth in her way; modelling that action of her face, as she has unconsciously modelled all its other expressions, on her pattern of sordid age. Such is Judy.

And her twin-brother couldn't wind up a top for his life. He knows no more of Jack the Giant Killer, or of Sinbad the Sailor, than he knows of the people in the stars. He could as soon play at leap-frog, or at cricket, as change into a cricket or a frog himself. But, he is so much the better off than his sister, that on his narrow world of fact an opening has dawned, into such broader regions as lie within the ken of Mr. Guppy. Hence, his admiration and his emulation of that shining enchanter.

Judy, with a gong-like clash and clatter, sets one of the sheet-iron tea-trays on the table, and arranges cups and saucers. The bread she puts on in an iron basket; and the butter (and not much of it) in a small pewter plate. Grandfather Smallweed looks hard after the tea as it is served out, and asks Judy where the girl is?

"Charley, do you mean?" says Judy.

"Hey?" from Grandfather Smallweed.

"Charley, do you mean?"

This touches a spring in Grandmother Smallweed, who, chuckling, as usual, at the trivets, cries—"Over the water! Charley over the water, Charley over the water, over the water to Charley, Charley over the water, over the water to Charley!" and becomes quite energetic about it. Grandfather looks at the cushion, but has not sufficiently recovered his late exertion.

"Ha!" he says, when there is silence—"if that's her name. She eats a deal. It would be better to allow her for her keep."

Judy, with her brother's wink, shakes her head, and purses up her mouth into No, without saying it.

"No?" returns the old man. "Why not?"

"She'd want sixpence a-day, and we can do it for less," says Judy.

"Sure?"

Judy answers with a nod of deepest meaning, and calls, as she scrapes the butter on the loaf with every precaution against waste, and cuts it into slices, "You Charley, where are you?" Timidly obedient to the summons, a little girl in a rough apron and a large bonnet, with her hands covered with soap and water, and a scrubbing brush in one of them, appears, and curtseys.

"What work are you about now?" says Judy, making an ancient snap at her, like a very sharp old beldame.

"I'm a-cleaning the up-stairs back room, miss," replies Charley.

"Mind you do it thoroughly, and don't loiter. Shirking won't do for me. Make haste! Go along!" cries Judy, with a stamp upon the ground. "You girls are more trouble than you're worth, by half."

On this severe matron, as she returns to her task of scraping the butter and cutting the bread, falls the shadow of her brother, looking in at the window. For whom, knife and loaf in hand, she opens the street-door.

"Ay, ay, Bart!" says Grandfather Smallweed. "Here you are, hey?"

"Here I am," says Bart.

"Been along with your friend again, Bart?"

Small nods.

"Dining at his expense, Bart?"

Small nods again.

"That's right. Live at his expense as much as you can, and take warning by his foolish example. That's the use of such a friend. The only use you can put him to," says the venerable sage.

His grandson, without receiving this good counsel as dutifully as he might, honours it with all such acceptance as may lie in a slight wink and a nod, and takes a chair at the tea-table. The four old faces then hover over teacups, like a company of ghastly cherubim; Mrs. Smallweed perpetually twitching her head and chattering at the trivets, and Mr. Smallweed requiring to be repeatedly shaken up like a large black draught.

"Yes, yes," says the good old gentleman, reverting to his lesson of wisdom. "That's such advice as your father would have given you, Bart. You never saw your father. More's the pity. He was my true son." Whether it is intended to be conveyed that he was particularly pleasant to look at, on that account, does not appear.

"He was my true son," repeats the old gentleman, folding his bread-and-butter on his knee; "a good accountant, and died fifteen years ago."

Mrs. Smallweed, following her usual instinct, breaks out with "Fifteen hundred pound. Fifteen hundred pound in a black box, fifteen hundred pound locked up, fifteen hundred pound put away and hid!" Her worthy husband, setting aside his bread-and-butter, immediately discharges the cushion at her, crushes her against the side of her chair, and falls back in his own, overpowered. His appearance, after visiting Mrs. Smallweed with one of these admonitions, is particularly impressive and not wholly prepossessing; firstly, because the exertion generally twists his black skull-cap over one eye and gives him an air of goblin rakishness; secondly, because he mutters violent imprecations against Mrs. Smallweed; and thirdly, because the contrast between those powerful expressions and his powerless figure is suggestive of a baleful old malignant, who would be very wicked if he could. All this, however, is so common in the Smallweed family circle, that it produces no impression. The old gentleman is merely shaken, and has his internal feathers beaten up; the cushion is restored to its usual place beside him; and the old lady,

The Smallweed Family

perhaps with her cap adjusted, and perhaps not, is planted in her chair again, ready to be bowled down like a ninepin.

Some time elapses, in the present instance, before the old gentleman is sufficiently cool to resume his discourse; and even then he mixes it up with several edifying expletives addressed to the unconscious partner of his bosom, who holds communication with nothing on earth but the trivets. As thus:

"If your father, Bart, had lived longer, he might have been worth a deal of money—you brimstone chatterer!—but just as he was beginning to build up the house that he had been making the foundations for, through many a year—you jade of a magpie, jackdaw, and poll-parrot, what do you mean!—he took ill and died of a low fever, always being a sparing and a spare man, full of business care—I should like to throw a cat at you instead of a cushion, and I will too if you. make such a confounded fool of yourself!—and your mother, who was a prudent woman as dry as a chip, just dwindled away like touchwood after you and Judy were born —You are an old pig. You are a brimstone pig. You're a head of swine!"

Judy, not interested in what she has often heard, begins to collect in a basin various tributary streams of tea, from the bottoms of cups and saucers and from the bottom of the tea-pot, for the little charwoman's evening meal. In like manner she gets together, in the iron bread-basket, as many outside fragments and worn-down heels of loaves as the rigid economy of the house has left in existence.

"But, your father and me were partners, Bart," says the old gentleman; "and when I am gone, you and Judy will have all there is. It's rare for you both, that you went out early in life—Judy to the flower business, and you to the law. You won't want to spend it. You'll get your living without it, and put more to it. When I am gone, Judy will go back to the flower business, and you'll still stick to the law."

One might infer, from Judy's appearance, that her business rather lay with the thorns than the flowers; but, she has, in her time, been apprenticed to the art and mystery of artificial flower-making. A close observer might perhaps detect both in her eye and her brother's, when their venerable grandsire anticipates his being gone, some little impatience to know when he may be going, and some resentful opinion that it is time he went.

"Now, if everybody has done," says Judy, completing her preparations, "I'll have that girl in to her tea. She would never leave off, if she took it by herself in the kitchen."

Charley is accordingly introduced, and, under a heavy fire of eyes, sits down to her basin and a Druidical ruin of bread-and-butter. In the active superintendence of this young person, Judy Smallweed appears to attain a perfectly geological age, and to date from the remotest periods. Her systematic manner of flying at her and pouncing on her, with or without pretence, whether or no, is wonderful; evincing an accomplishment in the art of girl-driving, seldom reached by the oldest practitioners.

"Now, don't stare about you all the afternoon," cries Judy, shaking her head and stamping her foot as she happens to catch the glance which has been previously sounding the basin of tea, "but take your victuals and get back to your work."

"Yes, miss," says Charley.

"Don't say yes," returns Miss Smallweed, "for I know what you girls are. Do it without saying it, and then I may begin to believe you."

Charley swallows a great gulp of tea in token of submission, and so disperses the Druidical ruins that Miss Smallweed charges her not to gormandize, which "in you girls," she observes, is disgusting. Charley might find some more difficulty in meeting her views on the general subject of girls, but for a knock at the door.

"See who it is, and don't chew when you open it!" cries Judy.

The object of her attentions withdrawing for the purpose, Miss Smallweed takes that opportunity of jumbling the remainder of the bread-and-butter together, and launching two or three dirty teacups into the ebb-tide of the basin of tea; as a hint that she considers the eating and drinking terminated.

"Now! Who is it, and what's wanted?" says the snappish Judy.

It is one "Mr. George," it appears. Without other announcement or ceremony, Mr. George walks in.

"Whew!" says Mr. George. "You are hot here. Always a fire, eh? Well! Perhaps you do right to get used to one." Mr. George makes the latter remark to himself, as he nods to Grandfather Smallweed.

"Ho! It's you!" cries the old gentleman. "How de do? How de do?"

"Middling," replies Mr. George, taking a chair. "Your grand-daughter I have had the honour of seeing before; my service to you, miss."

"This is my grandson," says Grandfather Smallweed. "You ha'n't seen him before. He is in the law, and not much at home."

"My service to him, too! He is like his sister. He is very like his sister. He is devilish like his sister," says Mr. George, laying a great and not altogether complimentary stress on his last adjective.

"And how does the world use you, Mr. George?" Grandfather Smallweed inquires, slowly rubbing his legs.

"Pretty much as usual. Like a football."

He is a swarthy brown man of fifty; well-made, and good-looking; with crisp dark hair, bright eyes, and a broad chest. His sinewy and powerful hands, as sunburnt as his face, have evidently been used to a pretty rough life. What is curious about him is, that he sits forward on his chair as if he were, from long habit, allowing space for some dress or accoutrements that he has altogether laid aside. His step too is measured and heavy, and would go well with a weighty clash and jingle of spurs. He is close-shaved now, but his mouth is set as if his upper lip had been for years familiar with a great moustache; and his manner of occasionally laying the open palm of his broad brown hand upon it, is to the same effect. Altogether, one might guess Mr. George to have been a trooper once upon a time.

A special contrast Mr. George makes to the Smallweed family. Trooper was never yet billeted upon a household more unlike him. It is a broadsword to an oyster-knife. His developed figure, and their stunted forms; his large manner, filling any amount of room, and their little narrow pinched ways; his sounding voice, and their sharp spare tones; are in the strongest and the strangest opposition. As he sits in the middle of the grim parlour, leaning a little forward, with his hands upon his thighs and his elbows squared, he looks as though, if he remained there long, he would absorb into himself the whole family and the whole four-roomed house, extra little back-kitchen and all.

"Do you rub your legs to rub life into 'em?" he asks of Grandfather Smallweed, after looking round the room.

"Why, it's partly a habit, Mr. George, and—yes—it partly helps the circulation," he replies.

"The cir-cu-la-tion!" repeats Mr. George, folding his arms upon his chest, and seeming to become two sizes larger. "Not much of that, I should think."

"Truly I'm old, Mr. George," says Grandfather Smallweed. "But I can carry my years. I'm older than *her*," nodding at his wife, "and see what she is?—You're a brimstone chatterer!" with a sudden revival of his late hostility.

"Unlucky old soul!" says Mr. George, turning his head in that direction. "Don't scold the old lady. Look at her here, with her poor cap half off her head, and her poor hair all in a muddle. Hold up, ma'am. That's better. There we are! Think of your mother, Mr. Smallweed," says Mr. George, coming back to his seat from assisting her, "if your wife an't enough."

"I suppose you were an excellent son, Mr. George?" the old man hints, with a leer.

The colour of Mr. George's face rather deepens, as he replies: "Why no. I wasn't."

"I am astonished at it."

"So am I. I ought to have been a good son, and I think I meant to have been one. But I wasn't. I was a thundering bad son, that's the long and the short of it, and never was a credit to anybody."

"Surprising!" cries the old man.

"However," Mr. George resumes, "the less said about it, the better now. Come! You know the agreement. Always a pipe out of the two months' interest! (Bosh! It's all correct. You needn't be afraid to order the pipe. Here's the new bill, and here's the two months' interest-money, and a devil-and-all of a scrape it is to get it together in my business)."

Mr. George sits, with his arms folded, consuming the family and the parlour, while Grandfather Smallweed is assisted by Judy to two black leathern cases out of a locked bureau; in one of which he secures the document he has just received, and from the other takes another similar document which he hands to Mr. George, who twists it up for a pipe-light. As the old man inspects, through his glasses, every up-stroke and down-stroke of both documents, before he releases them from their leathern prison; and as he counts the money three times over, and requires Judy to say every word she utters at least twice, and is as tremulously slow of speech and action as it is possible to be; this business is a long time in progress. When it is quite concluded, and not before, he disengages his ravenous eyes and fingers from it, and answers Mr. George's last remark by saying, "Afraid to order the pipe? We are not so mercenary as that, sir. Judy, see directly to the pipe and the glass of cold brandy-and-water for Mr. George."

The sportive twins, who have been looking straight before them all this time, except when they have been engrossed by

359

the black leathern cases, retire together, generally disdainful of the visitor, but leaving him to the old man, as two young cubs might leave a traveller to the parental bear.

" And there you sit, I suppose, all the day long, eh ? " says Mr. George, with folded arms.

" Just so, just so," the old man nods.

" And don't you occupy yourself at all ? "

" I watch the fire—and the boiling and the roasting—— "

" When there is any," says Mr. George, with great expression.

" Just so. When there is any."

" Don't you read, or get read to ? "

The old man shakes his head with sharp sly triumph. " No, no. We have never been readers in our family. It don't pay. Stuff. Idleness. Folly. No, no ! "

" There's not much to choose between your two states," says the visitor, in a key too low for the old man's dull hearing, as he looks from him to the old woman and back again. " I say ! " in a louder voice.

" I hear you."

" You'll sell me up at last, I suppose, when I am a day in arrear."

" My dear friend ! " cries Grandfather Smallweed, stretching out both hands to embrace him ! " Never ! Never, my dear friend ! But my friend in the city that I got to lend you the money—*he* might ! "

" O ! you can't answer for him ? " says Mr. George ; finishing the inquiry, in his lower key, with the words " you lying old rascal ! "

" My dear friend, he is not to be depended on. I wouldn't trust him. He will have his bond, my dear friend."

" Devil doubt him," says Mr. George. Charley appearing with a tray, on which are the pipe, a small paper of tobacco, and the brandy-and-water, he asks her, " How do you come here ! you haven't got the family face."

" I goes out to work, sir," returns Charley.

A GOOD SHAKING

The trooper (if trooper he be or have been) takes her bonnet off, with a light touch for so strong a hand, and pats her on the head. "You give the house almost a wholesome look. It wants a bit of youth as much as it wants fresh air." Then he dismisses her, lights his pipe, and drinks to Mr. Smallweed's friend in the city—the one solitary flight of that esteemed old gentleman's imagination.

"So you think he might be hard upon me, eh?"

"I think he might—I am afraid he would. I have known him do it," says Grandfather Smallweed, incautiously, "twenty times."

Incautiously, because his stricken better-half, who has been dozing over the fire for some time, is instantly aroused and jabbers "Twenty thousand pounds, twenty twenty-pound notes in a money-box, twenty guineas, twenty million twenty per cent. twenty—" and is then cut short by the flying cushion, which the visitor, to whom this singular experiment appears to be a novelty, snatches from her face as it crushes her in the usual manner.

"You're a brimstone idiot. You're a scorpion—a brimstone scorpion! You're a sweltering toad. You're a chattering clattering broomstick witch, that ought to be burnt!" gasps the old man, prostrate in his chair. "My dear friend, will you shake me up a little?"

Mr. George, who has been looking first at one of them and then at the other, as if he were demented, takes his venerable acquaintance by the throat on receiving this request, and dragging him upright in his chair as easily as if he were a doll, appears in two minds whether or no to shake all future power of cushioning out of him, and shake him into his grave. Resisting the temptation, but agitating him violently enough to make his head roll like a harlequin's, he puts him smartly down in his chair again, and adjusts his skull-cap with such a rub, that the old man winks with both eyes for a minute afterwards.

"O Lord!" gasps Mr. Smallweed. "That'll do. Thank

361

you, my dear friend, that'll do. O dear me, I'm out of breath. O Lord!" And Mr. Smallweed says it, not without evident apprehensions of his dear friend, who still stands over him looming larger than ever.

The alarming presence, however, gradually subsides into its chair, and falls to smoking in long puffs; consoling itself with the philosophical reflection, "The name of your friend in the city begins with a D, comrade, and you're about right respecting the bond."

"Did you speak, Mr. George?" inquires the old man.

The trooper shakes his head; and leaning forward with his right elbow on his right knee and his pipe supported in that hand, while his other hand, resting on his left leg, squares his left elbow in a martial manner, continues to smoke. Meanwhile he looks at Mr. Smallweed with grave attention, and now and then fans the cloud of smoke away, in order that he may see him the more clearly.

"I take it," he says, making just as much and as little change in his position as will enable him to reach the glass to his lips, with a round, full action, " that I am the only man alive (or dead either), that gets the value of a pipe out of *you?*"

"Well!" returns the old man, "it's true that I don't see company, Mr. George, and that I don't treat. I can't afford to it. But as you, in your pleasant way, made your pipe a condition——"

"Why, it's not for the value of it; that's no great thing. It was a fancy to get it out of you. To have something in for my money."

"Ha! You're prudent, prudent, sir!" cries Grandfather Smallweed, rubbing his legs.

"Very. I always was." Puff. "It's a sure sign of my prudence, that I ever found the way here." Puff. "Also, that I am what I am." Puff. "I am well known to be prudent," says Mr. George, composedly smoking. "I rose in life, that way."

"Don't be down-hearted, sir. You may rise yet."

Mr. George laughs and drinks.

"Ha'n't you no relations, now," asks Grandfather Small-weed, with a twinkle in his eyes, "who would pay off this little principal, or who would lend you a good name or two that I could persuade my friend in the city to make you a further advance upon? Two good names would be sufficient for my friend in the city. Ha'n't you no such relations, Mr. George?"

Mr. George, still composedly smoking, replies, "If I had, I shouldn't trouble them. I have been trouble enough to my belongings in my day. It *may* be a very good sort of penitence in a vagabond, who has wasted the best time of his life, to go back then to decent people that he never was a credit to, and live upon them; but it's not my sort. The best kind of amends then, for having gone away, is to keep away, in my opinion."

"But natural affection, Mr. George," hints Grandfather Smallweed.

"For two good names, hey?" says Mr. George, shaking his head, and still composedly smoking. "No. That's not my sort, either."

Grandfather Smallweed has been gradually sliding down in his chair since his last adjustment, and is now a bundle of clothes, with a voice in it calling for Judy. That Houri appearing, shakes him up in the usual manner, and is charged by the old gentleman to remain near him. For he seems chary of putting his visitor to the trouble of repeating his late attentions.

"Ha!" he observes, when he is in trim again. "If you could have traced out the Captain, Mr. George, it would have been the making of you. If, when you first came here, in consequence of our advertisements in the newspapers—when I say 'our,' I'm alluding to the advertisements of my friend in the city, and one or two others who embark their capital in the same way, and are so friendly towards me as sometimes to give me a lift with my little pittance—if, at that time, you could have helped us, Mr. George, it would have been the making of you."

"I was willing enough to be 'made,' as you call it," says Mr. George, smoking not quite so placidly as before, for since the entrance of Judy he has been in some measure disturbed by a fascination, not of the admiring kind, which obliges him to look at her as she stands by her grandfather's chair; "but, on the whole, I am glad I wasn't now."

"Why, Mr. George? In the name of—of Brimstone, why?" says Grandfather Smallweed, with a plain appearance of exasperation. (Brimstone apparently suggested by his eye lighting on Mrs. Smallweed in her slumber.)

"For two reasons, comrade."

"And what two reasons, Mr. George? In the name of the——"

"Of our friend in the city?" suggests Mr. George, composedly drinking.

"Ay, if you like. What two reasons?"

"In the first place," returns Mr. George; but still looking at Judy, as if, she being so old and so like her grandfather, it is indifferent which of the two he addresses; "you gentlemen took me in. You advertised that Mr. Hawdon (Captain Hawdon, if you hold to the saying, Once a captain always a captain) was to hear of something to his advantage."

"Well?" returns the old man, shrilly and sharply.

"Well!" says Mr. George, smoking on. "It wouldn't have been much to his advantage to have been clapped into prison by the whole bill and judgment trade of London."

"How do you know that? Some of his rich relations might have paid his debts, or compounded for 'em. Besides, he had taken *us* in. He owed us immense sums, all round. I would sooner have strangled him than had no return. If I sit here thinking of him," snarls the old man, holding up his impotent ten fingers, "I want to strangle him now." And in a sudden access of fury, he throws the cushion at the unoffending Mrs. Smallweed, but it passes harmlessly on one side of her chair.

"I don't need to be told," returns the trooper, taking his pipe from his lips for a moment, and carrying his eyes back from following the progress of the cushion, to the pipe-bowl which is burning low, "that he carried on heavily and went to ruin. I have been at his right hand many a day, when he was charging upon ruin full-gallop. I was with him, when he was sick and well, rich and poor. I laid this hand upon him, after he had run through everything and broken down everything beneath him—when he held a pistol to his head."

"I wish he had let it off!" says the benevolent old man, "and blown his head into as many pieces as he owed pounds!"

"That would have been a smash indeed," returns the trooper coolly; "any way, he had been young, hopeful, and handsome in the days gone by; and I am glad I never found him, when he was neither, to lead to a result so much to his advantage. That's reason number one."

"I hope number two's as good?" snarls the old man.

"Why, no. It's more of a selfish reason. If I had found him, I must have gone to the other world to look. He was there."

"How do you know he was there?"

"He wasn't here."

"How do you know he wasn't here?"

"Don't lose your temper as well as your money," says Mr. George, calmly knocking the ashes out of his pipe. "He was drowned long before. I am convinced of it. He went over a ship's side. Whether intentionally or accidentally, I don't know. Perhaps your friend in the city does.—Do you know what that tune is, Mr. Smallweed?" he adds, after breaking off to whistle one, accompanied on the table with the empty pipe.

365

"Tune!" replies the old man. "No. We never have tunes here."

"That's the Dead March in Saul. They bury soldiers to it; so it's the natural end of the subject. Now, if your pretty grand-daughter—excuse me, miss—will condescend to take care of this pipe for two months, we shall save the cost of one next time. Good evening, Mr. Smallweed!"

"My dear friend!" The old man gives him both his hands.

"So you think your friend in the city will be hard upon me, if I fail in a payment?" says the trooper, looking down upon him like a giant.

"My dear friend, I am afraid he will," returns the old man, looking up at him like a pigmy.

Mr. George laughs; and with a glance at Mr. Smallweed, and a parting salutation to the scornful Judy, strides out of the parlour, clashing imaginary sabres and other metallic appurtenances as he goes.

"You're a damned rogue," says the old gentleman, making a hideous grimace at the door as he shuts it. "But I'll lime you, you dog, I'll lime you!"

After this amiable remark, his spirit soars into those enchanting regions of reflection which its education and pursuits have opened to it; and again he and Mrs. Smallweed while away the rosy hours, two unrelieved sentinels forgotten as aforesaid by the Black Serjeant.

While the twain are faithful to their post, Mr. George strides through the streets with a massive kind of swagger and a grave-enough face. It is eight o'clock now, and the day is fast drawing in. He stops hard by Waterloo Bridge, and reads a playbill; decides to go to Astley's Theatre. Being there, is much delighted with the horses and the feats of strength; looks at the weapons with a critical eye; disapproves of the combats, as giving evidences of unskilful swordsmanship; but is touched home by the sentiments. In the last scene, when the Emperor of Tartary gets up into a cart and condescends to bless the united lovers by hovering over them with the Union-Jack, his eye-lashes are moistened with emotion.

The theatre over, Mr. George comes across the water again, and makes his way to that curious region lying about the Haymarket and Leicester Square, which is a centre of attraction to indifferent foreign hotels and indifferent foreigners, racket-courts, fighting-men, swordsmen, footguards, old china, gaming-houses, exhibitions, and a large medley of shabbiness and shrinking out of sight. Penetrating to the heart of this region, he arrives, by a court and a long whitewashed passage, at a great brick building, composed of bare walls, floors, roof-rafters, and skylights; on the front of which, if it can be said to have any front, is painted GEORGE'S SHOOTING GALLERY, &c.

Into George's Shooting Gallery, &c., he goes; and in it there are gas-lights (partly turned off now), and two whitened targets for rifle-shooting, and archery accommodation, and fencing appliances, and all necessaries for the British art of boxing. None of these sports or exercises being pursued in George's Shooting Gallery to-night; which is so devoid of company, that a little grotesque man, with a large head, has it all to himself, and lies asleep upon the floor.

The little man is dressed something like a gunsmith, in a green baize apron and cap; and his face and hands are dirty with gunpowder, and begrimed with the loading of guns. As he lies in the light, before a glaring white target, the black upon him shines again. Not far off, is the strong, rough, primitive table, with a vice upon it, at which he has been working. He is a little man with a face all crushed together, who appears, from a certain blue and speckled appearance that one of his cheeks presents, to have been blown up, in the way of business, at some odd time or times.

"Phil!" says the trooper, in a quiet voice.

"All right!" cries Phil, scrambling to his feet.

"Anything been doing?"

"Flat as ever so much swipes," says Phil. "Five dozen rifle and a dozen pistol. As to aim!" Phil gives a howl at the recollection.

"Shut up shop, Phil!"

As Phil moves about to execute this order, it appears that he is lame, though able to move very quickly. On the speckled side of his face he has no eyebrow, and on the other side he has a bushy black one, which want of uniformity gives him a very singular and rather sinister appearance. Everything seems to have happened to his hands that could possibly take place, consistently with the retention of all the fingers; for they are notched, and seamed, and crumpled all over. He appears to be very strong, and lifts heavy benches about as if he had no idea what weight was. He has a curious way of limping round the gallery with his shoulder against the wall, and tacking off at objects he wants to lay hold of, instead of going straight to them, which has left a smear all round the four walls, conventionally called "Phil's mark."

This custodian of George's Gallery in George's absence concludes his proceedings, when he has locked the great doors, and turned out all the lights but one, which he leaves to glimmer, by dragging out from a wooden cabin in a corner two mattresses and bedding. These being drawn to opposite ends of the gallery, the trooper makes his own bed, and Phil makes his.

"Phil!" says the master, walking towards him without his coat and waistcoat, and looking more soldierly than ever in his braces. "You were found in a doorway, weren't you?"

"Gutter," says Phil. "Watchman tumbled over me."

"Then, vagabondizing came natural to *you*, from the beginning."

"As nat'ral as possible," says Phil.

"Good night!"

"Good night, guv'ner."

RETIRING TO REST

Phil cannot even go straight to bed, but finds it necessary to shoulder round two sides of the gallery, and then tack off at his mattress. The trooper, after taking a turn or two in the rifle-distance, and looking up at the moon now shining through the skylights, strides to his own mattress by a shorter route, and goes to bed too.

CHAPTER XXII

ALLEGORY looks pretty cool in Lincoln's Inn Fields, though the evening is hot; for, both Mr. Tulkinghorn's windows are wide open, and the room is lofty, gusty, and gloomy. These may not be desirable characteristics when November comes with fog and sleet, or January with ice and snow; but they have their merits in the sultry long vacation weather. They enable Allegory, though it has cheeks like peaches, and knees like bunches of blossoms, and rosy swellings for calves to its legs and muscles to its arms, to look tolerably cool to-night.

Plenty of dust comes in at Mr. Tulkinghorn's windows, and plenty more has generated among his furniture and papers. It lies thick everywhere. When a breeze from the country that has lost its way, takes fright, and makes a blind hurry to rush out again, it flings as much dust in the eyes of Allegory as the law—or Mr. Tulkinghorn, one of its trustiest representatives—may scatter, on occasion, in the eyes of the laity.

In his lowering magazine of dust, the universal article into which his papers and himself, and all his clients, and all things of earth, animate and inanimate, are resolving, Mr. Tulkinghorn sits at one of the open windows, enjoying a bottle of old port. Though a hard-grained man, close, dry, and silent, he can enjoy old wine with the best. He has a priceless binn of port in some artful cellar under the Fields,

370

which is one of his many secrets. When he dines alone in chambers, as he has dined to-day, and has his bit of fish and his steak or chicken brought in from the coffee-house, he descends with a candle to the echoing regions below the deserted mansion, and, heralded by a remote reverberation of thundering doors, comes gravely back, encircled by an earthy atmosphere, and carrying a bottle from which he pours a radiant nectar, two score and ten years old, that blushes in the glass to find itself so famous, and fills the whole room with the fragrance of southern grapes.

Mr. Tulkinghorn, sitting in the twilight by the open window, enjoys his wine. As if it whispered to him of its fifty years of silence and seclusion, it shuts him up the closer. More impenetrable than ever, he sits, and drinks, and mellows as it were, in secrecy; pondering, at that twilight hour, on all the mysteries he knows, associated with darkening woods in the country, and vast blank shut-up houses in town: and perhaps sparing a thought or two for himself, and his family history, and his money, and his will—all a mystery to every one—and that one bachelor friend of his, a man of the same mould and a lawyer too, who lived the same kind of life until he was seventy-five years old, and then, suddenly conceiving (as it is supposed) an impression that it was too monotonous, gave his gold watch to his hair-dresser one summer evening, and walked leisurely home to the Temple, and hanged himself.

But, Mr. Tulkinghorn is not alone to-night, to ponder at his usual length. Seated at the same table, though with his chair modestly and uncomfortably drawn a little way from it, sits a bald, mild, shining man, who coughs respectfully behind his hand when the lawyer bids him fill his glass.

"Now, Snagsby," says Mr. Tulkinghorn, "to go over this odd story again."

"If you please, sir."

"You told me when you were so good as to step round here, last night—— "

"For which I must ask you to excuse me if it was a liberty, sir; but I remember that you had taken a sort of an interest in that person, and I thought it possible that you might—just—wish—to—— "

Mr. Tulkinghorn is not the man to help him to any conclusion, or to admit anything as to any possibility concerning himself. So Mr. Snagsby trails off into saying, with an awkward cough, "I must ask you to excuse the liberty, sir, I am sure."

"Not at all," says Mr. Tulkinghorn. "You told me, Snagsby, that you put on your hat and came round without mentioning your intention to your wife. That was prudent, I think, because it's not a matter of such importance that it requires to be mentioned."

"Well, sir," returns Mr. Snagsby, "you see my little woman is—not to put too fine a point upon it—inquisitive. She's inquisitive. Poor little thing, she's liable to spasms, and it's good for her to have her mind employed. In consequence of which she employs it—I should say upon every individual thing she can lay hold of, whether it concerns her or not—especially not. My little woman has a very active mind, sir."

Mr. Snagsby drinks, and murmurs with an admiring cough behind his hand, "Dear me, very fine wine indeed!"

"Therefore you kept your visit to yourself, last night?" says Mr. Tulkinghorn. "And to-night, too?"

"Yes, sir, and to-night, too. My little woman is at present in—not to put too fine a point on it—in a pious state, or in what she considers such, and attends the Evening Exertions (which is the name they go by) of a reverend party of the name of Chadband. He has a great deal of eloquence at his command, undoubtedly, but I am not quite favourable to his style myself. That's neither here nor there. My little woman being engaged in that way, made it easier for me to step round in a quiet manner."

Mr. Tulkinghorn assents. "Fill your glass, Snagsby."

"Thank you, sir, I am sure," returns the stationer, with

his cough of deference. "This is wonderfully fine wine, sir!"

"It is a rare wine now," says Mr. Tulkinghorn. "It is fifty years old."

"Is it indeed, sir? But I am not surprised to hear it, I am sure. It might be—any age almost." After rendering this general tribute to the port, Mr. Snagsby in his modesty coughs an apology behind his hand for drinking anything so precious.

"Will you run over, once again, what the boy said?" asks Mr. Tulkinghorn, putting his hands into the pockets of his rusty small-clothes and leaning quietly back in his chair.

"With pleasure, sir."

Then, with fidelity, though with some prolixity, the law-stationer repeats Jo's statement made to the assembled guests at his house. On coming to the end of his narrative, he gives a great start, and breaks off with—"Dear me, sir, I wasn't aware there was any other gentleman present!"

Mr. Snagsby is dismayed to see, standing with an attentive face between himself and the lawyer, at a little distance from the table, a person with a hat and stick in his hand, who was not there when he himself came in, and has not since entered by the door or by either of the windows. There is a press in the room, but its hinges have not creaked, nor has a step been audible upon the floor. Yet this third person stands there, with his attentive face, and his hat and stick in his hands, and his hands behind him, a composed and quiet listener. He is a stoutly built, steady-looking, sharp-eyed man in black, of about the middle-age. Except that he looks at Mr. Snagsby as if he were going to take his portrait, there is nothing remarkable about him at first sight but his ghostly manner of appearing.

"Don't mind this gentleman," says Mr. Tulkinghorn, in his quiet way. "This is only Mr. Bucket."

"O indeed, sir?" returns the stationer, expressing by a

373

cough that he is quite in the dark as to who Mr. Bucket may be.

"I wanted him to hear this story," says the lawyer, "because I have half a mind (for a reason) to know more of it, and he is very intelligent in such things. What do you say to this, Bucket?"

"It's very plain, sir. Since our people have moved this boy on, and he's not to be found on his old lay, if Mr. Snagsby don't object to go down with me to Tom-all-Alone's and point him out, we can have him here in less than a couple of hours' time. I can do it without Mr. Snagsby, of course; but this is the shortest way."

"Mr. Bucket is a detective officer, Snagsby," says the lawyer in explanation.

"Is he, indeed, sir?" says Mr. Snagsby, with a strong tendency in his clump of hair to stand on end.

"And if you have no real objection to accompany Mr. Bucket to the place in question," pursues the lawyer, "I shall feel obliged to you if you will do so."

In a moment's hesitation on the part of Mr. Snagsby, Bucket dips down to the bottom of his mind.

"Don't you be afraid of hurting the boy," he says. "You won't do that. It's all right as far as the boy's concerned. We shall only bring him here to ask him a question or so I want to put to him, and he'll be paid for his trouble, and sent away again. It'll be a good job for him. I promise you, as a man, that you shall see the boy sent away all right. Don't you be afraid of hurting him; you an't going to do that."

"Very well, Mr. Tulkinghorn!" cries Mr. Snagsby cheerfully, and reassured, "since that's the case——"

"Yes! and lookee here, Mr. Snagsby," resumes Bucket, taking him aside by the arm, tapping him familiarly on the breast, and speaking in a confidential tone. "You're a man of the world, you know, and a man of business, and a man of sense. That's what *you* are."

" I am sure I am much obliged to you for your good opinion," returns the stationer, with his cough of modesty, " but—— "

" That's what *you* are, you know," says Bucket. " Now, it an't necessary to say to a man like you, engaged in your business, which is a business of trust and requires a person to be wide awake and have his senses about him, and his head screwed on tight (I had an uncle in your business once) —it an't necessary to say to a man like you, that it's the best and wisest way to keep little matters like this quiet. Don't you see? Quiet! "

" Certainly, certainly," returns the other.

" I don't mind telling *you*," says Bucket, with an engaging appearance of frankness, " that as far as I can understand it, there seems to be a doubt whether this dead person wasn't entitled to a little property, and whether this female hasn't been up to some games respecting that property, don't you see? "

" O! " says Mr. Snagsby, but not appearing to see quite distinctly.

" Now, what *you* want," pursues Bucket, again tapping Mr. Snagsby on the chest in a comfortable and soothing manner, " is, that every person should have their rights according to justice. That's what *you* want."

" To be sure," returns Mr. Snagsby with a nod.

" On account of which, and at the same time to oblige a —do you call it, in your business, customer or client? I forget how my uncle used to call it."

" Why, I generally say customer myself," replies Mr. Snagsby.

" You're right! " returns Mr. Bucket, shaking hands with him quite affectionately,—" on account of which, and at the same time to oblige a real good customer, you mean to go down with me, in confidence, to Tom-all-Alone's, and to keep the whole thing quiet ever afterwards and never mention it to any one. That's about your intentions, if I understand you? "

"You are right, sir. You are right," says Mr. Snagsby.

"Then here's your hat," returns his new friend, quite as intimate with it as if he had made it; "and if you're ready, I am."

They leave Mr. Tulkinghorn, without a ruffle on the surface of his unfathomable depths, drinking his old wine, and go down into the streets.

"You don't happen to know a very good sort of person of the name of Gridley, do you?" says Bucket, in friendly converse as they descend the stairs.

"No," says Mr. Snagsby, considering, "I don't know anybody of that name. Why?"

"Nothing particular," says Bucket; "only, having allowed his temper to get a little the better of him, and having been threatening some respectable people, he is keeping out of the way of a warrant I have got against him—which it's a pity that a man of sense should do."

As they walk along, Mr. Snagsby observes, as a novelty, that, however quick their pace may be, his companion still seems in some undefinable manner to lurk and lounge; also, that whenever he is going to turn to the right or left, he pretends to have a fixed purpose in his mind of going straight ahead, and wheels off, sharply, at the very last moment. Now and then, when they pass a police-constable on his beat, Mr. Snagsby notices that both the constable and his guide fall into a deep abstraction as they come towards each other, and appear entirely to overlook each other, and to gaze into space. In a few instances, Mr. Bucket, coming behind some under-sized young man with a shining hat on, and his sleek hair twisted into one flat curl on each side of his head, almost without glancing at him touches him with his stick; upon which the young man, looking round, instantly evaporates. For the most part Mr. Bucket notices things in general, with a face as unchanging as the great mourning ring on his little finger, or the brooch, composed of not much diamond and a good deal of setting, which he wears in his shirt.

When they come at last to Tom-all-Alone's, Mr. Bucket stops for a moment at the corner, and takes a lighted bull's-eye from the constable on duty there, who then accompanies him with his own particular bull's-eye at his waist. Between his two conductors, Mr. Snagsby passes along the middle of a villainous street, undrained, unventilated, deep in black mud and corrupt water—though the roads are dry elsewhere —and reeking with such smells and sights that he, who has lived in London all his life, can scarce believe his senses. Branching from this street and its heaps of ruins, are other streets and courts so infamous that Mr. Snagsby sickens in body and mind, and feels as if he were going, every moment deeper down, into the infernal gulf.

"Draw off a bit here, Mr. Snagsby," says Bucket, as a kind of shabby palanquin is borne towards them, surrounded by a noisy crowd. "Here's the fever coming up the street!"

As the unseen wretch goes by, the crowd, leaving that object of attraction, hovers round the three visitors, like a dream of horrible faces, and fades away up alleys and into ruins, and behind walls ; and with occasional cries and shrill whistles of warning, thenceforth flits about them until they leave the place.

"Are those the fever-houses, Darby?" Mr. Bucket coolly asks, as he turns his bull's-eye on a line of stinking ruins.

Darby replies that "all them are," and further that in all, for months and months, the people "have been down by dozens," and have been carried out, dead and dying "like sheep with the rot." Bucket observing to Mr. Snagsby as they go on again, that he looks a little poorly, Mr. Snagsby answers that he feels as if he couldn't breathe the dreadful air.

There is inquiry made, at various houses, for a boy named Jo. As few people are known in Tom-all-Alone's by any Christian sign, there is much reference to Mr. Snagsby whether he means Carrots, or the Colonel, or Gallows, or Young Chisel, or Terrier Tip, or Lanky, or the Brick. Mr. Snagsby describes over and over again. There are conflicting opinions respecting the original of his picture. Some think it must be Carrots; some say the Brick. The Colonel is produced, but is not at all near the thing. Whenever Mr. Snagsby and his conductors are stationary, the crowd flows round, and from its squalid depths obsequious advice heaves up to Mr. Bucket. Whenever they move, and the angry bull's-eyes glare, it fades away, and flits about them up the alleys, and in the ruins, and behind the walls, as before.

At last there is a lair found out where Toughy, or the Tough Subject, lays him down at night; and it is thought that the Tough Subject may be Jo. Comparison of notes between Mr. Snagsby and the proprietress of the house—a drunken face tied up in a black bundle, and flaring out of a heap of rags on the floor of a dog-hutch which is her private apartment—leads to the establishment of this conclusion. Toughy has gone to the Doctor's to get a bottle of stuff for a sick woman, but will be here anon.

" And who have we got here to-night ? " says Mr. Bucket, opening another door and glaring in with his bull's-eye. " Two drunken men, eh ? And two women ? The men are sound enough," turning back each sleeper's arm from his face to look at him. " Are these your good men, my dears ? "

" Yes, sir," returns one of the women. " They are our husbands."

" Brickmakers, eh ? "

" Yes, sir."

" What are you doing here ? You don't belong to London."

" No, sir. We belong to Hertfordshire."

" Whereabouts in Hertfordshire ? "

" Saint Albans."

" Come up on the tramp ? "

" We walked up yesterday. There's no work down with us at present, but we have done no good by coming here, and shall do none, I expect."

" That's not the way to do much good," says Mr. Bucket,

turning his head in the direction of the unconscious figures on the ground.

"It an't indeed," replies the woman with a sigh. "Jenny and me knows it full well."

The room, though two or three feet higher than the door, is so low that the head of the tallest of the visitors would touch the blackened ceiling if he stood upright. It is offensive to every sense; even the gross candle burns pale and sickly in the polluted air. There are a couple of benches, and a higher bench by way of table. The men lie asleep where they stumbled down, but the women sit by the candle. Lying in the arms of the woman who has spoken, is a very young child.

"Why, what age do you call that little creature?" says Bucket. "It looks as if it was born yesterday." He is not at all rough about it; and as he turns his light gently on the infant, Mr. Snagsby is strangely reminded of another infant, encircled with light, that he has seen in pictures.

"He is not three weeks old yet, sir," says the woman.

"Is he your child?"

"Mine."

The other woman, who was bending over it when they came in, stoops down again, and kisses it as it lies asleep.

"You seem as fond of it as if you were the mother yourself," says Mr. Bucket.

"I was the mother of one like it, master, and it died."

"Ah, Jenny, Jenny!" says the other woman to her; "better so. Much better to think of dead than alive, Jenny! Much better!"

"Why, you an't such an unnatural woman, I hope," returns Bucket, sternly, "as to wish your own child dead?"

"God knows you are right, master," she returns. "I am not. I'd stand between it and death, with my own life if I could, as true as any pretty lady."

"Then don't talk in that wrong manner," says Mr. Bucket, mollified again. "Why do you do it?"

"It's brought into my head, master," returns the woman, her eyes filling with tears, "when I look down at the child lying so. If it was never to wake no more, you'd think me mad, I should take on so. I know that very well. I was with Jenny when she lost hers—warn't I, Jenny?—and I know how she grieved. But look around you, at this place. Look at them;" glancing at the sleepers on the ground. "Look at the boy you're waiting for, who's gone out to do me a good turn. Think of the children that your business lays with often and often, and that *you* see grow up!"

"Well, well," says Mr. Bucket, "you train him respect-able, and he'll be a comfort to you, and look after you in your old age, you know."

"I mean to try hard," she answers, wiping her eyes. "But I have been a-thinking, being over-tired to-night, and not well with the ague, of all the many things that'll come in his way. My master will be against it, and he'll be beat, and see me beat, and made to fear his home, and perhaps to stray wild. If I work for him ever so much, and ever so hard, there's no one to help me; and if he should be turned bad, 'spite of all I could do, and the time should come when I should sit by him in his sleep, made hard and changed, an't it likely I should think of him as he lies in my lap now, and wish he had died as Jenny's child died!"

"There, there!" says Jenny. "Liz, you're tired and ill. Let me take him."

In doing so, she displaces the mother's dress, but quickly readjusts it over the wounded and bruised bosom where the baby has been lying.

"It's my dead child," says Jenny, walking up and down as she nurses, "that makes me love this child so dear, and it's my dead child that makes her love it so dear too, as even to think of its being taken away from her now. While she thinks that, *I* think what fortune would I give to have my darling back. But we mean the same thing, if we knew how to say it, us two mothers does in our poor hearts!"

380

As Mr. Snagsby blows his nose, and coughs his cough of sympathy, a step is heard without. Mr. Bucket throws his light into the doorway, and says to Mr. Snagsby, "Now, what do you say to Toughy? Will *he* do?"

"That's Jo," says Mr. Snagsby.

Jo stands amazed in the disc of light, like a ragged figure in a magic-lanthorn, trembling to think that he has offended against the law in not having moved on far enough. Mr. Snagsby, however, giving him the consolatory assurance, "It's only a job you will be paid for, Jo," he recovers; and, on being taken outside by Mr. Bucket for a little private confabulation, tells his tale satisfactorily, though out of breath.

"I have squared it with the lad," says Mr. Bucket, returning, "and it's all right. Now, Mr. Snagsby, we're ready for you."

First, Jo has to complete his errand of good-nature by handing over the physic he has been to get, which he delivers with the laconic verbal direction that "it's to be all took d'rectly." Secondly, Mr. Snagsby has to lay upon the table half-a-crown, his usual panacea for an immense variety of afflictions. Thirdly, Mr. Bucket has to take Jo by the arm a little above the elbow and walk him on before him: without which observance, neither the Tough Subject nor any other Subject could be professionally conducted to Lincoln's Inn Fields. These arrangements completed, they give the women good night, and come out once more into black and foul Tom-all-Alone's.

By the noisome ways through which they descended into that pit, they gradually emerge from it; the crowd flitting, and whistling, and skulking about them, until they come to the verge, where restoration of the bull's-eyes is made to Darby. Here, the crowd, like a concourse of imprisoned demons, turns back, yelling, and is seen no more. Through the clearer and fresher streets, never so clear and fresh to Mr. Snagsby's mind as now, they walk and ride, until they come to Mr. Tulkinghorn's gate.

As they ascend the dim stairs (Mr. Tulkinghorn's chambers being on the first floor), Mr. Bucket mentions that he has the key of the outer door in his pocket, and that there is no need to ring. For a man so expert in most things of that kind, Bucket takes time to open the door, and makes some noise too. It may be that he sounds a note of preparation.

Howbeit, they come at last into the hall, where a lamp is burning, and so into Mr. Tulkinghorn's usual room—the room where he drank his old wine to-night. He is not there, but his two old-fashioned candlesticks are; and the room is tolerably light.

Mr. Bucket, still having his professional hold of Jo, and appearing to Mr. Snagsby to possess an unlimited number of eyes, makes a little way into this room, when Jo starts and stops.

" What's the matter?" says Bucket in a whisper.

" There she is!" cries Jo.

" Who!"

"The lady!"

A female figure, closely veiled, stands in the middle of the room, where the light falls upon it. It is quite still, and silent. The front of the figure is towards them, but it takes no notice of their entrance, and remains like a statue.

"Now, tell me," says Bucket aloud, "how you know that to be the lady."

"I know the wale," replies Jo, staring, "and the bonnet, and the gownd."

"Be quite sure of what you say, Tough," returns Bucket, narrowly observant of him. "Look again."

" I am a-looking as hard as ever I can look," says Jo, with starting eyes, "and that there's the wale, the bonnet, and the gownd."

"What about those rings you told me of?" asks Bucket.

" A-sparkling all over here," says Jo, rubbing the fingers of his left hand on the knuckles of his right, without taking his eyes from the figure.

382

The figure removes the right-hand glove, and shows the hand.

"Now, what do you say to that?" asks Bucket.

Jo shakes his head. "Not rings a bit like them. Not a hand like that."

"What are you talking of?" says Bucket; evidently pleased though, and well pleased too.

"Hand was a deal whiter, a deal delicater, and a deal smaller," returns Jo.

"Why, you'll tell me I'm my own mother next," says Mr. Bucket. "Do you recollect the lady's voice?"

"I think I does," says Jo.

The figure speaks. "Was it at all like this? I will speak as long as you like if you are not sure. Was it this voice, or at all like this voice?"

Jo looks aghast at Mr. Bucket. "Not a bit!"

"Then, what," retorts that worthy, pointing to the figure, "did you say it was the lady for?"

"Cos," says Jo, with a perplexed stare, but without being at all shaken in his certainty, "Cos that there's the wale, the bonnet, and the gownd. It is her and it an't her. It an't her hand, nor yet her rings, nor yet her woice. But that there's the wale, the bonnet, and the gownd, and they're wore the same way wot she wore 'em, and it's her height wot she wos, and she giv me a sov'ring and hooked it."

"Well!" says Mr. Bucket, slightly, "we haven't got much good out of *you*. But, however, here's five shillings for you. Take care how you spend it, and don't get yourself into trouble." Bucket stealthily tells the coins from one hand into the other like counters—which is a way he has, his principal use of them being in these games of skill—and then puts them, in a little pile, into the boy's hand, and takes him out to the door; leaving Mr. Snagsby, not by any means comfortable under these mysterious circumstances, alone with the veiled figure. But on Mr. Tulkinghorn's coming into the room, the veil is raised, and a sufficiently good-looking

383

Frenchwoman is revealed, though her expression is something of the intensest.

"Thank you, Mademoiselle Hortense," says Mr. Tulkinghorn, with his usual equanimity. "I will give you no further trouble about this little wager."

"You will do me the kindness to remember, sir, that I am not at present placed?" says Mademoiselle.

"Certainly, certainly!"

"And to confer upon me the favour of your distinguished recommendation?"

"By all means, Mademoiselle Hortense."

"A word from Mr. Tulkinghorn is so powerful."—"It shall not be wanting, Mademoiselle."—"Receive the assurance of my devoted gratitude, dear sir."—"Good night." Mademoiselle goes out with an air of native gentility; and Mr. Bucket, to whom it is, on an emergency, as natural to be groom of the ceremonies as it is to be anything else, shows her down-stairs, not without gallantry.

"Well, Bucket?" quoth Mr. Tulkinghorn, on his return.

"It's all squared, you see, as I squared it myself, sir. There an't a doubt that it was the other one with this one's dress on. The boy was exact respecting colours and everything. Mr. Snagsby, I promised you as a man that he should be sent away all right. Don't say it wasn't done!"

"You have kept your word, sir," returns the stationer; "and if I can be of no further use, Mr. Tulkinghorn, I think, as my little woman will be getting anxious——"

"Thank you, Snagsby, no further use," says Mr. Tulkinghorn. "I am quite indebted to you for the trouble you have taken already."

"Not at all, sir. I wish you good night."

"You see, Mr. Snagsby," says Mr. Bucket, accompanying him to the door, and shaking hands with him over and over again, "what I like in you is, that you're a man it's of no use pumping; that's what *you* are. When you know you have done a right thing, you put it away, and it's done with and gone, and there's an end of it. That's what *you* do."

"That is certainly what I endeavour to do, sir," returns Mr. Snagsby.

"No, you don't do yourself justice. It an't what you endeavour to do," says Mr. Bucket, shaking hands with him and blessing him in the tenderest manner, "it's what you *do*. That's what I estimate in a man in your way of business."

Mr. Snagsby makes a suitable response; and goes homeward so confused by the events of the evening, that he is doubtful of his being awake and out—doubtful of the reality of the streets through which he goes—doubtful of the reality of the moon that shines above him. He is presently reassured on these subjects, by the unchallengeable reality of Mrs. Snagsby, sitting up with her head in a perfect beehive of curl-papers and nightcap: who has despatched Guster to the police-station with official intelligence of her husband's being made away with, and who, within the last two hours, has passed through every stage of swooning with the greatest decorum. But, as the little woman feelingly says, many thanks she gets for it!

CHAPTER XXIII

WE came home from Mr. Boythorn's after six pleasant weeks. We were often in the park, and in the woods, and seldom passed the Lodge where we had taken shelter without looking in to speak to the keeper's wife; but we saw no more of Lady Dedlock, except at church on Sundays. There was company at Chesney Wold; and although several beautiful faces surrounded her, her face retained the same influence on me as at first. I do not quite know, even now, whether it was painful or pleasurable; whether it drew me towards her, or made me shrink from her. I think I admired her with a kind of fear; and I know that in her presence my thoughts always wandered back, as they had done at first, to that old time of my life.

I had a fancy, on more than one of these Sundays, that what this lady so curiously was to me, I was to her—I mean that I disturbed her thoughts as she influenced mine, though in some different way. But when I stole a glance at her, and saw her so composed and distant and unapproachable, I felt this to be a foolish weakness. Indeed, I felt the whole state of my mind in reference to her to be weak and unreasonable; and I remonstrated with myself about it as much as I could.

One incident that occurred before we quitted Mr. Boythorn's house, I had better mention in this place.

386

MADEMOISELLE HORTENSE

I was walking in the garden with Ada, when I was told that some one wished to see me. Going into the breakfast-room, where this person was waiting, I found it to be the French maid who had cast off her shoes and walked through the wet grass, on the day when it thundered and lightened.

"Mademoiselle," she began, looking fixedly at me with her too-eager eyes, though otherwise presenting an agreeable appearance, and speaking neither with boldness nor servility, "I have taken a great liberty in coming here, but you know how to excuse it, being so amiable, mademoiselle."

"No excuse is necessary," I returned, "if you wish to speak to me."

"That is my desire, mademoiselle. A thousand thanks for the permission. I have your leave to speak. Is it not?" she said, in a quick, natural way.

"Certainly," said I.

"Mademoiselle, you are so amiable! Listen then, if you please. I have left my Lady. We could not agree. My Lady is so high; so very high. Pardon! Mademoiselle, you are right!" Her quickness anticipated what I might have said presently, but as yet had only thought. "It is not for me to come here to complain of my Lady. But I say she is so high, so very high. I will not say a word more. All the world knows that."

"Go on, if you please," said I.

"Assuredly; mademoiselle, I am thankful for your polite-ness. Mademoiselle, I have an inexpressible desire to find service with a young lady who is good, accomplished, beauti-ful. You are good, accomplished, and beautiful as an angel. Ah, could I have the honour of being your domestic!"

"I am sorry—— " I began.

"Do not dismiss me so soon, mademoiselle!" she said, with an involuntary contraction of her fine black eyebrows. "Let me hope, a moment! Mademoiselle, I know this service would be more retired than that which I have quitted. Well! I wish that. I know this service would be less distinguished than that which I have quitted. Well! I wish that. I know that I should win less, as to wages here. Good. I am content."

"I assure you," said I, quite embarrassed by the mere idea of having such an attendant, "that I keep no maid——"

"Ah, mademoiselle, but why not? Why not, when you can have one so devoted to you! Who would be enchanted to serve you; who would be so true, so zealous, and so faithful, every day! Mademoiselle, I wish with all my heart to serve you. Do not speak of money at present. Take me as I am. For nothing!"

She was so singularly earnest that I drew back, almost afraid of her. Without appearing to notice it, in her ardour she still pressed herself upon me; speaking in a rapid subdued voice, though always with a certain grace and propriety.

"Mademoiselle, I come from the South country, where we are quick, and where we like and dislike very strong. My Lady was too high for me; I was too high for her. It is done—past—finished! Receive me as your domestic, and I will serve you well. I will do more for you, than you figure to yourself now. Chut! mademoiselle, I will—no matter, I will do my utmost possible, in all things. If you accept my service, you will not repent it. Mademoiselle, you will not repent it, and I will serve you well. You don't know how well!

There was a lowering energy in her face, as she stood looking at me while I explained the impossibility of my engaging her (without thinking it necessary to say how very little I desired to do so), which seemed to bring visibly before me some woman from the streets of Paris in the reign of terror. She heard me out without interruption; and then said, with her pretty accent, and in her mildest voice:

"Hey, mademoiselle, I have received my answer! I am sorry of it. But I must go elsewhere, and seek what I have not found here. Will you graciously let me kiss your hand?"

She looked at me more intently as she took it, and seemed to take note, with her momentary touch, of every vein in it. "I fear I surprised you, mademoiselle, on the day of the storm?" she said with a parting curtsey.

I confessed that she had surprised us all.

"I took an oath, mademoiselle," she said, smiling, "and I wanted to stamp it on my mind, so that I might keep it faithfully. And I will! Adieu, mademoiselle!"

So ended our conference, which I was very glad to bring to a close. I supposed she went away from the village, for I saw her no more; and nothing else occurred to disturb our tranquil summer pleasures, until six weeks were out, and we returned home as I began just now by saying.

At that time, and for a good many weeks after that time, Richard was constant in his visits. Besides coming every Saturday or Sunday, and remaining with us until Monday morning, he sometimes rode out on horseback unexpectedly, and passed the evening with us, and rode back again early next day. He was as vivacious as ever, and told us he was very industrious; but I was not easy in my mind about him. It appeared to me that his industry was all misdirected. I could not find that it led to anything but the formation of delusive hopes in connexion with the suit already the pernicious cause of so much sorrow and ruin. He had got at the core of that mystery now, he told us; and nothing could be plainer than that the will under which he and Ada were to take, I don't know how many thousands of pounds, must be finally established, if there were any sense or justice in the Court of Chancery—but O what a great *if* that sounded in my ears—and that this happy conclusion could not be much longer delayed. He proved this to himself by all the weary arguments on that side he had read, and every one of them sunk him deeper in the infatuation. He had even begun to haunt the Court. He told us how he saw Miss Flite there daily; how they talked together, and how he did her little kindnesses; and how, while he laughed at her, he pitied her from his heart. But he never thought—never, my poor, dear, sanguine Richard, capable of so much happiness then, and with such better things before him!—what a fatal link was riveting between his fresh youth and her faded age ; between his free hopes and her caged birds, and her hungry garret, and her wandering mind.

Ada loved him too well to mistrust him much in anything he said or did, and my guardian, though he frequently complained of the east wind and read more than usual in the Growlery, preserved a strict silence on the subject. So, I thought, one day when I went to London to meet Caddy Jellyby, at her solicitation, I would ask Richard to be in waiting for me at the coach-office, that we might have a little talk together. I found him there when I arrived, and we walked away arm in arm.

" Well, Richard," said I, as soon as I could begin to be grave with him, " are you beginning to feel more settled now ? "

" O yes, my dear ! " returned Richard. " I'm all right enough."

" But settled ? " said I.

" How do you mean, settled ? " returned Richard, with his gay laugh.

"Settled in the law," said I.

" O aye," replied Richard, " I'm all right enough."

" You said that before, my dear Richard."

" And you don't think it's an answer, eh ? Well ! Perhaps it's not. Settled ? You mean, do I feel as if I were settling down ? "

" Yes."

" Why, no, I can't say I am settling down," said Richard, strongly emphasising " down," as if that expressed the difficulty ; " because one can't settle down while this business remains in such an unsettled state. When I say this business, of course I mean the—forbidden subject."

" Do you think it will ever be in a settled state ? " said I.

"Not the least doubt of it," answered Richard.

We walked a little way without speaking; and presently Richard addressed me in his frankest and most feeling manner, thus:

"My dear Esther, I understand you, and I wish to Heaven I were a more constant sort of fellow. I don't mean constant to Ada, for I love her dearly—better and better every day—but constant to myself. (Somehow, I mean something that I can't very well express, but you'll make it out.) If I were a more constant sort of fellow, I should have held on, either to Badger, or to Kenge and Carboy, like grim Death; and should have begun to be steady and systematic by this time, and shouldn't be in debt, and——"

"*Are* you in debt, Richard?"

"Yes," said Richard, "I am a little so, my dear. Also, I have taken rather too much to billiards, and that sort of thing. Now the murder's out; you despise me, Esther, don't you?"

"You know I don't," said I.

"You are kinder to me than I often am to myself," he returned. "My dear Esther, I am a very unfortunate dog not to be more settled, but how *can* I be more settled? If you lived in an unfinished house, you couldn't settle down in it; if you were condemned to leave everything you undertook, unfinished, you would find it hard to apply yourself to anything; and yet that's my unhappy case. I was born into this unfinished contention with all its chances and changes, and it began to unsettle me before I quite knew the difference between a suit at law and a suit of clothes; and it has gone on unsettling me ever since; and here I am now, conscious sometimes that I am but a worthless fellow to love my confiding cousin Ada."

We were in a solitary place, and he put his hands before his eyes and sobbed as he said the words.

"O Richard!" said I, "do not be so moved. You have a noble nature, and Ada's love may make you worthier every day."

391

"I know, my dear," he replied, pressing my arm, "I know all that. You mustn't mind my being a little soft now, for I have had all this upon my mind for a long time; and have often meant to speak to you, and have sometimes wanted opportunity and sometimes courage. I know what the thought of Ada ought to do for me, but it doesn't do it. I am too unsettled even for that. I love her most devotedly; and yet I do her wrong, in doing myself wrong, every day and hour. But it can't last for ever. We shall come on for a final hearing, and get judgment in our favour; and then you and Ada shall see what I can really be!"

It had given me a pang to hear him sob, and see the tears start out between his fingers; but that was infinitely less affecting to me, than the hopeful animation with which he said these words.

"I have looked well into the papers, Esther—I have been deep in them for months"—he continued, recovering his cheerfulness in a moment, "and you may rely upon it that we shall come out triumphant. As to years of delay, there has been no want of them, Heaven knows! and there is the greater probability of our bringing the matter to a speedy close; in fact, it's on the paper now. It will be all right at last, and then you shall see!"

Recalling how he had just now placed Messrs. Kenge and Carboy in the same category with Mr. Badger, I asked him when he intended to be articled in Lincoln's Inn?

"There again! I think not at all, Esther," he returned with an effort. "I fancy I have had enough of it. Having worked at Jarndyce and Jarndyce like a galley slave, I have slaked my thirst for the law, and satisfied myself that I shouldn't like it. Besides, I find it unsettles me more and more to be so constantly upon the scene of action. So what," continued Richard, confident again by this time, "do I naturally turn my thoughts to?"

"I can't imagine," said I.

"Don't look so serious," returned Richard, "because it's

the best thing I can do, my dear Esther, I am certain. It's not as if I wanted a profession for life. These proceedings will come to a termination, and then I am provided for. No. I look upon it as a pursuit which is in its nature more or less unsettled, and therefore suited to my temporary condition— I may say, precisely suited. What is it that I naturally turn my thoughts to?"

I looked at him, and shook my head.

"What," said Richard, in a tone of perfect conviction, "but the army!"

"The army?" said I.

"The army, of course. What I have to do, is, to get a commission; and—there I am, you know!" said Richard.

And then he showed me, proved by elaborate calculations in his pocket-book, that supposing he had contracted, say two hundred pounds of debt in six months, out of the army; and that he contracted no debt at all within a corresponding period, in the army—as to which he had quite made up his mind; this step must involve a saving of four hundred pounds in a year, or two thousand pounds in five years —which was a considerable sum. And then he spoke so ingenuously and sincerely, of the sacrifice he made in withdrawing himself for a time from Ada, and of the earnestness with which he aspired—as in thought he always did, I know full well—to repay her love, and to ensure her happiness, and to conquer what was amiss in himself, and to acquire the very soul of decision, that he made my heart ache keenly, sorely. For, I thought how would this end, how could this end, when so soon and so surely all his manly qualities were touched by the fatal blight that ruined everything it rested on!

I spoke to Richard with all the earnestness I felt, and all the hope I could not quite feel then; and implored him, for Ada's sake, not to put any trust in Chancery. To all I said, Richard readily assented; riding over the Court and everything else in his easy way, and drawing the brightest pictures of the character he was to settle into—alas, when the grievous suit should loose its hold upon him! We had a long talk, but it always came back to that, in substance.

At last, we came to Soho Square, where Caddy Jellyby had appointed to wait for me, as a quiet place in the neighbourhood of Newman Street. Caddy was in the garden in the centre, and hurried out as soon as I appeared. After a few cheerful words, Richard left us together.

"Prince has a pupil over the way, Esther," said Caddy, "and got the key for us. So, if you will walk round and round here with me, we can lock ourselves in, and I can tell you comfortably what I wanted to see your dear good face about."

"Very well, my dear," said I. "Nothing could be better." So Caddy, after affectionately squeezing the dear good face as she called it, locked the gate, and took my arm, and we began to walk round the garden very cosily.

"You see, Esther," said Caddy, who thoroughly enjoyed a little confidence, "after you spoke to me about its being wrong to marry without Ma's knowledge, or even to keep Ma long in the dark respecting our engagement—though I don't believe Ma cares much for me, I must say—I thought it right to mention your opinions to Prince. In the first place, because I want to profit by everything you tell me; and in the second place, because I have no secrets from Prince."

"I hope he approved, Caddy?"

"O, my dear! I assure you he would approve of anything you could say. You have no idea what an opinion he has of you!"

"Indeed!"

"Esther, it's enough to make anybody but me jealous," said Caddy, laughing and shaking her head; "but it only makes me joyful, for you are the first friend I ever had, and the best friend I ever can have, and nobody can respect and love you too much to please me."

"Upon my word, Caddy," said I, "you are in the general conspiracy to keep me in a good humour. Well, my dear?

"Well! I am going to tell you," replied Caddy, crossing her hands confidentially upon my arm. "So we talked a good deal about it, and so I said to Prince, 'Prince, as Miss Summerson——'"

"I hope you didn't say 'Miss Summerson'?"

"No. I didn't!" cried Caddy, greatly pleased, and with the brightest of faces. "I said, 'Esther.' I said to Prince, 'As Esther is decidedly of that opinion, Prince, and has expressed it to me, and always hints it when she writes those kind notes, which you are so fond of hearing me read to you, I am prepared to disclose the truth to Ma whenever you think proper. And I think, Prince,' said I, 'that Esther thinks that I should be in a better, and truer, and more honourable position altogether, if you did the same to your Papa.'"

"Yes, my dear," said I. "Esther certainly does think so."

"So I was right, you see!" exclaimed Caddy. "Well! this troubled Prince a good deal; not because he had the least doubt about it, but because he is so considerate of the feelings of old Mr. Turveydrop; and he had his apprehensions that old Mr. Turveydrop might break his heart, or faint away, or be very much overcome in some affecting manner or other, if he made such an announcement. He feared old Mr. Turveydrop might consider it undutiful, and might receive too great a shock. For, old Mr. Turveydrop's deportment is very beautiful you know, Esther," said Caddy; "and his feelings are extremely sensitive."

"Are they, my dear?"

"O, extremely sensitive. Prince says so. Now, this has caused my darling child—I didn't mean to use the expression to you, Esther," Caddy apologised, her face suffused with blushes, "but I generally call Prince my darling child."

I laughed; and Caddy laughed and blushed, and went on.

"This has caused him, Esther——"

"Caused whom, my dear?"

"O you tiresome thing!" said Caddy, laughing, with her

pretty face on fire. " My darling child, if you insist upon it !
—This has caused him weeks of uneasiness, and has made
him delay, from day to day, in a very anxious manner. At
last he said to me, 'Caddy, if Miss Summerson, who is a
great favourite with my father, could be prevailed upon to
be present when I broke the subject, I think I could do it.'
So I promised I would ask you. And I made up my mind,
besides," said Caddy, looking at me hopefully, but timidly,
"that if you consented, I would ask you afterwards to come
with me to Ma. This is what I meant, when I said in my
note that I had a great favour and a great assistance to beg
of you. And if you thought you could grant it, Esther, we
should both be very grateful."

" Let me see, Caddy," said I, pretending to consider.
" Really I think I could do a greater thing than that, if the
need were pressing. I am at your service and the darling
child's, my dear, whenever you like."

Caddy was quite transported by this reply of mine ; being,
I believe, as susceptible to the least kindness or encouragement
as any tender heart that ever beat in this world ; and after
another turn or two round the garden, during which she
put on an entirely new pair of gloves, and made herself as
resplendent as possible that she might do no avoidable dis-
credit to the Master of Deportment, we went to Newman
Street direct.

Prince was teaching, of course. We found him engaged
with a not very hopeful pupil—a stubborn little girl with a
sulky forehead, a deep voice, and an inanimate dissatisfied
mamma—whose case was certainly not rendered more hopeful
by the confusion into which we threw her preceptor. The
lesson at last came to an end, after proceeding as discordantly
as possible ; and when the little girl had changed her shoes,
and had had her white muslin extinguished in shawls, she was
taken away. After a few words of preparation, we then
went in search of Mr. Turveydrop ; whom we found, grouped
with his hat and gloves, as a model of Deportment, on the

sofa in his private apartment—the only comfortable room in the house. He appeared to have dressed at his leisure, in the intervals of a light collation ; and his dressing-case, brushes, and so forth, all of quite an elegant kind, lay about.

"Father, Miss Summerson ; Miss Jellyby."

"Charmed ! Enchanted !" said Mr. Turveydrop, rising with his high-shouldered bow. "Permit me !" handing chairs. Be seated !" kissing the tips of his left fingers. "Overjoyed !" shutting his eyes and rolling. "My little retreat is made a Paradise." Recomposing himself on the sofa, like the second gentleman in Europe.

"Again you find us, Miss Summerson," said he, "using our little arts to polish, polish ! Again the sex stimulates us, and rewards us, by the condescension of its lovely presence. It is much in these times (and we have made an awfully degenerating business of it since the days of His Royal Highness the Prince Regent—my patron, if I may presume to say so) to experience that Deportment is not wholly trodden under foot by mechanics. That it can yet bask in the smile of Beauty, my dear madam."

I said nothing, which I thought a suitable reply ; and he took a pinch of snuff. .

"My dear son," said Mr. Turveydrop, "you have four schools this afternoon. I would recommend a hasty sandwich."

"Thank you, father," returned Prince, " I will be sure to be punctual. My dear father, may I beg you to prepare your mind for what I am going to say !"

"Good Heaven !" exclaimed the model, pale and aghast, as Prince and Caddy, hand in hand, bent down before him. "What is this ? Is this lunacy ! Or what is this ?"

"Father," returned Prince, with great submission, "I love this young lady, and we are engaged."

"Engaged !" cried Mr. Turveydrop, reclining on the sofa, and shutting out the sight with his hand. "An arrow launched at my brain, by my own child !"

"We have been engaged for some time, father," faltered Prince; "and Miss Summerson, hearing of it, advised that we should declare the fact to you, and was so very kind as to attend on the present occasion. Miss Jellyby is a young lady who deeply respects you, father."

Mr. Turveydrop uttered a groan.

"No, pray don't! Pray don't, father," urged his son. "Miss Jellyby is a young lady who deeply respects you, and our first desire is to consider your comfort."

Mr. Turveydrop sobbed.

"No, pray don't, father!" cried his son.

"Boy," said Mr. Turveydrop, "it is well that your sainted mother is spared this pang. Strike deep, and spare not. Strike home, sir, strike home!"

"Pray, don't say so, father," implored Prince, in tears. "It goes to my heart. I do assure you, father, that our first wish and intention is to consider your comfort. Caroline and I do not forget our duty—what is my duty is Caroline's, as we have often said together—and, with your approval and consent, father, we will devote ourselves to making your life agreeable."

"Strike home," murmured Mr. Turveydrop. "Strike home!"

But he seemed to listen, I thought, too.

"My dear father," returned Prince, "we well know what little comforts you are accustomed to, and have a right to; and it will always be our study, and our pride, to provide those before anything. If you will bless us with your approval and consent, father, we shall not think of being married until it is quite agreeable to you; and when we *are* married, we shall always make you—of course—our first consideration. You must ever be the Head and Master here, father; and we feel how truly unnatural it would be in us, if we failed to know it, or if we failed to exert ourselves in every possible way to please you.'

Mr. Turveydrop underwent a severe internal struggle, and

A Model of Parental Deportment

came upright on the sofa again, with his cheeks puffing over his stiff cravat: a perfect model of parental deportment.

"My son!" said Mr. Turveydrop. "My children! I cannot resist your prayer. Be happy!"

His benignity, as he raised his future daughter-in-law and stretched out his hand to his son (who kissed it with affectionate respect and gratitude), was the most confusing sight I ever saw.

"My children," said Mr. Turveydrop, paternally encircling Caddy with his left arm as she sat beside him, and putting his right hand gracefully on his hip. "My son and daughter, your happiness shall be my care. I will watch over you. You shall always live with me;" meaning, of course, I will always live with you; "this house is henceforth as much yours as mine; consider it your home. May you long live to share it with me!"

The power of his Deportment was such, that they really were as much overcome with thankfulness as if, instead of quartering himself upon them for the rest of his life, he were making some munificent sacrifice in their favour.

"For myself, my children," said Mr. Turveydrop, "I am falling into the sear and yellow leaf, and it is impossible to say how long the last feeble traces of gentlemanly Deportment may linger in this weaving and spinning age. But, so long, I will do my duty to society, and will show myself, as usual, about town. My wants are few and simple. My little apartment here, my few essentials for the toilet, my frugal morning meal, and my little dinner, will suffice. I charge your dutiful affection with the supply of these requirements, and I charge myself with all the rest."

They were overpowered afresh by his uncommon generosity.

"My son," said Mr. Turveydrop, "for those little points in which you are deficient—points of Deportment which are born with a man—which may be improved by cultivation, but can never be originated—you may still rely on me. I have been faithful to my post, since the days of His Royal Highness the Prince Regent; and I will not desert it now. No, my son. If you have ever contemplated your father's poor position with a feeling of pride, you may rest assured that he will do nothing to tarnish it. For yourself, Prince, whose character is different (we cannot be all alike, nor is it advisable that we should), work, be industrious, earn money, and extend the connexion as much as possible."

"That you may depend I will do, dear father, with all my heart," replied Prince.

"I have no doubt of it," said Mr. Turveydrop. "Your qualities are not shining, my dear child, but they are steady and useful. And to both of you, my dear children, I would merely observe, in the spirit of a sainted Wooman on whose path I had the happiness of casting, I believe, *some* ray of light,—take care of the establishment, take care of my simple wants, and bless you both!"

Old Mr. Turveydrop then became so very gallant, in honour of the occasion, that I told Caddy we must really go to Thavies Inn at once if we were to go at all that day. So we took our departure, after a very loving farewell between Caddy and her betrothed: and during our walk she was so happy, and so full of old Mr. Turveydrop's praises, that I would not have said a word in his disparagement for any consideration.

The house in Thavies Inn had bills in the windows announcing that it was to let, and it looked dirtier and gloomier and ghastlier than ever. The name of poor Mr. Jellyby had appeared in the list of Bankrupts, but a day or two before; and he was shut up in the dining-room with two gentlemen, and a heap of blue bags, account-books, and papers, making the most desperate endeavours to understand his affairs. They appeared to me to be quite beyond his comprehension; for when Caddy took me into the dining-room by mistake, and we came upon Mr. Jellyby in his spectacles, forlornly fenced into a corner by the great dining-table and the two gentlemen, he seemed to have given up the whole thing, and to be speechless and in-sensible.

Going up-stairs to Mrs. Jellyby's room (the children were all screaming in the kitchen, and there was no servant to be seen), we found that lady in the midst of a voluminous corre-spondence, opening, reading, and sorting letters, with a great accumulation of torn covers on the floor. She was so pre-occupied that at first she did not know me, though she sat looking at me with that curious, bright-eyed, far-off look of hers.

"Ah! Miss Summerson!" she said at last. "I was thinking of something so different! I hope you are well. I am happy to see you. Mr. Jarndyce and Miss Clare quite well?"

I hoped in return that Mr. Jellyby was quite well.

"Why, not quite, my dear," said Mrs. Jellyby, in the calmest manner. "He has been unfortunate in his affairs, and is a little out of spirits. Happily for me, I am so much engaged that I have no time to think about it. We have, at the present moment, one hundred and seventy families, Miss Summerson, averaging five persons in each, either gone or going to the left bank of the Niger."

I thought of the one family so near us, who were neither gone nor going to the left bank of the Niger, and wondered how she could be so placid.

"You have brought Caddy back, I see," observed Mrs. Jellyby, with a glance at her daughter. "It has become quite a novelty to see her here. She has almost deserted her old employment, and in fact obliges me to employ a boy."

"I am sure, Ma,—— " began Caddy.

"Now you know, Caddy," her mother mildly interposed, "that I *do* employ a boy, who is now at his dinner. What is the use of your contradicting?"

"I was not going to contradict, Ma," returned Caddy. "I was only going to say, that surely you wouldn't have me be a mere drudge all my life."

"I believe, my dear," said Mrs. Jellyby, still opening her letters, casting her bright eyes smilingly over them, and sorting them as she spoke, "that you have a business example before you in your mother. Besides. A mere drudge? If you had any sympathy with the destinies of the human race, it would raise you high above any such idea. But you have none. I have often told you, Caddy, you have no such sympathy."

"Not if it's Africa, Ma, I have not."

"Of course you have not. Now, if I were not happily so much engaged, Miss Summerson," said Mrs. Jellyby, sweetly casting her eyes for a moment on me, and considering where to put the particular letter she had just opened, "this would distress and disappoint me. But I have so much to think of, in connexion with Borrioboola-Gha, and it is so necessary I should concentrate myself, that there is my remedy, you see."

As Caddy gave me a glance of entreaty, and as Mrs. Jellyby was looking far away into Africa straight through my bonnet and head, I thought it a good opportunity to come to the subject of my visit, and to attract Mrs. Jellyby's attention.

"Perhaps," I began, "you will wonder what has brought me here to interrupt you."

"I am always delighted to see Miss Summerson," said Mrs. Jellyby, pursuing her employment with a placid smile. "Though I wish," and she shook her head, "she was more interested in the Borrioboolan project."

"I have come with Caddy," said I, "because Caddy justly thinks she ought not to have a secret from her mother; and fancies I shall encourage and aid her (though I am sure I don't know how), in imparting one."

"Caddy," said Mrs. Jellyby, pausing for a moment in her occupation, and then serenely pursuing it after shaking her head, "you are going to tell me some nonsense."

Caddy untied the strings of her bonnet, took her bonnet

off, and letting it dangle on the floor by the strings, and crying heartily, said, " Ma, I am engaged."

" O, you ridiculous child ! " observed Mrs. Jellyby, with an abstracted air, as she looked over the despatch last opened ; " what a goose you are ! "

" I am engaged, Ma," sobbed Caddy, " to young Mr. Turveydrop, at the Academy ; and old Mr. Turveydrop (who is a very gentlemanly man indeed) has given his consent, and I beg and pray you'll give us yours, Ma, because I never could be happy without it. I never, never could ! " sobbed Caddy, quite forgetful of her general complainings, and of everything but her natural affection.

" You see again, Miss Summerson," observed Mrs. Jellyby, serenely, " what a happiness it is to be so much occupied as I am, and to have this necessity for self-concentration that I have. Here is Caddy engaged to a dancing-master's son— mixed up with people who have no more sympathy with the destinies of the human race than she has herself ! This, too, when Mr. Quale, one of the first philanthropists of our time, has mentioned to me that he was really disposed to be interested in her ! "

" Ma, I always hated and detested Mr. Quale ! " sobbed Caddy.

" Caddy, Caddy ! " returned Mrs. Jellyby, opening another letter with the greatest complacency. " I have no doubt you did. How could you do otherwise, being totally destitute of the sympathies with which he overflows ! Now, if my public duties were not a favourite child to me, if I were not occupied with large measures on a vast scale, these petty details might grieve me very much, Miss Summerson. But can I permit the film of a silly proceeding on the part of Caddy (from whom I expect nothing else), to interpose between me and the great African continent ? No. No," repeated Mrs. Jellyby, in a calm clear voice, and with an agreeable smile, as she opened more letters and sorted them. " No, indeed."

I was so unprepared for the perfect coolness of this

reception, though I might have expected it, that I did not know what to say. Caddy seemed equally at a loss. Mrs. Jellyby continued to open and sort letters; and to repeat occasionally, in quite a charming tone of voice, and with a smile of perfect composure, "No, indeed."

"I hope, Ma," sobbed poor Caddy at last, "you are not angry?"

"O Caddy, you really are an absurd girl," returned Mrs. Jellyby, "to ask such questions, after what I have said of the preoccupation of my mind."

"And I hope, Ma, you give us your consent, and wish us well?" said Caddy.

"You are a nonsensical child to have done anything of this kind," said Mrs. Jellyby; "and a degenerate child, when you might have devoted yourself to the great public measure. But the step is taken, and I have engaged a boy, and there is no more to be said. Now, pray, Caddy," said Mrs. Jellyby —for Caddy was kissing her—"don't delay me in my work, but let me clear off this heavy batch of papers before the afternoon post comes in!"

I thought I could not do better than take my leave; I was detained for a moment by Caddy's saying,

"You won't object to my bringing him to see you, Ma?"

"O dear me, Caddy," cried Mrs. Jellyby, who had relapsed into that distant contemplation, "have you begun again? Bring whom?"

"Him, Ma."

"Caddy, Caddy!" said Mrs. Jellyby, quite weary of such little matters. "Then you must bring him some evening which is not a Parent Society night, or a Branch night, or a Ramification night. You must accommodate the visit to the demands upon my time. My dear Miss Summerson, it was very kind of you to come here to help out this silly chit. Good-bye! When I tell you that I have fifty-eight new letters from manufacturing families anxious to understand the details of the Native and Coffee Cultivation question, this morning, I need not apologise for having very little leisure."

I was not surprised by Caddy's being in low spirits, when we went down-stairs; or by her sobbing afresh on my neck, or by her saying she would far rather have been scolded than treated with such indifference, or by her confiding to me that she was so poor in clothes, that how she was ever to be married creditably she didn't know. I gradually cheered her up, by dwelling on the many things she would do for her unfortunate father, and for Peepy, when she had a home of her own; and finally we went down-stairs into the damp dark kitchen, where Peepy and his little brothers and sisters were grovelling on the stone floor, and where we had such a game of play with them, that to prevent myself from being quite torn to pieces I was obliged to fall back on my fairy tales. From time to time, I heard loud voices in the parlour overhead; and occasionally a violent tumbling about of the furniture. The last effect I am afraid was caused by poor Mr. Jellyby's breaking away from the dining-table, and making rushes at the window, with the intention of throwing himself into the area, whenever he made any new attempt to understand his affairs.

As I rode quietly home at night after the day's bustle, I thought a good deal of Caddy's engagement, and felt confirmed in my hopes (in spite of the elder Mr. Turveydrop) that she would be the happier and better for it. And if there seemed to be but a slender chance of her and her husband ever finding out what the model of Deportment really was, why that was all for the best too, and who would wish them to be wiser? I did not wish them to be any wiser, and indeed was half ashamed of not entirely believing in him myself. And I looked up at the stars, and thought about travellers in distant countries and the stars *they* saw, and hoped I might always be so blest and happy as to be useful to some one in my small way.

They were so glad to see me when I got home, as they

always were, that I could have sat down and cried for joy, if that had not been a method of making myself disagreeable. Everybody in the house, from the lowest to the highest, showed me such a bright face of welcome, and spoke so cheerily, and was so happy to do anything for me, that I suppose there never was such a fortunate little creature in the world.

We got into such a chatty state that night, through Ada and my guardian drawing me out to tell them all about Caddy, that I went on prose, prose, prosing, for a length of time. At last I got up to my own room, quite red to think how I had been holding forth; and then I heard a soft tap at my door. So I said, "Come in!" and there came in a pretty little girl, neatly dressed in mourning, who dropped a curtsey.

"If you please, miss," said the little girl, in a soft voice, "I am Charley."

"Why, so you are," said I, stooping down in astonishment, and giving her a kiss. "How glad am I to see you, Charley!"

"If you please, miss," pursued Charley, in the same soft voice, "I'm your maid."

"Charley?"

"If you please, miss, I'm a present to you, with Mr. Jarndyce's love."

I sat down with my hand on Charley's neck, and looked at Charley.

"And O, miss," says Charley, clapping her hands, with the tears starting down her dimpled cheeks, "Tom's at school, if you please, and learning so good! And little Emma, she's with Mrs. Blinder, miss, a being took such care of! And Tom, he would have been at school—and Emma, she would have been left with Mrs. Blinder—and me, I should have been here—all a deal sooner, miss; only Mr. Jarndyce thought that Tom and Emma and me had better get a little used to parting first, we was so small. Don't cry, if you please, miss!"

A PRESENT, WITH MR. JARNDYCE'S LOVE

" I can't help it, Charley."

" No, miss, nor I can't help it," says Charley. " And if you please, miss, Mr. Jarndyce's love, and he thinks you'll like to teach me now and then. And if you please, Tom and Emma and me is to see each other once a month. And I'm so happy and so thankful, miss," cried Charley with a heaving heart, " and I'll try to be such a good maid! "

" O Charley dear, never forget who did all this ! "

" No, miss, I never will. Nor Tom won't. Nor yet Emma. It was all you, miss."

" I have known nothing of it. It was Mr. Jarndyce, Charley."

" Yes, miss, but it was all done for the love of you, and that you might be my mistress. If you please, miss, I am a little present with his love, and it was all done for the love of you. Me and Tom was to be sure to remember it."

Charley dried her eyes, and entered on her functions : going in her matronly little way about and about the room, and folding up everything she could lay her hands upon. Presently, Charley came creeping back to my side, and said :

" O don't cry, if you please, miss."

And I said again, " I can't help it, Charley."

And Charley said again, " No, miss, nor I can't help it." And so, after all, I did cry for joy indeed, and so did she.

CHAPTER XXIV

AN APPEAL CASE

As soon as Richard and I had held the conversation of which
I have given an account, Richard communicated the state of
his mind to Mr. Jarndyce. I doubt if my guardian were
altogether taken by surprise, when he received the representation; though it caused him much uneasiness and disappointment. He and Richard were often closeted together, late at
night and early in the morning, and passed whole days in
London, and had innumerable appointments with Mr. Kenge,
and laboured through a quantity of disagreeable business.
While they were thus employed, my guardian, though he
underwent considerable inconvenience from the state of the
wind, and rubbed his head so constantly that not a single
hair upon it ever rested in its right place, was as genial with
Ada and me as at any other time, but maintained a steady
reserve on these matters. And as our utmost endeavours
could only elicit from Richard himself sweeping assurances
that everything was going on capitally, and that it really was
all right at last, our anxiety was not much relieved by him.

We learnt, however, as the time went on, that a new application was made to the Lord Chancellor on Richard's behalf,
as an Infant and a Ward, and I don't know what; and that
there was a quantity of talking; and that the Lord Chancellor
described him, in open court, as a vexatious and capricious
infant; and that the matter was adjourned and readjourned,

408

and referred, and reported on, and petitioned about, until Richard began to doubt (as he told us) whether, if he entered the army at all, it would not be as a veteran of seventy or eighty years of age. At last an appointment was made for him to see the Lord Chancellor again in his private room, and there the Lord Chancellor very seriously reproved him for trifling with time, and not knowing his mind—"a pretty good joke, I think," said Richard, "from that quarter!"— and at last it was settled that his application should be granted. His name was entered at the Horse Guards, as an applicant for an Ensign's commission; the purchase-money was deposited at an Agent's; and Richard, in his usual characteristic way, plunged into a violent course of military study, and got up at five o'clock every morning to practise the broadsword exercise.

Thus, vacation succeeded term, and term succeeded vacation. We sometimes heard of Jarndyce and Jarndyce, as being in the paper or out of the paper, or as being to be mentioned, or as being to be spoken to; and it came on, and it went off. Richard, who was now in a Professor's house in London, was able to be with us less frequently than before; my guardian still maintained the same reserve; and so time passed until the commission was obtained, and Richard received directions with it to join a regiment in Ireland.

He arrived post-haste with the intelligence one evening, and had a long conference with my guardian. Upwards of an hour elapsed before my guardian put his head into the room where Ada and I were sitting, and said, "Come in, my dears!" We went in, and found Richard, whom we had last seen in high spirits, leaning on the chimney-piece, looking mortified and angry.

"Rick and I, Ada," said Mr. Jarndyce, "are not quite of one mind. Come, come, Rick, put a brighter face upon it!"

"You are very hard with me, sir," said Richard. "The harder, because you have been so considerate to me in all other respects, and have done me kindnesses that I can never acknowledge. I never could have been set right without you, sir."

"Well, well!" said Mr. Jarndyce, "I want to set you more right yet. I want to set you more right with yourself."

"I hope you will excuse my saying, sir," returned Richard in a fiery way, but yet respectfully, "that I think I am the best judge about myself."

"I hope you will excuse my saying, my dear Rick," observed Mr. Jarndyce with the sweetest cheerfulness and good humour, "that it's quite natural in you to think so, but I don't think so. I must do my duty, Rick, or you could never care for me in cool blood; and I hope you will always care for me, cool and hot."

Ada had turned so pale, that he made her sit down in his reading-chair, and sat beside her.

"It's nothing, my dear," he said, "it's nothing. Rick and I have only had a friendly difference, which we must state to you, for you are the theme. Now you are afraid of what's coming."

"I am not indeed, cousin John," replied Ada, with a smile, "if it is to come from you."

"Thank you, my dear. Do you give me a minute's calm attention, without looking at Rick. And, little woman, do you likewise. My dear girl," putting his hand on hers, as it lay on the side of the easy-chair, "you recollect the talk we had, we four, when the little woman told me of a little love affair?"

"It is not likely that either Richard or I can ever forget your kindness, that day, cousin John."

"I can never forget it," said Richard.

"And I can never forget it," said Ada.

"So much the easier what I have to say, and so much the easier for us to agree," returned my guardian, his face irradiated by the gentleness and honour of his heart. "Ada, my bird, you should know that Rick has now chosen his profession for the last time. All that he has of certainty will be expended when he is fully equipped. He has exhausted his resources, and is bound henceforward to the tree he has planted."

"Quite true that I have exhausted my present resources, and I am quite content to know it. But what I have of certainty, sir," said Richard, "is not all I have."

"Rick, Rick!" cried my guardian, with a sudden terror in his manner, and in an altered voice, and putting up his hands as if he would have stopped his ears, "for the love of God, don't found a hope or expectation on the family curse! Whatever you do on this side the grave, never give one lingering glance towards the horrible phantom that has haunted us so many years. Better to borrow, better to beg, better to die!"

We were all startled by the fervour of this warning. Richard bit his lip and held his breath, and glanced at me, as if he felt, and knew that I felt too, how much he needed it.

"Ada, my dear," said Mr. Jarndyce, recovering his cheerfulness, "these are strong words of advice; but I live in Bleak House, and have seen a sight here. Enough of that. All Richard had, to start him in the race of life, is ventured. I recommend to him and you, for his sake and your own, that he should depart from us with the understanding that there is no sort of contract between you. I must go further. I will be plain with you both. You were to confide freely in me, and I will confide freely in you. I ask you wholly to relinquish, for the present, any tie but your relationship."

"Better to say at once, sir," returned Richard, "that you renounce all confidence in me, and that you advise Ada to do the same."

"Better to say nothing of the sort, Rick, because I don't mean it."

"You think I have begun ill, sir," retorted Richard. "I *have*, I know."

"How I hoped you would begin, and how go on, I told you when we spoke of these things last," said Mr. Jarndyce,

411

in a cordial and encouraging manner. "You have not made that beginning yet; but there is a time for all things, and yours is not gone by—rather, it is just now fully come. Make a clear beginning altogether. You two (very young, my dears) are cousins. As yet, you are nothing more. What more may come, must come of being worked out, Rick; and no sooner."

"You are very hard with me, sir," said Richard. "Harder than I could have supposed you would be."

"My dear boy," said Mr. Jarndyce, "I am harder with myself when I do anything that gives you pain. You have your remedy in your own hands. Ada, it is better for him that he should be free, and that there should be no youthful engagement between you. Rick, it is better for her, much better; you owe it to her. Come! Each of you will do what is best for the other, if not what is best for yourselves."

"Why is it best, sir?" returned Richard, hastily. "It was not, when we opened our hearts to you. You did not say so, then."

"I have had experience since. I don't blame you, Rick— but I have had experience since."

"You mean of me, sir."

"Well! Yes, of both of you," said Mr. Jarndyce, kindly. "The time is not come for your standing pledged to one another. It is not right, and I must not recognise it. Come, come, my young cousins, begin afresh! Byegones shall be byegones, and a new page turned for you to write your lives in."

Richard gave an anxious glance at Ada, but said nothing.

"I have avoided saying one word to either of you, or to Esther," said Mr. Jarndyce, "until now, in order that we might be open as the day, and all on equal terms. I now affectionately advise, I now most earnestly entreat, you two, to part as you came here. Leave all else to time, truth, and steadfastness. If you do otherwise, you will do wrong; and you will have made me do wrong, in ever bringing you together."

A long silence succeeded.

"Cousin Richard," said Ada, then, raising her blue eyes tenderly to his face, "after what our cousin John has said, I think no choice is left us. Your mind may be quite at ease about me; for you will leave me here under his care, and will be sure that I can have nothing to wish for; quite sure, if I guide myself by his advice. I—I don't doubt, cousin Richard," said Ada, a little confused, "that you are very fond of me, and I—I don't think you will fall in love with anybody else. But I should like you to consider well about it, too; as I should like you to be in all things very happy. You may trust in me, cousin Richard. I am not at all changeable; but I am not unreasonable, and should never blame you. Even cousins may be sorry to part; and in truth I am very, very sorry, Richard, though I know it's for your welfare. I shall always think of you affectionately, and often talk of you with Esther, and—and perhaps you will sometimes think a little of me, cousin Richard. So now," said Ada, going up to him and giving him her trembling hand, "we are only. cousins again, Richard—for the time perhaps—and I pray for a blessing on my dear cousin, wherever he goes!"

It was strange to me that Richard should not be able to forgive my guardian, for entertaining the very same opinion of him which he himself had expressed of himself in much stronger terms to me. But, it was certainly the case. I observed, with great regret, that from this hour he never was as free and open with Mr. Jarndyce as he had been before. He had every reason given him to be so, but he was not; and, solely on his side, an estrangement began to arise between them.

In the business of preparation and equipment he soon lost himself, and even his grief at parting from Ada, who remained in Hertfordshire, while he, Mr. Jarndyce, and I went up to

413

London for a week. He remembered her by fits and starts, even with bursts of tears; and at such times would confide to me the heaviest self-reproaches. But, in a few minutes he would recklessly conjure up some undefinable means by which they were both to be made rich and happy for ever, and would become as gay as possible.

It was a busy time, and I trotted about with him all day long, buying a variety of things, of which he stood in need. Of the things he would have bought, if he had been left to his own ways, I say nothing. He was perfectly confidential with me, and often talked so sensibly and feelingly about his faults and his vigorous resolutions, and dwelt so much upon the encouragement he derived from these conversations, that I could never have been tired if I had tried.

There used, in that week, to come backward and forward to our lodging, to fence with Richard, a person who had formerly been a cavalry soldier; he was a fine bluff-looking man, of a frank free bearing, with whom Richard had practised for some months. I heard so much about him, not only from Richard, but from my guardian too, that I was purposely in the room, with my work, one morning after breakfast when he came.

"Good morning, Mr. George," said my guardian, who happened to be alone with me. "Mr. Carstone will be here directly. Meanwhile, Miss Summerson is very happy to see you, I know. Sit down."

He sat down, a little disconcerted by my presence, I thought; and, without looking at me, drew his heavy sun-burnt hand across and across his upper lip.

"You are as punctual as the sun," said Mr. Jarndyce.

"Military time, sir," he replied. "Force of habit. A mere habit in me, sir. I am not at all business-like."

"Yet you have a large establishment, too, I am told?" said Mr. Jarndyce.

"Not much of a one, sir. I keep a shooting gallery, but not much of a one."

"And what kind of a shot, and what kind of a swordsman, do you make of Mr. Carstone?" said my guardian.

"Pretty good, sir," he replied, folding his arms upon his broad chest, and looking very large. "If Mr. Carstone was to give his full mind to it, he would come out very good."

"But he don't, I suppose?" said my guardian.

"He did at first, sir, but not afterwards. Not his full mind. Perhaps he has something else upon it—some young lady, perhaps." His bright dark eyes glanced at me for the first time.

"He has not me upon his mind, I assure you, Mr. George," said I, laughing, "though you seem to suspect me."

He reddened a little through his brown, and made me a trooper's bow. "No offence, I hope, miss. I am one of the Roughs."

"Not at all," said I. "I take it as a compliment."

If he had not looked at me before, he looked at me now, in three or four quick successive glances. "I beg your pardon, sir," he said to my guardian, with a manly kind of diffidence, "but you did me the honour to mention the young lady's name—— "

"Miss Summerson."

"Miss Summerson," he repeated, and looked at me again.

"Do you know the name?" I asked.

"No, miss. To my knowledge, I never heard it. I thought I had seen you somewhere."

"I think not," I returned, raising my head from my work to look at him; and there was something so genuine in his speech and manner that I was glad of the opportunity. "I remember faces very well."

"So do I, miss!" he returned, meeting my look with the fulness of his dark and broad forehead. "Humph! What set me off, now, upon that!"

His once more reddening through his brown, and being disconcerted by his efforts to remember the association, brought my guardian to his relief.

"Have you many pupils, Mr. George?"

"They vary in their number, sir. Mostly, they're but a small lot to live by."

"And what classes of chance people come to practise at your gallery?"

"All sorts, sir. Natives and foreigners. From gentlemen to 'prentices. I have had French women come, before now, and show themselves dabs at pistol-shooting. Mad people out of number, of course—but *they* go everywhere, where the doors stand open."

"People don't come with grudges, and schemes of finishing their practice with live targets, I hope?" said my guardian, smiling.

"Not much of that, sir, though that *has* happened. Mostly they come for skill—or idleness. Six of one, and half-a-dozen of the other. I beg your pardon," said Mr. George, sitting stiffly upright, and squaring an elbow on each knee, "but I believe you're a Chancery suitor, if I have heard correct?"

"I am sorry to say I am."

"I have had one of *your* compatriots in my time, sir."

"A Chancery suitor?" returned my guardian. "How was that?"

"Why, the man was so badgered, and worried, and tortured, by being knocked about from post to pillar, and from pillar to post," said Mr. George, "that he got out of sorts. I don't believe he had any idea of taking aim at anybody; but he was in that condition of resentment and violence, that he would come and pay for fifty shots, and fire away till he was red hot. One day I said to him when there was nobody by, and he had been talking to me angrily about his wrongs, 'If this practice is a safety-valve, comrade, well and good; but I don't altogether like your being so bent upon it, in your present state of mind; I'd rather you took to something else.' I was on my guard for a blow, he was that passionate; but he received it in very good part, and left off directly. We shook hands, and struck up a sort of friendship."

MR. GEORGE IN A BROWN STUDY

" What was that man ? " asked my guardian, in a new tone of interest.

'Why, he began by being a small Shropshire farmer, before they made a baited bull of him," said Mr. George.

" Was his name Gridley ? "

" It was, sir."

Mr. George directed another succession of quick bright glances at me, as my guardian and I exchanged a word or two of surprise at the coincidence ; and I therefore explained to him how we knew the name. He made me another of his soldierly bows, in acknowledgment of what he called my condescension.

"I don't know," he said, as he looked at me, " what it is that sets me off again—but bosh ! what's my head running against ! " He passed one of his heavy hands over his crisp dark hair, as if to sweep the broken thoughts out of his mind ; and sat a little forward, with one arm akimbo and the other resting on his leg, looking in a brown study at the ground.

" I am sorry to learn that the same state of mind has got this Gridley into new troubles, and that he is in hiding," said my guardian.

"So I am told, sir," returned Mr. George, still musing and looking on the ground. "So I am told."

" You don't know where ? "

"No, sir," returned the trooper, lifting up his eyes and coming out of his reverie. "I can't say anything about him. He will be worn out soon, I expect. You may file a strong man's heart away for a good many years, but it will tell all of a sudden at last."

Richard's entrance stopped the conversation. Mr. George rose, made me another of his soldierly bows, wished my guardian a good day, and strode heavily out of the room.

This was the morning of the day appointed for Richard's departure. We had no more purchases to make now ; I had completed all his packing early in the afternoon ; and our time was disengaged until night, when he was to go to

417

Liverpool for Holyhead. Jarndyce and Jarndyce being again expected to come on that day, Richard proposed to me that we should go down to the Court and hear what passed. As it was his last day, and he was eager to go, and I had never been there, I gave my consent, and we walked down to Westminster, where the Court was then sitting. We beguiled the way with arrangements concerning the letters that Richard was to write to me, and the letters that I was to write to him; and with a great many hopeful projects. My guardian knew where we were going, and therefore was not with us.

When we came to the Court, there was the Lord Chancellor —the same whom I had seen in his private room in Lincoln's Inn—sitting in great state and gravity, on the bench; with the mace and seals on a red table below him, and an immense flat nosegay, like a little garden, which scented the whole Court. Below the table, again, was a long row of solicitors, with bundles of papers on the matting at their feet; and then there were the gentlemen of the bar in wigs and gowns —some awake and some asleep, and one talking, and nobody paying much attention to what he said. The Lord Chancellor leaned back in his very easy chair, with his elbow on the cushioned arm, and his forehead resting on his hand; some of those who were present, dozed; some read the newspapers; some walked about, or whispered in groups: all seemed perfectly at their ease, by no means in a hurry, very unconcerned, and extremely comfortable.

To see everything going on so smoothly, and to think of the roughness of the suitors' lives and deaths; to see all that full dress and ceremony, and to think of the waste, and want, and beggared misery it represented; to consider that, while the sickness of hope deferred was raging in so many hearts, this polite show went calmly on from day to day, and year to year, in such good order and composure; to behold the Lord Chancellor, and the whole array of practitioners under him, looking at one another and at the spectators, as if nobody had ever heard that all over England the name in which they were assembled was a bitter jest: was held in universal horror, contempt, and indignation; was known for something so flagrant and bad, that little short of a miracle could bring any good out of it to any one: this was so curious and self-contradictory to me, who had no experience of it, that it was at first incredible, and I could not comprehend it. I sat where Richard put me, and tried to listen, and looked about me; but there seemed to be no reality in the whole scene, except poor little Miss Flite, the madwoman, standing on a bench, and nodding at it.

Miss Flite soon espied us, and came to where we sat. She gave me a gracious welcome to her domain, and indicated, with much gratification and pride, its principal attractions. Mr. Kenge also came to speak to us, and did the honours of the place in much the same way; with the bland modesty of a proprietor. It was not a very good day for a visit, he said; he would have preferred the first day of term; but it was imposing, it was imposing.

When we had been there half an hour or so, the case in progress—if I may use a phrase so ridiculous in such a connexion—seemed to die out of its own vapidity, without coming, or being by anybody expected to come, to any result. The Lord Chancellor then threw down a bundle of papers from his desk to the gentlemen below him, and somebody said, " JARNDYCE AND JARNDYCE." Upon this there was a buzz, and a laugh, and a general withdrawal of the by-standers, and a bringing in of great heaps, and piles, and bags and bags-full of papers.

I think it came on "for further directions,"—about some bill of costs, to the best of my understanding, which was confused enough. But I counted twenty-three gentlemen in wigs, who said they were " in it;" and none of them appeared to understand it much better than I. They chatted about it with the Lord Chancellor, and contradicted and ex- plained among themselves, and some of them said it was this way, and some of them said it was that way, and some of them jocosely proposed to read huge volumes of affidavits, and there was more buzzing and laughing, and everybody concerned was in a state of idle entertainment, and nothing could be made of it by anybody. After an hour or so of this, and a good many speeches being begun and cut short, it was "referred back for the present," as Mr. Kenge said, and the papers were bundled up again, before the clerks had finished bringing them in.

I glanced at Richard, on the termination of these hopeless proceedings, and was shocked to see the worn look of his handsome young face. "It can't last for ever, Dame Durden. Better luck next time!" was all he said.

I had seen Mr. Guppy bringing in papers, and arranging them for Mr. Kenge; and he had seen me and made me a forlorn bow, which rendered me desirous to get out of the Court. Richard had given me his arm, and was taking me away, when Mr. Guppy came up.

"I beg your pardon, Mr. Carstone," said he in a whisper, "and Miss Summerson's also; but there's a lady here, a friend of mine, who knows her, and wishes to have the pleasure of shaking hands." As he spoke, I saw before me, as if she had started into bodily shape from my remembrance, Mrs. Rachael of my godmother's house.

"How do you do, Esther?" said she. "Do you recollect me?"

I gave her my hand, and told her yes, and that she was very little altered.

"I wonder you remember those times, Esther," she returned with her old asperity. "They are changed now. Well! I am glad to see you, and glad you are not too proud to know me." But, indeed she seemed disappointed that I was not.

"Proud, Mrs. Rachael!" I remonstrated.

"I am married, Esther," she returned, coldly correcting me, "and am Mrs. Chadband. Well! I wish you good day, and I hope you'll do well."

Mr. Guppy, who had been attentive to this short dialogue,

heaved a sigh in my ear, and elbowed his own and Mrs. Rachael's way through the confused little crowd of people coming in and going out, which we were in the midst of, and which the change in the business had brought together. Richard and I were making our way through it, and I was yet in the first chill of the late unexpected recognition, when I saw, coming towards us, but not seeing us, no less a person than Mr. George. He made nothing of the people about him as he tramped on, staring over their heads into the body of the Court.

"George!" said Richard, as I called his attention to him.

"You are well met, sir," he returned. "And you, miss. Could you point a person out for me, I want? I don't understand these places."

Turning as he spoke, and making an easy way for us, he stopped when we were out of the press, in a corner behind a great red curtain.

"There's a little cracked old woman," he began, "that——"

I put up my finger, for Miss Flite was close by me; having kept beside me all the time, and having called the attention of several of her legal acquaintance to me (as I had overheard to my confusion), by whispering in their ears, "Hush! Fitz-Jarndyce on my left!"

"Hem!" said Mr. George. "You remember, miss, that we passed some conversation on a certain man this morning? —Gridley," in a low whisper behind his hand.

"Yes," said I.

"He is hiding at my place. I couldn't mention it. Hadn't his authority. He is on his last march, miss, and has a whim to see her. He says they can feel for one another, and she has been almost as good as a friend to him here. I came down to look for her; for when I sat by Gridley this afternoon, I seemed to hear the roll of the muffled drums."

"Shall I tell her?" said I.

"Would you be so good?" he returned, with a glance of something like apprehension at Miss Flite. "It's a Providence

I met you, miss; I doubt if I should have known how to get on with that lady." And he put one hand in his breast, and stood upright in a martial attitude, as I informed little Miss Flite, in her ear, of the purport of his kind errand.

"My angry friend from Shropshire! Almost as celebrated as myself!" she exclaimed. "Now really! My dear, I will wait upon him with the greatest pleasure."

"He is living concealed at Mr. George's," said I. "Hush! This is Mr. George."

"In—deed!" returned Miss Flite. "Very proud to have the honour! A military man, my dear. You know, a perfect General!" she whispered to me.

Poor Miss Flite deemed it necessary to be so courtly and polite, as a mark of her respect for the army, and to curtsey so very often, that it was no easy matter to get her out of the Court. When this was at last done, and addressing Mr. George, as "General," she gave him her arm, to the great entertainment of some idlers who were looking on, he was so discomposed, and begged me so respectfully "not to desert him," that I could not make up my mind to do it; especially as Miss Flite was always tractable with me, and as she too said, "Fitz-Jarndyce, my dear, you will accompany us, of course." As Richard seemed quite willing, and even anxious, that we should see them safely to their destination, we agreed to do so. And as Mr. George informed us that Gridley's mind had run on Mr. Jarndyce all the afternoon, after hearing of their interview in the morning, I wrote a hasty note in pencil to my guardian to say where we were gone, and why. Mr. George sealed it at a coffee-house, that it might lead to no discovery, and we sent it off by a ticket-porter.

We then took a hackney-coach, and drove away to the neighbourhood of Leicester Square. We walked through some narrow courts, for which Mr. George apologised, and soon came to the Shooting Gallery, the door of which was closed. As he pulled a bell-handle which hung by a chain to the door-post, a very respectable old gentleman, with grey hair, wearing spectacles, and dressed in a black spencer and gaiters and a broad-brimmed hat, and carrying a large gold-headed cane, addressed him.

"I ask your pardon, my good friend," said he; "but is this George's Shooting Gallery?"

"It is, sir," returned Mr. George, glancing up at the great letters in which that inscription was painted on the white-washed wall.

"Oh! To be sure!" said the old gentleman, following his eyes. "Thank you. Have you rung the bell?"

"My name is George, sir, and I have rung the bell."

"Oh, indeed?" said the old gentleman. "Your name is George? Then I am here as soon as you, you see. You came for me, no doubt?"

"No, sir. You have the advantage of me."

"Oh, indeed?" said the old gentleman. "Then it was your young man who came for me. I am a physician, and was requested—five minutes ago—to come and visit a sick man, at George's Shooting Gallery."

"The muffled drums," said Mr. George, turning to Richard and me, and gravely shaking his head. "It's quite correct, sir. Will you please to walk in?"

The door being at that moment opened, by a very singular-looking little man in a green baize cap and apron, whose face, and hands, and dress, were blackened all over, we passed along a dreary passage into a large building with bare brick walls; where there were targets, and guns, and swords, and other things of that kind. When we had all arrived here, the physician stopped, and, taking off his hat, appeared to vanish by magic, and to leave another and quite a different man in his place.

"Now look'ee here, George," said the man, turning quickly round upon him, and tapping him on the breast with a large forefinger. "You know me, and I know you. You're a man of the world, and I'm a man of the world. My name's Bucket, as you are aware, and I have got a peace-warrant against Gridley. You have kept him out of the way a long time, and you have been artful in it, and it does you credit."

Mr. George, looking hard at him, bit his lip and shook his head.

"Now, George," said the other, keeping close to him, "you're a sensible man, and a well-conducted man; that's what *you* are, beyond a doubt. And mind you, I don't talk to you as a common character, because you have served your country, and you know that when duty calls we must obey. Consequently, you're very far from wanting to give trouble. If I required assistance, you'd assist me; that's what *you*'d do. Phil Squod, don't you go a-sidling round the gallery like that;" the dirty little man was shuffling about with his shoulder against the wall, and his eyes on the intruder, in a manner that looked threatening: "because I know you, and won't have it."

"Phil!" said Mr. George.

"Yes, guv'ner."

"Be quiet."

The little man, with a low growl, stood still.

"Ladies and gentlemen," said Mr. Bucket, "you'll excuse anything that may appear to be disagreeable in this, for my name's Inspector Bucket of the Detective, and I have a duty to perform. George, I know where my man is, because I was on the roof last night, and saw him through the skylight, and you along with him. He is in there, you know," pointing; "that's where *he* is—on a sofy. Now I must see my man, and I must tell my man to consider himself in custody; but, you know me, and you know I don't want to take any uncomfortable measures. You give me your word, as from one man to another (and an old soldier, mind you, likewise!), that it's honourable between us two, and I'll accommodate you to the utmost of my power."

"I give it," was the reply. "But it wasn't handsome in you, Mr. Bucket."

"Gammon, George! Not handsome?" said Mr. Bucket, tapping him on his broad breast again, and shaking hands with him. "I don't say it wasn't handsome in you to keep my man so close, do I? Be equally good-tempered to me, old boy! Old William Tell, Old Shaw, the Life Guardsman! Why, he's a model of the whole British army in himself, ladies and gentlemen. I'd give a fifty-pun' note to be such a figure of a man!"

The affair being brought to this head, Mr. George, after a little consideration, proposed to go in first to his comrade (as he called him), taking Miss Flite with him. Mr. Bucket agreeing, they went away to the further end of the gallery, leaving us sitting and standing by a table covered with guns. Mr. Bucket took this opportunity of entering into a little light conversation: asking me if I were afraid of fire-arms, as most young ladies were; asking Richard if he were a good shot; asking Phil Squod which he considered the best of those rifles, and what it might be worth, first-hand; telling him, in return, that it was a pity he ever gave way to his temper, for he was naturally so amiable, that he might have been a young woman; and making himself generally agreeable.

After a time he followed us to the further end of the gallery, and Richard and I were going quietly away, when Mr. George came after us. He said that if we had no objection to see his comrade, he would take a visit from us very kindly. The words had hardly passed his lips, when the bell was rung, and my guardian appeared; "on the chance," he slightly observed, "of being able to do any little thing for a poor fellow involved in the same misfortune as himself." We all four went back together, and went into the place where Gridley was.

It was a bare room, partitioned off from the gallery with unpainted wood. As the screening was not more than eight or ten feet high, and only enclosed the sides, not the top, the rafters of the high gallery roof were overhead, and the skylight through which Mr. Bucket had looked down. The

425

sun was low—near setting—and its light came redly in above, without descending to the ground. Upon a plain canvas-covered sofa lay the man from Shropshire—dressed much as we had seen him last, but so changed, that at first I recognised no likeness in his colourless face to what I recollected.

He had been still writing in his hiding-place, and still dwelling on his grievances, hour after hour. A table and some shelves were covered with manuscript papers, and with worn pens, and a medley of such tokens. Touchingly and awfully drawn together, he and the little mad woman were side by side, and, as it were, alone. She sat on a chair holding his hand, and none of us went close to them.

His voice had faded, with the old expression of his face, with his strength, with his anger, with his resistance to the wrongs that had at last subdued him. The faintest shadow of an object full of form and colour, is such a picture of it, as he was of the man from Shropshire whom we had spoken with before.

He inclined his head to Richard and me, and spoke to my guardian.

"Mr. Jarndyce, it is very kind of you to come to see me. I am not long to be seen, I think. I am very glad to take your hand, sir. You are a good man, superior to injustice, and God knows I honour you."

They shook hands earnestly, and my guardian said some words of comfort to him.

"It may seem strange to you, sir," returned Gridley; "I should not have liked to see you, if this had been the first time of our meeting. But, you know I made a fight for it, you know I stood up with my single hand against them all, you know I told them the truth to the last, and told them what they were, and what they had done to me; so I don't mind your seeing me, this wreck."

"You have been courageous with them, many and many a time," returned my guardian.

"Sir, I have been ; " with a faint smile. "I told you what would come of it, when I ceased to be so ; and, see here ! Look at us—look at us ! " He drew the hand Miss Flite held, through her arm, and brought her something nearer to him.

"This ends it. Of all my old associations, of all my old pursuits and hopes, of all the living and the dead world, this one poor soul alone comes natural to me, and I am fit for. There is a tie of many suffering years between us two, and it is the only tie I ever had on earth that Chancery has not broken."

"Accept my blessing, Gridley," said Miss Flite, in tears. "Accept my blessing ! "

"I thought, boastfully, that they never could break my heart, Mr. Jarndyce. I was resolved that they should not. I did believe that I could, and would, charge them with being the mockery they were, until I died of some bodily disorder. But I am worn out. How long I have been wearing out, I don't know ; I seemed to break down in an hour. I hope they may never come to hear of it. I hope everybody, here, will lead them to believe that I died defying them, consistently and perseveringly, as I did through so many years."

Here Mr. Bucket, who was sitting in a corner, by the door, good-naturedly offered such consolation as he could administer.

"Come, come ! " he said from his corner. "Don't go on in that way, Mr. Gridley. You are only a little low. We are all of us a little low, sometimes. *I* am. Hold up, hold up ! You'll lose your temper with the whole round of 'em, again and again ; and I shall take you on a score of warrants yet, if I have luck."

He only shook his head.

"Don't shake your head," said Mr. Bucket. "Nod it ; that's what I want to see you do. Why, Lord bless your soul, what times we have had together ! Haven't I seen you in the Fleet over and over again, for contempt ? Haven't I come into Court, twen-ty afternoons, for no other purpose than to see you pin the Chancellor like a bull-dog? Don't you remember, when you first began to threaten the lawyers, and the peace was sworn against you two or three times a week? Ask the little old lady there; she has been always present. Hold up, Mr. Gridley, hold up, sir!"

"What are you going to do about him?" asked George, in a low voice.

"I don't know yet," said Bucket, in the same tone. Then resuming his encouragement, he pursued aloud:

"Worn out, Mr. Gridley? After dodging me for all these weeks, and forcing me to climb the roof here like a Tom Cat, and to come to see you as a Doctor? That ain't like being worn out. *I* should think not! Now I tell you what you want. You want excitement, you know, to keep *you* up; that's what *you* want. You're used to it, and you can't do without it. I couldn't myself. Very well, then; here's this warrant got by Mr. Tulkinghorn of Lincoln's Inn Fields, and backed into half-a-dozen counties since. What do you say to coming along with me, upon this warrant, and having a good angry argument before the Magistrates? It'll do you good; it'll freshen you up, and get you into training for another turn at the Chancellor. Give in? Why, I am surprised to hear a man of your energy talk of giving in. You mustn't do that. You're half the fun of the fair, in the Court of Chancery. George, you lend Mr. Gridley a hand, and let's see now whether he won't be better up than down."

"He is very weak," said the trooper, in a low voice.

"Is he?" returned Bucket, anxiously. "I only want to rouse him. I don't like to see an old acquaintance giving in like this. It would cheer him up more than anything, if I could make him a little waxy with me. He's welcome to drop into me, right and left, if he likes. I shall never take advantage of it."

The roof rang with a scream from Miss Flite, which still rings in my ears.

"O no, Gridley!" she cried, as he fell heavily and calmly back from before her, "not without my blessing. After so many years!"

The sun was down, the light had gradually stolen from the roof, and the shadow had crept upward. But, to me, the shadow of that pair, one living and one dead, fell heavier on Richard's departure, than the darkness of the darkest night. And through Richard's farewell words I heard it echoed:

"Of all my old associations, of all my old pursuits and hopes, of all the living and the dead world, this one poor soul alone comes natural to me, and I am fit for. There is a tie of many suffering years between us two, and it is the only tie I ever had on earth that Chancery has not broken!"

CHAPTER XXV

MRS. SNAGSBY SEES IT ALL

THERE is disquietude in Cook's Court, Cursitor Street. Black suspicion hides in that peaceful region. The mass of Cook's-Courtiers are in their usual state of mind, no better and no worse; but, Mr. Snagsby is changed, and his little woman knows it.

For, Tom-all-Alone's and Lincoln's Inn Fields persist in harnessing themselves, a pair of ungovernable coursers, to the chariot of Mr. Snagsby's imagination; and Mr. Bucket drives; and the passengers are Jo and Mr. Tulkinghorn; and the complete equipage whirls through the Law Stationery business at wild speed, all round the clock. Even in the little front kitchen where the family meals are taken, it rattles away at a smoking pace from the dinner-table, when Mr. Snagsby pauses in carving the first slice of the leg of mutton baked with potatoes, and stares at the kitchen wall.

Mr. Snagsby cannot make out what it is that he has had to do with. Something is wrong, somewhere; but what something, what may come of it, to whom, when, and from which unthought-of and unheard-of quarter, is the puzzle of his life. His remote impressions of the robes and coronets, the stars and garters, that sparkle through the surface-dust of Mr. Tulkinghorn's chambers; his veneration for the mysteries presided over by that best and closest of his customers, whom all the Inns of Court, all Chancery Lane,

430

and all the legal neighbourhood agree to hold in awe; his remembrance of Detective Mr. Bucket with his forefinger, and his confidential manner impossible to be evaded or declined; persuade him that he is a party to some dangerous secret, without knowing what it is. And it is the fearful peculiarity of this condition that, at any hour of his daily life, at any opening of the shop-door, at any pull of the bell, at any entrance of a messenger, or any delivery of a letter, the secret may take air and fire, explode, and blow up—Mr. Bucket only knows whom.

For which reason, whenever a man unknown comes into the shop (as many men unknown do), and says, "Is Mr. Snagsby in?" or words to that innocent effect, Mr. Snagsby's heart knocks hard at his guilty breast. He undergoes so much from such inquiries, that when they are made by boys he revenges himself by flipping at their ears over the counter, and asking the young dogs what they mean by it, and why they can't speak out at once? More impracticable men and boys persist in walking into Mr. Snagsby's sleep, and terrifying him with unaccountable questions; so that often, when the cock at the little dairy in Cursitor Street breaks out in his usual absurd way about the morning, Mr. Snagsby finds himself in a crisis of nightmare, with his little woman shaking him, and saying, "What's the matter with the man!"

The little woman herself is not the least item in his difficulty. To know that he is always keeping a secret from her; that he has, under all circumstances, to conceal and hold fast a tender double tooth, which her sharpness is ever ready to twist out of his head; gives Mr. Snagsby, in her dentistical presence, much of the air of a dog who has a reservation from his master, and will look anywhere rather than meet his eye.

These various signs and tokens, marked by the little woman, are not lost upon her. They impel her to say, "Snagsby has something on his mind!" And thus suspicion gets into Cook's Court, Cursitor Street. From suspicion to jealousy, Mrs. Snagsby finds the road as natural and short as from Cook's

Court to Chancery Lane. And thus jealousy gets into Cook's Court, Cursitor Street. Once there (and it was always lurking thereabout), it is very active and nimble in Mrs. Snagsby's breast—prompting her to nocturnal examinations of Mr. Snagsby's pockets; to secret perusals of Mr. Snagsby's letters; to private researches in the Day Book and Ledger, till, cashbox, and iron safe; to watchings at windows, listenings behind doors, and a general putting of this and that together by the wrong end.

Mrs. Snagsby is so perpetually on the alert, that the house becomes ghostly with creaking boards and rustling garments. The 'prentices think somebody may have been murdered there, in bygone times. Guster holds certain loose atoms of an idea (picked up at Tooting, where they were found floating among the orphans), that there is buried money underneath the cellar, guarded by an old man with a white beard, who cannot get out for seven thousand years, because he said the Lord's Prayer backwards.

"Who was Nimrod?" Mrs. Snagsby repeatedly inquires of herself. "Who was that lady—that creature? And who is that boy?" Now, Nimrod being as dead as the mighty hunter whose name Mrs. Snagsby has appropriated, and the lady being unproducible, she directs her mental eye, for the present, with redoubled vigilance, to the boy. "And who," quoth Mrs. Snagsby, for the thousand and first time, "is that boy? Who is that——!" And there Mrs. Snagsby is seized with an inspiration.

He has no respect for Mr. Chadband. No, to be sure, and he wouldn't have, of course. Naturally he wouldn't, under those contagious circumstances. He was invited and appointed by Mr. Chadband—why, Mrs. Snagsby heard it herself with her own ears!—to come back, and be told where he was to go, to be addressed by Mr. Chadband; and he never came! Why did he never come? Because he was told not to come. Who told him not to come? Who? Ha, ha! Mrs. Snagsby sees it all.

But happily (and Mrs. Snagsby tightly shakes her head and tightly smiles), that boy was met by Mr. Chadband yesterday in the streets; and that boy, as affording a subject which Mr. Chadband desires to improve for the spiritual delight of a select congregation, was seized by Mr. Chadband and threatened with being delivered over to the police, unless he showed the reverend gentleman where he lived, and unless he entered into, and fulfilled, an undertaking to appear in Cook's Court to-morrow night—" to—mor—row—night," Mrs. Snagsby repeats for mere emphasis, with another tight smile, and another tight shake of her head; and to-morrow night that boy will be here, and to-morrow night Mrs. Snagsby will have her eye upon him and upon some one else; and O you may walk a long while in your secret ways (says Mrs. Snagsby, with haughtiness and scorn), but you can't blind ME!

Mrs. Snagsby sounds no timbrel in anybody's ears, but holds her purpose quietly, and keeps her counsel. To-morrow comes, the savoury preparations for the Oil Trade come, the evening comes. Comes, Mr. Snagsby in his black coat; come, the Chadbands; come (when the gorging vessel is replete), the 'prentices and Guster, to be edified; comes, at last, with his slouching head, and his shuffle backward, and his shuffle forward, and his shuffle to the right, and his shuffle to the left, and his bit of fur cap in his muddy hand, which he picks as if it were some mangy bird he had caught, and was plucking before eating raw, Jo, the very, very tough subject Mr. Chadband is to improve.

Mrs. Snagsby screws a watchful glance on Jo, as he is brought into the little drawing-room by Guster. He looks at Mr. Snagsby the moment he comes in. Aha! Why does he look at Mr. Snagsby? Mr. Snagsby looks at him. Why should he do that, but that Mrs. Snagsby sees it all? Why else should that look pass between them, why else should Mr. Snagsby be confused, and cough a signal cough behind his hand? It is as clear as crystal that Mr. Snagsby is that boy's father.

"Peace, my friends," says Chadband, rising and wiping the

433

oily exudations from his reverend visage. "Peace be with us! My friends, why with us? Because," with his fat smile, "it cannot be against us, because it must be for us; because it is not hardening, because it is softening; because it does not make war like the hawk, but comes home untoe us like the dove. Therefore, my friends, peace be with us! My human boy, come forward!"

Stretching forth his flabby paw, Mr. Chadband lays the same on Jo's arm, and considers where to station him. Jo, very doubtful of his reverend friend's intentions, and not at all clear but that something practical and painful is going to be done to him, mutters, "You let me alone. I never said nothink to you. You let me alone."

"No, my young friend," says Chadband, smoothly, "I will not let you alone. And why? Because I am a harvest-labourer, because I am a toiler and a moiler, because you are delivered over untoe me, and are become as a precious instrument in my hands. My friends, may I so employ this instrument as to use it toe your advantage, toe your profit, toe your gain, toe your welfare, toe your enrichment! My young friend, sit upon this stool."

Jo, apparently possessed by an impression that the reverend gentleman wants to cut his hair, shields his head with both arms, and is got into the required position with great difficulty, and every possible manifestation of reluctance.

When he is at last adjusted like a lay-figure, Mr. Chadband, retiring behind the table, holds up his bear's-paw, and says, "My friends!" This is the signal for a general settlement of the audience. The 'prentices giggle internally, and nudge each other. Guster falls into a staring and vacant state, compounded of a stunned admiration of Mr. Chadband and pity for the friendless outcast whose condition touches her nearly. Mrs. Snagsby silently lays trains of gunpowder. Mrs. Chadband composes herself grimly by the fire, and warms her knees: finding that sensation favourable to the reception of eloquence.

434

Mr. Chadband "improving" a Tough Subject

A GENTILE AND A HEATHEN

It happens that Mr. Chadband has a pulpit habit of fixing some member of his congregation with his eye, and fatly arguing his points with that particular person; who is understood to be expected to be moved to an occasional grunt, groan, gasp, or other audible expression of inward working; which expression of inward working, being echoed by some elderly lady in the next pew, and so communicated, like a game of forfeits, through a circle of the more fermentable sinners present, serves the purpose of parliamentary cheering, and gets Mr. Chadband's steam up. From mere force of habit, Mr. Chadband in saying "My friends!" has rested his eye on Mr. Snagsby; and proceeds to make that ill-starred stationer, already sufficiently confused, the immediate recipient of his discourse.

"We have here among us, my friends," says Chadband, "a Gentile and a Heathen, a dweller in the tents of Tom-all-Alone's and a mover-on upon the surface of the earth. We have here among us, my friends," and Mr. Chadband, untwisting the point with his dirty thumb-nail, bestows an oily smile on Mr. Snagsby, signifying that he will throw him an argumentative back-fall presently if he be not already down, "a brother and a boy. Devoid of parents, devoid of relations, devoid of flocks and herds, devoid of gold and silver, and of precious stones. Now, my friends, why do I say he is devoid of these possessions? Why? Why is he?" Mr. Chadband states the question as if he were propounding an entirely new riddle, of much ingenuity and merit, to Mr. Snagsby, and entreating him not to give it up.

Mr. Snagsby, greatly perplexed by the mysterious look he received just now from his little woman—at about the period when Mr. Chadband mentioned the word parents—is tempted into modestly remarking, "I don't know, I'm sure, sir." On which interruption, Mrs. Chadband glares, and Mrs. Snagsby says, "For shame!"

"I hear a voice," says Chadband; "is it a still small voice, my friends? I fear not, though I fain would hope so——"

("Ah—h!" from Mrs. Snagsby.)

"Which says, I don't know. Then I will tell you why. I say this brother, present here among us, is devoid of parents, devoid of relations, devoid of flocks and herds, devoid of gold, of silver, and of precious stones, because he is devoid of the light that shines in upon some of us. What is that light? What is it? I ask you what is that light?"

Mr. Chadband draws back his head and pauses, but Mr. Snagsby is not to be lured on to his destruction again. Mr. Chadband, leaning forward over the table, pierces what he has got to follow, directly into Mr. Snagsby, with the thumb-nail already mentioned.

"It is," says Chadband, "the ray of rays, the sun of suns, the moon of moons, the star of stars. It is the light of Terewth."

Mr. Chadband draws himself up again, and looks triumphantly at Mr. Snagsby, as if he would be glad to know how he feels after that.

"Of Terewth," says Mr. Chadband, hitting him again. "Say not to me it is *not* the lamp of lamps. I say to you, it is. I say to you, a million times over, it is. It is! I say to you that I will proclaim it to you, whether you like it or not; nay, that the less you like it, the more I will proclaim it to you. With a speaking-trumpet! I say to you that if you rear yourself against it, you shall fall, you shall be bruised, you shall be battered, you shall be flayed, you shall be smashed."

The present effect of this flight of oratory—much admired for its general power by Mr. Chadband's followers—being not only to make Mr. Chadband unpleasantly warm, but to represent the innocent Mr. Snagsby in the light of a determined enemy to virtue, with a forehead of brass and a heart of adamant, that unfortunate tradesman becomes yet more disconcerted; and is in a very advanced state of low spirits and false position, when Mr. Chadband accidentally finishes him.

"My friends," he resumes, after dabbing his fat head for

some time—and it smokes to such an extent that he seems to light his pocket-handkerchief at it, which smokes, too, after every dab—" to pursue the subject we are endeavouring with our lowly gifts to improve, let us in a spirit of love inquire what is that Terewth to which I have alluded. For, my young friends," suddenly addressing the 'prentices and Guster, to their consternation, "if I am told by the doctor that calomel or castor-oil is good for me, I may naturally ask what is calomel, and what is castor-oil. I may wish to be informed of that, before I dose myself with either or with both. Now, my young friends, what is this Terewth, then? Firstly (in a spirit of love), what is the common sort of Terewth—the working clothes—the every-day wear, my young friends? Is it deception?"

("Ah—h!" from Mrs. Snagsby.)

"Is it suppression?"

(A shiver in the negative from Mrs. Snagsby.)

"Is it reservation?"

(A shake of the head from Mrs. Snagsby—very long and very tight.)

"No, my friends, it is neither of these. Neither of these names belongs to it. When this young Heathen now among us—who is now, my friends, asleep, the seal of indifference and perdition being set upon his eyelids; but do not wake him, for it is right that I should have to wrestle, and to combat and to struggle, and to conquer, for his sake—when this young hardened Heathen told us a story of a Cock, and of a Bull, and of a lady, and of a sovereign, was *that* the Terewth? No. Or, if it was partly, was it wholly, and entirely? No, my friends, no!"

If Mr. Snagsby could withstand his little woman's look, as it enters at his eyes, the windows of his soul, and searches the whole tenement, he were other than the man he is. He cowers and droops.

"Or, my juvenile friends," says Chadband, descending to the level of their comprehension, with a very obtrusive

demonstration, in his greasily meek smile, of coming a long
way down-stairs for the purpose, "if the master of this house
was to go forth into the city and there see an eel, and was
to come back, and was to call untoe him the mistress of this
house, and was to say, 'Sarah, rejoice with me, for I have
seen an elephant!' would *that* be Terewth?"

Mrs. Snagsby in tears.

"Or put it, my juvenile friends, that he saw an elephant,
and returning said, 'Lo, the city is barren, I have seen but
an eel,' would *that* be Terewth?"

Mrs. Snagsby sobbing loudly.

"Or put it, my juvenile friends," said Chadband, stimulated
by the sound, "that the unnatural parents of this slumbering
Heathen—for parents he had, my juvenile friends, beyond a
doubt—after casting him forth to the wolves and the vultures,
and the wild dogs and the young gazelles, and the serpents,
went back to their dwellings and had their pipes, and their
pots, and their flutings and their dancings, and their malt
liquors, and their butcher's meat and poultry, would *that* be
Terewth!"

Mrs. Snagsby replies by delivering herself a prey to spasms;
not an unresisting prey, but a crying and a tearing one, so that
Cook's Court re-echoes with her shrieks. Finally, becoming
cataleptic, she has to be carried up the narrow staircase like
a grand piano. After unspeakable suffering, productive of the
utmost consternation, she is pronounced, by expresses from
the bedroom, free from pain, though much exhausted; in
which state of affairs Mr. Snagsby, trampled and crushed in
the pianoforte removal, and extremely timid and feeble, ventures to come out from behind the door in the drawing-room.

All this time, Jo has been standing on the spot where he
woke up, ever picking his cap, and putting bits of fur in his
mouth. He spits them out with a remorseful air, for he feels
that it is in his nature to be an unimprovable reprobate, and
that it's no good *his* trying to keep awake, for *he* won't never
know nothink. Though it may be, Jo, that there is a history

so interesting and affecting even to minds as near the brutes as thine, recording deeds done on this earth for common men, that if the Chadbands, removing their own persons from the light, would but show it thee in simple reverence, would but leave it unimproved, would but regard it as being eloquent enough without their modest aid—it might hold thee awake, and thou might learn from it yet!

Jo never heard of any such book. Its compilers, and the Reverend Chadband, are all one to him—except that he knows the Reverend Chadband, and would rather run away from him for an hour than hear him talk for five minutes. "It an't no good my waiting here no longer," thinks Jo. "Mr. Snagsby an't a-going to say nothink to me to-night." And down-stairs he shuffles.

But down-stairs is the charitable Guster, holding by the handrail of the kitchen stairs, and warding off a fit, as yet doubtfully, the same having been induced by Mrs. Snagsby's screaming. She has her own supper of bread and cheese to hand to Jo; with whom she ventures to interchange a word or so, for the first time.

"Here's something to eat, poor boy," says Guster.

"Thank'ee, mum," says Jo.

"Are you hungry?"

"Jist!" says Jo.

"What's gone of your father and your mother, eh?"

Jo stops in the middle of a bite, and looks petrified. For this orphan charge of the Christian saint whose shrine was at Tooting, has patted him on the shoulder; and it is the first time in his life that any decent hand has been so laid upon him.

"I never know'd nothink about 'em," says Jo.

"No more didn't I of mine," cries Guster. She is repress, ing symptoms favourable to the fit, when she seems to take alarm at something, and vanishes down the stairs.

"Jo," whispers the law-stationer softly, as the boy lingers on the step.

"Here I am, Mr. Snagsby!"

"I didn't know you were gone—there's another half-crown, Jo. It was quite right of you to say nothing about the lady the other night when we were out together. It would breed trouble. You can't be too quiet, Jo."

"I am fly, master!"

And so, good night.

A ghostly shade, frilled and night-capped, follows the law-stationer to the room he came from, and glides higher up. And henceforth he begins, go where he will, to be attended by another shadow than his own, hardly less constant than his own, hardly less quiet than his own. And into whatsoever atmosphere of secrecy his own shadow may pass, let all concerned in the secrecy beware! For the watchful Mrs. Snagsby is there too—bone of his bone, flesh of his flesh, shadow of his shadow.

CHAPTER XXVI

SHARPSHOOTERS

WINTRY morning, looking with dull eyes and sallow face upon the neighbourhood of Leicester Square, finds its inhabitants unwilling to get out of bed. Many of them are not early risers at the brightest of times, being birds of night who roost when the sun is high, and are wide awake and keen for prey when the stars shine out. Behind dingy blind and curtain, in upper story and garret, skulking more or less under false names, false hair, false titles, false jewellery, and false histories, a colony of brigands lie in their first sleep. Gentlemen of the green baize road who could discourse, from personal experience, of foreign galleys and home treadmills; spies of strong governments that eternally quake with weakness and miserable fear, broken traitors, cowards, bullies, gamesters, shufflers, swindlers, and false witnesses; some not unmarked by the branding-iron, beneath their dirty braid; all with more cruelty in them than was in Nero, and more crime than is in Newgate. For, howsoever bad the devil can be in fustian or smock-frock (and he can be very bad in both), he is a more designing, callous, and intolerable devil when he sticks a pin in his shirt-front, calls himself a gentleman, backs a card or colour, plays a game or so of billiards, and knows a little about bills and promissory notes, than in any other form he wears. And in such form Mr. Bucket shall find him, when he will, still pervading the tributary channels of Leicester Square.

441

But the wintry morning wants him not and wakes him not. It wakes Mr. George of the Shooting Gallery, and his Familiar. They arise, roll up and stow away their mattresses. Mr. George, having shaved himself before a looking-glass of minute proportions, then marches out, bare-headed and bare-chested, to the Pump, in the little yard, and anon comes back shining with yellow soap, friction, drifting rain, and exceedingly cold water. As he rubs himself upon a large jack-towel, blowing like a military sort of diver just come up : his crisp hair curling tighter and tighter on his sunburnt temples, the more he rubs it, so that it looks as if it never could be loosened by any less coercive instrument than an iron rake or a curry-comb—as he rubs, and puffs, and polishes, and blows, turning his head from side to side, the more conveniently to excoriate his throat, and standing with his body well bent forward, to keep the wet from his martial legs—Phil, on his knees lighting a fire, looks round as if it were enough washing for him to see all that done, and sufficient renovation, for one day, to take in the superfluous health his master throws off.

When Mr. George is dry, he goes to work to brush his head with two hard brushes at once, to that unmerciful degree that Phil, shouldering his way round the gallery in the act of sweeping it, winks with sympathy. This chafing over, the ornamental part of Mr. George's toilet is soon performed. He fills his pipe, lights it, and marches up and down smoking, as his custom is, while Phil, raising a powerful odour of hot rolls and coffee, prepares breakfast. He smokes gravely, and marches in slow time. Perhaps this morning's pipe is devoted to the memory of Gridley in his grave.

" And so, Phil," says George of the Shooting Gallery, after several turns in silence ; " you were dreaming of the country last night ? "

Phil, by-the-bye, said as much, in a tone of surprise, as he scrambled out of bed.

" Yes, guv'ner."

442

" What was it like?"

" I hardly know what it was like, guv'ner," said Phil, considering.

" How did you know it was the country?"

" On account of the grass, I think. And the swans upon it," says Phil, after further consideration.

" What were the swans doing on the grass?"

"They was a-eating of it, I expect," says Phil.

The master resumes his march, and the man resumes his preparation of breakfast. It is not necessarily a lengthened preparation, being limited to the setting forth of very simple breakfast requisites for two, and the broiling of a rasher of bacon at the fire in the rusty grate; but as Phil has to sidle round a considerable part of the gallery for every object he wants, and never brings two objects at once, it takes time under the circumstances. At length the breakfast is ready. Phil announcing it, Mr. George knocks the ashes out of his pipe on the hob, stands his pipe itself in the chimney corner, and sits down to the meal. When he has helped himself, Phil follows suit; sitting at the extreme end of the little oblong table, and taking his plate on his knees. Either in humility, or to hide his blackened hands, or because it is his natural manner of eating.

" The country," says Mr. George, plying his knife and fork; " why, I suppose you never clapped your eyes on the country, Phil?"

"I see the marshes once," says Phil, contentedly eating his breakfast.

" What marshes?"

" *The* marshes, commander," returns Phil.

" Where are they?"

"I don't know where they are," says Phil; " but I see 'em, guv'ner. They was flat. And miste."

Governor and Commander are interchangeable terms with Phil, expressive of the same respect and deference, and applicable to nobody but Mr. George.

443

"I was born in the country, Phil."

"Was you indeed, commander?"

"Yes. And bred there."

Phil elevates his one eyebrow, and, after respectfully staring at his master to express interest, swallows a great gulp of coffee, still staring at him.

"There's not a bird's note that I don't know," says Mr. George. "Not many an English leaf or berry that I couldn't name. Not many a tree that I couldn't climb yet, if I was put to it. I was a real country boy, once. My good mother lived in the country."

"She must have been a fine old lady, guv'ner," Phil observes.

"Ay! and not so old either, five-and-thirty years ago," says Mr. George. "But I'll wager that at ninety she would be near as upright as me, and near as broad across the shoulders."

"Did she die at ninety, guv'ner?" inquires Phil.

"No. Bosh! Let her rest in peace, God bless her!" says the trooper. "What set me on about country boys, and runaways, and good-for-nothings? You, to be sure! So you never clapped your eyes upon the country—marshes and dreams excepted. Eh?"

Phil shakes his head.

"Do you want to see it?"

"N-no, I don't know as I do, particular," says Phil.

"The town's enough for you, eh?"

"Why, you see, commander," says Phil, "I ain't acquainted with anythink else, and I doubt if I ain't a-getting too old to take to novelties."

"How old *are* you, Phil?" asks the trooper, pausing as he conveys his smoking saucer to his lips.

"I'm something with a eight in it," says Phil. "It can't be eighty. Nor yet eighteen. It's betwixt 'em, somewheres."

Mr. George, slowly putting down his saucer without tasting

444

its contents, is laughingly beginning, " Why, what the deuce, Phil,"—when he stops, seeing that Phil is counting on his dirty fingers.

" I was just eight," says Phil, "agreeable to the parish calculation, when I went with the tinker. I was sent on a errand, and I see him a sittin under a old buildin with a fire all to himself wery comfortable, and he says, ' Would you like to come along a me, my man ? ' I says ' Yes,' and him and me and the fire goes home to Clerkenwell together. That was April Fool Day. I was able to count up to ten; and when April Fool Day come round again, I says to myself, ' Now, old chap, you're one and a eight in it.' April Fool Day after that, ' Now, old chap, you're two and a eight in it.' In course of time, I come to ten and a eight in it; two tens and a eight in it. When it got so high, it got the upper hand of me ; but this is how I always know there's a eight in it."

" Ah ! " says Mr. George, resuming his breakfast. " And where's the tinker ? "

" Drink put him in the hospital, guv'ner, and the hospital put him—in a glass case, I *have* heerd," Phil replies mysteriously.

" By that means you got promotion ? Took the business, Phil ? "

" Yes, commander, I took the business. Such as it was. It wasn't much of a beat—round Saffron Hill, Hatton Garden, Clerkenwell, Smiffeld, and there—poor neighbourhood, where they uses up the kettles till they're past mending. Most of the tramping tinkers used to come and lodge at our place ; that was the best part of my master's earnings. But they didn't come to me. I warn't like him. He could sing 'em a good song. *I* couldn't ! He could play 'em a tune on any sort of pot you please, so as it was iron or block tin. *I* never could do nothing with a pot, but mend it or bile it—never had a note of music in me. Besides, I was too ill-looking, and their wives complained of me."

" They were mighty particular. You would pass muster in a crowd, Phil ! " says the trooper with a pleasant smile.

" No, guv'ner," returns Phil, shaking his head. " No, I shouldn't. I was passable enough when I went with the tinker, though nothing to boast of then : but what with blowing the fire with my mouth when I was young, and spileing my complexion, and singeing my hair off, and swallering the smoke ; and what with being nat'rally unfort'nate in the way of running against hot metal, and marking myself by sich means ; and what with having turn-ups with the tinker as I got older, almost whenever he was too far gone in drink— which was almost always—my beauty was queer, wery queer, even at that time. As to since ; what with a dozen years in a dark forge, where the men was given to larking ; and what with being scorched in a accident at a gas-works ; and what with being blowed out of winder, case-filling at the firework business ; I am ugly enough to be made a show on ! "

Resigning himself to which condition with a perfectly satisfied manner, Phil begs the favour of another cup of coffee. While drinking it, he says :

" It was after the case-filling blow-up, when I first see you, commander. You remember ? "

" I remember, Phil. You were walking along in the sun."

" Crawling, guv'ner, again a wall—— "

" True, Phil—shouldering your way on—— "

" In a nightcap ! " exclaims Phil, excited.

" In a nightcap—— "

" And hobbling with a couple of sticks ! " cries Phil, still more excited.

" With a couple of sticks. When—— "

" When you stops, you know," cries Phil, putting down his cup and saucer, and hastily removing his plate from his knees, " and says to me, ' What, comrade ! You have been in the wars ! ' I didn't say much to you, commander, then, for I was took by surprise, that a person so strong and healthy and bold as you was, should stop to speak to such a limping

446

bag of bones as I was. But you says to me, says you, delivering it out of your chest as hearty as possible, so that it was like a glass of something hot, 'What accident have you met with? You have been badly hurt. What's amiss, old boy? Cheer up, and tell us about it!' Cheer up! I was cheered already! I says as much to you, you says more to me, I says more to you, you says more to me, and here I am, commander! Here I am, commander!" cries Phil, who has started from his chair and unaccountably begun to sidle away. "If a mark's wanted, or if it will improve the business, let the customers take aim at me. They can't spoil *my* beauty. *I*'m all right. Come on! If they want a man to box at, let 'em box at me. Let 'em knock me well about the head. *I* don't mind! If they want a light-weight, to be throwed for practice, Cornwall, Devonshire, or Lancashire, let 'em throw me. They won't hurt *me*. I have been throwed, all sorts of styles, all my life!"

With this unexpected speech, energetically delivered, and accompanied by action illustrative of the various exercises referred to, Phil Squod shoulders his way round three sides of the gallery, and abruptly tacking off at his commander, makes a butt at him with his head, intended to express devotion to his service. He then begins to clear away the breakfast.

Mr. George, after laughing cheerfully, and clapping him on the shoulder, assists in these arrangements, and helps to get the gallery into business order. That done, he takes a turn at the dumb-bells ; and afterwards weighing himself, and opining that he is getting "too fleshy," engages with great gravity in solitary broadsword practice. Meanwhile, Phil has fallen to work at his usual table, where he screws and unscrews, and cleans, and files, and whistles into small apertures, and blackens himself more and more, and seems to do and undo everything that can be done and undone about a gun.

Master and man are at length disturbed by footsteps in the passage, where they make an unusual sound, denoting the arrival of unusual company. These steps, advancing nearer and nearer to the gallery, bring into it a group, at first sight scarcely reconcilable with any day in the year but the fifth of November.

It consists of a limp and ugly figure carried in a chair by two bearers, and attended by a lean female with a face like a pinched mask, who might be expected immediately to recite the popular verses, commemorative of the time when they did contrive to blow Old England up alive, but for her keeping her lips tightly and defiantly closed as the chair is put down. At which point, the figure in it gasping, " O Lord! O dear me! I am shaken!" adds, "How de do, my dear friend, how de do?" Mr. George then descries, in the procession, the venerable Mr. Smallweed out for an airing, attended by his grand-daughter Judy as body-guard.

" Mr. George, my dear friend," says Grandfather Smallweed, removing his right arm from the neck of one of his bearers, whom he has nearly throttled coming along, " how de do? You're surprised to see me, my dear friend."

" I should hardly have been more surprised to have seen your friend in the city," returns Mr. George.

" I am very seldom out," pants Mr. Smallweed. " I haven't been out for many months. It's inconvenient—and it comes expensive. But I longed so much to see you, my dear Mr. George. How de do, sir?"

" I am well enough," says Mr. George. " I hope you are the same."

" You can't be too well, my dear friend." Mr. Smallweed takes him by both hands. " I have brought my grand-daughter Judy. I couldn't keep her away. She longed so much to see you."

" Hum! She bears it calmly!" mutters Mr. George.

" So we got a hackney-cab, and put a chair in it, and just round the corner they lifted me out of the cab and into the chair, and carried me here, that I might see my dear friend in his own establishment! This," says Grandfather Smallweed,

Visitors to the Shooting Gallery

alluding to the bearer, who has been in danger of strangulation, and who withdraws adjusting his windpipe, "is the driver of the cab. He has nothing extra. It is by agreement included in his fare. This person," the other bearer, "we engaged in the street outside for a pint of beer. Which is twopence. Judy, give the person twopence. I was not sure you had a workman of your own here, my dear friend, or we needn't have employed this person."

Grandfather Smallweed refers to Phil, with a glance of considerable terror, and a half-subdued "O Lord! O dear me!" Nor is his apprehension, on the surface of things, without some reason; for Phil, who has never beheld the apparition in the black velvet cap before, has stopped short with a gun in his hand, with much of the air of a dead shot, intent on picking Mr. Smallweed off as an ugly old bird of the crow species.

"Judy, my child," says Grandfather Smallweed, "give the person his twopence. It's a great deal for what he has done."

The person, who is one of those extraordinary specimens of human fungus that spring up spontaneously in the western streets of London, ready dressed in an old red jacket, with a "Mission" for holding horses and calling coaches, receives his twopence with anything but transport, tosses the money into the air, catches it over-handed, and retires.

"My dear Mr. George," says Grandfather Smallweed, "would you be so kind as help to carry me to the fire? I am accustomed to a fire, and I am an old man, and I soon chill. O dear me!"

His closing exclamation is jerked out of the venerable gentleman by the suddenness with which Mr. Squod, like a genie, catches him up, chair and all, and deposits him on the hearth-stone.

"O Lord!" says Mr. Smallweed, panting. "O dear me! O my stars! My dear friend, your workman is very strong —and very prompt. O Lord, he is very prompt! Judy, draw me back a little. I'm being scorched in the legs;"

which indeed is testified to the noses of all present by the smell of his worsted stockings.

The gentle Judy, having backed her grandfather a little way from the fire, and having shaken him up as usual, and having released his overshadowed eye from its black velvet extinguisher, Mr. Smallweed again says, "O dear me! O Lord!" and looking about, and meeting Mr. George's glance, again stretches out both hands.

"My dear friend! So happy in this meeting! And this is your establishment? It's a delightful place. It's a picture! You never find that anything goes off here, accidentally; do you, my dear friend?" adds Grandfather Smallweed, very ill at ease.

"No, no. No fear of that."

"And your workman. He—O dear me!—he never lets anything off without meaning it; does he, my dear friend?"

"He has never hurt anybody but himself," says Mr. George, smiling.

"But he might, you know. He seems to have hurt himself a good deal, and he might hurt somebody else," the old gentleman returns. "He mightn't mean it—or he even might. Mr. George, will you order him to leave his infernal fire-arms alone, and go away?"

Obedient to a nod from the trooper, Phil retires, empty-handed, to the other end of the gallery. Mr. Smallweed, reassured, falls to rubbing his legs.

"And you're doing well, Mr. George?" he says to the trooper, squarely standing faced about towards him with his broadsword in his hand. "You are prospering, please the Powers?"

Mr. George answers with a cool nod, adding, "Go on. You have not come to say that, I know."

"You are so sprightly, Mr. George," returns the venerable grandfather. "You are such good company."

"Ha ha! Go on!" says Mr. George.

"My dear friend!—But that sword looks awful gleaming

and sharp. It might cut somebody, by accident. It makes me shiver, Mr. George—Curse him!" says the excellent old gentleman apart to Judy, as the trooper takes a step or two away to lay it aside. "He owes me money, and might think of paying off old scores in this murdering place. I wish your brimstone grandmother was here, and he'd shave her head off."

Mr. George, returning, folds his arms, and looking down at the old man, sliding every moment lower and lower in his chair, says quietly, "Now for it!"

"Ho!" cries Mr. Smallweed, rubbing his hands with an artful chuckle. "Yes. Now for it. Now for what, my dear friend?"

"For a pipe," says Mr. George; who with great composure sets his chair in the chimney-corner, takes his pipe from the grate, fills it and lights it, and falls to smoking peacefully.

This tends to the discomfiture of Mr. Smallweed, who finds it so difficult to resume his object, whatever it may be, that he becomes exasperated, and secretly claws the air with an impotent vindictiveness expressive of an intense desire to tear and rend the visage of Mr. George. As the excellent old gentleman's nails are long and leaden, and his hands lean and veinous, and his eyes green and watery; and, over and above this, as he continues, while he claws, to slide down in his chair and to collapse into a shapeless bundle; he becomes such a ghastly spectacle, even in the accustomed eyes of Judy, that that young virgin pounces at him with something more than the ardour of affection, and so shakes him up, and pats and pokes him in divers parts of his body, but particularly in that part which the science of self-defence would call his wind, that in his grievous distress he utters enforced sounds like a paviour's rammer.

When Judy has by these means set him up again in his chair, with a white face and a frosty nose (but still clawing), she stretches out her weazen forefinger, and gives Mr. George one poke in the back. The trooper raising his head, she makes another poke at her esteemed grandfather; and, having thus brought them together, stares rigidly at the fire.

"Aye, aye! Ho, ho! U—u—u—ugh!" chatters Grandfather Smallweed, swallowing his rage. "My dear friend!" (still clawing).

"I tell you what," says Mr. George. "If you want to converse with me, you must speak out. I am one of the Roughs, and I can't go about and about. I haven't the art to do it. I am not clever enough. It don't suit me. When you go winding round and round me," says the trooper, putting his pipe between his lips again, "damme, if I don't feel as if I was being smothered!"

And he inflates his broad chest to its utmost extent, as if to assure himself that he is not smothered yet.

"If you have come to give me a friendly call," continues Mr. George, "I am obliged to you; how are you? If you have come to see whether there's any property on the premises, look about you; you are welcome. If you want to out with something, out with it!"

The blooming Judy, without removing her gaze from the fire, gives her grandfather one ghostly poke.

"You see! It's her opinion, too. And why the devil that young woman won't sit down like a Christian," says Mr. George, with his eyes musingly fixed on Judy, "I can't comprehend."

"She keeps at my side to attend to me, sir," says Grandfather Smallweed. "I am an old man, my dear Mr. George, and I need some attention. I can carry my years; I am not a Brimstone poll-parrot;" (snarling and looking unconsciously for the cushion;) "but I need attention, my dear friend."

"Well!" returns the trooper, wheeling his chair to face the old man. "Now then?"

"My friend in the city, Mr. George, has done a little business with a pupil of yours."

"Has he?" says Mr. George. "I am sorry to hear it."

"Yes, sir." Grandfather Smallweed rubs his legs. "He

is a fine young soldier now, Mr. George, by the name of Carstone. Friends came forward, and paid it all up, honourable."

"Did they?" returns Mr. George. "Do you think your friend in the city would like a piece of advice?"

"I think he would, my dear friend. From you."

"I advise him, then, to do no more business in that quarter. There's no more to be got by it. The young gentleman, to my knowledge, is brought to a dead halt."

"No, no, my dear friend. No, no, Mr. George. No, no, no, sir," remonstrates Grandfather Smallweed, cunningly rubbing his spare legs. "Not quite a dead halt, I think. He has good friends, and he is good for his pay, and he is good for the selling price of his commission, and he is good for his chance in a lawsuit, and he is good for his chance in a wife, and—oh, do you know, Mr. George, I think my friend would consider the young gentleman good for something yet?" says Grandfather Smallweed, turning up his velvet cap, and scratching his ear like a monkey.

Mr. George, who has put aside his pipe and sits with an arm on his chair-back, beats a tattoo on the ground with his right foot, as if he were not particularly pleased with the turn the conversation has taken.

"But to pass from one subject to another," resumes Mr. Smallweed. "To promote the conversation, as a joker might say. To pass, Mr. George, from the ensign to the captain."

"What are you up to, now?" asks Mr. George, pausing with a frown in stroking the recollection of his moustache. "What captain?"

"Our captain. The captain we know of. Captain Hawdon."

"O! that's it, is it?" says Mr. George, with a low whistle, as he sees both grandfather and grand-daughter looking hard at him; "you are there! Well? what about it? Come, I won't be smothered any more. Speak!"

"My dear friend," returns the old man, "I was applied—

453

Judy, shake me up a little!—I was applied to, yesterday, about the captain; and my opinion still is, that the captain is not dead."

"Bosh!" observes Mr. George.

"What was your remark, my dear friend?" inquires the old man with his hand to his ear.

"Bosh!"

"Ho!" says Grandfather Smallweed. "Mr. George, of my opinion you can judge for yourself, according to the questions asked of me, and the reasons given for asking 'em. Now, what do you think the lawyer making the inquiries wants?"

"A job," says Mr. George.

"Nothing of the kind!"

"Can't be a lawyer, then," says Mr. George, folding his arms with an air of confirmed resolution.

"My dear friend, he is a lawyer, and a famous one. He wants to see some fragment in Captain Hawdon's writing. He don't want to keep it. He only wants to see it, and compare it with a writing in his possession."

"Well?"

"Well, Mr. George. Happening to remember the advertisement concerning Captain Hawdon, and any information that could be given respecting him, he looked it up and came to me—just as you did, my dear friend. *Will* you shake hands? So glad you came, that day! I should have missed forming such a friendship, if you hadn't come!"

"Well, Mr. Smallweed?" says Mr. George again, after going through the ceremony with some stiffness.

"I had no such thing. I have nothing but his signature. Plague pestilence and famine, battle murder and sudden death upon him," says the old man, making a curse out of one of his few remembrances of a prayer, and squeezing up his velvet cap between his angry hands, "I have half a million of his signatures, I think! But you," breathlessly recovering his mildness of speech, as Judy readjusts the cap on his skittle-ball of a head; "you, my dear Mr. George, are likely to have some letter or paper that would suit the purpose. Anything would suit the purpose, written in the hand."

"Some writing in that hand," says the trooper, pondering, "may be, I have."

"My dearest friend!"

"May be, I have not."

"Ho!" says Grandfather Smallweed, crest-fallen.

"But if I had bushels of it, I would not show as much as would make a cartridge, without knowing why."

"Sir, I have told you why. My dear Mr. George, I have told you why."

"Not enough," says the trooper, shaking his head. "I must know more, and approve it."

"Then, will you come to the lawyer? My dear friend, will you come and see the gentleman?" urges Grandfather Smallweed, pulling out a lean old silver watch, with hands like the leg of a skeleton. "I told him it was probable I might call upon him, between ten and eleven this forenoon; and it's now half after ten. Will you come and see the gentleman, Mr. George?"

"Hum!" says he, gravely. "I don't mind that. Though why this should concern you so much, I don't know."

"Everything concerns me, that has a chance in it of bringing anything to light about him. Didn't he take us all in? Didn't he owe us immense sums, all round? Concern me? Who can anything about him concern, more than me? Not, my dear friend," says Grandfather Smallweed, lowering his tone, "that I want *you* to betray anything. Far from it. Are you ready to come, my dear friend?"

"Ay! I'll come in a moment. I promise nothing, you know."

"No, my dear Mr. George; no."

"And you mean to say you're going to give me a lift to this place, wherever it is, without charging for it?" Mr. George inquires, getting his hat, and thick wash-leather gloves.

This pleasantry so tickles Mr. Smallweed, that he laughs, long and low, before the fire. But ever while he laughs, he glances over his paralytic shoulder at Mr. George, and eagerly watches him as he unlocks the padlock of a homely cupboard at the distant end of the gallery, looks here and there upon the higher shelves, and ultimately takes something out with a rustling of paper, folds it, and puts it in his breast. Then Judy pokes Mr. Smallweed once, and Mr. Smallweed pokes Judy once.

"I am ready," says the trooper, coming back. "Phil, you can carry this old gentleman to his coach, and make nothing of him."

"O dear me! O Lord! Stop a moment!" says Mr. Smallweed. "He's so very prompt! Are you sure you can do it carefully, my worthy man?"

Phil makes no reply; but, seizing the chair and its load, sidles away, tightly hugged by the now speechless Mr. Smallweed, and bolts along the passage, as if he had an acceptable commission to carry the old gentleman to the nearest volcano. His shorter trust, however, terminating at the cab, he deposits him there; and the fair Judy takes her place beside him, and the chair embellishes the roof, and Mr. George takes the vacant place upon the box.

Mr. George is quite confounded by the spectacle he beholds from time to time as he peeps into the cab, through the window behind him; where the grim Judy is always motionless, and the old gentleman with his cap over one eye is always sliding off the seat into the straw, and looking upward at him, out of his other eye, with a helpless expression of being jolted in the back.

CHAPTER XXVII

Mr. George has not far to ride with folded arms upon the box, for their destination is Lincoln's Inn Fields. When the driver stops his horses, Mr. George alights, and looking in at the window, says:

"What, Mr. Tulkinghorn's your man, is he?"

"Yes, my dear friend. Do you know him, Mr. George?"

"Why, I have heard of him—seen him too, I think. But I don't know him, and he don't know me."

There ensues the carrying of Mr. Smallweed up-stairs; which is done to perfection with the trooper's help. He is borne into Mr. Tulkinghorn's great room, and deposited on the Turkey rug before the fire. Mr. Tulkinghorn is not within at the present moment, but will be back directly. The occupant of the pew in the hall, having said thus much, stirs the fire, and leaves the triumvirate to warm themselves.

Mr. George is mightily curious in respect of the room. He looks up at the painted ceiling, looks round at the old law-books, contemplates the portraits of the great clients, reads aloud the names on the boxes.

"'Sir Leicester Dedlock, Baronet,'" Mr. George reads thoughtfully. "Ha! 'Manor of Chesney Wold.' Humph!" Mr. George stands looking at these boxes a long while—as if they were pictures—and comes back to the fire repeating, "Sir Leicester Dedlock, Baronet, and Manor of Chesney Wold, hey?"

457

"Worth a mint of money, Mr. George!" whispers Grandfather Smallweed, rubbing his legs. "Powerfully rich!"

"Who do you mean? This old gentleman, or the Baronet?"

"This gentleman, this gentleman."

"So I have heard; and knows a thing or two, I'll hold a wager. Not bad quarters, either," says Mr. George, looking round again. "See the strong box, yonder!"

This reply is cut short by Mr. Tulkinghorn's arrival. There is no change in him, of course. Rustily drest, with his spectacles in his hand, and their very case worn threadbare. In manner, close and dry. In voice, husky and low. In face, watchful behind a blind; habitually not uncensorious and contemptuous perhaps. The peerage may have warmer worshippers and faithfuller believers than Mr. Tulkinghorn, after all, if everything were known.

"Good morning, Mr. Smallweed, good morning!" he says as he comes in. "You have brought the serjeant, I see. Sit down, serjeant."

As Mr. Tulkinghorn takes off his gloves and puts them in his hat, he looks with half-closed eyes across the room to where the trooper stands, and says within himself perchance, "You'll do, my friend!"

"Sit down, serjeant," he repeats, as he comes to his table, which is set on one side of the fire, and takes his easy-chair. "Cold and raw this morning, cold and raw!" Mr. Tulkinghorn warms before the bars, alternately, the palms and knuckles of his hands, and looks (from behind that blind which is always down) at the trio sitting in a little semicircle before him.

"Now, I can feel what I am about!" (as perhaps he can in two senses) "Mr. Smallweed." The old gentleman is newly shaken up by Judy, to bear his part in the conversation. "You have brought our good friend the serjeant, I see."

"Yes, sir," returns Mr. Smallweed, very servile to the lawyer's wealth and influence.

THE LAWYER AND THE TROOPER

"And what does the serjeant say about this business?"

"Mr. George," says Grandfather Smallweed, with a tremulous wave of his shrivelled hand, "this is the gentleman, sir."

Mr. George salutes the gentleman; but otherwise sits bolt upright and profoundly silent—very forward in his chair, as if the full complement of regulation appendages for a field-day hung about him.

Mr. Tulkinghorn proceeds: "Well, George?—I believe your name is George?"

"It is so, sir."

"What do you say, George?"

"I ask your pardon, sir," returns the trooper, "but I should wish to know what *you* say?"

"Do you mean in point of reward?"

"I mean in point of everything, sir."

This is so very trying to Mr. Smallweed's temper, that he suddenly breaks out with "You're a Brimstone beast!" and as suddenly asks pardon of Mr. Tulkinghorn; excusing himself for this slip of the tongue, by saying to Judy, "I was thinking of your grandmother, my dear."

"I supposed, serjeant," Mr. Tulkinghorn resumes, as he leans on one side of his chair and crosses his legs, "that Mr. Smallweed might have sufficiently explained the matter. It lies in the smallest compass, however. You served under Captain Hawdon at one time, and were his attendant in illness, and rendered him many little services, and were rather in his confidence, I am told. That is so, is it not?"

"Yes, sir, that is so," says Mr. George, with military brevity.

"Therefore you may happen to have in your possession something—anything, no matter what—accounts, instructions, orders, a letter, anything—in Captain Hawdon's writing. I wish to compare his writing with some that I have. If you can give me the opportunity, you shall be rewarded for your

459

trouble. Three, four, five, guineas, you would consider handsome, I dare say."

"Noble, my dear friend!" cries Grandfather Smallweed, screwing up his eyes.

"If not, say how much more, in your conscience as a soldier, you can demand. There is no need for you to part with the writing, against your inclination—though I should prefer to have it."

Mr. George sits squared in exactly the same attitude, looks at the painted ceiling, and says never a word. The irascible Mr. Smallweed scratches the air.

"The question is," says Mr. Tulkinghorn in his methodical, subdued, uninterested way, "first, whether you have any of Captain Hawdon's writing?"

"First, whether I have any of Captain Hawdon's writing, sir," repeats Mr. George.

"Secondly, what will satisfy you for the trouble of producing it?"

"Secondly, what will satisfy me for the trouble of producing it, sir," repeats Mr. George.

"Thirdly, you can judge for yourself whether it is at all like that," says Mr. Tulkinghorn, suddenly handing him some sheets of written paper tied together.

"Whether it is at all like that, sir. Just so," repeats Mr. George.

All three repetitions Mr. George pronounces in a mechanical manner, looking straight at Mr. Tulkinghorn; nor does he so much as glance at the affidavit in Jarndyce and Jarndyce, that has been given to him for his inspection (though he still holds it in his hand), but continues to look at the lawyer with an air of troubled meditation.

"Well?" says Mr. Tulkinghorn. "What do you say?"

"Well, sir," replies Mr. George, rising erect and looking immense, "I would rather, if you'll excuse me, have nothing to do with this."

Mr. Tulkinghorn, outwardly quite undisturbed, demands "Why not?"

"Why, sir," returns the trooper. "Except on military compulsion, I am not a man of business. Among civilians I am what they call in Scotland a ne'er-do-weel. I have no head for papers, sir. I can stand any fire better than a fire of cross questions. I mentioned to Mr. Smallweed, only an hour or so ago, that when I come into things of this kind I feel as if I was being smothered. And that is my sensation," says Mr. George, looking round upon the company, "at the present moment."

With that, he takes three strides forward to replace the papers on the lawyer's table, and three strides backward to resume his former station: where he stands perfectly upright, now looking at the ground, and now at the painted ceiling, with his hands behind him as if to prevent himself from accepting any other document whatever.

Under this provocation, Mr. Smallweed's favourite adjective of disparagement is so close to his tongue, that he begins the words "my dear friend" with the monosyllable "Brim;" thus converting the possessive pronoun into Brimmy, and appearing to have an impediment in his speech. Once past this difficulty, however, he exhorts his dear friend in the tenderest manner not to be rash, but to do what so eminent a gentleman requires, and to do it with a good grace: confident that it must be unobjectionable as well as profitable. Mr. Tulkinghorn merely utters an occasional sentence, as "You are the best judge of your own interest, serjeant." "Take care you do no harm by this." "Please yourself, please yourself." "If you know what you mean, that's quite enough." These he utters with an appearance of perfect indifference, as he looks over the papers on his table, and prepares to write a letter.

Mr. George looks distrustfully from the painted ceiling to the ground, from the ground to Mr. Smallweed, from Mr. Smallweed to Mr. Tulkinghorn, and from Mr. Tulkinghorn to the painted ceiling again; often in his perplexity changing the leg on which he rests.

"I do assure you, sir," says Mr. George, "not to say it offensively, that between you and Mr. Smallweed here, I really am being smothered fifty times over. I really am, sir. I am not a match for you gentlemen. Will you allow me to ask, why you want to see the captain's hand, in the case that I could find any specimen of it?"

Mr. Tulkinghorn quietly shakes his head. "No. If you were a man of business, serjeant, you would not need to be informed, that there are confidential reasons, very harmless in themselves, for many such wants, in the profession to which I belong. But if you are afraid of doing any injury to Captain Hawdon, you may set your mind at rest about that."

"Ay! he is dead, sir."

"*Is* he?" Mr. Tulkinghorn quietly sits down to write.

"Well, sir," says the trooper, looking into his hat after another disconcerted pause; "I am sorry not to have given you more satisfaction. If it would be any satisfaction to any one, that I should be confirmed in my judgment that I would rather have nothing to do with this, by a friend of mine, who has a better head for business than I have, and who is an old soldier, I am willing to consult with him. I—I really am so completely smothered myself at present," says Mr. George, passing his hand hopelessly across his brow, "that I don't know but what it might be a satisfaction to me."

Mr. Smallweed, hearing that this authority is an old soldier, so strongly inculcates the expediency of the trooper's taking counsel with him, and particularly informing him of its being a question of five guineas or more, that Mr. George engages to go and see him. Mr. Tulkinghorn says nothing either way.

"I'll consult my friend, then, by your leave, sir," says the trooper, "and I'll take the liberty of looking in again with the final answer in the course of the day. Mr. Smallweed, if you wish to be carried down-stairs——"

"In a moment, my dear friend, in a moment. Will you first let me speak half a word with this gentleman, in private?"

"Certainly, sir. Don't hurry yourself on my account." The trooper retires to a distant part of the room, and resumes his curious inspection of the boxes; strong and otherwise.

"If I wasn't as weak as a Brimstone Baby, sir," whispers Grandfather Smallweed, drawing the lawyer down to his level by the lappel of his coat, and flashing some half-quenched green fire out of his angry eyes, "I'd tear the writing away from him. He's got it buttoned in his breast. I saw him put it there. Judy saw him put it there. Speak up, you crabbed image for the sign of a walking-stick shop, and say you saw him put it there!"

This vehement conjuration the old gentleman accompanies with such a thrust at his grand-daughter, that it is too much for his strength, and he slips away out of his chair, drawing Mr. Tulkinghorn with him, until he is arrested by Judy, and well shaken.

"Violence will not do for me, my friend," Mr. Tulkinghorn then remarks coolly.

"No, no, I know, I know, sir. But it's chafing and galling —it's—it's worse than your smattering chattering Magpie of a grandmother," to the imperturbable Judy, who only looks at the fire, "to know he has got what's wanted, and won't give it up. He, not to give it up! *He!* A vagabond! But never mind, sir, never mind. At the most, he has only his own way for a little while. I have him periodically in a vice. I'll twist him, sir. I'll screw him, sir. If he won't do it with a good grace, I'll make him do it with a bad one, sir!—Now, my dear Mr. George," says Grandfather Smallweed, winking at the lawyer hideously, as he releases him, "I am ready for your kind assistance, my excellent friend!"

Mr. Tulkinghorn, with some shadowy sign of amusement manifesting itself through his self-possession, stands on the hearth-rug with his back to the fire, watching the disappearance of Mr. Smallweed, and acknowledging the trooper's parting salute with one slight nod.

It is more difficult to get rid of the old gentleman, Mr. George finds, than to bear a hand in carrying him down-stairs; for, when he is replaced in his conveyance, he is so loquacious on the subject of the guineas, and retains such an affectionate hold of his button—having, in truth, a secret longing to rip his coat open, and rob him—that some degree of force is necessary on the trooper's part to effect a separation. It is accomplished at last, and he proceeds alone in quest of his adviser.

By the cloisterly Temple, and by Whitefriars (there, not without a glance at Hanging-Sword Alley, which would seem to be something in his way), and by Blackfriars Bridge, and Blackfriars Road, Mr. George sedately marches to a street of little shops lying somewhere in that ganglion of roads from Kent and Surrey, and of streets from the bridges of London, centring in the far-famed Elephant who has lost his castle formed of a thousand four-horse coaches, to a stronger iron monster than he, ready to chop him into mince-meat any day he dares. To one of the little shops in this street, which is a musician's shop, having a few fiddles in the window, and some Pan's pipes and a tambourine, and a triangle, and certain elongated scraps of music, Mr. George directs his massive tread. And halting at a few paces from it, as he sees a soldierly-looking woman, with her outer skirts tucked up, come forth with a small wooden tub, and in that tub commence a whisking and a splashing on the margin of the pavement, Mr. George says to himself, "She's as usual, washing greens. I never saw her, except upon a baggage-waggon, when she wasn't washing greens!"

The subject of this reflection is at all events so occupied in washing greens at present, that she remains unsuspicious of Mr. George's approach; until, lifting up herself and her tub together, when she has poured the water off into the

464

gutter, she finds him standing near her. Her reception of him is not flattering.

"George, I never see you but I wish you was a hundred mile away!"

The trooper, without remarking on this welcome, follows into the musical instrument shop, where the lady places her tub of greens upon the counter, and having shaken hands with him, rests her arms upon it.

"I never," she says, "George, consider Matthew Bagnet safe a minute when you're near him. You are that restless and that roving——"

"Yes! I know I am, Mrs. Bagnet. I know I am."

"You know you are!" says Mrs. Bagnet. "What's the use of that? *Why* are you?"

"The nature of the animal, I suppose," returns the trooper good-humouredly.

"Ah!" cries Mrs. Bagnet, something shrilly, "but what satisfaction will the nature of the animal be to me, when the animal shall have tempted my Mat away from the musical business to New Zealand or Australey?"

Mrs. Bagnet is not at all an ill-looking woman. Rather large-boned, a little coarse in the grain, and freckled by the sun and wind which have tanned her hair upon the forehead; but healthy, wholesome, and bright-eyed. A strong, busy, active, honest-faced woman of from forty-five to fifty. Clean, hardy, and so economically dressed (though substantially), that the only article of ornament of which she stands possessed appears to be her wedding-ring; around which her finger has grown to be so large since it was put on, that it will never come off again until it shall mingle with Mrs. Bagnet's dust.

"Mrs. Bagnet," says the trooper, "I am on my parole with you. Mat will get no harm from me. You may trust me so far."

"Well, I think I may. But the very looks of you are unsettling," Mrs. Bagnet rejoins. "Ah, George, George! If you had only settled down, and married Joe Pouch's widow when he died in North America, *she'd* have combed your hair for you."

"It was a chance for me, certainly," returns the trooper, half-laughingly, half-seriously, " but I shall never settle down into a respectable man now. Joe Pouch's widow might have done me good—there was something in her—and something of her—but I couldn't make up my mind to it. If I had had the luck to meet with such a wife as Mat found!"

Mrs. Bagnet, who seems in a virtuous way to be under little reserve with a good sort of fellow, but to be another good sort of fellow herself for that matter, receives this compliment by flicking Mr. George in the face with a head of greens, and taking her tub into the little room behind the shop.

"Why, Quebec, my poppet," says George, following, on invitation, into that department. "And little Malta, too! Come and kiss your Bluffy!"

These young ladies—not supposed to have been actually christened by the names applied to them, though always so called in the family, from the places of their birth in barracks —are respectively employed on three-legged stools: the younger (some five or six years old), in learning her letters out of a penny primer; the elder (eight or nine perhaps), in teaching her, and sewing with great assiduity. Both hail Mr. George with acclamations as an old friend, and after some kissing and romping plant their stools beside him.

"And how's young Woolwich?" says Mr. George.

"Ah! There now!" cries Mrs. Bagnet, turning about from her saucepans (for she is cooking dinner), with a bright flush on her face. "Would you believe it? Got an engagement at the Theayter, with his father, to play the fife in a military piece."

"Well done, my godson!" cries Mr. George, slapping his thigh.

"I believe you!" says Mrs. Bagnet. "He's a Briton, That's what Woolwich is. A Briton!"

"And Mat blows away at his bassoon. and you're respectable civilians one and all," says Mr. George. "Family people. Children growing up. Mat's old mother in Scotland, and your old father somewhere else, corresponded with; and helped a little; and—well, well! To be sure, I don't know why I shouldn't be wished a hundred mile away, for I have not much to do with all this!"

Mr. George is becoming thoughtful; sitting before the fire in the whitewashed room, which has a sanded floor, and a barrack smell, and contains nothing superfluous, and has not a visible speck of dirt or dust in it, from the faces of Quebec and Malta to the bright tin pots and pannikins upon the dresser shelves,—Mr. George is becoming thoughtful, sitting here while Mrs. Bagnet is busy, when Mr. Bagnet and young Woolwich opportunely come home. Mr. Bagnet is an ex-artilleryman, tall and upright, with shaggy eyebrows, and whiskers like the fibres of a cocoa-nut, not a hair upon his head, and a torrid complexion. His voice, short, deep, and resonant, is not at all unlike the tones of the instrument to which he is devoted. Indeed there may be generally observed in him an unbending, unyielding, brass-bound air, as if he were himself the bassoon of the human orchestra. Young Woolwich is the type and model of a young drummer.

Both father and son salute the trooper heartily. He saying, in due season, that he has come to advise with Mr. Bagnet, Mr. Bagnet hospitably declares that he will hear of no business until after dinner; and that his friend shall not partake of his counsel, without first partaking of boiled pork and greens. The trooper yielding to this invitation, he and Mr. Bagnet, not to embarrass the domestic preparations, go forth to take a turn up and down the little street, which they promenade with measured tread and folded arms, as if it were a rampart.

"George," says Mr. Bagnet. "You know me. It's my old girl that advises. She has the head. But I never own to it before her. Discipline must be maintained. Wait till the greens is off her mind. Then, we'll consult. Whatever the old girl says, do—do it!"

"I intend to, Mat," replies the other. "I would sooner take her opinion than that of a college."

"College," returns Mr. Bagnet, in short sentences, bassoon-like. "What college could you leave—in another quarter of the world—with nothing but a grey cloak and an umbrella—to make its way home to Europe? The old girl would do it to-morrow. Did it once!"

"You are right," says Mr. George.

"What college," pursues Bagnet, "could you set up in life—with two penn'orth of white lime—a penn'orth of fuller's earth—a ha'porth of sand—and the rest of the change out of sixpence, in money? That's what the old girl started on. In the present business."

"I am rejoiced to hear it's thriving, Mat."

"The old girl," says Mr. Bagnet, acquiescing, "saves. Has a stocking somewhere. With money in it. I never saw it. But I know she's got it. Wait till the greens is off her mind. Then she'll set you up."

"She is a treasure!" exclaims Mr. George.

"She's more. But I never own to it before her. Discipline must be maintained. It was the old girl that brought out my musical abilities. I should have been in the artillery now, but for the old girl. Six years I hammered at the fiddle. Ten at the flute. The old girl said it wouldn't do; intention good, but want of flexibility; try the bassoon. The old girl borrowed a bassoon from the bandmaster of the Rifle Regiment. I practised in the trenches. Got on, got another, get a living by it!"

George remarks that she looks as fresh as a rose, and as sound as an apple.

"The old girl," says Mr. Bagnet in reply, "is a thoroughly fine woman. Consequently, she is like a thoroughly fine day. Gets finer as she gets on. I never saw the old girl's equal. But I never own to it before her. Discipline must be maintained!"

Proceeding to converse on indifferent matters, they walk up and down the little street, keeping step and time, until summoned by Quebec and Malta to do justice to the pork and greens; over which Mrs. Bagnet, like a military chaplain, says a short grace. In the distribution of these comestibles, as in every other household duty, Mrs. Bagnet develops an exact system; sitting with every dish before her; allotting to every portion of pork its own portion of pot-liquor, greens, potatoes, and even mustard! and serving it out complete. Having likewise served out the beer from a can, and thus supplied the mess with all things necessary, Mrs. Bagnet proceeds to satisfy her own hunger, which is in a healthy state. The kit of the mess, if the table furniture may be so denominated, is chiefly composed of utensils of horn and tin, that have done duty in several parts of the world. Young Woolwich's knife, in particular, which is of the oyster kind, with the additional feature of a strong shutting-up movement which frequently balks the appetite of that young musician, is mentioned as having gone in various hands the complete round of foreign service.

The dinner done, Mrs. Bagnet, assisted by the younger branches (who polish their own cups and platters, knives and forks), makes all the dinner garniture shine as brightly as before, and puts it all away; first sweeping the hearth, to the end that Mr. Bagnet and the visitor may not be retarded in the smoking of their pipes. These household cares involve much pattening and counter-pattening in the back yard, and considerable use of a pail, which is finally so happy as to assist in the ablutions of Mrs. Bagnet herself. That old girl re-appearing by-and-by, quite fresh, and sitting down to her needlework, then and only then—the greens being only then to be considered as entirely off her mind—Mr. Bagnet requests the trooper to state his case.

This, Mr. George does with great discretion; appearing to address himself to Mr. Bagnet, but having an eye solely on the old girl all the time, as Bagnet has himself. She,

469

equally discreet, busies herself with her needlework. The case fully stated, Mr. Bagnet resorts to his standard artifice for the maintenance of discipline.

"That's the whole of it, is it, George?" says he.

"That's the whole of it."

"You act according to my opinion?"

"I shall be guided," replies George, "entirely by it."

"Old girl," says Mr. Bagnet, "give him my opinion. You know it. Tell him what it is."

It is, that he cannot have too little to do with people who are too deep for him, and cannot be too careful of interference with matters he does not understand; that the plain rule, is to do nothing in the dark, to be a party to nothing underhanded or mysterious, and never to put his foot where he cannot see the ground. This, in effect, is Mr. Bagnet's opinion, as delivered through the old girl; and it so relieves Mr. George's mind, by confirming his own opinion and banishing his doubts, that he composes himself to smoke another pipe on that exceptional occasion, and to have a talk over old times with the whole Bagnet family, according to their various ranges of experience.

Through these means it comes to pass, that Mr. George does not again rise to his full height in that parlour until the time is drawing on when the bassoon and fife are expected by a British public at the theatre; and as it takes time even then for Mr. George, in his domestic character of Bluffy, to take leave of Quebec and Malta, and insinuate a sponsorial shilling into the pocket of his godson, with felicitations on his success in life, it is dark when Mr. George again turns his face towards Lincoln's Inn Fields.

"A family home," he ruminates, as he marches along, "however small it is, makes a man like me look lonely. But it's well I never made that evolution of matrimony. I shouldn't have been fit for it. I am such a vagabond still, even at my present time of life, that I couldn't hold to the gallery a month together, if it was a regular pursuit, or if I didn't camp there, gipsy fashion. Come! I disgrace nobody and cumber nobody; that's something. I have not done that, for many a long year!"

So he whistles it off, and marches on.

Arrived in Lincoln's Inn Fields, and mounting Mr. Tulkinghorn's stair, he finds the outer door closed, and the chambers shut; but the trooper not knowing much about outer doors, and the staircase being dark besides, he is yet fumbling and groping about, hoping to discover a bell-handle or to open the door for himself, when Mr. Tulkinghorn comes up the stairs (quietly, of course), and angrily asks:

"Who is that? What are you doing there?"

"I ask your pardon, sir. It's George. The serjeant."

"And couldn't George, the serjeant, see that my door was locked?"

"Why, no, sir, I couldn't. At any rate, I didn't," says the trooper, rather nettled.

"Have you changed your mind? or are you in the same mind?" Mr. Tulkinghorn demands. But he knows well enough at a glance.

"In the same mind, sir."

"I thought so. That's sufficient. You can go. So, you are the man," says Mr. Tulkinghorn, opening his door with the key, "in whose hiding-place Mr. Gridley was found?"

"Yes, I *am* the man," says the trooper, stopping two or three stairs down. "What then, sir?"

"What then? I don't like your associates. You should not have seen the inside of my door this morning, if I had thought of your being that man. Gridley? A threatening, murderous, dangerous fellow."

With these words, spoken in an unusually high tone for him, the lawyer goes into his rooms, and shuts the door with a thundering noise.

Mr. George takes his dismissal in great dudgeon; the greater, because a clerk coming up the stairs has heard the last words of all, and evidently applies them to him. "A

471

pretty character to bear," the trooper growls with a hasty oath, as he strides down-stairs. "A threatening, murderous, dangerous fellow!" and looking up, he sees the clerk looking down at him, and marking him as he passes a lamp. This so intensifies his dudgeon, that for five minutes he is in an ill-humour. But he whistles that off, like the rest of it; and marches home to the Shooting Gallery.

CHAPTER XXVIII

Sir Leicester Dedlock has got the better, for the time being, of the family gout; and is once more, in a literal no less than in a figurative point of view, upon his legs. He is at his place in Lincolnshire; but the waters are out again on the low-lying grounds, and the cold and damp steal into Chesney Wold, though well defended, and eke into Sir Leicester's bones. The blazing fires of faggot and coal—Dedlock timber and antediluvian forest—that blaze upon the broad wide hearths, and wink in the twilight on the frowning woods, sullen to see how trees are sacrificed, do not exclude the enemy. The hot-water pipes that trail themselves all over the house, the cushioned doors and windows, and the screens and curtains, fail to supply the fires' deficiencies, and to satisfy Sir Leicester's need. Hence the fashionable intelligence proclaims one morning to the listening earth, that Lady Dedlock is expected shortly to return to town for a few weeks.

It is a melancholy truth that even great men have their poor relations. Indeed great men have often more than their fair share of poor relations; inasmuch as very red blood of the superior quality, like inferior blood unlawfully shed, *will* cry aloud, and *will* be heard. Sir Leicester's cousins, in the remotest degree, are so many Murders, in the respect that they "will out." Among whom there are cousins who are

473

so poor, that one might almost dare to think it would have been the happier for them never to have been plated links upon the Dedlock chain of gold, but to have been made of common iron at first, and done base service.

Service, however (with a few limited reservations; genteel but not profitable), they may not do, being of the Dedlock dignity. So they visit their richer cousins, and get into debt when they can, and live but shabbily when they can't, and find—the women no husbands, and the men no wives—and ride in borrowed carriages, and sit at feasts that are never of their own making, and so go through high life. The rich family sum has been divided by so many figures, and they are the something over that nobody knows what to do with.

Everybody on Sir Leicester Dedlock's side of the question, and of his way of thinking, would appear to be his cousin more or less. From my Lord Boodle, through the Duke of Foodle, down to Noodle, Sir Leicester, like a glorious spider, stretches his threads of relationship. But while he is stately in the cousinship of the Everybodys, he is a kind and generous man, according to his dignified way, in the cousinship of the Nobodys; and at the present time, in despite of the damp, he stays out the visit of several such cousins at Chesney Wold, with the constancy of a martyr.

Of these, foremost in the front rank stands Volumnia Dedlock, a young lady (of sixty), who is doubly highly related; having the honour to be a poor relation, by the mother's side, to another great family. Miss Volumnia, displaying in early life a pretty talent for cutting ornaments out of coloured paper, and also for singing to the guitar in the Spanish tongue, and propounding French conundrums in country houses, passed the twenty years of her existence between twenty and forty in a sufficiently agreeable manner. Lapsing then out of date, and being considered to bore mankind by her vocal performances in the Spanish language, she retired to Bath; where she lives slenderly on an annual present from Sir Leicester, and whence she makes occasional resurrections in the country houses of her cousins. She has an extensive acquaintance at Bath among appalling old gentlemen with thin legs and nankeen trousers, and is of high standing in that dreary city. But she is a little dreaded elsewhere, in consequence of an indiscreet profusion in the article of rouge, and persistency in an obsolete pearl necklace like a rosary of little bird's-eggs.

In any country in a wholesome state, Volumnia would be a clear case for the pension list. Efforts have been made to get her on it; and when William Buffy came in, it was fully expected that her name would be put down for a couple of hundred a-year. But William Buffy somehow discovered, contrary to all expectation, that these were not the times when it could be done; and this was the first clear indication Sir Leicester Dedlock had conveyed to him, that the country was going to pieces.

There is likewise the Honourable Bob Stables, who can make warm mashes with the skill of a veterinary surgeon, and is a better shot than most gamekeepers. He has been for some time particularly desirous to serve his country in a post of good emoluments, unaccompanied by any trouble or responsibility. In a well-regulated body politic, this natural desire on the part of a spirited young gentleman so highly connected, would be speedily recognised; but somehow William Buffy found when he came in, that these were not times in which he could manage that little matter, either; and this was the second indication Sir Leicester Dedlock had conveyed to him, that the country was going to pieces.

The rest of the cousins are ladies and gentlemen of various ages and capacities; the major part, amiable and sensible, and likely to have done well enough in life if they could have overcome their cousinship; as it is, they are almost all a little worsted by it, and lounge in purposeless and listless paths, and seem to be quite as much at a loss how to dispose of themselves, as anybody else can be how to dispose of them.

In this society, and where not, my Lady Dedlock reigns

475

supreme. Beautiful, elegant, accomplished, and powerful in her little world (for the world of fashion does not stretch *all* the way from pole to pole), her influence in Sir Leicester's house, however haughty and indifferent her manner, is greatly to improve it and refine it. The cousins, even those older cousins who were paralysed when Sir Leicester married her, do her feudal homage; and the Honourable Bob Stables daily repeats to some chosen person, between breakfast and lunch, his favourite original remark, that she is the best-groomed woman in the whole stud.

Such the guests in the long drawing-room at Chesney Wold this dismal night, when the step on the Ghost's Walk (inaudible here, however), might be the step of a deceased cousin shut out in the cold. It is near bed-time. Bedroom fires blaze brightly all over the house, raising ghosts of grim furniture on wall and ceiling. Bedroom candlesticks bristle on the distant table by the door, and cousins yawn on ottomans. Cousins at the piano, cousins at the soda-water tray, cousins rising from the card-table, cousins gathered round the fire. Standing on one side of his own peculiar fire (for there are two), Sir Leicester. On the opposite side of the broad hearth, my Lady at her table. Volumnia, as one of the more privileged cousins, in a luxurious chair between them. Sir Leicester glancing, with magnificent displeasure, at the rouge and the pearl necklace.

"I occasionally meet on my staircase here," drawls Volumnia, whose thoughts perhaps are already hopping up it to bed, after a long evening of very desultory talk, "one of the prettiest girls, I think, that I ever saw in my life."

"A *protégée* of my Lady's," observes Sir Leicester.

"I thought so. I felt sure that some uncommon eye must have picked that girl out. She really is a marvel. A dolly sort of beauty perhaps," says Miss Volumnia, reserving her own sort, "but in its way, perfect; such bloom I never saw!"

Sir Leicester, with his magnificent glance of displeasure at the rouge, appears to say so too.

"Indeed," remarks my Lady, languidly, "if there is any uncommon eye in the case, it is Mrs. Rouncewell's, and not mine. Rosa is her discovery."

"Your maid, I suppose?"

"No. My anything; pet—secretary—messenger—I don't know what."

"You like to have her about you, as you would like to have a flower, or a bird, or a picture, or a poodle—no, not a poodle, though—or anything else that was equally pretty?" says Volumnia, sympathising. "Yes, how charming now! and how well that delightful old soul Mrs. Rouncewell is looking. She must be an immense age, and yet she is as active and handsome!—She is the dearest friend I have, positively!"

Sir Leicester feels it to be right and fitting that the housekeeper of Chesney Wold should be a remarkable person. Apart from that, he has a real regard for Mrs. Rouncewell, and likes to hear her praised. So he says, "You are right, Volumnia;" which Volumnia is extremely glad to hear.

"She has no daughter of her own, has she?"

"Mrs. Rouncewell? No, Volumnia. She has a son. Indeed, she had two."

My Lady, whose chronic malady of boredom has been sadly aggravated by Volumnia this evening, glances wearily towards the candlesticks and heaves a noiseless sigh.

"And it is a remarkable example of the confusion into which the present age has fallen; of the obliteration of landmarks, the opening of floodgates, and the uprooting of distinctions," says Sir Leicester with stately gloom; "that I have been informed, by Mr. Tulkinghorn, that Mrs. Rouncewell's son has been invited to go into Parliament."

Miss Volumnia utters a little sharp scream.

"Yes, indeed," repeats Sir Leicester. "Into Parliament."

"I never heard of such a thing! Good gracious, what is the man?" exclaimed Volumnia.

"He is called, I believe—an—Ironmaster." Sir Leicester

says it slowly, and with gravity and doubt, as not being sure
but that he is called a Lead-mistress; or that the right word
may be some other word expressive of some other relationship
to some other metal.

Volumnia utters another little scream.

"He has declined the proposal, if my information from
Mr. Tulkinghorn be correct, as I have no doubt it is, Mr.
Tulkinghorn being always correct and exact; still that does
not," says Sir Leicester, "that does not lessen the anomaly;
which is fraught with strange considerations—startling considerations, as it appears to me."

Miss Volumnia rising with a look candlestick-wards, Sir
Leicester politely performs the grand tour of the drawing-
room, brings one, and lights it at my Lady's shaded lamp.

"I must beg you, my Lady," he says while doing so, "to
remain a few moments; for this individual of whom I speak,
arrived this evening shortly before dinner, and requested—in
a very becoming note;" Sir Leicester, with his habitual regard
to truth, dwells upon it; "I am bound to say, in a very becoming and well-expressed note—the favour of a short interview with yourself and *my*self, on the subject of this young
girl. As it appeared that he wished to depart to-night, I
replied that we would see him before retiring."

Miss Volumnia with a third little scream takes flight, wishing her hosts—O Lud!—well rid of the—what is it?—Ironmaster!

The other cousins soon disperse, to the last cousin there.
Sir Leicester rings the bell. "Make my compliments to
Mr. Rouncewell, in the housekeeper's apartments, and say I
can receive him now."

My Lady, who has heard all this with slight attention
outwardly, looks towards Mr. Rouncewell as he comes in. He
is a little over fifty perhaps, of a good figure, like his mother;
and has a clear voice, a broad forehead from which his dark
hair has retired, and a shrewd, though open face. He is a
responsible-looking gentleman dressed in black, portly enough,

but strong and active. Has a perfectly natural and easy air, and is not in the least embarrassed by the great presence into which he comes.

"Sir Leicester and Lady Dedlock, as I have already apologised for intruding on you, I cannot do better than be very brief. I thank you, Sir Leicester."

The head of the Dedlocks has motioned towards a sofa between himself and my Lady. Mr. Rouncewell quietly takes his seat there.

"In these busy times, when so many great undertakings are in progress, people like myself have so many workmen in so many places, that we are always on the flight."

Sir Leicester is content enough that the ironmaster should feel that there is no hurry there; there, in that ancient house, rooted in that quiet park, where the ivy and the moss have had time to mature, and the gnarled and warted elms, and the umbrageous oaks, stand deep in the fern and leaves of a hundred years; and where the sun-dial on the terrace has dumbly recorded for centuries that Time, which was as much the property of every Dedlock—while he lasted—as the house and lands. Sir Leicester sits down in an easy-chair, opposing his repose and that of Chesney Wold to the restless flights of ironmasters.

"Lady Dedlock has been so kind," proceeds Mr. Rouncewell, with a respectful glance and a bow that way, "as to place near her a young beauty of the name of Rosa. Now, my son has fallen in love with Rosa; and has asked my consent to his proposing marriage to her, and to their becoming engaged if she will take him—which I suppose she will. I have never seen Rosa until to-day, but I have some confidence in my son's good sense—even in love. I find her what he represents her, to the best of my judgment; and my mother speaks of her with great commendation."

"She in all respects deserves it," says my Lady.

"I am happy, Lady Dedlock, that you say so; and I need not comment on the value to me of your kind opinion of her."

"That," observes Sir Leicester, with unspeakable grandeur; for he thinks the ironmaster a little too glib; "must be quite unnecessary."

"Quite unnecessary, Sir Leicester. Now, my son is a very young man, and Rosa is a very young woman. As I made my way, so my son must make his; and his being married at present is out of the question. But supposing I gave my consent to his engaging himself to this pretty girl, if this pretty girl will engage herself to him, I think it a piece of candour to say at once—I am sure, Sir Leicester and Lady Dedlock, you will understand and excuse me—I should make it a condition that she did not remain at Chesney Wold. Therefore, before communicating further with my son, I take the liberty of saying that if her removal would be in any way inconvenient or objectionable, I will hold the matter over with him for any reasonable time, and leave it precisely where it is."

Not remain at Chesney Wold! Make it a condition! All Sir Leicester's old misgivings relative to Wat Tyler, and the people in the iron districts who do nothing but turn out by torchlight, come in a shower upon his head: the fine grey hair of which, as well as of his whiskers, actually stirs with indignation.

"Am I to understand, sir," says Sir Leicester, "and is my Lady to understand;" he brings her in thus specially, first, as a point of gallantry, and next as a point of prudence, having great reliance on her sense; "am I to understand, Mr. Rouncewell, and is my Lady to understand, sir, that you consider this young woman too good for Chesney Wold, or likely to be injured by remaining here?"

"Certainly not, Sir Leicester."

"I am glad to hear it." Sir Leicester very lofty indeed.

"Pray, Mr. Rouncewell," says my Lady, warning Sir Leicester off with the slightest gesture of her pretty hand, as if he were a fly, "explain to me what you mean."

"Willingly, Lady Dedlock. There is nothing I could desire more."

Addressing her composed face, whose intelligence, however, is too quick and active to be concealed by any studied impassiveness, however habitual, to the strong Saxon face of the visitor, a picture of resolution and perseverance, my Lady listens with attention, occasionally slightly bending her head.

"I am the son of your housekeeper, Lady Dedlock, and passed my childhood about this house. My mother has lived here half a century, and will die here I have no doubt. She is one of those examples—perhaps as good a one as there is —of love, and attachment, and fidelity in such a station, which England may well be proud of; but of which no order can appropriate the whole pride or the whole merit, because such an instance bespeaks high worth on two sides; on the great side assuredly; on the small one, no less assuredly."

Sir Leicester snorts a little to hear the law laid down in this .way; but in his honour and his love of truth, he freely, though silently, admits the justice of the ironmaster's proposition.

"Pardon me for saying what is so obvious, but I wouldn't have it hastily supposed," with the least turn of his eyes towards Sir Leicester, "that I am ashamed of my mother's position here, or wanting in all just respect for Chesney Wold and the family. I certainly may have desired—I certainly have desired, Lady Dedlock—that my mother should retire after so many years, and end her days with me. But, as I have found that to sever this strong bond would be to break her heart, I have long abandoned that idea."

Sir Leicester very magnificent again, at the notion of Mrs. Rouncewell being spirited off from her natural home, to end her days with an ironmaster.

"I have been," proceeds the visitor, in a modest clear way, "an apprentice, and a workman. I have lived on workman's wages, years and years, and beyond a certain point have had to educate myself. My wife was a foreman's daughter, and

481

plainly brought up. We have three daughters, besides this son of whom I have spoken; and being fortunately able to give them greater advantages than we have had ourselves, we have educated them well; very well. It has been one of our great cares and pleasures to make them worthy of any station."

A little boastfulness in his fatherly tone here, as if he added in his heart, "even of the Chesney Wold station." Not a little more magnificence, therefore, on the part of Sir Leicester.

"All this is so frequent, Lady Dedlock, where I live, and among the class to which I belong, that what would be generally called unequal marriages are not of such rare occurrence with us as elsewhere. A son will sometimes make it known to his father that he has fallen in love, say with a young woman in the factory. The father, who once worked in a factory himself, will be a little disappointed at first, very possibly. It may be that he had other views for his son. However, the chances are, that having ascertained the young woman to be of unblemished character, he will say to his son, 'I must be quite sure you are in earnest here. This is a serious matter for both of you. Therefore I shall have this girl educated for two years'—or, it may be—'I shall place this girl at the same school with your sisters for such a time, during which you will give me your word and honour to see her only so often. If, at the expiration of that time, when she has so far profited by her advantages as that you may be upon a fair equality, you are both in the same mind, I will do my part to make you happy.' I know of several cases such as I describe, my Lady, and I think they indicate to me my own course now."

Sir Leicester's magnificence explodes. Calmly, but terribly.

"Mr. Rouncewell," says Sir Leicester, with his right hand in the breast of his blue coat—the attitude of state in which he is painted in the gallery: "do you draw a parallel between Chesney Wold, and a——" here he resists a disposition to choke—"a factory?"

"I need not reply, Sir Leicester, that the two places are very different; but, for the purposes of this case, I think a parallel may be justly drawn between them."

Sir Leicester directs his majestic glance down one side of the long drawing-room, and up the other, before he can believe that he is awake.

"Are you aware, sir, that this young woman whom my Lady—my Lady—has placed near her person, was brought up at the village school outside the gates?"

"Sir Leicester, I am quite aware of it. A very good school it is, and handsomely supported by this family."

"Then, Mr. Rouncewell," returns Sir Leicester, "the application of what you have said is, to me, incomprehensible."

"Will it be more comprehensible, Sir Leicester, if I say," the ironmaster is reddening a little, "that I do not regard the village school as teaching everything desirable to be known by my son's wife?"

From the village school of Chesney Wold, intact as it is this minute, to the whole framework of society: from the whole framework of society, to the aforesaid framework receiving tremendous cracks in consequence of people (ironmasters, lead-mistresses, and what not) not minding their catechism, and getting out of the station unto which they are called—necessarily and for ever, according to Sir Leicester's rapid logic, the first station in which they happen to find themselves; and from that, to their educating other people out of *their* stations, and so obliterating the landmarks, and opening the floodgates, and all the rest of it; this is the swift progress of the Dedlock mind.

"My Lady, I beg your pardon. Permit me, for one moment!" She has given a faint indication of intending to speak. "Mr. Rouncewell, our views of duty, and our views of station, and our views of education, and our views of—in short, *all* our views—are so diametrically opposed, that to prolong this discussion must be repellant to your feelings, and repellant to my own. This young woman is honoured with my Lady's notice and favour. If she wishes to withdraw herself from that notice and favour, or if she chooses to place herself under the influence of any one who may in his peculiar opinions—you will allow me to say, in his peculiar opinions, though I readily admit that he is not accountable for them to me—who may, in his peculiar opinions, withdraw her from that notice and favour, she is at any time at liberty to do so. We are obliged to you for the plainness with which you have spoken. It will have no effect of itself, one way or other, on the young woman's position here. Beyond this, we can make no terms; and here we beg—if you will be so good—to leave the subject."

The visitor pauses a moment to give my Lady an opportunity, but she says nothing. He then rises and replies:

"Sir Leicester and Lady Dedlock, allow me to thank you for your attention, and only to observe that I shall very seriously recommend my son to conquer his present inclinations. Good night!"

"Mr. Rouncewell," says Sir Leicester, with all the nature of a gentleman shining in him, "it is late, and the roads are dark. I hope your time is not so precious but that you will allow my Lady and myself to offer you the hospitality of Chesney Wold, for to-night at least."

"I hope so," adds my Lady.

"I am much obliged to you, but I have to travel all night, in order to reach a distant part of the country, punctually at an appointed time in the morning."

Therewith the ironmaster takes his departure; Sir Leicester ringing the bell, and my Lady rising as he leaves the room.

When my Lady goes to her boudoir, she sits down thoughtfully by the fire; and, inattentive to the Ghost's Walk, looks at Rosa, writing in an inner room. Presently my Lady calls her.

"Come to me, child. Tell me the truth. Are you in love?"

"O! My Lady!"

My Lady, looking at the downcast and blushing face, says smiling:

"Who is it? Is it Mrs. Rouncewell's grandson?"

"Yes, if you please, my Lady. But I don't know that I am in love with him—yet."

"Yet, you silly little thing! Do you know that he loves *you*, yet?"

"I think he likes me a little, my Lady." And Rosa burst into tears.

Is this Lady Dedlock standing beside the village beauty, smoothing her dark hair with that motherly touch, and watching her with eyes so full of musing interest? Aye, indeed it is!

"Listen to me, child. You are young and true, and I believe you are attached to me."

"Indeed I am, my Lady. Indeed there is nothing in the world I wouldn't do, to show how much."

"And I don't think you would wish to leave me just yet, Rosa, even for a lover?"

"No, my Lady! O no!" Rosa looks up for the first time, quite frightened at the thought.

"Confide in me, my child. Don't fear me. I wish you to be happy, and will make you so—if I can make anybody happy on this earth."

Rosa, with fresh tears, kneels at her feet and kisses her hand. My Lady takes the hand with which she has caught it, and, standing with her eyes fixed on the fire, puts it about and about between her own two hands, and gradually lets it fall. Seeing her so absorbed, Rosa softly withdraws; but still my Lady's eyes are on the fire.

In search of what? Of any hand that is no more, of any hand that never was, of any touch that might have magically changed her life? Or does she listen to the Ghost's Walk, and think what step does it most resemble? A man's? A woman's? The pattering of a little child's feet, ever coming on—on—on? Some melancholy influence is upon her; or

485

why should so proud a lady close the doors, and sit alone upon the hearth so desolate?

Volumnia is away next day, and all the cousins are scattered before dinner. Not a cousin of the batch but is amazed to hear from Sir Leicester, at breakfast-time, of the obliteration of landmarks, and opening of floodgates, and cracking of the framework of society, manifested through Mrs. Rouncewell's son. Not a cousin of the batch but is really indignant, and connects it with the feebleness of William Buffy when in office, and really does feel deprived of a stake in the country—or the pension list—or something—by fraud and wrong. As to Volumnia, she is handed down the great staircase by Sir Leicester, as eloquent upon the theme, as if there were a general rising in the North of England to obtain her rouge-pot and pearl necklace. And thus, with a clatter of maids and valets—for it is one appurtenance of their cousinship, that, however difficult they may find it to keep themselves, they *must* keep maids and valets—the cousins disperse to the four winds of heaven; and the one wintry wind that blows to-day shakes a shower from the trees near the deserted house, as if all the cousins had been changed into leaves.

CHAPTER XXIX

THE YOUNG MAN

CHESNEY WOLD is shut up, carpets are rolled into great scrolls in corners of comfortless rooms, bright damask does penance in brown holland, carving and gilding puts on mortification, and the Dedlock ancestors retire from the light of day again. Around and around the house the leaves fall thick—but never fast, for they come circling down with a dead lightness that is sombre and slow. Let the gardener sweep and sweep the turf as he will, and press the leaves into full barrows, and wheel them off, still they lie ankle-deep. Howls the shrill wind round Chesney Wold; the sharp rain beats, the windows rattle, and the chimneys growl. Mists hide in the avenues, veil the points of view, and move in funeral-wise across the rising grounds. On all the house there is a cold, blank smell, like the smell of a little church, though something dryer: suggesting that the dead and buried Dedlocks walk there in the long nights, and leave the flavour of their graves behind them.

But the house in town, which is rarely in the same mind as Chesney Wold at the same time; seldom rejoicing when it rejoices, or mourning when it mourns, excepting when a Dedlock dies; the house in town shines out awakened. As warm and bright as so much state may be, as delicately redolent of pleasant scents that bear no trace of winter as hothouse flowers can make it; soft and hushed, so that the ticking of the clocks and the crisp burning of the fires alone disturb the stillness in the rooms; it seems to wrap those chilled bones of Sir Leicester's in rainbow-coloured wool. And Sir Leicester is glad to repose in dignified contentment before the great fire in the library, condescendingly perusing the backs of his books, or honouring the fine arts with a glance of approbation. For he has his pictures, ancient and modern. Some of the Fancy Ball School in which Art occasionally condescends to become a master, which would be best catalogued like the miscellaneous articles in a sale. As, "Three high-backed chairs, a table and cover, long-necked bottle (containing wine), one flask, one Spanish female's costume, three-quarter face portrait of Miss Jogg the model, and a suit of armour containing Don Quixote." Or, "One stone terrace (cracked), one gondola in distance, one Venetian senator's dress complete, richly embroidered white satin costume with profile portrait of Miss Jogg the model, one scimetar superbly mounted in gold with jewelled handle, elaborate Moorish dress (very rare), and Othello."

Mr. Tulkinghorn comes and goes pretty often; there being estate business to do, leases to be renewed, and so on. He sees my Lady pretty often, too; and he and she are as composed, and as indifferent, and take as little heed of one another, as ever. Yet it may be that my Lady fears this Mr. Tulkinghorn, and that he knows it. It may be that he pursues her doggedly and steadily, with no touch of compunction, remorse, or pity. It may be that her beauty, and all the state and brilliancy surrounding her, only gives him the greater zest for what he is set upon, and makes him the more inflexible in it. Whether he be cold and cruel, whether immovable in what he has made his duty, whether absorbed in love of power, whether determined to have nothing hidden from him in ground where he has burrowed among secrets all his life, whether he in his heart despises the splendour of which he is a distant beam, whether he is always treasuring up slights and offences in the affability of his gorgeous clients —whether he be any of this, or all of this, it may be that my Lady had better have five thousand pairs of fashionable eyes upon her, in distrustful vigilance, than the two eyes of this rusty lawyer, with his wisp of neckcloth and his dull black breeches tied with ribbons at the knees.

Sir Leicester sits in my Lady's room—that room in which Mr. Tulkinghorn read the affidavit in Jarndyce and Jarndyce —particularly complacent. My Lady—as on that day—sits before the fire with her screen in her hand. Sir Leicester is particularly complacent, because he has found in his newspaper some congenial remarks bearing directly on the floodgates and the framework of society. They apply so happily to the late case, that Sir Leicester has come from the library to my Lady's room expressly to read them aloud. "The man who wrote this article," he observes by way of preface, nodding at the fire as if he were nodding down at the man from a Mount, "has a well-balanced mind."

The man's mind is not so well balanced but that he bores my Lady, who, after a languid effort to listen, or rather a languid resignation of herself to a show of listening, becomes distraught, and falls into a contemplation of the fire as if it were her fire at Chesney Wold, and she had never left it. Sir Leicester, quite unconscious, reads on through his double eye-glass, occasionally stopping to remove his glass and express approval, as "Very true indeed," "Very properly put," "I have frequently made the same remark myself;" invariably losing his place after each observation, and going up and down the column to find it again.

Sir Leicester is reading, with infinite gravity and state, when the door opens, and the Mercury in powder makes this strange announcement:

"The young man, my Lady, of the name of Guppy."

Sir Leicester pauses, stares, repeats in a killing voice:

"The young man of the name of Guppy?"

Looking round, he beholds the young man of the name of Guppy, much discomfited, and not presenting a very impressive letter of introduction in his manner and appearance.

" Pray," says Sir Leicester to Mercury, " what do you mean by announcing with this abruptness a young man of the name of Guppy ? "

"I beg your pardon, Sir Leicester, but my Lady said she would see the young man whenever he called. I was not aware that you were here, Sir Leicester."

With this apology, Mercury directs a scornful and indignant look at the young man of the name of Guppy, which plainly says, " What do you come calling here for, and getting *me* into a row ? "

" It's quite right. I gave him those directions," says my Lady. " Let the young man wait."

" By no means, my Lady. Since he has your orders to come, I will not interrupt you." Sir Leicester in his gallantry retires, rather declining to accept a bow from the young man as he goes out, and majestically supposing him to be some shoemaker of intrusive appearance.

Lady Dedlock looks imperiously at her visitor, when the servant has left the room ; casting her eyes over him from head to foot. She suffers him to stand by the door, and asks him what he wants ?

" That your ladyship would have the kindness to oblige me with a little conversation," returns Mr. Guppy, embarrassed.

" You are, of course, the person who has written me so many letters ? "

" Several, your ladyship. Several, before your ladyship condescended to favour me with an answer."

" And could you not take the same means of rendering a conversation unnecessary ? Can you not still ? "

Mr. Guppy screws his mouth into a silent " No ! " and shakes his head.

" You have been strangely importunate. If it should appear, after all, that what you have to say does not concern me—and I don't know how it can, and don't expect that it will—you will allow me to cut you short with but little ceremony. Say what you have to say, if you please."

The Young Man of the Name of Guppy

THE YOUNG MAN'S BUSINESS

My Lady, with a careless toss of her screen, turns herself towards the fire again, sitting almost with her back to the young man of the name of Guppy.

"With your ladyship's permission, then," says the young man, "I will now enter on my business. Hem! I am, as I told your ladyship in my first letter, in the law. Being in the law, I have learnt the habit of not committing myself in writing, and therefore I did not mention to your ladyship the name of the firm with which I am connected, and in which my standing—and I may add income—is tolerably good. I may now state to your ladyship, in confidence, that the name of that firm is Kenge and Carboy, of Lincoln's Inn; which may not be altogether unknown to your ladyship in connexion with the case in Chancery of Jarndyce and Jarndyce."

My Lady's figure begins to be expressive of some attention. She has ceased to toss the screen, and holds it as if she were listening.

"Now, I may say to your ladyship at once," says Mr. Guppy, a little emboldened, "it is no matter arising out of Jarndyce and Jarndyce that made me so desirous to speak to your ladyship, which conduct I have no doubt did appear, and does appear, obtrusive—in fact, almost blackguardly." After waiting for a moment to receive some assurance to the contrary, and not receiving any, Mr. Guppy proceeds. "If it had been Jarndyce and Jarndyce, I should have gone at once to your ladyship's solicitor, Mr. Tulkinghorn of the Fields. I have the pleasure of being acquainted with Mr. Tulkinghorn—at least we move when we meet one another —and if it had been any business of that sort, I should have gone to him."

My Lady turns a little round, and says, "You had better sit down."

"Thank your ladyship." Mr. Guppy does so. "Now, your ladyship;" Mr. Guppy refers to a little slip of paper on which he has made small notes of his line of argument,

491

and which seems to involve him in the densest obscurity whenever he looks at it; "I—O yes!—I place myself entirely in your ladyship's hands. If your ladyship was to make any complaint to Kenge and Carboy, or to Mr. Tulkinghorn, of the present visit, I should be placed in a very disagreeable situation. That, I openly admit. Consequently, I rely upon your ladyship's honour."

My Lady, with a disdainful gesture of the hand that holds the screen, assures him of his being worth no complaint from her.

"Thank your ladyship," says Mr. Guppy, "quite satisfactory. Now—I—dash it!—The fact is, that I put down a head or two here of the order of the points I thought of touching upon, and they're written short, and I can't quite make out what they mean. If your ladyship will excuse me taking it to the window half a moment, I—— "

Mr. Guppy going to the window, tumbles into a pair of love-birds, to whom he says in his confusion, "I beg your pardon, I am sure." This does not tend to the greater legibility of his notes. He murmurs, growing warm and red, and holding the slip of paper now close to his eyes, now a long way off, "C. S. What's C. S. for? O! 'E. S.!' O, I know! Yes, to be sure!" And comes back enlightened.

"I am not aware," says Mr. Guppy, standing midway between my Lady and his chair, "whether your ladyship ever happened to hear of, or to see, a young lady of the name of Miss Esther Summerson."

My Lady's eyes look at him full. "I saw a young lady of that name not long ago. This past autumn."

"Now, did it strike your ladyship that she was like anybody?" asks Mr. Guppy, crossing his arms, holding his head on one side, and scratching the corner of his mouth with his memoranda.

My Lady removes her eyes from him no more.

" No."

" Not like your ladyship's family ? "

"No."

"I think your ladyship," says Mr. Guppy, "can hardly remember Miss Summerson's face?"

"I remember the young lady very well. What has this to do with me?"

"Your ladyship, I do assure you, that having Miss Summerson's image imprinted on my art—which I mention in confidence—I found, when I had the honour of going over your ladyship's mansion of Chesney Wold, while on a short out in the county of Lincolnshire with a friend, such a resemblance between Miss Esther Summerson and your ladyship's own portrait, that it completely knocked me over; so much so, that I didn't at the moment even know what it *was* that knocked me over. And now I have the honour of beholding your ladyship near, (I have often, since that, taken the liberty of looking at your ladyship in your carriage in the park, when I dare say you was not aware of me, but I never saw your ladyship so near,) it's really more surprising than I thought it."

Young man of the name of Guppy! There have been times, when ladies lived in strongholds, and had unscrupulous attendants within call, when that poor life of yours would not have been worth a minute's purchase, with those beautiful eyes looking at you as they look at this moment.

My Lady, slowly using her little hand-screen as a fan, asks him again, what he supposes that his taste for likenesses has to do with her?

"Your ladyship," replies Mr. Guppy, again referring to his paper, "I am coming to that. Dash these notes! O! 'Mrs. Chadband.' Yes." Mr. Guppy draws his chair a little forward, and seats himself again. My Lady reclines in her chair composedly, though with a trifle less of graceful ease than usual, perhaps; and never falters in her steady gaze. "A—stop a minute, though!" Mr. Guppy refers again. "E. S. twice? O yes! yes, I see my way now, right on."

Rolling up the slip of paper as an instrument to point his speech with, Mr. Guppy proceeds.

"Your ladyship, there is a mystery about Miss Esther Summerson's birth and bringing up. I am informed of that fact, because—which I mention in confidence—I know it in the way of my profession at Kenge and Carboy's. Now, as I have already mentioned to your ladyship, Miss Summerson's image is imprinted on my art. If I could clear this mystery for her, or prove her to be well related, or find that having the honour to be a remote branch of your ladyship's family she had a right to be made a party in Jarndyce and Jarndyce, why, I might make a sort of a claim upon Miss Summerson to look with an eye of more decided favour on my proposals than she has exactly done as yet. In fact, as yet she hasn't favoured them at all."

A kind of angry smile just dawns upon my Lady's face.

"Now, it's a very singular circumstance, your ladyship," says Mr. Guppy, "though one of those circumstances that do fall in the way of us professional men—which I may call myself, for though not admitted, yet I have had a present of my articles made to me by Kenge and Carboy, on my mother's advancing from the principal of her little income the money for the stamp, which comes heavy—that I have encountered the person who lived as servant with the lady who brought Miss Summerson up, before Mr. Jarndyce took charge of her. That lady was a Miss Barbary, your ladyship."

Is the dead colour on my Lady's face, reflected from the screen which has a green silk ground, and which she holds in her raised hand as if she had forgotten it; or is it a dreadful paleness that has fallen on her?

"Did your ladyship," says Mr. Guppy, "ever happen to hear of Miss Barbary?"

"I don't know. I think so. Yes."

"Was Miss Barbary at all connected with your ladyship's family?"

494

My lady's lips move, but they utter nothing. She shakes her head.

"*Not* connected?" says Mr. Guppy. "O! Not to your ladyship's knowledge, perhaps? Ah! But might be? Yes." After each of these interrogatories, she has inclined her head. "Very good! Now, this Miss Barbary was extremely close —seems to have been extraordinarily close for a female, females being generally (in common life at least) rather given to conversation—and my witness never had an idea whether she possessed a single relative. On one occasion, and only one, she seems to have been confidential to my witness, on a single point; and she then told her that the little girl's real name was not Esther Summerson, but Esther Hawdon."

"My God!"

Mr. Guppy stares. Lady Dedlock sits before him, looking him through, with the same dark shade upon her face, in the same attitude even to the holding of the screen, with her lips a little apart, her brow a little contracted, but, for the moment, dead. He sees her consciousness return, sees a tremor pass across her frame like a ripple over water, sees her lips shake, sees her compose them by a great effort, sees her force herself back to the knowledge of his presence, and of what he has said. All this, so quickly, that her exclamation and her dead condition seem to have passed away like the features of those long-preserved dead bodies sometimes opened up in tombs, which, struck by the air like lightning, vanish in a breath.

"Your ladyship is acquainted with the name of Hawdon?"

"I have heard it before."

"Name of any collateral, or remote, branch of your lady-ship's family?"

"No."

"Now, your ladyship," says Mr. Guppy, "I come to the last point of the case, so far as I have got it up. It's going on, and I shall gather it up closer and closer as it goes on. Your ladyship must know—if your ladyship don't happen, by any chance, to know already—that there was found dead at the house of a person named Krook, near Chancery Lane, some time ago, a law-writer in great distress. Upon which law-writer there was an inquest; and which law-writer was an anonymous character, his name being unknown. But, your ladyship, I have discovered very lately, that that law-writer's name was Hawdon."

"And what is *that* to me?"

"Aye, your ladyship, that's the question! Now, your ladyship, a queer thing happened after that man's death. A lady started up; a disguised lady, your ladyship, who went to look at the scene of action, and went to look at his grave. She hired a crossing-sweeping boy to show it her. If your ladyship would wish to have the boy produced in corroboration of this statement, I can lay my hand upon him at any time."

The wretched boy is nothing to my Lady, and she does *not* wish to have him produced.

"Oh, I assure your ladyship it's a very queer start indeed," says Mr. Guppy. "If you was to hear him tell about the rings that sparkled on her fingers when she took her glove off, you'd think it quite romantic."

There are diamonds glittering on the hand that holds the screen. My Lady trifles with the screen, and makes them glitter more; again with that expression which in other times might have been so dangerous to the young man of the name of Guppy.

"It was supposed, your ladyship, that he left no rag or scrap behind him by which he could be possibly identified. But he did. He left a bundle of letters."

The screen still goes, as before. All this time, her eyes never once release him.

"They were taken and secreted. And to-morrow night, your ladyship, they will come into my possession."

"Still I ask you, what is this to me?"

"Your ladyship, I conclude with that." Mr. Guppy rises. "If you think there's enough, in this chain of circumstances

496

put together—in the undoubted strong likeness of this young lady to your ladyship, which is a positive fact for a jury— in her having been brought up by Miss Barbary—in Miss Barbary stating Miss Summerson's real name to be Hawdon —in your ladyship's knowing both these names *very well*— and in Hawdon's dying as he did—to give your ladyship a family interest in going further into the case, I will bring these papers here. I don't know what they are, except that they are old letters: I have never had them in my possession yet. I will bring those papers here, as soon as I get them; and go over them for the first time with your ladyship. I have told your ladyship my object. I have told your lady- ship that I should be placed in a very disagreeable situation, if any complaint was made; and all is in strict confidence."

Is this the full purpose of the young man of the name of Guppy, or has he any other? Do his words disclose the length, breadth, depth, of his object and suspicion in coming here; or, if not, what do they hide? He is a match for my Lady there. She may look at him, but he can look at the table, and keep that witness-box face of his from telling anything.

"You may bring the letters," says my Lady, "if you choose."

"Your Ladyship is not very encouraging, upon my word and honour," says Mr. Guppy, a little injured.

"You may bring the letters," she repeats, in the same tone, "if you——please."

"It shall be done. I wish your ladyship good day."

On a table near her is a rich bauble of a casket, barred and clasped like an old strong chest. She, looking at him still, takes it to her and unlocks it.

"Oh! I assure your ladyship I am not actuated by any motives of that sort," says Mr. Guppy; "and I couldn't accept anything of the kind. I wish your ladyship good day, and am much obliged to you all the same."

So the young man makes his bow, and goes down-stairs;

where the supercilious Mercury does not consider himself called upon to leave his Olympus by the hall-fire, to let the young man out.

As Sir Leicester basks in his library, and dozes over his newspaper, is there no influence in the house to startle him; not to say, to make the very trees at Chesney Wold fling up their knotted arms, the very portraits frown, the very armour stir?

No. Words, sobs, and cries, are but air; and air is so shut in and shut out throughout the house in town, that sounds need be uttered trumpet-tongued indeed by my Lady in her chamber, to carry any faint vibration to Sir Leicester's ears; and yet this cry is in the house, going upward from a wild figure on its knees.

"O my child, my child! Not dead in the first hours of her life, as my cruel sister told me; but sternly nurtured by her, after she had renounced me and my name! O my child, O my child!"

CHAPTER XXX

RICHARD had been gone away some time, when a visitor came to pass a few days with us. It was an elderly lady. It was Mrs. Woodcourt, who, having come from Wales to stay with Mrs. Bayham Badger, and having written to my guardian, "by her son Allan's desire," to report that she had heard from him and that he was well, "and sent his kind remembrances to all of us," had been invited by my guardian to make a visit to Bleak House. She stayed with us nearly three weeks. She took very kindly to me, and was extremely confidential : so much so that sometimes she almost made me uncomfortable. I had no right, I knew very well, to be uncomfortable because she confided in me, and I felt it was unreasonable ; still, with all I could do, I could not quite help it.

She was such a sharp little lady, and used to sit with her hands folded in each other, looking so very watchful while she talked to me, that perhaps I found that rather irksome. Or perhaps it was her being so upright and trim ; though I don't think it was that, because I thought that quaintly pleasant. Nor can it have been the general expression of her face, which was very sparkling and pretty for an old lady. I don't know what it was. Or at least if I do, now, I thought I did not then. Or at least—but it don't matter.

Of a night when I was going up-stairs to bed, she would

499

invite me into her room, where she sat before the fire in a great chair; and, dear me, she would tell me about Morgan ap Kerrig until I was quite low-spirited! Sometimes she recited a few verses from Crumlinwallinwer and the Mewlinwillinwodd (if those are the right names, which I dare say they are not), and would become quite fiery with the sentiments they expressed. Though I never knew what they were (being in Welsh), further than that they were highly eulogistic of the lineage of Morgan ap Kerrig.

"So, Miss Summerson," she would say to me with stately triumph, "this you see, is the fortune inherited by my son. Wherever my son goes, he can claim kindred with Ap Kerrig. He may not have money, but he always has what is much better—family, my dear."

I had my doubts of their caring so very much for Morgan ap Kerrig, in India and China; but of course I never expressed them. I used to say it was a great thing to be so highly connected.

"It *is*, my dear, a great thing," Mrs. Woodcourt would reply. "It has its disadvantages; my son's choice of a wife, for instance, is limited by it; but the matrimonial choice of the Royal family is limited, in much the same manner."

Then she would pat me on the arm and smooth my dress, as much as to assure me that she had a good opinion of me, the distance between us notwithstanding.

"Poor Mr. Woodcourt, my dear," she would say, and always with some emotion, for with her lofty pedigree she had a very affectionate heart, "was descended from a great Highland family, the Mac Coorts of Mac Coort. He served his king and country as an officer in the Royal Highlanders, and he died on the field. My son is one of the last representatives of two old families. With the blessing of Heaven he will set them up again, and unite them with another old family."

It was in vain for me to try to change the subject, as I used to try—only for the sake of novelty—or perhaps because

—but I need not be so particular. Mrs. Woodcourt never would let me change it.

"My dear," she said one night, "you have so much sense, and you look at the world in a quiet manner so superior to your time of life, that it is a comfort to me to talk to you about these family matters of mine. You don't know much of my son, my dear; but you know enough of him, I dare say, to recollect him?"

"Yes, ma'am. I recollect him."

"Yes, my dear. Now, my dear, I think you are a judge of character, and I should like to have your opinion of him?"

"O, Mrs. Woodcourt!" said I, "that is so difficult."

"Why is it so difficult, my dear," she returned. "I don't see it myself."

"To give an opinion——"

"On so slight an acquaintance, my dear. *That's* true."

I didn't mean that; because Mr. Woodcourt had been at our house a good deal altogether, and had become quite intimate with my guardian. I said so, and added that he seemed to be very clever in his profession—we thought—and that his kindness and gentleness to Miss Flite were above all praise.

"You do him justice!" said Mrs. Woodcourt, pressing my hand. "You define him exactly. Allan is a dear fellow, and in his profession faultless. I say it, though I am his mother. Still, I must confess he is not without faults, love."

"None of us are," said I.

"Ah! But his really are faults that he might correct, and ought to correct," returned the sharp old lady, sharply shaking her head. "I am so much attached to you, that I may confide in you, my dear, as a third party wholly disinterested, that he is fickleness itself."

I said, I should have thought it hardly possible that he could have been otherwise than constant to his profession, and zealous in the pursuit of it, judging from the reputation he had earned.

"You are right again, my dear," the old lady retorted; "but I don't refer to his profession, look you."

"O!" said I.

"No," said she. "I refer, my dear, to his social conduct. He is always paying trivial attentions to young ladies, and always has been, ever since he was eighteen. Now, my dear, he has never really cared for any one of them, and has never meant in doing this to do any harm, or to express anything but politeness and good nature. Still, it's not right, you know; is it?"

"No," said I, as she seemed to wait for me.

"And it might lead to mistaken notions, you see, my dear."

I supposed it might.

"Therefore, I have told him, many times, that he really should be more careful, both in justice to himself and in justice to others. And he has always said, 'Mother, I will be; but you know me better than anybody else does, and you know I mean no harm—in short, mean nothing.' All of which is very true, my dear, but is no justification. However, as he is now gone so far away, and for an indefinite time, and as he will have good opportunities and introductions, we may consider this past and gone. And you, my dear," said the old lady, who was now all nods and smiles; "regarding your dear self, my love?"

"Me, Mrs. Woodcourt?"

"Not to be always selfish, talking of my son, who has gone to seek his fortune, and to find a wife—when do you mean to seek *your* fortune and to find a husband, Miss Summerson? Hey, look you! Now you blush!"

I don't think I did blush—at all events, it was not important if I did—and I said, my present fortune perfectly contented me, and I had no wish to change it.

"Shall I tell you what I always think of you, and the fortune yet to come for you, my love?" said Mrs. Woodcourt.

"If you believe you are a good prophet," said I.

"Why, then, it is that you will marry some one, very rich and very worthy, much older—five-and-twenty years, perhaps —than yourself. And you will be an excellent wife, and much beloved, and very happy."

"That is a good fortune," said I. "But why is it to be mine?"

"My dear," she returned, "there's suitability in it—you are so busy, and so neat, and so peculiarly situated altogether, that there's suitability in it, and it will come to pass. And nobody, my love, will congratulate you more sincerely on such a marriage than I shall."

It was curious that this should make me uncomfortable, but I think it did. I know it did. It made me for some part of that night uncomfortable. I was so ashamed of my folly, that I did not like to confess it even to Ada; and that made me more uncomfortable still. I would have given anything not to have been so much in the bright old lady's confidence, if I could have possibly declined it. It gave me the most inconsistent opinions of her. At one time I thought she was a story-teller, and at another that she was the pink of truth. Now, I suspected that she was very cunning; next moment, I believed her honest Welsh heart to be perfectly innocent and simple. And, after all, what did it matter to me, and why did it matter to me? Why could not I, going up to bed with my basket of keys, stop to sit down by her fire, and accommodate myself for a little while to her, at least as well as to anybody else; and not trouble myself about the harmless things she said to me? Impelled towards her, as I certainly was, for I was very anxious that she should like me, and was very glad indeed that she did, why should I harp afterwards, with actual distress and pain, on every word she said, and weigh it over and over again in twenty scales? Why was it so worrying to me to have her in our house, and confidential to me every night, when I yet felt that it was better and safer, somehow, that she should be there than anywhere else? These were perplexities and contradictions

503

that I could not account for. At least, if I could—but I shall come to all that by-and-by, and it is mere idleness to go on about it now.

So, when Mrs. Woodcourt went away, I was sorry to lose her, but was relieved too. And then Caddy Jellyby came down; and Caddy brought such a packet of domestic news, that it gave us abundant occupation.

First, Caddy declared (and would at first declare nothing else) that I was the best adviser that ever was known. This, my pet said, was no news at all; and this, *I* said, of course, was nonsense. Then Caddy told us that she was going to be married in a month; and that if Ada and I would be her bridesmaids, she was the happiest girl in the world. To be sure, this was news indeed; and I thought we never should have done talking about it, we had so much to say to Caddy, and Caddy had so much to say to us.

It seemed that Caddy's unfortunate papa had got over his bankruptcy— "gone through the Gazette," was the expression Caddy used, as if it were a tunnel,—with the general clemency and commiseration of his creditors; and had got rid of his affairs in some blessed manner, without succeeding in understanding them; and had given up everything he possessed (which was not worth much, I should think, to judge from the state of the furniture), and had satisfied every one concerned that he could do no more, poor man. So, he had been honourably dismissed to "the office," to begin the world again. What he did at the office, I never knew: Caddy said he was a "Custom-House and General Agent," and the only thing I ever understood about that business was, that when he wanted money more than usual he went to the Docks to look for it, and hardly ever found it.

As soon as her papa had tranquillised his mind by becoming this shorn lamb, and they had removed to a furnished lodging in Hatton Garden (where I found the children, when I afterwards went there, cutting the horsehair out of the seats of the chairs, and choking themselves with it), Caddy had brought about a meeting between him and old Mr. Turveydrop; and poor Mr. Jellyby, being very humble and meek, had deferred to Mr. Turveydrop's Deportment so submissively, that they had become excellent friends. By degrees, old Mr. Turveydrop, thus familiarised with the idea of his son's marriage, had worked up his parental feelings to the height of contemplating that event as being near at hand; and had given his gracious consent to the young couple commencing housekeeping at the Academy in Newman Street, when they would.

"And your papa, Caddy. What did he say?"

"O! poor Pa," said Caddy, "only cried, and said he hoped we might get on better than he and Ma had got on. He didn't say so before Prince, he only said so to me. And he said, 'My poor girl, you have not been very well taught how to make a home for your husband; but unless you mean with all your heart to strive to do it, you had better murder him than marry him—if you really love him.'"

"And how did you reassure him, Caddy?"

"Why, it was very distressing, you know, to see poor Pa so low, and hear him say such terrible things, and I couldn't help crying myself. But I told him that I *did* mean it with all my heart; and that I hoped our house would be a place for him to come and find some comfort in, of an evening; and that I hoped and thought I could be a better daughter to him there, than at home. Then I mentioned Peepy's coming to stay with me; and then Pa began to cry again, and said the children were Indians."

"Indians, Caddy?"

"Yes," said Caddy, "Wild Indians. And Pa said,"— (here she began to sob, poor girl, not at all like the happiest girl in the world)—"that he was sensible the best thing that could happen to them was, their being all Tomahawked together."

Ada suggested that it was comfortable to know that Mr. Jellyby did not mean these destructive sentiments.

"No, of course I know Pa wouldn't like his family to be

weltering in their blood," said Caddy; "but he means that they are very unfortunate in being Ma's children, and that he is very unfortunate in being Ma's husband; and I am sure that's true, though it seems unnatural to say so."

I asked Caddy if Mrs. Jellyby knew that her wedding-day was fixed.

"O! you know what Ma is, Esther," she returned. "It's impossible to say whether she knows it or not. She has been told it often enough; and when she *is* told it, she only gives me a placid look, as if I was I don't know what—a steeple in the distance," said Caddy, with a sudden idea; "and then she shakes her head, and says 'O Caddy, Caddy, what a tease you are!' and goes on with the Borrioboola letters."

"And about your wardrobe, Caddy?" said I. For she was under no restraint with us.

"Well, my dear Esther," she returned, drying her eyes, "I must do the best I can, and trust to my dear Prince never to have an unkind remembrance of my coming so shabbily to him. If the question concerned an outfit for Borrioboola, Ma would know all about it, and would be quite excited. Being what it is, she neither knows nor cares."

Caddy was not at all deficient in natural affection for her mother, but mentioned this with tears, as an undeniable fact: which I am afraid it was. We were sorry for the poor dear girl, and found so much to admire in the good disposition which had survived under such discouragement, that we both at once (I mean Ada and I) proposed a little scheme, that made her perfectly joyful. This was, her staying with us for three weeks; my staying with her for one; and our all three contriving and cutting out, and repairing, and sewing, and saving, and doing the very best we could think of, to make the most of her stock. My guardian being as pleased with the idea as Caddy was, we took her home next day to arrange the matter; and brought her out again in triumph, with her boxes, and all the purchases that could be squeezed out of a ten-pound note, which Mr. Jellyby had found in the Docks I suppose, but which he at all events gave her. What my guardian would not have given her, if we had encouraged him, it would be difficult to say ; but we thought it right to compound for no more than her wedding-dress and bonnet. He agreed to this compromise ; and if Caddy had ever been happy in her life, she was happy when we sat down to work.

She was clumsy enough with her needle, poor girl, and pricked her fingers as much as she had been used to ink them. She could not help reddening a little, now and then : partly with the smart, and partly with vexation at being able to do no better ; but she soon got over that, and began to improve rapidly. So, day after day, she, and my darling, and my little maid Charley, and a milliner out of the town, and I, sat hard at work, as pleasantly as possible.

Over and above this, Caddy was very anxious " to learn housekeeping," as she said. Now, Mercy upon us ! the idea of her learning housekeeping of a person of my vast experience was such a joke, that I laughed, and coloured up, and fell into a comical confusion when she proposed it. However, I said, " Caddy, I am sure you are very welcome to learn anything that you can learn of *me*, my dear ; " and I showed her all my books and methods, and all my fidgety ways. You would have supposed that I was showing her some wonderful inventions, by her study of them ; and if you had seen her, whenever I jingled my housekeeping keys, get up and attend me, certainly you might have thought that there never was a greater impostor than I, with a blinder follower than Caddy Jellyby.

So, what with working and housekeeping, and lessons to Charley, and backgammon in the evening with my guardian, and duets with Ada, the three weeks slipped fast away. Then I went home with Caddy, to see what could be done there ; and Ada and Charley remained behind, to take care of my guardian.

507

When I say I went home with Caddy, I mean to the furnished lodging in Hatton Garden. We went to Newman Street two or three times, where preparations were in progress too; a good many, I observed, for enhancing the comforts of old Mr. Turveydrop, and a few for putting the newly married couple away cheaply at the top of the house; but our great point was to make the furnished lodging decent for the wedding-breakfast, and to imbue Mrs. Jellyby beforehand with some faint sense of the occasion.

The latter was the more difficult thing of the two, because Mrs. Jellyby and an unwholesome boy occupied the front sitting-room (the back one was a mere closet), and it was littered down with waste paper and Borrioboolan documents, as an untidy stable might be littered with straw. Mrs. Jellyby sat there all day, drinking strong coffee, dictating, and holding Borrioboolan interviews by appointment. The unwholesome boy, who seemed to me to be going into a decline, took his meals out of the house. When Mr. Jellyby came home, he usually groaned and went down into the kitchen. There he got something to eat, if the servant would give him anything; and then, feeling that he was in the way, went out and walked about Hatton Garden in the wet. The poor children scrambled up and tumbled down the house, as they had always been accustomed to do.

The production of these devoted little sacrifices, in any presentable condition, being quite out of the question at a week's notice, I proposed to Caddy that we should make them as happy as we could, on her marriage morning, in the attic where they all slept; and should confine our greatest efforts to her mama and her mama's room, and a clean breakfast. In truth Mrs. Jellyby required a good deal of attention, the lattice-work up her back having widened considerably since I first knew her, and her hair looking like the mane of a dust-man's horse.

Thinking that the display of Caddy's wardrobe would be the best means of approaching the subject, I invited Mrs.

Jellyby to come and look at it spread out on Caddy's bed, in the evening after the unwholesome boy was gone.

"My dear Miss Summerson," said she, rising from her desk, with her usual sweetness of temper, "these are really ridiculous preparations, though your assisting them is a proof of your kindness. There is something so inexpressibly absurd to me, in the idea of Caddy being married! O Caddy, you silly, silly, silly puss!"

She came up-stairs with us notwithstanding, and looked at the clothes in her customary far-off manner. They suggested one distinct idea to her; for she said, with her placid smile, and shaking her head, "My good Miss Summerson, at half the cost, this weak child might have been equipped for Africa!"

On our going down-stairs again, Mrs. Jellyby asked me whether this troublesome business was really to take place next Wednesday? And on my replying yes, she said, "Will my room be required, my dear Miss Summerson? For it's quite impossible that I can put my papers away."

I took the liberty of saying that the room would certainly be wanted, and that I thought we must put the papers away somewhere. "Well, my dear Miss Summerson," said Mrs. Jellyby, "you know best, I dare say. But by obliging me to employ a boy, Caddy has embarrassed me to that extent, over-whelmed as I am with public business, that I don't know which way to turn. We have a Ramification meeting, too, on Wednesday afternoon, and the inconvenience is very serious."

"It is not likely to occur again," said I, smiling. "Caddy will be married but once, probably."

"That's true," Mrs. Jellyby replied, "that's true, my dear. I suppose we must make the best of it!"

The next question was, how Mrs. Jellyby should be dressed on the occasion. I thought it very curious to see her looking on serenely from her writing-table, while Caddy and I discussed it; occasionally shaking her head at us with a half-reproachful smile, like a superior spirit who could just bear with our trifling.

The state in which her dresses were, and the extraordinary confusion in which she kept them, added not a little to our difficulty; but at length we devised something not very unlike what a common-place mother might wear on such an occasion. The abstracted manner in which Mrs. Jellyby would deliver herself up to having this attire tried on by the dressmaker, and the sweetness with which she would then observe to me how sorry she was that I had not turned my thoughts to Africa, were consistent with the rest of her behaviour.

The lodging was rather confined as to space, but I fancied that if Mrs. Jellyby's household had been the only lodgers in Saint Paul's or Saint Peter's, the sole advantage they would have found in the size of the building would have been its affording a great deal of room to be dirty in. I believe that nothing belonging to the family, which it had been possible to break, was unbroken at the time of those preparations for Caddy's marriage; that nothing which it had been possible to spoil in any way, was unspoilt; and that no domestic object which was capable of collecting dirt, from a dear child's knee to the door-plate, was without as much dirt as could well accumulate upon it.

Poor Mr. Jellyby, who very seldom spoke, and almost always sat when he was at home with his head against the wall, became interested when he saw that Caddy and I were attempting to establish some order among all this waste and ruin, and took off his coat to help. But such wonderful things came tumbling out of the closets when they were opened—bits of mouldy pie, sour bottles, Mrs. Jellyby's caps, letters, tea, forks, odd boots and shoes of children, firewood, wafers, saucepan-lids, damp sugar in odds and ends of paper bags, footstools, blacklead brushes, bread, Mrs. Jellyby's bonnets, books with butter sticking to the binding, guttered candle-ends put out by being turned upside down in broken candlesticks, nutshells, heads and tails of shrimps, dinner-mats, gloves, coffee-grounds, umbrellas—that he looked frightened, and left off again. But he came regularly every evening, and sat without his coat, with his head against the wall; as though he would have helped us, if he had known how.

"Poor Pa!" said Caddy to me, on the night before the great day, when we really had got things a little to rights. "It seems unkind to leave him, Esther. But what could I do, if I stayed! Since I first knew you, I have tidied and tidied over and over again; but it's useless. Ma and Africa, together, upset the whole house directly. We never have a servant who don't drink. Ma's ruinous to everything."

Mr. Jellyby could not hear what she said, but he seemed very low indeed, and shed tears, I thought.

"My heart aches for him; that it does!" sobbed Caddy. "I can't help thinking, to-night, Esther, how dearly I hope to be happy with Prince, and how dearly Pa hoped, I dare say, to be happy with Ma. What a disappointed life!"

"My dear Caddy!" said Mr. Jellyby, looking slowly round from the wall. It was the first time, I think, I ever heard him say three words together.

"Yes, Pa!" cried Caddy, going to him and embracing him affectionately.

"My dear Caddy," said Mr. Jellyby. "Never have——"

"Not Prince, Pa?" faltered Caddy. "Not have Prince?"

"Yes, my dear," said Mr. Jellyby. "Have him, certainly. But, never have——"

I mentioned, in my account of our first visit in Thavies Inn, that Richard described Mr. Jellyby as frequently opening his mouth after dinner without saying anything. It was a habit of his. He opened his mouth now, a great many times, and shook his head in a melancholy manner.

"What do you wish me not to have? Don't have what, dear Pa?" asked Caddy, coaxing him, with her arms round his neck.

"Never have a Mission, my dear child."

Mr. Jellyby groaned, and laid his head against the wall again; and this was the only time I ever heard him make an approach to expressing his sentiments on the Borrioboolan question. I suppose he had been more talkative and lively, once; but he seemed to have been completely exhausted long before I knew him.

I thought Mrs. Jellyby never would have left off serenely looking over her papers, and drinking coffee, that night. It was twelve o'clock before we could obtain possession of the room; and the clearance it required then, was so discouraging, that Caddy, who was almost tired out, sat down in the middle of the dust, and cried. But she soon cheered up, and we did wonders with it before we went to bed.

In the morning it looked, by the aid of a few flowers and a quantity of soap and water, and a little arrangement, quite gay. The plain breakfast made a cheerful show, and Caddy was perfectly charming. But when my darling came, I thought—and I think now—that I never had seen such a dear face as my beautiful pet's.

We made a little feast for the children up-stairs, and we put Peepy at the head of the table, and we showed them Caddy in her bridal dress, and they clapped their hands and hurrahed, and Caddy cried to think that she was going away from them, and hugged them over and over again, until we brought Prince up to fetch her away—when, I am sorry to say, Peepy bit him. Then there was old Mr. Turveydrop down-stairs, in a state of Deportment not to be expressed, benignly blessing Caddy, and giving my guardian to understand, that his son's happiness was his own parental work, and that he sacrificed personal considerations to ensure it. "My dear sir," said Mr. Turveydrop, "these young people will live with me; my house is large enough for their accommodation, and they shall not want the shelter of my roof. I could have wished—you will understand the illusion, Mr. Jarndyce, for you remember my illustrious patron the Prince Regent—I could have wished that my son had married into a family where there was more Deportment; but the will of Heaven be done!"

Mr. and Mrs. Pardiggle were of the party—Mr. Pardiggle, an obstinate-looking man with a large waistcoat and stubbly hair, who was always talking in a loud bass voice about his mite, or Mrs. Pardiggle's mite, or their five boys' mites. Mr. Quale, with his hair brushed back as usual, and his knobs of temples shining very much, was also there; not in the character of a disappointed lover, but as the Accepted of a young—at least, an unmarried—lady, a Miss Wisk, who was also there. Miss Wisk's mission, my guardian said, was to show the world that woman's mission was man's mission; and that the only genuine mission, of both man and woman, was to be always moving declaratory resolutions about things in general at public meetings. The guests were few; but were, as one might expect at Mrs. Jellyby's, all devoted to public objects only. Besides those I have mentioned, there was an extremely dirty lady, with her bonnet all awry, and the ticketed price of her dress still sticking on it, whose neglected home, Caddy told me, was like a filthy wilderness, but whose church was like a fancy fair. A very contentious gentleman, who said it was his mission to be everybody's brother, but who appeared to be on terms of coolness with the whole of his large family, completed the party.

A party, having less in common with such an occasion, could hardly have been got together by any ingenuity. Such a mean mission as the domestic mission, was the very last thing to be endured among them; indeed, Miss Wisk informed us, with great indignation, before we sat down to breakfast, that the idea of woman's mission lying chiefly in the narrow sphere of Home was an outrageous slander on the part of her Tyrant, Man. One other singularity was, that nobody with a mission—except Mr. Quale, whose mission, as I think I have formerly said, was to be in ecstasies with everybody's mission—cared at all for anybody's mission. Mrs. Pardiggle being as clear that the only one infallible course was her course of pouncing upon the poor, and applying benevolence to them like a strait-waistcoat; as Miss Wisk was that the only practical thing for the world was the emancipation of Woman from the thraldom of her Tyrant, Man. Mrs. Jellyby, all the while, sat smiling at the limited vision that could see anything but Borrioboola-Gha.

But I am anticipating now the purport of our conversation on the ride home, instead of first marrying Caddy. We all went to church, and Mr. Jellyby gave her away. Of the air with which old Mr. Turveydrop, with his hat under his left arm, (the inside presented at the clergyman like a cannon,) and his eyes creasing themselves up into his wig, stood, stiff and high-shouldered, behind us bridesmaids during the ceremony, and afterwards saluted us, I could never say enough to do it justice. Miss Wisk, whom I cannot report as prepossessing in appearance, and whose manner was grim, listened to the proceedings, as part of Woman's wrongs, with a disdainful face. Mrs. Jellyby, with her calm smile and her bright eyes, looked the least concerned of all the company.

We duly came back to breakfast, and Mrs. Jellyby sat at the head of the table, and Mr. Jellyby at the foot. Caddy had previously stolen up-stairs, to hug the children again, and tell them that her name was Turveydrop. But this piece of information, instead of being an agreeable surprise to Peepy, threw him on his back in such transports of kicking grief, that I could do nothing on being sent for, but accede to the proposal that he should be admitted to the breakfast table. So he came down, and sat in my lap; and Mrs. Jellyby, after saying, in reference to the state of his pinafore, "O you naughty Peepy, what a shocking little pig you are!" was not at all discomposed. He was very good, except that he brought down Noah with him (out of an ark I had given him before we went to church), and *would* dip him head first into the wine-glasses, and then put him in his mouth.

My guardian, with his sweet temper and his quick perception and his amiable face, made something agreeable even out of the ungenial company. None of them seemed able to talk about anything but his. or her, own one subject, and none of them seemed able to talk about even that, as part of a world in which there was anything else ; but my guardian turned it all to the merry encouragement of Caddy, and the honour of the occasion, and brought us through the breakfast nobly. What we should have done without him, I am afraid to think : for, all the company despising the bride and bridegroom, and old Mr. Turveydrop—and old Mr. Turveydrop, in virtue of his Deportment, considering himself vastly superior to all the company—it was a very unpromising case.

At last the time came when poor Caddy was to go, and when all her property was packed on the hired coach and pair that was to take her and her husband to Gravesend. It affected us to see Caddy clinging, then, to her deplorable home, and hanging on her mother's neck with the greatest tenderness.

"I am very sorry I couldn't go on writing from dictation, Ma," sobbed Caddy. "I hope you forgive me now ? "

"O Caddy, Caddy ! " said Mrs. Jellyby, "I have told you over and over again that I have engaged a boy, and there's an end of it."

"You are sure you are not the least angry with me, Ma ? Say you are sure before I go away, Ma ? "

"You foolish Caddy," returned Mrs. Jellyby, "do I look angry, or have I inclination to be angry, or time to be angry ? How *can* you ? "

"Take a little care of Pa while I am gone, mama ! "

Mrs. Jellyby positively laughed at the fancy. "You romantic child," said she, lightly patting Caddy's back. "Go along. I am excellent friends with you. Now, goodbye, Caddy, and be very happy ! "

Then Caddy hung upon her father, and nursed his cheek against hers as if he were some poor dull child in pain. All this took place in the hall. Her father released her, took

515

out his pocket-handkerchief, and sat down on the stairs with his head against the wall. I hope he found some consolation in walls. I almost think he did.

And then Prince took her arm in his, and turned with great emotion and respect to his father, whose Deportment at that moment was overwhelming.

"Thank you over and over again, father!" said Prince, kissing his hand. "I am very grateful for all your kindness and consideration regarding our marriage, and so, I can assure you, is Caddy."

"Very," sobbed Caddy. "Ve-ry!"

"My dear son," said Mr. Turveydrop, "and dear daughter, I have done my duty. If the spirit of a sainted Wooman hovers above us, and looks down on the occasion, that, and your constant affection, will be my recompense. You will not fail in *your* duty, my son and daughter, I believe?"

"Dear father, never!" cried Prince.

"Never, never, dear Mr. Turveydrop!" said Caddy.

"This," returned Mr. Turveydrop, "is as it should be. My children, my home is yours, my heart is yours, my all is yours. I will never leave you; nothing but Death shall part us. My dear son, you contemplate an absence of a week, I think?"

"A week, dear father. We shall return home this day week."

"My dear child," said Mr. Turveydrop, "let me, even under the present exceptional circumstances, recommend strict punctuality. It is highly important to keep the connexion together; and schools, if at all neglected, are apt to take offence."

"This day week, father, we shall be sure to be home to dinner."

"Good!" said Mr. Turveydrop. "You will find fires, my dear Caroline, in your own room, and dinner prepared in my apartment. Yes, yes, Prince!" anticipating some self-denying objection on his son's part with a great air. "You and our

Caroline will be strange in the upper part of the premises, and will, therefore, dine that day in my apartment. Now, bless ye!"

They drove away; and whether I wondered most at Mrs. Jellyby, or at Mr. Turveydrop, I did not know. Ada and my guardian were in the same condition when we came to talk it over. But before we drove away, too, I received a most unexpected and eloquent compliment from Mr. Jellyby. He came up to me in the hall, took both my hands, pressed them earnestly, and opened his mouth twice. I was so sure of his meaning, that I said, quite flurried, "You are very welcome, sir. Pray don't mention it!"

"I hope this marriage is for the best, Guardian?" said I, when we three were on our road home.

"I hope it is, little woman. Patience. We shall see."

"Is the wind in the East to-day?" I ventured to ask him. He laughed heartily, and answered "No."

"But it must have been this morning, I think," said I.

He answered, "No," again; and this time my dear girl confidently answered "No," too, and shook the lovely head which, with its blooming flowers against the golden hair, was like the very Spring. "Much *you* know of East winds, my ugly darling," said I, kissing her in my admiration—I couldn't help it.

Well! It was only their love for me, I know very well, and it is a long time ago. I must write it, even if I rub it out again, because it gives me so much pleasure. They said there could be no East wind where Somebody was; they said that wherever Dame Durden went, there was sunshine and summer air.

CHAPTER XXXI

I HAD not been at home again many days, when one evening
I went up-stairs into my own room to take a peep over
Charley's shoulder, and see how she was getting on with her
copy-book. Writing was a trying business to Charley, who
seemed to have no natural power over a pen, but in whose
hand every pen appeared to become perversely animated, and
to go wrong and crooked, and to stop, and splash, and sidle
into corners, like a saddle-donkey. It was very odd, to see
what old letters Charley's young hand had made; they, so
wrinkled, and shrivelled, and tottering; it, so plump and
round. Yet Charley was uncommonly expert at other things,
and had as nimble little fingers as I ever watched.

"Well, Charley," said I, looking over a copy of the letter
O in which it was represented as square, triangular, pear-
shaped, and collapsed in all kinds of ways, "we are improving. If we only get to make it round, we shall be
perfect, Charley."

Then I made one, and Charley made one, and the pen
wouldn't join Charley's neatly, but twisted it up into a knot.

"Never mind, Charley. We shall do it in time."

Charley laid down her pen, the copy being finished;
opened and shut her cramped little hand; looked gravely at
the page, half in pride and half in doubt; and got up, and
dropped me a curtsey.

"Thank you, miss. If you please, miss, did you know a poor person of the name of Jenny?"

"A brickmaker's wife, Charley? Yes."

"She came and spoke to me when I was out a little while ago, and said you knew her, miss. She asked me if I wasn't the young lady's little maid—meaning you for the young lady, miss—and I said yes, miss."

"I thought she had left this neighbourhood altogether, Charley."

"So she had, miss, but she's come back again to where she used to live—she and Liz. Did you know another poor person of the name of Liz, miss?"

"I think I do, Charley, though not by name."

"That's what she said!" returned Charley. "They have both come back, miss, and have been tramping high and low."

"Tramping high and low, have they, Charley?"

"Yes, miss." If Charley could only have made the letters in her copy as round as the eyes with which she looked into my face, they would have been excellent. "And this poor person came about the house three or four days, hoping to get a glimpse of you, miss—all she wanted, she said—but you were away. That was when she saw me. She saw me a-going about, miss," said Charley, with a short laugh of the greatest delight and pride, "and she thought I looked like your maid!"

"Did she though, really, Charley?"

"Yes, miss!" said Charley, "really and truly." And Charley, with another short laugh of the purest glee, made her eyes very round again, and looked as serious as became my maid. I was never tired of seeing Charley in the full enjoyment of that great dignity, standing before me with her youthful face and figure, and her steady manner, and her childish exultation breaking through it now and then in the pleasantest way.

"And where did you see her, Charley?" said I.

My little maid's countenance fell, as she replied, " By the doctor's shop, miss." For Charley wore her black frock yet.

I asked if the brickmaker's wife were ill, but Charley said No. It was some one else. Some one in her cottage who had tramped down to Saint Albans, and was tramping he didn't know where. A poor boy, Charley said. No father, no mother, no any one. " Like as Tom might have been, miss, if Emma and me had died after father," said Charley, her round eyes filling with tears.

" And she was getting medicine for him, Charley ? "

" She said, miss," returned Charley, " how that he had once done as much for her."

My little maid's face was so eager, and her quiet hands were folded so closely in one another as she stood looking at me, that I had no great difficulty in reading her thoughts. " Well, Charley," said I, " it appears to me that you and I can do no better than go round to Jenny's and see what's the matter."

The alacrity with which Charley brought my bonnet and veil, and, having dressed me, quaintly pinned herself into her warm shawl and made herself look like a little old woman, sufficiently expressed her readiness. So Charley and I, without saying anything to any one, went out.

It was a cold, wild night, and the trees shuddered in the wind. The rain had been thick and heavy all day, and with little intermission for many days. None was falling just then, however. The sky had partly cleared, but was very gloomy —even above us, where a few stars were shining. In the north and north-west, where the sun had set three hours before, there was a pale dead light both beautiful and awful; and into it long sullen lines of cloud waved up, like a sea stricken immovable as it was heaving. Towards London, a lurid glare overhung the whole dark waste; and the contrast between these two lights, and the fancy which the redder light engendered of an unearthly fire, gleaming on all the unseen buildings of the city, and on all the faces of its many thousands of wondering inhabitants, was as solemn as might be.

I had no thought, that night—none, I am quite sure—of what was soon to happen to me. But I have always remembered since, that when we had stopped at the garden-gate to look up at the sky, and when we went upon our way, I had for a moment an undefinable impression of myself as being something different from what I then was. I know it was then, and there, that I had it. I have ever since connected the feeling with that spot and time, and with everything associated with that spot and time, to the distant voices in the town, the barking of a dog, and the sound of wheels coming down the miry hill.

It was Saturday night; and most of the people belonging to the place where we were going, were drinking elsewhere. We found it quieter than I had previously seen it, though quite as miserable. The kilns were burning, and a stifling vapour set towards us with a pale blue glare.

We came to the cottage, where there was a feeble candle in the patched window. We tapped at the door, and went in. The mother of the little child who had died, was sitting in a chair on one side of the poor fire by the bed; and opposite to her, a wretched boy, supported by the chimney-piece, was cowering on the floor. He held under his arm like a little bundle, a fragment of a fur cap; and as he tried to warm himself, he shook until the crazy door and window shook. The place was closer than before, and had an unhealthy, and a very peculiar smell.

I had not lifted my veil when I first spoke to the woman, which was at the moment of our going in. The boy staggered up instantly, and stared at me with a remarkable expression of surprise and terror.

His action was so quick, and my being the cause of it was so evident, that I stood still, instead of advancing nearer.

"I won't go no more to the berryin ground," muttered the boy; "I ain't a-going there, so I tell you!"

521

I lifted my veil and spoke to the woman. She said to me in a low voice, "Don't mind him, ma'am. He'll soon come back to his head;" and said to him, "Jo, Jo, what's the matter?"

"I know wot she's come for!" cried the boy.

"Who?"

"The lady there. She's come to get me to go along with her to the berryin ground. I won't go to the berryin ground. I don't like the name on it. She might go a-berryin *me*." His shivering came on again, and as he leaned against the wall, he shook the hovel.

"He has been talking off and on about such like, all day, ma'am," said Jenny, softly. "Why, how you stare! This is *my* lady, Jo."

"Is it?" returned the boy, doubtfully, and surveying me with his arm held out above his burning eyes. "She looks to me the t'other one. It ain't the bonnet, nor yet it ain't the gownd, but she looks to me the t'other one."

My little Charley, with her premature experience of illness and trouble, had pulled off her bonnet and shawl, and now went quietly up to him with a chair, and sat him down in it like an old sick nurse. Except that no such attendant could have shown him Charley's youthful face, which seemed to engage his confidence.

"I say!" said the boy. "*You* tell me. Ain't the lady the t'other lady?"

Charley shook her head, as she methodically drew his rags about him and made him as warm as she could.

"O!" the boy muttered. "Then I 'spose she ain't."

"I came to see if I could do you any good," said I. "What is the matter with you?"

"I'm a-being froze," returned the boy, hoarsely, with his haggard gaze wandering about me, "and then burnt up, and then froze, and then burnt up, ever so many times in a hour. And my head's all sleepy, and all a-going mad-like—and I'm so dry—and my bones isn't half so much bones as pain."

"When did he come here?" I asked the woman.

"This morning, ma'am, I found him at the corner of the town. I had known him up in London yonder. Hadn't I, Jo?"

"Tom-all-Alone's," the boy replied.

Whenever he fixed his attention or his eyes, it was only for a very little while. He soon began to droop his head again, and roll it heavily, and speak as if he were half awake.

"When did he come from London?" I asked.

"I come from London yes'day," said the boy himself, now flushed and hot. "I'm a-going somewheres."

"Where is he going?" I asked.

"Somewheres," repeated the boy, in a louder tone. "I have been moved on, and moved on, more nor ever I was afore, since the t'other one giv' me the sov'ring. Mrs. Snagsby, she's always a-watching, and a-driving of me—what have I done to her?—and they're all a-watching and a-driving of me. Every one of 'em's doing of it, from the time when I don't get up, to the time when I don't go to bed. And I'm a-going somewheres. That's where I'm a-going. She told me, down in Tom-all-Alone's, as she came from Stolbuns, and so I took the Stolbuns Road. It's as good as another."

He always concluded by addressing Charley.

"What is to be done with him?" said I, taking the woman aside. "He could not travel in this state, even if he had a purpose, and knew where he was going!"

"I know no more, ma'am, than the dead," she replied, glancing compassionately at him. "Perhaps the dead know better, if they could only tell us. I've kept him here all day for pity's sake, and I've given him broth and physic, and Liz has gone to try if any one will take him in (here's my pretty in the bed—her child, but I call it mine); but I can't keep him long, for if my husband was to come home and find him here, he'd be rough in putting him out, and might do him a hurt. Hark! Here comes Liz back!"

The other woman came hurriedly in as she spoke, and the boy got up with a half-obscured sense that he was expected to be going. When the little child awoke, and when and how Charley got at it, took it out of bed, and began to walk about hushing it, I don't know. There she was, doing all this, in a quiet motherly manner, as if she were living in Mrs. Blinder's attic with Tom and Emma again.

The friend had been here and there, and had been played about from hand to hand, and had come back as she went. At first it was too early for the boy to be received into the proper refuge, and at last it was too late. One official sent her to another, and the other sent her back again to the first, and so backward and forward; until it appeared to me as if both must have been appointed for their skill in evading their duties, instead of performing them. And now, after all, she said, breathing quickly, for she had been running, and was frightened too, "Jenny, your master's on the road home, and mine's not far behind, and the Lord help the boy, for we can do no more for him!" They put a few half-pence together, and hurried them into his hand, and so, in an oblivious, half-thankful, half-insensible way, he shuffled out of the house.

"Give me the child, my dear!" said its mother to Charley, "and thank you kindly too! Jenny, woman dear, good night! Young lady, if my master don't fall out with me, I'll look down by the kiln by-and-by, where the boy will be most like, and again in the morning!" She hurried off; and presently we passed her hushing and singing to her child at her own door, and looking anxiously along the road for her drunken husband.

I was afraid of staying then, to speak to either woman, lest I should bring her into trouble. But I said to Charley that we must not leave the boy to die. Charley, who knew what to do much better than I did, and whose quickness equalled her presence of mind, glided on before me, and presently we came up with Jo, just short of the brick-kiln.

I think he must have begun his journey with some small bundle under his arm, and must have had it stolen, or lost

it. For he still carried his wretched fragment of fur cap like
a bundle, though he went bareheaded through the rain, which
now fell fast. He stopped when we called to him, and again
showed a dread of me when I came up; standing with his
lustrous eyes fixed upon me, and even arrested in his shivering fit.

I asked him to come with us, and we would take care that
he had some shelter for the night.

"I don't want no shelter," he said; "I can lay amongst the
warm bricks."

"But don't you know that people die there?" replied
Charley.

"They dies everywheres," said the boy. "They dies in
their lodgings—she knows where; I showed her—and they
dies down in Tom-all-Alone's in heaps. They dies more
than they lives, according to what *I* see." Then he hoarsely
whispered Charley. "If she ain't the t'other one, she ain't
the forrenner." Is there *three* of 'em then?"

Charley looked at me a little frightened. I felt half
frightened at myself when the boy glared on me so.

But he turned and followed, when I beckoned to him; and
finding that he acknowledged that influence in me, I led the
way straight home. It was not far; only at the summit of
the hill. We passed but one man. I doubted if we should
have got home without assistance; the boy's steps were so
uncertain and tremulous. He made no complaint, however,
and was strangely unconcerned about himself, if I may say
so strange a thing

Leaving him in the hall for a moment, shrunk into the
corner of the window-seat, and staring with an indifference
that scarcely could be called wonder, at the comfort and
brightness about him, I went into the drawing-room to speak
to my guardian. There I found Mr. Skimpole, who had come
down by the coach, as he frequently did without notice, and
never bringing any clothes with him, but always borrowing
everything he wanted.

They came out with me directly, to look at the boy. The servants had gathered in the hall, too; and he shivered in the window-seat with Charley standing by him, like some wounded animal that had been found in a ditch.

"This is a sorrowful case," said my guardian, after asking him a question or two, and touching him, and examining his eyes. "What do you say, Harold?"

"You had better turn him out," said Mr. Skimpole.

"What do you mean?" inquired my guardian, almost sternly.

"My dear Jarndyce," said Mr. Skimpole, "you know what I am: I am a child. Be cross to me, if I deserve it. But I have a constitutional objection to this sort of thing. I always had, when I was a medical man. He's not safe, you know. There's a very bad sort of fever about him."

Mr. Skimpole had retreated from the hall to the drawing-room again, and said this in his airy way, seated on the music-stool as we stood by.

"You'll say it's childish," observed Mr. Skimpole, looking gaily at us. "Well, I dare say it may be; but I *am* a child, and I never pretend to be anything else. If you put him out in the road, you only put him where he was before. He will be no worse off than he was, you know. Even make him better off, if you like. Give him sixpence, or five shillings, or five pound ten—you are arithmeticians, and I am not—and get rid of him!"

"And what is he to do then?" asked my guardian.

"Upon my life," said Mr. Skimpole, shrugging his shoulders with his engaging smile, "I have not the least idea what he is to do then. But I have no doubt he'll do it."

"Now, is it not a horrible reflection," said my guardian, to whom I had hastily explained the unavailing efforts of the two women, "is it not a horrible reflection," walking up and down and rumpling his hair, "that if this wretched creature were a convicted prisoner, his hospital would be wide open to him, and he would be as well taken care of as any sick boy in the kingdom?"

"My dear Jarndyce," returned Mr. Skimpole, "you'll pardon the simplicity of the question, coming as it does from a creature who is perfectly simple in worldly matters—but, why *isn't* he a prisoner then?"

My guardian stopped and looked at him with a whimsical mixture of amusement and indignation in his face.

"Our young friend is not to be suspected of any delicacy, I should imagine," said Mr. Skimpole, unabashed and candid. "It seems to me that it would be wiser, as well as in a certain kind of way more respectable, if he showed some misdirected energy that got him into prison. There would be more of an adventurous spirit in it, and consequently more of a certain sort of poetry."

"I believe," returned my guardian, resuming his uneasy walk, "that there is not such another child on earth as yourself."

"Do you really?" said Mr. Skimpole; "I dare say! But, I confess I don't see why our young friend, in his degree, should not seek to invest himself with such poetry as is open to him. He is no doubt born with an appetite—probably, when he is in a safer state of health, he has an excellent appetite. Very well. At our young friend's natural dinner hour, most likely about noon, our young friend says in effect to society, 'I am hungry; will you have the goodness to produce your spoon, and feed me?' Society, which has taken upon itself the general arrangement of the whole system of spoons, and professes to have a spoon for our young friend, does *not* produce that spoon; and our young friend, therefore, says, 'You really must excuse me if I seize it.' Now, this appears to me a case of misdirected energy, which has a certain amount of reason in it, and a certain amount of romance; and I don't know but what I should be more interested in our young friend, as an illustration of such a case, than merely as a poor vagabond—which any one can be."

"In the meantime," I ventured to observe, "he is getting worse."

"In the meantime," said Mr. Skimpole cheerfully, "as Miss Summerson, with her practical good sense, observes, he is getting worse. Therefore I recommend your turning him out before he gets still worse."

The amiable face with which he said it, I think I shall never forget.

"Of course, little woman," observed my guardian, turning to me, "I can ensure his admission into the proper place by merely going there to enforce it, though it's a bad state of things when, in his condition, that is necessary. But it's growing late, and is a very bad night, and the boy is worn out already. There is a bed in the wholesome loft-room by the stable; we had better keep him there till morning, when he can be wrapped up and removed. We'll do that."

"O!" said Mr. Skimpole, with his hands upon the keys of the piano, as we moved away. "Are you going back to our young friend?"

"Yes," said my guardian.

"How I envy you your constitution, Jarndyce!" returned Mr. Skimpole, with playful admiration. "You don't mind these things, neither does Miss Summerson. You are ready at all times to go anywhere, and do anything. Such is Will! I have no Will at all—and no Won't—simply Can't."

"You can't recommend anything for the boy, I suppose?" said my guardian, looking back over his shoulder, half angrily; only half angrily, for he never seemed to consider Mr. Skimpole an accountable being.

"My dear Jarndyce, I observed a bottle of cooling medicine in his pocket, and it's impossible for him to do better than take it. You can tell them to sprinkle a little vinegar about the place where he sleeps, and to keep it moderately cool, and him moderately warm. But it is mere impertinence in me to offer any recommendation. Miss Summerson has such a knowledge of detail, and such a capacity for the administration of detail, that she knows all about it."

We went back into the hall, and explained to Jo what we proposed to do, which Charley explained to him again, and which he received with the languid unconcern I had already noticed, wearily looking on at what was done, as if it were for somebody else. The servants compassionating his miserable state, and being very anxious to help, we soon got the loft-room ready; and some of the men about the house carried him across the wet yard, well wrapped up. It was pleasant to observe how kind they were to him, and how there appeared to be a general impression among them that frequently calling him "Old Chap" was likely to revive his spirits. Charley directed the operations, and went to and fro between the loft-room and the house with such little stimulants and comforts as we thought it safe to give him. My guardian himself saw him before he was left for the night, and reported to me, when he returned to the Growlery to write a letter on the boy's behalf, which a messenger was charged to deliver at daylight in the morning, that he seemed easier, and inclined to sleep. They had fastened his door on the outside, he said, in case of his being delirious; but had so arranged that he could not make any noise without being heard.

Ada being in our room with a cold, Mr. Skimpole was left alone all this time, and entertained himself by playing snatches of pathetic airs, and sometimes singing to them (as we heard at a distance) with great expression and feeling. When we rejoined him in the drawing-room he said he would give us a little ballad, which had come into his head, "apropos of our young friend;" and he sang one about a Peasant boy,

> "Thrown on the wide world, doom'd to wander and roam,
>   Bereft of his parents, bereft of a home,"

—quite exquisitely. It was a song that always made him cry, he told us.

He was extremely gay all the rest of the evening: "for he absolutely chirped," those were his delighted words; "when he thought by what a happy talent for business he was surrounded." He gave us, in his glass of negus, "Better health to our young friend!" and supposed, and gaily pursued, the case of his being reserved like Whittington to become Lord Mayor of London. In that event, no doubt, he would establish the Jarndyce Institution and the Summerson Almshouses, and a little annual Corporation Pilgrimage to St. Albans. He had no doubt, he said, that our young friend was an excellent boy in his way, but his way was not the Harold Skimpole way; what Harold Skimpole was, Harold Skimpole had found himself, to his considerable surprise, when he first made his own acquaintance; he had accepted himself with all his failings, and had thought it sound philosophy to make the best of the bargain; and he hoped we would do the same.

Charley's last report was, that the boy was quiet. I could see, from my window, the lantern they had left him burning quietly; and I went to bed very happy to think that he was sheltered.

There was more movement and more talking than usual a little before daybreak, and it awoke me. As I was dressing, I looked out of my window, and asked one of our men who had been among the active sympathisers last night, whether there was anything wrong about the house. The lantern was still burning in the loft-window.

" It's the boy, miss," said he.

" Is he worse? " I inquired.

" Gone, miss."

" Dead ! "

" Dead, miss? No. Gone clean off."

At what time of the night he had gone, or how, or why, it seemed hopeless ever to divine. The door remaining as it had been left, and the lantern standing in the window, it could only be supposed that he had got out by a trap in the floor which communicated with an empty cart-house below. But he had shut it down again, if that were so; and it looked as if it had not been raised. Nothing of any kind was missing. On this fact being clearly ascertained, we all yielded to the painful belief that delirium had come upon him in the night, and that, allured by some imaginary object, or pursued by some imaginary horror, he had strayed away in that worse than helpless state ;—all of us, that is to say, but Mr. Skimpole, who repeatedly suggested, in his usual easy light style, that it had occurred to our young friend that he was not a safe inmate, having a bad kind of fever upon him; and that he had, with great natural politeness, taken himself off.

Every possible inquiry was made, and every place was searched. The brick-kilns were examined, the cottages were visited, the two women were particularly questioned, but they knew nothing of him, and nobody could doubt that their wonder was genuine. The weather had for some time been too wet, and the night itself had been too wet, to admit of any tracing by footsteps. Hedge and ditch, and wall, and rick and stack, were examined by our men for a long distance round, lest the boy should be lying in such a place insensible or dead; but nothing was seen to indicate that he had ever been near. From the time when he was left in the loft-room, he vanished.

The search continued for five days. I do not mean that it ceased, even then; but that my attention was then diverted into a current very memorable to me.

As Charley was at her writing again in my room in the evening, and as I sat opposite to her at work, I felt the table tremble. Looking up, I saw my little maid shivering from head to foot.

"Charley," said I, "are you so cold?"

"I think I am, miss," she replied. "I don't know what it is. I can't hold myself still. I felt so, yesterday; at about this same time, miss. Don't be uneasy, I think I'm ill."

I heard Ada's voice outside, and I hurried to the door of communication between my room and our pretty sitting-room, and locked it. Just in time, for she tapped at it while my hand was yet upon the key.

Ada called to me to let her in; but I said, "Not now, my dearest. Go away. There's nothing the matter; I will come to you presently." Ah! it was a long, long time, before my darling girl and I were companions again.

Charley fell ill. In twelve hours she was very ill. I moved her to my room, and laid her in my bed, and sat down quietly to nurse her. I told my guardian all about it, and why I felt it was necessary that I should seclude myself, and my reason for not seeing my darling above all. At first she came very often to the door, and called to me, and even reproached me with sobs and tears; but I wrote her a long letter, saying that she made me anxious and unhappy, and imploring her, as she loved me, and wished my mind to be at peace, to come no nearer than the garden. After that, she came beneath the window, even oftener than she had come to the door; and, if I had learnt to love her dear sweet voice before when we were hardly ever apart, how did I learn to love it then, when I stood behind the window-curtain listening and replying, but not so much as looking out! How did I learn to love it afterwards, when the harder time came!

They put a bed for me in our sitting-room; and by keeping the door wide open, I turned the two rooms into one, now that Ada had vacated that part of the house, and kept them always fresh and airy. There was not a servant, in or about the house, but was so good that they would all most gladly have come to me at any hour of the day or night, without the least fear or unwillingness; but I thought it best to choose one worthy woman who was never to see Ada, and whom I could trust to come and go with all precaution. Through her means, I got out to take the air with my guardian, when there was no fear of meeting Ada; and

Nurse and Patient

wanted for nothing in the way of attendance, any more than in any other respect.

And thus poor Charley sickened and grew worse, and fell into heavy danger of death, and lay severely ill for many a long round of day and night. So patient she was, so uncomplaining, and inspired by such a gentle fortitude, that very often as I sat by Charley, holding her head in my arms— repose would come to her, so, when it would come to her in no other attitude—I silently prayed to our Father in heaven that I might not forget the lesson which this little sister taught me.

I was very sorrowful to think that Charley's pretty looks would change and be disfigured, even if she recovered—she was such a child with her dimpled face—but that thought was, for the greater part, lost in her greater peril. When she was at the worst, and her mind rambled again to the cares of her father's sick bed, and the little children, she still knew me so far as that she would be quiet in my arms when she could lie quiet nowhere else, and murmur out the wanderings of her mind less restlessly. At those times I used to think, how should I ever tell the two remaining babies that the baby. who had learned of her faithful heart to be a mother to them in their need, was dead!

There were other times when Charley knew me well, and talked to me; telling me that she sent her love to Tom and Emma, and that she was sure Tom would grow up to be a good man. At those times, Charley would speak to me of what she had read to her father as well as she could, to comfort him; of that young man carried out to be buried, who was the only son of his mother and she was a widow; of the ruler's daughter raised up by the gracious hand upon her bed of death. And Charley told me that when her father died, she had kneeled down and prayed in her first sorrow that he likewise might be raised up, and given back to his poor children; and that if she should never get better, and should die too, she thought it likely that it might come into

Tom's mind to offer the same prayer for her. Then would I show Tom how these people of old days had been brought back to life on earth, only that we might know our hope to be restored to Heaven !

But of all the various times there were in Charley's illness, there was not one when she lost the gentle qualities I have spoken of. And there were many, many, when I thought in the night of the last high belief in the watching Angel, and the last higher trust in God, on the part of her poor despised father.

And Charley did not die. She flutteringly and slowly turned the dangerous point, after long lingering there, and then began to mend. The hope that never had been given, from the first, of Charley being in outward appearance Charley any more, soon began to be encouraged ; and even that prospered, and I saw her growing into her old childish likeness again.

It was a great morning, when I could tell Ada all this as she stood out in the garden ; and it was a great evening, when Charley and I at last took tea together in the next room. But, on that same evening, I felt that I was stricken old.

Happily for both of us, it was not until Charley was safe in bed again and placidly asleep, that I began to think the contagion of her illness was upon me. I had been able easily to hide what I felt at tea-time, but I was past that already now, and I knew that I was rapidly following in Charley's steps.

I was well enough, however, to be up early in the morning, and to return my darling's cheerful blessing from the garden, and to talk with her as long as usual. But I was not free from an impression that I had been walking about the two rooms in the night, a little beside myself, though knowing where I was; and I felt confused at times—with a curious sense of fulness, as if I were becoming too large altogether.

In the evening I was so much worse, that I resolved to

prepare Charley; with which view, I said, "You're getting quite strong, Charley, are you not?"

"O quite!" said Charley.

"Strong enough to be told a secret, I think, Charley?"

"Quite strong enough for that, miss!" cried Charley. But Charley's face fell in the height of her delight, for she saw the secret in *my* face; and she came out of the great chair, and fell upon my bosom, and said, "O miss, it's my doing! It's my doing!" and a great deal more, out of the fulness of her grateful heart.

"Now, Charley," said I, after letting her go on for a little while, "if I am to be ill, my great trust, humanly speaking, is in you. And unless you are as quiet and composed for me, as you always were for yourself, you can never fulfil it, Charley."

"If you'll let me cry a little longer, miss," said Charley. "O my dear, my dear! if you'll only let me cry a little longer, O my dear!"—how affectionately and devotedly she poured this out, as she clung to my neck, I never can remember without tears—"I'll be good."

So I let Charley cry a little longer, and it did us both good.

"Trust in me now, if you please, miss," said Charley, quietly. "I am listening to everything you say."

"It's very little at present, Charley. I shall tell your doctor to-night that I don't think I am well, and that you are going to nurse me."

For that the poor child thanked me with her whole heart.

"And in the morning, when you hear Miss Ada in the garden, if I should not be quite able to go to the window-curtain as usual, do you go, Charley, and say I am asleep —that I have rather tired myself, and am asleep. At all times keep the room as I have kept it, Charley, and let no one come."

Charley promised, and I lay down, for I was very heavy. I saw the doctor that night, and asked the favour of him that I wished to ask, relative to his saying nothing of my illness in the house as yet. I have a very indistinct remembrance of that night melting into day, and of day melting into night again; but I was just able, on the first morning, to get to the window, and speak to my darling.

On the second morning I heard her dear voice—O how dear now!—outside; and I asked Charley, with some difficulty (speech being painful to me), to go and say I was asleep. I heard her answer softly, "Don't disturb her, Charley, for the world!"

"How does my own Pride look, Charley?" I inquired.

"Disappointed, miss," said Charley, peeping through the curtain.

"But I know she is very beautiful this morning."

"She is indeed, miss," answered Charley, peeping. "Still looking up at the window."

With her blue clear eyes, God bless them, always loveliest when raised like that!

I called Charley to me, and gave her her last charge.

"Now, Charley, when she knows I am ill, she will try to make her way into the room. Keep her out, Charley, if you love me truly, to the last! Charley, if you let her in but once, only to look upon me for one moment as I lie here, I shall die."

"I never will! I never will!" she promised me.

"I believe it, my dear Charley. And now come and sit beside me for a little while, and touch me with your hand. For I cannot see you, Charley; I am blind."

NOTES ON BLEAK HOUSE

CHAPTER I

" High Court of Chancery."

Bleak House does not contain Dickens's first assault on Chancery. The popular reputation of the Court is conspicuous in the phrase of the Fancy, " The Chicken's head was in Chancery," that is, tucked under an opponent's left arm and punished by his right. In *Household Words*, 1850 51, " Martyrs of Chancery," Dickens exposed the cases of men who were practically prisoners for life on a charge of " contempt," because they were unable to pay sums, or comply with orders, in the obscure and intricate cases that entangled them. Sir Edward Sugden (Lord St. Leonards), who had instituted reforms, replied in the *Times*, the gist of his contention being that the Court was overworked. Dickens replied in his journal, and carried on the war in *Bleak House*. The endless Jennings case is said to have suggested that of Jarndyce. A missing will, and executors *non inventi*, was the basis of the action. The case of Gridley (Chapter XV.) was borrowed, says Mr. Ketton, from one set forth in a pamphlet by Mr. Challiner, of Leek. " In reality there was only one defendant, but in the bill, by the rule of the Court, there were seventeen ; and, after two years had been occupied over the seventeen answers, everything had to begin over again because an eighteenth had been accidentally omitted." The legacy was of £300, in five years the costs were about £900 ; the defenders were nearly ruined. Forster gives details. The plaintiff would have been glad to escape from the legacy if he could thereby evade paying costs. Dickens cited examples of denunciation of the system by eminent lawyers, in his *Household Words* articles. The Nemesis which attended the will of Lord St. Leonards himself cannot have been forgotten.

CHAPTER II

" A face of a character that would be rather called very pretty than handsome, but improved into classicality by the acquired expression of her fashionable state."

These lines probably aim at forestalling a criticism already hinted, that Lady Dedlock's face can scarcely have had such a striking resemblance to that of Esther—that is as the modest Esther leads us to think of "Dame Durden." The reader may compare Esther in "Caddy's Flowers," with Lady Dedlock in "The Young Man of the name of Guppy." Neither is remarkable for "classicality," original or acquired.

CHAPTER V

"I can neither read nor write."

This odd scene of the man who can draw letters, but cannot read, really contains the *mot d'énigme* of the plot, though to detect it might almost have puzzled the ingenuity of Edgar Poe.

CHAPTER VI

"Harold Skimpole's children have tumbled up somehow or other."

A glance at Mr. Carlyle's sketch of Leigh Hunt's household does rather suggest that this "tumbling up" was not drawn wholly from the unaided imagination. Skimpole's "I don't feel any vulgar gratitude" may also be studied in the light of Leigh Hunt's work on Byron. "He relies upon everybody," as Mr. Jarndyce says. It was not a very rare condition of mind among men of letters. Godwin relied on everybody ; and an unpublished but well-attested anecdote of another eminent writer, not Leigh Hunt, leaves Skimpole in the shade. But *this* tale (which involved family plate) demanded the existence of yet another author, who gave as recklessly as Skimpole received.

CHAPTER VII

The Ghost's Walk.

A viewless tread is, perhaps, the commonest phenomenon in "haunted houses," and, "evidentially," the least satisfactory. That ghosts are, in popular opinion, appurtenances of the great, was clearly set forth by the head housekeeper of a party who, in 1897, resided in a "haunted house" for purposes of investigation. "I have lived in the best families, and am accustomed to it," said the young woman, when asked not to be timid.

CHAPTER VIII

"They wanted everything."

One of the innumerable "askers" (as beggars call themselves, *inter se*) who haunted Dickens, asked that a donkey might be "left out for him." This was the last straw, and Dickens did not supply the animal.

NOTES ON BLEAK HOUSE

CHAPTER IX

Boythorn.

Landor said that he had not read *Bleak House*, and does not seem to have appreciated the honour of suggesting the roaring Boythorn.

CHAPTER XII

" The Vulgar wanting faith."

" The New England party " is, no doubt, satirised, for " putting back the hands upon the Clock of Time, and cancelling a few hundred years of history." Thackeray's ballad of " A Bareacre " is better-humoured banter. In *Coningsby*, Mr. Rigby (Croker) talks a good deal in the manner of " you are dependent on the caprice of Puffy."

CHAPTER XVI

" The Burial Ground."

This is fondly localised in the churchyard of St. Mary-le-Strand, and a gate at the end of a passage near Drury Lane seems to resemble that in Phiz's design, " Consecrated Ground." There are other claimants. The places have been more or less humanised, and are certainly no longer " picturesque."

CHAPTER XVIII

" I make four pounds—in a lump—by the transaction."

Richard's theory of finance practically recurs in *Great Expectations*, where Herbert and Pip practise the system of " leaving a margin," and spending up to it.

CHAPTER XIX

" Are you a beast of the field ? No ! "

Mr. Chadband's rhetorical practice suggests that of the Scottish minister on the fish that swallowed Jonah : " Was it a herring, my brethren ? No, it was not a herring ! "—with what follows.

CHAPTER XXV

" Terewth."

Judging from his spelling, in his *History of the Reformation*, John Knox pronounced this important word in the accent of Mr. Chadband.

NOTES ON BLEAK HOUSE

CHAPTER XXIX

" O my child, my child ! Not dead in the first hours of her life, as my cruel sister told me ; but sternly nurtured by her, after she had renounced me and my name ! "

The explicit and categorical character of this " cry " is rather useful as an *éclaircissement*, than characterised by passionate maternal emotion. The inevitable convention of the stage is intruded in the romance.

*This book
designed by William B. Taylor
is a production of
Heron Books, London*

**The introduction to this book
was originally published for the
Oxford Illustrated Dickens,
published by
the Oxford University Press**

*Printed in England by
Hazell Watson and Viney Limited
Aylesbury, Bucks*